Legends of
Power

Legends of Power

By

Andrea Sharkey

McClain Printing Company
212 Main Street
Parsons, WV 26287
www.mcclainprinting.com

ISBN 1-58721-102-5

1stBooks - rev. 9/22/00

About the book

Power is a magnet, as bees are drawn to nectar so are we drawn to power. It is what makes us so desirous of that sensual star on the big screen or makes us blindly follow the golden voice at the podium. Escape into a world where you can share the most intimate moments with such people whose passion erupts in spite of the many gods they worship, two people who must have met while the Gods turned their heads. Read on as these people take their world down a path only they could envision. This is the experience you will have as you read Legends of Power.

Power
Always there
A sword in the sky
The steed on the hill
Power
Ultimate freedom
Ultimate enslavement
An alluring trap
A tempting nymph
Power
There for the taking
There for the losing
Power
Never given
Never sold
Power
For those with the courage to wield it
and the strength to harness it
For those with hate to steal it
And corruption to bind it
Power
Always there

Preface

Traveling through the universe, one encounters beings of all shapes, sizes and colors, each group developing according to its needs. One thread runs through each star and culture, legends of people and places.

The oddest fact is that no matter how far apart the planets or how different the cultures or beings, the legends are the same. The names and deeds differ, but the characters shine as mirror images through the galaxies.

Chapter 1
The Beginning

Expectant faces crowded the oversized doorway. Tall forms craned and stretched over short ones, red-cheeked youths braving the chill twilight air. Anticipation painted their eyes, then, as if not one more breath could pass, a violet streak split the night. Its tail patched the sky in blues, corals and greens. The gods' hands made thunder louder than a thousand horses rumbling down a cobblestone way. Satisfied, the crowd cheered and retired to the main room where blazing fires and hot tea warmed chilled bones.

All settled into place, some alone cross-legged, others in pairs leaning on the large feathery pillows from a time long gone.

While the floor filled with people, Ezra Mowatt, eldest of his family, walked slowly to the podium, eased himself into the overstuffed gold chair, placing his knobby wooden cane behind him.

His wise and melodic voice began the spell of the tale:

On this first night of spring, as on all other first nights of spring, we shall hear the tale of the Duke and his Lady.

In the year 1123, a violent medieval time, when blood was drawn by swords and earthy bedroom lust spilled to open affection in the parlor, Lord Duke Atan Ishtba was born. The proud parents, Duke Ulfan and Duchess Marita, were kind and loving and Castle Cordan was as comfortable as any stone castle could be.

Duke Ulfan ruled a province that could be covered in no less than three days of riding, but as time passed, Ulfan grew weary of ruling.

Ulfan's neighbors, sensing this lassitude, did not hesitate to expand their borders and to compress his. It was not a violent expansion, simply a walking through and taking more crop than was one's own, or allowing animals to graze beyond one's pasture.

Though Ulfan did not raise more than an eyebrow or sigh lightly when such events occurred, young Atan brooded over them in silence.

Silence was certainly young Atan's mark. He spoke when necessary and necessary was usually to gather information. His pragmatic ways and inner drive led him to books, preoccupying himself with the tales of great kings and strategies of conquerors. When he had enough of his lessons, he took to the land.

As a youth, into his early teens, Atan would walk to digest information and to clear his mind. So, a daily hike was Atan's way.

A scent of winter mingled in with the autumn breeze as Atan rambled over the grounds. By the castle, Ulfan grazed korobs to keep the grass short. Though it was mostly still green and lush, occasionally a prickly brown patch appeared, just as a reminder of the season.

Atan walked past the first boundary, the stables. He allowed the odor of rameks to sift through his nostrils. The beasts, wild and powerful, whinnied as he passed and although most people were sufficiently repelled by the stable stench to walk around it, Atan drifted to it. The power of it excited him and enhanced his walk as he approached the outer fields.

There the grass tickled at his knees and Atan breathed deeply as he surveyed the acreage. Despite those nibbling neighbors it pushed beyond eye view. As he perused the amber and green blades of the meadow, he caught sight of something that did not belong.

Atan squinted and tried to define the image, but to no avail. His lanky body straightened to its full height and stiffened, resting his hand lightly on the small dagger at his waist.

With self-taught care he approached the unknown, sorting possibilities with each noiseless footstep. It was not a beast, hunting experience and instinct told him that. Yet no servant or town dweller would roam this land. So, what was left, a wild nomad? Perhaps. Though most young teens would have moved forward with both fear, and courage born of pride, Atan did neither. This was his land, he would clear it of all trespassers, by force if necessary, and that was all.

And yet, when he reached his goal the intruder who crouched at his feet was only a boy dressed in servant's clothes. Atan, hand still on his dagger, waited until the boy turned from his preoccupation and saw the brown leather boots of a lord. He stood in silence and faced Atan, head up, eyes forward, not staring, but not cowering.

Atan studied the boy, whom he now recognized as a servant child of the castle. *Built like a soldier* Atan thought, and as his eyes moved down. Something gleamed in the grass. At the boy's feet lay a sharp, bloody blade and beside it, well. . .

Atan, with cold curiosity pushed the creature with his toe. Its smooth, shiny skin flapped away from the fibrous inner organs that glistened in the sun. Atan's eyes widened. The creature's heart still beat. Its muscles twitched, in what must have been agony yet its movement was paralyzed. The deft hand that skinned the animal alive had cut muscles at its joints leaving it helpless. Atan allowed himself an unseen shiver.

A sadistic glint flashed into the boy's eyes but disappeared when Atan met his gaze. The only movement from the boy was the nervous twitching of his blade hand,

Atan stared into the boy who held onto a calm and courage that did not really exist, but the facade held well.

"What's your name, boy?"

"Mahtso, sir." Spoken like a soldier to his commander. Atan's countenance, even more than his station created the aura of control.

"Do you enjoy doing this?" The question requested information, but passed no judgment.

"Yes." Mahtso tried not to swallow and failed, but eyes did not leave Atan's.

"Have you ever used another type of creature?"

"No!" The definitive answer seemed to state values. Whether natural or pounded in by his very humanitarian surroundings Atan could not tell, but the value existed.

"Pick up the knife Mahtso."

Mahtso did so and proceeded to give it to Atan, who finally showed some expression, a brief smile.

"It's yours. I'll take you to a nearby stream where it can be cleaned."

So began a relationship. As they walked Atan saw he had found a peer, one on his intellectual level who was obedient and, who offered unspoken devotion and unquestioning loyalty to the death.

What of Mahtso's preoccupation? Guided and controlled, it too could serve a purpose.

"Mother, I see no reason not to take him." Atan did not whine, he was incapable of that.

"Atan, he is with you constantly. You don't need him there. Anyway there should be more than a few lovely young women there to occupy your time." Duchess Marita smiled, surely that thought would deter her son.

Atan rolled his eyes in annoyance.

The discussion continued and soon Duke Ulfan discovered them.

"What is going on here?" Ulfan stared at his wife, who was close to tears and at his son, though calm, betrayed well-controlled anger.

"Father, I wish to bring Mahtso to the king's gala, mother says he may not come."

"Bring Mahtso? As a guest?"

"No, as . . . "

Ulfan cut off his son, perhaps intentionally. "Well, Marita, Atan wishes a valet. At 15 he is certainly old enough."

Though Marita disliked Mahtso, she could accept him as Atan's valet.

Atan's mouth opened, his face and eyes contorted with disgust but his voice stayed calm. "Mahtso will stay home." Each word was said as if cast in stone. Square-shouldered as ever he left the room.

Ulfan and Marita said nothing. Somehow, Atan had his way without getting it.

4

Morning's mist blanketed the ground and framed the carriage as it stood by the castle doors.

Two rameks (beasts similar to horses), their bridles firmly tied to the carriage, stamped the ground anxious to run. The carriage was a shiny black box with rounded corners, two doors and a seat for a driver. This particular carriage's inner compartment was quite comfortable by the day's standards, with well-padded seating, storage for blankets, and a small hollow pedestal for storing lumpglows (stones that glowed) and holding one on its top.

Before the mist dissipated the family Ishtba was seated in the conveyance and on their way to the king's autumn gala.

Once the sun warmed the morning chill, Atan opened the shutters and gazed upon the land.

Marita watched him, the small gray eyes in her fleshy face full of hope and worry. Her hand flattened a bolt of hair that needed no attention, then jerked back as he moved but didn't turn.

Ulfan shook his head, "Poor Marita," he thought, taking the offending hand, "She'll never understand how he cares."

The ride continued with little ado and the passengers dozed on and off over the two day journey.

The reins snapped lightly on the rameks' backs and a soft clicking sound left the driver's mouth as family Ishtba entered King Samed's grounds, Calcoran Castle.

By noon they were settled in their rooms and ready to join the other guests. Over the next two days Marita flitted among the women, gathering gossip and spreading some. Ulfan met with his peers and shared views on politics and such things as Dukes and Lords discuss.

Atan wandered through the castle and its grounds, taking notes in his journal for later discussion with Mahtso.

"The stables are large and well organized, there must be over 200 rameks here. Guards are set equidistant from each other and there are many, however they are easily distracted and quite informative."

Atan's discussion with the friendly sentinels taught him about their training techniques, actual quantity and weaponry.

The men even joked about how little they knew of weapons, as it was a time of peace.

The Nomadic Wars had ended more than a century before in the days of King Samed's great grandfather. Since then peace had reigned and the methods of defense and the very standards of living had changed little.

New knowledge was usually greeted with fear, due to the mass superstition that change was the bearer of destruction. Men approached new knowledge gingerly and women prayed to the 6 nameless ones for protection.

Atan knew all this, but understood neither superstition nor that kind of fear. He ignored both and learned what he could from everyone.

While Atan spent most of his time alone, the other teenage guests were not so inclined. In a field by the castle a group of boys romped, the matted grass and loosed soil evidence of rough play. Atan approached slowly, noting the dirt-smudged sweaty bodies rolling and struggling in adolescent battles of physical prowess. He watched silently and wrote in his journal` *"I have noted the techniques each boy uses, I believe it will be an indication as to how they will react as adults, I have listened to their words and tones, and made cloudy guesses as to what their interests and goals might be. "* At this point a grimy young boy grabbed Atan by the shoulder and he quickly stashed away his notes.

"Come on, join us." The boy invited breathlessly with a good-natured grin.

Atan remained still and stone-faced. "No, I'll just watch."

By now a circle of boys formed around him.

"Think you're too good for us?"

"What's the matter Ishtba, scared?"

The taunts varied and the voices rose. Atan felt himself being shoved and pushed. Though it took a great deal of self-control he did not react. He had no intention of showing any of himself to these boys. So, with great resolve he shouldered his way through the crowd and when they saw he would provide no entertainment, they returned to their games, unsure about Atan Ishtba but generally passing him off as a coward.

Twilight arrived and so did the grand ball. The hall was dotted with pyramids of lumpglows, sitting on tables just large enough to frame the pyramid bases, and the light pale blue walls inlaid with patterns of white and gold lace. Each depicted a king or some event in the history Calcoran. The western half of the room was empty except for the musicians and the lumpglows, but the eastern half was a maze of tables laden with meats, fruits, dainties, and wines, all for the pleasure of the guests.

At the eastern wall itself stood King Samed's throne and that of his first wife.

The gold chairs studded with rubies and sapphires represented the Calcoran colors. The floor was row upon row of red and blue stone from entrance to walls.

Atan entered with his parents but separated from them quickly. At first he observed dress, it told a little of people's financial status. He walked around casually, his nose rather overwhelmed by the variety of scents worn by the women. He nodded as required and listened with diligence. Most conversations were repetitions of another, but one made him stop, it centered around his mother. Some women were evaluating the guests and one made note of Duchess Marita. "Have you seen her? Such a dowdy old woman, no wonder Ulfan keeps so many concubines."

Atan turned to face the speaker. His eyes bored into her, as his nostrils slightly flared just a bit. She turned away first, face flushed and crimson.

Soon the guests were being introduced to the king, for many young men, such as Atan; it would be the first time. He watched as the girls tittered and curtsied and blushed.

The boys made their appearances, some tripping over themselves or over swords worn just for the occasion. Others made loud noises and long speeches of bravery and good deeds. The king took all in stride.

Finally, Ulfan and Marita bowed before the king, exchanged social amenities and with parental pride presented Atan.

As with the others, King Samed studied his subject. Atan did not fumble or boast. He bowed his head and waited for the king to speak rather than break the silence himself as all the others before him had done.

"You look like a fine young man Atan Ishtba."

Atan raised his head and again broke tradition; he met the king's glance with his own.

Samed's eyes opened and his back straightened to give him full height in his chair and the crowd felt the difference occurring here. Samed spoke again, "Indeed you are a fine young man and a credit to the continuance of the Ishtban name."

Atan heard the words and their subtle meaning. Samed recognized and feared the ambition in Atan's eyes, and said so in his own way.

Atan lowered his wiry form to one knee, right hand and closed fist upon his heart. With his eyes fixed on the king just loudly and firmly enough. "My lord King, I swear my loyalty to you and your heirs for as long as I shall live."

King Samed leaned back. For as much as he ignored the boasts of the others, he took Atan Ishtba's words to be an oath and as inexplicably as he feared the ambition he saw, he also trusted the oath he heard. "May Ishtban prosper and you with it"

The brief scene ended, but it left a chill with most adults and confusion in the youth. Ulfan and Marita beamed with pride.

The music began when the greetings were done. Atan was forced to dance with a few of the young female royals. It wasn't that he disliked women; he used the castle's concubines, as necessary to satisfy his needs, but he had no interest in females beyond such activities, at this point.

However, Ulfan had been approached with a number of betrothal offers and although past discussions proved useless, he hoped tonight would be different. He took Atan away from the crowd.

Under the cold starlight of fall Atan felt his best -- free, clear and energetic. Ulfan wrapped his coat tight around his torso as a shield against the chill air. "You made quite a deep impression tonight son, not just on the king, but everyone else as well."

8

Ulfan dug his hands deep into his pockets. "Atan, we have two excellent offers of betrothal, one should be accepted."

Distracted by his stargazing it took a moment for Atan to register the gentle suggestion. "Father, there is not a girl or woman here I would have as a concubine, much less, a wife."

Ulfan paced and rubbed his hands together. "Atan, you should be grateful you have so many choices. I don't understand your reluctance."

How does one explain something that needs so few words in their mind, when words are so hard in the first place? "Father." Atan said gently, "I cannot choose a wife, simply because society expects me too. I'm sure all those girls will find husbands and they will all be happy, and their parents will be happy too. I do not seek love, but if I am to be wed, it will be to a mate, not a showpiece. It will be to someone who understands my ways and is worthy of bearing a child of mine. The girls here are frivolous mindless fools and would give me children just like them. I shudder at the thought of living with that. I'm sorry, but I choose no one, at least for now."

Ulfan, frustrated and still finding Atan's thoughts incomprehensible, was also proud. Not many young men would stand by a principle so strongly. Then again, Atan always had, even if it meant punishment, which was rare.

"I will tell them you need time to decide, it is easier that way."

"As you wish father."

Father and son returned to the ball and completed the evening that also ended the trip.

The next morning the guests began their journeys home.

Over the next five years Atan and Mahtso planned and schemed. They spent time organizing large groups of young men to do something, just what, no one, except Atan and Mahtso really knew.

As Atan approached his 20th year, Ulfan's his life began fading quickly. By spring his death was imminent, but Atan could wait no longer to take action.

At sunrise he appeared beside his father's bed dressed in battle gear.

Ulfan, his limbs almost useless, bade Atan to prop him sit and sit by him.

"Where are you going?" He asked weakly.

"Father, Ishtba has been gnawed at long enough. I go to retrieve what is ours."

"So this is what you've been planning. All the maps and exercises." Ulfan closed his eyes, even speaking was a strain. "Do well my son, my pride." Atan rose but Ulfan beckoned him to come close. "Does your mother know?"

Atan frowned and sighed. He did not like leaving his father now, but he knew his father understood. "I did not want to tell her, but she insisted. She is in her room crying."

"Of course. Send her to me. I can't make her understand. I really don't either, but we can comfort each other."

"As you wish." Atan turned to go but felt his father's fingers reach out. Atan in his youth and determination could not understand the emotion filling his parents, but respect commanded him to cooperate.

"Come close." Ulfan said. Atan bent near to his father's face and felt the dry lips on his cheek. "Should I not see you again, remember my love and pride are always with you."

In his discomfort Atan was silent, moving away to find his mother and send her to Ulfan.

By noon, the Ishtban troops were afoot, anxious and determined, their intended victim a day away.

Only the element of surprise stood in their favor. Training and exercise were no match for real battle, the lesson was hard but victory tasted good.

After two days Atan and the bulk of his troops began a relaxed journey home, leaving a small occupation force behind. The morning sun colored the clouds pink amid the violet sky as the men walked through strange lands.

All looked for the differences, there were few, trees and birds are the same wherever, and few people traveled anywhere. The path the Ishtban army took, they created.

About midmorning the lead man stopped and pointed silently to movement in the tall grass. Atan nodded his head and two soldiers crept forward to investigate. When one signaled, Atan dismounted and walked toward him.

There by the soldier was a man, kneeling and quivering in his tattered clothes, bones shaking as much from malnutrition and cold as fear. Behind cowered a woman and child.

"Please sire" he stammered before the young general, as he eyed the sword hanging from Atan's belt. "We meant no trespass, no harm. I have no weapon. I only wish to find food and shelter for my family." The bony figure bowed low as if waiting for the ax to fall. The child peeked from behind his mother, eyes wide in fear and wonder. The woman did not raise her head. Even the birds were silent.

As he turned away Atan spoke to the lead man. "Bring them food and blankets."

The man and child ate ravenously not allowing even a crumb to reach the ground. The woman pressed bread into her cloak and as she did, a wail arose, one so sad and shrill as to stop the wind.

Atan turned to and saw a child's limp body, limp, pale and lifeless. Her wail spoke of his death as salvation arrived.

Gently two men took the body away. All gave a silent prayer for the child's soul.

The family, once fed and rested, was sent to the new fief, and the Ishtban army continued homeward. No one was untouched by the incident, especially Atan Ishtba.

It struck a fiery chord in his icy veins. Duke Ulfan and Duchess Marita were self-indulgent, but not selfish. They would not hesitate to feed a beggar or to take in an orphaned child. No matter how cold and indifferent, Atan could not escape that compassion in himself, though he denied it through a thin veil of pragmatism. (A waste of human life is a loss of potential productivity he told himself). He privately vowed that when he ruled the world people would not starve nor waste their days in homeless wandering.

The next day Castle Cordan's grounds loomed before the Ishtban troops and by afternoon the men were in their homes. Atan and Mahtso put the rameks in their stalls and strode

11

leisurely towards the main door, ignoring the dirt and grime that covered them, breathing the fresh air of home. Their legs handled the hill with ease and soon the stables faded behind them.

"Well Atan, how does it feel?' Mahtso was in good spirits. He had enjoyed the battle and taken advantage of the opportunity to pursue his private pleasures.

"How does what feel?"

"Victory."

"Not as sweet as it should. Our losses were high. That will not happen again." Atan reprimanded himself for the losses.

"Perhaps, but we learned a lot and the next will be better." Mahtso spoke hungrily.

"Indeed it will." Atan was already planning.

"Atan."

"Yes."

Apparently changing his mind Mahtso shrugged.

"Are you sure?" Atan watched the chain hanging at Mahtso's side run in and out of his fingers like a snake searching for prey.

"Yes, it's nothing." Mahtso buried his thought, unsure of why it came to mind.

Atan let it pass. When Mahtso was ready the question would be asked. "Well Mahtso, I'm looking forward to a hot bath and a good meal.

"Me too, I hope Fatell is . . ." Mahtso stopped his words as they reached the main door and saw the white ribbon that framed the door and flapped gently in the wind.

Mahtso's hand rested on Atan's shoulder and he bowed his head, "I'm sorry, I shall miss him." Mahtso's eyes filled and he allowed a tear to meet the stones at his feet and mumbled a quiet prayer.

Atan stared at the white ribbon and searched for grief, that would not come. He had known his father was near death and there was nothing he could do about it. He had said his good-byes and paid his respect while his father lived. Atan offered a prayer for Ulfan's soul to please the gods, then opened the door and for the first time entered as Lord Duke Atan Ishtba.

After comforting his mother as best he could, Atan returned to his plans.

Atan and Mahtso spent hours off in the solitude of the upstairs family room. Often Fatell would pass by, and sometimes, when the mood struck, she would stand in the bedroom to watch and to listen to her love, and to her master as they planned.

Atan's tall lean form paced back and forth as he threw ideas for battle plans and new weapons at Mahtso. Sometimes Fatell could see him drawing a route on a map, each line specific in its beginning and ending. On occasion Fatell glimpsed into Mahtso's ice blue eyes as he looked up from his notes. Always she heard the soft clicking of his chain as it ran through his fingers, sometimes gently, when the discussion was at a lull or sometimes fast as the heartbeat of a rabbit when a new concept surfaced.

Fatell never interfered, never spoke of what she heard or saw. She would finish her work and leave, sometimes unnoticed, sometimes not.

The plans led to actual battle. Each spring the troops had Castle Cordan at their back and by fall they returned with larger boundaries for the Ishtban province and more power for Lord Duke Atan Ishtba.

As his plans entered their fifth year, Atan clothed in a green woolen sweater, dark britches and smooth leather boots, stood at the open door of his Castle thinking. Hands clasped behind his back, his face reached toward the crisp winter air. He smiled as it embraced him. Lady winter had not shed a flurry of white for six days, a sure sign that her time was ending and that energetic spring was pushing her way in.

Atan ran his fingers through the snow that reached his knees. His eyes were a book that he let no one read. Within a few days the next takeover would begin, and with that in mind he turned inside and waited.

Three days later both he and Mahtso stood at the same doorway watching the last of many white hoods disappear past the Castle gate. Mahtso's chain was like the pendulum of an overwound clock, moving too fast and losing a beat. He felt Atan's long fingers on his shoulder.

"What's wrong?"

Mahtso sighed, "I'm concerned. Were they really ready for this?"

Atan leaned casually against the doorframe. He was confident and always felt better when he took action. "You are an odd one," he chuckled. I've watched you at work and don't hesitate to admit that I wouldn't wish to be your enemy and here you are clucking like an old mother bird."

Mahtso lowered his head, confused and embarrassed.

"Mahtso, those men trained all winter for this, and they all volunteered. They have provisions to last twice as long as they will need and they're so heavily laden with fur I half fear it will bury them in the snow."

Mahtso half smiled, "You're right. Let's get everyone else ready."

As Atan expected the snow melted quickly, but not before the well camouflaged troops formed an unseen frame around their prey.

Inside the castle, that was their target Atan's spies roamed free. Their positions as groundskeepers and servants opened all rooms and passages. Their training gave them access to information and gossip, which had found its way to Atan.

Had the inhabitants of the fief been keen observers, they might have sensed something different, as if the trees were closer or perhaps a few sensitive people would have felt, claustrophobic. But instead on a cool spring afternoon, as the gardeners began to seed their plots of spices, the people found themselves engulfed. The noose had tightened. Methodically all royalty and military personnel were executed. Escape was impossible. All exits were sealed and double guarded.

With victory at hand, the inspection began, nothing was taken for granted. Thoroughness was imperative to success as far as Duke Ishtba was concerned, and Mahtso understood.

"Mahtso, are the executions complete?" Atan asked, scanning his acquisition.

"Yes, except those left for me." Mahtso's chain swung with excitement.

Atan ignored Mahtso's mood. "All the children as well?"

Mahtso nodded. "Anyone with an ounce of royal blood or military connection is now a fleshless and charred skeleton in the entrance yard.

It would be two days before the last whimper signaled the end of Mahtso's work. He appeared sweaty, fingertips smelling of blood in Atan's temporary bedroom. As he shifted from foot to foot the chain circled wildly. Atan sighed a bittersweet sound. Although he knew Mahtso would have valuable information, his methods were a bit disturbing. "I suppose you're done."

"Yes, I have learned much this time."

"Good. You will have to share it with me."

"Atan, I have seen many fresh young women. I will be taking one, why don't you? This is a good victory, true?"

Atan hesitated a moment. He never took a woman outside his castle, but, this time . . . "All right, but find me a willing one I have had enough battles for the moment."

Mahtso nearly leapt from the room and reappeared shortly with a willing woman.

She chattered on while they undressed, doling out compliments to her new master. Atan was silent. He fulfilled his need, put on his clothes and pierced her heart. She fell, without so much as a whimper.

Atan cleaned the sword on her gown, taking a minute to reflect, "It is a pity to waste life, but I'll chance no unwanted heirs." A dead fly in his soup would have received equal compassion.

As he left to meet Mahtso, Atan ordered one of his men to clean the mess.

Mahtso stood outside the main hall, observing the survivors, their nervous murmurs, shuffling feet and the occasional sigh of fear.

Atan arrived, knowing all would be ready for his speech.

Before he entered, he pulled Mahtso to the side. "In the future, I wish to avoid these women. Murder after lust is irritating."

"As you wish." Mahtso shook his head and accepted the order without understanding his master's reasoning.

The Lord Duke entered the main hall and so did silence. Even the grains of dirt that speckled the floor, feared to move. Side by side he and Mahtso stood before the crowd, dressed in full military gear. Mahtso's hand absentmindedly stroked the whip at his waist and his eyes still gleamed with recent pleasures. Atan probed the scene with his eyes and instincts. Though it only took a moment, to the crowd it was an eternity. Finally he spoke, " I am your leader, Duke Atan Ishtba."

To his discomfort they all bowed in unison. "Your show of respect is noted, but not necessary." His hand rested lightly on his sword while he waited for all eyes to raise and then he spoke, again. "Beside me is Mahtso, my second in command. A quick hand signal and another man joined them. "This is Sidno, he will administer this fief. You will obey him, as if he were me." If a voice could sound like a blade being sharpened, then Atan's did. "If you cannot live by my rules and Sidno's administration, then Mahtso will teach you the folly of your ways."

Atan hid a smile as Mahtso's eyes still shone like a beast fresh from the kill as he fondled his whip.

Atan continued. "Production of herbs and spices is of first importance. If your methods are effective, you may continue in your usual manner. If not, we will find another way." His voice and gaze softened.

"You will notice that all whipping posts have been removed, it will remain that way." These objects of discipline, hated and feared by servants, were common in most fiefs. They disappeared when the Ishtban crest rose. There hadn't been any at Castle Cordan in the Duke's lifetime and he realized that whipping a cook for a poor meal or servants for inadequate service, produced only contempt, not better quality.

"Mahtso will post the rules I expect you to obey. There are a few here who can read, correct?" Two or three men nodded their

16

heads. "Good, you may relate these rules to your peers. I will return every summer to verify that all is as it should be."

Ishtban rules were clear, direct and strict. Punishment matched crime. Should a man steal an animal, he would be forced to return it and pay the owner its value. The only reason for corporal punishment was malicious destruction of Ishtban property, and then only with the Duke's approval.

The people stared in silent bewilderment. ,The boldest man stepped forward, swallowing hard, "Is that all m'lord?"

"You act as if you expect more."

"To be honest sire, we heard that you took much harsher measures with the, um, survivors of your new acquisitions." The servant, brave as he was, still quivered before his new master.

"What is you name?"

"Alato sire."

"Well Alato, you will find I try to be fair -- strict, but fair."

"Yes m'lord." Alato bowed his head.

Atan did his best to relax the scene, he leaned on a nearby table. "What else?"

Alato looked behind him for support before speaking. "We have heard that each time you take a fief..." He paused and croaked, Mahtso had his way with every person left alive."

"And you believed this?"

"M'lord, when Orian, the previous master came of age and took over from his father, every servant over the age of fifteen was whipped as a lesson for future disobedience. Your reputation spoke of worse."

"You have given me good information. It is appreciated. But, while the whip has mostly vanished, beware that should a whisper of treason reach my ears, the whipping post will seem a child's spanking in comparison."

Treason was the one unforgivable sin. Even Atan did not understand his obsession with it, he simply knew that destruction, from within was a far deadlier sword than that of the stranger.

There was no trial, no second chance. With accusation came conviction and that spelled terror -- as a beginning. Mahtso, or his special corps of men exercised a form of torture that demanded the victim announce the pain emanating from your

17

shredded skin and fractured limbs. The exercise lasted at least a day, more for the stronger. But eventually, the watching crowd, heard prayers and pleas for death.

Despite this example, every new acquisition had a traitor, once in a while two.

Atan spent a day longer to assure the new fief was conforming to Ishtban standards. He was a ruler as much as an owner. Centralized government was nonexistent. Most fief owners collected taxes and offered only protection or less. Ishtba created a loose confederation, encouraging trade between his properties and keeping a balance of wealth. This balance kept all his fiefs working to potential and avoided the childish arguments of who has more. He rewarded productivity, and, as he expected the rewards brought greater yields.

On the road back to Castle Cordan, Mahtso rode beside his Duke, twitching in uneasy silence. As dusk approached the Ishtban troops made camp for the night.

Atan sat down and leaned against a tree, eyes closed, enjoying the night air. Mahtso stood over him a few moments before Atan realized he was there. "Yes Mahtso, what is it?"

"May I ask a question?" Mahtso spoke to the ground.

"Sit down Mahtso. Why are you being so shy about this, whatever it is?" Atan moved toward Mahtso.

Mahtso sat down and the chain in his hand jerked like a hangman's noose with its job completed.

"Mahtso, what is bothering you?" Atan snapped out the words.

"The children."

"Children? What are you talking about?"

"The ones we kill at every battle."

"Oh, those children, what about them?" Atan leaned back once again.

"Why must we kill them?" Mahtso's gentle humane side had surfaced.

"Are you questioning my orders?" He teased.

"No. I just don't understand. He lowered his head more out of embarrassment, than fear.

"Mahtso, children grow up. They may not remember where their cloaks are, but they will remember who killed their parents. I cannot chance one of them coming out for revenge. I see no other way to avoid that future potential problem. Do you understand?"

Atan wanted the volatile Mahtso's unwavering confidence.

"Yes, it makes sense."

That question settled, both men rested easy under the sheltering leaves of the strong oak tree.

The years passed and Atan reached 28. That autumn as all others, King Samed held his gala. Atan was required to attend now, much as he had been 14 years before.

The people remained the same, the pageantry was still grand, but Samed seemed faded.

The king sat at the eastern wall of the room. The gold throne embellished with a rainbow of precious stones, dwarfed the weary man. Though not physically bent and gnarled with age, his eyes lacked the spark of power a king needs. His heart was preoccupied with his offspring to the point of obsession. Samed's interest in the world outside a day's ride of his castle was nominal. Yet, Duke Ishtba could not be ignored, could not be covered like an unpleasant statue or changed like an eerie painting, it was too late for that.

"Duke Ishtba, why must you continue this aggression against your neighbors? Soon their fear will subside and they will be the aggressors." Samed voiced a mandatory concern for the world.

"Your highness, my aggressions will stop when Ishtban province has filled its needs for growth." As always Atan's eyes met the King's.

"Have you not grown enough? Why do you need more?" King Samed leaned forward and shook his staff.

The Duke stood tall and did not move away from the king. His tone cool and determined did not change. "It is not a question of *more*, but of *what*, sire. Under my rule the fiefs

19

produce more and the people fare well. I need a greater variety of fiefs to make Ishtban reach its peak. Your highness, my loyalty to you and your sons remains unchanged. You have my sworn vow." It was small comfort to the world, but Samed felt safe again, and made do with that.

Guests gathered in small groups, each conversation an echo of the others.

"Tell me Fakrash, has Ishtba been to see you of late?"

The query was posed by a young fiefholder in King Samed's half of the world.

Fakrash stuffed a third piece of meat into his mouth before answering. "No, but I wait, and if he doesn't come to me," Fakrash snickered and gulped his wine, "perhaps I will go to him."

"You scoff at a powerful man."

"He doesn't frighten me." Fakrash's sleeve mopped his greasy face.

While the men spoke of power and property and women, the women spoke of men. Each was perused and categorized, the bachelors coming under the heaviest scrutiny; and who was nominated as most fascinating? Atan Ishtba; of course.

The women standing not far from this object of interest discussed it in just those terms.

"I wonder what he's like? I mean, underneath the indifferent exterior? A young single woman began the conversation.

"Who knows. He is as distant as the sun and as cold as the space between here and there."

A third woman joined the chat. "I don't want to know, he frightens me."

"He frightens everyone, even the men. Still, a night in his bed would be different." She smiled and took a moment to fantasize the statement.

"You would never be the same." This from an older woman speaking, who studied the Duke as he spoke.

"Why? We have no tales of horror from Castle Cordan, no butchered or beaten women. Although, very little comes out or goes in there."

"You have a point. And, all in all, better a dull bed every night than one where the outcome is in question."

The women laughed. Each held that secret desire, whether they chose to admit it or not.

Atan and Mahtso spent a good deal of time talking with the men, very little time, dancing with the ladies and most by themselves, observing and learning. Mahtso saw avenues Atan neglected.

"M'lord, would not one of the women here do as a wife?"

"Shall I pick a name from a hat Mahtso?"

M'lord, a Duke of your age should be wed by now, it is time." Mahtso rarely pressed, but he felt the need.

"When the proper woman appears, I will take her." Atan was only half listening.

"Sire, there are many beautiful women here, some with intelligence as well." Mahtso's chain rolled between his fingers with increasing speed.

"Beautiful? Tell me Mahtso, is that why you care so much for Fatell, beauty?"

Mahtso took a moment to reflect on his love. She was as plain as a gray winter's day, yet he could love no woman more. .

"My lord, I admit, beauty is not everything."

"Good, I'm glad you see that, and the intelligence you see in these women they waste on frivolous decorations and foolish games."

"Sire, perhaps you expect too much."

Atan became somber. "Mahtso, the women here tremble at my touch. There is not one who does not fear me."

"Once they know you, it could change." Mahtso grasped for reasons. His friend looked at him and put a hand on his shoulder.

"Mahtso, everyone fears me, even you, true?"

Mahtso nodded. He knew that while there were those who had cause to fear, he had none. Still there lived in a small corner of his heart, a piece of that universal fear.

21

Atan looked in Mahtso's eyes. "I cannot share a lifelong bed with a woman who fears me. I am not so old or desperate yet to choose wantonly. I can live with my loneliness a bit longer."

Mahtso felt a strange tinge of icy emptiness go through him. He dropped his queries, as Atan wished.

The two men left the gala with more knowledge of others and themselves.

Two more years passed, and with them more wins for Ishtba. By now, Lord Duke Atan Ishtba reigned over just less than half the known world, his dominion second only to King Samed's.

As happens after years of travel, a man tires and can ache for home. When victory comes to easy, boredom sets in. Even the Lord Duke was not immune from such feelings.

The pale violet of Raaleken twilight framed Castle Cordan as Duke Atan Ishtba returned home from another victory. The stone monster, his castle, was ominous and reassuring all at the same time. Like eyes the turrets windows, saw all but allowed no viewer to trespass inside. At the right turret the Ishtban crest flew, green on the right for growth, black on the left for power and guarding both a Golden Gilfon, lion headed, dragon winged beast of mythical lore.

Snug inside these walls lay a hollow tube used for storage in case of siege. Beyond that were two great circular levels of rooms, the lower for guests, dining and entertaining, servants quarters and the kitchens. At the lowest level was the basement, or perhaps dungeon was a better term. There, Mahtso did his investigations. Also were tunnels, whose ends were a mystery.

The highest level held a host of twelve rooms, 2 rooms for the guards (at either side of the stairwell), one for the Duke, (with an anteroom) one for his chosen mate, one dining room and the remaining seven for the children. There was also a large family room between them all. Except for the guards' rooms and that of the Duke, the level was barren, a silent painful echo of the master of the house.

Atan passed through the anteroom and entered his room. His sense of security deepened. The tall dresser stood solidly to his left, a patient guard awaiting orders and by the window across the wide expanse was a faded green couch his father had built.

The walls echoed the feeling of patience and power. By the bed was hook on which Atan hung his sword. The wall facing the four-poster bed held some dusty history. Hand chains and a small whip, one strong enough to do damage to any one. These sat unused for two generations, neither Atan nor his father had seen need for them. But it was a reminder of Atan's grandfather, so it remained. Atan lay down, stared at the ceiling. closed his eyes closed and ignored the emptiness beside him.

Castle Cordan had its master back. Life would continue on.

Chapter 2

While Duke Ishtba was building his empire, a girl child was born to the cloth merchant Goran, in Milson, the village not half a day's journey from Castle Cordan. Raphela as she was named, was the eldest of five daughters.

Being such, her parents gave her the honor and opportunity at age 7 to run errands for them throughout the small village and her already unusual nature blossomed.

The errands, which started as short trips, minutes long became excursions taking hours. Raphela would stay at a shop longer than necessary to watch and learn and after a time found others besides her destination to visit.

No one seemed to mind the child's presence. Her silent wide-eyed intelligent face caused no disturbance, questions came at the appropriate moments, and she wallowed in the knowledge.

Although Raphela enjoyed her freedom and the shopkeepers her company, her parents were disturbed. Her help was needed at home. But scolding, even the occasional spanking, did not change her. Keeping her from errands was the only answer, yet Raphela's charm usually eliminated that problem. For some reason, these kind people felt powerless against the child.

At twelve, Raphela decided her life was lacking something, and her father could help. One evening, when the house was dark and quiet, she spoke with him.

"Papa," she whispered, "I must talk to you."

"What about Raphela?" He yawned and sat on a chair.

"Papa, I must learn to read and write." She spoke earnestly as if her life depended on it.

"Must!?" he laughed, " Girls must not learn any such thing."

"Other girls."

"Umhm, why must you learn?" He could never take his daughter too lightly.

"Just because I must." Raphela was sitting beside him and moved in closer, smiling. "Anyway, then I could help you, right?"

Goran heaved a sigh. "I suppose."

"Then you'll teach me." Raphela's eyes lit and before Goran could utter another word she hugged him. "Thank you Papa, thank you."

"Oh Raphela," he stroked her hair, "what will become of you, I worry about that. You are beautiful, but what man will keep such an independent, wench?"

"I will become whatever I choose to be and no man will keep me. I will find one I can share a life with, not serve as a slave."

Goran's heart trembled a bit at her words, but he hugged her tight and kissed her on the forehead. "Somehow, I believe that."

In two months time, Raphela did learn to read and write and began sneaking about the town borrowing books she knew would not be missed. Eventually her father taught her to keep his business records, since she failed miserably at domestic duties.

Though Raphela knew many people, her world was still lonely. The only woman to befriend her was Sarah, the deaf seamstress. Their mutual loneliness created a bond even though Sarah was old enough to be Raphela's mother.

Sarah could read lips so they shared secrets and in time developed a sign language to expedite their conversations. One day with a book tucked under a loose bodice, Raphela slipped away in the early hours of the day and appeared at Sarah's door.

The small shop, where the seamstress lived alone, was filled with neatly arranged tables of cloth and thread, the colors brightened what would have been a dismal room.

"Sarah" Raphela tapped her on the shoulder.

Sarah's graying head raised from the hem in her hands. "Don't you look excited."

"I am." Raphela's effervescence bubbled over as she spoke.

"What about?"

Patience comes hard with most children, Sarah's eyes returned to the cloth, but Raphela couldn't wait. She shoved the book into Sarah's lap.

"Ouch!" Sarah's finger met the sharp needle just hard enough to draw blood. She looked reprovingly at Raphela whose enthusiasm was diluted, but only a bit.

"What is it child?" Even when she stood, Sarah's tiny form was overwhelmed by the table. Raphela practically pulled Sarah over the barrier between them. "Look, look at what I have!"

The woman complied. "So, you have a book. You might as well have a ramek. There is nothing you can do with either one." Sarah was not usually short-tempered, but her delicate features showed annoyance.

"That's where you're wrong. I can do something with this book."

Raphela looked around to make sure they were alone, opened the book to the first page, and read it aloud to Sarah, who sank back in her seat. Anyone else she would have accused of lying, of faking, but with Raphela, that was impossible.

"Who taught you?!" Envy and desire filled her voice.

"My papa." Raphela's eyes gleamed. "Would you like me to read more. I can read the whole thing and it's a wonderful story."

Sarah's first reaction was to say no, but Raphela was hard to refuse. "Go ahead, the mending will wait."

For three weeks Raphela read to Sarah, until one rainy afternoon when she stopped Raphela in midsentence. "Raphela, what you're doing is very nice..." she paused. "But could I ask a favor? Perhaps, you could teach me to read."

Raphela's eyes lit. "Why not? I'd love to. I'll bring my books and scribes tomorrow. We'll have a great time."

On the way home that evening she thought about Sarah's request. "How sad it is. So many people not permitted to read and enjoy books. It's not fair. If everyone could read and write, we'd all know so much more, and faster too. Something needs to be done." All the way home her mind churned with the changes such a thing could mean.

In 1148, Raphela turned 16 and looked 20, standing as tall as many men. Her softly curved form radiated sensuality with full bosoms and buttocks and a slender waist, a flowing together like a rainbow of pastel ribbons on a summer breeze. Her face crowned the appealing form, the creamy olive skin, enticing brown eyes and full lips, all surrounded by black hair cascading just below her waist. Underneath it all her deep intelligence, created a mystique, which, by choice or not, beckoned to most men.

She walked through the town enjoying the dawn hours on a cool spring day, her dress moving in harmony with her body. Her firm youthful body expressed both an interest and a need.

As she expected, the shop door was unlocked. He always started before dawn.

Quietly she entered the small shop. The place was just large enough for the table under the window, two stools and a second table.

Raphela found her way to the stool and observed. Nabus was preoccupied, polishing a charm and humming softly. His hands moved easily, gliding over the gold with a sensual touch. He did not greet her, and it was not expected. But minutes passed and the easy quiet changed to uncomfortable silence.

Although Raphela did not stare or peer over his shoulder Nabus sensed something. He, like the other merchants had known Raphela since early childhood. He didn't raise his head but his voice edged the silence as mist wets the dry land. "Your questions must be difficult to answer today."

Raphela, lost in thought, drew back to reality. "What do you mean?"

"They seem difficult to ask." Nabus' eyes still rested on the piece, but caught the warm blush on the girl's face.

"You know I hate to disturb anyone when they work."

He placed gold and cloth to the side and faced her. Her hair glistened in the morning sun and her eyes were a dance waiting for the music. "All right, what is today's question? Nabus smiled.

"I need to learn something." Raphela found herself suddenly shy.

"Raphela you always need to learn something. How do I shape the stones, hammer silver, polish the gold? Where does it come from? And who? What, when, where, why..."

She broke his good-natured tirade. "How, is today's query." Her eyes met his and they locked in place.

"How what?"

"How to make love."

28

"Raphela, child, that will be answered on your wedding night." He thought no less of her, but the question puzzled him.

"First of all, in case you haven't noticed, I'm not a child! She stood and whirled about with arms spread. "And second, you say learn on my wedding night. What makes you so sure I will have one? And if I do, I should not want to spend it groping and scouring for what feels right." The music had started and Raphela danced.

Nabus held back a smile. "If I were your father I'd have to spank you for that."

Raphela came closer to him, her innocence and desire inescapably intertwined. "Nabus," she said softly and took his hand in her two. His heart pumped a bit faster. "I don't want to seduce you. It's a cheap trick. I want your help." She backed away and returned to the stool.

He was stunned. Raphela always had a power over everyone, even him. But never before had he realized its strength. "Why me? There are so many others, who willingly, I'm married, happily married. Why . . ." His voice trailed.

"Why? The others are too willing, married or not. They would take what they wanted and leave me with a bitter taste. They lack intelligence and humanity. I have no desire to steal you from Falle. But I trust you and believe you would teach me well."

You're not a child and I apologize for saying so. I do find it hard to refuse you." He did not avoid her eyes.

"Then don't." Those eyes pushed, prodded, but she remained seated.

"I'll think about it. But you should think of all the risks involved, beyond reputation." It was a weak attempt at rebuttal.

Raphela smiled deep, "A woman at the right time can avoid these risks. That much I learned."

"I'm not surprised." He sighed. "Come back in a few days, I'll let you know."

Raphela left and as Nabus watched the door close he sank onto a stool and poured himself a glass of wine. It was noon when she left. The light faded, moved into twilight and still he could not form any real thoughts. Words and phrases rose in his

29

mind like swift birds, and fluttered away. *What of Falle, she'll feel something's amiss, what will I say?* These were the only clear words, and as they passed through his mind for the millionth time, he realized that the stars were shining into the window. He forced himself out of the workshop and into the house.

Falle heard the door and as usual left the kitchen to greet her husband. She turned the corner to see a dazed man walking through habit, not conscious effort.

Falle took his hand and guided him to the couch. "What's wrong Nabus?"

Nabus stared at his wife. Though she lacked Raphela's exceptional features, Falle was everything to him. The lumpglow on the table created soft shadows and a relaxed Falle waited.

Finally Nabus spoke. "Raphela came to see me today."

Falle wanted to say that there was nothing unusual in that but instinctively held her tongue.

"Falle, she asked me to teach her lovemaking." Nabus breathed deeply and sank back into the couch.

"Why?" Falle was neither shocked nor angry.

"Why lovemaking or why me?"

"Both".

"She says she needs to learn. And she trusts me."

Falle kissed him and squeezed his hand. "Why shouldn't she trust you? You're a good man. Now, what are you going to do?"

"What?! Falle, I don't...."

Did you expect a fit of blue jealousy? Ranting and raving? Nabus, you should know me better by now."

Nabus knew Falle was as unpossessive and secure as people come. He wasn't bothered that she didn't think he would accept the offer, but why she would expect him to accept it.

"Don't be hurt my love. If it makes you feel better her beauty is painful. But what will you do?"

"You're pushing me to say yes. Why?"

"Call it instinct. Raphela is destined for power and while she'd do you no harm for saying no, yes, could reap greater rewards.

30

"Aren't you afraid of what could develop?"

"You mean that the two of you would fall in love? Does it frighten me? No. I believe you will. But I also believe that the three of us are strong enough to deal with it and turn it to its best advantage." Falle caressed his cheek and nibbled at his ear. "Any way, I'm complimented that she chose you and if I am ever going to compete for you who better than Raphela to compete against."

Nabus pulled Falle close. The passion behind her icy words stirred him. Falle saw a future, and a way to make the most of it for their whole family.

Nabus and Falle rested easy that night, in a marriage built on solid foundations. The lessons began two weeks later.

She appeared in the early afternoon, closing and locking the workshop door, at the same time. Raphela sat on the recently installed bed.

Nabus ignored her, at first, but as soon as she sat, her fingers moved to the buttons on her blouse and began undoing them. Before the blouse bared more than one soft shoulder, Nabus joined Raphela and refastened it.

"I don't understand, what's wrong?" For the first time, Raphela was caught off guard and the beauty of her naiveté shone around her.

"Nothing is wrong, but if I am to teach you, you will learn more than what goes between your legs."

Raphela blushed lightly.

"Sweet young girl, you can be a whore after you're in bed, until then be a lady. I'll give you ample opportunity to be aggressive."

She leaned back on the bed, allowing her hair to brush against his arm and her bosoms to peek above her bodice. "Teach me." she purred. Nabus the neighbor faded and the man came to surface.

It began with a caress, velvety adept fingers testing the smooth skin of her arms. His handsome face buried itself in hair that smelled of sunshine. He cupped his hand behind her neck. "Have you ever been kissed?"

Raphela, entranced, shook her head before greeting his lips.

Passion and gentility possessed the afternoon that ended in no more than simple petting and kissing, as did the next few lessons. It took four to reach a consummation. As pleasurable as all of it was, by the third time they were together Nabus realized that something was missing. Raphela learned quickly and even improvised, but her touch was empty and Nabus knew her soul was not.

Raphela lay naked on the bed, hair just covering her nipples.

Nabus also nude, sat beside her. He didn't touch her. After a few minutes of silence he got up and threw a blanket at Raphela.

"What are you feeling Raphela?" He asked coldly.

"What are you talking about?" Raphela stared at the blanket lying across her.

Nabus grabbed her arm. "I mean what is going on inside you?"

Raphela turned and saw a face no less serious than a judge ready to pass sentence. "I don't understand. What do you mean? I feel fine." She pulled back without even realizing it.

He got up and wrapped a robe tightly around himself. "Are you happy, are you sad? What makes you happy, what makes you sad? He put his face an inch away from hers.

"What difference does it make?"

Nabus moaned. "What difference? Raphela your lessons are over. I have failed as a teacher and you as a student have also failed."

Raphela stood and caressed his shoulder. Nabus kept his back to her and walked stiffly away.

"I don't see the failure, please explain it to me." Although Raphela was obviously concerned, he had not yet broken through to her.

"Raphela, if you keep your distance so that I won't fall in love with you, you're wasting your time. That happened long ago. But if you have nothing else to show, than go. You have learned to be a prostitute, but you have not learned lovemaking.

Raphela's barriers began to crumble. Not because of his words but because he was angry with her and despite her best efforts, it hurt. The tears stung her eyes though she remained silent.

32

Nabus, eyes red with pain faced her and though her tears seared him, he knew it wasn't enough. "Listen to me, you have to let someone inside, just a little. To deny yourself any intimacy is to be half a person. You think you've suffered, the loneliness, you have, but you must learn the other side too, the joy and pain of friendship. If you don't your heart will turn to stone. And when the time comes when you meet that special man, you will have nothing to give and no way to receive. Let me be your friend. I can be your lover only in bed, but I can be your friend in all places and times."

Raphela curled up and reflected on the barrage of feelings thrown at her and welling up inside. No pain had ever been this deep or this good. Before her lay the road of friendship. She stepped forward with care, as a child with a new doll. Ever so gently she moved so as not to break anything. "Nabus," she whispered, "be my friend."

His arms opened and she buried her head in his chest, allowing her tears to flow and her emptiness to fill.

They talked till dusk when Raphela had to return home. The day gave them a rare and eternal friendship, one with no rules, no bounds. This first day they shared memories, opened and healed some old wounds. Sexually, they lived in a fantasy land exploring things only lovers can do.

One afternoon as Raphela prepared for a visit to Nabus, unusual sounds drew her outside her father's shop. As she looked up, a man passed by-- tall, lean, bordering harsh. Although he didn't see Raphela, a silent electricity passed between them and Raphela stood frozen, staring. After a moment, she grabbed her father.

"Papa, who was that?"

"That was Duke Ishtba and I fear he would disapprove of your gaping." Goran pulled her back.

"Nonsense Papa, I'll stare at who I choose."

Goran just shook his head.

"I'll see you later Papa."

"Raphela, wait, for just one minute." Goran studied his child, I don't know what you do, but please, be careful."

"I am." She kissed his cheek and went on her way.

The walk to Nabus' shop seemed never-ending, so her arrival was marked by a slam of the door that was followed by arms around Nabus' neck and a sensual kiss planted on his surprised lips. When Raphela finally released him, their arms were still wrapped about each other.

The glow of excitement flushed her face, tingling Nabus' senses and curiosity. "All right Raphela, what is it, what happened?"

She took a deep breath. "I saw a man today."

"Who?

"The Duke, Duke Ishtba."

"Oh." Although Raphela had said little, Nabus felt jealous, even though he knew he had no right.

"Please Nabus, don't be upset. Share this with me."

"He didn't answer, so she began to speak. While she talked, Nabus watched and listened, but like bees to flowers he was drawn to touch. Raphela had no objections. Nabus made love to a woman experiencing her first taste of lust, and Raphela rolled in the covers with a tall lean stranger with piercing eyes.

As they lay in bed, their physical love exhausted, Raphela began her interrogation. "Nabus, you must tell me all about him. How old is he? Is he married? Does he have any children?"

"Slow down. I know you're excited, but why haven't you asked before?"

Raphela calmed down and grew thoughtful. I suppose, until today, he was a name, almost a myth. Today he became real."

"Good point. Well, first, he is about 27 or 28. Second, as far as I know, he is not married, nor does he have any children. But it's hard to tell. Unlike Duke Ulfan, he is extremely private. But if he were to wed, someone in town would have known. A new wife would have required something, cloth, furniture, things.

Raphela nodded her head, listening, and planning. Nabus knew and reluctantly he did not intervene. She dressed, kissed him on the cheek and left.

By the next morning her plans had taken shape. Every merchant knew of Raphela's new project. She dug and scraped for knowledge, but with no more or less fervor than any other time. The men laughed. What would she do with all she learned? But not one refused her a morsel of information.

Only Nabus could guess what she had in mind and even he only had vague outlines.

He watched as Raphela approached his shop. The fall air blew her hair like a banner, and even through the heavy clothes her figure was impressive.

As she entered he placed warm a cup of tea in her hand, she sipped it slowly allowing the heat to remove the tingle from her cold fingers. Her cheeks at first raw with the cold grew rosy with the warmth.

With every passing moment Nabus inched toward her, only to jerk himself back. Raphela stared at the floor.

"It's cold today." She forced the words even as the tears streamed down her face.

Nabus held back no more, holding her tight. "My love, please, please, seeing you cry..."

She sniffed and they rubbed tear stained cheeks. "What you said was right. I needed to learn the pain of friendship. And I hate seeing you so sad. But, it's time."

"I know." And he did know for she was beginning to take control and he couldn't stop it.

"Nabus, you taught me well. I think we both passed." She smiled weakly. He nodded, and she continued. "You will always be with me and I with you, no matter where we are."

Nabus swore the winds warmed as she spoke and they embraced sharing a whispered "I love you."

Raphela did not return for some time, it was more than either of them could bear.

Two years later Raphela was still unattached when most women her age had a child. Her sisters were engaged or wed. Raphela spent her days working for her father, apparently undisturbed by her situation. She remained friendly with the merchants, whom she questioned especially those who traveled. So, on the day she stopped Sarek, one of those traveling merchants neither he nor her father thought much of it.

She broached him outside her father's shop.

"Hello Sarek, how are you today?"

"Fine Raphela, and you?"

"Fine."

"Is that all you can ask? He laughed at the commonplace exchange. I'm disappointed."

"Raphela pulled him away from the shop, her eyes hard and determined. "No, I have one more. Will you take me to Castle Cordan?"

"Raphela, I'm afraid you're investigating is going to far. The Castle is not Milson." He reacted almost as a father would, especially one familiar with the Castle, where he sold goods. And knew it was not a place with a welcome sign painted on the front door.

"I don't go there to investigate, I go there to live."

"To what?" He asked sure his ears had deceived him.

"To live."

"Raphela, you would not make a good serving girl. Sarek couldn't imagine any other possibility for her existence there.

"Sarek, you are a good man, but you can't see. I have no intentions of being a serving girl, I plan to be the Duke's concubine."

He laughed. "Oh well that's a different story, of course. Just walk in and say Here I am your lordship, your new concubine." His sarcasm was kind, but he continued. "Besides the fact that he already has quite a few, I haven't heard of any that are that excited about holding that position."

"Good," she said, "less competition for me."

"Raphela, you're serious."

"Yes, I am."

"You shouldn't feel so desperate, you'll find a husband." Sarek patted her shoulder sympathetically. He could only believe his thoughts, why else would she go.

"Desperate? Desperate!" She controlled a sneer. "Sarek, I am not desperate. I have received more proposals than any of my sisters, none of which would I allow my father to accept. For him I am sorry." Her tone softened. "I made plans for my life long ago. The time has come to put those plans in motion."

Sarek's mind reeled as he began to understand and it frightened him.

36

"Raphela, I don't think you know what you're getting into. The Duke is not like other people, he will not bend to your will because you smile at him."

"I know. All the more reason I wish to go." Her arrogance subsided and the rational woman took control. "Sarek, there is no life here I wish to live."

"But at least you know you'll"

Raphela finished his sentence. "Stay alive. Perhaps, but it is not worth the frustration. I know some of the chances I'm taking, the others I will learn. So please, take me."

"What about your father? He'll never forgive me."

"That's a weak point and you know it. He knows you would never volunteer for such a thing."

"True, but what excuse to arrive with you?

Raphela smiled, produced a gray scarf and covered her head and face. "I am a gift for the Lord Duke Ishtba, for so many years of being a good customer. Certainly that is not that unusual."

Sarek lowered his head. "No, it's not, though I have never...."

Raphela would hear no more arguments. "Let's go, now. My father will not be back for a few more minutes and I will not torture him with good-byes."

Midafternoon turned to dusk as Sarek and Raphela entered Castle Cordan.

Chapter 3

Sarek presented a veiled and fully covered Raphela to the Duke. Atan Ishtba was curious, he received few gifts of this sort. He did not start with the body, but his hands reached for the veil, which he brushed aside. To his surprise he was met not by the eyes of property, but the face of a willing temptress. The veil was not lowered immediately.

As he let those eyes go, he thanked Sarek who breathed a quiet sigh of relief. She at least had a chance. Fatell who had already been summoned awaited orders.

"Fatell, dress her properly and then take her to my chambers."

"Yes m'lord."

Fatell brought Raphela to the concubines' rooms where the women lounged comfortably comparing and sharing experiences. Raphela was noticed and given more than the usual attention, though no one spoke to her. Fatell dressed her and delivered her as ordered.

When Fatell returned alone she was surrounded by the others.

"Does she have any idea of what awaits her?"

"Somehow Sonja, I think she does," Fatell answered, thinking of the young woman she had just sent to her master.

"Well, I for one don't envy her." Sonja was young, her words concerned, not bitter.

"That's true," another agreed.

Sarina leaned forward as she brushed her hair. "I don't know what you girls are so upset about, he's really not so bad." Sarina threw her hair over her shoulder and smoothed her eyebrows.

Marquesa shook her head. "Sarina, you fear him as much as any of us do. You're simply afraid to admit it."

"I am not," she pouted. "Anyway, who are you to talk about being afraid, considering that monster Mahtso you and Fatell sleep with."

"We all have our interests. And the last time the Duke took you, you shook when you slept and that was after downing a decanter of wine."

"I was tired and thirsty. He is energetic."

Marquesa lost patience. "Energetic, yes. And before you say it, no he's not cruel. But his power grows every day and consumes anyone near him."

"You don't know what you're talking about. It was all the answer Sarina could muster, but the conversations continued on into the night.

While the women talked, Raphela waited in the Duke's outer chamber. When he arrived, Atan Ishtba marched right past her, closing his inner door. A few moments passed, the door opened and Duke Ishtba motioned for her to enter. He waited and closed the door behind her.

No words were exchanged at first. Raphela felt no tension, what this man would want or do was a total mystery, one she enjoyed.

Then it began, with her hair. He brushed against it and the scent only he noticed waved through his senses. "And what brings you to me?" he asked.

"I am a gift my lord." Her eyes were downcast, but her voice held a note of amusement.

"And, who gives the gift?" He played the game.

"Why Sarek, my lord," she paused for a moment, "upon my request." Raphela met his eyes.

"Your request?! You wish to be a Duke's property?" His fascination deepened.

"It is certainly better than being pauper's property, my lord." Raphela stood by the bed where he sat. She controlled the urge to lean towards him.

"Perhaps, yet one as lovely as yourself should have been wed by now." He stroked her hair.

"Most men in my village found me to be too troublesome."

"You speak honestly." He stood and spoke gravely. "Do you know the consequences if I find you to be too troublesome?"

"Yes my lord, I do." Her face told him she understood.

"Does death not frighten you?" His body responded to this bold creature, it warmed and his pulse quickened. "What does frighten you?" His hands studied her form.

After a moment's consideration she answered, "I can think of nothing at this time, sire."

"Perhaps that will change."

"Yes my lord." Raphela smiled, her eyes beckoned for him to continue his touch.

No encouragement was needed, yet she purred to his caress. When he stopped for a moment to look at what was before him, she spoke. "My lord, may I remove your robe?"

He nodded and Raphela gently slid the robe off and they both lay on the bed. Her hands caressed skin exposed to all weathers. She could picture his back facing a winter storm with no shield between it and the biting snow. As Atan lay back, Raphela's body leaned on him, every muscle supporting her with ease. Her hands explored and traversed and tingled with each touch. Finally her eyes having soaked in his form, met his face, a dark thin face, framed with straight black hair. And as their eyes met, time froze. They were not two lovers, young and infatuated, or even two sexual mates overcome by lust, but two generals, analyzing, learning. For an instant, they allowed their power to pass between them. It ended with a kiss so electric, all control was gone.

With her hair wrapped around his hand and her breasts pressing against his chest the kiss broke. Control was back and he took it. "Tell me your name!" He commanded.

"Raphela, my lord," came the unintimidated reply.

"Raphela." He rolled it over in his mind. "Raphela, you are a different sort of woman."

She did not answer. The conversation of words rolled into conversation of the skin. The small flame of interest grew to a blaze. Atan's hands explored her body and pressed down and around her thighs. She responded with a nibble and her hand on his, sliding it with him.

Atan stopped, surprised at the move and almost angry. "Does that not please you?"

41

"My lord, it pleases me a great deal, I simply want more of it."

Before he could reply, she found his lips and received no argument. The passion rolled and completed itself with a great deal more than simple satisfaction as the end result.

After the interrogation from the concubines Fatell headed back to her room.

As she walked a figure appeared at the stairs. She smiled. "Mahtso, were you looking for me or him?"

"Well, I was looking for a sweet little thing to share some time with me." His blue eyes, filled with a playful stare, brought her close.

"I think I can help."

They walked hand in hand to her room.

"So my love, tell me of this new woman our Duke has found." Mahtso caressed her hand.

"Different. " Fatell kept the stare of her love as she spoke. "I believe she was not only unafraid, but anxious to meet him."

"That will change," Mahtso purred in her ear.

"Perhaps."

As usual Atan breakfasted in the small dining room on the family level. Steam from the teapot rose and filled the air with the pungent aroma of munden spice. Atan's feet stretched out beside the table and his back angled in the chair. He sipped the tea, almost unaware that it was in his hand.

Mahtso saw him like this and smiled. "Good morning Atan."

"Oh, good morning Mahtso. Sit down."

Mahtso poured himself some tea. "I understand you received a gift last night."

"Yes I did." Atan was oblivious.

Mahtso's smile faded. "She seems to have made a deep impression."

"Yes she did."

Raphela rose with the sun. After finding a robe she quietly passed the other women, still sleeping and strolled about the castle's lower level, until she bumped into Fatell.

"Well child, are you an early riser?"

"Yes"

Both women hedged, wanting to continue, but unsure. Fatell followed her feelings. "Come, join me for some tea in the kitchen. The cooks are just waking, we'll have a few minutes."

The kitchen was quiet, as Fatell had said. She set cups of hot drink on the table and found some sweetcakes from the day before. Raphela warmed her hands on the cup and Fatell nibbled at a cake.

"Did you sleep well Raphela?"

"Yes, quite. The bed was comfortable, and the other women were asleep when I arrived." She fought blurting out her thoughts. *Not yet, only if she asks*.

Fatell touched her hand. "It's all right child if he frightened you. You can tell me. I understand." No pillow could have been softer and no pillar stronger or more reliable than Fatell's voice.

"Frightened? Oh no Fatell, I am not frightened." Raphela beamed and leaned close to Fatell. "Never have I met any one so exciting, so powerful, so complex. He's like a finely woven cloth, laden with color and texture. But not frightening," Raphela stopped and considered, "at least not to me."

Fatell smiled easily. "I thought you might feel that way."

Three weeks passed with many a night finding Raphela in Atan's quarter's. Finally one morning while Atan breakfasted he called for Mahtso. Atan finished his tea as Mahtso entered.

"What can I do for you?" Mahtso was distant.

"I'll tell you, but sit down and tell me what's bothering you."

"It's my business." Mahtso stared at the walls, his chain slipping through his fingers quicker than a rabbit's heartbeat.

"As I suspected. Hmmm." Atan wanted to be severe, but his mood was too good. "It's Raphela, isn't it?"

Mahtso didn't answer. Atan sensed a danger level and a jealousy he wouldn't have expected.

"Am I right?"

"Yes, it's Raphela. She spends so much time with you." Atan swore he heard a whine in Mahtso's voice.

"Didn't you tell me to find a woman?"

"Yes, but..." Mahtso shook his head.

43

"Mahtso, calm down and listen. Raphela is different and I enjoy that. But I too feel the need for caution. I'd like you to investigate."

Mahtso leapt from the table and cut Atan's words. "I'll bring her downstairs right now."

Atan let only a fraction of his anger show. "Sit down!"

"Yes." Mahtso lowered his head like a naughty puppy.

"I said investigate, not interrogate. She has substance and though I believe she could withstand your queries, I'd rather not chance it. Go to Milson; see if she really is who and what she claims. Keep it simple and gentle."

"As you wish." He rose to go, feeling empty.

"Mahtso wait." Atan now felt obligated to express thoughts and feelings so hard for him.

"You are my friend. That will not change. I don't know who or what she is, but she obviously has struck a chord I cannot ignore. But it will not change our friendship. Do you understand?"

Mahtso nodded, embarrassed at his outburst of jealousy. "I'll find the truth."

While Mahtso spent his time in Milson, Raphela continued to learn about life in the harem. In the four bedrooms, dining room, and gossip hall, Raphela learned the Duke had never spent an entire night with any woman, including herself. He had no children.

Fatell, though never in the Duke's room, was responsible for the women. She was a small woman, usually bent over as if guarding a secret. Although about the same age as the Duke, she seemed years older. Coarse graying hair surrounded a plain face whose eyes tried to hide the sadness within. She was treated with the respect she deserved.

Then there was Marquesa, experienced and strong, Sonja, young, naive and a few others. But Sarina, treated Fatell like a servant and Raphela like poison. On this particular afternoon the venom was evident as always.

"So tell me Raphela what potion do you pour in his wine?" Sarina brushed her hair and faced the wall as she spoke.

"I don't understand Sarina, what potion? Raphela feigned no innocence; she honestly did not comprehend Sarina's thought.

"Don't put on an act, the potion you use to make him take you so often to the point of neglecting us.

Raphela felt all eyes turn to her and pushed away the sudden uneasiness. She leaned back into the pillows and crossed her hands calmly on her chest. "I need no potion to hold his interest. I am sufficient by myself."

Sarina wheeled, putting her face an inch away from Raphela's. "Liar! You drug him, you must." The hairbrush slammed on a table. "And I will prove it!" Raphela rose like a queen turning on a disobedient servant, Her eyes meeting Sarina's as she began a slow walk that pushed Sarina against a nearby wall. Raphela's left arm pressed Sarina's shoulders against the flat surface and her right hand pulled a small blade from her bodice. Its point tickled Sarina's white and trembling throat. Raphela sneered. "I've had no quarrel with you Sarina, but you are becoming a nuisance. Should you irritate me too much, I'll slit your throat as if I were crushing a fly."

Sarina's eyes begged the women for support.

Someone shifted but Marquesa motioned for the group to stay still.

Raphela didn't need to look around to assess the situation. "And I don't think there would be an over-abundance of grief at your loss. Do you understand me?"

Sarina froze wide-eyed.

"Just nod dear." Raphela ran the blade under Sarina's ear as the woman forced her head up and down.

"That's better. Now go back and brush your hair, it's gotten all messed up."

Raphela backed away, replacing the blade, in her bodice as Sarina slinked to her table and began stroking her hair, mumbling something about revenge. One of the women tried to soothe her but was quickly shoved away.

Raphela decided to go for a walk. As she headed out the harem door Marquesa followed, not stopping her until they were well out of earshot of the others.

"Are you all right?"

45

Raphela leaned against the wall, trying not to tremble. "I'll be fine, thank you."

Marquesa looked her over. "You're a strong one. If Fatell had been there, it would never have gone that far."

"I know, it's good that she wasn't." Raphela was grateful for the experienced woman's shoulder, she seemed to understand.

"Now child, where did you get that knife and why do you carry it?"

Raphela touched the blade for reassurance and smiled. "I bought it in town years ago since I had a tendency to be out by myself lot. As far as here is concerned, I'm not sure, except maybe that I'm not quite home yet."

"I have a feeling you'll know soon enough. Under normal circumstances I'd say our good Duke would offer a verbal reprimand or even turn you over to Mahtso. Somehow I think you'll be treated a bit differently. Now come back to the room and relax."

Marquesa and Raphela walked back arm in arm. Raphela stopped before the doorway. "Marquesa, how will the Duke find out?" Raphela wasn't really afraid, but certainly curious.

Marquesa smiled. "Mahtso will tell him."

"Who's going to tell Mahtso?"

"As a favor to you, I will."

Raphela entered the harem and though she could see the respect and tinge of fear in the women; she couldn't help but wonder what reaction her action would elicit from the Duke

The next day Mahtso returned from town and reported to Atan.

"Sit down Mahtso." Atan pointed to a nearby chair.

The library was uncomfortably quiet for Mahtso as he joined Atan, and his chain circled his fingers in broken rhythm.

"You have a report on Raphela?"

"I've learned what I could."

"You sound disappointed." Atan felt his palms moisten.

"She is all she claims to be, born and raised in Milson, well traveled within town limits, but no further, except for her talks with strangers."

"This disturbs you. Why?" Atan never discounted Mahtso's instincts.

"She also knows how to read and write. It seems so wrong." Mahtso's chain wound faster.

Atan leaned back and controlled a smile. "She has not wasted her intelligence."

"That is true." The chain struck the table at a quickening pace.

"You think she's a spy?" Atan bated.

"I'm not sure." The chain stopped. "But I could verify." Mahtso felt the saliva reach the corners of his mouth. Atan did not need to see it fall to know how the man felt.

"No, my friend. Though she could possibly withstand your, verification, I do not wish to risk leaving a shell where a woman once existed."

"As you wish." Mahtso moped.

"Anyway, you don't really believe she's a spy."

Mahtso sighed. "You're right."

Atan changed the subject. "By the way, how is she faring with the women?"

"Funny you should ask." Mahtso's chain returned to a slow steady rate as he repeated Marquesa's tale.

"Raphela handled it well, wouldn't you say?" Atan did his best to hide his pride.

"Yes she did." Mahtso felt icy and insecure. The chain tightened around his hand.

"Go get her, it's time I made some changes."

Mahtso did as required and for no particular reason walked with her back to Atan's quarters. Though he clung to his jealousy, Mahtso felt it slipping through his fingers. Raphela's beauty and intelligence aside, he sensed a quality that eased him.

Raphela took the opportunity to consider Mahtso. He had a firm comfortable gait, but seemed ready for anything. The man's thick legs and body reminded her of the strong oaks that withstood the harshest winters. When they reached Atan's rooms, he turned to her. He neither smiled nor frowned. His thick sandy hair, tied neatly behind his head, did not interfere with his eyes, and there lay his tale. Raphela saw the inner turbulence, a violent storm of two souls locked in an eternal raging battle. To be his friend was imperative to her goals, but she also wanted his friendship.

As he walked away Raphela was drawn to the chain that swung from his hand and recurrently tapped his leg. She realized it had been doing so during the entire trip.

In the midst of this fascination Atan appeared. "Raphela, come in."

It took her a moment to respond and Atan realized the object of her interest. "Does the chain disturb you?" Raphela shook her head, still in thought. "No m'lord, it's not disturbing."

"Then what?" Atan guided her to a seat in his chamber.

"Sire, it's a mystery. There must be a reason he carries it, I just can't understand its significance."

Atan sighed, but was glad that Raphela was curious and not upset.

"Mahtso possesses some less than socially acceptable quirks to his personality, as I'm sure you've heard. These characteristics had a tendency to display themselves in an unsavory fashion, such as the dissection of live insects during the course of a conversation. So, I gave him the chain to occupy his hands and it has also come to serve as a good indicator of his mood."

"I think I understand sire."

Atan studied her eyes; Raphela understood. "Good, now for the reason I brought you here today. It has come to my attention that you can read and write."

"That is true my lord." Raphela smiled with broad satisfaction.

"Why do you smile?" He made a weak attempt at anger.

"I'm honored sire."

"Honored, at what?"

"That you would take so much time and trouble to find out about me."

"Time and trouble?"

"Yes m'lord. This information was not spilled by anyone at the Castle, as no one here has known this, until now." As her elbows rested on the table she exercised great effort not to lean towards him and he, in turn, forced his hands in his lap.

But their eyes indulged in what their hands wouldn't do.

Atan nodded to certify that her assumption was correct, and then stood. "Now that we have established that your skills exist, they will be put to use."

He went on to describe the bookkeeping tasks he wished her to perform. She listened intently, this was business and both took it seriously.

When he finished, Raphela could say little. She hoped her face did not expose her exuberance at the opportunity. "I'll do my best sire." She rose to go.

Atan watched her hair flowing across her back as she approached the doorway.

"Raphela." It was a croaked whisper, but she spun to face him.

"Yes my lord." Expectation and curiosity played in her eyes.

He didn't look up at first. "Raphela have you ever ridden a ramek?"

"No sire."

"Would you like to try?" Now his eyes met hers and despite all efforts, the twinge of fear that she would refuse swept through him.

Raphela's face lit and she swore her heart beat hard enough to show through her gown. "Oh yes my lord, that would be wonderful."

"Good" Atan regained his composure. "Be at the stables at dawn. Oh, have Fatell find something suitable for you to wear."

"Yes my lord."

Raphela controlled her walk as she left, doing her best to hide her excitement. Atan stared blankly at the book in his hands and let his mind wander.

As the moons left their last rays in the sky Raphela rose from an anxious sleep. She rubbed her eyes and noticed a small form checking the clothes that had been laid out for her. The form moved, took a seat and sipped a drink.

As Raphela moved close, she realized that Fatell was sitting at the nearby table.

"What are you doing here?" Raphela asked.

"Just making last minute preparations." Even in the dark, Raphela could see Fatell blush.

Raphela smiled. "As long as you're here, why don't you help me, I've never worn men's clothes before."

Fatell gladly assisted the young woman, tightening the pants as best as possible.

"Why are you here Fatell?" Raphela asked again.

"It?s my job." Fatell attempted an official tone.

"It's above and beyond. You fawn me over as if I were a child. There's no need. So why?"

"Perhaps because the Duke favors you so."

Raphela pressed the point no further just gave Fatell a kiss on the cheek and a whispered thank you.

"How do I look?" Raphela's hands held her hips as she posed.

"Lovely, as always." Still, she straightened Raphela's hair, one last time. "Have you ever been near a ramek?"

"Once or twice. Why?"

" I know you're brave, but these are beasts, not people. They are difficult to handle, even for many men."

"So I've heard."

"A long time ago, Mahtso told me that if the reins did not control the animal, pulling its mane would, or so he says. Fatell tried to believe the words, yet the fear inside rose as she envisioned the young woman near the beasts.

"Thank you, but don't worry. I'm sure the beasties and I will come to understand each other." Raphela's voice changed and Fatell sensed a power that comforted her.

"I'll try not to, now hurry up, the sun is about to show its face."

"Yes mother." Raphela teased.

Atan arrived at the stables first, allowing time for a brief inspection. All the stalls were filled with clean, dry grass. The animals were well groomed and on each stall hung reins and a saddle.

Casually he examined the rameks, choosing one here and there for a closer check. Soon he returned to his steed, the largest of the herd. Its chin lowered and brushed against the top of Atan's head. Atan stroked the long brown neck feeling muscles strong and tight as the sword by his side. Slowly Atan led the animal from its stall, its bony legs holding the solid body with ease. The beasts were not domesticated, barely tamed, Duke Atan Ishtba felt at ease with the animals.

While Atan studied his ramek, the door cracked open and Raphela slipped in. She took a quick survey of the barn. She found the odor that most people called stench, surprisingly inoffensive and shared Atan's perception of it as the essence of wild and powerful steeds.

Atan motioned for Raphela to approach and noticed with appreciation how feminine she looked in men's attire. "Raphela, you'll ride with me. We can share a beast."

"As you wish m'lord."

While they waited for the stable man to find a larger saddle Raphela strolled around and brushed against the steed Atan held. Atan's hand jerked her away from it, despite the fact that instead of trying to chomp on her flesh, it ignored her.

Raphela knew the animals to be fierce, but saw no reason for his reaction.

"I'm sorry my lord, I don't think I caused any damage."

Atan let her go, and lowered his head a moment before looking in her eyes. "Raphela, do you think me that cold?"

"Cold, sire?" Cold was a side of him that Raphela saw, but never personally experienced.

"That I would be more concerned for a beast than the woman about to ride it?"

Raphela smiled. "M'lord, you are not cold, at least not to me."

"Then why react as you did? You are not in the habit of donning false modesty."

"Sire, I know you favor me above the other women, but I do not presume to be of greater worth than appearances allow. The rameks are very valuable. Also, I noticed you have a personal liking for them. You almost treat them with affection. I confess

51

to sneaking down and watching you on occasion." She cracked open his locked emotions, and let a bit of musty air to escape.

"You're very observant, but you may believe that in this instance, I am more concerned about you than the beast." Atan toyed with her hair and whispered. "Tell me, why do other women cower at my glance, yet you blossom at my touch?"

Raphela pulled his hand away, kissed and held it. "My lord, other women fear your power, but I, if I may be so bold as to say. I like it. It excites me."

"Other men have had power, and more than I, yet they have not frightened people." Atan felt his soul stretch out a shaky hand.

"I have read the stories of the great kings and generals, you are different. At best they struggled with power to keep it from controlling them. You, my lord, just as you handle the rameks with strength and compassion, take power as a friend; even bend it to your will. Other men do not take it to bed, for fear that their women will use it too. But it is a fine bedmate for you, and I don't mind sharing." Raphela glowed as she spoke and Atan found her insight a comforting and exhilarating reminder of his power. They felt the need to touch and their hands met in an unconscious gesture.

"You know much about me, for one who has been here such a short time," he said.

Raphela blushed and smiled. At that moment the stableman could be heard turning the corner. They released hands; such a romantic stance did not befit public view for the Duke.

When the saddle was strapped on, Atan mounted and Raphela joined him with the help of the stableman. They took off slowly, but once Atan felt Raphela was secure, he let the beast go at full speed, partially because he wanted to, and also because he wanted to test her, she held fast.

They rode until the castle was well out of sight and with it every other sign of civilization. Atan stopped by a tree and tied the animal to it. Raphela dismounted without help and surveyed the grassy meadow where the morning dew filled her nostrils with its fresh scent. A semi-circle of trees provided a natural fence to protect the rainbow of flowers that dotted the landscape.

52

The air was cool and clear and the land beckoned to those with vitality and strength to become a part of it.

Raphela and Atan found their ride intoxicating. Neither spoke. Atan took her hand and they walked, occasionally stopping to share a view. Never before had Atan Ishtba been so relaxed with anyone. Raphela silently echoed the feeling.

After a time, Atan realized that Raphela had flowers in her arms, so many that she began to put them in her hair.

"I didn't know that you were so fond of my "jewels of the soil."

"What?" Her eyes were taking in the clouds and she heard only half the words.

"The flowers, "jewels of the soil", was a term my mother used."

"It's a beautiful way of saying it, and yes I do like them. The colors are so vibrant."

"Perhaps a few around the castle would brighten it up?" *Did I read your mind*, he hoped? To please her felt right.

"Oh yes! Large obenums for the hall, gold cloudbursts for your anteroom, green beast teeth for . . ."

"Enough, I'll have the gardener get what you like." He laughed, whirled her around, and kissed her in the joy of the day.

Raphela felt his soul touch hers and she radiated what they shared. When he put her down she took his hands and spoke.

"My lord,.." she hesitated.

"What? What do you want?" At that moment he wished to honor all her desires.

"My lord, may I ride the ramek? Alone."

"Alone?! That's very dangerous." Though taken aback the idea excited him.

"Oh please sire, it would be such an adventure for me." Her eyes searched his and pleaded for a yes.

Atan held her hair in his hands while he considered and did not refuse her gaze. "All right, should I help you mount."

"Yes, oh thank you my lord." Raphela hugged him and planted a girlish kiss on his cheek. He blushed.

He handed her the reins. "Go slowly, at least at first."

She listened, taking the beast in circles for a while, but once her confidence grew, Raphela let all inhibitions go. She rode as if born to it and Atan watched, his skin tingling with excitement. She held the ramek, but did not cling and guided it with little trouble.

Raphela felt strong and free, as if a ton of chains had been lifted off her spirit and the wind blushed her cheeks and waved her hair like a flag. She rode until her breath was all but gone, she returned to the waiting Atan Ishtba. She thought` "So strong, so different, why do I tingle at the mere thought of him?"

When she arrived at the tree, he helped her off and tied the animal to it. "Raphela, you ride like an experienced warrior." A rare broad smile joined the words.

"Thank you my lord," she breathed heavily. "We communicated, the beast and I."

Atan realized that she had. Rameks understood only one thing; power and this woman had it.

"You look exuberant." He said, skin tingling.

"You make me feel it, m'lord." Truth was truth.

A sudden somber look came upon his face. "Tell me Raphela, if I were to lose my power, would you be so energetic?"

"You could no more lose your power, than the sky could lose the sun."

"Yet if I did?"

"She wrapped her arms around his waist, pulled herself close to him and her voice demanded that his eyes meet hers. "I would be terribly sad, for you are your power and it is you, it cannot be lost or chased away or stolen."

He took her face in his hands and kissed it hard, the kiss melting into a warm secure embrace.

Without a word they rode back to the castle. Raphela nearly ran to the women's quarters where Fatell anxiously awaited her return.

"Raphela, you smell of animals, go bathe." Fatell issued the good-natured order and wrinkled her nose as she disposed of Raphela's riding clothes.

54

Raphela laid back in a warm tub, caring little about the odor, only concentrating on the pleasant ache she was beginning to experience.

"And, how was the ride?" Fatell let the question blurt out.

"Oh Fatell, it was great, fantastic." Raphela sat up splashing water on the other woman.

Fatell stepped back holding out a towel. Raphela's fingers grasped the soft full cloth. "You know, Sarina was brought to see them once. She was so frightened that the beast roared beyond control and she had to leave."

"If you handle them properly they're fine and the land is, magnificent." Raphela beamed.

"I know, we live in a lovely place." Fatell smiled while Raphela dried her hair and dressed. "The Duke tries to keep it that way."

"He is an unusual man." Raphela's voice relayed more affection than she intended.

"I imagine you will get to know him well."

"Perhaps."

While Raphela dressed, Mahtso met with the Duke in one of the meeting rooms. "Here are the books Atan. Tell me, how did she do? "

Atan stood up and walked around, a twinkle in his eye. "Mahtso, she rode by herself, at full gallop." He spoke with pride.

"She pleases you a great deal, doesn't she?"

"That she does. Not only does she not fear my touch, she welcomes it, with a warmth and power of her own."

Mahtso studied his friend; the man was alive, so much of his emptiness filled.

"It's good to see you like this."

"It is good to be like this. For the first time in my life I feel as if I'm not alone."

Mahtso smiled and the ever present chain hung motionless in his hand.

A few moments later Raphela joined them and learned her duties. The basic act of bookkeeping was a simple task that Raphela mastered quickly. She took it upon herself to ask for new responsibilities, which the Duke let slip easily from his hands to hers. She began to keep an eye on all castle business, whether assigned to her or not.

One such domain was the food supply. She observed deliveries many times, noting who the merchants were and how they handled the transactions, as well as how Rabi, the head cook, handled the situations. When she saw a possible discrepancy, not in the Duke's favor, she would bring it to Rabi's attention. Rabi took her advice and found it useful. Mahtso, perhaps intentionally, perhaps not, listened in.

"Rabi, the grain merchant will be coming today, right?"

Raphela helped him move some pots while she spoke. Rabi unconsciously accepted the assistance. "Yes, so what?"

"I believe he has a problem with weights, perhaps you should check his bags." Raphela could not come out and call the man a thief, though she felt he was one.

"Thank you, I will." Rabi handed her a last pan and she left.

Mahtso waited for the grain merchant and as Raphela suspected his goods were not as described. Rabi corrected him and Mahtso, developed a new respect for this unusual woman.

As the weeks passed, Raphela's position solidified in the business of Ishtba and with the Duke personally. The night before he chose to ride with her again, they both found sleep elusive.

He lay on his back and stared at the ceiling. "Tomorrow I'll see her again. It's terribly confusing. Raphela is an addiction. What end will this lead to? Addiction and these thoughts are equally dangerous; both are as difficult to control as Raphela. But not dangerous enough to make me stop, yet."

Raphela wrapped herself in a blanket and ignored the women around her. "These weeks have been like living a dream, each day something new. It's been three days since I've seen him, I should be satisfied. Yet the more time we spend together, the more I want, it makes no sense. To be the chosen lady-- I want it now more than ever. But something stops him, and me, but what?"

The morning came and they rode. Atan felt his power flow and even balloon, his occasional glance at Raphela, now on her own steed, increased his feelings as he drank from her free spirit.

Once the beasts were tied, Atan held out his hands to Raphela. "Come here woman, I want you." The good-natured command enticed her, but a devilish glint came to her eyes. He wanted her, but how much? She sought the answer with the same single-mindedness that had brought her life to that point.

"Come and get me." She ran to the open field, every step increasing their desire. He pinned her to the grass after a short run.

Victory and lust shone in her eyes as his body pressed against hers. *He wants me, enough to chase; I am more than a bedwench or secretary.*

Atan watched the rise and fall of her chest as she caught her breath and looked in her eyes. Her reverie was broken by the back of his hand, hard across her cheek. "I don't like the look in your eyes." The harsh cold Duke was here. He rose and walked away.

The stunned woman leaned on her elbows and rubbed her cheek, in confusion.

She knew she had somehow stepped beyond her bounds, she responded, apologetically, but without subservience.

"I am sorry my lord, I shall remember who and what I am."

He did his best to ignore the cold words. "Yes you shall." He kept his back to her.

Raphela could not be that still. "Would you have me whimper and grovel as the others do? I wish to be a woman for you, not a trained animal."

Damn you woman he thought, *why must you be like this*

"You will be what I . . .he turned as he spoke and found her naked and vulnerable . . . "wish you to be," he finished softly.

Raphela took a step closer, as did Atan and he wrapped his arms around her. They exhausted an angry lust under the warm sun.

Their differences were left unsolved, while each wondered why, they could not resist the other's touch long enough to win the point.

57

Despite any misgivings, Atan continued to spend time with Raphela. After a few more weeks, he opened another avenue of his life for her to share.

The sun warmed Atan as he and Mahtso walked around Castle Cordan, and the flowers had begun to peek through the soil.

"Well Mahtso, do you think he will be a problem?"

Mahtso's face beamed desire, "No, the battle should be easy."

"I agree." They walked in silence until the front doors shadowed over them. "Tonight Raphela will join us for dinner." Atan said.

Earlier in the year Mahtso's chain would have beat his leg black and blue, but now it ran lazily through his fingers. "A good idea. I'm sure she'll be pleasant company."

Atan looked at the buds breaking through the ground. "Indeed."

Mahtso found Fatell quickly.

"You there, the lovely wench, come here." His eyes lit when she approached.

She giggled and warmed inside. "What is it you want of me?"

Mahtso held her tight. "What I want of you will have to wait. Our Duke wants Raphela to dine with him, so prepare her."

"Easier said than done."

"I know, but inform her."

"That's better. He's really taken with Raphela."

"Yes, perhaps more than he realizes." A cloud momentarily passed over Mahtso's face.

"And she with him."

"Good. Now, we both better get to work."

They kissed good-bye and headed to their duties. Fatell found Raphela pouring over some book and dragged her to a private dressing room.

"Fatell, I was really trying to learn something. What is so important?" Raphela did not hide her irritation well.

Fatell shook her head. "The Lord Duke Atan Ishtba requires your presence at dinner tonight."

Raphela froze. "Dinner, with him? Are you serious?"

"Yes." Fatell laughed and proceeded to find a dress appropriate for the occasion.

Raphela thought for a minute. "This is important, isn't it?"

Fatell didn't bother to look up. "I suppose. The only person he's dined with since his parents' deaths is Mahtso." Fatell pulled out an exotic violet gown, sheer and tempting.

Raphela took a look and cast it aside. "Not tonight. "She chose a conservative deep red gown, low cut, but not showy.

"Raphela, you are not the lady of Castle Cordan. What I have chosen, fits your station." Fatell knew it was futile to argue, but she felt required to attempt to hold her ground.

"I will not be a harlot at dinner, at least not from the neck down. From the neck up I will reek of sensuality."

Fatell shook her head. "Raphela, when Duke Ulfan had a concubine, she dressed in what was chosen. Why not you?'

"Duke Ulfan had a wife, Duke Atan does not." Raphela held the red gown in front of her.

"Surely you don't plan to play the role of wife?" Even Raphela could not be so bold, or so Fatell thought.

"Why not? Part wife, part aide, part temptress." To Raphela it was a matter of fact, to Fatell it was playing with fire.

"You walk a thin line. The Duke will certainly read the message of your dress. It would not be difficult for him to think you too presumptuous."

The red dress was laid carefully on a chair and Raphela rested her fingers on Fatell's shoulders. "I take many risks to get what I want. I try to include some safety factors, like being a concubine with my face. I have plans. The Duke is a powerful, intelligent and interesting man, to be by his side, would be, well . . . I think you understand. If you help me, I'll always be there for you. If you fight me, then I'll just use you. I would like you on my side."

Fatell saw Raphela was attempting to gain a great deal more than matrimony, and found it compelling. "I like you. You're honest and direct. I'd be honored to help. Anyway, the Duke seems to be opening the path for you, so let's make it a pretty one."

59

"Thank you Fatell." Raphela said, sealing the bond of friendship. "Now, should the Duke question my attire, I will take full responsibility."

Fatell had no doubt that she would.

The Duke and Mahtso had just been seated when Raphela appeared. The gown was unexpected, but her face left little room for arguments. Raphela's thick black hair was pulled back, leaving a few curls to dangle by her cheek. The top was laced with gold ribbon and her makeup accented her deep eyes and full mouth. Atan nodded and Mahtso rose to hold her chair.

The first course of dinner passed with a minimum of conversation. Atan finished his soup and took a moment to stretch his legs, leaving Raphela and Mahtso to entertain themselves.

Mahtso studied her, with some desire. "You look lovely tonight."

"Thank you."

"But you tread dangerously close to disaster." He grinned, a friendly gesture.

"I know." Confidence surrounded her as surely as the walls surrounded the castle.

"Why?"

"It keeps life interesting."

"I'm impressed. Do you play Tralfag?"

"Tralfag? Isn't that a game of military strategy? No, but I'd like to learn." Raphela met his eyes and felt at ease.

"I believe you know more than you realize, but I'll teach you the technical side of it."

Atan returned and felt the comfortable mood, it pleased him.

The trio spoke of politics and history, fitting together, like a puzzle finally completed.

After the meal Raphela was dismissed to Atan's chamber's, Mahtso rose to go, but Atan held him. "What do you think of her now?"

"She's quite bright."

"And desirable."

"Of course, but somehow I cannot imagine her in my bed."
Mahtso didn't know why, except that she felt more like a sister
than anything else.

"I think I understand." Both left for their women. Raphela
was standing near the bed as Atan entered. A piece of gold
ribbon hung from her hair, a tease that seemed to cry out, "Pull
me!" Atan did, and Raphela's hair cascaded into his hands and
stayed there in a firm hold until she pulled away.

"That is an interesting gown Fatell chose for you." He
smiled and absentmindedly twirled her hair.

"I chose it my lord." Friendly, defiant eyes matched her
tone.

"You?!" he mocked surprise.

She nodded and began undoing her bodice.

"I could punish you severely for such boldness."

"Yes sire, you could." Raphela continued as if discussing
the weather and removed her outer layer of clothes.

The game of conversation and her slow steady movements
whetted an already excited appetite. "What reason have I for
not?" His sword and daggers now hung on the walls and his
shirt was open to his waist as he stepped closer.

Raphela leaned her right leg on the chair in front of Atan and
rolled down her second stocking, calmly placing it on the arm,
wondering how much longer he would tolerate her impudence,
sensual as it was. She faced him. "Because my lord, there are
better things to do with me." Raphela's breasts pressed at his
chest.

Atan grabbed her arms and drew her to him, feeling the
warmth of her breast. He looked in her eyes and made her
wonder what was to follow. The glance lasted half a minute then
Atan Ishtba kissed his harlot in lady's clothes. What they
engaged in was not passion, or lovemaking, but sheer
unadulterated lust. Their inexplicable desires took them long
into the night and they parted only because of Atan's promise to
himself.

Over the following weeks, while Raphela performed her
tasks as recordkeeper, etc. a mild reorganization took place. She
streamlined the general operation and rearranged the library, all

61

with the Duke's permission, granted with a wave of the hand or an absentminded nod of the head.

Every week Atan and Mahtso reviewed the records. On this their chosen day the library door was shut.

"Mahtso, where are the tax books? Atan looked around the table.

"Raphela put them away."

"Away? Where?" He spoke as if she had stolen them.

"In the second bookcase just as you agreed." Mahtso's chain began a nervous agitation in his pocket.

"Oh yes." Atan attempted to brush off his statement. "When do we need to complete the linen inventory?"

"Raphela has already taken care of it."

"Quite efficient, isn't she?" Somehow the compliment did not come out as such, and that added to Atan's growing feelings of confusion and frustration. He waved his hand at Mahtso. "You may go."

As was becoming a weekly occurrence, Raphela dined with Atan and Mahtso that evening, but the Duke only pushed at his food and gulped the wine that he usually ignored.

Raphela and Mahtso sat like two children; unsure of what had they had done wrong, but knowing something was definitely amiss. They said nothing.

Silence was a cold rod administering unseen punishment to all three.

After Atan growled at the servant over some cold pudding, he finally spoke to his dinner mates.

"Raphela, the labeling system you devised lacks clarity, fix it. I will not spend hours searching for information that should be at my fingertips."

"Yes my lord." Raphela bowed her head, not wishing to make his mood any worse, though she knew he was wrong.

"Mahtso, the troops are getting sloppy, they must be perfectly tuned. Fakrash will have to be dealt with soon.

"Yes sir." Mahtso's chain dug deep into his palm.

Atan paced around the table, not looking at either Raphela or Mahtso as he spoke. "Fakrash claims to be visiting on business, but I don't believe it, as Mahtso knows. Raphela, I wish to know what he really plans. Considering his lust for women, I will give you to him for the evening. Do you think you can extract the necessary information?"

Raphela fought sarcasm and tears. "I'll do my best."

"Yes, you will." He commanded it. "Now both of you may go."

They left the room quickly and quietly, leaving Atan to brood. Once out of earshot, both breathed.

"Mahtso, has he ever been like this before?" Raphela prayed for Mahtso's friendship.

"No, no he hasn't."

Raphela leaned against the wall. "As much as I'd like to believe it is that pig Fakrash that disturbs him so, we both know it is not."

"I see you know about Fakrash."

"I've been doing some research, he has a bad reputation here."

"True, Ulfan hated him."

"So I've heard."

They walked again, in anxious quiet, avoiding the subject until Raphela spoke. "All right Mahtso, can I talk to you?"

"Of course." He said with relief.

They found an empty room. "It's me, isn't it?" Raphela held Mahtso with her eyes, he couldn't turn away.

His chain circled in his hand. "Yes, I believe it is."

"I've moved too fast. His life has changed so much, so quickly." Raphela wanted to hold Mahtso's hand for support but held back.

Mahtso hesitated to speak, but he knew Raphela was strong. "He can't be like this when Fakrash arrives, you know that."

Raphela swallowed. "I know."

"Raphela..." Mahtso felt lost for words.

She forced a smile, a grimace. "I am the only one who can cure his mood, I created it."

"How?"

Raphela patted his hand. "The same way I started it."

"Do you have no fear?" Mahtso trembled for her. Atan's troubled soul emanated through the walls of Castle Cordan, no one was untouched.

"Not yet, I was careless. I should have expected this, at least I'm not all alone." He kissed her hand. "That's true."

"Now I'm going to put together a brew for the cure. You straighten out your troops." she teased.

"You take this too lightly Raphela," Mahtso wagged his finger like a big brother.

Raphela turned somber. "Not at all my friend."

She left for the women's quarters. Mahtso sat for a while longer.

Late the next afternoon Atan called for Raphela in his chambers.

She took her time and dressed exotically.

He paced, waiting for her. When she arrived, he viewed her with disgust.

"Have you not yet learned how to dress?"

"Oh, I'm so sorry, but your call was not specific my lord." Her sarcasm bit like a cornered beast.

"How dare you speak to me like that!" Atan felt his anger rise, his blood felt like lava burning his insides, and ballooned to stretch his skin. His fingers flexed in frustration.

"I'll speak to you as I choose sire!" Raphela spoke the words and winced.

The back of his hand knocked her down. She offered little resistance as he dragged her to the chains on the wall. With the rings clipped on her hands, what little control she had was gone. Her eyes watched the wall as she heard her gown being ripped away from her back.

"Now you shall learn fear, woman, and perhaps die with it."

Raphela wasn't sure if the sound or pain struck first, but the second lash certainly was felt first. Atan's eyes flamed and his hand continued the strokes, each crack a bit louder. There was no torturer's rhythm, only a man's anger. Raphela closed her eyes and let the silent tears fall; Atan saw the blood and worked the whip again and again.

Raphela's head bobbed back and forth in pain, but no sound escaped from her lips.

He continued, indulging in his control, "speak as I choose" he muttered, the whip stroked harder.

After sometime passed, he looked to see what his hand was doing. He saw it raise the whip and watched as the leather made one more tear on soft flesh.

Atan's eyes no longer held fire, only shock. Raphela hung unconscious before him. He forced the whip from his hand and sank to his bed.

"By the gods, what have I done?" Atan sat, for how long, he didn't know.

Raphela's limp blood-stained body was all that he could see. Finally, he walked out and sent a guard for Mahtso and then returned to the bed and stared on.

Though Raphela had been the only one to feel the whip, no one in Castle Cordan was shielded from the anger, unseen but it hung on the walls and in the ground. No one did not fear the outcome.

Mahtso arrived quickly. He had expected trouble, but this was more than he could imagine. This was not his Duke, his friend. He was not sure who was worse for the experience." Atan?"

"Mahtso, you're here, good." The words were emotionless.

"Is she alive?"

Atan stared at his hand, before turning his pleading eyes to a friend. "I don't know."

Mahtso pressed his fingers against her throat, and breathed a sigh of relief. "She's hurt pretty bad, but she's alive. Should I take her down?" He began to undo the chains.

Atan stopped him. "I don't know."

"What?!" Mahtso didn't think he could be more shocked.

"Look what she drove me to. If she lives, what more will she do?" His eyes welled and grew red.

"Atan, I can't tell you. Either you trust her or you don't. She is not a battle or a fief. There is no plan for this." Mahtso, sensing the possibilities, gritted his teeth and pulled the dagger from his waist, raising it towards her throat.

Ever so gently Atan stroked her hair. "Raphela, you will be my ultimate destruction or my overwhelming glory. But which?" He caressed her face. "You have spoiled me, the loneliness I clung to is dissipating and I can't rebuild it." He stared at Raphela and then at Mahtso. "Mahtso, help me take her down, gently."

The two men placed her on the bed. Mahtso got salve and they dressed her wounds as best they could.

"Mahtso, see to it that we are not disturbed. Except for Fatell, no one is to know of this, do you understand?"

"Yes."

Mahtso left, and for all his other side could do. He felt pained at Atan's treatment of Raphela.

And so for the first time in his life, Duke Atan Ishtba slept the full night with a woman. As the sun rose Raphela's eyes opened. Her back ached, almost too much to move, the previous day still a blur in her mind. When Atan's robe caught her eye, the shock of where she was set in.

"It's about time you woke up."

"Yes my lord."

Atan helped her to sit, leaning her with the greatest care against a wall of satin down-filled pillows. He sat down beside her on the bed. He brushed the back of his hand against her cheek and then held her hand He searched her eyes, for the anger, the scorn, neither was there. "Raphela, the lady's chamber is being readied for you, if you would take it."

Now it was her turn to study. Was it guilt or the solidified base of their relationship that earned her this honor? Their faces held no secrets, no veils. Neither would speak the feelings. She caressed his face and engaged him in a long kiss, he held her as tightly as her battered body would allow. Their tears mixed paths as their lips parted.

"Who would you choose as your personal side? Atan attempted the official question.

Both laughed at the weak attempt at protocol, then Raphela smiled. "Fatell, of course."

"Of course."

By midafternoon Atan carried Raphela to her new quarters and both took some time alone. Later in the day Mahtso checked on her.

She allowed him to move her to a chair. He studied her face.

"So this was a cure?" Mahtso taunted as any big brother would.

"It worked." Raphela hid her pain, as best she could.

"Oh yes, it worked. It nearly got you killed."

"It was a bit more than I expected." She tried to laugh and Mahtso jumped to her side as she almost slipped from the chair.

"Did you think he'd say naughty girl and take you over his knee to spank you?" He couldn't help the admonishment; she had taken so great a chance.

"No, of course not, neither did you."

He softened as she winced. "I also didn't think it could go this far. You took a terrible risk."

"But look at my reward." Despite any physical discomfort, she beamed. "Look where I am, Mahtso. The only permanent damage I've suffered is cosmetic and if the gods are willing I may bear the scars with pride one day."

Mahtso just stared. "You know Raphela, I believe you'd meet a demon in his den and welcome the battle, if the reward were right."

"If the reward were right." She managed a grin.

Mahtso shook his head. "Would you like to get back into bed?"

She nodded.

By dinnertime Fatell found her way to Raphela's chambers, she approached the bed quietly. Raphela lay on her stomach and Fatell held back a gasp as she sank into the chair.

Though the men had tried to help, their attempt was clumsy. Beside the purple bruises where the whip did not cut, clumps of hair intermingled with closing wounds. Fatell wept in silence before waking Raphela.

Fatell's hand moved the hair from her face. "Raphela, child."

Raphela's eyes opened and she smiled weakly upon seeing her friend. "It's good to see you."

"Lay still. I'm going to clean up this mess."

"All right." Raphela closed her eyes. Fatell could see her muscles relax.

With utmost care Fatell sponged the lacerations with warm water, loosening the hair and cleansing the wounds. Then she tied Raphela's tresses up and away from her back.

Raphela flinched on occasion.

"Are you all right?" Fatell swabbed Raphela's face, which was a bit too gray for her liking.

A sniffle escaped and a salty tear burned down Raphela's cheek. "How long before the pain subsides?"

"Considering your fortitude, I expect you'll feel well enough to walk around in a day or two."

"Not too bad I guess."

"No and I'll see that you are not disturbed, even by our grand Duke." Sarcasm was not Fatell's nature, but the word "grand" cut deeply.

"You can't mean . . ." Raphela stopped. Tears drowned themselves escaping from her eyes. "Maybe it is best." She leaned on her elbows and held Fatell's hand. "But not too long."

Fatell heard the door click behind her for the third night, Raphela slept.

In the kitchen, two cups of tea sat on the table, Fatell sat by hers.

"How is she?" Mahtso asked it gingerly. His chain remained in his pocket.

"Better." Fatell glared and kept her hands tightly wrapped around her teacup.

Mahtso felt lost and wounded. His friend Atan, though calm, was sulking in guilt, his new friend was putting her energy into healing and Fatell, his love, was angry. "Please, don't be angry with me."

"You could have stopped him."

"Fatell" He stretched an arm that was neither greeted nor turned away. "You know I couldn't. What control could I have between them?"

Fatell broke and moved to rest in his arms. "I know, it just seems so unfair. She didn't deserve that."

"True, but she provoked it."

"That I believe."

Mahtso held her close all night. "I love you Fatell."

Two weeks passed. Atan felt the chill from Fatell and Mahtso dissipate, while the bond with Raphela, continued to solidify. And so it was on the day of Fakrash's visit.

Castle Cordan was as ready and polished as its hosts were, the stones in the entrance reflected the afternoon sun, sending beams of light through the hall where Lord Duke Atan Ishtba and the faithful Mahtso took their places.

They were an imposing pair, even standing at ease, the two trim bodies in well-tailored black garb. Mahtso's green waistband and gold shoulder braids highlighted his insignia by which the world knew him.

Atan stood as a solid tower, his belt holding the sash that crossed his chest, his eyes as unmoving as his lips. Not only was he unquestionable, he seemed unapproachable.

Shortly the light that shone in was blocked as Fakrash squeezed through the doorway, his servants scrambling behind him, brushing the dirt off the heavy velvet cape he dragged from his shoulders.

Fakrash nodded at his host, noting the somewhat austere surroundings. "It is a pleasure to see you again Ishtba." He slapped some lackey who tripped beside him.

"Welcome to Castle Cordan." Atan moved forward and spread his arm in a welcoming gesture. Mahtso shadowed his footsteps, his chain wrapped tightly, but hanging enough to make short quick half turns around his hand.

"Thank you."

"I'm sure you'd like to rest before dinner. You've had a long trip." Atan was firmly polite.

"I most certainly do. These carriages are very uncomfortable and make me ache." Fakrash snapped his fingers and a silk cloth was placed in his hands which immediately wiped the sweat which formed rapidly and heavily all over his face.

"If you will follow my man, he will show you to your quarters." Atan nodded to one of his servants.

Fakrash followed him, mumbling something about stairs.

Once their guest was out of sight, Mahtso's chain loosened allowing the blood to circulate in his hand again.

Atan sighed. "Dinner should prove interesting."

When Fakrash arrived in the dining room, the hosts were standing behind their chairs, Atan at the head of the table, Mahtso to his right and Raphela beside Mahtso. A place to Atan's left was set for Fakrash.

Fakrash openly ogled Raphela, whose violet gown accentuated her attributes, without revealing them. He attacked the first course while he leered. "Ishtba, you have provided a pleasant decoration for the dining hour."

"You mean Raphela?" His cold tone was lost on Fakrash.

"Raphela, is that her name, not that it's important. A woman's name never is." He placed his greasy napkin beside the plate.

Raphela ate and watched in silence, grateful for Mahtso and Atan's company while she grew accustomed to the overloaded sack of gruel that drooled at her.

"Lord Fakrash, you said you'd like to engage in trade with me. What commodity did you have in mind?" Atan worked at redirecting Fakrash's attention.

Mahtso sat as easily as a hungry cat watching a bird.

"Commodity? Oh yes, well, uh, commodity, yes. I was considering your donags. I realize that your herd is young, but I believe in a year or two that each head might be worth a sack of grain. It would provide a buffer for me, not a necessity you see."

Dessert ended. Fakrash brushed the crumbs off his tunic and belched loudly. Atan gritted his teeth and stared at his guest. Raphela hoped Atan would change the plan, as did Mahtso. Atan weighed the thought.

"Lord Fakrash, would you like some company in your bed tonight?"

No faces changed, not an out of place breath could be heard.

Fakrash smiled slyly and thought to himself. He needs me, he will offer his little trollop. Good, she may prove useful. Then he spoke to Atan. "I would be pleased."

"Then Raphela will be in your chambers when you arrive there."

Atan nodded to Raphela and she did as bid.

Shortly after the post-dinner drink Fakrash headed hungrily to his chambers.

Atan sat in solemn silence, watching the wine make gentle waves in his cup.

"She'll be all right." Mahtso put out as much confidence as he could muster.

Atan simply raised his eyes.

Mahtso left Atan to his mood and searched for Fatell and his comfort.

Atan lay in his bed, trying to shake the unfamiliar feelings that clung to him like sand on wet skin.

Raphela sat, fully dressed in the seat near Fakrash's bed.

She heard him thumping towards the room shoving away servants. He slammed the door and began undressing even before he looked at Raphela. As he stood half-naked before her, he realized she was dressed, a fat but strong arm jerked her up from the chair and threw her on the bed. His hand raised, but stopped. "I'll forgive your insolence this time. Since you do not know my ways. Now get naked."

"Yes my lord." She spoke with head bowed. "I beg your forgiveness."

"That's better."

Raphela undressed and poured Fakrash a full goblet of wine. He gulped it down, with the excess making a path on his chin.

Raphela held calm as he inspected her body, squeezing her arms and breasts with his fleshy hands and discovering the scars on her back. "I see your Duke understands discipline." He turned her around and studied her back. Raphela said nothing.

"Now, tell me woman, what tales of glory does your Duke share with you? What great battles does he plan?" Fakrash swallowed another half goblet of wine.

"Battles, my lord?" Raphela met his look with wide-eyed innocence, as she refilled his cup.

"Yes you fool, battles, conquering. He's certainly done enough of that." His words began to slur.

"Why would my master speak to me of such things sire?"

"Because men do. You are such an idiot."

71

"Yes sire, but would you tell me? I would like so very much to hear." The subservient frightened child appealed to Fakrash.

He grabbed her arms and squinted into her face. Raphela's stomach curdled. "Battles, I will tell you of battles. In two weeks I will march through the back gates of Duke Ishtba's precious land and take him down as if he were a tired old steer."

Raphela continued the act. "Why would you do that sire?"

"Why?! You are a fool." His hand flew out and met her face, she allowed the tears to fall "Don't cry in my presence woman." He struck again. She sniffled and controlled the tears, but felt her face puff and knew his idiocy would leave its temporary mark.

Fakrash mounted her, forcing his body to work. She fought the urge to shove him onto the floor. When done, he fell asleep. Raphela sat like a stone in the chair, trying not to think of all that had happened. She only lay in the bed as he stirred to wake in the morning. He left her and joined the Duke for breakfast.

Atan sipped at his tea while Fakrash stuffed his mouth with morning cakes, the crumbs spilling from his mouth as he spoke.

"Fakrash, I hope Raphela was satisfactory."

"She is stupid, but satisfied the need."

"I see. Is she still in bed?"

"The bitch still sleeps."

Atan controlled his desire to leap across the table and throttle his guest. Instead he called for Mahtso.

"Yes my lord." Mahtso responded quickly.

"Arouse Raphela and send her about her chores."

"Yes my lord." Mahtso understood all too well, Fakrash's irrational violence concerned them both.

Mahtso found Raphela and one look at her face explained her absence. Mahtso's chain swung wildly striking a nearby wall. "That bastard."

Raphela was unnaturally calm. "Yes, he is."

"If Atan saw that . . ."

"I know, he might forget the plan. I assumed it was best to handle it this way."

"You're right." He felt uneasy; she was taking this too well. "Are you going to be all right?"

"Of course. For now I'm going to take a long, hot bath and try to get Fakrash off my skin."

"That's fine."

Mahtso returned to Atan and let him know that Raphela was all right.

Fakrash noticed no mention of the woman's bruise He left soon after breakfast.

Atan took one look at Raphela's face and exploded. "So this is why you avoided me, to protect that, that thing, and you too Mahtso."

Raphela glared at Atan and leaned close to his face. She spoke with the kind of venomous whisper that chilled even Mahtso. "I have information that should assure your victory over that thing and his entire army, not just eliminate him. I allowed myself to be used by that pig. You have no right to accuse me of betrayal."

Atan stared. His voice started harshly but faded into apologetic tones. "Raphela, you come dangerously close to disrespect."

She said nothing.

"I will make him pay Raphela, you can be sure."

"Take full payment, he and his army."

Raphela disclosed her information and left.

Atan and Mahtso spent most of the day devising and refining battle plans. That night, when the first moon rose Atan knocked gently on Raphela's door. She joined him in the family room. They said nothing, but he ached knowing the horror she had gone through the night before. She lay in his arms, and he caressed her hair, while she sobbed herself to sleep.

Fakrash returned two weeks later, as promised, and attacked exactly as promised.

The Ishtban troops were waiting to begin the slaughter. It was a brief conflict, lasting but a few hours. Neither Atan nor Mahtso needed to be directly involved for more than a few minutes. By dusk, the land was strewn with the bodies of Fakrash's army and he was tied to a stake in courtyard.

Although Raphela had stayed inside as ordered, she was by now a hypnotized observer; Atan saw her and called her out. He paced around Fakrash, slicing his clothes, scraping his skin. Raphela stood by Atan's side. He handed her a blade. "Fakrash, I thought perhaps you'd like to see a pleasant decoration before you die." Atan laughed. Mahtso watched his eyes aflame with delight.

"She's a witch." Fakrash spat when he spoke.

"Tch, tch. What a thing to say. Raphela, I hope you're not too offended."

"A witch eh? That doesn't offend me. However his existence does." She raised the blade and drew but a tiny line of blood from behind his ear.

Fakrash trembled. "Do not fear, I will not take your life, but.." Raphela lowered the sword and mutilated his manhood.

He howled in pain and shame.

Atan took the blade from her hand, noticing the respect and fear she now commanded from his men. It exhilarated him. He pointed his sword at Fakrash's throat. "You claim to be a man, strong and brave. Yet you quiver and beg for life. I shall show you courage, strength." Atan pulled Raphela towards him and turned her so Fakrash would see her back. Atan ripped her dress and the scars shown clear to all. "You questioned these, they were by my hand, but not for the discipline you have so little of. She did not offer a whisper, a cry, though I nearly killed her. You are not a man, you are not worth the words I spend on you." And with that, Duke Ishtba beheaded Fakrash and as the head hit the ground a cry of victory arose. Atan Ishtba raised his sword "Holiday for all till midnight tomorrow!"

Atan and Raphela entered his chambers and slammed the door.

Their eyes shared an animal excitement. They rolled in lusty victory. Their bodies pumped with frenzied energy, lips moving too quickly to meet or stopping so long that breath was lost. Their sweat mingled as the moons watched triumph come to life. Their sleep was a peaceful basking of glory and a cleared pathway to future victories.

Chapter 4

Victorious spring blossomed into fruitful summer. The land of Ishtban bore plentiful crops, the trees laden down fruit and the donags growing fat on the rich grass.

At Castle Cordan Duke Ishtba once more concentrated on planning his future and Raphela's new found importance gave her the opportunity to make improvements. She began with the dining hall. The spacious room had dingy walls, with dreary linens and the curtains a melancholy cousin to the walls. The intricately carved wood, gold table, deserved better. Raphela chose deep beige, for the walls and a mosaic of burnt orange tiles for the floor. Chairs were built to match the table, upholstered in green velvet. New curtains and linens completed a picture of good spirits.

Turning to the more formal of the two parlors, Raphela sought to create a room that would make a lasting impression. She stood alone at the doorway, gazing upon the time worn red and black decor. Within a week, workmen had removed every stick of furniture. The walls were scraped and the carpet replaced with one bearing the Ishtban crest woven in of gold, green and black. Raphela selected high back chairs and firm couches, all in gold and green matching gold drapes. The walls bore pictures of Ishtban ancestry. One chair stood out; its black iron frame, seat pad and Golden Gilfon emblazoned on the back proclaimed, its only resident would be Duke Atan Ishtba.

The informal parlor was metamorphosed from drab green to light and dark blue, deep cushioned chairs and couches scattered around for easy movement, atop animal skin rugs. Small wooden tables placed by the seating added to the comfort, giving the room a warm glow.

The castle's entrance way, now well polished and filled with hanging plants glowed with light and life.

Though Raphela reported the progress of refurbishment with the accounts of her other duties, and Atan had little interest in decoration, he took time to observe. Many times he silently gravitated to a chamber where Raphela was planning or directing. Equally as often, Raphela found reason to seek him out, to ask an unimportant question.

Atan traveled a great deal during the summer, assuring his profits from good relations with his fiefs. In the past he returned to his castle and steadfast servants, and a backrub by an obliging concubine and perhaps a warm bath and his bed.

But this summer he learned that he returned to a bit more

It was midsummer and his trip had only lasted a few days. The servants nodded his arrival and attempted to anticipate his needs. Sonja, a bright young girl stood in front of him, "A bath my lord or perhaps some tea?"

Atan's eyes searched the hall while she patiently waited for an answer to a question that he barely heard. "No, no nothing."

"Yes, my lord." Sonja left, knowing that his eyes were looking for something besides dust.

He climbed the stairs, still searching as he neared the top he looked in the family room, he saw only furniture. But then he caught a glimpse of a green gown. Raphela leaned at his doorway, smiling. Though neither would ever say it, even two days seemed a long time to be apart.

First he caressed her face and they shared a simple touching of the lips. Then her arms wrapped around his neck and his hands fondled the hair behind her head and their kiss deepened. After staring for a while he broke the silence. "Raphela, have Rabi prepare a picnic dinner, I'll get a blanket. Meet me by the stable."

"Oh, yes, my lord." She smiled wickedly and he patted her bottom as she turned to fulfill his command.

Raalek's summers were as beautiful as the winters were harsh. Raphela and Atan walked in the breeze, taking in every sweet flower's smell, every color of the trees and after a time walked barefoot to feel the cool and rich ground under their feet.

They stopped at a large boulder sitting on the edge of a hill. Raphela swore she could touch the sunset that was beginning to fill the sky and the town below looked like a dollhouse. For Atan, no matter how often he strolled his grounds, he always felt refreshed and peaceful.

"How was your trip?" She asked.

Atan finished chewing the last of his cold meat and downed a homemade brew that Rabi concocted out of the grains. "Quite productive."

"How?"

"Not why, when and where as well, my wench?"

Raphela's hands were on her hips, "You haven't given me the opportunity to ask those questions yet."

She took his tease in good stride as he pulled her close. "Perhaps I won't." He lightly nibbled on her neck.

"In fact, Raphela, I was in Milson these past two days. I had some business to complete. There is a merchant there who was commissioned to do some work for me."

"Oh." Her voice turned a bit melancholy and he did not want that just now.

"Raphela, much has changed here at the castle, most for the better and most because of you. You have touched my life." The words were so gentle and so strong Raphela was taken aback.

"I..." Atan brushed her lips with his long fingers.

"Sh, and listen, for once."

"I wanted something for you." He reached inside the pouch on his hip and pulled out a box.

The sunset was at its most brilliant point, still light enough to see anything and dramatic in its stature as it framed the two people standing on the hill. Atan opened the box, ever so gingerly and presented his gift to Raphela. He watched her eyes, and for a man, who, with but a sweep of his hand could command ten score of men to die, his look was so hopeful, that those men would not have believed it was the same man.

Raphela was stunned. Tiny diamonds and rubies shone from the box like the sun at midnight, bright and clear as raindrops on delicate strong threads of gold woven into a rope of intricate detail.

As Atan placed it around her neck, she felt the cool stones on her throat, and could only whisper her thanks.

He stared and shook his head.

"Atan, is something wrong?"

"Wrong, oh no, it looks more exquisite on you than I could have imagined, though the jeweler, an artist, said that no other woman would give it justice. I'd swear, he knew you, almost intimately, though my description was vague."

"Nabus created this, only he is capable of such craftsmanship and yes, I know him." She said it almost with fear.

"I think I'm grateful."

Raphela hugged him and let the tears of joy flow. He held her close and realized in that moment what courage it took for Raphela to leave her town and come to his castle. He also saw how lonely she must have been, and as he looked in her eyes and then laid her head against his chest, as he admitted to himself, how empty his life had been before she arrived.

They walked back to the Castle, arms around each other and slept very close that night appreciating the companionship more than ever. The next morning a groggy Raphela joined Fatell in the kitchen.

Fatell poured tea for both and wrapped her robe more tightly around her waist, then warmed her hands on the teacup. "Drink the tea, it's a cold morning." She said as she nibbled on a biscuit.

Raphela stared into the cup and made a sour face, yawning as she spoke. "I'm not cold and I think I'll skip breakfast. To be honest, the sight of food makes me feel, oh I don't know, queasy." She pushed everything away from her.

"Hmm, you do look pale." Fatell leaned forward and rested her fingertips on Raphela's cheek, it was cool, normal. She shook her head in confusion.

"Don't worry, Fatell, I'm sure it's nothing."

"Maybe, but you've hardly eaten anything all week. Let the healers take a look at you."

"What for? They can't do anything except put herbs in my tea." An irrational irritability crept over Raphela.

"Whatever you say. I have work to do. I'll see you later." Fatell knew better than to push Raphela.

"All right." Raphela sat for a while, pondering the imbalance inside her, unsettling her body and her mind. The inability to find the cause increased her disturbance all the more.

Fatell was troubled all day, she knew the answer to Raphela's problem, yet it eluded her. She sat in her room sewing a dress. The needle rose up and down through the cloth with even, unconscious strokes. Fatell paid little attention to either needle or gown, over and over Raphela's condition rolled through her mind. Finally, as she neared the end of the seam, it all became clear. The gown dropped to the floor as she rose and rushed to find Mahtso.

She found him speaking with a guard. Fatell ran her hand down Mahtso's back and whispered in his ear, "We need to talk."

Mahtso excused himself and followed Fatell to her room, a little annoyed. "Fatell, this is not like you, surely you could have exercised a little discretion." Mahtso undid his shirt as he spoke.

Fatell closed Mahtso's shirt. "I'm sorry, but this has little to do with either of us and I did not wish to expose the subject, yet."

Mahtso sensed her seriousness. "What is it?"

"It's Raphela. Have you noticed her of late?"

Mahtso smirked, Raphela was always noticed. "If you mean, do I think she's been moody lately, yes, what of it?"

"I think she's pregnant." Fatell heard Mahtso's chain begin its journey, slow and uncertain.

"Are you sure?"

"Not fully. But I must speak with Raphela and possibly the healers. I was hoping you'd be with me when I told Raphela."

They sat in silence. How does one go about telling a woman that she may be carrying the heir to Ishtba? And that if she is, she may have to let it die. If, the Duke feels she is not worthy of being the child's mother.

Mahtso took Fatell's hand. "Let's go, she needs to know, if it is true."

They found Raphela inventorying linen and dragged her to an unused bedroom. "What is wrong with you two? I have work

79

to do." Raphela stood with her hands on her hips and towered over her friends who sat on the bed before her.

"Sit down, Raphela." Mahtso commanded as well as he could, though it sounded feeble at best. Yet, Raphela obeyed.

Fatell broke the uncomfortable silence that followed. "Raphela, when was your last cycle?"

"My last cycle? Fatell, what is going on here?"

"Please, Raphela."

"Two months ago, exactly six weeks after Fakrash's defeat."

Mahtso and Fatell shared a glance and suddenly Raphela understood. She sank back in the chair. "Fatell," she whispered, "Fatell, am I pregnant?"

"That seems the obvious conclusion."

"Does the Duke know?"

"No."

"I see." Raphela sighed. "I suppose I must tell him." A piece of her searched Mahtso's eyes, hoping he would offer to take on the task, but he lowered his head.

"When will the child be born?"

"I believe in early spring." Fatell answered gently.

"Do you think he'll accept ..."

Mahtso offered the support she so rarely sought. "I don't think anyone else on all Raalek would have the honor."

"Thank you. Now, we all have things to do. I'll tell him tonight."

Fatell and Mahtso left and prayed silently that what they believed would be truth. Raphela planned as best she could. After dinner when the second moon was peeking in Atan's window, she knocked on his door.

He saw her framed by the doorway, clothed in a simple deep gold gown, her hair lying over her breast. He gently pulled her in the room.

"I hope I'm not disturbing you." She said tentatively.

"Of course not." Atan sensed her discomfort, allowing her time to speak while he toyed with hair.

"My lord, there is something I must tell you."

"My lord? Raphela, what's wrong?" Despite his best efforts, Atan felt a tinge of fear.

"Atan, I carry your child." There, it was out, she lowered her head.

His hand loosened from Raphela's locks, he stood and paced by the bed. No one thought came to him, no word. At last, for it seemed an eternity to Raphela, standing more than an arm's length from her, he spoke.

"Are you sure?"

"Fatell and Mahtso are fairly confident." She could not raise her head.

Atan stared at her for another moment. He felt his heart beat, and that inner joy, the one that reminds you that life is more than getting up in the morning, the kind that makes you cry for no reason, welled up inside him. He held Raphela's face in his strong hands and kissed her, first a gentle press of the lips, then with the passion that he felt.

Raphela cried.

He carried her to the bed. "I would let no other woman bear my child. When will the rest of Raalek see it?"

"Early spring." She relaxed and lay in his arms.

"How do you feel?" Atan wrapped her hair around his hand and inebriated himself on its scent.

"Better now."

"Now?" He pulled away from her. "Were you really not sure?"

She ducked her head sheepishly then felt a deep kiss titillate the nape of her neck.

"I'm not good at saying what ..." he began.

Raphela did not need the words he didn't have, but immersed himself in what he shared so well.

Though Raphela stayed in bed, at Atan's insistence, he rose with the sun, as usual. By the time he had finished his second cup of tea, Mahtso joined him.

Mahtso entered cautiously, Atan's relaxed form stiffened as he heard the footsteps, and his face took on a grim mask.

"Good morning, Atan." Mahtso avoided looking at him and poured himself a cup of tea.

Atan did not answer at first. They sat in silence until he quietly said, "Mahtso".

"Yes." Mahtso stared into his teacup.

"I understand you are aware of Raphela's condition." Atan maintained the grimace and cold tone.

"Yes, I know."

"Well, speak to me, you are an advisor, are you not? Should I allow her to keep the child?" He raised his tone in apparent annoyance.

Mahtso, though not bent towards fear, was terribly unsure. "Atan," he raised his head, "is there another woman on this entire planet who is worthy of being mother to your child?" He didn't give Atan the opportunity to answer. "I think not."

"You're getting quite defensive of her, aren't you?"

Mahtso didn't answer, but in his mind he knew if he could have chosen a sister, Raphela would have been it.

Suddenly, Atan grabbed Mahtso and pulled him out of the chair. His hands grasped Mahtso's shoulders almost hard enough to cause pain. "Mahtso," Atan smiled broadly, "I am excited beyond belief, I look forward to every minute of her pregnancy, the birth and to the raising of our child."

A relieved Mahtso returned the embrace. "I'm so happy for you, and Raphela. What can I do to help?"

"Do whatever she asks." "I know so little of these affairs. Help me to learn."

"My unabounded pleasure, my lord."

"Good, now tell Fatell she may announce the upcoming birth."

After Raphela rose she headed for the kitchen. She still wasn't hungry, but she definitely needed something warm. As she walked by the meeting room she noticed people sitting and realized that Fatell was about to speak.

Fatell waited for silence and every member of Castle Cordan had his or her eyes on her. Despite her diminutive stature and quiet nature, her position and proven ability commanded respect.

"I asked you to be here this morning for a very special reason. As you well know Raphela has become the Duke's only consort. I'm sure you all realize that this means more than sharing a meal or a riding lesson or even a battle. The Duke and Raphela are proud to announce that they are expecting a child."

Glances of shock and then delight passed around the room. Then the questions began. When was it due? What was needed? Could real plans for a royal birth be made? If Castle Cordan bloomed when Raphela was made consort, then the impending birth of an heir was like fodder from the gods.

Raphela left the doorway unnoticed and went on to the kitchen to wait for Fatell. She glowed. Never before had so many wished her so well and wanted so much to be right. She only hoped that as a mother she could produce the proper heir and meet all the expectations.

When Fatell finally arrived, Raphela jumped from her seat and threw her arms around her, nearly knocking the poor woman down. After catching her breath, Fatell returned the overwhelming hug and took Raphela's hands in hers. "I'm so glad for you, and so is everyone else. Ever since you arrived I hoped this would be. No one can do enough for you, whatever you want is yours."

Raphela let the tears flow, "I know, I heard."

The morning rolled on and it seemed that every moment brought another person offering congratulations and help. Rabi, the cook, sent for Raphela's favorite foods and any others he knew pregnant women craved. The seamstresses worked to create the most elegant and comfortable dresses imaginable. The healers dug up every potion and herb they could find to assure Raphela's health.

Only two people seemed uneasy, Sarina, for the usual reasons, but also Sari, the midwife, despite the encouragement of Corin, the chief healer, Sari remained edgy and Raphela had to know why.

She found Sari in the empty healing chamber, a room with a few beds, for those with fevers or extensive injuries and needing constant care.

Raphela noticed how clean and refreshing the room smelled, so bright and cheery, not like the healer's rooms in town which were reminiscent of the gray shadows of death. "Sari, may I speak with you?"

"It is probably a wise idea."

Sari stared at the beautiful and powerful woman sitting by her. She realized that if any would understand, Raphela would. "Raphela, do you know what is inside you?"

"A child," Raphela answered cautiously, feeling as naive about the pregnancy as the Duke.

Sari smiled sadly, "Yes, my dear, but not just any child, the child that will be given the rights as heir to all of Ishtba, the child that will belong to Lord Duke Atan Ishtba." Sari spoke the words with such reverence and solemnity that Raphela was taken aback and it took a moment to realize just what Sari was saying. "You're afraid, aren't you? If something goes wrong during the birth, or the pregnancy. Do you think he would hold you responsible?"

"I'm glad you understand."

"Don't you think the Duke would understand, if, may the gods prevent it, if, something goes wrong." Raphela could not imagine him blaming anyone, unless he could see that neglect and malice were intentional.

"Raphela, Duke Ishtba has no other women or children. Even if he regretted it afterwards, I would not want to be near, if the child died at birth. His frustration could easily overrule his sense."

Raphela was reminded of his frustration and a brief memory of pain ran through her back, but she also knew no one else would suffer such a fate. "Sari, I perhaps understand better than any one our Duke's temperament, but I believe in all my heart you have nothing to fear. And, I will tell you this, I need your help and guidance more than any other woman ever has. I desperately want to know what is happening to me now and what it is I should expect."

Though all Sari's fears were not erased, such a plea could not be ignored. "As you wish. The first order of business is to have Corin examine you and then we will establish a proper diet for you. I know you have not eaten right for weeks." Sari wagged her finger at Raphela who hung her head in mock shame, but gladly accepted the advice and followed Sari to Corin's quarters.

Corin, a frail looking old man with absorbing green eyes and a shirt that needed pressing, greeted Sari with a friendly smirk that seemed to say, "I knew you'd help when asked." The two took a moment to confer and Raphela studied Corin's workplace.

She sat down on the clean but loosely made bed and breathed the aromas seeping out of the array of bottles lined up on the shelves. The scent of herbs and remedies created an aura of calm and satisfaction. Raphela had always felt nervous around healers as a child; their stark surroundings and vile smells reminded her of death. But like all of Castle Cordan, this healer's room was different. Beyond the colorful bottles of potions and the table laden with towels and basins was an immaculate cabinet, it held books, all written in the ancient language. She had to know what knowledge they possessed, in this room were secrets of a special kind.

Her thoughts were interrupted by a hand on her shoulder. "Raphela, lay down and let's see if we can determine just how old this baby is now." Raphela lay back as ordered. "Corin, I. . ."

"Shhh, be still. Babies this young are hard to find."

Corin ran his hand along her abdomen and pressed carefully a few times, mumbling something about women being examined before this happened so he could know for sure what the differences were in the body. He made some notes in a book, talked with Sari and finally spoke to Raphela who was about to burst with curiosity. "I believe that Fatell was correct in her guess of an early spring birth." He sat on a stool by the bed and leaned towards her. "Now, how do you feel?"

"Good." His matter of fact answers might have been distant, but Raphela realized that he was more frustrated than distant.

"Sari will have Rabi prepare your meals to my recommendations and your tastes, I doubt it will vary greatly from your usual diet."

"Thank you."

Corin turned away from her and Sari left the room when Rabi was mentioned. Raphela sat on the bed, silently watching Corin return to whatever he was doing before she arrived.

His attention was on one of those well-preserved books, and it was quite a few minutes before he realized she hadn't left. "Raphela, did I forget something?"

"No, my dear healer, but I must talk to you. There are a million questions and I need some answers."

"I'm sure Sari can answer all your questions." He was being as patient as possible, unlike most others at the castle, he showed little concern in offending or upsetting Raphela and thereby the Duke. Raphela liked that, it made for some honest replies.

"I'm sure she can't, I think what we both want to know is in your cabinet."

"You didn't even know you were pregnant, how can you think of attempting to approach what is in those books."

"I can't without your help. Tell me what is really happening inside me. Tell me how I got pregnant and don't give me some stupid answer about that's what happens when men and women sleep together. I won't ask you about what it's like to give birth, that is Sari's job. But, why I should or shouldn't eat something or why I feel a certain way-- explain that to me. Tell me why people get sick, tell me why some live and some die."

Corin took her hands and placed them on the book he was studying. "My child, I learned the old language, but not very well. I have been a healer all my life and with all modesty have been told I am better than the king's healers. But I can't answer those questions. The knowledge you seek, the knowledge I seek, is in these books as you said, but I'm getting old and it is more and more difficult to concentrate and to learn."

"Then let me help you, work with you. Please, it can only be for the best." Raphela asked him in the same way she had asked her father to teach her to read. She could have easily used her influence and commanded it.

Corin probed deep into her eyes. "Yes, yes, I think that would be a good idea," he said, be here tomorrow morning and we shall begin."

"Why not today?"

"Because, young lady, you and I have other things planned for today."

Raphela smiled and left.

She sought out Sari, who was once again sitting alone in her workplace.

"Sari, tell me about birthing. What is it like? What should I expect? I was young when my sisters were born, I only remember that my mother was in pain. What else do I need to know? Is there some way of avoiding the pain?"

"Raphela, the pain is there, and there is little you can do about it. I can't tell you about giving birth. You must see it, experience it."

"Sari, what aren't you telling me? I have a right to know all that can happen to me."

"So you do. You could die, Raphela, many, many women do and sometimes for no rhyme or reason. It never gets any easier."

"Sari, if it is a fact, then I must accept it. But please, you said to see would help. Who will be giving birth before me?"

"Dorina is due about midwinter, you are welcome to help and maybe she will tell you how she feels as her pregnancy progresses."

"Oh, yes, that would be wonderful. When can I talk to her?"

"Raphela, are you always this impatient and energetic?"

Raphela bowed her head. "Yes."

"All right let's see if Dorina is available."

Dorina worked in the laundry. The bleaching solution irritated Raphela's nose almost to the point of burning. As she and Sari entered the stone room lined with shallow basins, it seemed quite cold, for summer.

"Sari, couldn't this work be done outside?" Raphela's eyes burned as she passed the bleach. The room had but a slit of an opening to the outdoors even though it was on ground level. Light was provided by lumpglows sitting beside the basins and a few around the room.

"Too much flying dirt."

"I see. Well, I do think even a room this large needs fresh air. I will see to that."

Sari smiled, although she had just met Raphela that day, she understood why Castle Cordan had changed.

Dorina was at the last basin and cool as it was, sweat poured down her forehead, despite the cloth tied around her head. Raphela noticed the large woman's muscular arms as they scrubbed the clothes against the ribbed board in the tub. Dorina's belly pressed against the basin making her work a little more difficult, but she seemed content and undisturbed.

"Sari, should she be working so hard?" Raphela watched the water splash around the side of the tub and noticed how very little spilled out.

"Hard? It is hard if you've never done it before. Dorina has scrubbed our clothes for years, her body is quite accustomed to the labor."

"Even so, she is pregnant."

"I don't notice you lying in bed." Sari began to feel as if she had a child with her and not a woman as worldly as Raphela.

"Sari, my work is not that strenuous."

"True, but the hard work should not harm Dorina or the baby. Her constitution allows for it. Although I will admit some women must do very little if they wish to carry a baby and deliver it. Those are the ones for whom I fear."

Dorina sat up and realized she had company. "Sari, it's nice to see you. Oh, Raphela, I'm sorry, did you want something?" Dorina wiped her hands on a cloth nearby and straightened her dress as she stood, doing everything short of a curtsy.

"Relax, Dorina, I only want to talk with you. Since I'm going to have a baby, I need to learn a few things and you're just a few months ahead of me. Would you help?"

"Um, oh, my, yes, yes, of course. I would love to help you, but I'm not sure what I can do."

"Wonderful, when can we talk, I don't want to interrupt your routine."

"After lunch, would that be all right?" Raphela spoke to the washerwoman like a peer and it would take Dorina a while to get used to it.

"Perfect. Save some room for whatever Sari and Rabi let us snack on in the afternoon.

Dorina smiled, "As you wish."

Sari and Raphela returned to the main hall. Raphela thanked Sari and left to continue the linen inventory she hadn't completed the day before, but Sari called to her. "Raphela."

"Yes"

"Raphela, I owe you an apology."

"Why?"

"Despite what I had heard, I expected you to be a spoiled, inconsiderate brat. To my delight you have proven me wrong. Even in a place as open minded as Castle Cordan, women who do laundry and scrub floors are often treated with disdain, especially by women who get the Duke's favor. You have made a devoted and steadfast friend in Dorina."

Raphela stared at Sari in wide-eyed wonder and innocence. As Atan Ishtba made very little distinction in stations among people, neither did Raphela. "Sari, she is a person, no more, no less. I can't imagine treating her any other way. But, I am always grateful for a good friend."

"Good, I think you two will learn much from each other."

"Me, too."

Dorina and Raphela met in the kitchen and talked for hours. Dorina knew she couldn't match Raphela's intelligence, but she had the advantage of experience. This was her second child.

Raphela felt Dorina's stomach and swore the baby moved. They discussed how different their bodies felt and finally Dorina mentioned childbirth but said very little.

"Raphela, when my time comes, would you please be there?"

Raphela took her hand. "I wouldn't miss it and we must talk again before that. All right?"

"I'd love to. Now, I think my husband would like to see me."

"Oh, I'm sorry, I shouldn't have kept you so long. I hope he won't be angry with you.".

"Oh, no, he'll be terribly excited for me, having spent an afternoon with you. Almost as excited as I am. Thank you."

"Dorina, thank you."

Dorina couldn't hold back a clumsy curtsy as she left and it was Raphela's turn to blush.

Summer played into fall. Atan kept his travels to a minimum. Raphela decorated the nursery, using bright yellow and green. She dragged Fatell to some old storage rooms and insisted that they find some pleasant artifacts to add some history to the child's nursery.

"Fatell, let's open that trunk. It must have some old treasure, a rattle or blanket that belonged to the Duke or even his father or grandfather."

"Raphela, it's been years since anyone has been here. I don't even think Duke Atan's mother saw the contents of these boxes." Fatell blew some dust off one and sat down, watching Raphela delve into her pleasures. But Raphela noticed a melancholy veil in the woman's eyes.

"What's wrong, Fatell?" Raphela was moving a little more slowly than before and hesitated to sit. Getting up was becoming difficult.

"Nothing, nothing, child, let's see what you've found."

Raphela didn't push. They pulled out a lovely blanket, perfect for the baby's cradle. In another box were some booties and intricately knitted sweaters. Fatell gently folded everything and put the items aside for Dorina to wash.

"Raphela, let's go, it's getting late and this room grows cold."

"If you think we should go." Raphela was a little hurt.

Raphela walked silently with Fatell, trying to understand her friend, her surrogate mother. Finally, Raphela saw and it burned inside her with the quickness and strength of lightning. "Fatell, I am sorry. You have been so kind and giving, I forgot that you have no children of your own. This must be so painful for you. Please forgive me for drowning you with this pregnancy."

Fatell hung her head, part in shame, part in pain. "Raphela, I don't deserve an apology. I feel the agony and shame of being childless, though none would say a word to me, least of all Mahtso. Still, I have no right shadowing your joy, it has been selfish of me."

"We can both bend. What do you think?" Raphela smiled at her friend.

Fatell hugged Raphela and they both cried.

Atan watched Raphela's body change and found it strangely exhilarating. Though she was only about half through her pregnancy, her belly was large and round. He smiled when she climbed into the bed moving close for warmth as much as anything else. Atan stroked her hair and placed a gentle kiss on her neck. "I think I like sharing a bed with two. I've never had a woman with child in my bed

"Is it so different?" Raphela, for all her confidence, could still be unsure.

"Yes, it's quite exciting." Atan's tongue found hers and Raphela melted accordingly. As their clothes left their bodies and his joined hers, a flame sparked that was felt through the Castle, no one missed it. As the night progressed and Raphela lay next to Atan to sleep, and he suddenly jumped up and demanded, "Raphela, what's wrong, what did I do?"

"Nothing, why?"

"You kicked me."

"I did no such thing." She was irritated, it was late and she was tired.

"Raphela, I know when I've been kicked in the back."

"Well, maybe the baby did it." As the words left her lips, they realized what she said and they both sat up. He brought the lumpglow by the bed close to her and they stared at her stomach.

"Raphela, could it have been?"

Raphela thought about her talks with Dorina and Sari and realized that it was about the right time for the baby to be able to do this. "Yes, definitely."

Atan felt her round form and waited, she placed her hand on his. They sat like two children, waiting.

The lumpglow began to fade, their eyelids grew heavy, but not a hand moved. As the lumpglow died and Raphela's eyes closed, it came. A strong solid kick, enough to make both parents jump.

"It is real! Alive! Raphela, this is a wonder." Atan was elated.

Raphela kissed his cheek. "Yes, very real. Now as excited as this makes me, please may I go to sleep."

"Good night, Raphela. He said sheepishly.

"Good night, Atan."

Raphela lay down and feel into a deep sleep. Atan lay next to her, hand glued to his heir.

Fall was beautiful but short, so Raphela spent a great deal of time indoors with Corin and Sari, learning all she could. She and Corin spent innumerable hours in the library, translating the old medical books, discussing what little they had translated. Most of the information seemed as foreign as the language. Though both were often frustrated with the slow, tedious and often unrewarding work, they believed with their hearts that a door would open.

Dorina's pregnancy progressed well and she willingly shared every feeling and movement and past experience with Raphela. Raphela came to know Dorina's husband, Edwar and son, Metzek. Still with all this activity, Raphela did not neglect her other duties around the castle. Everyone was kept quite busy, so much so that winter crept upon Ishtban without much notice.

The window shutters opened easily this winter morning and Raphela sat by the open air, hot tea in her hand and fully wrapped in layers of robes.

She studied the snow, so often a cruel cape suffocating the land. Today it seemed like a thick, gentle blanket protecting the soil from the biting wind that ripped the skins from the trees.

Ishtban's heir had grown. Raphela's swollen belly was accompanied by breasts filling with sweet nourishing milk.

All told, winter had reached its peak and Raphela considered the year as she absentmindedly ran her fingers through the snow that rested on the windowsill. During this reverie a young woman entered the kitchen and tapped Raphela on the shoulder startling her. It was Sonja, petite and pretty a sweet harem girl, lacking only in confidence, but not intelligence or loyalty to Raphela.

"I'm sorry, Raphela, I didn't mean to bother you." Sonja twisted her head nervously in either direction.

"What is it, you seem so jumpy?"

Sonja sat down and took a deep breath looking into Raphela's eyes for strength. "It's about Sarina."

"Yes."

92

"It's what she plans on doing."

Raphela took Sonja's hand. "Sonja, who do you fear, me or her?"

Sonja swallowed and smiled nervously. "Maybe both."

"I wouldn't harm the bearer of ill news."

"I know." Sonja stared at the table. "Raphela, she plans on seeing the Duke."

Raphela nodded. "And on offering her, um, services?"

"Yes."

"I see." Raphela was calm, stony.

"Aren't you angry?"

"Angry? No, Sarina disturbs me at times. I dislike people who prey on other's weaknesses instead of relying on their own strengths. One day Sarina will pay for all her treachery and cruelty. I know how she's treated the women, especially Fatell and that angers me."

Sonja saw Raphela's eyes light for just a moment, and was grateful Sarina had earned the woman's wrath and not her.

"Well, I just wanted you to know."

"Thank you, I will remember this."

Sonja went about her business knowing that Raphela would remember, everything.

Later that day Raphela worked with Dorina, doing her best to keep the woman from working too hard. Mahtso caught both of them dragging clothes around the castle and threatened to whip them both if he were not allowed to carry the baskets. The women giggled and allowed Mahtso his gallantry. He was amazed and almost furious at the weight of the clothes.

Raphela made a point of avoiding Atan all day, Sarina, however, as expected, did not.

She knocked on Atan's door. "Come." Atan was expecting a servant with tea, not Sarina in a temptress' gown and a carafe of wine. He raised his eyes. "What is it, Sarina?"

"M'lord, I have come to offer myself to you." Sarina swayed with all the sensuality she could muster, and that was a good bit.

Atan wasn't interested, he had chosen to spend a few minutes in pleasant solitude and didn't appreciate the intrusion. "What are you talking about?"

"M'lord, with Raphela in her present condition, I thought you might need some, companionship." She smiled and rested her firm buttocks on the bed.

"You mean in my bed?" Atan asked, bemused.

"Yes, my lord."

"Sarina, I find Raphela quite satisfying and her condition not in the least repulsive. But your offer is appreciated. You may go." His words were definitive but not punitive. Raphela could deal with this at her leisure.

"Yes, my lord." Sarina left, her hate for Raphela festering like a witch's poison.

Raphela waited until nightfall to see Atan. He had even begun to wonder why she waited so long to arrive for dinner, especially since they had barely seen each other for a week.

A fire blazed in the family room, and a bottle of wine waited on the table. Raphela kept herself from falling into him as she sat amidst the deep pillows on the couch. She casually filled both their glasses and then leaned into him. They watched the fire dance around the logs. His hand, in gentle habit, wrapped around her hair. "Raphela, I had a visitor today."

She could not look at him yet. "I know."

"You do?"

"Yes, Sarina came to see you."

His hand let go of her hair and he turned to face her. "How did you know?"

"I have friends." Raphela's quiet confidence etched new respect in Atan.

"Atan, if I may be so bold, did you accept?" Raphela knew there was a chance and she risked her ego for the truth. He wouldn't lie. They slept together often, but sex was less frequent, often because he feared hurting her and the baby.

Atan's large hand caressed Raphela's cheek, his lips passionately meshed with hers and he whispered, "I wouldn't know how."

Raphela allowed a tear to escape and whispered back a thank you. The fire burned long after they fell asleep on the soft pillows.

A few weeks later, Dorina's time came. Her son raced around the castle, bumping into this one and that, looking for Raphela. Finally, the breathless boy, guided by many pointing fingers, found her and urgently tugged at her gown.

"Raphela!"

"Oh, Metzek, what is it?" Raphela laid a calm hand on the boy's shoulder.

"My mommy, she's gonna have the baby."

"You mean now?!" Raphela's heart skipped a beat.

"Yes!" He tugged at her hand, and she followed.

Metzek dragged Raphela to his mother's room. Sari was already there and Metzek was ordered to leave which he did unhappily.

Dorina was on the bed, leaning against her husband, Edwar, who held his wife firmly. Her hands squeezed around his with every contraction. Despite the cold and her half-naked form, Dorina's forehead and neck were drenched in sweat.

"Raphela, so glad to see you." She panted.

"I wouldn't miss this. Sari, how long has she been in labor?"

"Since noon and I'd say by the first moon, this child will be born." Sari was crisp and efficient. "Now, Raphela, since you've chosen to be my assistant, get to work."

Raphela, tutored by Sari over the past season did as ordered. She wiped Dorina's face, which turned redder and wetter by the second, but Dorina did not seem to be in the horrendous pain Raphela expected.

Sari rubbed Dorina's stomach and watched for the baby's head, wiping her hands on a nearby cloth. She made sure that hot water was readily available and that the towels on the table by her side stayed clean.

Edwar comforted his wife every time she grimaced and the tension began to balloon. Raphela paced as Sari nervously counted the towels.

95

Raphela could sense that night was approaching. As she leaned down to brush a line of sweat from Dorina's cheek, the woman's lips parted and let forth that unmistakable signal that a new child was about to show its face. Raphela threw the cloth at Edwar and pushed on Dorina's stomach at Sari's command. Dorina pushed the child through and within minutes a red and wrinkled baby was born.

Sari cleared its mouth and the baby announced her arrival with a lusty cry. As she cut the umbilical cord and Raphela cleaned the baby, Sari said. "Dorina, Edwar, you have a beautiful baby girl. Congratulations."

Raphela handed them the baby wrapped in blankets, "Congratulations."

When Metzek arrived to stare at the baby. Raphela and Sari left them.

"Sari, was this a typical birth?" Raphela had found it all too quick, almost too easy.

"Don't be fooled, for a second birth, it was about normal. First time around the labor is rarely that short."

"I see." Raphela's mind looked back to the bloody sheets and Dorina's bloodstained legs. "How long will she bleed?"

Sari sighed, "As far as I can tell most of the bleeding has stopped. Dorina bled very little with Metzek. I will check her before I go to sleep. But in better answer to your question, there is some bleeding for about two weeks."

"Oh." A million questions popped into Raphela's head but she was too tired to ask. The second moon had already risen, so, too tired to climb the stairs, she found an empty guest room and fell asleep.

In the morning, as she often did, Raphela went to the kitchen for tea. At the table Fatell sat with Mahtso, neither looking particularly excited.

Raphela rubbed her eyes and poured herself the tea. "What's wrong with the two of you?

Neither answered. Raphela felt her back stiffen, her eyes opened wide. "Is it Atan? Is he sick, hurt?"

Fatell took her hand. "No Raphela, the Duke is fine."

Mahtso's chain ran through his fingers as he watched the tea leaves float in his cup. His eyes raised and lowered. "Raphela," he paused, "Dorina died last night."

Raphela's face went pale and her breathing became suddenly shallow. Mahtso rushed to her side in fear she would fall from the chair. Her eyes darted back and forth from Fatell to Mahtso. "I, I don't understand. Dorina was fine. Where's Sari?" Raphela's accusatory tone took them by surprise.

"Sari was with her all night. She and Corin did all they could." Fatell's tone was motherly.

Raphela felt childish. "I'm sorry. What happened?"

She bled to death."

Frustration and helplessness built inside Raphela, but she stepped around it to get the answers she needed. "Fatell, what about the baby, who will take care of her?"

Fatell softened. Lolita, has just finished nursing her own baby and volunteered to care for Dorina's.

"How wonderful."

"You seem surprised."

Raphela sighed, "My friends, this castle is a haven, the rest of the world is not so. In Milson, unless a sister or cousin were available, the baby met the same fate as the mother."

Fatell lowered her head in pity for the world and then explained the ways of orphaned children at Castle Cordan, Mahtso being a prime example. Temporarily it moved the topic from Dorina, but while Fatell and Mahtso went about their business, Raphela buried herself in her chambers. Mahtso sought out the Duke. They met in the library.

"Atan, you look well." Mahtso's chain swung back and forth, hitting the table at irregular intervals.

"What's wrong?" He had seen Raphela slip into her room, but she was all right.

"Do you remember Dorina?"

"Dorina? Yes the woman that Raphela has spent so much time with this winter. What about her?"

"She gave birth yesterday."

"Really, boy or girl?" Atan asked out of a master's required curiosity.

"A girl." Mahtso's chain swung faster.

"Mahtso, obviously something went wrong. What?" Atan felt his patience pushed.

"Dorina died, she bled to death."

Atan sat down. "I am sorry. Is there something I can or should do?" Atan did not get involved in the daily lives of his people, but his concern was genuine.

"No, not for her family, the routine for all that is well established. But Raphela is upset. I would suggest that if by nightfall she hasn't left her room, you go in."

"Nightfall. I'll do no such thing. I will see her now." Atan's face was flushed as he rose to go.

Mahtso beat him to the door. "Atan, please sit down." It was a difficult for him and Mahtso felt his chain dig deep into his hand.

"Mahtso, she can't be left alone. What if something goes wrong, if she gets sick?" Atan protested.

Mahtso smiled gently, "Fatell has made arrangements for Sonja to bring her food and check her every few hours."

"Sonja is a child. Raphela can push her away like a feather."

Mahtso took a deep breath and pushed his friend back into his chair. "Sonja is young, but bright and devoted. She will watch and report. That's all we need."

Atan took a few deep breaths. "I'll take your word, but keep me apprised."

Mahtso nodded and left.

Atan paced through the castle all day grumbling and groaning and Mahtso kept everyone out of his way. Raphela stayed in her room ignoring Sonja and the meals she brought. Sometimes she paced, sometimes she sat. Very few clear thoughts came into her mind. Raphela felt like a child kidnapped and dropped in a strange place, not knowing where to turn.

When Atan finally arrived she was sitting on the bed, knees drawnup, thighs pressing against her stomach. Atan sat on the bed, not too close and he did not offer a hand. Raphela ignored him, staring straight ahead. Words were always difficult for him, now they seemed nonexistent.

The lumpglow on the table by her bed shadowed her face. Finally, Atan caught the glistening of a tear. Raphela's head didn't move, but her lips parted. "Why? Why did it happen? I don't understand. It's so useless, so senseless." She got up and began to pace.

Atan jumped up and stood by the bed. His arms by his side but ready.

Raphela looked out her window. "Why? What could we have done?" She turned to Atan. "Oh, great Duke, master of all, why did Dorina die? Are the gods so callous that they turn their backs or are they so disgusted by human frailty?" She cried as she spoke and her sarcasm cut deep into him, but her tears were worse. He remained silent and still as she rambled on. "Dorina was healthy, strong. Sari said the bleeding stopped, so why? Why is there so much that we don't know? Atan, tell me."

"Death is a fact of life, I can offer no other answers." He felt helpless and hated it.

"This death is not an acceptable fact of life. It cannot happen again. I've been lazy. The answers are here, they will be found." She wiped the tears that rolled freely down her face. "I'm going to find Corin and we will do research the right way." She headed for the door.

Atan more than stepped in her way, he lifted her up.

Raphela pushed at his chest. "Put me down, I have work to do."

Atan ignored her demand and carried her to his bed. "Young woman, you can find any answer you want, but, first you will sleep and then eat a healthy breakfast or you will hang by the shackles on my wall and be force fed." Atan's command held the fury of a worried mother threatening to spank a sick child too stubborn to admit illness.

Raphela seethed for a few minutes and then realized the wisdom of his words. "Atan." Quiet tears lined her checks. "Hold me."

Atan lay beside her and she crawled into him. His arms were a soothing brace and blanket. He stroked her hair as she fell asleep. His eyes did not close until he felt sure she would not wake until morning.

Although Atan did not want Raphela exerting herself, he knew she could only be limited to a very small extent. When they finished breakfast, he walked her to Corin's workplace. At least there, Atan knew that Raphela was with someone who would keep her from getting too tired.

Corin expected Raphela and allowed her to begin the conversation, "We've been handling this all wrong."

His weary face and tired eyes matched his voice. "Raphela, am I not plagued with enough guilt for every death?"

She took both his hands. "There is no blame, but we can make it better."

"How? We have searched and dissected every book I own. No answers, just more questions. It's all still a mystery."

Raphela remained calm. "We've done nothing with the books. Translating a word on a page or two has proven useless. We've approached it all wrong. We must crawl before we walk."

"What do you mean?"

"I mean, before we so much as look at the cover of one of your books, we will become fluent in the ancient tongue. I have Mahtso searching the library now for a primer. You and I will begin as children do. If there is no dictionary, we'll create one. If you know anyone who is knowledgeable, find him."

Corin's head raised and his body felt a wave of energy that he hadn't experienced for years and with it a surge of respect. No longer were they student and teacher, they were a team. He knew she was right and hoped he could keep up with her.

"As you wish, but your health is of prime concern. At the first sign of fatigue you rest. You will eat properly and if you don't follow those guidelines, I will tell the Duke." Corin wagged a grandfatherly finger.

"Of course." Raphela smiled.

They walked to the library, where three primers were out on the table. The lessons began. Winter wore on and slowly passed, Raphela's belly reached its maximum size and as the snow stopped falling, she climbed the stairs less often.

The family room was set up as an auxiliary library, to the Duke's great satisfaction. By the last week of winter, Raphela did not attempt the stairs at all.

Raphela woke knowing the last day of winter had arrived. A bird chirped outside and when Atan opened the curtains, the sun warmed her face. He insisted that she not sleep alone.

"Atan, how can you stand me? I can't even stand me." She moaned as her bottom slid around and her hands reached for a pole to grab onto so that she could sit.

Atan, standing a foot away, watched in amusement, his hands folded across his chest. He had learned that she was simply a pregnant woman, not a delicate vase precariously balanced on a ledge.

"To be honest, I think your condition disturbs only you. Although, at this moment, lying on the bed, you rather look like a large melon sprouting limbs." He laughed and helped her up.

Raphela gave his shin a good-natured kick. "Large melon?"

"Yes, and quite tasty, too." Atan surprised her with a long engaging kiss.

"You don't taste too bad either."

Atan dressed and helped Raphela with her clothes. They shared a light breakfast.

"Mahtso said the fiefs were well prepared for the spring planting, what do you think?" Raphela's palms rested against the warm teacup.

"Most, but I wish we could get better yields. It seems that the land is hiding a secret." Atan got lost in the thought.

Raphela waited until he appeared to return. "You'll find the secret, maybe the books will help."

"Perhaps." Atan said still preoccupied.

Raphela placed a kiss on his cheek. "Corin is waiting, I'll see you later."

Corin had just settled on the couch and asked one of the boys, who kept close to summon Sari when Raphela's labor began, to stoke the fires.

Raphela waddled over to him and carefully fell into the couch. Corin saw the impression of a little foot kick from inside her.

"Shhh, child, we have work to do." Raphela rubbed her belly and smiled.

They reviewed the winter's studies. The primers were completed and they had reached the equivalent a fifth year student's work. Raphela was more and more uncomfortable as the morning wore on. Around noon she was about to suggest a break. Her hand reached over to Corin and suddenly she squeezed his arm, her eyes opened wide and her right hand went to her stomach.

"Corin," she caught her breath, "I'm no expert, but I think it's time."

Corin agreed and sent the children to get Sari, Fatell and the Duke.

All arrived quickly. Atan did not ask if Raphela could walk, he just carried her to his bed.

Fatell, Sari and Corin made the necessary preparation. Since the labor was in its early stages, time was taken to do everything right. Mahtso came up and dragged Atan from his room.

"Mahtso, this is not the time for a discussion of any kind." Atan protested

Mahtso brought Atan to the family dining room and poured tea for both of them.

"Atan, I'm here as a friend. Raphela won't need you for some time. For now, let me help you." Mahtso was as forceful as he knew how to be with his master.

"What is it?"

"First, this can last for days, so be patient. Second, think carefully whether or not you want to be there. Watching someone you care for go through that kind of pain can push a man to his limits. Sari is a good midwife, the best. Remember that she will do all she can. Unleashing any frustration on her will only cause harm." Mahtso's blue eyes locked on Atan's face and Atan knew that his speech was to be burned deep into his mind. "Raphela will need your strength. Forgive and forget what she says, if what she says hurts."

Mahtso let all that sink in and then spoke again. "There is one more thing you should be prepared for. You may be forced to choose between Raphela and the baby. One may have to die so that the other can live. You have some time to consider it, you must. It is 'The Question' and you will not have time to weigh the factors if it is asked."

Atan stared at Mahtso, hating him for bringing up the subject, yet grateful for the concern. He was not unaware of the possibility but had avoided thinking about it. "I understand." They sat for a few more minutes and finished their tea in silence before he said. "Mahtso."

"Yes."

"Thank you."

Atan returned to the room and saw that Raphela was covered with a blanket. Fatell, Sari and Corin were making the final preparations. When Atan realized that Corin was to be present during the birth, he began to object, but Raphela stopped him.

"Atan, he can learn here. It's very important."

"Yes, but it has not been a place for men, so close to a woman, when she is ..."

Atan did not like the idea of another man touching his woman, especially where Corin would be touching and Raphela realized this. But before she could respond, a wave of pain crossed inside her and her teeth clenched enough to turn her face white. Atan looked to Fatell for instructions, but the pain passed quickly and Raphela relaxed.

"Atan," she panted, "perhaps if the gods are not kind and there is a problem, he can solve it."

At that point he could not and would not argue. Raphela's birthing room was ready. Atan and she were on the bed, Fatell stood by and Sari and Corin waited at the foot of the bed.

The contractions came closer together, by the first moon they were five minutes apart.

As Sari predicted, it was a long labor. Fatell, Sari and Corin took turns leaving for a few minutes, to Atan's quiet frustration. He refused to leave.

Shortly after the second moon appeared, Raphela's contractions became much stronger and more frequent. Earlier, she had instructed Corin to study and to make detailed notes as to what happened to her body. Corin reached between Raphela's legs during the contractions, finally reaching his hand up into her and feeling the difference in the opening and exactly where the baby was located. It took every ounce of self-control Atan had to keep from tossing the small man across the room.

But within minutes Raphela's labor became so intense she was all that mattered.

Fatell could not keep her dry, the woman's body was encased in salty sweat that filled the sheets. Sari and Corin concentrated on the baby, their faces grim and voices low.

Atan leaned against the headboard, Raphela's body soaking his shirt. He didn't feel her nails digging into his skin or see the blood they drew. He only heard her pain. The cries burned and scarred him with their intensity. Each time she cried out, he wanted to scream and demand help, but Mahtso's words stuck with him.

Raphela was overcome with the pain. When a contraction was done, she tried to catch her breath for the next one. She felt as if the baby was going to break through her body and destroy it in the process. The looks on Sari's and Corin's faces spoke of the same thing. At one point, Sari was ready to ask "The Question" but Corin held her back.

Raphela's blood coated her thighs and dyed the sheets, the smell permeated the room along with her pain. Fatell prayed to the gods.

As the sun of spring's first day peeked in the window, Sari commanded an exhausted Raphela to push one more time. Raphela pulled strength from Atan, closed her eyes and did as told.

Corin heard her skin rip with the wail of agony, but the baby's head was through and with his wrinkled old hands he delivered his first child. Raphela could barely breathe, but she seemed all right, and Atan's attention was fully on her. Sari cut the umbilical cord and washed the baby. Then held it up, stark naked for all to see. "My lord, you have a son" "You did it, Raphela, a boy." Atan kissed her lightly on the forehead.

The baby was none too happy at being waved around in this cold new place and cried loudly to make sure everyone knew it. But the cry made for a good sign of a healthy child.

Fatell kissed Raphela on the cheek and congratulated both parents. "What is his name?"

Atan and Raphela had discussed this before. Atan spoke. "His name is Vanar Ulfan Ishtba."

Vanar, having seen his mother seemed a little happier. Now wrapped in a blanket, was handed to his father. Atan held his miracle with more warmth and strength than anyone except Raphela knew existed. A glow crossed his face and Vanar obviously approved of his father.

All this time, Corin had been cleaning Raphela and with Fatell's help changed the sheets. Corin grabbed Sari. "Sari, the skin on her bottom that tore when the baby was born, do you ever sew it up?"

His clinical attitude took Sari by surprise but she managed an answer. "No, I wouldn't know how."

"Well, I do I'll show you."

Raphela was far too tired to feel the stitching and Atan had left the room for a few minutes.

Vanar suckled comfortably at his mother's breast. A cradle sat by the bed.

Fatell found Mahtso leaving his room, strangely calm and unconcerned. "Mahtso."

"Fatell, what is it? A boy or a girl?"

"How did you know that everything was all right?" Fatell expected him to be nervous, but even his chain was still.

"I will tell you something, every one in the Castle knows that the birth went well. You can feel it, the walls speak it."

Fatell took a moment and realized that the Castle did feel good, as if nothing could possibly be wrong. "You're right."

"Of course, but what is it?"

"It's a boy, Vanar Ulfan Ishtba."

"That is marvelous news." Mahtso picked up Fatell and whirled her around. "Come, let's gather everyone and tell them."

All eyes were on Mahtso, everyone knew that Raphela had been in labor, without hearing about it. As Mahtso had said everyone also knew that all was well, but he spelled out the details. "Ishtba has an heir. His name is Vanar Ulfan Ishtba and I hear he is a large as a calf."

The crowd applauded and a new purpose for being now existed at Castle Cordan.

Upstairs, Raphela, now cleaned and patched nestled close to Atan, feeling quite exhausted. Atan, though tired, was still concerned. "Raphela, how are you?" Some color had returned to her cheeks as he stroked her face and hair.

"Tired, and you, papa?"

Atan just held her close, occasionally peeking over to the cradle to catch a glimpse of his son.

In the family room, Corin slept fitfully, hoping that Raphela's body would restore itself quickly. He checked on her every few minutes until nightfall and felt satisfied that Ishtba not only had an heir, but someone to mother him as well.

Chapter 5

Three days passed. Raphela rested and recovered. She felt some pain from the stitches, but overall did well. Vanar ate, cried, ate, and slept--all the usual things newborns do Atan spent time with his family and then a day by himself. On the third day of Vanar's life, he watched Raphela place the yawning infant into his cradle and then slowly walk to her room to bathe and change clothes. When she was ready he walked her to the couch in the family room. It was evening and the fire blazed.

"Atan, that is one hungry baby." Raphela sat slowly, trying to find a comfortable position.

Atan sipped his wine and stared at the fire. "Raphela, I think it's time you became my wife." It was a simple statement, given the same consideration and feeling as an offer for a prize bull.

Raphela replied just as matter of factly. "I agree."

"Good, make the arrangements."

When Fatell came by the next morning Raphela told her of the upcoming wedding with the same nonchalance, but Fatell was not so calm, engulfing Raphela in a hug as tears streamed down her face. "I'm so happy for you both."

"The arrangement does have its advantages. I'm glad it makes you so happy, but there are a thousand things to do. I've never planned a wedding or announced a birth.

Raphela's total calm took Fatell aback but she said nothing. "Fatell, we will make a list of all the things we will need, people to invite, and whatever else."

"As you wish," And as Raphela walked away, Fatell whispered "my lady".

While Raphela broke the news to Fatell, Atan reviewed the troops with Mahtso.

"The men are looking good, but they seem edgy, let's get them outdoors. The snow has melted enough for a good hike." Atan commented.

"All right." Mahtso's chain jiggled loosely in his palm.

"Oh, by the way, Raphela and I have decided to marry."

Both the chain and his jaw dropped. He stopped walking as Atan went on with the inspection. It took him a few seconds to catch up with his friend and say, "Well, congratulations and it's about time."

Atan didn't even bother to turn and look at Mahtso. "It seemed the wise thing to do." As they continued the inspection he added "Raphela is handling all the arrangements. I am sure this is unnecessary, but help and guide her as you see fit."

"With pleasure, my lord."

By day's end, every living thing in Castle Cordan knew of the upcoming event and all anxiously waited for instructions.

Fatell and Mahtso met late in the evening after answering the same questions more times than there were people to ask them. They sat on her bed, taking turns rubbing each other's back.

"So Fatell, when is the wedding?" Mahtso laughed.

"The 45th day of spring." Fatell eased back and let Mahtso's strong fingers work at the tension in her shoulders.

"Any particular reason?"

"It was the earliest feasible date she felt comfortable setting."

"Then Raphela was excited?"

"No, she acted as if she were ordering tapestries for the halls." Fatell turned to Mahtso and kissed the palms of his hands. "I don't understand, he didn't seem to care, did he?"

"No."

"Your turn, do you have any idea why, they seem so... I'm not sure what I'd call it."

Mahtso laid his head in Fatell's lap and sighed. "It did bother me at first, but in truth, it's just a political necessity, at least to them. Could any vow change them? He married her the first night she slept with him till dawn. But this wedding and Vanar establishes him as a viable leader, not just a conqueror. A wife and a child solidified his respectability. One can only guess what it will do for Raphela."

"Mm, I see." Fatell lay down and slept peaceably in her man's arms. Mahtso's soul found its moment of calm with Fatell near his heart.

To Raphela's frustration, her studies with Corin were put on hold, but for the all important wedding. She spent a day considering everything she wanted for the affair and who should attend. By dinner time she was ready to talk about it with Atan.

In the family room a cook removed fresh spice bread from the hearth, the aroma wafted through the air. It added a warmth to the evening. Atan fell to its hypnotic aroma. Raphela joined him and dipped the bread in the rich brown meat sauce that filled her plate.

"I believe that the cooks are getting better." Atan said as he finished chewing the steamed vegetable mixture in his bowl.

"I agree." Raphela brushed a napkin across her lips and pushed her plate away. "And if I'm not careful I will always look pregnant."

Atan just smiled and shook his head, Raphela's occasional vanity interested him.

"Atan, I'd like to discuss the wedding."

"What about it?"

"I believe we should invite all the fiefmasters, the King and..." she hesitated and watched his face, "Lord Rayna and Baron Akar." Raphela knew that Rayna and Akar were the last two men who owned the property besides Atan and the King. She also knew that Atan did not plan to allow that to continue.

Atan leaned back and spoke quietly, watching the steam rise in lazy columns from the teapot, Why?"

"I want to know who they are."

"I understand. Invite whom you wish." Atan resisted the lustful urges that arose and Raphela did the same, as her body could not handle the passion.

"Thank you." She poured more tea for both of them. " I have another request." Her tone moved to apprehension.

Atan could not imagine what would bring about such a change. "Yes."

"I would like my parents to spend a few days here. I don't know if they would feel comfortable at the wedding, but, I would like them to know how well I am, to see their grandson and maybe even meet their future son-in-law."

Atan's eyes lit. He grabbed her arms. "Why would you even ask? Your family is always welcome and I am looking forward to meeting them. I could never understand why you never mentioned seeing them before this."

"To be honest, I was afraid."

"Impossible. Raphela does not know fear."

"Oh, Atan, I'm afraid they won't come because they're angry and hurt. I never said goodbye, I just left. And poor Sarek, he must have borne a terrible burden."

"Raphela, they will come."

"I hope so." She sniffled.

They changed the conversation to the lighter topics of food and sleeping arrangements. But as they slipped under the covers and their skin made sure to touch and Vanar's tiny breath was close enough to be heard, Atan and Raphela brushed a melancholy of being alone in the world.

Over the next few days Raphela and Fatell doled out responsibilities to everyone, even the harem women, all of whom cooperated gladly, except Sarina. Raphela did find a need for Mahtso and pulled him, with little effort, away from a game of Tralfag, and into a meeting room. After the door was closed, Mahtso, to Raphela's surprise, picked her up, whirled her around, planted a big kiss on her forehead, and then sat her down on a large table.

Raphela crossed her arms and stared for a moment at this totally out-of-character Mahtso. "Would you care to explain?"

"I'm very happy for you. You're like a sister to me. And I'm ecstatic for Atan. Though I realize that personally the ceremony means little to the relationship you both share, to the rest of the world, it's a tremendous event. Any ounce of respect that was lacking for Lord Duke Atan Ishtba will be erased. He is now more than a warrior, he is a man with a support system that all must envy. And he is a man with a future, a future named Vanar."

"Perhaps if he knew how pleased you'd be, it would have happened sooner." She smiled.

"No, the timing is perfect. Now, what can I do for you?"

"Find Sarek and bring him here."

110

"Who is Sarek?"

"The man who brought me to Castle Cordan."

Mahtso sat down and stared up quizzically at Raphela. "If you wish, but why?"

"Because I owe him a great deal." Raphela held out her hand for Mahtso to help her off the table and into a chair. "I'm sure my father took out a great deal of frustration on him. Now I want him to bring the news of my marriage and Vanar's birth to my parents and all of Milson."

"Consider it done. My men will find him within three days."

Raphela smiled warmly. "Thank you, my friend."

As promised, within three days Sarek was delivered to Raphela. She waited in a cozy room lined with tapestries. Beside her comfortable chair lay Vanar, well covered in his basket and sleeping after a good meal. She did not rise when Sarek entered. He sat in a nearby chair, not hiding the surprise in his face.

"Raphela, did you bring me here?"

"Yes. How are you faring?" She held onto a cool professionalism, almost bating him.

Sarek's nostrils flared. "Financially, quite well. But certain friendships have been strained, leaving me with donag steaks, fine wine and an empty table. Soup and bread combined with good company taste much better than steak.

Raphela cringed and would have preferred a beating instead of the words. Her cool attitude melted and though a tear escaped, She looked Sarek in the eye. "I deserve all you have said and more. But perhaps I can make it up to you."

"You think so," he sneered. Though a kind man, his hurt pushed him to lash out further. "Make me richer. I hear the Duke is to take a bride, maybe I can have the business that goes with that affair.

"It's all yours."

Sarek stared at her, beautiful as ever, perhaps more so and more serious than he had ever seen her. "Is it yours to give?" He asked.

"Yes."

"You are the bride?"

"That and the mother of his child." She lifted Vanar from his basket and walked over to Sarek, who rose to look.

"I'd like you to bring the news to my parents. A carriage will bring you to town and bring them back to the castle to stay for a few days, if they are willing. And you can tell the whole town. Let them know about me. Take the credit, not the blame. I need Milson to help with the wedding supplies and who knows what else. You will be the broker to Castle Cordan."

"I don't know that anyone will believe me."

"You will go with a note from me to my father and to the town with an order for.goods with the Duke's seal on it." Raphela handed him some papers and covered his hand with hers. "Please."

Sarek studied her hopeful face. "Raphela, has anyone ever said no to you?"

She just smiled. "Each note has a name on it. There are three special papers, one for my father, one for Sara, and one for Nabus.

Sarek tucked them in his cloak. "This should keep me busy. And now, I should be on my way."

Raphela shook her head. "I'll hear of no such thing, it's past sundown. I've made arrangements for you to dine here and spend the night, even with a woman, if you choose."

"Thank you, Raphela, that would all be very kind." He felt warm for the first time in more than a year.

In the morning the Ishtban carriage rode slowly down the hill to Milson. By midday Sarek arrived at Goran's store. Goran's strained politeness still hurt, but Sarek pushed it aside.

"Goran, stop fooling around with that cloth and look at me. Goran did all but sneer. Sarek closed his eyes a moment and then continued. "I have some news for you."

Goran did not alter his expression.

"By the Gods, Goran, I have word from your precious Raphela. She is fine and doing quite well as a matter of fact." Sarek's exasperation meant nothing to Goran, but at Raphela's name, he softened.

"What do you mean?"

"Well, Grandpa, she is the mother of a fine young man, barely a week old."

"What?!"

Sarek smiled and put his arm around his friend. "And, she is to marry Duke Ishtba."

Goran brought his hand to his chest, but he retained his calm. "My Raphela, are you sure? How do you know?"

Sarek showed him the letters.

Goran hugged Sarek and spun him around. Raalek's sun sat inside Goran and no man felt more pride. He ran into the house and grabbed Batya, his wife, dancing her around the room saying, "Our Raphela is going to be Lady Ishtba."

"You have had too much wine, sit down."

Goran laughed and grabbed her hand. "Come here, woman, let Sarek tell you."

Raphela's mother was soon convinced and the word spread quickly through Milson. Sarek brought Sara her note. She cried and thanked him. Raphela was sending her an assistant and her measurements so that she could create Raphela's wedding gown.

Nabus read his note alone, sitting by his worktable.

Dearest Nabus,

How I have missed you. So many nights when I first came to Castle Cordan I wept and wished I was back in Milson, sharing time with you.

But, I will tell you this, your lesson of friendship gave birth to what has happened in my life. In case you have not been drowned in the news, I am the mother of the Duke's son and will soon be Duke Ishtba's wife.

The necklace you created for me has no compliment high enough, but I must ask you to delve inside yourself once more and create a piece for the Duke. On a golden chain, hang a golden Gilfon with eyes as black and rich as the soil below our feet and his wings should be laden with the fertile greenstone of Raalek's belly and give it strength befitting Duke Atan Ishtba. I could ask this only of an artist and my friend.

I love you.

Raphela

113

Nabus stared at the paper, now stained with his tears. Carefully he folded it and put it in his safe box and then drank until he fell asleep. Falle came at moonrise and dragged him to bed, allowing herself a moment's jealousy.

When Goran and Batya reached Castle Cordan stared in wide eyed wonder at the beauty and size of the structure. Raphela and Atan met them at the doorway, Atan carrying Vanar in his basket.

Batya could not raise her head but allowed Atan to hug her and she felt his strength ooze through every fiber of her soul. Atan offered his hand in friendship to Goran. The men's hands locked on each others' wrists and their eyes locked as well. For this one moment in time Atan allowed himself to be what Goran saw, a man about to steal away a precious child. The silent exchange lasted less time than it took to open and close a door, but long enough to satisfy Goran, and Atan.

Batya's eyes rested on the basket that emitted the sweetest of cries, at least as far as she was concerned. Raphela smiled and lifted Vanar from his resting place, gently placing him in his grandmother's anxious arms.

Goran and Batya gazed at the cherubic face which stared back at them. Goran's hand brushed against Vanar's soft cheek and the baby turned. His lips drew together and he began to suckle the empty air.

"You have a hungry baby Raphela, a big healthy hungry baby." Goran laughed. Goran and Batya cooed over the baby a while longer and were then shown to their quarters and fed a handsome dinner.

Over the next few days Raphela's parents came to know where she lived and the people who shared the castle with her. As the day came for them to return home, Goran and Raphela walked around the Castle, her hand in his.

"Papa, I am so glad you came to see Vanar and me."

"Raphela, as angry as I was, I couldn't stay away. But I still think you deserve a good spanking for running away like that."

Raphela blushed. "You're right."

"Mmmm," Goran smirked.

They walked a little more and came to the front door. Raphela opened it. The sun shone brightly, warming them on the cool spring day.

"Tell me, Raphela, are you really happy? Does he take care of you? I mean, you truly are more than one of those harem women to him?" It was Goran's turn to blush.

Raphela took both his hands. "Papa, he has had no other woman since a month after I got here. And, yes, I am very happy. Atan treats me well, as does everyone else. I have been welcomed and it's a very warm feeling. You've met Fatell, I'm sure you can tell."

Goran remembered speaking alone with Fatell and smiled. "Take care of yourself, the Duke and of course, my grandson."

"Yes, Papa." Raphela smiled back and then cried as they shared a hug that bound and broke them all at the same time.

Later that day Goran and Batya returned to Milson.

Batya spoke of the wondrous rooms and food. Goran boasted of the fine cloth his daughter chose for the Castle and what a fine man Duke Ishtba turned out to be and both rambled on endlessly about their beautiful grandson.

Responses to the invitations returned quickly. No one was going to miss this occasion.

The king's reply however, was not delivered by an Ishtban messenger. It was hand delivered by the king's nephew, Jivad.

Fatell greeted him and saw him settled in quarters and before he dined with the Duke, Raphela and Mahtso.

Atan sat at the head of the table, Raphela to his right and Mahtso on the left. Jivad sat beside Mahtso and studied his hosts and they him. The uneasy silence was finally broken by a polite toast, offered by Jivad, to the Duke and his fiancee.

The servants removed the soup bowls and allowed some time to pass before bringing in the next course. Atan spoke.

"Tell me, Jivad, why did the King send you to Castle Cordan?"

"Duke Ishtba, the King always sends an emissary ahead to assure his comfort for a stay. In addition, the King felt that since your bride was unknown among the royalty that she might need some assistance in protocol." Jivad was professional in his delivery, but something was not right.

Atan's face turned stern, both Raphela and Mahtso sat up straight in response. Mahtso's chain moved from a slow pace to a quick march, as Atan continued.

"Does the King believe that my hospitality is lacking?" Atan asked, acting offended though he really didn't care what the king thought.

"Oh, no, my lord! He will tell you himself that he is set in his ways and only wishes to sleep and eat as is his habit. It is no reflection on you or Castle Cordan." Jivad's quick response and honest tone impressed the trio, especially since he did not cower.

"Then the king thinks my bride to be incompetent to handle her own wedding and that I would choose someone incapable of such a task."

"Sire, King Samed could not think in such a way, his respect for you is immeasurable. He is concerned only that you and your bride make the best possible impression." Jivad felt somehow that his words were not yet right, if they ever would be.

Mahtso felt a surge rise inside him and Raphela saw the cruel but necessary game reaching a height. "My lord, I think the King insults you. Perhaps his emissary should return with the message that his attitude displeases you." Mahtso stood as he spoke and stroked the whip that always lay on his hip.

Atan allowed Mahtso to pace around Jivad, who remained calm.

"Raphela, it seems that you have borne the largest portion of the insult. Should the king's emissary relay the message Mahtso has suggested?" Atan enjoyed the game.

Raphela stared into Jivad's eyes, "My lord, does the king's emissary feel he should bear the burden of the king's thoughts?"

"Good point, Raphela. Jivad, what do you think?"

Now Atan stared at Jivad, who was almost able to meet the man's eyes.

Jivad stood by Mahtso and turned to Atan. "My lord, if I have not been able to convince you of King Samed's good intentions then whatever message you choose to send I will bring back without argument."

Raphela rewarded the strength, courage and honesty of the answer. "My lord, perhaps it would be more fair to ask what Jivad thinks, rather than what the King thinks."

"Mmm. Sit down, Jivad."

"Speak for yourself."

Jivad was silent for a few minutes.

He studied Raphela's eyes and even Mahtso's, he had not the strength for Atan, but he made his decision. "In the few minutes I have spent with all of you, I believe that if you three could not do something, then it could not be done. I would be honored if you would allow me to assist in your wedding plans".

The game was over and everyone won.

With Jivad at the castle, Atan and Mahtso were able to devote their time to security procedures for the wedding. Fatell was busy finalizing arrangements with vendors, organizing the staff and in general wallowing in the joy of her friends' upcoming union. Working together Raphela and Jivad learned much of each other's worlds.

Raphela kept Vanar with her most of the time and had chosen Sonja to be her right hand with the baby. When Jivad entered the room, Raphela could not miss Sonja's blush, or the way he fumbled the minute Sonja moved. Raphela took to leaving them alone, which grew to them finding time by themselves.

One evening, under the sparkling spring sky, Raphela watched as they strolled the castle grounds.

Jivad and Sonja walked in silence. Before long they stopped. Their hands slipped apart and their eyes melded. Jivad held Sonja's face in his hands, his heart pounded, Sonja prayed.

Jivad's lips parted, spilling a soft "I love you."

Sonja felt his kiss and swore nothing else existed.

A few days later they approached Raphela and asked to speak with her.

"Of course, sit down." Raphela acted nonchalant, playing with Vanar.

Jivad and Sonja sat down, got lost in a stare and then returned to the patient Raphela.

"Raphela, Sonja and I would like to marry. Would the duke allow this?"

Two sets of hopeful eyes turned to her. "Much as I would hate to lose an assistant as good as Sonja, I suppose I might convince him. Though I doubt it will be difficult." Raphela smiled at the glowing couple.

"Jivad, what of the king? Will he permit you to choose your own wife?"

"A realistic concern, Raphela, thank you. But, I have been given permission to choose a bride at any time or place.

That night Raphela and Atan discussed the matter and he agreed to the marriage with no argument.

Fatell heard the steady clicking of the wheels first. Before long the first carriage, full of guests, stood before Castle Cordan's doorstep. Over the next two days the carriages formed a caravan of activity, not seen by Ishtban in more than a quarter of a century. For all its chosen solitude, Cordan beamed its welcome. The walls absorbed the clamor of voices and the floor rang with footsteps. Every guest was treated like royalty. Every bed was made to perfection, the floor shone like a mirror, even the snacks for the children echoed of thought and care.

Fatell tended to the organizing. Mahtso and his men watched every being, taking care to guard without insulting the guest.

The day before the wedding Raphela held a luncheon so that all the women could meet (really inspect) her and Vanar. She, of course, could do the same. Scattered around the room at various tables were the sixty or seventy women who were connected to all the important men on Raalek. Lise, the king's first wife, sat with Raphela.

"Raphela, you have turned the world around, or so it seems." Lise's kind and wise face leaned towards Raphela, gray eyes studying the younger woman.

"My lady, I am honored, but I'm sure you exaggerate."

"Oh, no, Raphela, she doesn't," said a consort of one of the king's fiefholders, a bubbly young thing. "You are the talk of all

118

the world. Everyone wanted to know what kind of woman Duke Ishtba would marry."

"I'm just a person." Raphela was taken aback at the unabashed curiosity and respect .

Soon she just sat back and answered questions as briefly as possible.

When the luncheon ended and the women left to explore, Lise stayed behind. "Raphela, can we speak, alone?"

"Of course, my lady."

Lise studied the bride to be and Raphela took the opportunity to do the same with her guest. Lise was short, slender and still quite attractive for her age. She carried a gracious air of position. Raphela liked her.

"Raphela, all I know about you is your name and that you are to be Atan Ishtba's wife. I will guess that your parents are townspeople, merchants, perhaps?"

"Yes."

Lise squinted and stared deep into Raphela. "You are educated, I will venture to say that you can read and write."

"How do you know that?"

"Your eyes sparkle with intellect. You possess the same power as your betrothed. If I were twenty years younger, I'd be in a jealous rage, but fortunately, I've passed that time."

Lise placed her hand on Raphela's. "I wish you much health and happiness. I warn you to use your power with wisdom and consideration. You will never choose the easy road, though many here believe you already have. I know better."

Raphela wished for a moment, that this woman could stay with her and guide her. "Thank you my ..."

Lise held her hands to Raphela's lips. "To you, I am Lise."

Raphela smiled. "Thank you, Lise."

That evening Atan entertained the men in what most would call a bachelor party. Wine and women abounded, though Atan took advantage of neither. Mahtso still on guard, unofficially, followed his master's lead in self control. The male guests however, imbibed in both freely.

Many of the men complimented Atan on his taste in women. Atan nodded and smiled, enjoying the compliments but knowing they had no real concept of Raphela's real quality. Just as well, he thought.

Raphela and Atan had seen little of each other since Vanar's birth, and since the guests arrived, had been totally apart. They determined it to stay that way until the wedding.

Raalek's sun knocked on the windows in full dress the morning of the wedding. It lit a fuse of excitement that spread like fire on dry grass.

Castle Cordan literally buzzed. Women dressed and primped for hours. Even the men took extra care that day. By midafternoon guests flowed into the hall. After a time the room was a mass of color and noise. As the wine flowed, so did the conversation. Boundaries of station and politics dissipated. Even the guards went unnoticed. The tweeting of flutes and tapping of drums acted as a frame for the human sound.

Raphela dressed in her chambers with Fatell at her side. Fatell buttoned the golden gown. The threads shimmered in the sunlight and the low cut bodice and well-designed seam lines gave Raphela's body room to exhibit its beauty.

"How do I look?" She asked as she spread her arms and spun around. "Magnificent," Fatell's eyes welled with tears as she fastened Raphela's necklace.

"Are you nervous?"

"I, well, YES. I don't know why, but I am." Raphela checked herself in the mirror one more time.

"It's just a few more minutes, we just have to wait for the Duke to enter the hall," Fatell said, fussing with Raphela's hair.

Next door, Atan tightened the wide black belt around his tunic, placed a small bracelet in his pocket and then carefully sheathed his sword.

Mahtso primped his master's sleeves and handed him the box that sat on the dresser. With his back to Mahtso, Atan held the black velvet box in his hand and fondled the rounded lid before opening it. Raphela had pressed it in his hand a week before and bade him not open it until the wedding day. And, as she had put it, "If it does not offend you, wear it during the ceremony." Such meekness amazed him. What could she give that would offend? His long fingers opened the box. Before him

120

was a golden disk, embellished with a gilfon, created with such detail he could count the hairs of the mane. Its black eyes pierced the viewer and greenstone gave it life. Atan placed the heavy gold rope around his neck and faced Mahtso. "Well, Mahtso, am I presentable to become a man among Raaleken royalty?" Mahtso stared at the man who in his eyes was still more than mortal, he saw no less than a king. Yet, he sensed the desire and anxiety that any man should feel, but Atan had so persistently denied. "Presentable? The only person who could stand next to you and be seen is Raphela."

Atan allowed himself a smile. "Let's not keep her waiting."

As Atan left his chambers, two servant children scampered from the door. One flew down the stairs to announce the arrival of the Duke. The other knocked on Raphela's door.

The musicians let their flutes and tiny drums fade. Deep-hearted drums pounded a slow march, trumpets began a rising blare. Soon the floor was covered with anxious guests, the only open space a path from the doorway to the elderman.

Atan walked the path, never glancing at the hundreds of eyes that stared with hypnotic entrancement.

When he reached the eldermen, the music stopped. Atan turned and faced the doorway.

Trumpets started a lighter but firm tune, the drums still a strong beat and Raphela made her way slowly to Atan.

Not even a whisper, escaped the crowd.

Enchanted silence filled the hall as Raphela and Atan stood before the elderman who raised his hands and began.

"Lord Duke Atan Ishtba, it is said that you have chosen the woman beside you Raphela of Milson, to be your wife. Do you stand by this?"

Atan took Raphela's hair and encased his hand with it, their eyes locked. "Without question."

"Raphela of Milson, it is said that you are not commanded to this marriage, but do so by choice, yea, willingly."

Raphela's fingers made a sensual path down Atan's chest. They moved a step closer to each other, eyes still engaged. "No doubts."

121

"Then, Raphela of Milson, you agree to be his." The elderman nodded to Atan.

"I agree to be the wife of Atan Ishtba."

The elderman did not ask if she chose to be property, he told her she was to be Atan's chattel. Raphela obviously disagreed, to the quiet astonishment of the elderman and the guests. All waited with bated breath. The elderman, lips quivering, began to repeat the statement.

Atan smiled at Raphela and put his arm around her waist, pulling her close. His lips whispered, a soft wisp of sound in her ear, "Tempestuous wench."

Raphela's chest heaved up and down, allowing her breasts to come within a hair's breadth of his chin. Atan released her waist. "Elderman, Raphela of Milson is to be my wife."

The elderman breathed a sigh of relief and nodded. Atan raised Raphela's hand and turned it to the crowd. "Raphela wears the bracelet of Ishtba. Only Lady Ishtba may adorn herself with it."

Even those at a distance could not miss the golden glimmer on Raphela's wrist, and those close by caught the magnificence of the green and black gilfon inlaid in gold. It, and Atan's firm tone, told outsiders that ownership existed as far a they were concerned.

Two young boys brought in a simple clay pot filled with soil. The elderman placed Atan's and Raphela's hands in the soil. "May your union be as Ishtban soil, rich and fruitful."

Both hands delved into the cool soil and were raised together from the pot, few grains escaped their palms. Once high enough above the pot for all to see, the hands turned downward and returned to the soil.

Now on the table by the clay pot was set an empty bowl. Mahtso and Fatell each carried a goblet of wine. Fatell handed hers to Raphela and Fatell his to Atan.

The elderman recited, "As the wine is poured from your cups, the bowl shall hold and blend it."

Like waterfalls the wine fell from the goblets and made easy waves in the bowl as the contents mixed. The elderman continued. "As you exchange goblets and share the blend of wine."

Raphela and Atan dipped the goblets into the bowl and raised them for all to see, the cups brimming over and dripping into the Ishtban soil, mixing the land and the people.

"Know now that you have chosen to enmesh your lives."

Their hands entwined.

"As you drink the mixture your decision to be husband and wife is sealed by the Six Nameless ones above and witnessed by those before you." Atan's and Raphela's glances did not waver as they wine simultaneously met their lips. A roar of approval rose from the crowd, the musicians began a slow but powerful rhythm, accompanied by equally powerful and rhythmic foot stomping and hand clapping. To Raphela and Atan the noise was as distant as the stars. They saw only each other, felt their skin tingling as they touched. The foot stomping and hand clapping was unnecessary encouragement. Atan's hand fondled Raphela's hair close to her head and her fingers caressed his waist. Their lips met, their tongues met, silence filled the hall.

Sonja found herself leaning into Jivad and his arms wrapped tightly around her. Mahtso's hand grasped Fatell's. Baron Akar moved close to one of his boys. Rayna sat alone, shoving the women away as he glared at the couple. All felt the kiss, but all knew it was not meant for an audience. As the kiss reached its end, the clapping began again. Atan Ishtba lifted his bride and carried her to his chambers.

The celebration in the hall ran long into the night, the last guest falling asleep shortly before sunrise.

How their clothes fell to the ground was unknown and unimportant.

Raalek's moon shed enough light for Raphela to see that Atan's heart burned with a passion like her own.

Warm sweaty skin brushed close, anxious lips pressed feverish kisses on necks. Their tongues danced in harmony with fingers touching and enticing every pore.

Atan's long fingers pulled her buttocks and she felt him tease her and she returned a tempting glide of fingers across his

123

side. Ecstasy rolled down their bodies before the bed could reach out to them.

Atan's mouth encompassed her breasts and Raphela felt her temperature rise. Waves of lightning coursed through his body with each lick of her tongue from his calves to the hair on his neck. His hand wrapped around her hair as he lay on top of her. Already wet with desire her thighs welcomed him. Their bodies rocked in perfect time. She felt him push inside her and wallowed in his strength. With every pump of his body Atan reveled in the passion he felt for his woman. Long into the night they rolled in their reveries.

And the morning sun aroused a new lust that touched every living thing in Castle Cordan.

Before letting go of the sheets, Atan held Raphela in his arms and their eyes traveled deep into their souls to say what their voices could never utter.

Breakfast was shared quietly and then, as duty called, they bathed and dressed for the day's events. Amidst thunderous applause Atan and Raphela walked to their seats, with each step a path opened before them and quickly closed as they passed.

Atan's hand wrapped around Raphela's as he led them to the chairs, still virgin until the newlyweds were seated.

Again the crowd applauded. Atan rose, thanked the guests for sharing their joy and invited them to continue partaking of the food and wine.

A variety of toasts were made. Then gifts were presented. Jivad did the honor of announcing the gifts while a scribe recorded the item and its donor. Raphela and Atan and Mahtso half focused on the gifts but paid a lot of attention to their guests. Lips that whispered too close to an ear, company that was kept too long or too often, or not enough was all noted.

Jivad drew attention to the king when his gift was announced. King Samed gave a pair of breeding rameks, to match the fertility and ongoing fortune with animal husbandry that Ishtban seemed to possess. Not forgetting to mention that such fortune could be shared.

Most fief owners gave household items or extra services for the future. One presented an oddity. Gani apologized for the

124

small gift, but hoped its uniqueness would compensate for its seemingly low value. In his hand was a long wooden tube, with glass at both ends. If you looked in one side, the opposite end appeared a great deal closer than it actually was. Atan congratulated Gani on his ingenuity and made mental note of the man's creativity.

Akar laid upon a long table a set of dinnerware, stunning white porcelain plates inlaid with gold and greenstone. He seemed quite proud of his gift.

Raphela watched as Rayna stood to announce his gift. She saw him push away one of his women. In his eyes was an infinite blackness, almost appealing, yet it echoed of a willingness to cast away the soul of anyone he touched so as to own the pliable shell that remained. Rayna raised his wine glass and toasted the couple and handed Jivad a scroll stating that he had given five acres of land, adjacent to Ishtban property, to the Duke and his Lady. It struck all as an extremely generous gift.

His gift was the last. Atan thanked everyone for their generosity.

For the first time Raphela realized just what position she held as Atan's wife. King Samed, though given the proper honors by all the guests, was obviously past his prime and was treated as such.

Atan was the strength, the world centered around him, people hung on his words. Even those who clung to their fear and black-hearted hatred and jealousy could not deny him respect, and those who believed in him, believed almost to the point of reverence. Never before had Raphela been exposed to the powers of Raalek. Never before had she seen a stranger bow to her husband or cower at his possible anger.

Even Atan was surprised, but now understood why Mahtso's heart had burned for this moment.

Mahtso stood by Fatell and near the Duke, his chain still, his eyes aflame. All he wished for his Duke seemed to be here and the Gods pity any who would venture to douse one sparkle of enthusiasm or darken one degree of respect.

Fatell soaked in Castle Cordan's glory and the excellent beginning to this marriage.

Jivad strained to hear each word uttered by the Duke and his Lady, his eyes glued to each gesture, he hoped for perfection. After the thank yous Atan returned to his chair and Raphela. Jivad watched and waited. Atan still sat. Jivad walked to King Samed, spoke with him quietly and then approached Mahtso.

"Jivad, are you enjoying yourself?" Mahtso's chain remained still.

"Yes, but ..."

"But what concerns you?" Now the chain began a slow swirl.

Jivad laughed. "Don't worry, nothing dangerous, at least not physically. But the Duke should introduce his bride personally to his guests, starting with the king."

Mahtso, no better at protocol or socialization than anyone else at Castle Cordan, considered asking why, but, bent to Jivad's judgment.

"All right, tell them."

Jivad's expression told Mahtso that he could not and that Mahtso must make the announcement to the Duke. Mahtso sighed, he definitely disliked this, but approached Atan

"Yes, Mahtso."

"Jivad suggests that protocol would be satisfied if you personally introduced Lady Raphela to your guests."

"Hmmm, I'm sure he's right. Raphela, shall we?" Atan held out his arm for her, his mood light.

Raphela was a bit insecure about dealing with the crowd but knew it would give her a chance to meet everyone.

Mahtso nodded to a man across the room and with amazing deftness the man was suddenly by Raphela's side. Logan towered above Atan, his tunic outlined a muscular body and his deep blue eyes indicated ecstasy at being chosen to guard Lady Raphela.

Atan looked at him and gave Mahtso a half smile, "Good choice."

Logan, Mahtso, Atan and Raphela began their social trek. Jivad brought them to the king. "King Samed, I bring Duke Ishtba and his Lady, Raphela."

Duke Ishtba bowed and Raphela curtsied, both raised their heads to meet Samed's eyes. Samed rose and placed a gentle kiss on Raphela's cheek. "Ishtba, you have chosen well. May the rest of your lives be as pleasant as these past few days." His words were kind but possessed a bittersweet tone as he glanced at his son.

"I know that Raalek has on it a strong leader. I hope he will be wise and just."

Atan recognized Samed's silent request for eventual leniency with his son.

"I have learned from a good king, may his throne remain strong."

Raphela walked with the three men, nodding mostly at first, but after a few introductions she felt at ease enough to make light conversation.

They came to Baron Akar. He stood as they approached, his slight body seemed to sway and not from the wine.

He congratulated Atan and told Raphela how beautiful she looked and what a lovely gown she wore. But Raphela noticed Logan shift uneasily behind her and realized that although Akar spoke to her he looked at Logan.

Poor Logan, she thought. She touched Akar's hand. "Oh, Baron, your gift was so elegant, I've never seen porcelain like that before. Wherever did you get it?" The spell was broken and the Ishtban group moved on. Logan muttered a quiet thank you to Raphela. She just smiled. Soon all the faces and names became a blur and Atan was tied up with some boring old fiefmaster. Raphela caught sight of Sonja, walked over and grabbed her.

"Sonja."

"Oh, my lady."

"Sonja, are you having a good time?"

"Yes, my lady, a wonderful time." Sonja glowed.

Raphela sighed. "Raphela, all by itself, would sound good about now, but I understand."

"Yes, my lady."

"Sonja, I haven't seen Vanar for a day and a half. How is he?"

"Just fine, my lady."

"Do you think Jivad would find it appropriate to bring him here?" Raphela was anxious for her son's presence and knew Atan felt the same.

"I don't know, but I'll ask."

"If he says yes, make sure you have a guard with you at all times."

"Yes, my lady."

"Well my lady must flit off to her guests." Raphela raised her hand in a gesture of mock snobbery. Before she could lower it, long strong fingers were wrapped around her own.

"Who gave you permission to leave my side?" Atan was truly stern.

Raphela glanced at Mahtso. "Forgive me, I did not know I was on a leash." Her sarcasm bit the air.

Though their voices were soft, they were audible.

"I have warned you not to take that tone with me."

"Oh, so your wife may not speak as she wishes. I would be better off as a harem woman."

"That's enough!" The whisper was venomous.

Atan grabbed her hand and the foursome, with as little ado as possible, headed for the door

Logan was sent back inside the hall.

Voices with incomprehensible words passed through the doorway and the crowd's sound diminished, enough for everyone to catch the last moment "You will obey". Atan's harsh tone was a perfect match for the clap, hard on her cheek.

Atan stared at her and used his hands to verify the lack of tears on her face.

The incident was not announced, but not really hidden either. Most were aware, all said nothing. The party of four returned to their rounds.

Raphela chatted pleasantly with the fiefmasters, learning about the types of farms and livestock Atan owned. She was never more than an arm's distance from him. Logan stood a step closer, or so it seemed. No guest moved without Mahtso being aware of it.

Soon the wedding couple reached Lord Rayna's table. He untethered himself from the women by this side and stood to greet the Duke and Raphela.

"Lord Rayna, may I present my wife, Lady Raphela." Atan made no gesture at a handshake.

Rayna's coal black eyes peered deep into Raphela, he took her hand. Logan stiffened and moved close enough to hear Raphela breathe. Mahtso's chain beat his leg. Atan held her other arm.

Rayna raised his eyes, first to the men, then to Raphela. Then her hand was at his lips which delivered something more like a nibble than a kiss. She returned a smile to match the gesture. Inside she cringed and yet felt drawn.

Rayna held her hand a moment longer. "Duke Ishtba, you have quite a prize. Lady Raphela, you shed light on the once somber Castle Cordan. Your Duke is a lucky man, I envy him."

"I am fortunate to be his bride."

"Such devotion Ishtba, hmmp."

"She is a good woman." Atan's arm found its way around Raphela's waist and she leaned into him.

"Indeed, she must be."

"My lord, perhaps Lord Rayna could pay us a visit this summer?"

"Hmm, well, Raphela, I suppose it's time we had visitors on a more regular basis. Rayna, would you care to visit?" Professionalism ruled Atan's tongue.

Rayna's eyes sparkled. "I would be honored."

"So be it. The fifth week of summer you shall spend a day or two at Castle Cordan."

"Thank you, until this summer, Lady Raphela."

Raphela nodded. The Ishtban foursome continued on. Sonja arrived with Vanar, who seemed as happy to be with his parents as they with him. All attention focused on Vanar for the remainder of the afternoon. By dawn the next day, all the guests had departed or were doing so as the sun rose.

Chapter 6

Vanar's hand explored the air and landed on his father's chest, locking onto the curly hair attached to it. Raphela chortled as Atan winced and then looked to her for help. Slowly her fingers pried Vanar's tiny hand loose.

"I hope he retains that grip." Atan's fingers caressed Vanar's hand and then reached to Raphela's face. Her soft skin contrasted his toughened hand, comforting it. He leaned over and let his kiss speak his feelings. "I'll be leaving in the morning for the spring spot check."

"Umhm."

Atan lay back and stared at the ceiling. "Mahtso will remain here."

Raalek's moons hung in the sky as all drifted to sleep and by dawn Atan was on his way. After Raphela turned Vanar over to Loren, his new nurse, she sent them downstairs. Raphela paced the family room. Her irregular steps and expressive hand motions caught Mahtso off guard as he reached the landing. A quick nod and he and Raphela were alone. Mahtso's chain kept time with Raphela's feet. He stood by the fireplace in silence, until she realized he was there.

"When did you get here?" She asked.

"A short time ago. What's the problem?

"Sarina is the problem."

"And what do you want to do about solving it?"

Raphela dropped to the couch and Mahtso joined her. Taking a deep breath before she spoke again. "Mahtso, she's a drastic problem. We all know that."

Mahtso nodded.

"She requires drastic measures."

Mahtso's chain spun.

Raphela whispered. "Offer her a choice, death or mutilation. In other words, if she chooses life, it will be without a tongue and without a right arm. I want her helpless and solitary. You can do this and keep her alive. Right?"

"Yes." Mahtso's blue eyes bore deep into Raphela. "But are you sure?"

"Quite."

"Atan may not approve." Mahtso shivered lightly at the thought.

"It's the chance I'm willing to take."

Mahtso stood and bowed. "As you wish, my lady."

That night as Raphela walked the stairs to her room a shriek of agony reverberated through Castle Cordan. She stopped to cringe and ice ran through her veins.

The next morning Mahtso reported, "She chose life."

Raphela swallowed. "Good, I had hoped she would."

Raphela avoided contact with almost everyone. Logan kept close watch on his solemn lady, only allowing himself short periods of rest when Marceno would take over.

A few nights later Atan returned. Sleeping alone that first night, meeting with Raphela and Mahtso in the family room the next morning

Atan discussed his findings and listened to the events that occurred in his absence. Raphela took full responsibility for Sarina.

"You followed her command?!" Atan's voice rose as he stood and pointed to Raphela who also stood.

Mahtso looked between them. "My lord, she is lady of the house."

The guards listened and did their best to be invisible.

"Lady. She is not a lady! She is a spoiled child and obviously one who ignores my rules and abuses my property." Atan's hand clenched around Raphela's wrist drawing her near. His lips were not two inches from hers. "Obviously simple embarrassment is not enough."

Atan dragged Raphela to his chambers. "And do not lag behind, Mahtso." Such a venomous sound filled Atan's voice that Mahtso bent his head in shame and followed. No doors were closed.

"Chain her!"

The cold iron cuffs locked onto Raphela's wrist and she clung to the chains. Atan moved her hair and ripped the back of her dress. Mahtso's hand reached for the whip but Atan's eyes stopped him.

The strokes were loud and searing, but controlled. Ten bloody lines scored her back. Mahtso took her down.

Marceno moved his head from the doorway as footsteps approached.

"Take care to remember who is the ruler in this castle. Go to your room, Raphela, and lick your wounds, alone. Mahtso, you leave me, too."

Atan remained alone for the day. Sunrise brought little change, nor did many of the following days. He made his plans and kept mostly to himself. On occasion he would command the staff that he not be disturbed. Sometimes Mahtso joined him. Often neither could be found.

Raphela maintained the household. Her work with Corin resumed and she was swallowed by it. The ancient tongue beckoned to her, tempting her with knowledge. Even Corin became enmeshed in her fascination.

At times, however, she too would demand solitude and was unreachable. She spoke with few people -- Fatell, Mahtso, Logan and on a number of occasions, Marceno.

When the Duke and Lady were together, rare as it was, voices were raised and anyone near Mahtso could see his chain bruising his leg with its beat.

Raalek's summer began and rolled on, its fifth week arrived and with it Lord Rayna to Castle Cordan. He noted how the castle looked and operated like a well-trained army, even if it lacked the spirit of the wedding. Certainly that kind of fervor could not last for long, he imagined. A young servant woman showed him to his quarters where he stayed until dinner.

Atan and Mahtso were waiting in the dining hall. Logan escorted Raphela to her seat and stood guard at the end of the room. Marceno escorted Rayna and his guard. Dinner was cordial. Rayna offered a toast to the newlyweds.

"Thank you. Tell me, has the spring's lack of rain hurt your crops?" Atan sipped his wine.

"Only a little. Yet if only we could harness the snow, drought could be laughed at." Rayna briefly studied Mahtso, who did not retreat from the gaze.

"Indeed, a good thought."

"Lady Raphela, you are as lovely as ever." Rayna's eyes traveled over her.

"Thank you, my lord." Her lips broke into only the tiniest and politest of smiles.

Little of substance was discussed. Often Rayna spoke to Atan yet his eyes were on Raphela.

Rayna spent a few days at the Castle. By the third he asked that Raphela show him her perspective. Atan coldly gave permission. Raphela took him through the kitchen, laundry, and Corin's office, and of course the library. Here they stopped to talk.

"Castle Cordan is quite a place. Yet not quite so militarily oriented as I would have expected."

"I have nothing to compare it to, so I will take your word for it." Raphela laughed lightly.

Rayna observed all the books. "Raphela, can you read?"

"Yes."

He reached out to touch her face but she flinched back. "I wouldn't strike you."

"I'm sorry." Raphela sunk into a chair.

Rayna knew it was time. Marceno had fed him the information. He slithered toward her and grasped her hand. "I've heard that all is not well between you and your Duke. Perhaps I could help."

She smiled. "That's kind, but what can you do?"

"I don't know until I have more information." His gentle manner took her by surprise.

A tear rolled down her cheek as she sniffled. "Lord Rayna, it simply appears that I had more freedom and rights as his consort than as his wife." She relayed her problems with Sarina. "For breaking a rule like this, he punished me as you can see." She was wearing a dress cut low enough in the back to show scars both old and new. Rayna stared blankly.

"Raphela, my castle would flourish if you were my lady. Help me defeat this savage and you shall rule Ishtba and my lands as well."

Rayna's black eyes glistened and his pulse raced. Raphela felt a certain tingle, but she said, "What you ask is treason and beyond. Should I fail, my death would last almost as long as my life."

"But if you succeed . . .And, you are not alone." He took her hand in his. "Consider it."

"I will. Tomorrow before you leave you shall have an answer."

They finished their tour. After dinner Raphela met with Atan and the now constant battle of sound raged on again. Both slept alone.

By noon the next day Rayna was stepping into his carriage. Raphela came close to bid him goodbye. "Rayna, I am with you. What is your wish?"

He studied her eyes just to be sure. "In three weeks I shall return. Keep him mellow, off guard and here. I must take him by surprise and my army will crush the Ishtban forces like ants beneath my boots."

"It will be done."

"Good. Keep Marceno close to you, he is sworn to protect you."

"Thank you."

Rayna took her hand and kissed the palm. "Till the next moon." He entered his carriage and was off.

Two weeks wore on. The Duke and his lady had no more incidents of raised voices and the tension faded to routines.

Raphela found reason to send Fatell and Vanar on a visit to Jivad and Sonja. Despite Fatell's pleadings for an explanation Raphela remained silent. "My lady, why are you doing this? Is the Duke aware? What wrath will you bring upon yourself now?" Fatell quivered as Raphela wrapped a strong arm around her.

"Don't fear, the Duke knows that a dreadfully contagious little illness is going about the castle. Neither one of us wish to expose Vanar. Perhaps we're being overprotective but bear with us."

Fatell sighed. "As you wish." She believed not a word and hesitated with every step toward the carriage.

Logan and Raphela made sure all was secure and as the second moon rose Fatell and Vanar began their journey. Raphela slipped quietly under the covers trying not to disturb Atan who opened one eye, which quickly shut before she could see.

Raalek's sun broke Atan from his sleep and by the time he was dressed Raphela welcomed the new day. Mahtso and Atan began early with a ramek inspection.

Before the sun reached its peak, Raphela felt it-- a steady rhythm, row upon row of single-minded movement and thought. It sifted through her skin before her ears picked up.

Yet it wasn't long before she heard a stranger's sword banged against the gate. In the kitchen, Raphela sat, then walked, then sat. Her eyes and hands moved in every direction.

Soon the door opened and Rayna's form filled the doorway. Raphela walked toward him, her breasts inviting more than a glance and her eyes more than a kiss. His arms locked together around her waist and his lips dug into her neck. Raphela's left arm retained the embrace as her right raised behind his neck. Seconds later Rayna's lips lost their grip and his eyes stared in bewilderment. Raphela's blade had plunged deftly into the tender spot at the base of his neck. He slid to the floor. She pushed at him with her toe. "You snake, you died too quickly. What I have had to bear because of you ... I should have left you to Mahtso."

Knife still in hand, she called for Logan and Marceno. Once in the room Logan's arms closed around Marceno. Raphela sneered. "Spy, traitor, the house of Ishtban spits upon you. May the gods pity your soul for I curse it." Her whispered hiss matched the sound of her blade cutting across his throat. She stood stone-faced as the blood sprayed across her face and dress as he gurgled to lifelessness.

Blade still in hand she ordered Logan to bring Rayna's body outside where once again a battle raged. Heavy metal swords clashed stinging the air with their noise. Smaller blades found their way into soft bellies and pumping hearts with little sound.

Both sides fought well, but Mahtso's men had belief and more. If one blow were not enough to kill, then piece by piece a man would be hacked to death, leaving arms and legs to writhe in the blood-soaked grass.

Mahtso found one man so stubborn in his desire to cling to life and so brave that even when a sword swept by his heart the grip on his weapon did not falter. Mahtso took pride in his work, first were the man's feet, one at a time, each limb took several blows and finally as he was on the stubs of his knees the shrieks of pain sputtered out, turning to a howl that chilled most men to the marrow of their bones, but not Mahtso. Mahtso's blood turned hot, his eyes flamed and his blade worked until the man was a puzzle scattered on the ground.

Raphela picked her way through the furor, Logan right behind, until they appeared before Mahtso and Atan. Logan dropped Rayna's limp form at Atan's feet. Ishtban's trio stood together drinking in their victory. In silence, Atan's eyes moved from his wife's face to Rayna's body, to the blade still tight in Raphela's grasped.

"He died by your hand?"

"Yes."

Neither voice held emotion, no joy, no anger, just simple fact. Mahtso observed the scene and gently pried the weapon from Raphela's fingers, while ordering Logan to post Rayna on a stake for all to see. By dusk Ishtban forces had assured their victory.

Mahtso organized search parties to capture any lost sheep of Rayna's and created an overall cleanup plan. Then he and Atan and Raphela mounted their rameks and headed to a cabin far from the battle scene.

They rode in silence as Raalek's sun made its slow journey across the sky. Soon it surpassed the trio and their shadows changed shape as the first moon took its place above.

All three rameks matched paces, though the beasts would quite frequently turn their heads to glance about. The riders were not so inclined, except Mahtso.

Raphela's eyes moved from the ground to her bodice and up to the sky. Marceno's blood almost stung as it sat upon her skin. Her hand grasped the reins tightly lest it be driven again to raise a blade.

Atan stared at Raphela for the first half of the trip. His eyes did not move, they rested on her bloody gown. Never before had he been with a woman who could kill. It was not natural. The deed shook his very soul. Men kill because it is their nature to do so. Women give life, not take it. And what power has she now? What will she plot to do next?

Mahtso rode between the two. He watched as Atan's growing anxiety worked its way to the beast he straddled, making it whinny and eager to stray. Mahtso watched as Raphela's depression drove down her ramek's head almost forcing the pace to slow. Mahtso drowned in the silence and prayed to the nameless ones, in hope they would listen and solve the problem that was festering all too quickly and intensely. Their moods felt like winter winds dragging the icy snow around, destroying anything they passed. Only Mahtso's friends were capable of such intensity and destruction.

Finally the cabin showed itself and all entered without a word. Atan and Mahtso stripped down to comfortable clothes, but Atan began to pace, each footstep louder.

"She killed a man today, no two men." he said finally.

"That she did, as we expected could happen. Atan, my friend, you should be proud." Mahtso was proud of Raphela and also understood what she was now feeling. But to make Atan understand, that was something else.

"A woman who kills, that's not good. Especially a woman as ambitious as her." Atan's long fingers slid a small knife from the sheath at his leg.

Mahtso's chain, which had beat hard and fast, dropped to his side.

He moved next to his Duke. "Atan, this is your wife. She killed for you."

"She killed in cold blood. Could not that delicate hand find its way to my throat? I have my heir, I no longer need her." Atan saw and heard nothing but his own thoughts as he walked toward the bedroom, his knife solidly clasped between his fingers.

Mahtso fell to a chair and buried his head in his hands.

Raphela, now scrubbed from head to foot and in clean garb, heard the door open and turned to face Atan. Gray ice eyes looked past her. Raphela took a deep breath and struggled not to let the tears flow. She stood before the tall lean form, father of her child, husband, friend and knew he only saw a killer, a threat to his empire.

She dropped to her knees and opened her robe just enough to bare her chest. She couldn't help the tears as they flowed silently down her face. "My lord, if you cannot accept what I have done as part of your victory, as a gift to see you rise to ultimate power, then plunge your knife deep, for I cannot live without your trust and belief."

Atan's breath was barely audible. Both hands held the blade and it found its way to Raphela's skin. She felt the pressure, the prick and she watched the first stream of blood. Yet she still looked to his eyes and offered all she could to his heart. For just a moment, he saw her face, her eyes.

The blade fell to the floor and Atan to his knees. His hands held her face as the Ishtban couple planted feverish kisses on each other. He carried her to the bed. Raphela's body started to shake, tears filled her eyes and soaked her robe. Even Atan's strong arms were not enough to calm her. At Atan's shout Mahtso brought wine. Three or four glasses later she dozed off and Mahtso smiled and left them alone.

Atan slid down on the bed, not letting Raphela out of his arms. He placed a gentle kiss on her forehead.

She squeezed him a little tighter.

"Atan," she whispered.

"Yes."

"I love you."

Atan pulled her close enough to hear her heartbeat. In the dark peaceful night Raphela found sleep and Atan found his cheeks stained with his tears as he drifted into slumber.

Summer's blossom soaked and sifted through the cabin, but as Atan awoke his nostrils sensed something more.

His feet guided him towards the aromas and stopped in the kitchen just as Raphela was placing the last of the breakfast platters on the table. Surrounded by red mangine fruit and green berries was a pile of freshly baked biscuits. Beside that plate sat a tray filled with cheeses and smoked meat.

"Well, my wife, I didn't know you could cook."

Raphela didn't turn to look at Atan. "Hmmph. A skill that was shoved at me in childhood. But don't look too pleased yet. I never mastered it."

Mahtso stood at the doorway and laughed. "Rumor at the castle says she speaks the truth."

Atan moved to put his arms around her, but she sat too quickly. "Mahtso, would you bring the tea and, Atan, come sit and nourish yourself."

Pleasant chatter of unimportant things filled the breakfast time. After the meal, Raphela sent the men to wander and relax as she cleaned up. Her eyes spotted every speck of dust that clung to the cabin and its contents and her hands removed each one. Every pot was scrubbed and every cloth washed. The dishes sparkled enough to reflect the sunlight. The small rugs were taken out and beaten.

Mahtso and Atan strolled the grounds surrounding the cabin. By noon they stopped to lunch on the meat and bread that Raphela had packed. A light breeze stirred the trees above the ground where they sat. On occasion some small furry creature would pause to study them and then move on.

Mahtso rambled on about the battle. "It would have been more difficult if not for our plans." He swallowed some spring water.

"Mm, I suppose." Atan gazed at the tree behind Mahtso, scrutinizing some insect that made its way up the bark.

"Rayna's men were well trained." Mahtso tried to maintain a cheerful repose, despite Atan's distance. But the chain in his hand beat more and more quickly against the rock beside him.

A small rodent scampered by Atan. He flinched.

"Is it Raphela?"

Atan just stared into Mahtso's clear blue eyes.

"She needs a little time, my friend. She'll be with you soon."

Atan sighed and began a purposeless stroll.

Raphela continued to scrub and polish, her mind a mottled cloud of feelings and thoughts so confused and intense, that words had no place.

By dusk the men returned. Raphela served a decent meal, they all talked and went to sleep.

At sunrise Atan awoke and held a sleeping Raphela in his arms. The back of his hand caressed her cheek. Raphela's eyes opened, her lips placed a gentle kiss on his neck and then she popped out of bed.

"Atan, I miss Vanar, can we please go today?"

"Is that what's troubling you? Of course we can leave as soon as you're ready." Atan felt better, convinced Raphela would be relaxed once she had whole family back together again.

Breakfast was a quick affair. The beasts were packed and the trio headed to Jivad and Sonja's house. By midafternoon they arrived.

Jivad heard them first, as the rameks beat the ground stirring tiny pebbles from comfortable spots and sending clouds of dust into the air. As the trio approached the door, Fatell, Jivad and Sonja with Vanar in her arms, crowded the doorway.

Jivad tied the beasts to a strong post. Fatell ran to Mahtso who held her tight in his arms. Both cried. Raphela took Vanar from Sonja and pressed him close to her. He smelled so sweet, like the spring air. Atan stroked his son's head and smiled.

Once inside, Sonja made tea. Raphela put a sleepy Vanar in his cradle. When she walked back to her seat, she stumbled. Atan jumped to catch her. As her head raised, he saw the daggers of flame in her eyes leap out at him. Anguish filled Atan's heart. He felt the pain of the first whip strokes he laid upon her back. And he felt her anger at him for the blade that nearly pierced her heart. She castigated him. Atan's knees wobbled. Her eyes said, "Why bother to help me, my death would suit you just as well."

Atan's arms wrapped around Raphela's waist while her hands pushed against his chest. "Forgive me," he whispered. "I swear to you, never again."

In that moment their lives were as tossed as if torrential rain and winds ripped the trees from the soil and birds were sent hurtling towards the clouds despite the desperate flapping of their wings. Atan waited in the eye of the storm, for Raphela held the clouds and the winds in her eyes. Eternity seemed to pass, everyone heard and felt their own hearts beat, Atan most of all.

Raphela heard and felt only Atan, the storm that raged inside her found a door and dissipated. Her arms found his waist and their lips met in a long warm greeting that put the sun back in the sky and rerooted the trees. Raalek saw a rainbow fill its sky. After dinner Fatell could wait no longer.

"Please tell us what happened, Raphela. I feared for your life."

Though drained, Raphela knew she could best relate the tale. She leaned forward, away from Atan's strong shoulder and began. "In truth, my friends, it started at the wedding. The three of us noticed how close Sarina and Marceno were to Rayna. It showed us that he was a threat that could strike far sooner than anticipated. So a plan was formed. The Duke and I had to appear less settled than reality allowed, starting with the wedding reception."

Everyone nodded, remembering the Duke's disciplinary measures.

"What about Sarina?" Fatell squeezed Mahtso's hand.

"Sarina needed to be eliminated and so did Marceno. Marceno we felt might serve a temporary purpose, but Sarina, was trouble. My previous experiences with her were enough excuse for her punishment. She was offered that or death.

"As for Marceno, we felt that he was a spy, and was proven such when the Duke returned from his trip. Marceno stood outside the Duke's room and listened to every angry word.

142

When he saw the Duke raise the whip, I believe he was convinced I could turn.

"The scars, Marceno's tale and the Duke's general attitude towards me convinced Rayna that I was ripe for betrayal."

Jivad and Sonja looked around their cozy home, with its comfortable furniture, full cupboard, fireplace stacked with wood and thick rugs to keep the chill out in the winter. They looked then at each other, with the same thought. How much of this life rests on the Duke's kindness and good will? What if he was to be angered or threatened?

"Why send me away?" Fatell asked.

Raphela took her hand. "Oh, Fatell, who would Rayna seek if we failed? You and Vanar. Keeping either of you in the castle was too great a risk, and the less you knew the better."

Fatell shuddered at the thought of Rayna ruling Ishtba.

Rayna told me when he would plan his attack and that I was to keep the Duke happy and off guard, to which I agreed. When Rayna and his men arrived, Castle Cordan was ready. Rayna's defeat and death were the end to the tale and here we are."

Raphela carefully omitted her part in Rayna's death and what followed. The three listeners sensed the missing piece but knew better than to ask.

By the next morning Jivad and Sonja bid their friends farewell.

Castle Cordan waited like an anxious mistress, primped and ready for all that made life whole. As the party rode up the path all the souls felt peace arriving. The enormous doors opened and a gleaming floor and spotless hall filled with anxious people greeted the royal family and friends. The structure itself seemed to smile. Warmth and satisfaction seeped through the walls like steam from fresh bread on a winter's day.

Mahtso's first task upon returning was to verify that his orders had been carried out.

Even before retiring for the night he received reports from his captains, all neatly written and organized. Despite his exhaustion, Mahtso felt compelled to read them. So, by the light of two lumpglows at the kitchen table and with Fatell by his side he settled into his work.

Fatell poured his tea, massaged his shoulders and just contentedly waited on him, glad to have him back.

The chain in his pocket lay calm most of the night. His eyes caught every word, he glowed inside at the thoroughness of his men.

When not lavishing attention on Mahtso, Fatell busied herself around the kitchen, taking stock of supplies and handling a general check up.

Mahtso yawned as he reviewed the last few pages.

Fatell nodded as he yawned, and then jumped, spilling a bag of flour on the floor as Mahtso slammed the teacup on the table. Fatell saw pieces of the cup fly and the tea made a dripping puddle on the table. As she cleaned the mess, Mahtso's chain pounded the table.

"Mahtso," Fatell spoke softly. "Is it very bad?" Meaning, dangerous.

Mahtso turned his blue eyes to her. No love, not hate, just purpose filled them. "It will be remedied."

Atan and Raphela cuddled Vanar, put him to sleep and then wrapped around each other, confident that all was well, drifted into peaceful slumber.

Breakfast in the family dining room smelled of spice bread and fired meat.

Mahtso, bloodshot eyes and tousled hair, appeared at the doorway, and even he was soothed by the aromas and contentment of the Ishtban family.

But Atan responded quickly to his disheveled friend. "What is it, Mahtso?"

Mahtso lowered his head and fingered the chain in his pocket, and his speech was almost a mumbling stutter. "In our absence, my men discovered a spy."

Atan heaved a sigh. "I see." The pause was torture and Atan played it out, looking at Raphela the next time he spoke. "Where is he now?"

"In the dungeon, kept alive for interrogation."

"Get some rest and take care of it." Atan's cool tone relayed a strange sense of power.

Mahtso shrunk back. "Yes, sire."

Raphela watched, knowing only the surface, but sensing Mahtso's agony as he shuffled out of the room. Once out of earshot, she spoke.

"What was that all about?"

"Mahtso made a mistake."

"A mistake?!" Raphela gritted her teeth. "How could you be so cruel about a mistake. After all the spy was captured."

"Raphela, a spy could be the end to all we know. It's Mahtso's job to keep Castle Cordan free from such vermin. He failed at an important task. If not for the stressful circumstances of the past weeks, I would have been a great deal harsher."

"Atan, he was punishing himself fairly well." Raphela's robes flowed around her as she put the teapot on the hearth.

As she turned back her waist felt Atan's arms closing around it and his lips were but an inch from hers. He whispered, "Are you my conscience, too?"

She melted in his embrace. "If need be."

"Mmmmm."

Atan's lips and tongue meshed in perfect harmony with hers. They had little trouble finding a short path to his bed.

They rolled in their love, hands holding and squeezing, noses buried in hair and rubbing against the lusty scent of passion embroiled skin as tongues opened the sensitive pores and continued the feverish cycle.

It was midmorning before they could stop; too many nights had passed, too many long painful, lonely nights since they had last shared each other.

Clearheaded and satisfied they returned to Castle Cordan's routine.

As Raphela went about her routines she thought about Mahtso and what he was about to do.

This side of him that instilled terror in most living things, remained well tamed at the castle. Yet, Raphela always felt it near. Now was the perfect opportunity, if she were allowed.

As Mahtso passed her on his way to the dungeon she grabbed his arm.

Intense concentration flowed from his eyes, so much that few words, quickly stated were best.

"May I watch?"

Mahtso wrapped his fingers around her wrist and squeezed hard. "Are you mad?" He breathed as if flames were tearing at his throat.

Whatever demon that resided in Raphela took stage in her eyes and answered him.

"If he allows." With that, Mahtso resumed his journey to the dungeon.

And Raphela, titillated by the possibilities found Atan. "Please, Atan, it would explain so much." Her pleas were almost demands.

Atan sighed. "Raphela, you have no idea what lies in wait for you."

"All the better." She panted.

"You will do it anyway, go ahead." Atan shook his head as Raphela laid a thankful kiss on his cheek and headed towards the dungeon.

Despite the lumpglows along the wall, darkness prevailed on the thin stairway. Raphela could feel the dampness creep under he skin as she clutched the cold railing. Her feet felt every inch of ragged stone and the slippery spots of mildewed algae. Odors of decaying animals echoed in the air, speaking of decades past.

But Raphela ignored it all to reach her goal. That Room. As she left the stairs, her eyes caught a glimmer of light. Using cold walls as a guide, she made her way to Mahtso.

The room was oddly lit. A few feet past the doorway and to her right was a stone table, laden with tools, clean, shiny and deadly. Beside the tools was an array of bottles containing things living and otherwise. Everything was quite in order.

An incredibly large place, the walls were shadowed, except for one, directly in front of her. For there he was, an average looking man, no leaner or fatter than most. Perhaps a shade taller than Mahtso. His head was recently shaved, but not his bare chest and he was remarkably clean. Around his wrist and legs were shackles, much like those in the Duke's chambers, and in spite of the dampness they showed no signs of rust. Around his forehead was a metal band, keeping his head up and straight.

So far no sound escaped his lips. The room seemed to itch at the silence.

"They all look so pretty to start." Mahtso crept out from the shadows and his hiss startled her, but Raphela showed no reaction. "I do believe he will last, for a while anyway." Mahtso's blue eyes looked black and he reeked of something foul.

The man on the wall froze as Mahtso's eyes turned on him.

Raphela felt an icy finger slither down her arm. "Come, my love, let us learn together," Mahtso purred. She was torn between disgust, terror and excitement, but followed.

Mahtso's hands examined every inch of the man, his fingers much like a spider, weaving a web. Raphela saw no pain inflicted, yet she knew the captive's skin crawled with each touch. She could see his muscles tighten in discomfort. Mahtso stepped away, and from a dark corner pulled a stool and a long thin stick with soft bristles at its end. He sat on the stool and toyed with the stick, gently stroking it and occasionally grinning up from lowered eyes. Gently he rubbed the soles of his captive's feet and watched the man's toes curl and twist.

"Tell me," Mahtso's tone was almost conversational, "do you know who I am?"

The captive's eyes opened wide, his head seemed to nod, but no words were spoken.

"Now, now, I asked you a question, answer me." Mahtso's firm schoolmaster tone was accompanied by a stroke of the stick that just missed the man's ear.

Raphela flinched.

The captive shivered. "I believe you are Mahtso."

"Good, that wasn't so hard, was it?"

"No, sir."

"Sir, I like that. You're polite." Mahtso turned his back and returned to stroking the stick. "Oh, my. I do feel awful. I have been terribly rude." Mahtso's self chastisement, a grasp at opportunity, did not ease the captive. Mahtso turned to Raphela, and held out his hand. Raphela held out hers and walked to Mahtso, slowly.

"Now, for a proper introduction. Lady Raphela, mistress of Castle Cordan, I'd like you to meet," Mahtso stopped in mock surprise. "Oh, I'm afraid I didn't catch your name." Mahtso's eyes peered out from under a furrowed brow.

The captive squirmed at first, then straightened as much as his position would allow, even his chest stuck out a bit, but his lips were sealed.

Mahtso stamped his stick on the floor and laughed with great satisfaction. "My lady Raphela, we have a professional. This will be a pleasure, a test of my skills."

Raphela kept her distance from Mahtso more because of the odor than anything else, but she shook her head in confusion. "I don't understand."

"There are two kinds of spies, a soldier spy and a professional spy. Both have advantages and disadvantages. The former generally gathers one small bit of information and spits it back to his captain and never questions why. He is limited to whatever task is given. The professional," Mahtso wagged his finger at his captive, who felt the cold stones irritate his back and tried to keep away from them, "the professional assembles the whole picture and reports his analysis, a far more creative and intricate fellow. A solder spy immediately offers his name, but that is all, for it is all he has to give. The professional spy reveals nothing. For a name, one's identity." Mahtso emphasized the word, "that opens the door. Who can resist responding to one's own name, and from there it is a matter of time. You see, Raphela, the professional knows both sides of the tale, his capture could mean doom for those who sent him."

Mahtso returned to the stool, picking up his stick as he sat. The captive maintained his courageous stance.

Mahtso brushed the edge of his tool under the captive's chin. "Brave soul aren't you? I respect that."

Mahtso slithered off the stool and stood directly under the man's nose. The man tried to move his head away from the stench, but Mahtso's strong fingers locked his chin in place. "Respect," he hissed, "goes just so far. I too have a job and I am not a patient man."

Even Raphela recoiled. The captive's eyes were like saucers and the lump in his throat grew, but he remained silent. Mahtso backed away. "Very well." He shrugged his shoulders. "Are you thirsty?"

"Yes, sir."

Mahtso gave him a drink and offered him a piece of bread, both of which the man readily downed.

"Have you reconsidered, sir? I'm sure Lady Raphela would like to know your name."

The silence echoed through the room and into Raphela's heart. Mahtso heaved a sigh. "I grow bored, what can I do? Ah, here we go." His hand reached out and picked up a large winged insect.

Mahtso held its wings and blew on it. "Interesting creatures, quite strong." His fingers caressed the bug and then he jerked out one of its four wings, which he lay on the stool for the captive to see. Mahtso grinned as he pulled off a leg and laid it perpendicular to the wing. Piece by piece, slowly enough to seem like hours, and directly in the captive's view, Mahtso disassembled the insect until all that was left was a writhing head and body sitting on the stool amidst its wriggling appendages. Mahtso was quite insistent that his captive watch every move and stare at the bug until it died. After which Mahtso ate it, one appendage at a time.

Raphela stayed in the shadows. The captive turned pale, almost yellow, gagged more than once, yet remained silent.

Mahtso shook his head. His hand reached out for a soft white loci a gentle sweet creature, totally harmless. The captive watched as Mahtso nuzzled the creature and stroked it, more and more harshly. The captive's mouth opened. "Elat," he croaked.

Slowly Mahtso put down the creature. "Elat, so that's your name."

"Yes."

"Well, Elat, where are you from?" Elat stiffened once more, still believing that he could outlast his captor. Silence ruled for the moment.

Raphela leaned against the wall, its cold moist stone made her muscles tighten. As she pushed herself away, her fingers felt a bite of pain. She brought them to her face and saw the tiny trickle of blood escape her fingertips. She sucked on it to stop the bleeding.

Mahtso caught the scent of her blood and felt a lust grow inside himself. Raphela and Elat shifted uneasily. Mahtso beckoned for Raphela to come near. Her slow steps gave her time to recompose and consider Elat's very uncomfortable position.

"My lady, we must continue the questioning. Stay close, so that you hear all he has to say." Mahtso's eyes danced and his nostrils flared.

His hands, gently placed on her shoulders, guided her to the stool and traveled her back before returning to his pockets. He then began a new line of questioning. "For whom do you work?"

Though Elat felt every cut the stones had made in his back and his body ached, his lips were still.

Mahtso maintained his calm. The room grew frosty, darker, one could only assume that the sun was setting. Neither Raphela nor Mahtso had any desire for food or drink. But Raphela noticed that Elat was offered both, frequently. Why, she did not understand. But now that hours had passed, that action became more clear. Elat would have to relieve himself, eventually. Soon enough, the time came. Elat requested privacy; the use of his hands, Mahtso snickered and took his methodical steps away from Elat.

Mahtso busied himself with some lizard, that died slowly, while Raphela observed both men. Elat, very soon had to choose between allowing the poisons that circulated inside his body, eating at the inner linings of him, to continue their path, or suffer the embarrassment and discomfort of relieving himself. The latter choice, seemed more logical, at least for the moment.

Mahtso jumped at this chance, turning on him like a cat on a mouse. "You child, the slightest discomfort and you lose control, what would your master think?" At first, Elat bravely listened, and then shut his eyes as if it would shut out the voice.

When Mahtso bored of this and became silent, the room overtook the people. It echoed with the sound of caged insects, helpless beating wings furiously against solid walls.

Raphela noticed that Mahtso's chain was motionless, carefully tucked away. This sent a moment of terror through Raphela, for it meant that Mahtso was truly content. His frequent glances and half smiles in her direction created an even stranger feeling.

At one point. Mahtso asked Raphela to place an object on a shelf beside Elat's ear. The object, a wooden triangle was fitted with a long thin needle. It moved back and forth at an incredibly steady pace, enough to drive one mad after a few minutes, much less the hours intended for Elat.

Raphela was fascinated by it and took her time to study the thing, as she placed it on the shelf, Mahtso watched her fluid movements and tempting form. His hand stroked a small switch. Elat's eyes opened wide, would this maniac, take on the lady of the house?

Raphela didn't see Mahtso, but sensed him and for a split second understood and shared his urge. She raised her arms and leaned towards the wall.

Mahtso felt the blood rush. His hand caressed Raphela's shoulder, but she felt the switch caressing her leg. She lowered her arms and turned around. Mahtso's arm briskly moved and the switch drew first blood from Elat's leg.

Raphela returned to the safety of the shadows and Mahtso to the job at hand.

In the polite vampirish tone he so enjoyed, Mahtso began. "Now, I believe we were discussing your employer."

"I was not." Temporarily distracted from his own situation, Elat spoke.

"That's a shame. It's getting late and I really do need to know."

"I will die first." Elat hoped his bravery would touch Raphela and so spare him any additional agony.

Mahtso leaned his foul breathed face into Elat's. "It is well that you pray for death, for you will welcome it. But not until..." Mahtso stopped and took a deep breath. His eyes turned darker

151

and his stench more foul. Raphela almost gave in to Elat's plea, but knew better.

Mahtso continued. "Enough games, I need information." Mahtso walked to his table, his steps never changing rhythm, matching that of the object on the wall. His fingers wrapped around a shiny well honed-blade. Deft hands brought the blood to Elat's knee, with precise incisions.

Once the cries of agony ceased, Raphela chanced taking a closer look. Despite the bloody mess, she could see that Mahtso had cut that portion of the man's leg that controlled movement. The ankle and foot swung in uselessness. Elat stared in horror.

Mahtso questioned him again. Elat did not respond. Mahtso cut the other leg, making sure that loss of blood was minimal to avoid wasting time in reviving the captive.

Elat's chest heaved in anguish, tears rolled down his red face, yet he did not answer. Mahtso's knowledge of anatomy proved remarkable, and the sight and scent of blood just seemed to push him farther. One by one, he slit the muscles in Elat's fingers, and wrist of his left hand. He almost drooled as the blood dripped from the man's shoulder, so lost was he, that Elat's hoarse scrams reverberated through the castle before he listened for any more answers. Raphela learned respect for both men.

Finally, Elat's screams were heard, his body shaking with the loss of his life's fluid, "AKAR, BARON AKAR, I work for Baron Akar."

Mahtso cleaned the blade and replaced it exactly to where it had been before, then held out his hand to Raphela. "My lady, the rest will be simple. You will miss nothing if you leave now."

Raphela had had enough anyway. "Thank you, Mahtso, I'll let you complete your work alone."

Mahtso nodded.

Raphela heard the door close behind her. She walked calmly to Atan's bedroom, carefully avoiding any human contact.

It was just past dusk. The sun had set, leaving only its last rays in the sky. Atan followed them as Raphela entered.

She said nothing, but her ashen face and icy hands spoke the tale. He wrapped a blanket around them both and held her close, keeping her warm with his body, and calm with his strength.

She woke a few times in a cold sweat, and nestled in tighter to Atan.

As always, Atan woke with the sun, and Raphela was not far behind.

"Are you all right?"

"Yes." She smiled sheepishly, "But I deserve the lecture."

"Obviously not needed."

"Thank you. I have never seen him so calm, so content. Mahtso really enjoyed what he did."

Atan tied his robe. "He always has, yet today, he will be ecstatic."

"What do you mean?"

Atan sighed. "Raphela, yesterday he exercised self control in order to retrieve information. Very shortly he will appear and regurgitate it to me."

As he spoke, Mahtso appeared in the doorway. Atan nodded. Mahtso methodically laid out all the information, Atan took notes.

Mahtso didn't glance at Raphela, his sweaty forehead remained in Atan's direction and his chain jiggled furiously.

"You've done well, Mahtso, very well."

"Thank you." Mahtso was strangely short of breath.

Raphela noticed the eye contact between the two men.

"Yes, Mahtso, I have enough."

"Thank you sire."

As Mahtso scurried out the door, Raphela couldn't help but feel that the master had just thrown his faithful dog a meaty bone. It chilled her, just a bit.

And just what was Mahtso's bone?

It wasn't long before Raphela knew.

Long wails and pleadings for mercy resounded through the castle, till just past noon.

Raphela, Atan and Vanar spent the day together, as did most families.

Fatell took a long walk, out of earshot of the castle.
By dawn Castle Cordan returned to its status quo.

Chapter 7

Warm rays of sun broke Atan from his sleep, but the scent of Raphela's hair kept him in bed just a bit longer. Her voluptuous form, heightened by Vanar's birth, was a pleasant sight for the day's beginning. He laid a kiss on her cheek and entered into his morning routine.

The handle of the water pitcher was cold against his skin, refreshing as he poured the clear cold liquid into the bowl. His long fingers squeezed the water soaked cloth and then Atan began to bathe himself from head to toe.

Unbeknownst to him, Raphela awoke. After shaking the hair away from her face, she leaned on her elbows and watched her husband's lean form. As he reached to wash his back, her hands took the cloth and did it for him. She didn't miss an inch, from his strong shoulders, to his tight cheeks and muscular calves. Before she had a chance to put the cloth away, Atan turned and wrapped his arms around her. They shared a passionate and loving kiss. Then Raphela handed Atan his pants, which he slid into, and then his shirt, a loose comfortable affair, light in weight and color. One more kiss and Atan was off for a morning ride.

Raphela started her similar routine of bathing, after which she donned a summery blue dress with sleeves ending just above the elbow and a hem just below the knees. Her form gave it shape, but no more. Once dressed, it was time for Vanar. She leaned down to get the smiling baby from his cradle. The smile turned to a gurgle of joy at the sight of his mother. Mother and son shared silly noises and faces and lots of cuddles. He didn't even mind the bath.

Raphela placed him in the basket and headed toward the stairs. There Logan, ever faithful, patiently waited. Taking Vanar from Raphela, he led the way down the stairs. Atan, back from his ride and waiting for Mahtso, nodded his approval to Logan.

Castle Cordan's long stairway, took as much time to descend as ascend. Raphela walked slowly, passing Mahtso along the way.

155

They shared a brief but potent glance that sealed their bond.

What little fear she had had evolved into respect-- not so much for what he could do, as that most of the time he didn't. This solid respect was reflected with equal admiration. Never before had a woman watched. If Mahtso had searched the world for a sister, none better than Raphela could be found. If she had scoured for a brother, only Mahtso would have surfaced. Now it was done, the bond was beyond words and beyond comprehension.

Mahtso found Atan. The lord and master rested comfortably in the family room, a faint smile on his face. He gazed at the dying embers in the fireplace, feeling a contentment he didn't understand. Then he caught the sound of Mahtso's footsteps. The man's easy gait and clear eyes were a good sign. His chain jingling ever so slightly in his hand.

"Sit, my friend."

Mahtso laid his notes on the table and took a seat near Atan on the couch. "Atan, we retrieved quite a bit of helpful information from Elat."

"Good. Even though we feel at peace with the world right now, I am still anxious to be rid of the last pest. So, remind me why I should wait." Atan stood and paced, he was not edgy, but his words were accurate.

"Atan," he smiled. "The men are ready for rest, not war. Winter will be here sooner than we think. Business needs attention. Shall I go on?"

"No." Atan squeezed Mahtso's shoulder. "I needed to hear it, that's all. I just want to be free of those who wish me harm." Atan held back for a moment, then began. "Mahtso, life should be better, less pain, more comfort. Longer life, better ways of living. Why is tilling the land so hard? Why must everything we do require such intense labor. Will my son waste hours traveling from one place to another? There is so much, my friend. And we waste time, conquering, just because everyone fears the change." Atan shook his head and sighed. "Oh, well, on to the battle. What of Akar?"

Mahtso pulled out his notes, slowly trying to digest Atan's thoughts. But for all the years they had spent together, Atan was still a mystery, one to be blindly followed. But Mahtso knew that Raphela understood. How, he knew not, perhaps some invisible link, perhaps by the gods' wishes. But Raphela shared the dreams. Atan and Raphela fed and seeded the other, both embraced a future no one else could envision.

"Mahtso, are you ready?"

"Sorry, lost in thought for a moment. Anyway, Akar. He is not as much a barbarian as the others. Elat spoke of tools and instruments that do men's work, such as I've never heard." Mahtso stopped for a moment. "You know, your desire to improve could be sitting in his castle. Perhaps already in use, perhaps gathering dust. Only Akar and his people know."

"An excellent point. It sounds like we need a spy over there."

"Yes."

"Yes," Atan nodded, and considered Elat's fate. "But it is a delicate matter, one to be handled with great care. Let's take some time, the winter, to think it over and then plan."

"As you wish, especially since Akar has no immediate plans."

"Good. But will he not miss hearing from Elat?"

Mahtso grinned, "No. Elat was not to report until next spring. As a matter of fact, Akar does not even know if Elat arrived safely. It appears that he arrived amidst our battle with Rayna."

"I see. That eases my mind. What about Akar's army? That is, does one exist? If so, any details?"

"Yes, it exists and according to Elat, is fairly well trained."

"Hmmmm."

Atan and Mahtso continued on for many hours.

In the meantime, Raphela sought out Fatell and dragged her through every inch of the castle. Despite the excitement of the past few months, Castle Cordan still operated as well as the Duke's army. Raphela noted Fatell's skillful organization and knowledge of everyone's task. Many times during their walk Fatell would be asked to give instructions or directions, which she did with little effort. But Raphela noticed how often Fatell assigned frivolous jobs to keep people busy, because the

157

substantive work had been done. This played on Raphela's mind. By noon they had traversed the castle, almost from top to bottom. Raphela was ready for a change.

"Logan, would you please bring Vanar back from the nurse. Fatell, have someone bring us lunch in the informal living room." Raphela didn't wait for a reply, she headed straight for the room.

Fatell did as told, as did Logan, who was sent off to other duties after fetching Vanar. The warm colors and comfortable setting put both women at ease. Raphela sat on the floor and nursed Vanar while Fatell spread out the plates and food.

Vanar suckled hard and long, while his mother lavished him with affection. Finally, he was sated and placed in a small curved rocker, made especially for him. There he studied the world. Raphela rolled a leafy vegetable around a piece of cold fowl and proceeded to nibble away at that and the other finger foods before her. Fatell indulged along with her.

"Fatell, the castle is running incredibly well. You're doing a wonderful job." Raphela sincere, and excited was grateful for the smooth operation that gave her more time to devote to her studies with Corin.

Fatell blushed. "Raphela, years of established routine make it simple and your minor changes have made it that much easier."

Raphela chuckled. "Thank you." Her hands caressed Vanar's face and she bent down to kiss him and whisper at him. Without looking up, she spoke, "Who taught Atan how to read and write?"

"One of the elders."

"Hmmm. And the other men? Who taught them?" Raphela rubbed her nose against Vanar's.

"Their fathers or uncles, I suppose." Fatell sat up straight, growing curious.

"That's logical." Vanar's fingers wrapped around Raphela's hair, pulling her close.

"And you, Fatell, who taught you?" Raphela buried a grin in Vanar's tummy.

Fatell almost choked on her water. "Me? I don't, my lady, why would you think, women don't..."

Raphela laid a gentle hand on her flustered friend. "Why do you babble so? I know you can. And it's certainly no crime."

Fatell lowered her head. "It's the only thing that my father faulted me for and it still hurts. He believed that women should not do such things."

"May the gods protect your father's soul, but I'm glad you learned. It's valuable to me."

"Why?" Fatell's eyes scrutinized her friend without trying hide her own fear.

Raphela ignored the question. "Fatell, I want every man, woman and child to learn to read, write, add, subtract, everything."

"What?! Raphela, it just isn't done." Fatell's plate clattered under the dropped fork.

"Where? The rest of the world? Castle Cordan is different." Raphela sat up and stared hard at her friend.

"Raphela, the Duke - - - are you sure?" Fatell sunk back, knowing the uselessness of the argument.

Raphela leaned on her knees and grabbed Fatell by the shoulders. "The Duke would be ecstatic."

Fatell's small frame, usually bent over anyway, seemed to shrink and turn in, as she shook her head in confusion. Raphela spoke softly, "For all the years you've lived here, you still don't understand. My poor, Fatell."

Raphela stood up and made Fatell rise with her. She walked her to an open shutter that looked out on the castle's garden. "Look around you. Is not everything the best?"

"Yes, but..."

"But you think it's simply wealth. No, even before I came here, I learned about Duke Atan Ishtba. The merchants who traveled would speak of all the castles and homes. Cordan was special. The food always plentiful and better. The people wiser, kinder, more learned and trained than anywhere else. Everything at Cordan was the best. Many met the king and other barons and dukes, very few met Atan Ishtba. But nowhere else would they rather stay than at his home. Atan Ishtba believes in making things better. I've read his reports. Always seeking a way for life to be lived at its best. Education makes it better. He strives for excellence, and I, for one, will give it to him."

Her friend was easily caught in the mood, though she still did not understand all the need for growth and change. Raphela picked up a vegetable. "You see this. It must be the greenest, strongest and tastiest that can be grown. Because, people will enjoy it more, maybe even be healthier. I don't know. But his ideas are right."

"I'm beginning to see. But how do we teach everyone? There aren't enough men to teach one at a time. It would take centuries."

Raphela sat down and put her chin in her hands. "I know." Silence held them both, then Raphela lifted her head, eyes aflame, heart beating almost loud enough to hear. "Groups, learning in groups. Just like soldiers learn in a group. Why not everything else?"

"What?"

"Mahtso and Atan trained their soldiers together, not one by one. Why can't reading and writing be taught the same way?" Raphela went on. "Definitely. It can be done. Here's the plan. First, we must find someone capable and willing to organize the men who will be the teachers. So many of our elders are begging for something to do. And those men too injured to work, let them teach as well. Also, we must put together a nursery. No one will miss the opportunity to learn, because they have no help in caring for a child. Children, children age 7 and older must start to learn as well." Raphela stopped to catch her breath. "Now, let's think about who, what, when, where and how."

The two women spent the rest of the day making plans.

Summer turned to autumn. Leaves on the trees reached the climax of their lives by showing their shades of red, orange and purple, while the bark deepened to the color of wine.

Atan traveled, inspecting the fiefs and levying whatever taxes he felt appropriate. Back at the castle Raphela and Fatell pursued their project. Mahtso verified the receipt of taxes, in the form of goods. Also, with some persuasion, sought out teachers.

Raphela did not neglect Vanar or her time with Corin. By summer's end they had learned the ancient tongue well enough to read many of the books in Corin's collection and the Ishtban library. Raphela marveled at the tales and wondrous life of the past. Corin drank in the medical knowledge with an unending thirst.

One day Raphela came upon a book that seemed to call her name. She finished it in an afternoon and then raced through the entire castle looking for Corin. Finally, out of breath and panting, Raphela stopped, just to catch her wind, and then popped in front of Corin, who was peacefully sitting under a tree. The poor man was so startled his skin turned white.

"What is it, child? You scared me half to death."

"I'm sorry, but you must look at this, read it, make sure I understand it." She shoved the book in front of him.

He read a few pages, occasionally glancing at Raphela, whom paced back and forth, shivering in the cool autumn air. "This is very interesting." Corin closed the book. "But why are you so excited?"

Raphela grabbed him. "Corin, can it work, Trancestate? Will it work?"

"I really don't know."

"I must know. It speaks of people being put to sleep, but not really, just in a trance and then they are given a suggestion of something to do, upon a specific signal. They are taken out of the trance, not remembering being in it, but responding properly to the signal. It even speaks of people being told they are someone else. This could be invaluable to the Duke."

"I know I don't understand why, but I have learned not to question. I will read it tonight and tomorrow we will discuss it further."

"All right. I'll see you in the morning."

Obsessed as she was, Raphela found a way to occupy herself. Fatell was interviewing the last of today's group of men when Raphela arrived. Fatell's hair was straying from its band and she shook her hand from the stiffness of taking notes, but her eyes did not stray from the work and her voice was amazingly calm and strong. Finally the last man passed through the

161

doorway and Raphela took a seat next to her friend. They stared at each other for just a moment, a check on the mood. Fatell shaped her lips in a mock scowl and shook a finger at Raphela. "I should be angry with you for this. It is quite a task."

Raphela smiled widely. "And you love every minute of it."

"Perhaps," Fatell allowed herself a grin.

"Are these men to teach or administrate?"

"Administrate. I think I've narrowed it down to three. I'd like you to meet with them."

"Wonderful. Set up a time and I'll be there." Raphela rose to go.

"Thank you, Raphela." The thanks was more for the task than the help.

By dawn Raphela was anxious to find Corin. It was not long after that she was knocking on his door. Now, as every time Raphela entered Corin's office, she was overtaken by the variety of herbal scents and the rows upon rows of jars lining his shelves. She had come to believe healers arranged their surroundings to keep a veil of mystery about their work.

"Well, Corin, did you read it?"

"Good morning to you, too, my lady."

Raphela lowered her head. "I'm sorry, you're right, good morning."

"And, yes, Raphela, I did. Fascinating, truly fascinating."

"Yes, yes." Raphela could not keep her impatience at bay. "But can it work?"

Corin shook his head, exposing his annoyance. "I believe so."

"Good."

The day passed in heavy discussion of the book's contents, procedures and potential. By dusk they knew the next step was to find a subject.

"Try it on me, Corin. I trust you." No child could have begged more sweetly, than Raphela.

Corin did not need to consider long. His old speckled hand patted Raphela's soft cheek and grabbed her chin. "Young lady, you might trust me, but the Duke would not be so willing. And should an accident happen, his rage might get the better of him and of me."

"I suppose you're right," she conceded.

"In any case, I'd like to start with someone who is more expendable and equally amenable to the situation, while understanding the dangers. I'll speak to some of the men. I'll find the right person."

Raphela was still anxious, but knew this was the best way. "Fine. Let me know, soon."

Over the next few days Raphela played with Vanar, worked with Fatell and did as much as she could to keep herself busy. The nights were becoming increasingly lonely. Atan's travels kept him away for many weeks this time. Raphela longed for his touch, his words, his company. The bed was flat desert, even with Vanar in it.

Atan made his rounds, but he too found an emptiness in his days. He missed listening to her voice, sharing his thoughts. He ached for the scent of her hair and touch of her skin. And he missed his son.

Corin found his subject, an older man whose body was ravaged by age, but whose mind was clear. His name was Cusat.

Raphela had a soft comfortable chair brought in for him. Corin explained very vaguely what was to happen. Cusat nodded his understanding and Raphela smiled kindly in his direction which put the old man at ease.

Corin sat directly in front of Cusat and picked up a chain, wrapped half of it around his hand, while half dangled down weighted by a shiny gold ring.

"Cusat, are you relaxed?"

"Yes."

"Good. Just watch the gold ring."

Cusat's eyes rested on the ring, which began a slow steady movement, a pendulum taking its time to reach each peak. It traveled a never changing path, so steady, so calm, so thoughtless, yet so enticing. The shiny ring was easy to watch. Cusat, with little coaxing concentrated on the ring.

Raphela sat back, clenching her gown as Cusat's head began to nod.

Corin whispered, "Are you feeling sleepy?"

Cusat blinked his eyes. "Um, yes."

"Good, your eyes should be closing, very soon." Corin dragged out the whispered words, maintaining a monotone. But Cusat's eyes did not close, they opened and he yawned. The almost spell was broken. They tried from noon until dinnertime, but never got past that point.

Cusat was brought to his room to rest. Corin, exhausted, retired for the night.

Raphela took the book and paced the castle, until Mahtso insisted she go upstairs and limit herself to the safety of the family room. There she fell asleep on the couch, book across her lap, fire dying in the hearth. Logan covered his lady in blankets and placed a pillow behind her head.

When Raphela woke, her body ached from the odd position in which she'd slept. She rubbed her eyes and looked down at the book. The paragraph that she thought had been tattooed in her brain struck her like cold water on a hot summer's day. She rushed through her morning routine and then found Corin, in the kitchen. He sipped his tea and moaned when Raphela approached. "My lady, I have no answer so early."

Raphela grabbed a teacup and found it full before she had a chance to pour. A young servant girl curtsied and scurried away. Raphela gulped some tea.

"But I do, Corin. Our mistake is simple. You cannot ask him if he's sleepy. You must wait until his eyes are closed and then verify he can hear you. You may tell him he's sleepy. Ask him, and he must think and that breaks the spell. In the book they do not ask."

Corin laughed at Raphela's ability to mix such exuberance with such seriousness. "I am almost too old for this, but I am willing to try again."

Raphela had Cusat returned to the same chair. Corin began again. "Just concentrate, on the ring and my voice. Nothing else exists."

The ring swung back and forth, Cusat concentrated, Corin held the chain and periodically encouraged Cusat into an increasingly relaxed state. Raphela held her breath and watched.

Finally, Corin saw Cusat's eyes close. Corin looked to Raphela who nodded.

Corin spoke. "Can you hear me?"

Cusat nodded, but his eyes remained closed.

"Whenever you hear the word 'moon,' you will clap your hands three times. Do you understand?" Cusat nodded.

Raphela and Corin took deep breaths. Corin spoke it, "Moon." Raphela bit her finger. Cusat raised his hands and clapped, once, twice, three times.

It took all they had not to leap for joy. Corin continued. "That was good. I will count to three and snap my fingers. When I do, you will wake, feeling refreshed and not remember that you were asleep. Do you understand?"

Cusat nodded. Corin did as he said. Cusat opened his eyes and looked around. "When will you begin?"

Raphela just smiled. "How are you feeling?"

"Rather well."

"Good. Moon." Cusat clapped is hands three times.

"Why did you do that?" Raphela was gentle.

"Do what, my lady?"

"Oh, nothing, I guess. I thought you tried to stand."

"No, my lady."

"Very well, I'll have someone bring you to the kitchen for lunch."

"Yes, my lady."

As Cusat was being walked to the kitchen Raphela stopped him. "Cusat."

"Yes, my lady."

"Thank you very much for your help. The Duke will be pleased." Cusat smiled. It had been a long time since the Duke had any reason to even know he existed.

Raphela and Corin walked around the castle grounds breathing in the cool autumn air. "Was it real?" Raphela's excitement was laced with a healthy skepticism.

"I think so. I did check his eyes while he was under and they were not normal. Still, our assistants will let us know for certain."

"If it worked on Cusat, I'm going to find someone young and headstrong as our next subject, just to be sure."

"As you wish."

For the next two days, periodically, people would say "moon" to Cusat and he reacted as hoped. All seemed well. But the long-term effects, if any, were an unknown. Knowing Atan would be home soon. Raphela pursued the continuation of the project. Fatell found her a young woman who met the basic qualifications. Raphela interviewed her in what was now Raphela's office.

The petite young girl barely reached Raphela's shoulders and she was so thin Raphela wondered if she ate. But her dark eyes spoke a determination that Raphela liked. "What is your name?"

"Nalab, my lady."

"Have a seat, Nalab." Raphela pointed to a chair beside her.

"Nalab, I have a job for you. But it is potentially dangerous. The damage could be permanent. So I am offering you the choice of taking the risk or not."

Nalab nodded and thought for a moment. "My lady, may I be direct."

"Of course."

"I have lived at Castle Cordan all my life and I know that should harm come to me I will be cared for, but, what if all is well? Will I be dismissed with a, a, thank you?"

"You wish to be paid or rewarded?" Raphela tried to sound severe.

"Yes, my lady." Nalab did cower, but only a little.

"I see. What did you have in mind?"

Nalab did not hesitate, for weeks she had prayed for such an opportunity. "I have heard that everyone in the castle will learn to read, write and use numbers."

"It is my plan."

"I wish to be one of the first, and I wish to be allowed to pursue," Nalab hesitated, took a breath, "my own interests."

"And what might those be?" The girl, her forthrightness and decisiveness, intrigued Raphela.

"I wish to make things."

166

"What kinds of things?"

Nalab stood, filled with a feeling that had been cultivated over years. "Nothing so foolish as dresses or shoes. But things that work, that makes people's work easier. I have scrubbed enough clothes to know that there has to be a better way. I need to draw the plans that are in my mind. And water, why is it so troublesome to move something so vital? We lose so much. Buckets spill as they swing back and forth. My lady, if only I could read. The old books maybe, maybe there are answers, or at least ideas to match my own."

"Why have you not come to me before?"

"I don't know, I guess I was afraid. It seems foolish, but I'm only 17 and I could be all wrong."

Raphela laid a strong and gentle hand on Nalab's shoulder. "Let's hope the experiment goes well. I'd like to see your ideas blossom."

"Really?" Nalab's composure dissipated to pure ecstasy. "Oh, my lady, I will do my best for you. Thank you. Thank you."

"You're welcome. Be here after lunch."

"Yes, my lady."

As planned the next day found Nalab with Raphela and Corin. Nalab took her place in the large plush chair, but did not sink into its comfort. Her hands rubbed her arms and her eyes darted from Raphela to Corin, to the door, the floor, every inch of space was inspected. Even the few bits of dust hiding in a deep corner were captured.

Raphela sat in front of her, stroking Nalab's hands as she spoke. "Relax, I intend no harm."

Nalab sighed. "I know, my lady, but just what is it that you expect of me?"

Raphela ignored the question. "Nalab, what five things do you like most, at least one should be food."

Nalab squinted her eyes in confusion and then closed them to concentrate on the answer. Corin studied a book, Raphela the room, while a scribe seesawed in her hand. "Donag steak!" The words blurted out.

Raphela flinched.

"Sorry, my lady." Nalab smiled. "But I remembered how much I like donag steak."

"Quite all right." Raphela wrote the words. "Now, continue."

Once Nalab completed that list, Raphela requested a second, those things, which Nalab hated and feared most. Nalab sucked on her right forefinger. Her eyes shared a brief encounter with Raphela and then rested on the wall. The time that elapsed was short, not for thought but for courage and the faith to trust a stranger. "Fire," she whispered.

"Fire," the word glided across the page. Nalab finished her list quickly.

"Thank you." Raphela rubbed the girl's shoulder and watched the tension dissipate.

"Nalab, take a deep breath and relax. There is no possible way to fail at this task." Raphela's tone, worked like a thick blanket on a shivering child. Nalab's tiny form released its grip on the chair and sunk into the soft comfort it offered.

Corin took over. Nalab was, as expected, more difficult to trance, but it worked. As before a suggestion was placed successfully.

The second stage, to have her reverse likes or fears was achieved with limited success. Changing tastes or the enjoyment of something was far easier than changing any of the fears or hatreds. It was a valuable even vital lesson.

Those suggestions that worked were left to use for demonstration with the Duke. For he had to see and believe. Raphela knew he was back even before she heard the click of the carriage wheels being walked into place by the tired rameks.

Atan slept until noon and by afternoon the family Ishtba was picnicking on the grounds. It was a day spent away from the routine of rule. With dawn came a return of that routine.

Mahtso arrived first, opening the shutters of the meeting room and gazing upon the expanse below. Distant property glowed in the morning sun, echoing back to Castle Cordan the hearty colors of autumn and of well-tended fields of bountiful crops. Birds sang the seasonal warning of the cold to come and the brisk fresh air gave life to the room.

The well-polished round table was structured and set specifically for Atan. His chair, the largest, was set between the others and by his spot at the table was a carved out area for his teacup.

Mahtso took his place to the left of Atan and waited. The chain swinging carelessly from his hand. Raphela brought her scribe. "Good morning, Mahtso."

"Good morning. I see..."

Mahtso didn't get to finish as Atan entered and took his seat, setting the teacup in its place. Mahtso turned to face Atan while Raphela passed a warm glance in her husband's direction.

"Mahtso, begin." Atan leaned back, sipped his tea and turned his attention to Mahtso.

"Most taxes are flowing in well. We've had less reports of marauders than in the past. As a matter of fact, every year there are less."

Atan smiled. "A sign of increasing civilization."

"I suppose."

Mahtso continued with his report. Raphela gave a cursory glance to the notes Atan had placed in front of her. While Mahtso rambled on, Raphela stared blankly out the window. Both men noticed her preoccupation but chose to ignore it.

"Thank you, Mahtso, well done. I found most of the fiefs to be in good order. Rayna's property proved most interesting. His herd of donags is far larger and healthier than I anticipated. Though his surroundings lacked substance, his business was well run. "Merej handles the cattle exceptionally well. I'm considering moving him to Rayna's castle. What do you think?" Atan sipped his tea and left the question open to both parties.

Mahtso's chain made lazy circles around his hand. "I think he should remain where he is. To uproot his family would be difficult and costly, especially with winter coming."

"Mm. Raphela, what do you think?"

Raphela continued her empty gaze. Atan tapped her shoulder. "Are you with us or the nameless ones?"

"What? Oh, I'm sorry."

"Now, should we move Merej and his family to Rayna's estate to farm the donags?"

"No."

"Why not?" Raphela could hear the exasperation creep into his voice. She sighed and came to matters at hand.

"First, as Mahtso said, uprooting his family is laborious, especially since his wife is pregnant. And anyway, isn't moving the donags to him more logical?" Raphela had said her peace and attempted to return to her thoughts.

But Atan and Mahtso were taken aback. "Raphela, what do you mean?"

"Mean about what?"

"Moving the donags?" Mahtso's chain beat against the table.

Raphela looked between the two men and wrapped her shawl tighter around her shoulders. "Have I spoken of some wild act? What is so amazing about moving donags?"

"It's never been done!" Atan was adamant.

Raphela sat up and moved her chair closer to the table. "It most certainly has. The ancients moved donags all the time. I expected that it was commonplace today."

Atan squeezed her hand. "Raising donags has been limited to a small number of men, as feeding them became expensive when..." Atan's voice began to trail, "when the land could no longer support the animals' needs." Silence was the speaker for the moment.

"Raphela, the ancient ones, did they give written instruction on how to move the donags?"

"Yes, I found it quite fascinating. Would you like me to get the book so that you can read it?"

"No, I'd like you to translate it. My knowledge of the ancient tongue is rusty. I want a full report as soon as possible."

"As you wish."

"Good. Now, what news do you have?"

"The school is almost ready to start. Fatell has found a dozen men anxious and capable to educate Ishtba."

"Anything else?" Atan noted his pleasure at the progress but also noticed the excitement waving in Raphela's eyes.

"Yes. I have found something too amazing. It regards your concern about sending a spy to Akar for fear he will be caught."

"Yes?" Both men were attentive.

"What if his identity could not be discovered?"

"Go on."

"There is a thing, the ancients called it Trancestate. You place someone in a trance and the suggestion you place while they are in that state remains, even after the trance is broken. Corin and I have learned the method and proven it works."

"I don't understand. How can this help?" Mahtso's curiosity peaked.

Raphela moved like a gilded bird, strutting all her colors. "Corin and I can give someone a new identity. A name, history, everything. Without the proper code word the person's true identity is," she paused, "unreachable."

Holding back his excitement at its potential. Atan pressed Raphela further. "You say you've proven this."

"Yes"

"Show me."

Raphela beamed and jumped up. "Gladly."

She moved so quickly Atan swore she created a wind as she walked past him.

Having anticipated Atan's request Raphela had Logan waiting nearby to retrieve Nalab.

Raphela paced as she watched Nalab and Logan climb the stairs. Nalab walked slowly, her stomach turning with each step. Never had she gotten close to the Duke, or even Mahtso. That inexplicable fear, which rested in everyone began to overwhelm her. Logan could see her face pale and knees tremble. He placed a supportive arm around her waist. Nalab buried her head in his chest, for just a moment.

"They are not monsters." He whispered. "No harm will come to you."

Such gentility and sweetness arising from this gargantuan almost made Nalab laugh.

"Thank you, you're very kind." She planted a shy kiss on his cheek.

His blush matched the red fire in the kitchen stove.

Raphela greeted Nalab and guided her to a chair, making sure Nalab felt the constant and reassuring hand on her shoulder.

171

The girl did not venture to meet Atan's glance or even Mahtso's. So Raphela took her through the routine, proving how likes and dislikes can be altered with Trancestate.

Even her fears were muted, though not totally dissipated.

The proof complete, Nalab was sent one her way, with Logan's welcome assistance.

Mahtso's chain beat steadily against the chair leg.

Atan stared at his wife.

"Raphela, how?"

"How what?"

"How did you find this method and more important, how did you learn it?"

Raphela's back stiffened as Atan leaned towards her, his eyes accused what his words could not. "Did you think I would harm anyone? Have you so little faith" Do you think my appetite for knowledge exceeds all bounds of decency?"

Dragon's fire would have crawled in shame at Raphela's voice.

Mahtso closed his eyes and prayed, not sure for whom.

Atan did not take his eyes off his wife. "Mahtso, you may go."

Quickly and silently Mahtso left.

Atan heard the massive door meet the frame, shutting the world out. Rising from the chair, his body shadowed over Raphela. She felt his hands wrap tightly around her arms, almost cutting the flow of blood. He jerked her out of the chair.

His words spun out in a secretish whisper. "I believe your appetite for knowledge makes you the most dangerous and desirable woman I've ever known."

Their lips engulfed not just each other, but all of Castle Cordan felt the power and shivered in awe at the passion of a kiss.

When it broke and hot breath steamed the air, their eyes bound and their lust reigned supreme. Control belonged to passion and nothing else. Raphela flew in the ecstasy of Atan inside her and he wallowed in her scent, hands caressing with such intensity that even the nameless ones could not have broken that spell.

172

It seemed instantaneous and yet forever, but finally the lust was spent. A final kiss, fingers against skin and hair. "Your appetites and methods are in excess, in only the right direction." He whispered as she closed the bodice of her dress.

Raphela smiled. "Perhaps its time for Mahtso to return so that all the possibilities can be explored.

Mahtso returned and the trio created many scenarios, finally deciding that Raphela and Mahtso would find a suitable person for the role of spy.

Raalek's sky was turning from light violet to sleepy gray, a sure sign of winter's approach. Every day carts rolled in with grains and supplies.

Ishtban had operated in the same way for almost six years and so far it had worked well.

After delivering tax payment in the form of goods, each fief's representative would take with him his fief's share of bounty from the Ishtban pool of goods, occasionally trading with someone for more of this or less of that. But Atan had put great emphasis on the concept that all his properties would be well supplied. Shortages and unbalanced wealth led to an overabundance of rivalry and poor production. Exceptional production was rewarded with luxuries, minimal production meant receiving the basics and nothing more, but no fief went hungry or cold.

Halius, supervisor of receiving and disbursement of taxes shivered slightly in the cold air. "You there, the spice man, move your cart in line. Margo, could we get some hot tea out here?"

Margo directed the women to bring hot tea to all the cart drivers and delivered a mug to Halius personally.

Halius shaded his eyes and tried to ascertain just how long this line ran. Rubbing his hands together he began to walk, perusing the containers, most of wood, tightly constructed, wheels hugging the sides, canvas carpeting the tops to protect the precious cargo. Within minutes he realized that he would not see the end of the trail. Three rows of carts circled the castle and a long tail looking more like children's toys than wagons of goods led halfway down the hill. It would take three or four days to acknowledge receiving all this and weeks more to categorize it.

At sunset, the remaining carts were brought as close to the castle as possible and the men all given shelter until the morning when the counting of bags of beans and sides of meat would continue.

Halius' fingers ached from cold and his toes barely moved. Once in the cozy warmth of his room, his mind tracked the day's events and he recalled the ease of his job six years before, a third or half a day for three or four days and the job was complete. Now from dawn to dusk for two weeks the cart wheels creaked up the hill. The method of receiving hadn't changed, but it must. He would think of a way this winter.

As the days passed the last carts headed for home and winter's face embroidered the sky. The rameks were settled into their stalls, the storage barns locked tight and shutters on Castle Cordan could be heard through the still night, softly closing, one by one. The castle outlined the sky as a massive shadow not sharing any of the light or warmth that glowed inside.

Chapter 8

Though people don't hibernate, most of Raalek came close. Inside the castles and houses, there was much sleep, the minimum accomplishment of daily tasks, just enough for survival and incidental repairs. For at least a century, Raalek had lived as such.

Castle Cordan, true to its recent history, broke with this winter tradition. Raphela's study groups blossomed, learning became the theme of the season. Atan's never-ending desire to improve and grow, swept through like fire. Not a day passed when someone hadn't created a new and better way of doing something.

Raphela still found time for tea with Fatell, it was a wonderful way to explore her thoughts and get a feel for what the rest of the castle was experiencing.

"Good morning Fatell."

"Hmm, oh Raphela, good morning." Fatell yawned and pulled the hair away from her eyes. "And you too Vanar."

Raphela wrapped her hand around his waist as she sat. "I see you have an admirer Fatell."

"One of unswerving fidelity." Fatell stroked Vanar's soft hand.

"How true." Raphela sipped her tea. "It seems so long since we last spoke. Tell me, how is everything moving along?"

"At an incredible rate. The children learn so quickly and the adults compete to maintain superiority. I'm amazed. It's all so quick, as if the sun can't push the moon out of its place fast enough." Fatell had started vibrantly, but wound down to a barely audible thought.

"What's wrong?" Do you feel left out, pushed aside? Please Fatell, tell me?" Her friend, so obviously distraught it was hard to bear.

"No my friend, I certainly don't feel left out, perhaps..." Fatell searched for the word, "overwhelmed." She stirred her tea and watched the ripples bump into the rim of the cup and dissipate.

"Then get some more help. Use anyone." Raphela overcome with concern could not see all that Fatell was saying.

"The work load is fine. It's just, well, life has changed so much. Three years ago a new supply of linens was cause for excitement. Today its how to weave a new kind of cloth. Just yesterday Atan Ishtba chose the mother of his child, deliberately, with care, giving women a status unknown for centuries. And tomorrow, women will be teaching children to read." Fatell's eyes opened wide. "Everyday something new, a better way, a faster way. Is it right? What's wrong with the old ways?"

"I'm sorry Fatell. Now I see and you can't be the only one to feel this. But you can't deny the changes are for the better. Knowledge will help us live stronger and longer. And if Atan Ishtba is to rule, should he not make it the best it can be? Something to take pride in? To wake up knowing that you've done your best. Even more than that, should not the children find a solid foundation on which to build and to give their children more? It is our duty and our joy." Raphela more than believed her words, she lived and breathed them and no one could escape the power of her thoughts.

Fatell smiled. "Thank you. Just what I needed."

"Me too." How about you Va..." Raphela couldn't finish or move quickly enough.

Vanar had no interest in the conversation, but his eyes had rested on a large flaky biscuit, just barely in arm's reach. His stubby fingers grabbed it and made short work to his mouth. Fatell roared with laughter.

A six-month baby's perception is limited and the biscuit landed in his mouth and all over his face. The brown crust hung on his eyebrows and white crumbs covered his chin and cheeks like a beard. Vanar seeing Fatell, joined in the laughter, not having the vaguest idea of what was funny. It was simply joyful to join his friend. As he laughed, the crumbs fell from his face, like snow being shaken from a tree.

Raphela sat him on the table, attempted a scowl but quickly retreated to a smile. "Now you've done it young man, look at you." Vanar smiled at his mama, every bit of him covered in crumbs.

One of the servants had already fetched clean clothes and a warm damp towel. Vanar's smile disappeared as his soft hands battled with mama as she washed him down and changed his clothes.

"Now you're ready to meet with your new friends." Raphela picked him up, Fatell followed as she walked from the kitchen.

"Has the Duke finally agreed to allow Vanar into group care?" Her question was mildly sarcastic.

"Begrudgingly."

"I'm sure. Bye Vanar." Fatell planted a kiss on his cheek.

Raphela walked to the play group, remembering her discussion with Atan, just a few nights before. Vanar was in his crib. She and Atan had crawled under the thick covers while the lumpglow faded.

"No, he is the duke's son. He should remain separate." Atan sounded like a schoolmaster repeating a necessary lesson.

"Separate?! Is that why you married me?" Her words meant to cut and did.

"That's different." Atan rolled over and leaned his back on her, curling his shoulder down like a shield.

"Why?" Raphela lay on her back, directing her voice to the ceiling.

"Because he's just an infant." Annoyed defensiveness never spoke so clearly.

"What better time for him to learn about people and how to interact. He will come to know everyone and they him."

"Not important."

"Atan," Raphela gently tugged him. "look at me."

His eyes rested on hers. She took his hand. "He must know his people. He will not make this garden you are planting flourish if he doesn't understand the seeds. Your power is unique. Vanar will need to prove himself in other ways. He will have a difficult man to follow."

"I know. All too well I know." He half spoke to himself. "All right, but his nurse is to be there, the children are to keep their distance. What if a child is ill, and. . . "

"Atan."

He kissed her palm. "Do what's best."

Raphela's smile was caught by the last glow of light.

"But the nurse remains,"

"As you wish, my lord."

Raphela finished her reverie in time to hand Vanar to his nurse. The children surrounded Vanar as he was placed in his special seat, created so that he could watch. He lapped up the attention like a kitten after warm milk. Raphela left smiling.

Her feet led her through the castle Despite the cold of Raalek's winter, Castle Cordan barely had a chill in the air. Strategically placed cast iron stoves, regularly fueled with slow burning stones, dotted the castle. The concept had been learned from Fakrash, perhaps the only decent thing he did.

She checked various and sundry activities, but found herself at the room of an old friend. He had aged greatly this past year. His skin was wrinkled and dry and his hands moved ever so slowly. It took more than a moment for him to notice Raphela.

"Well my lady, it is good to see you." He attempted to rise from the chair, but Raphela stopped him.

"Sit down." She drew a chair and sat beside him. "would you like some tea?" Before he could answer, she had motioned to a servant girl to bring a pot and two cups.

"Still making decisions for people, eh Raphela."

She blushed. "Corin, how are you?"

Steady old eyes peered at her. "My child, I believe the nameless ones think I am old. My body yearns to rest but my mind screams out that it is not ready. I live in battle."

"Then you need some warriors on your side. As of now you will have a personal aide. She will attend to your physical survival."

Corin raised his hand in protest.

"Don't argue with me."

Corin let the matter drop, his pride had never overridden common sense.

"Have you found an assistant?" It was a gentle question.

"Don't mince words Raphela, someone to carry on for me. The answer is no."

"Would you mind if Fatell and I interviewed some candidates and presented them to you so you could pick from that group?"

"Thank you."

The tea arrived and the young girl bringing it was assigned to Corin, together they shared the tea and some companionship.

Raphela continued her travels through the castle and stopped by the informal dining room, temporarily transposed for Atan's winter project. The large table was now a base for a model of Ishtban lands. Atan stood at one end, his books stacked neatly on a chair, the top one spread open. On either side of the table were the two men chosen for this project. On Atan's right was Merej's top donagmaster and on his left, one from the king's territory.

Atan's tall form leaned over the table, his deep voice rippling the air as he spoke and motioned to the man on his right.

"Trasta, are these hills, mountains or small mounds?"

Trasta, a head shorter and even thinner than Atan studied the area. The model, made to scale, was well constructed and borders were incredibly accurate, but topography was left to the men in this room.

"My lord, it is a fair size hill, one to go around, not climb with donags."

"mm"

Vorsi, about as tall as Trasta but quite a bit plumper looked on making mental notes.

"Trasta, you seem unsure about the animals. Why?"

Trasta and Vorsi shared a glance and Vorsi answered. "Sire, it's simply so new. You brought us here and for weeks have told us that the ancients moved donags between properties, but how? We can devise many paths, but in all honesty, we wouldn't know what to do."

Atan sank down into a chair and sighed, his eyes darting back and forth between the men. "Gentlemen, I obviously made the incorrect assumption that you would know. Well, let's stop this portion of our work, Do either of you read and or write?"

Both men lowered their heads in embarrassment. "Then you shall listen and before you leave this castle, both of you will

179

learn to read and write. There are daily lessons. Yours will begin tomorrow. But for now, I will read to you."

Raphela left, unnoticed as Atan began to read aloud. He had taken the time to relearn the ancient language.

By midday she felt comfortable that all was well. Knowing that it would be a few more days until Mahtso found a suitable candidate for spy, she indulged in her personal thirst for knowledge. The library served up some intriguing books on medicine and she dove right in, not stopping until dinnertime.

So the winter days passed. Castle Cordan's walls soaked in the noise of voices learning, chanting with the energy of bees bringing honey to the hive. People busily scurried about, as they created for tomorrow. Though night did fall, it seemed that even the moons were able to watch Castle Cordan at work. Day or night the enticing aroma of growth filled the air.

By midwinter 30% of the castle had basic reading skills. Trasta and Vorsi had begun to draw plans for moving the donags. Mahtso had narrowed his candidates down to three. Raphela's interviews with the men drew it down to one, Kito.

He stood before Raphela and Mahtso, slender and pale, so attractive he bordered on the feminine. Curly locks of blond hair were carefully trimmed to accentuate his best features, like the hazel eyes that glimmered above a mischievous smile.

"You do the face well Kito, but I'd maintain a slightly more serious attitude with the Duke." Raphela offered the light reprimand.

Kito's expression dissipated to obedience, but the good looks and fresh clean scent of him did not fade.

"Better. Mahtso, you've chosen well. I hope the Duke agrees."

Mahtso's chain met his leg in slow rhythmic beats. "He is waiting. Are you ready Kito?"

Feeling like a delicate new vase, easily smashed if not liked, Kito nodded and followed his leaders to the Duke's library. There, with little more than an introduction, Kito was deposited to a waiting Atan.

Kito stood at ease, staring at the bookshelf at the far end of the room, carefully avoiding his Duke's intense inspection.

"Sit down Kito." Gently spoken, Atan did his best not to alarm the young man.

"Do you know why you're here?" Atan seated himself diagonally from Kito. It was hoped that the small room and comfortable setting would encourage total honesty unbound by fear.

"Yes my lord. You have an important task to be done, and with your approval, I will have the honor of completing it." Though Kito could not meet his Duke's eyes, he made every attempt and his sincerity was solid.

"Do you know the task at hand?"

"Only that I must retrieve information vital to the security of Ishtba."

"Hmm. Is there risk to yourself on this mission?"

"Yes my lord, according to Mahtso and Lady Raphela my life could be in jeopardy and I would have no immediate support." His answers were planned but not rehearsed.

"Are you willing to take this risk?"

"Of course my lord." Kito held his ground, but did not hide his surprise at the abrasive tone of the question.

"Why?" Atan demanded.

Pain crossed Kito's face as if he had been accused of some awful act. "Sire, though I am not well traveled, I believe with all my soul and the nameless ones as my witness, that Ishtba is the best and greatest of all lands on Raalek. My life could not be better. Surely defense and protection of this land have no equals in duty. I would die to preserve what is Ishtba." Kito's passion touched Atan, the man's devotion was real.

"When the job is done, what reward would you choose?"

Kito's hazel eyes shone and his hands moved as he spoke. "To travel sire, to bring Ishtba to the world and the world back to Ishtba."

"Why?" Atan's curiosity was piqued.

"My lord, all my years I have listened to the merchants and their tales. Even they thought no one from the Castle could hear. All prayed to settle in Ishtba some day. So I know that the world must know more of Ishtba. And the merchants tales spoke of wonders we haven't seen, why not bring them here. For whatever it is, Ishtba would make better use of it."

"Kito, if you are prepared to accept the risks and maintain your fidelity, then you have my permission to engage in the upcoming task. And, if you succeed, then travel all you wish."

"I will my lord and thank you." He nearly ran from the room, overwhelmed with joy.

Raphela and Mahtso, close at hand, smiled. Their work had just begun.

Raalek's winter sun oozed through the crack's in the shutters and Atan, ever sensitive to day's beginning, awoke.

Raphela slept soundly, while Atan found a thick long robe, wrapped it around his waist, slipped his feet into fur slippers by the bed and padded his way to Vanar's room.

Vanar stood in his crib, grasping the rails, waiting for any break in the monotony. Atan's face brought instantaneous, wide-eyed excitement. Vanar's small form bounced up and down, rattling his crib against the stone floor. As Atan got closer Vanar's joy exploded, his fingers released their grip and as with all infants, balance being most precarious, fell back onto his bottom.

For a moment the happy gurgle and high pitched squeal of glee stopped. Vanar tried to decide if the fall was worth a tear. But Papa was at the crib now, so the immediate decision was to stand and get as close as possible.

Atan reached down and swept his young son from his station. Now, despite babies sweet scents, a night's worth of diapers can be unsettling. So, with minor trouble, Atan changed the diaper and bundled his son into warm and cozy clothes and carried him as they snuck toward the dining room.

"Vanar," he whispered, "we must be quiet and not wake mama. But let's see what treats are hidden in the cupboards."

The dining room fireplace blazed keeping the black pot of water hot for tea. Atan looked around to find some small snack as Vanar grasped his collar.

Vanar's eyes studied the room. He'd been here before. Yes, yes, food, sweet hard sticks that felt good against his gums. They were hiding. He tried calling to them, but the only response was a "Shh" from papa. Then he remembered and began bouncing in Papa's arms. His grasp turned to a tug and his other arm pointed, definitively at a cabinet.

"So, you know where things are kept." Atan opened the cupboard and found exactly what Vanar wanted and a snack for himself.

As father and son shared the quiet moments of morning, Raphela stirred in her sleep. Soon she appeared at the dining room doorway, just in time to watch Vanar dribble warm tea down his face and hear Atan laugh with his son about nothing at all.

"May I join the party, or is this men only?"

Vanar, perched comfortably on the table, began to crawl to mama.

"Need we say more?" Atan placed a gentle kiss on Raphela's lips and Vanar grabbed on tight to his mother's robes.

Breakfast continued as a quiet warm affair. Raphela brushed the crumbs from Vanar's clothes while he wriggled in Atan's firm grip. Once done Atan placed Vanar in a chair. Before either parent imagined that such a thing was possible, they were watching Vanar's bottom scurrying out the door towards the family room.

Atan's long sinewy form strode quickly, Vanar didn't get far, and the stern glance he received had little effect on his adventurous desires. Atan shook his head. "Here Raphela." His outstretched arms attempted to hand Vanar over.

Raphela placed her hands on her hips. "Just where do you think you're going?" Her eyes twinkled.

"To work?" Was the sheepish reply.

"Not today. Today we spend together, the three of us."

"Well Vanar, what's your opinion?"

The baby just giggled and reached to grab Atan's chest. "As you both wish" the lord and master conceded.

Vanar wallowed in the spent time with mama and papa together, his adventurous spirit a guide to their every move. He seemed anxious to escape the confines of the castle walls in spite of the cold and snow. The family Ishtba bundled up and entered the realm where even Atan had no control.

Vanar stared in wonder at the white expanse. Each tree was cocooned in snow and the bright crystalline vastness stirred Vanar to unforeseen excitement. Even the cold against his soft skin, did not deter him from straining to touch and see. No other child seemed so born to the heart of Raalek.

Only when his eyelids drooped against his gallant efforts to keep them open could Atan and Raphela bring him inside.

While he slept, they took time together. For two hours Vanar slept. Neither Atan nor Raphela spoke a word. Tea led to the comfort of a warm fire, gazed at without thought. Raphela's head rested comfortably on Atan's firm shoulder as his arm wrapped around her. An occasional kiss, gentle and thoughtful would break the stillness, but that was all. The fibers of emotion and thought that drew them together, took over. When Vanar awoke, he demanded food and more adventure.

"Raphela, our little man wants to explore. I think it's time for a new venture."

Vanar holding lightly onto the couch walked around to play peekaboo.

Raphela swept him up. "I agree. Vanar, let's see how brave you really are."

Raphela sat on the floor. Five feet away Atan sat facing her. Vanar stood in front of Raphela, looking at his Papa, who beckoned and cajoled. Vanar's eyes lit. His little foot moved forward and his hands waved the air, then his other foot moved and his heart beat so fast. As he moved that right foot again, his balance was overwhelmed by excitement and he plopped down on his bottom. Undaunted and sensing well what his parents intended, he got up and tried again.

It took some time, but after four or five or ten attempts Vanar figured out the method of one foot in front of the other. Finally he made it to papa's anxious arms, where he was rewarded with a big hug. Eager to show his new skill he walked to mama, only falling once on the way, but received the same wonderful reward. An eventful day led to a quiet night, a simple dinner and early bed for Vanar. Raphela and Atan took a few moments to study the stars and then crawled into their warm bed feeling revived and content.

As his pale slender arms and legs moved evenly around the track.

Kito's blond hair was framed with beads of sweat as his pale slender arms and legs moved evenly around the track as Mahtso monitored his exercise. Endurance and concentration were the objectives. Mahtso trained Kito for escape and emergency.

Raphela watched his development. As Kito ran, objects would appear in his way. In the early weeks he'd lose a second or two deciding what to do. Now his reactions were instantaneous so Mahtso created more subtle distractions. Kito moved on, as if he were encased and untouchable.

"He's doing well." Raphela commented.

Mahtso's chain missed a beat as she spoke. "Yes."

Kito slowed his pace, gradually coming to a halt in front of Raphela. Undisturbed by the salty beads of water that dripped from his eyebrows. He stood at attention awaiting further instruction.

Mahtso let him stand for a moment before throwing a towel at him. "At ease."

Raphela took Mahtso to one side. "I'd like to do some in-depth teaching. He needs to learn about Akar before he becomes someone else. But is he ready?"

Mahtso peered over his shoulder. Kito was practicing some defensive techniques. It was a joy to have all that energy to harness. "Yes, he needs a new challenge."

"Kito,"

"Yes m'lady?"

"Tomorrow morning, the library, after breakfast, be there."

The next morning Raphela laid a stack of papers in front of Kito. "This is the information on Akar. Learn it. Learn him."

"He will be destroyed."

Raphela's hand gently grasped his fist. "Kito, Akar is not evil. He's only in the way. His wants and desires are the same as ours. We simply must want the prize more and be better at getting it. Don't let emotion litter the path of success."

"Yes, my lady. But Ishtba will succeed, it must."

"Indeed. Now learn what you can and I will see you later."

185

Kito absorbed every word until he believed he could see Akar standing before him. He could hear his voice, feel his hand, and perhaps know his thoughts. Over the weeks Raphela drilled his mind as Mahtso had drilled his body. Soon the new personality was introduced.

Raphela and Corin worked to develop intricacies of a total personality,--from nuances of speech, to facial and hand gestures. Mika, had no training from Mahtso. He was permitted to pursue a side interest of Kito's, room design. He was given materials and workers. Weeks were spent on the meeting rooms moving furniture or replacing fabrics. Raphela allowed the interest to develop into a skill.

As far as Mika knew, he was on the king's land visiting with a friendly lord. And around him life went on. Atan continued with the cattle project, Fatell guided the school, and Vanar grew. As winter's end approached, many goals neared completion.

"Lord Neeley, may I present to you Mika, of the north line." Raphela stood back as Mika stepped forward with bowed head.

"Good day Mika." said Atan in his guise as Lord Neeley.

"Oh my, Lord Neeley, it is such an honor. I have heard so much about you. I am so pleased to meet you." Mika's words spilled like beans clattering over the edge of an overloaded pail.

"Where are you headed?"

Mika sighed. "I have heard" a smile lit his lips, "that Baron Akar is looking for some help." Mika's hand took a sensuous glide across his chest. His eyes turned flirtatiously towards Mahtso. "After all, Akar does have a most delightful lifestyle."

Mahtso smiled. Raphela had done well. Atan cringed, but appreciated the accomplishment. Mika was sent to his quarters to prepare for his journey.

The demands of rule temporarily completed Atan and Raphela gladly gave in to the urge to be parents and leave leadership behind. They strolled towards the learning center to pick up Vanar for the noon meal.

A strange quiet emanated from the room. Atan and Raphela stood at the door, invisible to all inside and watched.

Vanar stood up and turned his attention to a small red ball hopping in the hands of a playmate about ten feet from him.

"Come on Vanar, come and get it." The sweet voice enticed him but that red ball was all that mattered. For a moment he grasped onto a child by his side, but his burning desire for that ball, out-weighed his fears. His tiny legs sped forward and, with barely a wobble, he was there. The red ball jumped into his waiting hands amidst the cheers of his playmates. Vanar laughed with pride, grasping tightly onto the ball.

The proud parents exercised restraint and waited for things to calm down, but soon Raphela found herself holding Atan as one of the children picked up the happy baby and brought him to a nursemaid. Vanar bounced with joy as he caught sight of Mama and Papa and showed them his prize. Rewarded with hugs and kisses Vanar reluctantly gave up the ball and wallowed in affection.

After lunch Vanar took a nap and mama and papa spent a quiet afternoon by the fire in the family room.

A week before spring, Kito/Mika departed from the castle with open good wishes and silent prayers. In a small meeting room Fatell pulled together her reports for Raphela who smiled at the neat stacks of paper laid out in a row and waited patiently for Fatell to explain her progress.

Fatell ignored the steaming tea by her hand, and stood by the table, anxious to begin. "Raphela, so very much has happened."

"Tell me, my friend."

Fatell picked up the first stack of sheets. "I have compiled a list of students in the winter class. Of all the people in the castle, nearly all were students, and only a very few of the children over age 6 were not involved with the learning sessions.

The majority of the adults stayed with the studies until the end of the session. More learned the basics of reading, counting, adding and subtracting than I could have imagined. And of the children even more successfully learned the alphabet, numbers and reading to their level of age and ability." Fatell glowed.

"That's unbelievable, an incredible success. How did you do it?"

Fatell sat down and looked directly at Raphela. "I caught your spark and spread it. The first time is always the hardest but also the most exciting. We've discovered other avenues. A number of the older children, teenagers have shown an interest in pursuing their studies. With the help of the teachers and your approval, school will continue throughout the year."

Fatell handed Raphela the second stack of papers Here's a list of names of students and teachers. In addition, some of the teenagers have offered to work with the little ones." Fatell had maintained composure but now exploded.

She began to pace, her breathing became rapid and her hands began a story.

"The project has blossomed.. Everyone is wrapped up in it. I can hardly keep up with the requests." She handed Raphela a third stack, her tiny frame nearly shaking. "Here, here are names upon names, requests to teach and learn. Different focuses of study, from history to math and science."

A wide grin filled Raphela's face. "Congratulations. Do it, make it happen. Make this your life. You obviously do it well."

"You believe that the Duke will approve?" Fatell saw this as hope beyond hope.

"Yes" Raphela's simple reply was enough.

Chapter 9

As Atan peered out the window he could see winter's icy grasp losing its grip. Snowy wigs and icicle earrings faded off the trees. The branches looked bare from a distance, but up close the first bumps of spring's buds could be seen. Though the air was brisk, he left the shutters open.

Raphela and Mahtso arrived simultaneously and the meeting began. It had been a season teeming with success. Not only was Kito trained and sent on his way, but word came that he arrived safely and was immediately drawn to Akar's side.

Mahtso's chain took a brief respite, it was good news.

Atan's work with the cattle had equally good results. Vorsi and Trasta had devised a method for moving the donags and even started compiling a manual. Raphela's news of the school pleased everyone and permission to operate all year was readily granted. It was a brief meeting, all good news.

Within a week Atan was ready for his spring tour of Ishtba. He left with some reluctance. Vanar waved goodbye from Raphela's arms as Atan climbed into the carriage.

Slowly the rameks pulled it away from Castle Cordan. Raphela prepared herself for the lonely weeks ahead.

Atan's first stop the Spice fief, lay about a day and a half away from the castle. The rameks were drawn to a halt at the edge of the fief's entrance. Just far enough to arrive unnoticed. At the edge of the fief the carriage halted so Atan could stretch his lean frame.

He strolled around the colorful patchwork of spices and herbs, each variety dominating its territory, the sweet acla, boasted deep purple textured leaves and a scent that intoxicated even the insects. Plants lined up in neat rows, some stretching toward the last rays of sun, others shying away, waiting for the darkness. Yet as he walked Atan could not help but notice a few more brown leaves than expected, a few feet of the short fences, in disrepair. Nothing extraordinarily wrong, just not as he would have liked it.

Soon Atan was surrounded by tiny plants and the smell made him feel a tinge of remembrance of days past. The first time he visited this place with his father, the smell then overpowered him; he had reeled from it, running to an open spot to breathe. Now, it was like a taste of strong wine, a momentary jolt to the palate and head, but no long lasting effect.

At the front door of the house, framed by colorful flowers and a scattering of garden tools, Atan knocked and was greeted by a scantily clad young woman who curtsied and guided him to the fief administrator, Sidno.

They walked down a long hall lined with dusty lumpglows and closed doors. It was not long before Atan saw light from an open doorway and heard voices babbling inside. Sidno's dining hall housed a rectangular table and walls covered by tasteful tapestries. Against the right wall sat a heavy wooden sideboard laden with platters of fruits, cheeses, smoked meats, loaves of fresh baked bread and pitchers of wine.

Sidno sat at the table with his back to the door. Seven or eight attractive young women littered the room. A few sipped wine or tea by the sideboard, a pair conversed by the window overlooking a garden, and three surrounded Sidno. One rubbed his neck, another sat on his lap giggling as he nibbled her neck, and a third flinched as she received a good natured slap on her bottom.

"You are becoming well padded Alicia, I like that." Sidno laughed and popped a small bundle of fruit into his mouth. The girl on his lap looked up and saw Atan. She whispered in Sidno's ear. Sidno gently pushed her off, stood and straightened his clothes. "Welcome my lord, please come in."

The Duke walked past Sidno, noting the heavy scent of wine on the man's breath. Sidno raised his hand to lay a welcoming pat on his Duke's back, but found it stopped in midair. A strong hand wrapped around Sidno's wrist. Sidno looked up to a man more than a head taller than him and twice his weight. The man just shook his head as if a child had attempted a naughty deed.

Atan ignored the situation. Mahtso had remained at Castle Cordan at Atan's request, but Mahtso insisted on sending a guard. Sidno's women crowded together behind his chair, all wide-eyed. Atan nibbled at the overflowing plate of food before him. Sidno shifted in his seat. "How was your trip, my lord? Was the weather warm enough for travel?"

"Uneventful and yes." Atan's grey eyes studied the room.

"I'm glad you had no trouble." Sidno shooed the women away. Atan sipped his wine and tore gently at a bit of roast donag. "The winter ended early here." He observed

"Yes sire, we were able to begin planting nearly four weeks ago.

"I see."

Atan finished his meal. "I'd like to see my quarters."

"Of course sire. If you would like someone to, oh, keep you warm, Melita would be quite willing."

A slender girl, perhaps 16, lowered her head and trembled.

Atan just stared at Sidno. No conversation could have been more punishing. Atan's fidelity was well known. Sidno shivered and the relieved girl simply guided the Duke to his room. It was clean and amply furnished.

Once settled, Atan roamed the house which was overall in good order. As the second moon rose Atan stared out his window into the cold clear night. For years he had traveled, it was routine, just part of life. But tonight, for the first time, he felt something new. Loneliness. He missed his wife and son. It almost felt good.

As always he rose with the sun, had breakfast alone, and waited until midmorning before seeing a groggy Sidno arrive to begin work. Sidno took his Duke through every field, twice and introduced him to the foreman of the work crews. Sidno managed to spend a great deal of time returning to the house to "attend to business" while his Duke inspected the fief. For two days Atan interviewed workers, dug his hands in the soil, sniffed the plants, and checked the tools. At night he studied the records of the fief with meticulous care. By the third morning Atan was ready to discuss his findings with Sidno, who managed to arise a little closer to sunrise, but not much.

The dining hall, where they met, was free of other people. Atan sipped tea as he spoke. "Sidno, how do you feel you've handled business in the past few years?" The question was presented innocently enough.

"Adequately sire."

"Mmm. I would agree with you. *Adequate* is an excellent term. I have noticed a certain carelessness and indiscretion in priorities, however I noted that you have replaced more than half your tools since two years ago. It seems a bit excessive."

Sidno just sat, speechless.

"You also seem to have a problem staffing the fields whereas you have an abundance of help for the house."

"My lord, the men are difficult to handle and unreliable. I have tried." Beads of sweat formed on Sidno's brow.

"Yes. I'm sure you have." Atan presented the echo of cruelty so readily opened by the weaker members of his regime. "I believe you need some help. I'm sending an assistant administrator. Your knowledge of your business, is without question, formidable, however accomplishing a top quality product seems difficult for you. There is obviously too much work for one man."

Sidno thought about arguing but knew better. By next year his control and many of his luxuries would be gone. He would always have a place to live and a few niceties, but never again would he be a fief master. "As you wish my lord."

While Atan traveled, Castle Cordan opened up for spring, the shutters spreading wide to invite in light and warm air. Merchants began to stop by with their newest and finest items.

Fatell gave everyone a two-week recess from school. Mahtso, however, trained his men rigorously and Raphela often worked until late in the night, keeping Vanar by her side, to stave off the loneliness.

A large rock jolted the carriage, rousing Atan from a dreamless slumber. Sleep was difficult at night, but he nodded off often during the days ride. He stretched as best he could and peeked through the slats of the carriage door. Bright sunlight filled the sky. He tapped on the carriage roof for the driver to stop. " It's only a few miles from here. I'll walk."

As he walked, his guard keeping his distance, Atan felt his body wake and his mind begin to work. The last stop had been a good one. After a disastrous first year, Ethan spent the next three years laboring to improve. The fief now produced some of the finest fowl Atan had seen and tasted. The situation brought a brief smile to Atan's face.

A little after the sun hit its peak, Atan was faced with a tall well-sanded wood fence, accompanied by a different kind of scent, clean crisp and unusual.

As he walked through the gate he heard his carriage behind him and signaled for the driver to wait.

Inside the fence the flat ground was free of stones. A well-defined pathway led to the front door.

Atan however, walked to the right off the path, toward the fields and the smell. Large green squash and bright orange berries stood proud in the spring air. The fields from afar were a rainbow of colors and textures.

In the distance Atan could see a group of laborers. All heads wore the same hat and backs the same shirt. They seemed to move as a unit, as evenly spaced as the plants for which they cared. Their arms moved hoes in exacting harmony, no one broke the rhythm. A supervisor stood by, wearing the same hat, but a different color shirt. Compared to the hunched backs of the workers, he appeared like a giant statue. His hands rested on his hips, where the only movement was his fingers toying with something hanging from the right side of his belt. Atan could find nothing wrong. Every leaf was green, the paths raked and free of stones.

He headed towards the house finding the same orderly well manicured grounds by the front door as out in the field. The front door opened, without a creak, into a small hall.

Atan entered and was immediately met by Gellen and Anya, the fiefmaster and his wife. Beside them stood their daughter and behind them the motionless servants all wearing black shirts and gray pants.

The young girl stepped forward, curtsied without a giggle and returned to her mother's side. Anya nodded her approval.

"Welcome to our home, Duke Atan Ishtba." Gellen's words were crisp and matched his trim form. Both he and his wife had short hair, and clothes cut from the same pattern.

Atan nodded. A brief silence came and went, broken by Anya. "I will give you a tour of our house." Her words bore a resemblance to a command.

Atan noted her tone. "First this man," he pointed to the one who had opened the door "will take me to my room, where he will wait until I'm ready to go. At that time, HE will take me on a tour of the house."

Anya's lips moved to argue but Gellen's moved faster. "As you wish sire." He shot Anya a reproachful glance and directed Oram to assist Atan.

Anya waited until they were out of earshot. "How dare he argue with me in my house."

Gellen stared blankly at his wife. "Anya, it is not our house, it is his. We are allowed to live here. I'd forgotten him, it's been two years since we came here. Duke Ishtba always gives a season or two for new administrators to get their footing and see how they really operate." Gellen's words trailed and Anya stomped away in stubborn defiance.

Atan studied the starkly furnished room. It consisted of a tightly made bed with a single pillow, two sheets, and a blanket. Beyond the bed and an unadorned dresser, the only items were his two bags, now empty, neatly placed by the dresser.

Oram stood motionless by the closed door and flinched when it opened.

The hallway was empty as Oram guided Atan through the house. It was immaculate. Despite the 20 or so servants, Atan saw no sign of children, if any existed besides Gellen's one. All rooms were in perfect symmetry with color schemes of black, gray and white. As Atan walked, he realized that a sanitary smell permeated the air. Even near the kitchen, there were no cooking aromas. It was also apparent that except for the people there were no living things in the house.

Overall Oram took him on an orderly tour of an orderly house, but the inner courtyard was carefully avoided. "Oram, I'd like to see the courtyard." Atan was casual but Oram stiffened and turned pale.

"My lord, Master Gellen forbids entry there without he or Mistress Anya present or by his direct command." The fear

194

welling inside Oram exhibited itself in his sweaty palms and lowered head. But all the more reason for Atan to look. "Oram, I am the Duke of this house and land. My desires override any of Gellen's orders and I will personally explain that to him since he has obviously forgotten."

Oram swallowed hard. "As you wish my lord." Oram opened the door to a small yard.

The dirt floor was raked and there were no miscellaneous objects on the ground. In the center of the yard was a post about 10 feet high. As Atan approached it, a feeling rose inside him that would soon overpower him.

Attached to either side of the post was a hook and chain welded to a wrist clamp. The smell of blood and fear filled Atan's nose. Without looking, he could see that blood spattered the ground. Red stained whips lay dormant in a tray. Atan's blood throbbed in his temples and his whispered order to Oram to leave and set up a meeting with Gellen was venomous.

Atan kicked over the tray and headed to the chosen room.

Gellen and Anya waited.

Atan slammed the door behind him. His eyes burned into Gellen and the nearby table lifted in the air when Atan's fist struck it. "Gellen, you have lived in Ishtba all your life, there is no excuse for what is here."

"My lord, what is wrong?" Gellen trembled while Anya stood impatiently.

"The post, how dare you use a whipping post on my land."

"Well, of all things to be angry about, Anya was cut short, when Atan grabbed her arm squeezing it until it was white. "Out of self respect only, I will not touch you, but one more word and my wrath will be all I have," he snapped. Turning back to Gellen, he said "You are responsible."

"My lord, I must control the help. It is necessary," he pleaded.

Atan flung Gellen across the room, then strode over to the cowering man, lifted him up and held him against the wall. "If it is necessary to whip a servant to achieve obedience than the servant has been given the wrong task or the master is incompetent to give correct orders. In either case it is your fault."

Gellen's sweaty face was now filled with tears, pain, and defeat. "Sire," he rasped, it will stop. I will find another way."

Anya still whimpering cringed at Gellen's words. Atan forced himself to listen despite the cloud of anger that surrounded him. He released Gellen who shook uncontrollably. "See that you do, or next time I will not be so kind." He turned away and walked towards the door, stopping by Anya. His form created a dark shadow over her. "I'll dine alone in my room."

Atan walked around outside, not seeing anything, just reeling in a tidal wave of emotion, waiting for it to subside. By dark he could return to his room and deal with the situation rationally. His dinner was acceptable though he barely touched it. Sleeping was even harder than usual. He rose before the sun.

Anya and Gellen ate in silence and climbed into bed early. Anya, now removed from the situation felt better. "He can't be serious! Remove the posts! How does he expect to maintain control? There must be a post at the Castle."

"I don't remember seeing one."

"Well we must keep it."

"You tell him," Gellen snapped.

Anya stopped her chatter and recoiled into a restless sleep.

In the morning Atan toured the fields alone. He saw what he expected, excellent crops, but a scent of fear that hung over the fields. Sadly he knew, that while Gellen ran this fief, never again would a melon from this place be sweet. He concluded business by noon and headed towards his final stop, taking Oram with him as a new member of his staff.

The carriage pulled into a clearing ringed by knee-high stalks of lilac plants. Atan breathed in the scent of new grass as the men laid out blankets to sit on. Although it was barely past midday, Atan chose to stop and continue the rest of his journey tomorrow.

Behind the clearing a forest beckoned. Sturdy old trees whose leaves teased the clouds seemed to watch the intruders, and their branches whispered secrets to one another. Atan felt drawn. He removed the gold and green cloak that bespoke his position and laid it neatly on the blanket. Beside it, he put the sword that rarely left his side. Gently he bade Oram to guard them and ordered his guard to stay behind while he accepted the forest's invitation.

Atan walked between the rocks and stopped to take in the wonders of the land. Ants marching in perfect order, carrying crumbs ten times their size to who knows where. The intricately woven sounds and scents helped him clear his mind of the past days events. Atan rested against an old tree, his still form soon blending with the forest life. Birds flew close enough to touch and small furry creatures rubbed against his leg.

By nightfall he felt cleansed and returned to a compatible but concerned group of men. Atan ate his dinner in silence and fell asleep staring at the stars.

His company relaxed at his return and continued their conversation. Oram marveled at the freedoms of Castle Cordan while the other two shuddered at Oram's tales. Raalek's sun's first rays shone into an empty clearing and the branches whispered about the carriage that left before the sun could offer her greeting.

Lehcar, Merej's eldest saw him first, and the news spread quickly.

It was past dusk, and Atan could see little as he rode up to the front gate. A lumpglow by the doorway shed enough light to see the door, a little worn in spots, but bearing a wreath of branches and berries.

Atan had barely tapped on the door when it opened slowly, creaking a bit along the way. He heard the scurrying of feet.

Merej and Norana stood proudly in the hall, their three children close beside. The middle child, about 6 years old giggled and her big sister offered a sly kick while the youngest worked at staying awake. Merej bowed, Norana curtsied and the girls followed suit.

Lehcar, almost a teenager, broke the silence, as she pushed her carefully combed brown curls away from her face. "Duke Ishtba, we welcome you to our home." She blushed and the other two, Marya and Ruda presented him with a basket of fruit.

Ruda, the youngest, whispered to him as he bent down to receive the gift. "It's in case you get hungry after dinner." Atan smiled and whispered a thank you and the parents beamed their pride.

"My lord, we have readied rooms for you and your aides. I hope they will be sufficient."

"I'm sure they will Norana." Atan followed the short plump woman as she led the way to his room. It was a small affair, with a bed and dresser. Very clean, though the bed dressing was worn, almost frayed. Since it was late he chose to spend the evening alone.

Despite the trip, he could not sleep, so he walked through the dark house. A few lumpglows placed in key positions provided dim light. Throughout his tour, Atan found no signs of house servants. This became particularly obvious when he stepped on a toy of some sort near one of the girls' room.

From his room he could stare at the moons, which he did as he nibbled on a very sweet fruit. He finally dozed off to sleep. As he rose in the morning the scent of fresh bread wound its way to his room and led him to the nearby kitchen.

Soon Norana was in view. She had obviously taken great care to set the table as properly as she thought it was to be, and placed a breakfast adequate for three families on it.

"The setting is lovely Norana."

She blushed. "Thank you my lord. Would you like some tea?"

"Yes." Atan ate some biscuits and fruit in silence and sipped his tea while he watched Norana work. As he finished another woman, in her early thirties, arrived. Norana relaxed.

They did not speak until he left the room, but he was not out of earshot. "Susa, I'm so glad you're here. There is so much to do."

Susa peeked around the corner. "Is he as bad as they say?"

Norana smiled. "I don't think so. He hasn't been here long, but so far he's been a true gentleman."

Raalek's morning air was cool enough for even Atan to need a cloak. It stayed wrapped around him as he wandered away from the house. The strong scent of the cattle seeped into the misty morning air, it filled Atan with the same sense of strength as the scent of rameks bucking in their stalls. There was a healthy feel to this place.

He headed towards some commotion from a nearby structure. As he got closer and the morning mist lifted he could see the barn. The floor was immaculate. Each cow had its own stall, and each stall was well maintained, not a nail out of place or a loose splinter on the floor.

Deep contented bellows reverberated through the stone walls. The cows had all been brushed and cleaned so well, that the flies took little interest in them. A group of women and young boys nervously filed past the Duke. Within minutes the cows were munching on fresh stacks of hay and the milking process had begun. Soon the Duke's presence was ignored and amidst the friendly chatter was the steady streams of milk flowing into the pails by the milker's feet.

In the fields Atan could see Merej and his men. Slowly he strolled in their direction, noting the lush green fields and fat satisfied donags corralled in one spot.

Merej instructed his men for the day and listened to their suggestions, by the time the chill air slipped away, Merej's field hands were about their business.

Atan rode with Merej for the day, watching some of the winter's plan take effect. He marveled at what could be done. Five men on rameks, each dressed in protective leather and carrying ropes, surrounded hundreds of the beasts, herding them together. They shouted meaningless words at the animals, creating one massive blanket of black and brown bodies spreading over the land. One man moved to the right to open the gate and the push began.

A thousand hoofed feet rumbled over the fields, guided by the whooping voices and watchful eyes of the men. By dusk all one could see were black dots fading into the sunset and the trail of donag odor mingling with the cows in the barn.

Atan followed Merej back to the house. The young man's short muscular form filled his work well. As Atan handed his ramek over to one of Merej's men he noticed a large building about 100 yards from the barn. "What is that?"

Merej closed the gate behind the rameks and stroked the beast before leaving it. "My lord, that is where the field hands live."

"I see, I'll meet you in the house shortly." Atan headed towards the large building.

Merej fidgeted with his clothes and returned home.

From the large house Atan could hear the conversations. A few unhappy voices, mostly about inconsequential matters. For the most part the men and women spoke of the day's accomplishments and what could be done tomorrow. Peeking through an opening Atan saw plenty of food and drink. Stoves and fireplaces were well fueled, he even caught a glimpse of a bed supplied with clean sheets and warm blankets.

At the main house Norana had everyone wait for the guest of honor before sitting down to eat around the large wooden table. Steaming bowls of vegetables and fresh bread adorned the table along with a platter of thick grilled and well seasoned donag steaks.

When Atan sat down, dinner began. At first silence ruled, but soon the girls giggled and whispered. Atan smiled and the conversations flowed.

"My lord, how was your trip?" Merej tore open a hot roll.

"Yesterday's journey was pleasant and uneventful. Norana, your dinner is fit for a king."

Norana bowed her head.

"Lehcar, how old are you?"

With the air of a typical girl her age, proud to have lived so long, she said twelve, my lord."

"Umhmm. I noticed you reading a book."

Instant fear froze everyone but Atan. They did not know the extent of the Castle's winter endeavor. Lehcar bowed her head. "Yes my lord."

"Excellent. What is it about?" Sighs of relief passed around the table.

"Healing my lord. It is so interesting. I have learned a lot. I fixed a man's hand the other day." She glowed with pride as Merej nodded his agreement and approval.

"Perhaps when you are a little older you'd like to visit Castle Cordan and study with our healers. Maybe, just maybe, even Lady Raphela could spend some time with you, as it is one of her most heartfelt interests."

"Could I really?" In her excitement Lehcar forgot the protocol of his title, which Atan ignored.

"If your parents approve."

"We will discuss it." Norana was honored, but would not let Lehcar fly off the handle.

By now all had adjourned to the living room. The fireplace blazed, shedding its warmth toward the couch, where the adults sat. The children sat cross-legged on pillows staring at the wonder of the man called Duke Atan Ishtba.

"Duke Atan, tell us about Lady Raphela, is she really as beautiful as everyone says?" Maria let the words spill honestly from her lips before Merej could tell her to hush.

Atan gave in to the thought of his wife and son. "Yes, she is as beautiful as you can imagine."

The children dominated the conversation with questions, and finally begging for a tale from the great traveler and master.

Finally Atan obliged and told a happy tale of Ishtba as he saw it. As the tale came to an end Ruda nodded off to sleep and the others marched sleepily and happily to bed.

Soon the adults followed, and Atan slept well that night.

Much as he enjoyed his stay by noon it was time for him to go. "Merej I am pleased, continue with your work."

"Norana, have you provided Oram with the list I requested?"

"Yes my lord, but these things really are not necessary."

"They are and you will have them."

"Yes m'lord."

Atan waved goodbye to all the children and reminded Lehcar to come visit and was soon on his way home.

In the carriage he looked over Norana's list and added a variety of items. "Oram, be sure Lady Raphela gets this list. Merej and his family deserve far more creature comforts than they take."

Chapter 10

Raphela brushed her hair and fidgeted with her dress before she left the sleeping Vanar and joined Fatell for breakfast. The two women shared a pot of hot tea and a basket of scones in the cool quiet kitchen. Fatell rambled on about the school as Raphela's eyes stared blankly at the kitchen door.

"The students are begging for more paper and writing tools, I don't know what to do."

"Really" Raphela's distant voice matched her eyes.

Fatell let go a smile. "And green spotted donags will be mating with the king's sons next week."

"That's nice," The words were out before Raphela realized Fatell was teasing. She blushed. "Sorry, I guess I'm not very good company lately."

Fatell patted Raphela's hand. "Its all right, he'll be home soon."

"I know. It's just been so long."

"So it seems." Amidst the growing bustle in the kitchen, Fatell offered the support of a woman long accustomed to such separations.

Morning dragged into afternoon but then dusk fell. Raphela brushed her hair again and as the moon rose she knew, long before the gates opened, she knew.

Atan stepped out of the carriage pushing all anticipation as far from his mind as he could. The front door opened to a dim empty hallway. Before it closed Raphela appeared to fly down the stairs.

For a moment they just stared, in wonder that the other was so close. And then, they wrapped around each other like a butterfly in a cocoon. Their breathless kisses planted from head to neck and deep inside warm lips, ruled for a pleasant eternity. As they climbed the stairs, peace settled over Castle Cordan.

Atan was asleep as soon as his head hit the pillow. Raphela smiled and fell into a comfortable world of dreams, beside him.

Raalek's sun had barely yawned its first rays when Atan awoke to the fresh smell of his wife's hair. And as his fingers wallowed in that rich mane, Raphela stirred and rolled to face him.

"Am I dreaming, or are you really here?"

Atan buried his tongue deep inside her mouth while she pulled him closer. Her chin raised inviting him to nibble on her smooth skin as she massaged and titillated his firm buttocks. Long fingers aroused her nipples, keeping their interest until a wet and skillful tongue took over the pleasant task and her body moved in harmony to its gentle swirls. Warm teasing kisses carefully placed, sent shivers of ecstasy down his spine and being one with each other was all they could imagine. He pumped his body inside her and welcomed it with the warm ooze of lust.

The innocent sheets of sleep were soaked in sweat of love and its scent, exhilarating the couple even more, driving the rise and fall of muscle and curve, until their energy was spent. And then they slept some more, with her hair wrapped gently around his hand.

Raalek's sun continued its slow path, warming the castle and waking the inhabitants. By midmorning everyone woke feeling more than refreshed. Atan dressed quickly, quietly anxious and left as a smiling Raphela finished buttoning her gown.

Atan's feet turned not towards the stairs but towards the nursery. Vanar dropped whatever trinket that had occupied his hand. Much like his mother, he knew who was coming and shook his crib with glee. Atan swept his son up into his arms, his soul melting as he took in the baby's clean and fresh scent. Vanar hugged his papa almost as hard as papa hugged him.

Raphela leaned against the doorway, basking in it all, especially Atan's blush of embarrassment. Her hand caressed his cheek. "Now my lord, did you think I didn't know where you'd gone?"

Atan, holding Vanar in one hand, wrapped the other around Raphela, pulled her close, and planted a loving kiss on her lips.

After his reunion with his family, Atan, took firm even steps down the stairs. No one scurried or bowed as he reached the main level, yet the atmosphere did change. A certain sense of pride unfolded. Faces glowed if the Duke nodded his approval.

This was not an inspection, no, not an inspection, just a simple passing through towards his destination, but his presence was enough to put them all on display.

As Atan entered the courtyard the men were engaged in training. It was a technique Corin discovered, during his research along with others that were buried in the dusty records of centuries past.

The Duke smiled, his grey eyes studying each man until dusk. Only the flurrying rainbow of clouds, announcing a strong storm, ended the activities, just as the sky threw down its first lightning bolts.

While Atan observed his troops, Raphela gathered her staff, to prepare the progress report due the next day. Corin, Fatell and others circled around Raphela in the meeting room. Each presented his or her information verbally and turned in a written report. Much of the winter's plans and work had come to fruition. Only when rich scents of thick gravies and stews, and fresh bread wafted through the castle, announcing dinner did Raphela close the meeting, with deep acknowledgment and appreciation for jobs well done.

The next day Atan did inspect the castle and, as he expected, all was well. By midafternoon he, Raphela and Mahtso gathered in the family room.

"Mahtso you begin. What happened while I was gone?" Atan sat back on the couch and toyed with Raphela's hair.

"We received word from Kito, all is well with him. Akar has shown him some favor. Two new men were recruited for the troops and one retired. Sadly, Lencko, the oldest member of the guard, died. Though we knew it was coming, it was still difficult and we lost a day of training, out of respect." Mahtso's chain beat hard and steady against the table and his blue eyes stared into the flickering flames.

Atan leaned forward. "Is his widow taken care of? If I remember, she was quite dependent on him." The concern was genuine and deep.

"Yes, one of harem women is caring for her."

"Good. Go on."

Mahtso's chain circled lazily around his hand. "I started sending the men on trips to the town. All is quiet and Milson appears to be prospering. The two scouts I sent on a long exploratory trek have not returned, but I believe they will before the summer is done.

After a few more questions, Atan turned to Raphela and smiled. She handed him a yawning Vanar, and began her own account. "Corin and I have uncovered a wealth of knowledge from ancient times. One thing we've begun to explore is diet. We're experimenting with some specific food combinations to see how they affect energy, stamina and growth." Raphela paused for a sip of tea and added, "Fatell has been pushed to the limit with the schools."

"What do you mean?"

"The interest is so strong that there are people waiting to learn. We're trying to devise a way to mass produce writing materials and books. I've assigned a task force to come up with a solution. We are very open to suggestion.

"Mmm. Go on."

Raphela checked off the items she had covered and continued. "Nalab has completed her plans for the waterways inside the castle. We'd like your nod of approval, so that the actual work can begin."

"How long will it take to complete?"

"Our estimate is about two years."

He nodded his head as a nurse arrived to put Vanar to bed. "Begin whenever you're ready."

Raphela completed her report and Atan began his own, reviewing the changes that needed to be made at the various fiefs. "Sidno needs to retire. Let's send him an aide. The northern grain fief needs more laborers. See what can be done. " He mentioned each fief, coming to Gellen last. The teacups on the table had been filled and emptied many times and dinner had passed with simple finger foods.

"Gellen is a problem and much as I wish to believe he will change, I know he will not." Atan sighed as he described the conditions he'd found.

The knife on Mahtso's chain dug deep into the leather bag at his side and Raphela dug her nails deep into the pillows of the couch. Atan had already decided what was to be. "Mahtso, watch them. He will fall, but I will not devour my own people unless I must." On that somber note the meeting ended.

Mahtso sought out Fatell. They shared some wine and the warmth of sleep.

Raphela watched Atan pace by their bedroom window, lean on the sill and peer out at the landscape.

She moved behind him and with soft hands firmly massaged his tense shoulders. He relaxed a little and sat down on the bench by the window and leaned into Raphela. She continued making gentle circles with her fingers and until she drew him next to her. His fingers closed tightly around hers. Grey eyes stared at the stars.

Why must my own people do this?"

Raphela placed a gentle kiss on his cheek, it was the only answer she had. They slept close that night, her hair ever circling his hand.

As summer wore on Raphela found herself struggling to find time for Vanar and even for Atan. Though Ishtba and the castle flourished, she sensed something missing. One night as she allowed herself the luxury of a long hot bath. Warm bubbles of soap rode the gentle waves of the tub. She closed her eyes and looked to her childhood, when life seemed simpler. Her mind lazily wandered through summers past. Gradually she came to a realization, something that existed in her youth, but did not now, not here. But it should she thought.

Though it was late and Atan would soon reach out for her in his sleep, she needed to resolve this immediately. She dressed and found Fatell cradling a snoring Mahtso in her lap. Fatell stroked his hair as she watched the last embers of a fire fade away.

"I'm sorry to bother you Fatell." Raphela said softly. Fatell started to move, but Raphela stopped her. "Sit still, it's just a question."

Mahtso stirred momentarily and then settled back to sleep.

"Fatell, has the castle ever had a day of rest?"

"I'm not sure what you mean."

Raphela made some helpless gestures with her hands in an attempt to describe what she meant. Both women giggled at her attempts. "I mean a standard, once a month, once a week, a day of rest. Do you understand?"

"No, I don't think so."

"Well, in Milson, once a week, all the shops closed. It was the same day for everyone. It was a tradition that began even before my parents were born."

"All right. What of it?"

"I think we need it here. No one has time for anything except work. I've barely seen my son or husband in weeks. Frankly, I miss them, and I can't be alone."

"Family units, are a somewhat new idea here. The Duke's parents didn't discourage the idea, just ignored it. You have changed all that. The time is right for such a thing. See if your husband agrees."

She kissed Fatell on the cheek and then headed towards the bedroom and crawled under the covers, falling into a deep sleep.

During breakfast the next day Raphela broached the subject to Atan.

"A day of rest, once a week? Hmm" Atan finished his tea and poured another cup while Raphela removed biscuit crumbs from Vanar's hair.

"Yes, why not?" Her large anxious eyes were enough to convince him, but his mood was playful.

"I don't know. What would people do if they weren't working?" Atan's eyes glistened and Raphela jumped right in.

"I don't know about anyone else," her sensuous well-rounded bottom was suddenly on Atan's lap, "but I could think of something."

"Is that a fact?" Warm lips sucked teasingly at her neck, evoking more than a little moan. To Vanar's surprise he was promptly put in his crib.

His Mama and Papa considered the possible activities of a day of rest. Their passion for each other grew stronger and sweeter each day. Although this morning's affair was brief, it was satisfying and more than convincing to both that a full day to do what they pleased was in order.

The last day of the week no one would work. Those tasks that could not be set aside would have rotating schedules among the staff.

Even those on duty found ways to have more free time, preparing meals in advance so that they too could escape to the green hills and fields.

On a particularly warm day, Atan, carrying Vanar on his shoulders, climbed to a favorite hilltop spot with Raphela. She laid out a picnic in the shade of a thick tree where a convenient rock served as a table.

Vanar made a dash for the open space as soon as his legs touched the ground, and Atan leaned against the tree, watching his son. He also kept an eye on his shapely wife as she settled them in for the afternoon.

Vanar's giggles of glee and grunts of frustration filled the sky. His round eyes stared in amazement at a colorful butterfly, hovering beside his curly hair. The creature wisely fluttered away when a curious hand reached for its wings.

Raphela watched with pride and her senses opened to the summer air. Every sweet flower sent a signal, and she swore she could hear the ants in a nearby hill.

Disappointed, Vanar found his way back to his parents. He plopped down on the plush grass, studied the fine blades and in the tradition of all toddlers, pulled a handful from the ground and attempted to further study it with his mouth.

Raphela, with more than a little trouble pried open his tiny fingers and took it away. "No, Vanar, no." The verbal admonishment and theft of his discovery produced a frown, but mama turned to quick for the tears to be of use, so he stood up and went towards papa.

Atan was still leaning against the tree, staring at the clouds, lost in some unimportant thought. Small pieces of tree bark sprinkled into his straight black hair.

Vanar came upon his papa, looked him over and then hit is leg. "No papa, no papa." Startled, Atan looked down. "No papa, no papa."

Atan picked Vanar up, Raphela already kneeling by their side.

"What Vanar, what is it?" Atan's concern bordered panic.

Vanar reached up and pulled a piece of grass from Atan's lips, one that he had been chewing lazily.

Both parents laughed in comprehension

"He told you, now...." Suddenly Raphela stopped, and stared at Vanar. "Atan, he spoke! Do you realize, he spoke!"

Shock plastered Atan's face. "You're right. He's never done that before. Never a real word, just babble. Raphela, our son can speak. Isn't he too young though?"

Raphela thought about it for a minute. "Yes, he's not even a year and a half old. Well, he is your son," he finished indulgently.

Atan's face lost its elation. He turned and pinned Raphela to the ground. "OUR son, I didn't make him by myself."

A special smile and look passed between them ending in a loving kiss, interrupted by a hungry child, who was quickly grabbed and made part of the hug.

Towards the end of summer, an invitation arrived, to the King's Gala, now held every other harvest season. Raphela read it carefully:

> King Samed hereby requests the presence of Duke Atan Ishtba to the Harvest Gala The Ishtban Family is welcome to the fold of Calcoran as well.

She placed the rainbow-trimmed parchment on the breakfast table. Affairs of state were rare. The only one she had attended had been her own wedding. Her role in this affair was a mystery to her.

Atan seemed unconcerned and studied some financial report while a silent Raphela busied herself with cleaning the table. Finally he noticed her discomfort. "What's wrong?"

"Nothing," she said to the table.

Atan put down the papers and motioned for Raphela to sit on his lap. "Now, don't study the cracks in the ceiling or dust on the floor. Look at me." Embarrassed eyes met his. "Raphela what's wrong?"

She breathed deeply. "The gala."

"What about it?"

"What is my place beyond Ishtba?"

"Beyond Ishtba?" For Raphela it was an eternity until he understood her concern, for Atan it was only a few seconds.

A caress more loving did not exist, or a smile more honest. "Beyond Ishtban borders, you are the queen of Ishtba and its most important representative."

Lips opened to argue, but a long finger pressed for silence. "I am known, but you represent what the world cannot see. They will never see Ishtba through me, you are the doorway."

His words were meant to be comforting, but the statement was also brutally honest, and laid some pressure on Raphela neither realized existed until that moment.

"Will Vanar come also?" she asked.

"I don't know, what do you think?"

Raphela toyed with a teacup. "I'm not sure. I'd hate to be away from him."

"True and for the world to see how he has grown would bring us both a great deal of pride."

"Could he handle the trip?"

"Indeed. More importantly, can we guarantee it?"

"Atan."

"Yes"

"We can't guarantee anything."

"I know." He said, feeling an unfamiliar inadequacy. "I suppose the real question is, is it worth the risk?"

Neither could answer.

Two nights after the question was posed, Raphela and Atan crawled under the covers, looked into each others eyes and simultaneously answered, "No, it's not worth the risk."

When the day of their departure arrived Raphela stroked Vanar's hand. "Be a good boy for Fatell."

Vanar's curly haired head tipped to one side. "Mama go bye bye?"

211

"Yes, but we'll be back soon." Tiny salty tears began forming in her eyes.

Vanar stretched out his arms. "Vanar go, Vanar go." His sweet little voice forced Atan to retreat into the carriage.

"No baby, stay here, Mama and Papa will be back soon." With one last kiss above the big blue eyes Raphela hurried into the carriage so she would not have to listen to him cry. Little did she know Vanar's tears stopped soon after the castle door closed.

By noon of the second day they arrived in Calcoran and at the King's castle.

The castle spread over a vast area. Well beyond the main gates, rugged hills glistened in the noon day sun. The gardens maze of flora and fauna delicately balanced for sight and scent, matched almost to the leaf, the description of the King's land, of a hundred years before. Raphela had envisioned it as such from the books she read.

The heavily adorned door slowly opened to reveal old Gerig, the castle master, standing in the great hall.

He bowed low. "Welcome Duke Ishtba, it is good to have you here again."

"Thank you, Gerig."

"You must be Lady Raphela Ishtba." Gerig smiled and after a moment's pause added, "My lord, if I may be so bold, you have chosen well." A brief flush of pride swept Atan's face. Gerig snapped his fingers and two boys appeared to show the Duke and his Lady to their room. Logan and Balin, the Ishtban guards, were placed on either side of the couple.

Once unpacked and settled in, Raphela and Atan strolled through the castle. Incredible art from past ages covered the walls. Intricate metallic sculptures, sat poised on solid black bases by almost every doorway. The household bustled with activity. Dukes, barons, counts and their mates chatted in small rooms over spice tea and biscuits or simply passed in the hallways with a simple nod. As they walked Raphela became increasingly uncomfortable, her silence gave her away.

"What's wrong Raphela?" Atan asked.

"It's foolish."

"Not likely."

"I don't know anyone here," she said turning to stare at a painting on the wall, to hide the tears in her eyes.

Vanar's tiny hand could have knocked Atan to the ground. "So?" He said.

"So," she sniffled, "I feel out of place."

"Just a minute. Is this the same woman who blindly, left her home and family to hopefully live in a strange castle and be favored by the mysterious Duke who lived within its walls?"

"That was different." She sniffed.

"Indeed it was, you could have been killed back then." His tone softened. "And what about the wedding, you didn't know anyone there either?"

Finally she looked at him. "It was my territory, my rules. I don't even know the rules here. The people walk past us and look at me so strangely."

Atan took her hand and guided her to a bench outside the castle. Raalek's sun cast deep shadows off the glistening hills. "Raphela, I apologize. I've been here so often and think so little of the social value, it escapes me. This was almost true, except that Atan glowed every time someone noticed his wife.

"Shall I tell you about this place?" She nodded. "Many of the women here were offered to me for marriage. I turned them all down. And for what it may be worth, Ishtba is now larger than Calcoran. All of this makes us very special guests. For example, the man that greeted us at the front door greets only one other person, the king's brother. The strange looks you receive are jealousy, respect and fear. As I've said before, you are the Queen of Ishtba and share that rule with no one. The king has a first wife, but five others as well. You are unique. You can't break any rules, because you and I are the rules."

The power that made Atan Ishtba what he was, struck Raphela with renewed force. It was a mixed bag of blessings and curses.

Small groups met for dinner. To Raphela's delight, Sonja and Jivad appeared at the Ishtban table. They dined with one other couple from the King's land and enjoyed a pleasant and relaxing evening.

Atan spent the first full day of official activities meeting with representatives from various fiefs in the Calcoran kingdom. The King's first son, a young man about 23 years old, conferred with Atan as well.

"You look well Ishtba." Dahlek's forced and phony arrogance made Atan sigh silently.

"As do you. What responsibilities has your father assigned to you?" An innocent question.

"I monitor all the financial activities of the land."

"A task requiring great care. You should be proud. The last time I spoke with your father he mentioned selling a herd of Rameks, is that offer still open?" At that sign of respect and trust the younger man relaxed and business talk began.

Unlike Atan, Raphela was free to explore the castle. When she walked into the main kitchen as if walking into her own, a startled servant asked, "My lady, is there a problem? Have we prepared food incorrectly?"

"No, I was simply curious. I just wondered if your operations differed any from our own?

"Would you like someone to explain our methods to you?"

"Yes, that would be wonderful."

A young cook was taken from his duties and given the task of escorting Raphela. She watched them prepare raw food, choose ingredients, even butcher meat. Some of the methods had been eliminated at Castle Cordan even before Raphela arrived there, simply because there were better ways.

"Tell me, how long have you been preparing food this way?"

The young man stopped walking and stuck out his chest with pride. "My lady, these traditions have existed since before my great-grandfather's time."

"I see. I must mention some of them to the cooks at Castle Cordan." She offered it as a compliment, but all of the conversation around her stopped. The kitchen director approached her. "Pardon my asking, but are you Lady Raphela?"

"Yes."

A white pallor of fear covered the woman's face. "My lady, I hope we did not offend you in any way."

"Of course not. I appreciated the courtesy of your time and hope I have not interfered too much with your routine," she said graciously.

"You are more than welcome my lady and were no trouble at all."

Raphela left a stunned and buzzing kitchen staff.

And to her delight found a library and a librarian. The old man poured over his book with such a religious attention that he jumped when Raphela came close.

"May I look at your books?" She asked.

The old man squinted. "Are you a woman?"

She smiled. "Yes."

He looked around and whispered "You can read?"

When she nodded his wrinkled skin cracked into a wise smile and a wrinkled finger wagged at her. "You must be Lady Raphela of Ishtba."

"That I am," She laughed.

He stood and bowed. "Please, look, peruse, study, devour! I welcome you to it."

Raphela walked towards the bookshelves and understood his glee at her request.

Despite a recent cleaning for Gala, it was obvious that this room was rarely used and the same could be said for the man. Carefully she pulled a book from its place, waving the dust from its leaves away from her nose. Amazingly, she found it written in the same ancient language as the books at Ishtba. This one, like so many others, spoke of contraptions and events so foreign it was beyond comprehension, but Raphela leafed through a few and found two about healing.

"Sir, would you and the king allow me to borrow these, take them back to Ishtba and return them next spring?"

The old man threw up his hands and shrugged his shoulders, "My lady, you could borrow this whole room and the King wouldn't notice its absence. You have my permission and with it the King's, as he has given me total control of this room."

Raphela continued her explorations questioning gardeners and guards, seamstresses and winemakers. Atan found her interrogating a carpenter. Gently he tapped her on the shoulder.

215

She turned to see him cross-armed and trying to look severe, which terrified the poor workman who froze in his spot, but didn't bother Raphela at all.

"Would you care to join me for dinner?"

She shot him a devilish grin before turning to the quaking carpenter. "Thank you for your time. My Duke and I must attend to affairs of state."

As the workman scurried away Atan placed a loving smack on her bottom. Raphela chortled, shrugged her shoulders and held out her arm for Atan to walk her to dinner.

The next day, as tradition demanded, the King held open court. The great hall, lined with wall-length tapestries, placed between equally long windows, held the two hundred people in attendance.

King Samed sat on his throne, Lise, standing to his right and on his left, his young sons, fidgeting and jockeying for position. A great semicircle formed around the throne, each member of the court took his place with his wife or consort beside him. One by one, they paid their respects to the King. It was a simple process, kneel before King Samed, when acknowledged stand, present your gift, accept the King's thanks and return to your place.

Years ago, this process, would have lasted from a little past dawn, until dusk, but now it began after the noon meal and ended just before sunset. Atan Ishtba was the last presenter and although King Samed did not cower before him, Atan's power emanated well beyond the small square in which he stood. The general chitchat and whispers that dotted the room came to a dead halt when he stood before the King. Even among the King's subjects, Atan Ishtba had control. Raphela was amazed. Atan finished his tribute; King Samed rose, made a brief speech and signaled for the festivities to begin.

Four musicians began a light tune and servants circulated around the room with trays of hors d'oevres. Delicate scents floated through the air and goblets of wine appeared in every hand.

Deftly, Atan, with Raphela at his side, wound his way through the crowd. Not one eye missed the couple's perfectly designed clothes, in Ishtban gold green and black. An old woman, a soothsayer, followed them with her deep violet eyes. She blended in with the crowd, and after a time muttered to herself, "they are the power, legends they will be, legends of power."

Atan proudly introduced Raphela to a variety of royal couples. She quickly grasped the politics of the situation, smiling often and listening a great deal. King Samed and Lise approached the Ishtban couple.

The King offered his hand to Atan in friendship and respect. "You look well, married life agrees with you."

"Indeed it does." Atan squeezed Raphela's hand, then released it as Samed drew him to the side.

"Ishtba, you have but one man left not under my direct rule. Once you finish him off, will your loyalty still stand?"

Although unafraid, Samed had lived long enough to know that success can feed on itself and push even good men beyond their principles.

Atan was not offended, but he did choose to let Samed know he expected no aggression from him either. "My word will not waver. I expect to remain at peace with you and your sons for as long as I live."

It was not lost on Samed that the powerful duke had not used a formal form of address. And the gesture was not lost on Atan when Samed took two goblets from a passing servant and offered one to him with a slight tilt of his head.

Lise took Raphela's hand. "How are you dear?"

"A little overwhelmed I suppose, but other than that, quite well." She was grateful for the older woman's attention.

"I did not believe your husband could grow stronger, but he has. Marriage and fatherhood serve him well."

"Both of us."

"Yes. I understand you took quite a tour yesterday."

"Oh, I hope you don't mind."

"Not at all."

"Thank you. I did have a lovely time. I borrowed two books from your library."

"I know." She smiled and Raphela saw a woman whose prime had come and gone and with it the opportunity to achieve the greatness belonging to a King and his wife. "As the librarian said, they will not be missed. So please, keep them, as a gift from the King."

"Thank you." Raphela felt saddened. Lise and Samed were good people, who had simply fallen into the trap of tradition and routine and never escaped.

"Keep on growing Raphela, now is your time." Lise kissed her on the cheek and left.

A group of women stared at Raphela and driven by curiosity, she joined them.

"How do you do. I am Raphela of Ishtba and who might you be?"

"Lauren of Calcor West."

"Margo of Dunsen Calcor."

"Petra of North Calcor."

"A pleasure to meet all of you," Raphela smiled.

A momentary silence fell, which Lauren finally broke. "How is it to be married to the great Atan Ishtba?" The question was biting.

"It's good for me, but you seem to have a problem, is it with me or my husband?" Raphela answered calmly.

"I, I, I, just, umm, don't understand," she stammered.

"You don't understand what?"

"Why he chose you?" Lauren was relieved to say it. The other women hungered for the answer as well.

"Instead of you?" Raphela asked, bemused.

"Well, yes."

"Are you married?"

"Yes."

"Are you happy?"

"Yes."

"Then what difference does it make?" Gentility pervaded every fiber of her words.

"I'm sorry. I didn't mean to attack you. Please understand, many of us were offered to him and he chose a woman not even of royal blood. What did you do?"

218

"I don't know. Perhaps I just looked him straight in the eye when we met."

Amazed glances shot between the other women.

"You can look him straight in the eye?" Petra asked.

"If I couldn't, then I certainly couldn't live with him."

"But he is Atan Ishtba! No one except the King and that strange man Mahtso look him in the eye," Margo protested.

"I do, I must, it is the only way we can be." Raphela's firm conviction spoke to the power of her own being.

At that moment Atan appeared to escort her to dinner. As they joined the guests filing toward the shimmering blue and silver tables. The women continued to stare.

"What was that all about?" Atan asked under his breath.

"You," Raphela said, hiding a smile when he arched a brow.

They found themselves seated with Akar, who nodded, but appeared quite preoccupied. His head turned from side to side and his foot nervously tapped the floor. Sonja and Jivad were also seated at the table. Sonja's petite frame sank into the cushiony chair and she laughed with Raphela at how childlike she seemed. Atan and Jivad simply shook their heads.

Two other couples, cousins of Jivad, joined the party. Akar's fidgeting increased. He stood occasionally, craning his neck, searching for something or someone. Finally he sat down. A young man took the seat beside him.

"Where have you been?" He asked in a motherly tone that fitted his lithe form and exaggerated movements.

The young man whispered in Akar's ear. Akar sighed resignedly and then noticed the commotion he had caused. "Forgive my rudeness. I am Baron Elthen Akar, and this is my," he hesitated, "companion, Mika."

King Samed made a brief speech about good futures, loyal friends, etc. As he concluded, the smell of fine meats and vegetables permeated the air. Dinner had five courses and the wine flowed without end.

"Akar, how are you faring these days?" Atan made an attempt at camaraderie. "Quite well, the land is good and Mika has been so very helpful in sprucing up the castle. I'd be honored to show it to Lady Raphela."

"Perhaps I will come in the spring," Raphela said as she toyed with her goblet.

"Mika, make a note to contact Lady Raphela in the spring."

Mika pulled a device from his shirt and wrote a note as ordered. As he moved to return it, Raphela's hand reached over to stop him. "What is that? I've never seen anything like it."

Akar's head cocked in confusion. "This is new to you?"

"Yes."

"Mika, give it to Lady Raphela. Consider it a gift."

Gingerly Raphela accepted it. There were two pieces, one a hollow oblong shell, about the length of a finger, which acted as a cover to the other piece, twice its length, tipped with a triangular metal point. She turned the pieces over in her hand, rolled them between her fingers, allowing the polished wood casing to become warm in her palm. "Akar, where is the writing fluid? How does this work?"

Curiosity overwhelmed her. Atan was not thoroughly pleased, but knew it would be for the best.

Akar, now proud of this wondrous item, pulled one from his own vest. Gently he untwisted the long piece and revealed a well inside holding the fluid. Carefully he twisted it together.

"Thank you. One more question, how do you make the fluid for this . . ."

"Stylus."

"Stylus."

"It's a recipe handed down from generation to generation among our scribes. I will see if our head scribe will part with it."

"I would be grateful."

Akar nodded courteously and whispered something in Mika's ear. Mika glanced at Raphela.

"Akar, what do you write on?" She asked.

"Animal skin."

"So do we." Raphela was disappointed.

"My lady," a young voice at the end of the table cracked as it spoke.

"Yes."

"We use something different." One of Jivad's cousins, Zed, had joined in the conversation.

"Really, what do you use?" Raphela's interest was aroused.

Servants cleared the table from the third course. Zed waited for them to leave before speaking.

"Woodsheets."

"Woodsheets? What are they?"

Atan leaned back and listened. This young man was anxious to share his bounty.

"They are made from trees. Thin sheets, thinner than animal skin, but sturdy enough for writing. We have an abundance. Very little writing is done in Calcoran."

Zed shrugged his shoulders and a seam from his shirt showed itself, and the fact that his fief was not one of the more favored of the land.

"Is this the major product of your fief" Atan asked.

"Yes. But most of it is used for burning in fireplaces."

"And you still have an abundance?" Raphela nearly drooled at the wealth in Zed's possession. The young man bowed his head in shame.

"Winter is coming, there is always need for more fuel, perhaps you'd be interested in selling some of your stock?" Atan's offhand remark brought a deep smile to Zed's face.

"Oh yes, my lord, thank you."

"Fine, we'll discuss the price later and perhaps to satisfy Lady Raphela's curiosity someone could teach one of our woodsman to make these Woodsheets."

"Of course my lord."

Raphela was momentarily offended and then realized her curiosity and desire to solve a problem overlooked her common sense. It is never wise to express one's desires in public.

After dinner musicians played and everyone danced to the rhythmic melodies of the lutes and harps. When Raalek's second moon waned, the last of the guests retired. At dawn Atan and Raphela left Calcoran.

"Atan, why do those hills shine?" She asked as they drove away.

Atan peered out the carriage window. "I don't know, but we will find out." He smiled, Raphela's thirst for knowledge never ceased.

221

"Good." She stared at the hills a moment longer. "I'm anxious to speak with Logan. He and Kito talked for a long time."

"So am I. I was concerned that Akar would see them." Atan made notes of what needed to be done.

The journey back took less time than expected, much to the delight of the royal couple.

Vanar sat in a warm tub of water as his nurse washed him down. His soft hand slapped the water and drops flew in the air landing on the nurse and himself. He was so thrilled with himself he used both hands to send water splashing over the tub's rim. Vanar giggled at his accomplishment, sharing it with the warm rays of sun that peeked through the shutters.

His nurse shook her head and after trying to stop him, just waited until he tired of his fun. Suddenly he stopped and raised his hands to the nurse. "Mama, Papa, home, Mama, Papa, home."

He stood up and demanded to be removed from the tub. The girl gratefully obliged, wrapping him in a warm blanket and trying to reason with the toddler as she dried him. "Vanar, mama and papa are not home, not yet."

"Yes! Home! Mama, Papa, home!" He twisted towards the door.

"If you keep on moving, I can't dress you."

Vanar forced himself to be still until she'd dressed him in green pants and a yellow sweater.

Before they reached the top of the stairs, the nurse stopped in astonishment. Atan and Raphela were climbing the stairs. Vanar struggled desperately to reach them.

Atan's long strides gave him first arrival and he whisked Vanar from the nurse's hands.

"Papa, Papa." Vanar hugged Atan and Raphela who joined them a few seconds later.

After receiving a warm thank you, the nurse went to her room and shared the experience with no one, until she understood it herself.

Vanar ruled the day. Atan and Raphela were prisoners of their offspring and gladly so, not leaving his side until the moon rose.

It was nearly noon when Atan headed to the meeting room. His hands brushed against the textured walls as two children ran past arguing about some game. His castle lacked the luster and sophistication of Calcoran, but its warmth and spirit were welcome substitutes. He realized what a well-woven piece of work his abode had become; he decided he liked it.

Raphela's footsteps and thoughts echoed right behind him. This was home, no place had ever been as much. Her hand slipped into Atan's for a moment before they entered the room, where Mahtso paced, anxious for news and anxious to see his master.

"Have you been here long Mahtso?" Atan's baritone voice startled him.

"Long enough. How are you?" Mahtso's chain beat lightly against his leg.

"I'm fine." Atan put a fatherly hand on Mahtso's shoulder, and felt the man relax at his touch.

"Good to see you, Mahtso," her comfortable tone put him even more at ease.

"Did all go well while we were away?" Atan leaned back in his chair and soaked in the fresh fall air.

"Quiet and incident free I'm pleased to say," Mahtso answered with a touch of pride.

"Excellent. I believe the first order of business is to debrief Logan."

Raphela signaled for Logan to enter. The young man nearly bounced into the room, grinning from ear to ear.

"You look very happy." Raphela addressed the obvious.

"Nalab has agreed to marry me."

"Congratulations, we are very happy for you."

"Best of luck Logan." Atan, although glad to see his staff content, still had work to do. "Now, tell us what information Kito divulged."

Mahtso, Raphela and Atan turned to Logan who shrank back. "Akar's main interest is in his castle. He spends only enough time, money and effort on his lands to support his lifestyle."

"Which is what?" Raphela pressed.

"Kito said his castle is very different from Cordan, almost no children or even married couples. The rooms and halls are filled with paintings and sculptures, some elaborate and detailed, and others so simplistic they are childish. Such a wide variety of colors of paints and cloth are used, that there is one man, whose sole task it is to catalog all the colors. Most curious of all are the men who design buildings." Logan stopped.

"Buildings?" Mahtso wasn't sure what designing a building meant.

"Yes, not castles, but structures made mostly of wood and bricks. He gave me a picture of one." Logan passed it around but no one was quite sure what to make of it.

But, it meant that creativity was alive and well at Baron Akar's castle. For a moment, the three leaders silently questioned their plans for Akar.

"How many people live in the castle?" Atan began taking notes.

"About 120."

"Size of the army?"

"It's small and poorly trained according to Kito." Logan said.

An assortment of mixed feelings and glances spread around the room. Logan picked up on them.

"My lord, may I tell of something Balin overheard?"

Atan returned from his thoughts. "Of course."

"While at the Gala, Balin saw Akar with the King, they were discussing, umm, you."

"Go on."

"Akar told the King he'd heard rumors that you questioned your decision of loyalty."

Atan began to stir in his seat.

"Akar's words also, were, "Can you be sure that he will be satisfied with only half the world. Does not the beast once tasting blood seek more, despite a full stomach?"

Mahtso's chain wrapped hard around the arm of the chair. Atan's nostrils' flared.

"What a shame, such appreciation of beauty to be married to such stupidity." Raphela sneered. Akar had sealed his fate with his backstabbing ways. "Did Kito provide any information on the layout of the castle grounds?"

Logan gnawed on his lip, "Akar's superstition has guided him to build strong walls around the castle, but Kito discovered ancient tunnels that end outside the walls. Akar has sealed most of them, but the seals are weak." Logan produced a map, drawn by Kito, marking each tunnel. He continued. "Mika told me that Akar will not leave his room the day after the moons' cycle ends. Akar's starguide has warned him of danger every month on that day."

"Mika told you?" Mahtso missed nothing, not a word, not an inflection, not even a raised eyebrow.

"Yes, I thought speaking with Mika would provide a different perspective on the man."

By now Raphela and Atan were paying full attention. It appeared that Logan had more than simple brawn as an attribute.

"Excellent job Logan, continue." Atan prodded.

When Logan was done, Raphela posed some questions about Calcoran. "Would it be possible, to send two emissaries to Calcoran? To collect Woodsheets and whatever other knowledge they can discover?"

"Woodsheets?" Mahtso looked up from his notes.

"Material for writing. It comes from trees, replaces animal skin." Atan explained.

Atan rubbed a finger across his upper lip. "Just how important is this?"

Raphela stared into his eyes. "How important is it that Ishtban people know more than any other?"

"Your point is made. Mahtso, find two men to travel and to return with a supply of Woodsheets."

Raphela's victorious smile irritated and excited her husband.

Other minor concerns were discussed before the trio returned to the daily routines Raphela walked at a leisurely pace away from the room, mulling over the information discussed. Long strong fingers suddenly wrapped around her wrist and pulled her towards the body to which they belonged.

"You test me woman!" Raphela's arms were encased in Atan's firm grasp.

"Someone must." She wrapped her arms around his waist.

"I suppose," he sighed and returned the hug as he stroked her thick hair.

After breakfast the next morning Fatell greeted Raphela with a warm hug. "It is good to see you. You must tell me all about it." Her eyes lit with anticipation. For all the gala's that had been attended, Fatell never saw them from a woman's point of view, she relished the opportunity. Raphela obliged, beginning and ending with the stylus.

Chapter 11

Zed checked the knots one last time as the cart made ready to leave. Both driver and rider were well supplied with clothes and food for the journey. Slowly the cart moved away down the path, its wheels hobbling over the stone road. After closing the door behind him and hanging up his cloak, Zed walked towards the kitchen where his wife Kellen handed him a hot cup of tea.

"I don't understand why you're doing this." She said

Zed sighed. She sounded like his mother when he left home. "Jivad recommended it." He allowed steam from the tea to warm his face before the liquid warmed his throat.

"Jivad, always Jivad!" Kellen threw the cleaning rag down in frustration.

"He has always provided good counsel." Zed said gingerly.

"Good counsel! Is that why we live in this magnificent palace? Does Sonja wash her own dishes?" Kellen's upper lip curled in disgust.

Zed leaned his head into his hands and fought back tears. "I am very sorry Kellen that this marriage was arranged for you, and that I lack Jivad's ability to be a better provider." He stopped and looked at her. "Even though there is no love, can we not share some respect? I do the best I can. And if not for Jivad, we'd be servants somewhere instead of this poor little fief where at least we have some control of our lives." Zed did not raise his voice, he pleaded an old and tired case.

Kellen picked up the rag and lowered her head in embarrassment. He was right. "So why did you send that waste to Ishtba?"

"The Woodsheets were sent because it would please Lady Raphela."

"Why please someone that you barely know, and who may even be an enemy?"

"Kellen, Atan Ishtba is the most powerful man in the world."

"Not more powerful than the king." Kellen insisted.

227

"You may not understand why I listen to Jivad, but he knows. If Duke Ishtba wished to conquer King Samed, he could. Is it not wise to be on the man's good side?"

"So you buy his friendship with waste? Excuse me a *gift* of Woodsheets and the method to make them. Then he has no use for you at all." She threw up her hands in frustration.

Zed shook his head. "Ishtba cannot be bought. I am extending to him my friendship and loyalty. I assure you, he would acquire the knowledge with or without my help."

"I just don't understand you." Kellen stormed out of the kitchen and Zed buried himself in his tea.

A week after the meeting, Mahtso dispatched two men to Zed's fief. One day into the journey the Ishtban emissaries encountered them. They all returned to Castle Cordan. Fatell was ecstatic. She dragged Mahtso to the school. Ivory stacks of Woodsheets created a border around each of the classrooms.

"Mahtso, look at them. Isn't it amazing?" Fatell's eyes were wide as saucers. Between her fingers now hung a woodsheet, about twice as long as a man's hand and 3/4 as wide and so thin one could almost see through it. Mahtso wallowed in Fatell's glee, the Woodsheets meant little to him. Fatell rambled on. "Look, you can write on it and it doesn't tear, as thin as it is. And there is so much of it. Raphela says we are learning to make more." Mahtso just smiled, his blue eyes calm. Fatell bounced from stack to stack and in her mind from plan to plan.

Zed's men toured Castle Cordan, awed at the inhabitants' busy lives. Confident shining children passed them in the halls, and the servants were more like fiefmasters. The pace and feeling overwhelmed both men. While they enjoyed a brief rest at the castle, another visitor arrived, this one from Akar's castle. Raphela and Logan met with him.

"My lady, Baron Akar has asked me to deliver this gift to you." He held out a container and a scroll. "It is the writing liquid and its recipe." The man bowed low as Raphela took the gifts. As he stood, something fell from his shirt. "Oh, my lady, I'd almost forgotten, Mika sent these for you." He held out three styli, one with Raphela's name engraved on the side.

"Thank you. Tell Baron Akar I appreciate his generosity. And tell Mika the same."

"Yes my lady. The baron wishes to invite you to his castle on the first day of the second week of spring."

Raphela stared at the small frightened man. "I will discuss it with the Duke. You will have an answer before you leave."

"Yes, m'lady."

Raphela chose to give one stylus to Atan and one to Mahtso, who she found in a nearby room. "Mahtso, I have something for you." Raphela stuck out her hand, displaying the stylus. He took it and while he examined it, she studied the one marked for her.

Carefully Raphela took it apart. The fine grained wood felt smooth in her hand and the silver tip was finely constructed. As she separated the body into two, instead of liquid she found a tiny scroll.

She reassembled the writing tool and with great care unrolled and read the message. When her eyes grew wide, Mahtso took it from her, his chain beating with greater fervor at each word.

"Greetings, Lady Raphela, I must warn you that Baron Akar's invitation is a ruse. It is his intention to hold you hostage until the Duke agrees to abort any hostile plans against him."

Mahtso shook his head. "I don't relish giving Atan this note."

"Let's do it together.

That evening after Vanar went to bed, Raphela and Atan sat in the family room relaxing by the fire.

Mahtso's chain announced his approach halfway up the stairs. Atan didn't get up, he turned his head and motioned for Mahtso to join them.

When Raphela and Mahtso looked at each other like guilty children. Atan chuckled. "What are you two conspiring about now?"

Mahtso pulled the note from his pocket and stood up as he handed it to Atan.

Who read it, then crumpled the note in his fist which he slammed down on the wooden table. Small chips flew from its surface and a river of cracks spread from beneath his hand. He uncoiled himself from the couch and grabbed Mahtso's shirt almost lifting him from the floor. "Why is this man Akar, still alive?" Castle Cordan's walls shook at the commanding thought, besides the tone.

Atan's chest heaved up and down.

Beads of sweat formed on Mahtso's forehead, his chain hung limp at his side, and his ice blue eyes met Atan's cold grey stare. Raphela moved towards Atan and gently stroked his back. "My lord" she whispered, "release him."

Less than gently Atan let Mahtso go. "Leave me, both of you." He growled.

Stopping at the top of the stairs Raphela grinned sheepishly. "That went well."

"Oh quite!" He said sarcastically.

"It could have been worse."

"True."

They both considered that thought.

"Yet, while I was prisoner of his grasp, I finally understood everyone else's fear of him. I believe the nameless ones took form as Atan Ishtba and stared their wrath into my soul." Mahtso shivered.

Raphela warmed, it was just that power that enticed her.

"Good night Mahtso."

"Good night Raphela."

Mahtso spent the night curled up with Fatell.

Raphela waited patiently for Atan to come to bed.

His anger at Akar was boundless, but his anger that there was something he could take was maddening. "Why did I marry her, let her bear me a child. What danger have I put both of them in?" These thoughts circled his mind, a cruel blanket for the night. Finally exhaustion forced him to bed. As he pulled the covers up to his neck and without thinking wrapped Raphela's hair around his hand, the blanket lost its sting and the thoughts faded as he held her close that night.

In the morning Akar's man was told that Lady Raphela gratefully accepted his invitation.

Within a few days Castle Cordan was free of visitors and within a few weeks it readied for winter, curling up like a dog readying for sleep.

Unlike the sleepy dog, Cordan bustled all winter long, with all exploring their own interests.

Atan concentrated on Akar, the intensity of his thoughts and plans grew as winter came to its end. And the day after Vanar's second birthday, (year 1156) Atan Ishtba and his troops left on their journey.

Atan rose before the sun and dressed quietly. As he reached for his belt and sword a soft hand stopped him. Raphela wrapped the belt around his waist. Her arms lingered there.

Silent lips shared what words could not and so farewell was spoken.

Fatell wasn't surprised when Raphela joined her for breakfast.

Raphela said nothing, just toyed with her teacup.

"Frightened?" Fatell's tone was gentle.

"No. Worried." Raphela sipped the tea. "Doesn't it bother you?"

"Of course it does, but I've grown accustomed to the leaving" she paused, "and the waiting."

Now Fatell stared into the silent cup. "What will they do?"

Raphela's jaw dropped in shock. "I thought you never wanted to know."

"That's true, but somehow it's different now."

"All right. Last week men were sent ahead for final training at the other fiefs. Men close to Akar's fief were dispatched to seal and guard the tunnels."

"Other fiefs?"

"Yes, Atan has men training at all his fiefs between here and Akar's. No one place is without guards and there will be a far larger army than if we just used the men from Castle Cordan."

As Raphela had spoken they finished their tea and went upstairs to the family room.

"That makes sense. But why not destroy the tunnels instead of sealing them?"

Fatell's childlike innocence and curiosity brought the storyteller and teacher in Raphela. "Why destroy what you wish to use?"

Fatell nodded. "Go on, tell me more."

Raphela wove the tale.

As she did Ishtban forces traveled in the bitter Raaleken cold. Spring meant only the first storm had come. The wind was still biting. But Ishtban clothes were coveted for their warmth and durability. And the Ishtban men seemed immune to the wind and snows deadly effects. (Rumor had it, that Ishtban land sprung plants in the snow, just a rumor)

Mahtso insisted that Atan ride in the middle of the group, and despite his desire to lead from beginning to end, Atan knew Mahtso was right. Mahtso brought up the rear, and throughout the journey the other men changed positions, resembling a ballet of beast and man carefully choreographed to the beat of the wind. The men welcomed the warmth and fresh food at each fief. Atan refused to stop in a town.

The plans had been well laid. Kito had been removed from Akar's castle on a familial pretense. Camouflaged in white furs that made them disappear into the snow Atan's men waited outside the castle while "Lady Raphela' -- a young man in disguise-- entered with a small entourage. As the gates closed the guards were quietly overpowered.

When he came to greet his guest, Akar was trapped, two strong arms held him on each side. Every man beside him lay in a pool of blood on the floor.

Atan entered the castle and Akar lowered his head. Atan nodded to the men who held him. They took him to his room, tied him to a chair and gagged him.

Atan's long held anger, aching to escape, echoed menacingly in firm footsteps down the hallway. The two guards nodded as he entered Akar's sweet smelling room.

Atan removed the gag. Akar spat out the pieces of cloth that remained on his tongue. "What do you want Ishtba?"

"To be done with this." Atan said nonchalantly.

"Do you think it will be that easy?" Akar taunted.

Blackness filled Atan's eyes. "It doesn't matter" he sneered. A small blade scraped against Akar's neck.

"Be done with it then." Akar demanded.

An ogre of a man turned on Akar, bearing down with the strength of a storm, and single-mindedness of a beast.

"You will not be let off that easy. Trying to turn Samed against me, that was wrong." Atan wagged a long finger in his face. "But, to think that you could hold Raphela hostage!" Atan's hand wrapped around Akar's throat, squeezing until the man's face was blue. "No, you shall not die so easy."

Akar choked and gasped for air. "How did you know?"

"All in good time, all in good time." Atan toyed with Akar, bringing him to the brink of death, torturing him with words, but never spilling a drop of blood.

Akar pleaded for death.

Atan laughed, even the Ishtban guards quivered at the laughter.

The next morning Akar was brought outside to view his dead soldiers.

He begged one more time. "How did you know?"

Atan whispered in his ear. 'Your lover, Mika, he was one of my men, specially trained for you."

Akar hung his head in shame, for he loved Mika "Ishtba, one question before I die. What now, who's left to conquer?"

"Who? There never was a who. People were not the object, only the obstacles. The land will share its bounty and we will learn to use it well, with respect and without obstruction from people like you."

Akar, now broken, welcomed the blade that ended his life.

When Atan addressed the conquered inhabitants, he sensed these people feared the loss of their lifestyle more than that of their lives, a fact Atan could use to his advantage.

"There is little here I can use, right now," Atan began and the assembly rippled with uneasiness. "But I am a man who believes in the future. You may continue your activities in art and design, if that is what you choose. But do it well, I demand the best." He saw the faces placated with relief and still some fear. Just what he wanted. "Are there any among you who have an interest in agriculture or animal husbandry?" Heads turned from side to side, and three young men, stepped forward, as if breaking ranks. Atan assigned them to one of his soldiers. "If any of you have other interests, besides what you do now, inform the fiefmaster, Molosco." No one else spoke. "You are dismissed."

As the crowd dispersed, Atan pointed to a man a little older than himself "You, come here."

With his head held high and a crispness in his walk the man approached Atan and bowed slightly. "Yes, my lord?"

"Did you handle the day-to-day operations of this castle?"

"How do you mean sire?"

Atan's tone softened. "The necessities, ensure that the cooks ordered the meat, maids changed the sheets, and so forth. Did Akar rely on you for this?"

"Yes my lord." A tone of sadness touched his voice.

"Your name."

"Omer, sire."

"Omer, the new fiefmaster will need you to do the same."

"But my lord, don't you wish everything to be done in Ishtban fashion?"

Atan smiled. "Do you question my decision?"

Omer looked at his feet. "Sorry my lord."

"Don't be, it is apparent that you do operate in Ishtban fashion. Akar chose well."

Atan had studied Kito's reports of the castle's operation and he knew Omer ran things efficiently.

"Thank you my lord." Omer's response was polite but laced with confusion.

"Omer, I knew much about this place before I arrived. Now, how many men are literate?"

"About half, sire."

"Once the week of mourning is past, the other half will begin to learn, I will rely on you to see that this is accomplished."

"As you wish my lord."

"Work with Molosco, it will benefit all."

"Yes my lord." Omer bowed with respect and new found pride.

The next morning Ishtban troops began the trek home.

Mahtso rode beside Atan for a while, chatting amiably about the battle and its victory. Atan nodded absentmindedly as they trotted over the bumpy paths outside the castle's main gate.

In the days that it took to return Atan became more and more silent. Even at night the others could hear Mahtso's chain beating incessantly, like a faithful dog pacing around a sick master.

Cold and tired troops rode into Castle Cordan's gates. With achy limbs and dry cold skin they brought their beasts to the barn and there the rameks, glad to be home, ate heartily on Ishtban feed.

Raphela waited at the door for Atan, to no avail. Frantically she sought out Mahtso. "Where is he?" she demanded.

"He went straight to the mausoleum after returning his ramek to the barn. I don't know what's wrong." He skulked away, a failure at pleasing his master.

Raphela waited until almost dusk. Well wrapped in furs, she walked the distance beyond the barn to the mausoleum.

Atan's lean body sat hunched over the cold stone, his back to the entrance, hand on his father's crypt. Raphela took off her hood and draped a fur around his shoulders, knelt beside him and waited.

"It has taken me so long Raphela," he said, "but now it's done." Atan's eyes were red. "I have honored them, returned all that was theirs, and more. Now I can mourn. I never could please them, never give them what they needed from me in life. I disappointed them, hurt them. I was so cruel."

Raphela's warm hand brushed his cheek. "Don't be so harsh on yourself, you are a good man and a good son." Pain welled inside her.

"They would have liked you, so much and the life you brought here and their grandson."

Raphela forced a smile.

Atan continued. "But I never gave my mother the affection, the warmth that she wanted. And all she ever really wanted was for me to be successful, happy, have a family. I was so selfish. I couldn't make her happy, couldn't change my ways for her, it was unfair. My father was so disappointed he couldn't see me become a member of Raaleken society before he died." Atan buried his head in his hands and then reached out his arms to Raphela's shoulders. "Do I make you happy?" Such desperation was so foreign to him that Raphela cried. She hugged him as hard as she knew how. "Happy beyond words" she whispered in his ear.

"Atan, you haven't disappointed your parents, you have achieved what they wanted for you. And if they were as good as I've heard, they understood you gave them all you could."

He held her hand. "They did not need this victory to rest," he said, "I know that, much as I deny it. It was my own desire. Their souls were free the moment I married you. That gave them all they wanted, a good wife for their son, a legitimate grandson and their son a place as a man in the world, at least in their eyes." He walked between the two crypts and placed a hand on each one. "I miss them." Those were the hardest words he'd spoken in years.

He placed a pot of rock and soil on each crypt, took one more moment to reflect and walked hand in hand with Raphela back to the castle.

Raphela ordered a hot bath, some wine and bread. Together they climbed into the steamy tub, gently washing each other, wrapping themselves in warm robes when the bath cooled too much.

They left the outer room, closing the bedroom door behind them to first nibble on bread and sip wine, which turned to tender kisses, and loving strokes. Entwined in love and pain they shared the night. The pain inside Atan was so powerful; even Raphela struggled with it.

Children and adults wept in their sleep. Vanar twisted and turned all night. Even the beasts whinnied in their stalls and the wild dogs howled at the nameless ones demanding peace.

In the morning Atan stared down at his wife and cursed himself for not being able to say what he felt. Raphela squeezed his hand and demanded the deep passionate kiss that replaced words. They cuddled until well after sunrise.

Weather warmed and people healed.

Raphela watched the flowers bloom, and when the gray days brought her inside, she read and practiced healing. Vanar grew like a weed. His very nature drawing him to people and all they did and saw.

Atan buried himself in the plans he had so long waited to begin, until the snows melted away and then he traveled.

Fatell managed an ever increasing number of students, monitoring the advanced learning she soon could not understand. Mahtso's men exercised.

As the weeks passed, during Atan's absence, a quiet sour seed sprouted. Time fed it, and it grew lungs and arms. Most people tried to ignore it, in hopes it would go away.

It did not.

Mahtso sat in the kitchen with Fatell. His finger toyed with a round squirming object, just smaller than his thumb. When he realized her eyes were elsewhere he sneered, "Come now Fatell, can't you watch? Or is it that dry gray hair of yours in your eyes?"

Fatell felt her eyes turn red.

"What's wrong, didn't you believe what everyone said. Poor innocent Fatell." Mahtso's bloodstained fingers wiggled in front of Fatell's eyes. "Do you still want me my love, or should I find a stronger stomach and a prettier face?" Mahtso drooled over his fingers.

Fatell ran from the kitchen in tears and ran straight into Raphela who caught the sobbing woman in her arms. "Fatell, what's wrong?"

Fatell stared at her friend, wordlessly ran to her room, and locked the door.

Raphela went into the kitchen.

The cook was cleaning the table, mumbling about the mess. He relayed the incident to Raphela. She went in search of Mahtso, but he had disappeared.

The next day she finally found him at the training grounds. As she entered, a foul stench almost overwhelmed her. The typically immaculate place was littered with food, waste and drunken bodies. Mahtso sat at a table, sharing crude tales with his men, over many tankards of ale. None of them had bathed

237

in days, including Mahtso. His hair was loose and stuck to his forehead.

Raphela stood in the doorway. "Mahtso, could I see you." She spoke as pleasantly as she could.

"Go away woman, I'm busy." he snapped.

Raphela took a deep breath, "Mahtso, there is a stranger here. I thought you might want to question him."

Mahtso responded with a hungry smile, "Work calls." He staggered down the hall, following Raphela to a meeting room. She closed the door.

"All right Raphela," Mahtso wiped the drool from his chin and looked around. "Where is he?" The usually sweet sound of flesh being struck burned Mahtso as Raphela's hand hit hard against his face.

"You disgust me. You are a disgrace to Ishtba," she said icily.

Mahtso moved to strike back, but the alcohol slowed his movements. Raphela landed another blow and shoved him into a chair. "Just what do you think you're doing?" She towered over him like a school marm over a tardy child.

He lowered his head, and controlled the nausea that began to attack his stomach, as the reality of his condition became clearer.

"You will get cleaned up, sobered up and report to me in the morning."

"Yes, my lady," he mumbled and stumbled off to his quarters, head down.

In the morning he bathed, a headache reminding him of the previous day. Word got to Fatell that he would need clean clothes after his bath, She came in while he washed and laid the clothes on a chair. He asked her to stay. With lowered head she sat and waited.

Mahtso scrubbed, concentrating much more than was necessary. He winced as silent tears rolled down Fatell's cheeks. Her small hand presented a towel to him as he got out of the tub. He dried himself and once wrapped in the towel around him opened his arms to her, and pleaded. "Fatell, please."

As his arms closed around her, she sobbed and he with her. "I am so sorry. Somehow, someday, please forgive me. You are the best, most wonderful beautiful thing in my life. Without you I am a demon. I beg you to forgive me."

She held him tight. "I love you so much Mahtso."

Raphela paced around her office. She had pushed Mahtso hard. Fear did not come easy to her, but Mahtso could bring her a slow painful death before Atan returned. She hoped she'd chosen the right path.

Mahtso appeared at the door. "May I enter, my lady?" He bowed respectfully.

Raphela breathed a silent sigh of relief. "Come in and sit." She poured hot tea for both of them. He sipped his and smiled, a dose of medication for "foolish soldiers who drank too much" had been stirred in the brew.

Raphela proceeded gently. "Tell me what's wrong?"

Mahtso stared into his teacup. "I'm sorry Raphela."

"I know. What's wrong?"

He sighed deeply. "Boredom, fear, a combination of both."

"Fear?"

He met her eyes. "Raphela, we are soldiers, there are no more battles. What will we do?"

"I don't know. But you can't believe that Atan would simply desert his men, leave them with no other purpose." Raphela was shocked that Mahtso, of all people, would allow himself to be drawn into such desperate thinking.

"In my heart I know that, but somehow I've been blinded." He stared back into the cup. "And I still can't see."

"Open your eyes Mahtso. There must be a way out of this emotional dungeon."

Mahtso fondled his chain and began to sway in his chair while Raphela paced.

"Raphela" he said finally what if I were to ask the men what they would do if they were not soldiers. They have all mentioned other tasks they would enjoy. Now could be the perfect opportunity to explore the options." His mood brightened with each word.

"Yes! Make a list of things they'd like to be. We have a whole new world to conquer, in many different ways besides with a sword."

Mahtso smiled. "Yes my lady."

He bowed and left Raphela to her thoughts as he rounded up his men.

The training ground was clean and neat by the next afternoon and the men gladly looked at all avenues of work.

The day after Atan returned, rain pattered lightly against the shutters. Raphela nodded to the servant as he left a pot of tea on the meeting room table where she sat with her husband and Mahtso.

"The troops look good," Atan said, but I sense a different attitude"

Mahtso's blue eyes peered at Raphela from underneath a concerned brow.

Raphela's innocent and silent response slowed Mahtso's chain. It only took a few seconds for this to pass and Atan decided to investigate later.

Mahtso suddenly spoke "The men have been considering what they will do now that the battles are done."

"Really?" Atan asked with interest.

"Yes" Mahtso handed Atan a written list and Raphela a copy.

After studying the sheet Atan said appreciatively, "This is fascinating. The interest in metalwork I expected. I would have hoped for more thoughts on agriculture. The issue of transportation seems strong. Any idea why?"

"I believe, after their years of travel, they know there could be a more efficient and comfortable way to get from place to place." Mild sarcasm blended well with the trio.

"Good point. Do you have any plans for putting these ideas in motion?"

Mahtso had worked all night to structure plans in anticipation of that question. "Yes. Besides releasing the men to fields of interest that are presently active, I'd like to create three new groups, land and water transportation and exploration."

Raphela's ears perked up and the teacup in her hand gently rattled the plate as she put it down. "Exploration?"

"Yes."

"How far?"

Atan smiled and patted his wife's hand. "Just what is it that you want to know this time?"

Raphela pulled her hand away. "Everything, of course. What is at the end of Ishtba? Has anyone ever seen it?"

"I have." Atan sighed, as he was possessed by a faraway glance and distant tone. "At the end of land, far to the east, is the *Bath of the Gods*."

"The what?" Mahtso asked.

"The Bath of the Gods. I saw it as I was standing on a cliff. It was a body of water so vast I could not see its end in any direction."

"A large river?" Raphela pressed.

"No, no it was magnificent. When I reached the shore, the soil lost its rich feel and black color and turned brown and grainy. The water was bitter, yet many creatures moved in its depth. It didn't flow like a river or sit calm like a lake. The water moved back and forth, up and down, as the water in a tub when you sit to bathe. Towards dusk, great walls of water would rise and crash onto the shore. It reminded me of dropping a stone in a tub of water and have the liquid rise up and spill from the tub. But mostly, the gentle movement and smell of life captured me." Atan spent a moment in silent reverie.

"Why call it the *Bath of the Gods*?" Mahtso asked.

"All I could imagine was that only the Gods could have use for something so vast and amazing. And, it seemed as if the water moved as if someone were taking a bath at the other end. Hence, *Bath of the Gods*."

Raphela who had lost herself in the imagery of the tale quickly recovered. "There must be another end, somewhere, and I'm sorry, but I don't believe it's the home of the gods."

Gray eyes pierced deep into her. "I know. Perhaps with the right vehicle, we'll know one day."

"Hmm." Raphela smiled at all the possibilities.

Chapter 12

Towards the end of that summer Raphela received word that her father had taken ill.

Plans were made for a visit.

Hand in hand Raphela and Atan walked in the afternoon sun, climbing the hill whose top gave a view to the first vast steps of Ishtba.

Raphela lifted her head to embrace the clean breeze. "Will you come with us?"

Atan stared at the clouds. "I considered it, but it seemed foolish. No one in town would feel comfortable, and neither would we. There will be enough commotion with just the two of you." Atan's melancholy tone sent a shiver through Raphela. "You're right," she agreed "We'll be back before first moonrise."

Atan pulled her close; his gray eyes demanded her attention. A passionate kiss was the word of the moment, he held her close. She relaxed into his strength.

They sat by a tree and studied the traveling white fluffs making passage across the ever-changing horizon. "You know Vanar will need his own bodyguard." Atan tossed a leafy branch towards his toes.

"I know." Raphela sighed, the reality of Vanar's life was upon them.

"I've told Mahtso to bring a candidate to me and I'd like your input in the selection."

"Of course and we'll need Vanar's approval as well."

"He's just a baby. How could he possibly..."

"Yes, and if he doesn't like his guard he will avoid the man at all possible costs."

"Point well made, Mama." Atan conceded.

"Thank you." Raphela said, grinning.

Following breakfast the next day the family Ishtba gathered in the family room. Vanar played peekaboo with his Papa and Mama made sure lots of toys were available. When steady footsteps climbed the stairs Vanar looked toward the door.

Though Bertram's easy confident gait did not alarm Vanar, the toddler still backed off. When the stranger entered, his tiny hands rustled Mama's long skirt and he peered out from his safe position. The adults chose to sit, forcing Vanar to squeeze between Mama and Papa. Atan began the interview and Raphela joined in on occasion. Bertram's gentle, brown eyes rested easily on Raphela and lowered slightly with Atan. Vanar, no longer the center of attention, took to playing with a ball. He climbed off the couch and threw the toy, chasing after it, carefully avoiding the stranger.

Bertram seemed to ignore him, concentrating on the conversation. Raphela probed the young man about his family, his likes, his dislikes. Mahtso stood by Atan, his chain beating rhythmically against his leg. Vanar, now behind the couch, tossed the ball high into the air, as it began its descent an arm reached up and surrounded it with firm support, and laid it on the couch. Bertram's quick and silent response interested Vanar, who gingerly approached the young man. Bertram ignored Vanar as the toddler came closer. A tiny hand grabbed the ball and moved quickly away. Once at a safe distance, Vanar turned to see who followed, to his surprise no one had. Cautiously Vanar rolled the ball towards Bertram who gently pushed it back. This continued until Vanar was brave enough to meet the man, eye to eye. When he did, he studied the stranger with an innocence befitting his age and a seriousness befitting his position. Then, without a word, Vanar climbed on Bertram's lap, ball in hand and chirped "Mama, want a cookie."

"Say please"

"Please"

Raphela brought out a tray of cookies. Vanar took one for himself and stuffed one in Bertram's mouth. "Thank you Vanar." Bertram mumbled as he brushed the crumbs off his lip and Vanar's lap.

The interview was complete, travel plans were made.

Raphela dressed a sleepy Vanar as the sun tiptoed into the morning. Logan and Bertram waited by the front door.

"Logan, is it a long trip to Milson?" Bertram asked.

"We should be there long before noon." Logan checked his weapons and laid a hand on Bertram's shoulder. "I believe you have the most difficult and important job in Ishtba."

Bertram turned his head up to the man who was a head taller than himself. "I think I got it because I believe that too. Although guarding Lady Raphela is no easy task. She does not exactly sit in her room and sew all day."

Both men laughed.

They continued in easy chatter, as Raphela came down the stairs. Atan followed, carrying a sleepy Vanar in his arms. Silently Atan returned up the stairs and the party began their journey.

During the short ride Vanar woke and divided his attention between Raphela and Bertram.

When Raphela heard people walking she knew they had entered Milson. As the carriage doors opened, Logan transformed from a gentle giant to an ominous protective wall. With arms wrapped tight around Vanar Bertram stepped out of the carriage. He stood calm and faced the small group but his eyes covered the terrain like a cat watching for prey.

A path opened through the small crowd that had formed. Raphela's mother and sisters approached, hugs and kisses were exchanged. Then family and friends strolled back to the house.

Familiar smells greeted Raphela, her favorite bread sat on the kitchen table.

Amidst the noise and commotion Vanar got to know his Grandma and aunts and uncles. With reluctance Bertram allowed the relatives to hold and touch the toddler, but never moved more than an arm's distance,

"Mother, where's Papa? Raphela asked as she nibbled on the bread.

"Sleeping." Her mother's pained response brought hot tears to Raphela's eyes. She wrapped her arms around the older woman and there they made their silent peace.

"I'll see him later. Raphela said. "I've got some friends I want to visit."

Raphela and Logan slipped out quietly. Milson hadn't changed and Raphela felt comfortable with its sights and sounds.

Instinctually she made her way to Sarah's door.

Sarah responded to the flickering change in light created by Raphela as she moved the outer shade, and greeted Raphela with a hug. "I was just about to visit your parents house. Come in, come in."

Raphela entered and noticed a pair of men's boots by the doorway. Sarah caught the glimpse and pulled Raphela into the sitting room. Logan shuffled in behind. "Are you well?" Sarah signed and mouthed at once.

"Yes, quite."

"And the baby?" Sarah's pleasant anxiety made Raphela giggle.

"He's wonderful, big and strong, just like his Papa. Now, tell me, what is new in your life?"

Sarah blushed. "Well, I guess you noticed,"

"Yes, whose boots are they?"

"Sarek's." Sarah bit her lip, looking for approval.

"Sarek?! That's wonderful, but when, how?" Raphela was ecstatic for her friend's new companionship.

"After you brought him to the castle. When he came to see me, we began to talk and it grew from there. As a matter of fact, we found ways to write each other while he was traveling. It has brought a comfort to both of our lives." Sarah glowed.

They chatted like schoolgirls for some time.

"Sarah, I have one more place to visit, if he's home."

"Very well, I'm going to your parents house, I believe Sarek is already there."

"Probably, I'll see you later."

Raphela and Logan walked slowly. Soon they heard the small metal sign, swaying in the morning breeze. It glistened in the sun.

As usual the door was open. Raphela bade Logan guard the doorway.

Her footsteps were soft and Nabus, lost in his world of creation, did not hear her. Soft warm fingers began a gentle massage at his neck and ran through his hair. His hands laid the tools on the table. His lungs filled with air and slowly released it. "Raphela" The word flowed from his lips as his eyes rested on her.

She felt his gentle touch on her face. Their arms wrapped so tightly around each other that Logan thought they would melt together.

Nabus handed Raphela a cloth to wipe the tears from her face as he did the same.

"You are as beautiful as ever." He said.

"I've missed you." She answered simply.

Nabus turned away. "Is he treating you well?"

"Yes." Raphela felt a wall of ice growing.

"I heard rumors." Nabus said, turning to face her.

"I'm sure they're all true." In the silence that followed Raphela gathered her emotions. "Come to my parents house, see my baby." The last was almost a plea.

"No, I can't."

She grabbed his hands. "Are you that angry with me? Why?"

"Why? I've missed you! When you left, a gray mist hung over this town. Hard to believe that a child so shunned and taunted should be so missed. Your parents cried for weeks. Sarah moped. I tormented my family and myself. And poor Sarek, he was the villain of the age. All this you, yes you, brought upon this town. If indeed your Duke laid his whip upon you, then perhaps it paid for a bit of the pain you caused." Nabus didn't shout, but his tone was as acidic as his words.

Raphela stared in disbelief.

"Yes, I see the scars around your neck."

"Nabus, I, I..."

"You're sorry, I'm sure. And if you think I miss your touch," his outburst mellowed, "you are right, but more I miss the little girl who had to know how much gold I need to make a necklace. And I miss the young woman who had to know the dark stranger that ruled the land. You left a gap my lady, and although Milson prospers now, financially, and your parents can take pride in their daughter and grandson, those of us left, who love you so much, miss you and always will."

Tears rolled down his face and Raphela was curled up in a chair, sobbing. He picked her up and held her on his lap.

"I love you too Nabus. So many nights I cried myself to sleep wishing you were there, to hold my hand and guide me. But I am happy now and without you I could not have been, you taught me well."

"I'm sorry Raphela, I shouldn't have, I..." Nabus fumbled for words.

"It's all right" she sniffled. They sat for a while longer, hugged and parted with a friendship renewed.

A rainbow of voices filtered from the house, oohs and aahs, gossip and joy and woe. Almost everyone in town was there. Logan sighed as they walked up the path. "So many people."

Raphela smiled. "It's a safe place. Take a little break and take Bertram with you. Enjoy the food."

"My lady, I must protest."

"Logan, consider it an order," she said firmly.

"Yes, my lady." He reluctantly obeyed.

Raphela saw Vanar in a sea of friends and relatives. Poor Bertram was trying to keep up, as Vanar sensed his mother's presence and ran to her crying, "Mama, mama" he bounced into her arms.

"I love you too, Vanar." She held him close.

"Bertram, join Logan, get something to eat and take a rest. Vanar and I will be fine."

A weary Bertram nodded and gratefully did as told.

Raphela and Vanar slid off to Goran's room.

Raphela held her gasp at the sight of his gray skin and frail form.

"Hello Papa," she said bending down to kiss him. Vanar sat quietly on the bed next to his Grandpa.

"He's magnificent, Raphela. A healthy smart boy, just look at him." Goran's eyes lit with pride as he stroked Vanar's thick hair. The toddler yawned and was soon curled up by his Grandpa asleep by his side.

"You look happy Raphela."

"I am, Papa."

"The Duke is a good man, you chose well."

Both laughed, for as she had said, she would be the one to choose. Goran coughed and wheezed, holding Raphela's hand tightly. Soon he too fell into slumber. Raphela put Vanar in a crib and had Bertram keep an eye on the tired child, so she could rejoin her mother, but when Raphela asked for her sister, Reba, their mother carefully avoided eye contact and mumbled, "In the kitchen, with Darlena."

Raphela saw her sister from behind and called her name.

"What?" Reba answered but didn't turn.

Raphela moved close and forced Reba to look at her. Raphela's stomach turned at the sight of Reba's swollen purple cheeks, bruised arms and cut lip. "That animal Donan, he did this, didn't he?" she demanded.

Reba wept and nodded in shame.

"How often?"

Darlena, just looked at Raphela as if to say this was not unusual.

"It will not happen again," Raphela's nostrils flared and she could feel the blood flush her cheeks. On her way out she grabbed Logan. If not for his long stride he'd have had a difficult time keeping up with her.

"My lady, are you all right?"

Raphela stopped for a moment and reviewed Logan. "Be prepared to defend me, it may be necessary."

Towards the end of town they slowed. From a nearby building came the stench of ale and wine. Raphela headed towards the door. Logan sighed and followed.

In the dim, dingy tavern she walked to the bar. "Bartender, where is Donan?"

An uncaring finger pointed towards a table in the center of the room. Logan stayed within inches of his mistress, her hair hanging perfectly on her back and every thread of clothes in place.

"Donan" Raphela's voice sent a shiver through Logan's spine.

Donan raised his dark unshaven faced and moved the unkempt hair from his eyes. "Oh, its Lady Raphela", he mocked, "do you come to protest my treatment of that trollop, your sister."

Raphela ignored both the words and his ugly breath. "Never, never raise a finger to my sister again."

"Perhaps it's you who needs a hand raised." Donan got as far as lifting his hand and barely closing his fist before Logan buried his sword in the man's heart. He pulled it out as the drunkard, fell, shock his final expression.

Shock at defeat was Donan's last expression.

Raphela stared down at the body. "I don't think so," she said.

No one stirred, or even seemed to care. The bartender merely shrugged his shoulders.

Raphela and Logan left without another word.

Once in the street Logan said, "My lady?"

"You did well Logan. Perfect as a matter of fact, thank you. Now we have one more stop," She took him to a small house, a bit run down, but pleasant. A young man answered the door.

"Yani, that is you isn't it?" she asked.

"Raphela, by the gods..."

Logan shifted uneasily and the young man realized his mistake.

"Sorry, so sorry, Lady Raphela" Yani bowed.

"Stop." She smiled and took his hand. "Yani, do you still care for Reba?"

"With all my heart."

Then go to her, she's a widow now."

"Raphela, I'm so poor, I could never provide for her..."

"Yani, was her life with Donan so rich?"

Yani lowered his head. "I hated that monster and what he did to her."

"Then go care for her."

Raphela and Logan arrived shortly before Yani. "Reba, we must talk."

"I'm sorry Raphela."

"You poor child, you've done nothing wrong, you never have." Raphela gently raised Reba's chin. "He's dead Reba, he can't hurt you anymore."

250

"But now I'm alone. Is that a blessing?" Reba was so battered emotionally she couldn't see the blessing. Then came a gentle tap on the shoulder. She turned to see wildflowers and Yani. "I'll take care of you. I don't have much. But I will share it all with you."

Reba wrapped her arms around his neck and cried. "After all this time, you'd still have me?"

"You never wanted Donan, I know that, I would have waited for you forever."

Raphela walked out and stared into the afternoon sun, not sure what or how to feel. She heard footsteps.

"Oh, its you."

"Just me." Nabus rubbed her shoulders. "Care to talk?"

"Hmmm." Raphela took his hand. "I love you, but I have someone to share my secrets and my pain with now. He waits for me."

Much as it hurt his pride, it also pleased him. She kissed his cheek and by nightfall was back at the castle. When Vanar was in bed, Raphela joined Atan in the family room.

"How was the trip?" He asked

"It was all right."

"What's wrong?" He said softly.

She spoke to the fire. "Logan had to kill a man today."

"I see." Atan held his curiosity and let Raphela go on.

"It was my sister's husband."

"Why?"

"He hurt her badly. I found him and told him never again to harm her. He raised his hand to me."

Atan felt his blood rise but kept silent.

"Logan settled it before he had a chance to swing." She sniffled.

"Are you all right?"

Raphela crawled into his arms. "Hold me, hold me tight."

That he did and carried her bed and held her as they slept, with her hair wrapped around his hand.

Chapter 13

"Vanar, finish your breakfast."

Vanar shoved the last spoonful of cereal into his mouth and giggled. Raphela handed him a napkin to wipe the milk that slipped from his lips.

"Where's Papa?"

"He went for a ride."

"Can I go for a ride?" Vanar bounced in his seat as five-year-old boys do.

"Not until you're older."

"But that's what you said last week." He didn't whine, but he did pursue.

"I know, but I mean, years older."

"Maybe when I'm ten?"

"I think not." The deep-voiced reply took them both by surprise.

Atan kissed Raphela's cheek. He smelled of beasts and trees. She squirmed in her seat.

"But Papa, why not?"

"Because you must take my place someday and I need to keep you in one piece for that long."

Vanar knew it was a mixed blessing and he began to respond but Bertram appeared at the door. So, with brief hugs to parents Vanar was on his way to school.

Atan blindly reached for a biscuit while watching Vanar leave and discovered soft warm flesh under his hand instead. Raphela's robe opened slightly, revealing just a tease of cleavage. Atan tightened his grip around her hand. "Come here wench."

A purrish growl accompanied a slinking walk around the table. She straddled Atan's lap, spreading open her robe, revealing all of her wonder. Atan held her hands behind her back and grinned. "Just what excites you so about a man who stinks of the beasts?"

Raphela sucked on his neck before answering. "Just that my lord, perhaps because they are what excite you most" deep brown eyes taunted him, "except me."

He released her hands and stood to make the most of her. "You are as the rameks, untamable, except by the strongest hand."

As they buried themselves in unbridled passion, his foot slammed the dining room door shut. Raphela felt her blood rise as she undid his vest and belt. Panting and clawing they moved about the room, skin tingling, mouths wet with desire no portion left untouched. No floor or table was necessary. Raphela felt her buttocks press against the cool wall and Atan pushed so deep inside her, it hurt. Excitement oozed down her leg. He felt her warmth. Neither had a thought, both worked the power like beasts until the energy subsided with a powerful thrust and a kiss. As she turned away to get her robe from the floor he landed a smack on her rump. "You, are a naughty girl."

"So spank me." she offered a mock sneer.

Tempted as they were for another round of play, a warm and gentle kiss sufficed as both went about the day's duties.

Once warmly dressed, Raphela headed toward Fatell's new domain, the school and playground that sprawled beyond the castle's front gate. The new facility had been needed after basic education had been made compulsory. The round two-story building housed classrooms and a daycare center all bright and colorful, that evolved with each day of use.

Raphela wandered through the halls, passing children forced to walk not run as they chatted. The walls displayed works of art by the children and other accomplishments. Eventually she reached Fatell's organized office, efficient and full of flowers.

"Do you have time for me?" Raphela asked from the door.

Fatell grinned from ear to ear. "I'll make some."

"The school looks great. How about a real tour?"

Fatell proudly walked Raphela through the building and out to the playground, which held various climbing apparatus, tunnels and blunt tools in a fenced area. Behind the playground a group of students and a teacher were involved in something, but Raphela couldn't fathom what.

Fatell offered the answer, "They're planting a tree."

Raphela's puzzled look gave Fatell reason to explain. "It seems that one of the children asked where the woodsheets come from. When the teacher explained, a discussion ensued with the children considering what would happen if all the trees got used up. So they plant a tree every spring and visit the woodsheet forest during the summer. As a matter of fact, it resulted in two more forests being planted, so they could be used on a rotating basis."

"Incredible what children can create, isn't it? Raphela marveled.

Raphela continued on to the castle.

Mahtso's hands were on his knees as the sweat poured from his forehead. Atan's hand on his shoulder took him by surprise. "Trying to keep up with the young ones?" he teased.

Mahtso wiped his forehead. "No, forcing them to keep up with me."

"They look good."

"Indeed. We'll be ready for the 'Games' this summer. Each summer the fiefs and even the king sent representatives to the 'Games', a series of mock battles and tests of strengths and endurance that had been created to replace actual battle.

They walked to a nearby bench and continued the light discussion. Important matters of the fiefs were not yet pertinent. "When will you leave for Porath's event?" Mahtso studied the men while he spoke.

"Tomorrow morning. Vanar is quite excited about visiting a new place and Raphela feels its good 'politics' that we all go".

Mahtso laughed. "That is what wives are supposed to do, tell you what's right and wrong. I believe she is domesticating you my friend."

Atan nodded. "I think she was better prepared for peace than any of us."

Mahtso pushed his chain gently to make small circles. "That is a fact."

Tiny gardens dotted the grounds by Porath's main house, displaying a wondrous variety of fruits and vegetables. Beyond this, rows and rows of golden grain swayed to and fro at the whim of the spring wind.

Vanar, under Bertram's watchful eye, spent the remainder of the day with the other children. Atan and Raphela strolled the grounds taking in the sights and smells, catching interesting tidbits of conversation from those who didn't know them or believed them to be out of earshot. Many people with red armbands circulated among the guests. These turned out to be townspeople hired to aid the house staff.

The house was old and quite large, housing the sixty or so guests was not overly taxing.

Voices worked in harmony and feet moved slowly, arms placed hugs for distant friendships, overall a warm and welcome feeling dominated the arrival day.

Dinner was served to the individual families in their rooms and the tired travelers bedded down early.

Breakfast was a buffet of fruits, biscuits, and tea. Afterwards the children were ushered into an indoor play area as the weather was not cooperative enough for anything else. Bertram stood inside the door, out of the way but close at hand. Vanar ignored him and studied the room. He played with different groups of children, sometimes just rolling a ball, sometimes playing at sword fighting and sometimes just talking.

Towards the end of the morning he found himself involved in a game of royalty and servants, he being one of the servants. Vanar had no trouble with this, since no one knew who he was. His parents had strongly suggested that he not announce his position, unless absolutely necessary, he would learn more that way.

The boy playing the "Duke" was tall and talkative, friendly, giving speeches about taxes and planting and such. The girl playing "Duchess," was short and thin, spending her time ordering servants to bring her tea or biscuits and finding fault with most everything. She must have asked for three different robes in just a few minutes.

One small child, anxious to play and to please carried over a tray of cookies, which fell from the plate and crumbled on the floor. The little boy's eyes welled with tears.

The "Duke" fluffed it off, but the "Duchess" stood and pointed a long finger at him. "You will be punished for this, guards take him to the whipping post."

Every mouth stopped moving, most hung open and all eyes stared at the "Duchess." The "Duke" spoke, "What are you talking about?"

"The whipping post,"she said with exasperation.

"What's a whipping post?"

"Oh, you know, the post in the courtyard where disobedient servants are taken, chained and whipped. Everyone has one."

"I've never seen one." The boy was puzzled.

"Your parents just don't want you to see it."

Another girl spoke up. "I don't think the real Duke lets people have those things."

"Of course he does. Anyway, my parents told me the only way to keep servants in line is with the whip."

"Who are your parents?"

"Anya and Gellen."

"I'm sure the real Duke doesn't let people have whipping posts. My father told me the Duke doesn't believe in hurting people."

"I don't believe you."

Vanar felt it was time to speak. "Maybe we should ask the Duke?" Everyone's eyes were on him now.

The "duchess" opened her sarcasm, "And who will ask, you?"

Vanar was calm, despite his desire to tell her who he was, "Yes, is there a reason not to ask him?"

She just shook her head. "You're just a baby. How would you know anything? No one talks to the Duke, except maybe Mahtso and Lady Raphela."

"You don't know as much as you think you do." His father's unapproachability was something he heard about often, but never understood.

She began a retort, but it was time for lunch and everyone was being called to the main room. Bertram complimented Vanar on how well he handled himself. But Vanar was sullen and moped through lunch.

At the end of the meal an old man dressed in shimmering robes, was escorted by two young women, to a stage, and behind him a boy, perhaps 12 or 13 caught Vanar's attention.

To his lips, the boy placed the narrow end of a twisted funnel, an animal horn, and lifted his head up and blew into the funnel creating a unique sound, loud and full, yet bittersweet, it echoed throughout the room, demanding silence.

The old man cleared his throat and began reading from the large book on the podium. Much of it was in the ancient tongue and the children were soon twisting and turning, the adults politely listened. Another sound from the funnel and a path from the back of the room opened up. All eyes watched as proud parents walked through the crowd behind another man in robes who carried the quiet baby girl. She was placed in her mother's arms and the father found her tiny hand wrapped around his finger.

Again the old man began to speak. He blessed the child, asking the gods for protection and biding the parents to care for her well. By now the children were anxious to see this new creature and the parents hoped for a quick end to the ceremony. Finally a shower of sweetly scented flower petals sprinkled down on the infant and parents signifying the completion of the rites.

The parents moved into the center of the room and were quickly surrounded by the other guests. Children crawled through the crowd to see the little thing that caused so much commotion.

Vanar stared at the tiny, pink form that stared back and yawned, stretched and latched onto his hand. Vanar felt quite important, though why, he didn't know. Finally the baby fell asleep and loosened her grip. The festivities and food lasted well into the second moonrise, when sleepy children and worn out parents went to bed.

With sunrise the guests began to leave. Atan left a generous gift with the parents and the family Ishtba climbed into the carriage and headed for home.

Vanar was full of questions. "Mama, can I have a baby sister? Could I, please, soon?"

Raphela stroked his head. "Perhaps."

Atan stared into nothingness.

It was a question unasked by Raphela, yet burned deep inside her. "Why were there no others, was she now barren, what was wrong with her? Atan would never question and he trusted no one else to be mother of his offspring. Yes, a big WHY hung over them all.

Vanar prattled on and tired only as they pulled up the road to Castle Cordan.

Raphela put him to bed, took a long hot bath and found Atan in their bedroom staring at the stars.

Her gentle touch was coldly shrugged off. To Raphela, it was if a hot iron had been shoved onto her heart and branded her failure as a woman and as a wife. She crawled into bed and curled up in a ball. There was too much pain for tears. Raphela listened to Atan breathe and pace. She wished he would yell or even strike her, but this icy wall was worse than she ever endured. She took a moment to curse Nabus for teaching her to feel.

Atan paced, feeling haunted and cold. Finally as the second moon began its exit from the night sky Atan climbed into bed. Raphela lay in a state of half sleep. She felt his hand stroke her arm. "Raphela" he whispered.

She turned and saw in the waning moonlight his tear stained face. They lay face to face, his palm caressed her cheek. "You know, I may be the most powerful man on Raalek. A thousand men would die at my command, the beasts go calm at my touch" his voice got louder and stung in his ears, he felt his grip tighten around Raphela's arms as they sat up. "Mahtso "the terrible" bows in loyalty to me, even the great Lady Raphela obeys me on occasion."

She managed a laugh through the tears.

"But, one thing is beyond my control," facing the window, he shouted, raising his fists to the sky. "That one thing, that makes a peasant a king, and the gods bridle me in like a beast under the whip."

He turned back to Raphela and whispered "I'm sorry."

Raphela allowed large tears to form and fall. He brushed them away. "It's not your fault. Vanar is a miracle. I've had enough women, none ever carried a child. The gods gave me you and Vanar, but that will be all. You don't need to bear that pain, it isn't yours."

If Atan Ishtba could be embarrassed, he was and the castle reverberated with his pain. Raphela relieved of guilt, still anguished with him. They fell asleep quietly crying in each other's arms. The matter closed forever.

A few days later Vanar became withdrawn. Raphela noticed it at dinnertime. Atan sipped some wine and Raphela cut meat on Vanar's plate.

"Merej sent word that he found a new breeding donag, first calf is due this month." Atan took a whiff of the fresh bread before soaking it in gravy.

"Is it for meat or milk?"

"Meat. He said something about more muscles. Merej has become quite an expert."

"Mmm. Nalab is almost done designing the waterways for the healers building. I know you're looking forward to that."

At this point both parents noticed Vanar pushing around the food on his plate and saying nothing.

Atan held his hand. "What's wrong son?"

Vanar stared up with big sad eyes and all attention was on him. Atan tried to take him on his lap, but Vanar avoided him.

"Vanar?" Raphela prodded

His lower lip trembled and he swallowed hard.

"Vanar, tell us what's wrong."

"Mama, some girl said that Papa whips his servants. I said it wasn't true, but she said I was too little and he wouldn't let me see anyway."

Dinner was over. The family, with Vanar in Raphela's arms adjourned to the family room. It took some time to calm Vanar down and to convince him the girl was lying.

He hugged Atan, who was more than happy to hug back. As Vanar sniffled, an important question was asked. "Who was this girl?"

"Tory, Anya and Gellen's daughter"

Raphela squeezed Atan's hand, praying he would hold his feelings until Vanar finished his whole story and went to sleep.

In the dwindling light of day Atan's long anxious legs brought him to the barn. Instinctively he saddled his ramek and headed toward the hills. Trees passed his sight looking like twigs. The ramek grabbed at the freedom to run at full speed. Man and beast joined in flight, the ground a jump off point for the next gallop. Atan needed all his strength to maintain control and that was what he wanted, to pour his anger into the ride and not onto one he cared for so much. He rode, even as the darkness took hold, he rode.

Raphela twisted and turned in bed, aching for no physical reason. How many times she got out of bed to look out the window she didn't know. As the moons took their places in the sky, she lay in bed and stared at the ceiling.

Finally Atan returned quietly, entering so as not to disturb her. She heard but lay still. Neither spoke. He climbed into bed, wrapped her hair around his hand and both fell into uneasy sleep. Morning's light brought them together with Mahtso.

Atan stood at the table in the small meeting room, while Raphela and Mahtso waited in their seats. "We have a problem."

Mahtso and his aching leg, sore from the deep incessant movement of his chain, didn't know what the problem was, just that it was bad.

Atan continued. "Anya and Gellen have not changed their ways." He relayed Vanar's tale.

"Atan, you're taking the word of a child. Children exaggerate, misunderstand." Mahtso had not seen evidence on his last tour.

Atan placed his hands on the table and leaned into Mahtso. "Children repeat what they see and hear, and according to

261

Bertram, who I spoke with this morning, the child was quite adamant. By the way," Atan stood up and pointed a long menacing finger at Mahtso, "the next time Bertram witnesses an altercation like this and does not report it immediately, he will spend his life protecting the vegetable garden. Do you understand?"

Mahtso nodded.

"Now, we must solve this problem, permanently."

"We do need proof," Raphela said gently.

"Get it and soon. Once we have it, the masters will be brought down," he paused "by the servants."

"What are you saying?" Mahtso's chain stopped in midbeat.

Anger and anguish filled Atan's voice. "Revolution, within the fief, with our support and guidance, but not our direct action."

"Why Atan?" Raphela asked.

Atan finally sat and sighed, "Because no one must think that I would do this to my own people and more importantly, the servants need to cleanse themselves and release their anger. Unfortunately death and destruction will be the only way and still maintain loyalty to Ishtba." Mahtso broke the silence. "I have a spy. He will draw no attention to himself, but can verify the situation." His chain beat sadly against the chair.

"Good. Once we have proof we will have to choose a leader from amongst the servants. Oram should be able to give us some direction." He turned to Raphela. "I must ask something of you now. I would like you to visit Anya and Gellen, to arrange for the leader to do his job. Fatell should travel with you." His stoic speech was a poor cover for the guilt he felt at sending his wife on this mission.

"If that is what you need, then that is what I'll do." Her support was open.

"So be it. Mahtso tell me who you will use."

Mahtso watched his friend's pained expression as Raphela left.

"Atan"

"What?"

"Raphela knew that marrying Duke Ishtba did not mean choosing linens for dinner parties. She'll be fine."

Before summer was over the spy verified Vanar's story and Raphela and Fatell set out for a surprise visit to Anya and Gellen. Fatell sat stiffly in the carriage, flinching every time they hit a bump. It was the last leg of the journey to the fief.

"Is it the dress?" Raphela asked smoothing her own.

The small woman blushed. Her new dress, crisp and designed for this trip was on her mind, but it played only a small part of her concern. "It's a little uncomfortable, but what we are doing is...."

"Different." Raphela finished it for her.

"For lack of a better word, I suppose." Fatell pondered the cracks in the door. "In truth, I don't know if I can do this."

"You worry too much, just be yourself." Raphela exuded all the confidence she could muster, in the hopes that Fatell would not see her own concerns.

A tall, stately, gray-haired gentleman opened the front door, perhaps 40 or so. Though he had never seen Raphela he knew her immediately. "Lady Raphela?!"

"Yes, you recognize me." She was impressed.

But the man's real attention turned to Fatell. Instant attraction held them both. Fatell curtsied and whispered, "Fatell of Ishtba."

The man bowed to both women, "Barin at your service."

Raphela nodded to Fatell. This was the second choice of three given by Oram. Barin had motioned to one of the servant boys, dressed in a severe uniform similar to his own, to bring the master and mistress immediately. Raphela hoped the connection between Barin and Fatell would show itself in front of Anya and Gellen.

Anya's brisk pace announced her arrival. Doing her best to hide her annoyance, she curtsied in front of Raphela. "My lady, what brings you to our humble home?"

"The Duke suggested I tour Ishtba."

Gellen out of breath, showed up and stood behind Anya, and caught the glances being exchanged by Barin and Fatell, just as

Anya said, "My lady, you are welcome to stay as long as you wish."

"Thank you. Perhaps you could show my servants where to put my things." She purposely made little acknowledgment of Fatell and the others, as the less important they appeared, hopefully the more freedom they would possess. Raphela had also learned long ago that assuming the mannerisms and attitudes of those around you created an openness and often allowed otherwise guarded speech to flow.

Anya immediately picked up on Raphela's intentions and believed them. "Barin show the servant woman and others to quarters, I will take care of the Lady."

Barin nodded. Fatell both lost and found, remained close to Barin, who delivered Logan and the others first.

Raphela's room was large and clean. During her carefully guided tour of the house however she noticed the barren walls and lack of movement. Everything was stationary, even the people held to minimal movement within their stations. The children (about a dozen) were limited to a large enclosed area, closely supervised by two stern women. One little boy, with a glint of mischief in his eyes, watched the women and when he saw a clear path, made a dash to the neatly aligned row of toys and attempted to exchange one he had for another. His attempt failed and was met with a solid stroke across his bottom and time in the corner, Obviously freedom of movement was not encouraged, There was no learning here, simply control. The tour ended at the dining room, just in time for dinner.

Fatell dined with the servants. There was little conversation and most eyes were concentrating on the plates.

Raphela found the dinner table atmosphere to be polite, crisp and stiff. Servants brought each course to the table. Every plate looked identical, carefully portioned, planned, and bland. There were no platters of fruit or bread. Tosco, Oram's other choice, was the head server, obedient and exacting, but the spirit needed for the task ahead showed itself in a gentle knowing smile when the master and mistress could not see.

Raphela considered trying to speak to him, but soon realized his life would be torture and more of a prison than existed now, which wouldn't serve her purpose either. Every word he spoke was guarded and Anya listened to every syllable.

Somehow Barin convinced Gellen that time alone with Fatell would be proper and useful. He took Fatell's arm and walked her outside into the fields. "Tell me about Castle Cordan. What do you do there? Obviously you are not waiting hand and foot on Lady Raphela."

Fatell bit her lip and laughed. "You're very perceptive. I'm in charge of the school."

"School? What's a school?"

Fatell wasn't sure if he really cared about the answer or if he just wanted her to talk. Even Mahtso didn't make her feel this good. "Everyone at Castle Cordan must learn to read and write. The school is where the teaching is done. We have many levels of classes."

"Required knowledge, for everyone?"

"Yes."

"If you don't learn, then what?"

"Not much. The only people avoiding it are very old and we respect their age. Everyone else is anxious, the more you learn, the better position you can hold."

"You have a choice in position." Barin was amazed.

"Well, you can't be the Duke or the Lady but other than that it's a fairly open field."

"You can go anywhere in the castle, anytime?"

"As long as you're not invading anyone's privacy."

"To lead such a life." He muttered enviously.

Fatell, though drawn into the romance of the moment, remembered her reason for being there, she had been thoroughly briefed. "Would you like to have that here?" It was half statement, half question.

Barin kissed her hand. "Dear lady, I do believe I would risk a week at the whipping post if I knew at the end I would be free. But such things are a dream."

Fatell took a deep breath and asked her most difficult question. "Would you kill for it?"

Barin stared in disbelief at the tiny serious woman before him. "What do you suggest?"

"Barin, if you organize the servants and you are capable of inspiring them, the Duke would turn his head at certain breaks of rank."

Barin stumbled back and sat down. "Is that why you and Lady Raphela are here?"

"Yes"

"But why?"

Fatell put her arms around Barin and placed her hands under his shirt. Her fingers easily found the scars, old and new, on his back. Tears came to both sets of eyes, he was embarrassed, she simply felt lost. But as her fingers caressed the scars she spoke. "Because of these. Duke Ishtba can no longer tolerate the abuse."

Barin looked in her eyes and hugged her, then walked away and stared at the stars. He thought, "Indeed a week at the post would be gentle punishment if I fail, but if I succeed, the prize." He studied the stars and weighed all the issues, the scars on his back ached.

Finally, he took Fatell's hand. "What do I do?"

Now more than ever Fatell wished Raphela were there, but that couldn't be. Fatell explained the plans.

"I must turn all of them against Anya and Gellen, it won't be easy. Everyone is so afraid." Barin said.

Fatell squeezed his hand. "I know. But you know that the laborers and house staff outnumber the guards four to one."

"But we are not trained. They know how to defend themselves." Barin protested.

"Then turn them too." Fatell began to understand. "Have not all of them tasted the whip at one time or another? Remind them of the scars and that even they do not have freedom."

"Do you have that much faith in me?"

"Yes, I know these people will follow you because you believe."

Barin cupped her face in his hands. She allowed, even enjoyed the kiss. Though this attractive man warmed her soul, her words brought her closer to Mahtso. "Good luck Barin." Fatell slipped away and Barin walked slowly back to his room, his life changed forever.

Raphela and Fatell began the trip back in silence.

266

Raphela worked at warming herself, not from the weather, for the sun generously laid its rays on the carriage, but from the people and place she had just visited.

For all the people who called Atan cold, they had no concept of real cold. Her first site of Atan drew her to the passion, well guarded from a world incapable of dealing with it. But these people, Gellen and Anya, had no passion, no dreams, only a need for control and a deep, deep fear of the loss of it. This created the void which Raphela found so painful. She wrapped herself in the warm thoughts of home until the chill slowed to a dull ache.

Fatell was lost in a clouded reverie. She had a piece of life that didn't fit in her personal puzzle. It was oddly shaped and the colors were all wrong, but it was special. As the trip moved on, she found a shelf in her mind on which to store it, someplace dark and quiet, where only she could go.

Raphela warmed enough to speak. "You seem calmer than before we arrived."

"I suppose I am."

"Barin must have been something special." Raphela had a girlish curiosity to know what had happened between them.

Fatell shrugged and squirmed.

"How did you convince Gellen to allow the two of you time alone"

"He has certain information which Gellen would rather not reveal to Anya, prior history as it were. Barin has been there a long time."

"Interesting. Barin obviously used his knowledge carefully."

"He wants this Raphela, I could feel it." Fatell held Raphela's hands.

"You trust him?" she asked, peering into Fatell's eyes.

"Yes."

"Then it will be successful. But what about your personal feelings."

Fatell sighed. "No man ever made me feel pretty and feminine except him and that charm will work well with others. But it was real and it gave me a feeling I will never forget. Yet it also gave me new insight into Mahtso. For the cruel monster I know he can be, I know that the murder he has committed has

267

often been against his nature and that agony plays on him, I feel for him now more than before. Our love is too deep to be destroyed by a distraction, even one as strong as Barin." Fatell sounded a little sad, but Raphela didn't press, this was Fatell's bed to make.

Fatell knew her life would return to normal, but she clung to the past few days as her bed eased the pain in her back from the long ride.

When Mahtso discovered she was back he hurried to her room, each step increasing his concern for her condition, for what horrible things they might have done. By the time he stepped over the threshold his breath was coming out in short bursts. "Fatell," he panted, "are you all right? I was worried about you in that house."

Fatell's smiled softly and her glow of confidence made Mahtso's chain swing nervously.

"It wasn't that bad. Raphela kept Anya and Gellen occupied.

"Where were you?"

"With the servants"

Mahtso breathed out hard of his nose. Though Fatell treated her placement as a matter of fact, he found it demeaning.

Fatell went on. "They were quiet and timid. But the few that Oram said had spirit truly did."

"Then someone was found for the job."

"Yes, Barin should do a good job." Fatell's voice floated for just a split second, arousing Mahtso's suspicion, as the chain bruised his leg and the piece of him that gets answers infiltrated his mood.

"Then Raphela instructed him well?"

Fatell now had a decision to make, to live in her days of adventure and create a maze of deceit or to return to her life and to her love. She put her arms around him and looked up into his troubled blue eyes.

"I instructed him."

Mahtso didn't know exactly what had passed between Fatell and Barin, only that for the first time in his life, he felt he could lose her. Her touch was all that kept his sanity for the moment.

Strong fingers squeezed her arms, lifting her up. "I love you Fatell, I need you. I...."

Fatell put her fingers to his lips. "I know. I love you too."

Mahtso made love to her and prayed she really knew.

Raphela undressed in the quiet bedroom. She didn't know where Atan was at the time. Wrapping a warm robe around her, she went to take a bath. To her surprise, Atan was climbing into the steaming tub and faced her as he sat. "I thought you were back," he said. "Just a little while ago." Atan's heart burned at her sullen response and the sight of her pale skin. "Come." She stepped into the tub and rested her head on his chest. Long fingers made large relaxing circles on her shoulders. Slowly she relaxed and sank down into the warm bubbly water. Atan brushed his chin against the hair wrapped around her head, his guilt reformed itself into a warm blanket for his wife. As the water cooled they found the warmth of their bed. Raphela slept well. Atan surrounded her like a cocoon, resting only when her peace was secure.

Chapter 14

Summer rolled to the winter that cast its heavy blanket on Raalek. Deep snows and biting wind demanded respect and to venture out when the sun didn't shine was to stretch a beckoning finger to death.

Castle Cordan kept warm, but its inhabitants had their desires. By the front door a mass of fur and feet jostled impatiently. The children waited anxiously for their teachers to arrive and guide them through the protected walkway to the school.

Finally the adults showed, larger versions of furbound beings, and marched the children to school.

The hall emptied and Raphela stood alone, staring at the door.

Quietly, from behind, she heard, yet did not hear, the echo of footsteps.

A voice whispered in her ear. "What's on your mind?"

"The weather" Raphela said distantly.

"The weather?"

"Yes Mahtso, the weather." She snapped.

"What about it?"

"It is so confining. Look at how the children must dress, for the brief walk to school and still they freeze along the way."

"Next year we'll encase the walkway in stone, that should help

"I suppose" she sighed. Raphela stared at the door for a minute more. "But there must be a better way." She envisioned stone walkways spiraling the land like water filling holes, there would be little place to walk or ride. No, there must be a better way.

Aharon, the healer who replaced Corin after his death, met Raphela in the "Get Well" room, as Vanar called the chamber. It contained eight beds lined up in two rows against the walls. Only three were occupied, the first by a woman expecting a child and feeling more tired than she normally did, the second by an old

271

man, soon to die and resting out his last days. The third was filled by a teenage boy.

Aharon, having checked the other two, turned his attention to the boy. Aharon massaged the muscles in the boy's injured ankle and then referred to a book for wrapping cloth around it. He did so in a criss-cross fashion, tight enough for support but still comfortable. The boy hobbled out of bed and limped around the room.

"There you go, now leave the bandage on until tomorrow when I will check it again." The boy nodded and limped away.

"Well done Aharon," Raphela smiled.

"Thank you, my lady."

"Now, I've been studying the newest book we found. Come look."

They sat at an empty table, side by side. Colorful pictures showing the inner workings of an animal, all the parts labeled, easy to identify.

Raphela felt her face flush, Aharon's forehead beaded with sweat and a chill ran down both their spines with each turn of the page. It was dusk before they could drag themselves away.

"Aharon, this is just the beginning, I promise." Raphela's vision began to take shape and Aharon could only hope to be there when she fully opened the door.

At dinner Vanar expounded on all the wonderful things he did. "Mama, today I taught the little children about colors, they don't know very much at all. But they learned red and blue and yellow." Vanar beamed with pride and wisdom.

Atan and Raphela shared a smile.

"That's very good Vanar. What did you learn today?" Atan pushed away his plate.

A sheepish grin accompanied shrugging shoulders. "I don't remember Papa."

"Perhaps tomorrow you will." Atan attempted to be stern but to no avail.

"Yes Papa, I promise." Vanar jumped on his lap and hugged him hard.

In the hearth, the fire flickered in jealousy at the warmth of family Ishtba. Vanar ran off to his room to play before bedtime.

"What did you learn today Papa?" Raphela teased, as she watched her son leave.

"Very little, but I made some progress."

"In what?"

Grey eyes studied the floor and a face much like Vanar's reached Raphela's curious glance. "I suppose I hadn't mentioned it before. My experiment."

Raphela attempted a stern glance and failed miserably. Her childish curiosity surfaced. "Can I see?"

He held out his hand. With the aid of a newly designed torch they crept down the stairs to the kitchen, like errant school children. Both ignored the teasing scent of spices and hot tea wandering around the empty room.

Raphela moved closer to Atan, "hold the torch," he said as he gently picked up a glass bowl and held it up to the light.

Raphela squinted her eyes to see the contents but nothing impressed her. Large brown eyes turned to Atan, lost and confused.

"Put the torch on the wall."

She did so and watched his finger point to a fragile green leaf topping an almost transparent stem no longer than Vanar's thumbnail. It barely poked its point out of a mass of sand curiously buried under water at least twice its height. Raphela turned the bowl and stared. Her breath clouded the glass. Atan rubbed it clear. "It's amazing, to grow plants under water. Why? How?"

Atan beamed with pride. "It is wonderful isn't it."

Raphela swore the room warmed at his pleasure, for she certainly did.

"Yes, tell me all about it." Never before had she seen him with a personal hobby or project. Everything was large and involved masses of people. This tiny plant was intimate with him, he saw it as a child of his creation and Raphela gloried in his pleasure.

"I too have read the old books. Growing plants can be done many ways. This is one we haven't tried before."

"That is a fact."

They talked long into the night. When the torch died they opened a lumpglow. A tingle spread through the castle as master and mistress plotted the future on a plane of fantasy and hope, a luxury they were rarely afforded.

Towards winter's end Raphela and Aharon finished reading their book of anatomy and visited Mahtso in his dungeon. Aharon shuddered as he walked through the door.

Raphela and Mahtso stood by a small square table, clean instruments gleaming in the abundant torchlight. " Come closer Aharon." Raphela's easy and vibrant tone relaxed him. He looked down and saw the small, smooth-skinned creature.

"Aharon, did you bring the potion?"

"What?" He broke out of the trance created by the room. "Oh yes, here it is." He produced a small vial of liquid, which was fed to the creature. It quickly became drowsy and slowed its movements to a halt. Raphela prodded it with a pin the creature did not respond.

"I think he's ready. Mahtso, if you please," she handed him a small knife.

Mahtso deftly turned the creature on its back and slit open its skin. The smell of blood and life tantalized him, but he held back and allowed Raphela and Aharon access to the creature. Raphela opened the book to the page showing what they should expect to find. Aharon, at first taken aback by the smell and sight, regained his composure and found the first organ.

"My lady, the heart, look right here." He prodded a small roundish piece that pumped ever so slowly and seemed to be the center of activity. Carefully, without disturbing the position of anything Raphela and Aharon searched inside the creature, naming each piece, noting what had no match in the book.

Mahtso stood by, swallowing hard, feeling like a caged beast. His chain made deep bruises in his hands. The scent of Raphela and her excitement drove him to a private madness controlled only by respect and love.

As the creature began to stir Raphela handed needle and thread to Aharon, who sewed the open skin back together, as he had done for injured people. The creature lived for only a few moments after being repaired. While this saddened Raphela and Aharon, they were still ecstatic with what they learned.

Raphela raced to find Atan. Though it was night she easily found her way up the stairs. He was just undressing for sleep and stood by the bed, tunic off. Even in the dark he could see Raphela's flushed face and she smelled of excitement.

"Atan, I have had the most incredible day!"

He wrapped his arms around her waist and firmly grabbed her bottom, "Is that so?"

Raphela ran her fingers through his hairy chest and placed an intense but brief kiss. "Yes, yes. We finally did it."

"Did what?" Atan laid her on the bed and unlaced her bodice.

"First, we put a small lizard to sleep."

"With one of your magic potions I suppose."

"Yes, with one of our magic po..." she gasped a moment as his hands ran up her leg and explored. "Potions"

"And the what?"

Raphela leaned back, baring her neck and pressing her breasts together, inviting more of what was offered. "Then we opened it and explored." she panted.

Atan stood up, cold and stiff. "You what?" he demanded.

"We explored, we looked at everything inside. It was phenomenal." She leaned on her elbows.

"I don't want to hear any more about it." He turned and finished readying for sleep.

"What is wrong with you? This is a great stride in healing."

"It's wrong, simply wrong."

Raphela's ecstasy turned to anger. "Is it right for Mahtso to do what he does? For no purpose except his pleasure?" Raphela faced him now.

Atan raised his hand, the back coming close to her cheek, but he held back. "Raphela, I don't approve, drop the matter." Frustration and anger boiled inside him, Why he didn't approve even he didn't know, but he didn't and not knowing why made it worse.

"Such blindness! How can someone so anxious to create a standard of life beyond what we've ever known be so unyielding, so closed."

This time he hit the mark. "I said enough."

Raphela rubbed her cheek but did not cry. "Indeed it is," was her chilling reply.

She left the room and went to her quarters. It had been years since she slept in that bed, not that either of them slept that night. Night rolled into day and days into a week. Castle Cordan's vibrant life took on a sick pallor. Children waited for school on solid silence, no typical complaints of "he touched me, "she took my things", feet remained still until told to move. Conversations between people were limited to as few words as possible and the kitchen lost its pungent inviting smell.

Atan and Raphela ate together for Vanar's sake, though not a word passed over the table. During the day all were buried in work, escaping the harsh feelings. At night, in the dark, it was not so easy.

Vanar cried himself to sleep, not having "the" bed to crawl into when a nightmare struck. Raphela lay in a cold dark void and it grew colder and deeper each night. Atan rolled in a sea of confusion, unable to deny his feelings, yet knowing what she had done was best.

One week turned to two. Mahtso and Fatell held each other every night, as did all the couples except the most important.

In the cloudy skies the gods watched in cold envy, unable to warm the castle walls, much less the souls inside. Empty routines continued, the wound lay open another week. Spring's first storm pounded its way into the middle of a starry night.

Atan and Raphela separately watched the webs of lightning layer the dark sky. After a time, while the storm still danced, Atan, barefoot and scantily clad traveled easily down the dark hallway to her room. Raphela still watched the show outside her window as he stood half a room away. She didn't turn as he spoke; her blood heard the honesty and pain.

"I cannot change what I feel."

Raphela remained motionless.

"Yet, I would not ask you to do so either. More important, progress, for which we have battled so hard to create, must continue."

Salty tears made a path down Raphela's cheeks. "You know, I believe the view is better in our room."

Atan smiled.

The storm did not subside; snow blew like waves on the sea.

As their door closed, his skin rubbed hers. Atan lost himself in the scent of Raphela's hair and her fingers renewed their acquaintance with his muscles. Fingers of lightning peeked in the window and from the first gentle kiss through the constant rustle of sheet and muscle, to the sweaty passionate fulfilling climax, the storm worked in harmony with the Duke and his Lady.

Castle Cordan's walls drew on the heat and dispersed it to the residents.

Everyone slept well past sunrise and woke feeling refreshed and warm, ready for spring.

In the cool of an early spring night a traveler knocked on Castle Cordan's door. The young man had a message for the Duke, but assured Fatell it could wait until morning.

Raphela welcomed the pleasant aroma of hot tea while Atan poured more juice for Vanar. A young servant girl shyly knocked at the dining room door. Raphela motioned for her to enter. With bowed head and shaky voice she told them of the messenger's presence.

"Send him here." Atan was as gentle as he knew to be.

The poor girl still trembled. "Yes, my lord." She scurried out of the room.

Moments later the messenger arrived. He dropped to one knee, eyes on the floor. Raphela and Atan sighed at such annoying subservience.

"You may stand," Raphela said.

The boy rose but still watched the floor. "My Lord Duke Ishtba, I bring you the sad news that our beloved King Samed has passed on and is by the gods' will traveling with them. Prince Dahlek requests your presence at the funeral, followed by his coronation and wedding to Altira of Calcoran North. May I return with a positive reply?"

Atan nodded to Raphela. She spoke for them. "Of course, tell Prince Dahlek we are saddened by his loss and will be honored to attend all ceremonies."

"Thank you, my lady." He said and left.

"It's a shame about King Samed." Raphela broke a biscuit in half and began nibbling.

"Yes, but not unexpected."

"True I suppose we'll leave tomorrow?" This interrupted many plans, but nothing crucial.

"Today. Have everything packed and ready by noon. " Atan felt a momentary chill as he left. Raphela watched and shared his chill.

"Mama," Vanar tugged at her sleeve. "Mama!"

"Yes Vanar?"

"Mama, can I go too?"

"No dear, this is for grown up people only." She was distant, Vanar knew pursuit was useless.

"Mama"

"Yes?"

"I'm going to school now."

"Go ahead."

By noon Atan and Raphela were in the carriage and bound for Calcoran.

They arrived amid a jumble of movement. Servants bowed nervously to anyone they didn't know. Guests, wandered aimlessly in the entrance hall and nearby corridors. Dahlek barked orders at whoever was close by.

Atan and Raphela stood quietly at a hallway entrance. If not for the sad occasion they would have been amused at the lack of structure as servants actually bumped into each other by following contradictory orders. Atan watched Dahlek's tall thin form, topped with a mass of straight blond hair, work its way towards him.

"Duke Ishtba, have you been here long? I must reprimand my servants for being so lazy as not to take you to a room."

"It's quite all right. We understand it is a difficult time." Raphela was calm and matronly, doing her best to relieve any pressure he felt.

278

"That's generous of you, but still you will be taken care of immediately." He turned in all directions and then grabbed a young boy by the shoulder. "You boy, take the Duke and Lady to a room in the west wing."

"Yes sire."

"Thank you, Prince Dahlek."

Once settled Raphela and Atan walked around the castle, going their separate ways and observing different things. Raphela bumped into Sonja. "You look wonderful." Sonja's tiny form echoed a happy life.

"And you as well my lady." They shared a hug and walked together through the main hall.

"Are the children here?" Raphela asked as she studied a nearby couple.

"No, we left them with Colin and Marta. Even though I told Jivad I didn't want servants he insisted. Colin and Marta love the boys, so I don't mind leaving them."

"Vanar is at home too. There is certainly enough white draping." Each doorway and hall entrance was framed in three layers of sheer white drapes.

"Poor Altira was terrified that she wouldn't show enough respect."

"Altira?"

Sonja nodded. "Yes, Dahlek has her running the household."

Raphela's eyes opened wide. "How old is she?"

"Sixteen."

"Is she the daughter of royalty?"

"Yes. And in answer to the unasked question, She has never been given an ounce of responsibility before this. She's trying." Sonja honestly felt bad for the girl.

"I see."

"Here she comes."

Altira walked stiffly, clutching her gown, long blond hair flowing down her back, delicate skin obviously paler than normal. She curtsied with bowed head in front of Raphela. "My lady, it was kind of you to come. Dahlek and I appreciate your presence." Her speech was as stiff as her walk.

"Altira, you may call me Raphela. How are you?" Raphela stressed the you.

"I'm fine." Her voice began to tremble.

"This is a great deal of responsibility to handle on short notice. Can I help?"

"Oh no, it's fine really. Anyway, Dahlek would be angry if anyone else got involved. I have the older women here." Altira's eyes brimmed with tears.

Sonja and Raphela each took an arm and walked her outside to a bench. "Tell me what's wrong?" Raphela said as she put a strong arm around the girl.

"There's so much to do, I'm so afraid I'll do it wrong." She sniffled and buried her head in Raphela's chest. Raphela stroked her hair, let her cry and gave her a cloth to wipe her eyes when she calmed down.

"Now, what are you afraid of?"

"I don't know."

"Is it Dahlek. Will he execute you for a mistake?" Raphela was being facetious but needed to show the girl a little of her foolishness.

Altira's eyes opened wide. "Oh! Never!"

"Then you're afraid he will beat you?"

"Oh no, Dahlek would never hurt me. He loves me." She sounded like what she was, a teenager in love.

"Then he'll banish you?"

"No" Altira was now calm.

"Then what are you afraid of?"

She shrugged in embarrassment. "That everyone will think I'm foolish and laugh at me. I don't know anything about being a queen. I'll say and do all the wrong things."

Raphela sighed, thinking what a shame it was that Lise had died and couldn't help this child. "Altira, as queen you determine what is right and wrong. If you choose to start dinner with dessert and end with soup, then it is right because you say so."

Altira giggled. "I suppose you're right. But I'm not good at telling people what to do, especially when I don't know what to do myself."

"Well, I'll tell you a secret. Nobody knows how to do everything. Find two people. One who knows how to get things done and the other, to talk too. Someone who can see things a little differently than you. They're called advisors and all rulers have them.

"Thank you," she smiled and studied the ground a minute. "Lady Raphela, would you help me now? I know the castle is running so poorly."

"Of course, let's find the first person, the one who can run things."

The three women strolled back to the castle, still a haphazard stream of activity. Upon entering they saw Dahlek, engaged in a heated discussion with a young guard. "Where is Altira?" He grabbed the guard's tunic forcing him to stand.

"She went with Lady Raphela and some other woman. They took a walk." His answer was matter of fact.

"Why weren't you with her?" Dahlek demanded.

"She was with Lady Raphela, why did she need me?" His intention that Logan was sufficient.

Dahlek threw the man against the wall. "It is your responsibility to be with Altira any time that I am not. Does that wall of a man Logan leave Lady Raphela's side? NEVER! Now go find Altira before you are guarding the flowers."

The man straightened his clothes, seemingly unmoved by the outburst and took but two steps before Dahlek saw Altira.

"You are fortunate that she is unharmed." Dahlek growled and took long quick strides to his woman.

"I was worried about you." Dahlek hugged her tight and caressed her cheek.

"I was just with Sonja and Lady Raphela. We"

He cut her off. 'I'm sure you ladies had a nice chat. But I need you now, it's getting late." He was gentle.

"All right, but Lady"

"Altira, it's time to go. Lady Raphela, thank you for your time." He was curtly polite and took Altira's arm as he left.

"Altira, why did you leave without your bodyguard?"

Innocent blue eyes turned to him. "I was safe, Lady Raphela's guard protected us."

281

Dahlek shook his head and slowed his pace. "Don't you see, perhaps it is Lady Raphela we should be concerned about." He turned back for a quick look.

"Oh no. I cannot believe Lady Raphela would ever do me harm."

Dahlek sighed as they walked.

Raphela watched and listened.

"That can be dangerous."

Sonja jumped at the deep voice. Raphela smiled, she knew Atan was behind her, she felt him half a room away and she didn't turn when he spoke or when she answered.

"Yes, it's sad."

Though Sonja was taken aback at Atan's presence, Raphela's instinctive knowledge of it, sent chills down Sonja's spine. Jivad was there too, but she didn't know it until he tapped her shoulder and then joined in the conversation.

"He's been like that since childhood, always looking over his shoulder. It's probably why I didn't mind being sent away."

Under the pale moonlight in a large clearing the crowd began to form. King Samed's widows formed a semicircle around a stone altar mounted on a slab of well packed soil. Resting on top, shrouded in sheer white cloth was Samed's lifeless form. The cool spring wind billowed the cloth like a sail. Surrounding the altar were brown pots overflowing with sweet incense. Two rows of torches made a frame around the guests. A path opened as the slow family processional moved forward, each step matched by the lighting of a torch. Dahlek led his brothers to the stone altar. Silence born of respect and tradition dominated the night.

The widows laid a frame of wildflowers around Samed's body and then stepped back into the crowd. Dahlek and his brothers formed a tight circle around the altar with Dahlek by Samed's head and the rest in age order so that the youngest, age nine, was by his side.

Calcoran's high priest raised his hands and blessed the royal family. He began a liturgy of Samed's life and deeds. Many wept. Raphela now understood Atan's silence at the news. She felt a tiny scorch of loss as the priest's stories were not mere recounting of old worn tales, but warm and loving vignettes of a man cherished and respected by those around him.

As the memories were closing, young boys lit the pots of incense and handed the torches to the sons. The priest ended his speech as all priests did "May the Gods make a place for him at their table" (This was a prayer that the dead be a part of eternity in the sky)

As his words ended Dahlek placed the first torch on the altar, each brother followed in turn and all stepped down.

The flames made quick business of their work, the orange-blue fingers making tiny skyward leaps as if to invite the attention of the Nameless Ones. Women continued to weep. Altira sobbed openly and Dahlek, despite his best attempts of control, found tears burning through his eyes,

From the west, a burst of wind whirled the flames on the altar. All eyes rested on the fire, but nothing looked different. Atan and Raphela however, felt the change. Samed's soul no longer made home in the body, but found peace in a cloud beneath the Gods. Neither spoke of this, neither understood why they knew, but they did know.

The incense covered the smell of the flames and as the fire dwindled, the last sparks were put to rest by a cold wind. The guests filed back inside and retired for the night.

At noon the next day guests were quickly ushered into the great hall, still lined with white drapes. People shuffled about, yawning and nodding. Atan and Raphela noted the casual dress. What little conversation existed wove a strange cloudy fabric over the room. Some complained of a lack of respect for Samed, but most felt this "coronation ceremony" was unnecessary. Everyone knew who was to be king, few seemed to care. Altira stood by the throne, surrounded by old women, primping and preening and "guiding" her. She looked pale and frightened, eyes searching for the comfort of Dahlek.

Atan took a casual walk around the room, getting close to the doorway where he could observe Dahlek. With mild success Dahlek organized an awkward congregation of guards and when the priest arrived mumbled his way into the room, guards escorted Dahlek to the throne. His brothers stood to the left and Altira to the right.

Dahlek knelt before the priest, solely out of protocol. His eyes darted back and forth around the room. Even Atan began to wonder if a threat really did exist. The ceremony was more than quick, it was hasty, and was followed by a satisfying buffet lunch. Dahlek's shoulders no longer looked as if pulled by a harness and Altira no longer shook. It didn't take long for Altira's "handmaidens" to whisk her away to prepare for the wedding, that evening.

As Raalek's sun finally began to exit from the sky. Atan and Raphela dressed in silence. As he buckled the belt on his tunic, Atan's eyes turned to Raphela. He remembered the bevy of women offered to him, he was glad he had waited. Raphela didn't need to hear him say it, she placed a kiss on his cheek. A warm flush rose to his face. Raphela pretended not to see.

They joined ceremony-weary guests as they filtered into the great hall one more time. Carefully designed bouquets of pastel flowers made a wavy pattern on the drapes. Colorful trees formed of cloth and wood made archways around the room. Musicians played out a lively but gentle tune and the crowd's mood brightened a bit. Conversations began, the weather and fashion the most appropriate topics if an uninvited ear listened.

Dahlek dressed in Calcoran colors, as did Altira. The wedding ceremony flowed easily and broke a bit more tension. After the ceremony a receiving line was formed and the new couple received congratulations and gifts from all. A fine dinner was served and the musicians continued to play. No one lingered past the second moonrise and all left early the next morning.

Dahlek's insistence on accomplishing everything at once diminished all and left a mottled feel to a wedding that should have brought new blossom to Calcoran.

Chapter 15

"Mother" Vanar tapped Raphela on her shoulder.

"Yes Vanar" She didn't look up from the task at hand.

"Mother, Father said I could travel with him this spring " Vanar paused "if I have your permission.

Raphela put down her scalpel and faced Vanar. He looked so much like Atan, tall and lean for his 9 years. He even began exercising to develop a well-toned body like his father. There he stood, wide-eyed and hopeful. "So, you and your father have discussed this matter?"

Vanar was too excited and perhaps consciously blind to pay attention to his mother's annoyance.

"You know, it's not an easy trip."

"Yes Mother, I know."

"Umm. Well, after I speak with your father, if he still agrees, then I give my permission."

"Thank you mama." He hugged her and ran off to his friends.

Later that day Raphela caught Atan while walking by the kitchen. "My lord Duke, may I have a word with you." Raphela's school marm tone said a great deal more than the words.

Atan closed his eyes and took a deep breath "As you wish my lady"

They went to a small room and shut the door.

Atan attempted innocence. "What do you need?"

"Vanar came to see me today, something about traveling this spring. Do you know about it?"

"Well, yes. He asked and I thought he might enjoy the trip. Don't you?" Atan had mellowed and if he could be sheepish, he was now.

"So, now I must risk both of my men, for weeks at a time." Her annoyance no longer covered her concern.

Atan wrapped his arms around her waist. "I'll take only the safest routes." His hand caressed her cheek.

She rested her head on his chest. "I suppose I'm being foolish, but the two of you are..."

"Shhh."

Their kiss was long and warm.

As they left the room she did pose one more statement. "By the way, just because you sent Vanar to ask permission didn't guarantee I would say yes. That was naughty of you." She landed a playful slap on his bottom.

"Yes my lady."

"Atan."

"Yes."

"Next time, talk to me first."

He kissed her hand and they went off to their separate tasks.

Three weeks later Raphela watched the shiny new carriage slowly roll down the hill.

The rameks did not have to work as hard as before. Mahtso's men had redesigned the carriages. Square clumsy boxes were transformed to sleek rounded forms, no longer riding on unbending axles but a bed of springs, so that the well polished wheels didn't jolt the passengers at every bump.

Vanar peered out the window, soaking in every new sight. Bertram rested comfortably beside him.

Atan stretched out his legs, while his bodyguard (Nahal) joined Bertram in rest.

"Father, which fief will we visit first?" Vanar lost interest in the trees and the road had no companions, it stretched out long and lonely.

"The spice fief."

"Is it your favorite?"

"No."

"Which is your favorite?"

Atan considered the question, no one had ever asked it before. "I don't believe I have one Vanar."

"Will it take long to get there?"

Atan chuckled. "Much longer than you would like it to take."

Vanar sighed, he had so many questions but he had to use the right words. He listened to the wheels of the carriage and watched the land pass by. After a time he took out his book of woodsheets and drew pictures of what he saw along the way.

Raphela do not want Vanar receiving any special favor regarding supplies, but Fatell doted on his every request. Raphela could not keep her from spoiling the boy. So, he had quite a supply of woodsheets for the journey.

They arrived at the spice fief the next morning.

Vanar observed the roads and pathways as he walked around, before joining the other children at the fief.

Atan paid a visit to Sidno, now living in a small house near the west side of the main building.

"How are you Sidno?" Atan took the military at ease position while standing on Sidno's doorstep.

Sidno bowed his freckled bald head and ushered the Duke and his guard inside. A delicate sprinkling of the fief's bounty laced the room, Atan enjoyed it.

"I'm doing well my lord. I've been treated quite fairly."

A young girl, perhaps 17 or 18 entered the room and delivered a trained curtsy, and giggled.

"Be a dear Lara and get us some tea."

The girl stopped a moment to think about the order, quietly and clearly given. Once understood she walked to the kitchen and made tea.

Atan shuddered at the thought of sleeping with a woman so empty. But it pleased Sidno and she was an inexpensive retirement gift.

They chatted for a while and then Atan began his unguided inspection. He was pleased, all looked neat and clean and in order. Overall conditions had improved over the years, production increased to meet the growing demand.

He noticed that Vanar was not overcome at the initial encounter with the gardens and when he approached he noted a dilution of aroma, still pungent, but different.

Meals were served in a well-lit room with Zorba, his wife Cassatra and their 4 year old twin sons.

Vanar sat by his father during dinner, following his lead as much as possible.

"Zorba, I like the conditions I've seen so far. But the aroma from the gardens has changed, it is less potent than in the past. He sipped some cold water flavored with spice leaves.

Vanar sipped as well.

"My lord, we have bred the herbs and spices to be less powerful, more palatable to more people." He hedged a bit, concerned he had made an error in judgment.

"A good decision."

Vanar watched the people and listened to words and tones, and compared them to the physical surroundings. The table was covered in a light cloth, delicately painted with pastel colored flowers. Cassatra, wore a lacy dress with many layers of ribbon and the boys clothes were sturdy yet light in color. They did their best to be still during dinner, only having to be reprimanded once.

"Vanar, are you enjoying your trip?" Cassatra's tone was directed to a 4 year old, which Vanar ignored.

"We have just begun, but it is very interesting so far. You have made a very good dinner." His answer, mature and honest pleased Atan.

Cassatra blushed a thank you.

They left a day later, although Atan had no complaints, he missed the aroma, wild untamed and powerful.

The next stop was a grain fief.

A short plump man greeted them at the door, along with four zorel pups, domesticated animals with four legs and lots of hair and strongly devoted to people.)

The pups, to Vanar's delight, knocked him down and placed a multitude of long wet tongued kisses all over him.

Barlow gently shooed them away. "I'm sorry my lord."

Atan checked Vanar who stood up and brushed himself off.

"No harm done"

They walked through a small building to a cluttered sitting room

"Where is your wife?" Atan looked around and posed the question out of sheer curiosity.

Barlow lowered his head and sniffed. "She passed on this winter, sire."

Atan felt for this man. He and his wife were kind gentle people, unable to have children. Over the past twenty years they took in every stray animal and child that walked by their door. It was a house full of life and the couple was very close. Many of the strays had stayed on to help. One of them, Theo, a teenager looked after Barlow as if he were his own father and called him such.

"May she rest with the Gods."

"Thank you my lord."

Theo entered the room and kneeled before Atan. "My lord I am at your service."

"Please stand. I appreciate your offer. Perhaps you can take me for a walk around the grounds."

"As you wish my lord."

Vanar spent some time with Barlow and then wandered off into the yard, followed by Bertram and one of the pups.

Barlow smiled, it was good having a young one in the house, even if only for a while.

Atan took his time with Theo. He could see a problem sprouting.

"Theo, how has Barlow been since his wife's death?" Atan dissected a stalk of wheat while he spoke. Tiny grains took flight on wings of a gentle wind of the sunny day.

"Badly my lord. He loved mother so much. He can hardly do anything. He spends a great deal of time staring at her clothes, which I am not allowed to destroy or give away. I'm worried about him." Theo's voice cracked and a sense of relief at finally telling someone all of this, spilled out.

"I see. Have you learned from Barlow? Do you know anything of this business?"

"Sire, father has taught me everything he could. I have kept the records for two years now and last fall was permitted to work with the foremen." The boy was proud.

Atan stared at the bright sun as Theo shifted back and forth.

"Theo, take care of Barlow and let him rely on you for anything he needs. Should the burden become to heavy, do not hesitate to ask for help. Pride is a good thing until it is the only

289

thing and then it is a corrupt disease eating its way through everything It touches."

Atan's point was well taken. Theo knew what was to be and was grateful for the Duke's understanding.

Vanar ran with the pup and rolled on the ground with him. Before they got up, Vanar noticed a small black insect crawling across his hand and for some reason his eye followed it.

Six black legs, thin as hair, supporting three thick bulbs, it walked undaunted towards something. Vanar made the pup sit still as he observed. Not far was a hole and the insect, with two hair like protrusions apparently guiding it, made its way down the hole.

Vanar peeped down the tiny opening and saw moving darkness. Curiosity drove him. His fingers gently pulled away at the layers of dirt, he ignored the pup pulling at his leg.

Eyes opened in wonder at the teeming life. He turned and looked for Bertram who was but a step away.

"Come, look, look at what I found."

Bertram looked and saw the mass of insects crawling around, he had seen it before.

"Bertram, isn't it wondrous."

Vanar glowed.

Bertram was lost, he didn't understand the excitement.

Vanar noticed a shadow.

"Father look."

Atan kneeled down next to his son and soon both were bellies to the ground.

"What is it that fascinates you so?"

Vanar realized that no one knew what he really saw. He took Atan's finger and placed it by a row of insects. "They are working together, they have roads. But where are they going?"

"I don't know, shall we dig deeper? His son's interest lit a fire in him.

"Yes. Yes let's."

They dug and found a central area. Surrounded by other insects was a large one, being fed and cared for with what appeared to be undying vigilance.

290

"Father, this is a community, all these small creatures have built so many roads and worked out this system, just to care for this one being."

Vanar closed his eyes and made a mental note as dusk was arriving and the winding tunnels and crosspaths would soon be to small to see in the dark. By torchlight he drew an accurate picture of his discovery and then wrote notes.

Atan wasn't quite sure what drove his son, but the boy's passion reminded him of his own and he warmed at the thought.

The next fief was a fair distance away. Barlow and Theo packed an enormous box with food for the Duke and his party. Vanar was given the pup as a gift. Vanar named it Posa, the ancient word for friend.

Once Posa settled in for a nap, Vanar turned to his father with the mountain of questions befitting a boy.

"Father, what do you think that one insect does, besides eat? Is it the king? Do other insects behave that way? DO they meet with others like them near our castle? Wouldn't it be wonderful if their road were that long? Isn't it amazing how their roads crossed each other, but every one seemed to know which road to take. Why father?"

Atan, tired and preoccupied stared at his son. "Vanar, I do believe you have your Mother's curiosity."

Vanar thought for a moment. "Is that good?"

Atan heaved a sigh. "Vanar"

"I'm sorry Father, I didn't mean to disturb you."

Atan's shoulders drooped as he shook his head and pulled Vanar on his lap. "My son, you cannot disturb me, and yes it is good to have your mother's curiosity. It's probably why you're here today."

"Really! Why?" Vanar now had a new diversion.

Atan smiled.

"How did you meet Mother?"

This question had to be answered carefully. Vanar did not know the recent past. "A mutual acquaintance introduced us."

"Did you marry her right away?"

"No."

Vanar went back to his seat.

291

"When did you marry her?"

"A year later."

"Oh." Obviously his father was not going to speak much, not that he ever did. No matter, Vanar turned to his books.

He had insisted on learning the ancient language and by the time he was 8, he could speak both fluently and by now he was more adept than most at reading the old books. It was these that he had, books on communication and business. How and why people interacted, fascinated him as much as the warriors of long ago took hold of his father.

Raphela sighed as she squinted toward the morning sun. Unraveling her leg from the twisted bed sheets, she turned and sat, stared at the pillows scattered on the floor, instead of the bed and considered laying her head back down on the one that remained on the bed.

Eventually she would have to leave the bed, so, she shoved the covers away and took another long look towards the window before bathing and breakfasting.

The servant girl sighed as she cleared another half-eaten meal from the table. "Poor Lady Raphela," she thought.

Raphela brushed against Fatell as they passed in the main hall.

"Raphela are you all right?'

Fatell grabbed her friend's arm and couldn't help but notice the usually shiny hair crowning Raphela's head seemed so dull and almost messy.

"I'm fine." She snapped and kept on walking.

Fatell rushed to catch up. "You don't look fine."

"Just leave me alone." Her tone would have carved stone.

Fatell's face revealed shock and hurt as Raphela shook off Fatell's light grasp and continued on to her chosen task of the day.

At dusk Raphela returned to the family quarters and poked at the food on her plate before sitting by the open window in the bedroom and staring at the stars.

Fatell and Mahtso strolled to a hilltop. Mahtso leaned against a wide oak tree and as he slid slowly to the ground he heard the light crackle of loose bark attach itself to his vest. Fatell laughed as he grabbed her and she landed in his lap. A few warm kisses and gentle strokes were all they needed. She lay back and they both gazed through the leaves to the stars.

"He acts like that too" Mahtso made circles with her hair.

Fatell turned to look at him, at first confused, then she leaned back into his chest and sighed.

Atan and Vanar camped in an open field. Vanar slept soundly.

Atan watched a moon shrouded in a veil of clouds and fought the loneliness inside him.

Travels continued. The carriage took a road parallel to the river.

The water entranced father and son. Atan studied the life waving beneath the surface and the life that poked above. Communities of long stems crawling with infinitesimal leaves swayed to the movement of the fish. The first time they stopped he knelt down and breathed in the unique scent of fish and fauna. He wondered at schools of scaly beings weaving in and out of the rocky divides. At one point he even speared one of the fish and they feasted on it for lunch (thought it needed quite a few side dishes to fill them up.)

Later in their journey they came upon men building a boat and Vanar demanded they stop, for he had watched the water flow. It's movement making slippery business for the creatures that tried to cross. He noted how constant and reliable the movement of this river. So when he saw the boat, he had to see how it worked.

Vanar dragged out his book on travel and with a maturity beyond his years discussed the design of the boat with the men. They listened, at first because he was heir apparent. But soon the burly men, sweat dried to their skin and shirts half open, sat around the boy and spoke of what was growing by the riverbank and how it began. Vanar had a vision of what was to be and these men would make it so.

Once the river veered from their path Atan took to staring out the window, encased in a quiet solitude and sadness. Vanar knew no reason for this and after a sunset and sunrise of silence, tapped his father's knee.

"Father, what's wrong?" Concerned and innocent eyes prodded Atan. He sighed, sometime Vanar would need to know.

"The next fief we will visit has been a problem in the past." It had been 2 years since Gellen's demise, the servants had done well. Barin proved to be an exceptional leader.

Mahtso had verified the work and tied up the loose ends. Mostly the children, which, understandably, no one had the stomach to do.

"What do you mean Father?"

Posa lay a tired head in Vanar's lap.

"The people that were in charge could not live by my rules." Atan stared out the window. The wind sneaking through small separations between door and carriage gently tossed a few hairs by his temple.

Bertram knew the tale and wondered if he should stop Vanar's questions now.

"Father?"

Atan now turned to Vanar, he spoke softly and with the wisdom of pain. "They betrayed my trust."

These words ran through Vanar like fire on a dry bed of leaves. Once he had "Betrayed his father's trust", the result was the only spanking his father ever gave him and a disappointed frown from both parents. Frowns and spanking left a deep impression, he never lied again.

He could not imagine anyone betraying a trust more than once, for his father did allow a second chance.

"Father, did they betray you more than once?"

"Yes"

Vanar leaned back into the seat, his hand stroked Posa's head and the puppy returned with soft kisses.

Vanar had heard tales of battle when he passed soldiers as they trained, but his parents preferred not to advertise those actions. Vanar knew violence and bloodshed were a strong part of the recent past. He felt ready for reality.

"What did they do?"

Thick obedient silence wove its fabric in the carriage, even the wind held its tongue.

How much to tell a boy of 9, even one who will rule one day.

"They abused their power and the people who worked for them. I gave the servants permission for and instruction on how to" Atan paused, "eliminate their masters." Atan's tongue barely breathed life into the word "eliminate" which added to its power.

Vanar swallowed hard and for the first time understood the "fear" of his father, "Duke Ishtba".

The last leg of the trip was done in silence.

Green and yellow flowers were laid in a pattern of winding circles on the gates of Barin's fief.

Gratitude greeted them at the door. Children with bright shiny faces carefully choreographed in a semicircle, kneeling and waiting, laden with gifts of fruit and flowers

Barin waved open his arm and bade them enter. "My lord, we are so pleased you've chosen to visit us.

The children rose, bowed and placed the gifts in the hands of all members of the Duke's party.

Thank yous were given and the children scurried away. Teenagers were close at hand to unburden the guests and take them to their rooms.

Most of the cold had left this place. Atan no longer felt choked by the walls.

Vanar felt a strange sense of excitement, relief and sadness all around him.

That evening Atan and Barin shared quiet conversation and wine,

Barin's eyes held the pain of victory and its rewards. "My lord, the freedom you have afforded us cannot be measured. We only hope to make this place even more fruitful than before."

"It appears that all is well." Atan leaned back into his chair and sipped the wine,

"Barin, do you sleep?" Atan's concern regarded Barin's state of mind. The concern was for the man, yet also the business. If Barin could not function, neither would this fief. The balance was still fragile, even with the many sided support of Duke Ishtba.

"Better every day sire. Better every day." Barin could see the faces of those he killed, even in his pain and hatred it was hard.

In the morning Vanar joined the children who doted on him beyond words.

One of the older children took Vanar on a tour.

Vanar's hand brushed against the walls, now carefully painted in rainbows of bright colors. The house was immaculate, even cleaner than the castle. Children bowed as he walked by, even adults nodded to him. After a while the attention was annoying, but he said nothing. The guide spoke endlessly, describing rooms and their uses. Most of the rooms were full of color, well placed plants, nothing was out of place.

As they came to the courtyard the guide slowed his pace.

His hand turned the knob and the door opened slowly, now the boy said nothing.

Vanar felt something. He looked down and saw the dirt, spotted with flakes of dried matter, dark against the loose soil.

His eyes were drawn to the center of the yard. From a thin pole hung a whip, above it a sign read:

Here hangs the whip

To tear the flesh of the servant

And the soul of the master

Beside it was a thick post, solemn and dark. Clinging to its sides were chains, rusty and spotted with stains and resting on top, a wooden sign, carved with precision.

"Behold the post, hard and unbending

Like the ground and its stones

Behold the chains, ever prisoners to the past

Remember the servants
Encased in the chains
And as their hands were bound
So are the souls of the masters
Bound to the ground
Never to touch the sky
Never to meet the nameless ones
Never to rest on a cloud
Bound to wander
Trapped in the torture they created"

The words were deep and difficult, but the hatred and fear chilled Vanar, yet the respect and pride in survival touched him as well. This was a strange place.

They stayed for two days and as they left the gates closed, Atan could only think of the place as a hurt animal, now healing, but not remembering how to live without the pain.

They rode to a clearing Atan had become comfortable with years before.

He walked to the woods alone, Vanar knew why, but didn't understand.

In the cool evening Vanar sat around the fire with the men. Posa stood guard by his young master and all watched for the return of the Duke, not staring, but an occasional turn of the head and stretching to stand.

Atan wandered the forest, first to remove himself from the fief, it was not evil, just painful.

Soon he found a tree and leaned against it as he stared at the stars. Something was missing in him. Every year it was a little worse. At first only the smell, and touch or the voice, but now....

By the time he returned to the camp the fire was a mere smolder and everyone slept. Posa lifted his head and quickly snuggled near Vanar. Atan lay down on the other side of Vanar and closed his eyes till dawn.

Mahtso took Raphela's arm as she walked down the stairs. She didn't notice as he guided her outside the castle until the sunlight struck her face. She squinted, her pale skin heated quickly in the bright sun.

"Is it because he's away?" Mahtso tried breaking through.

Raphela stared at him blankly.

"He'll be home in a week or so, you know that."

Raphela sighed. "You're very kind Mahtso."

Mahtso left her, pained at whatever she felt.

Raphela picked at a flower and its petals. The castle had been quiet these last few weeks. Fatell closed the school, as the children needed a break.

Family units were beginning to blossom and time was spent with children and mates.

Castle Cordan's library had been exhausted of its supply of books on healing so Raphela sent Aharon to Calcoran to see what he could gather.

Fatell and Mahtso were spending more and more time together,

Raphela had little to do except build on the hollow inside her, it was beyond loneliness, it was....

Atan's carriage pulled through the open gates of the next fief. As the rameks walked up the path, Vanar saw children and his eyes lit. He and Posa bolted from the carriage, Bertram only a few steps behind.

Giggling and yelling echoed around the nearby trees and a mass of small forms moved in one direction which Vanar easily followed.

Down a small hill covered in rich green grass, the children ran, ending the journey in a splash.

At the bottom of the hill lay a clear pond. Some dove in head first, others feet first, others, leery of the cold, tiptoed and tried to avoid the massive walls of water being thrown by playmates.

Vanar quickly removed his shirt and shoes and jumped into the fray. Posa barked, then turned his head and floppy ears in puzzlement and finally gave up and joined Vanar in the water.

No one noticed the newcomer until Posa, placed a friendly wet tongue on someone's hand. Of course he got the initial attention and then Vanar was acknowledged.

Children exchange names and often leave other details to quieter times when fun is less important. So Vanar's position was not mentioned.

Merej left the barn as Atan's carriage continued its journey to the main house.

Both arrived at the same time.

Merej wiped his forehead and hands then returned the cloth to his back pocket.

"My lord, its good to have you back."

Atan allowed himself a small smile and patted Merej on the back. "It is good to be here."

They went into the house and found Norana in the kitchen amidst an army of aromas and women.

The other women scattered as the Duke entered. Norana curtsied. "My lord"

Atan breathed in the assorted smells of breads and meats and gravies.

A little boy ran in and tugged at Norana's skirt.

"Mama. Valeria says I can't play anymore. And I want to play. I wasn't being bad. Tell Valeria I can play."

"Coty, why don't you sit here and help me, I've got your favorite candy."

Coty settled for the candy but grumbled as he sat.

"My lord, I'm sorry. Would you like some tea?"

"Yes, that would do well right now and perhaps one of your famous biscuits."

Norana blushed at the compliment and laid out tea and biscuits for Merej and Atan who fell into easy chatter.

Wet footed children pitter-pattered in and out all afternoon. At dusk as the fireflies began their dance and the blanket of the days aromas were carried away on an evening breeze the children returned home.

The workers children to their houses and Merej and Norana's to the main house with Vanar and Posa tagging along. Four wet bodies entered the kitchen door, clothes sticking like a second skin on well-tanned bodies with mud splattered feet and grinning faces.

Drops of water fell from hair and noses. As if to be sure the adults didn't miss out on the fun, Posa shook vigorously spraying everyone close by.

Norana stood with hands on hips and shook her head. "All of you, go to your rooms, dry off and change clothes and make sure Vanar has a towel and dry clothes as well."

Atan nodded his approval.

Posa pranced behind the children as if one of them.

Dinner was served in the dining room. Although there were three children plus Vanar, they were not the same ones that Atan had told stories to, many years before.

Lehcar was at Castle Cordan, studying with the healers and the second oldest was married and living at another fief.

Formerly the youngest, now the oldest at home, took charge of the children as older sisters do. The chatter bantered back and forth around the table amongst everyone. Vanar felt more at home than ever before. Valeria, the second youngest and a year younger than himself, was pretty, he chastised himself for this thought, for at this age, girls were the enemy, but she was pretty.

Atan's inspection the following day found the donags healthy, with a new breed coming along well.

While Atan took his time with the cattle, Merej helped Norana bring supplies to the house.

"The Duke seems preoccupied" Norana walked backwards lifting a load of vegetables while Merej lifted the other end.

"He's always distant."

"I don't know, every year it's more intense."

Merej turned to the barn as the vegetables were loaded into a bin by the kitchen door. "I suppose you're right."

Atan lost himself in the donags and rameks for just a while.

Vanar spent another day in the pond and even came to tolerate Coty.

They left early the next morning.

That day Raphela spent in the sun, warming body and soul, allowing the light to lift the pain inside.

By nightfall her hair shone and she crawled into bed for a good night's sleep.

Noon the next day the rameks beat their hooves up Cordan's pathway.

Vanar jumped from the carriage and hugged his mother briefly.

He panted with excitement. "Oh Mother, it was a wonderful trip. I got a present." At this moment Posa brushed up against Raphela and looked up for her approval. A pat on the head was sufficient and he and Vanar went off with tales of wonder.

Atan walked through the doorway. His grey eyes turned to meet her. Raphela stood, frozen.

Atan's palm brushed a tear from Raphela's cheek and hand in hand they climbed the stairs to their room.

Their chests heaved in pain as their clothes fell to the floor. But passion would wait. First, life pulsed through them and the castle itself, as if a river broke its dam.

Two long bodies, intertwined rested on the bench, fingers caressed hungry skin and lips brushed against lonely wisps of hair.

Atan felt his blood course through him again, he had not felt it for so long.

Raphela's skin tingled and she began to remember she was alive.

After a long time, past dusk, when the moons blocked the starlight they took to the bed.

There they danced. Tongues buried in warm wet mouths, hands pressing bodies together. Atan burst inside her so hard, it hurt them both, but the pain was an incredible joy. Her breasts lapped up every touch of tongue and squeeze of hand,

His neck reached up for her soft full lips sucking hard on his skin.

As the moons began their descent, the gods watched in envy, unable to taste or control the passion in that room.

Castle Cordan bloomed like a flower in the rain.

He slept with her hair wrapped around his hand and even the sun could not disturb their slumber.

When they did wake up and stared into each other's eyes, a million words raced through their minds. Hands caressed cheeks and a passionate kiss were sufficient to say all.

Aharon returned two weeks later with books and news.

Gilt-edged pages in leather-bound covers were stacked neatly at the end of the table.

Raphela sat beside Aharon. Mahtso and Atan occupied the other seats around the library table.

"Was Dahlek concerned with your request for the books?" Atan opened the meeting.

"My lord, he seemed anxious to be rid of them. He felt their presence and use could give people "unnecessary thoughts." As a matter of fact, he offered his entire library. I took what I could carry in the carriage and a cart the King readily offered."

"That's good. Are all the books on healing?" Mahtso's chain picked up its pace as he spoke.

"No, I found that Calcoran's strength of knowledge was in metalcraft and machinery. I chose many books relating to transportation." Aharon leaned forward as he spoke, excited about relating his tale.

"What else do you bring from Calcoran?"

All eyes focused on Aharon. "There is to be a new heir to Calcoran."

"Altira is with child?" Raphela's voice rose.

"Yes my lady."

"How is she feeling?"

"I don't really know my lady. I saw her for a moment. She looked quite pale, but I've heard she is generally that way." Aharon shrugged his shoulders.

Raphela nodded. "Did you offer your services?" Much as Raphela would have missed him, Aharon would have been very useful to Altira.

"Yes my lady, of course. But King Dahlek would not hear of it. I tried speaking to their healers but they insisted they needed no outside interference. They were almost secretive in the way they guarded her."

Mahtso and Atan turned their heads and stared at each other.

"Secretive? How do you mean? Do you think he's building an army?" Mahtso had the chill to his voice meant for interrogation, a tone he immediately regretted, even without the sharp glances from Atan and Raphela.

Aharon shrank back in his chair and quivered inside.

Raphela took up the silence. "Aharon, was there anything unusual?"

He considered all questions. His training had been in healing, not as a soldier, but the study of human nature covered everything. "I saw no building of anything my lord, yet there should have been."

"What do you mean?" Raphela leaned forward.

"My lady, when you carried Vanar there was celebration, excitement. At Calcoran there was relief, perhaps with the execution of the brothers."

"Execution! Then it's true, he eliminated all of them." Mahtso turned to Atan.

"A shame, he doesn't realize the treasure he's destroyed." Strong words for the man of few, it brought silence to the table.

"Continue Aharon." Atan waved his hand,

"All seemed relieved that the line could continue. And if it was unusually secretive, I believe they were hiding internal troubles, not troubles they could cause elsewhere."

Shoulders relaxed and backs leaned into the seats. Aharon had always been a good judge of character and situations and his evaluation fell into place with the other reports.

"Are these all the books?" Mahtso tried to be casual as his chain wrapped and unwrapped around the chair leg.

"No, the books for the men are in the training room library, the others are in the Healers Building, except for these few."

Aharon pulled the books close to him. "I thought these would be of special interest." He handed each of them one and noted one for Vanar. They were labeled as diaries, but they were written in an ancient tongue long forgotten.

Raphela smiled. "You bring us puzzles."

"My lady, it is what you enjoy."

Atan nodded.

Aharon and Raphela left to review their books. As they walked Aharon began. "My lady, there is something else."

Raphela stopped. "What?"

"The healers at Calcoran were not interested in the knowledge they had, but one very old man and one very young man whispered to me a message. Far to the east there is a land, brimming with knowledge of healing and potions." "Is it legend?" I asked. The old man took an amulet from his neck and placed it in my hand. "It is legend if this is," he said. I have not opened it, I thought we might try together." Aharon dangled the chain and its glass ball surrounding a pale purple liquid.

"Why didn't you say this before?" Her eyes followed the swinging ball.

"I don't know, the time wasn't right I suppose."

"Hmm."

They walked on to the healers building and put the amulet safely away, then attacked the new books.

Atan leafed through his gift and spent more than a few minutes looking for a familiar mark before returning to work.

Chapter 16

During the dwindling color of fall Raphela often stared at the makeshift walkways between the buildings. Each day she found them more disturbing, even the carefully woven covers that matched the fabric of the land, did not belong. She would sigh and return to the work at hand, knowing this concern would not be a priority for a long time.

As fall passed to winter Castle Cordan continued its tradition of intense learning and development. Atan often found his fingers traveling through the pages of the gilt-edged book. Vanar absorbed writings on transportation and roads and as always he was drawn to insects and their tunnels. He felt that a wealth of information and progress taunted him from their world, but refused to reveal itself.

Spring arrived at dusk on a cold grey day. The colorful storm battled for its place in the sky against thick black clouds. Two days later, when the storm was gone and the wind didn't even whisper, a guard, just leaving his post for dinner, noticed the snow fly up from the ground. Immediately, the Duke and his lady were notified and the new guard watched from the turret as two long-necked rameks emerged from the tree lined path. They struggled through the snow, pulling a large carriage similar to Ishtban's old models.

Guards were sent to greet or halt the carriage. Two drivers, blue with cold peered bravely out from snow-laden hats and attempted to sit straight. The Ishtban guards saw no threat and guided the carriage to the front door of the castle. The drivers were carefully carried in and brought to the warmth of a blazing fire.

Mahtso greeted the riders, and by now everyone knew their identity, as a tall thin man stumbled from the carriage, Mahtso looked inside and pushed the man away. The tall man struggled briefly and then let Mahtso climb in. Within moments Dahlek walked through the front door, skin ashen under wet blond hair.

Mahtso followed, Altira draped across his arms, cold, fragile and barely breathing. Her bloodstained gown told most of the tale.

"Raphela, I beseech you, save her, save my wife, anything you can do, anything." Dahlek pleaded.

A rolling bed had arrived and Altira was placed on it, Aharon and Raphela by her side.

"We'll do what we can." She nodded to Atan who took Dahlek to privacy where he could change clothes and warm himself with some hot tea.

They wrapped Altira in blankets and made quick work of the makeshift walkway to the healers building. She moaned as they walked. The room was bright and warm. With the greatest of care Raphela and Aharon moved Altira to a bed and removed her gown. Raphela fed the girl tea while Aharon cleaned her. Blood stained her legs down to her ankles and her belly, swollen with child, was also bloated with fluid. Altira breathed hard as Aharon spread her legs. Raphela wiped her forehead and held her hand.

Aharon rested his hand on her belly, moving it gently from side to side, hoping for a faint sign of life, a weak turn or kick, but all was still. As he looked in the dark crevice between her legs, he saw the infant and without further ado pulled the child out. Raphela gasped at the tiny, mangled, and lifeless form. It had obviously struggled for life and sadly failed. The damage to Altira was irreparable. Her blood loss was so extensive they knew nothing could help.

Avoiding any feelings of her own, Raphela sat with Altira and fed her herbal tea, to at least ease the pain. Dahlek was brought in and knelt by the bed, encompassing Altira's cold white hand in his own. "She looks better already." False hope he knew but he had to have it.

Aharon left to go to bed.

Raphela felt a chill inside her. "Spend these moments together." She slouched down in a soft chair right outside the door.

Dahlek relaxed in the bright fresh room. Everything sparkled and it smelled different, like fresh herbs. Altira stirred. Dahlek stroked her forehead. "Altira, I'm here."

306

Altira turned her head and smiled. "My king, I'm sorry for so much trouble."

Dahlek felt tears welling his eyes. "My love, it's my foolishness that caused this. But you'll be well soon, you'll see."

Most people grow up at one time or another, even when it seems to late, now was Altira's time. She stroked Dahlek's head as he knelt by the bed. "My King, my love, I think not, but I would ask this of you."

"Anything."

"I always wanted to see the life inside me, before it arrived to the rest of the world. Aharon told the Calcoran healers that the Ishtban healers dream of the same thing, to see the workings of a person." Altira took a few breaths and continued, in crackled tones and whispers, "If I cannot give Calcoran an heir, at least let my death mean something. Give me to Raphela and her healers. Let them learn. Maybe your next wife will not suffer."

"I want no other wife and it will be a long time before the healers will be learning from you," he said hoarsely.

"As you wish my lord. For now, hold me."

Dahlek climbed onto the bed and held her in his arms. Both fell into a deep slumber. Dahlek awoke to Altira's cold limp body. "Altira," he whispered and caressed her face. "Altira!" his voice grew as panic set in. He shook her, to no avail. Raphela awoke to the shouting and sent a messenger to get Atan.

Dahlek sat on the bed, Altira laying in his arms like a rag doll. His body swayed back and forth to no rhythm except his anguish. "Do something, fix her!" he demanded.

Raphela came to the bed and Dahlek lay the girl down on a pillow and stood aside. No breath came from Altira's lips and the blood no longer pumped inside her, this much Raphela knew. Death had won.

"Dahlek, there is nothing that can be done. It's too late."

He turned on Raphela. "No, no you just won't try, you can fix her." His fingers wrapped tightly around Raphela's arms and he began to shake her.

At this point Atan walked through the doorway and used every ounce of self-control he had not to destroy Dahlek. Very firmly he removed the man's hands from Raphela. "This will not bring back your wife."

Dahlek's head lowered in shame. "May I say good-bye?"

Raphela and Atan left the room. "Are you all right?" Atan rubbed her arms. She nodded.

Dahlek laid his head on Altira's chest and wept. "I loved you so." His tears stained her gown, and by dawn he had none left. His knees ached as he rose from the floor. He spent the day in the room provided for him, sending away servants and ignoring the food left by the door. After dinner he met with Atan. One torch leaned against the wall, casting an odd shadow of the grieving man.

"Atan, I have destroyed everything I touched and everything I love." Calm blue eyes, totally at peace matched the voice. Atan found it disturbing.

"Before any more damage is done, I must leave."

"Where are you going?"

"That's not important." Dahlek pushed a stack of woodsheets towards Atan. "But, my people and my land cannot be left to wither and die without a leader either. Treat them well Duke Ishtba."

Atan looked at the work before him. Each sheet had a seal and they all spelled out very clearly that Duke Atan Ishtba was to be the new ruler of Calcoran. The people should cooperate and put their trust in him as the King had already done so. The lands belonged to Duke Atan Ishtba unless he chose otherwise. Dahlek felt the grey eyes rest on him and almost met their gaze. "Are you sure Dahlek. This is very serious."

"Yes."

"As you wish. But should you change your mind, I will return it to you."

Deep creases made a bittersweet smile on Dahlek's young face. "I suppose that is why I chose you, always honorable." He sighed. "I have sent for Jivad, he works well with you."

With that Dahlek left and Atan fingered the pages. Always knowing it would come to this in one fashion or another, he felt uncomfortable with this fashion.

In the morning guards lowered Dahlek's limp, broken body from a beam in the ceiling. Altira was placed in the snow, a box built around her. There she would stay until the ceremonies were done. Atan considered arguing the point but knew he would lose. He just pretended it didn't exist. Jivad and his family arrived later that day.

Cordan's great hallway was warm after the long ride and all four family members soaked in the strength of this place as Raphela and Atan greeted them. "My lord, King Dahlek has asked us to join him here." Jivad looked around for the King.

Atan placed a hand on Jivad's shoulder. "We need to talk. Raphela will join us."

Sonja looked at Raphela who said, "Vanar, take Falor and Geho to the playroom. I'm sure you boys will get along quite well."

"Yes Mother." Vanar knew what had happened, but it meant little to him. Falor was about his age so having a new playmate was an advantage for him.

Once settled in a cozy room with just chairs and a fireplace Atan explained the events of the last two days. Sonja wept quietly and held Jivad's hand.

"Has there been a funeral yet?" Jivad believed in getting the ceremonies out of the way so that life could proceed.

"No. I wanted your feelings on the matter. Should it be done here or in Calcoran." Atan spoke with the utmost respect.

Jivad and Sonja looked to each other for silent advice. They felt like children thrust into a grown-up world. Suddenly, they were dealing with Duke Ishtba and being held responsible for the remains of a King. Jivad took a deep breath. "My lord, I must be honest. King Dahlek, while not despised, was not revered either. To have the matter settled and for life to go on would probably be best. Atan nodded. That night a quiet ceremony shared the darkness. A small fire blazed in the night sky. A lock of Altira's hair and her clothes were placed on Dahlek's chest. White and orange flames did a sad dance on the mound that lasted only brief moments.

Each couple spent the next day alone until dinnertime when a large table was set for all seven people. Vanar and Falor bounded in together, Geho, Falor's younger brother shuffling in behind. The boys sat together, watching the full platters of meat and vegetables and breads take places on the table. Mothers doled out portions to the children, while fathers helped themselves. Geho exploded with an "ouch" and all adults turned their eyes to him. "He hit me," he said pointing to Falor, whose brown eyes complained as much as his voice as his thick curly hair bounced as he spoke.

"He touched my plate."

"No I didn't"

"Yes you did."

Raphela stifled a grin, remembering similar experiences as a child. Atan was lost. Sonja and Jivad shook their heads. "Boys, we are guests, behave yourselves. " Sonja's firm tone and Jivad's equal stare temporarily settled matters.

Falor changed the topic. "Mother, are we spending another night?" Vanar and Falor shifted in their chairs and held their breaths for an answer.

"Yes. Why?"

Now Vanar spoke up. "Could Falor and I set up a spare bedroom and spend the night together. Please Mother."

All parents shared a glance before Raphela answered. "Under two conditions."

"Yes Mother?"

"One, no damage to anything, and two, you must be asleep before the second moon rise."

"Yes Mother, we promise. Thank you." The boys shook hands under the table.

"Me too?" Geho piped up.

"No, you're too young." Falor said quickly. Sonja had to agree, much to her younger son's disappointment.

"May we leave the table?" Vanar pushed away his plate.

"You've barely eaten your dinner," Atan said.

"Please Father, we're not hungry now."

"Go ahead."

All three boys raced from the table. Atan stared. "I'm sure they're still hungry." Being an only child, this phenomenon was new to him.

Raphela patted his hand. "It's all right, we'll have a snack prepared for later."

Atan and Jivad shrugged their shoulders as fathers do. Adult conversation continued. "How was your trip?" Raphela nibbled at a bowl of leafy greens.

"Much easier than expected. Your roads have made a big difference." Sonja's response brought a little uplift to Atan's serious lips.

"This is an excellent meal, Lady Raphela. Cordan's cooks never cease to amaze me." Jivad poured another glass of wine for himself and one for Atan. "By the way, what of Altira?"

Raphela sighed before answering. Atan occupied himself with wine and a piece of meat. "She is being preserved." No one pursued the topic.

"My lord, who will be going to Calcoran?" Jivad the ambassador, revealed the confidence of a leader. Atan stared at him. Although Jivad did not return the look, he did not shrink into the chair either.

"Jivad, in these informal surroundings you and Sonja do not need to use titles, my lord and sire will not be necessary." Under the table Raphela rubbed Atan's leg in support of his statement.

"Thank you."

"Now, to answer your question. I think it best that the four of us at this table go to Calcoran."

"I see," Jivad's voice skimmed disappointment.

A servant cleared the table and the foursome adjourned to a comfortable sitting room. "Jivad, I must assess the situation before I leave it in your hands. Each of us has strengths, they must all be used in evaluation of the condition of Calcoran. The people will trust you, but they need to know that Ishtba will support them and you.

Jivad blushed in embarrassment. Atan looked at Raphela and she understood, taking Sonja out of the room. "Jivad, Dahlek and I have thrust this upon you. Your actions speak that you want this responsibility, at least that is what I see. If this is not so, tell me now."

"To govern Calcoran, while under your wing, has been but a dream until today. Except for my family, there is nothing more that I could want."

"Good." Atan offered his hand and they shook as leaders do. A silent bond that began years before was now sealed. Jivad realized he had just become part of a very small circle and felt the power of it race through him yet he brushed against something not meant for him and to strong for his imagination

Raphela felt the seal and placed a strong arm around Sonja's shoulder. "Things are as they should be." Sonja didn't understand but felt the meaning.

That night Sonja and Jivad whispered of the strange events in their lives.

Atan stared at the ceiling, Raphela twisted and turned, kicking the covers and struggling for sleep while the castle's inhabitants rustled in bed with mysterious aches and pains.

Finally, a little after midnight Atan put on his robe and stood at the end of the bed. "Well, will you join me for tea or not?"

Raphela leaned on her elbows "Why not, obviously this bed doesn't want us here."

After checking on the boys, and covering them as they slept on the floor, they sat in the family room and stared at the fire.

"She was too young." Raphela broke the awkward silence, her back straight and stiff as she sat on the soft couch.

Atan had been leaning back, eyes closed. "They both were."

Raphela's nostrils flared. "It was his fault, his stupid pride." Her teacup clattered as it hit the table.

Atan raised his eyebrows and sat up. "Indeed?"

"Yes," Raphela began to pace. "He waited so long, why, why so long?" Large tears began to well in her eyes, blurring the light of the fire. "Aharon could have stayed, but Dahlek would have none of Ishtba's help." Her arm waved as she sobbed.

"Could Aharon have saved her?"

"I don't know, maybe." Raphela rubbed her eyes, her heart beat hard in her chest. Atan had hit the problem. She sat on the couch, rested her head in her hands and cried. Once her tears slowed to a drizzled, she wiped her nose and moved closer to Atan. He brushed a tear from her cheek and stroked her hair as

312

she put her head in his lap. After a while she regained composure and got up to stoke the fire and pour fresh tea.

Atan turned a vacant stare to the flames. "It shouldn't have happened this way." He turned to Raphela. "I would have preferred killing him myself than to see the self destruction of an entire line. It's wrong. Brother should not turn against brother. They were not evil people, lost and confused, but not evil. He should have abdicated long ago. Yes, that would have been right, or at least battled his brothers." Atan shook his fist at the ceiling, while his voice stretched to reach the sky. "But not executed them!" Atan realized he had been shouting and reverted to a whisper. "Eventually, it would have fallen to me, but not like this."

Even to Raphela he could not openly admit what he knew he felt. Was it his doing? Dahlek's obsessive fear of Ishtba? Did it drive him to this? Was it because he knew Atan would take control, without ever attacking? Was it that kind of despair, the defeat existed before the battle. Was he Atan, responsible for the death of the royal Calcoran line, to whom he swore his loyalty? Did he break his oath, unwittingly or not?

Raphela cringed at his pain. Her fingers caressed his hands as she knelt before him. "Atan."

He ignored her.

"Atan, you were true to everyone, you could be no other way."

He searched her eyes for deception, grabbed her arms and pulled her close. Raphela embraced his questions and pain. Atan's hands began to bruise her arms, she didn't feel it.

Castle Cordan rocked in agony until he knew she believed what she said and he could believe it too.

Atan lay on top of her, pressing her down into the soft pillows of the couch. Clothes were on but lips and tongues were locked in passionate fury of healing. Their heavy breaths eased the aches and pains of all that rested. Raphela's tears melted away the final ragged edges of his doubt and his power closed the wound of her helplessness.

Sleep was brief but solid, he woke with her hair wrapped around his hand.

It was decided that the children would remain at Castle Cordan while both couples went to Calcoran. They took separate carriages and began the journey after breakfast.

Sonja twisted the rings on her hand and stared down at the shimmering blue cloth of her gown. Jivad, was at first occupied with writing new plans, but then she felt a finger gently lift her chin.

"Is the answer to all the world's problems in your gown?"

"Just the questions." Jivad sat back and listened, the delicate woman he called his wife meant a great deal more than plans. She attempted a smile. "I miss the boys already."

"Enjoy the peace while you can."

"I know." She paused. "Jivad" her green eyes turned to him, "I'm afraid."

"Of what?"

"I'm not Raphela."

"For that, I'm grateful," he smiled.

Sonja's quizzical expression gave him cause to explain. "She's a beautiful woman, but so are you and she is more than I could ever handle."

"I can't do what she does."

"And I can't do what the Duke does. We are not expected to rule, just govern by the standards they set. Our responsibilities will be shared with many and help will always be available."

"You're right. I just never imagined Calcoran as my home and me as its mistress. It's a bit overwhelming."

In the other carriage Raphela and Atan drew separate and then combined plans. Raphela would assess the educational and health systems as well as basic accounting procedures. Atan's first task was to discover just where every fief was located, what they produced, and then how to do it better.

He looked at her as she carefully categorized each job, with the ease of a seasoned ruler.

"What are you looking at?" Raphela felt the stare.

"I remember many years ago, when you first entered Calcoran Castle and how you felt."

Raphela flushed. She had been so unsure. Atan had called her a queen and the word struck them at the same moment.

314

"Raphela" His voice had no lilt.

"Yes?"

"Do you wish to be queen?"

"Can I not pose the same question to you. Do you wish to be king?"

"We could be."

Both laughed.

"I think not, too many people bow and grovel now." Atan was light.

"True."

About now Calcoran's mountains glistened at them and soon they were at the front door.

Jivad knocked and waited. Spring's chill air made Sonja's teeth chatter and Raphela's fingers were stiff, even inside the fur muff.

It took some time for the door of the castle to open. When it did, a tiny, white-haired man peeped through the crack and quickly ushered them in when he saw Jivad. "Jivad, my apologies for the wait, the King and Queen are not here, we've had few instructions."

"I understand Monty. If you would be so kind as to arrange rooms for us and at dusk gather all the servants in the great hall."

"As you wish."

Monty signaled to a few boys standing by and gave a distrustful look over his shoulder to the Duke. Atan and Raphela took no offense, they understood. Once warmed and settled they met with the servants. No one sat on the throne. Atan and Raphela were dressed in Ishtban colors, formal but not military.

Jivad looked around the room, many wrinkled tired faces, a few young ones. They all looked to him. "My friends, King Dahlek and Queen Altira left Calcoran to seek help. The queen's condition was critical and Ishtban offered the most hope. Queen Altira survived the journey, but her body was beyond repair. Ishtban healers did what they could." Sobs sprinkled the crowd. Jivad took a deep breath. "We mourn the death of our queen. But there is heavier news." Heads turned and ears lifted. "King's Dahlek's love for his wife was boundless. To live without her was not life in his mind. He and his queen rest with the gods."

The silent crowd did not move or change. Jivad allowed the news to sink in. A voice piped up. "What of the baby?"

"It did not live long enough to reach Ishtban land."

A thick, tall man with a rough voice stood and pointed an accusing finger at Atan. "Is that why he is here?"

Jivad turned to Atan, who answered. "Yes."

Mumblings through the crowd, talk of assassination, nothing that Atan did not expect.

"Before I say anything of my own, I would ask who among you can read?"

Four men stood, turning to see if they were alone.

"Come forward."

Cautiously the men approached. Atan produced four scrolls. The man who pointed at Atan was given the first. Atan had him face the crowd. "King Dahlek requested these scrolls be given and read at this time. You may read out loud."

The man trembled and swallowed hard, but he opened the scroll and looked for Dahlek's personal mark, it was there. So he began:

"Loyal subjects and servants, you now know of my death. Do not blame Duke Ishtba. His honor is more than I am worthy of having. I have done a great disservice to you and all of Calcoran. I cannot change the past, but the future is yet to be. Follow the Duke, he will guide you to the greatness I never could. Farewell."

Atan looked out upon a mass of bowed heads, blond hair and grey created a blanket in the room. Red eyes and wet cheeks looked back at him. He sighed, it was sad. "I will do for Calcoran as I do for Ishtba. Jivad will be regent. You will turn to him with your questions. Lady Raphela and I will stay until Calcoran is ready for us to leave."

Atan wanted no enemies and he could see these people wanted a leader.

They spent few weeks, set up the systems and left Calcoran in the competent hands of Jivad and Sonja. The great hall was still shrouded in white when the door closed behind them and the throne, in a white veil, would never to used again.

316

During the parents absence Falor and Vanar sealed a strong friendship. Posa, now a large beastie, accepted the knot and protected both with a ferociousness befitting his position.

"That animal will kill someone if you're not careful Vanar." Falor rubbed Posa's belly.

"Maybe, but then if I want to explore let's say, the cave, my parents don't need to send Bertram" Vanar's eyes lit with boyish mischief.

"I see your plan."

Both boys lay on their backs and stared at the ceiling, no words passed for a while and then Falor sat up and wrapped his arms around his knees. "Wouldn't it be great if I could spend the summer?" He said it quietly but his brown eyes sparkled.

Vanar shot up. "What a good idea. Then we could explore and have some real fun."

Falor fell into the excitement for a moment and then sobered. "My parents will want me at the new castle. Maybe you could visit?"

"If my parents let me," Vanar sighed. Being heir apparent often seemed disadvantageous.

"Well, it's worth a try." Falor shrugged his shoulders. "Maybe by winter I can stay."

"Maybe"

By the time Raphela and Atan returned the boys had laid plans upon plans which they thrust upon Duke and Lady almost immediately. Both agreed to Falor spending the winter if Sonja and Jivad agreed as well.

Chapter 17

Falor did spend the winter with Vanar, in fact, the next several winters.

The boys worked in their "office," a spare bedroom they had transformed. The bed, covered with a well-wrinkled spread, rested against a bare wall to serve as a couch. Two desks sat side by side, surrounded by bookcases and faced 'the board'. 'The board,' a wooden plaque as long as Falor was tall and almost as wide. It rested against the wall by the door and listed all their plans, past, present and future.

Vanar looked up at it before returning to his homework.

"If you don't stop watching the board we'll never get done and Fatell will hang both of us," Falor complained.

"I know, but there's so much more to do." Vanar pushed his scribe hard, determined to finish the work correctly, but quickly. Falor closed his book and tossed a bone to Posa. Vanar put his work away. "There, it's done, now let's do some real work."

Vanar pulled out a long wide woodsheet and laid it on the floor. Posa lay down at the other end of the room having been scolded enough for approaching. The boys lay on the floor and studied their design. It was labeled "The Marketplace." Vanar had discovered the word and its infinite possibilities in one of the ancient books. Skillfully drawn lines created the image of a many sided building sporting innumerable entrances and sitting as the hub of many long roads.

Vanar picked up a scribe and pointed to the roads. "These should do well."

"I agree. Have you decided on a location?" Falor filled in a shadow to complete one road.

"It has to be centrally placed. Equidistant from all fiefs, as much as possible."

"Good idea. Do you think it's big enough?"

They smoothed out the sheet and checked their measurements. "It's twice the size of Cordan's and Calcoran's great halls combined. I hope it's big enough."

"Have you told your father yet?"

"No, but I'm going to soon. We're almost done." Vanar stood up and stared at the plans. Every road was calculated for direction and connection with existing routes. Every interior room was given a size and place. They had written a small book on their plan and its operation.

"Will we keep it open all year?" Falor, though a year younger had a unique way of prodding Vanar.

"I wish we could, but no one will travel in the snow." Vanar turned his head and looked at his glass case of insects. He watched them tunnel through the dirt and as he did he realized they did very little on the surface. Why, he didn't know. Perhaps predators or a sensitivity to the weather?

His long hand reached for the scribe and he turned to "The Board". The word "tunnels," appeared in large dark letters.

"Tunnels?" Falor asked.

"Yes, just like these insects. If we can figure out how to build tunnels, then the snow won't be a problem."

Falor stared at the word. "I suppose that's our next project?"

Vanar grinned.

"I just remembered something." Falor's usually studious mood lightened. "Aren't the men preparing for the games?"

"Yes, let's go."

They put away the plans and threw a bone to Posa so that he wouldn't follow them out the door. Closing the door quietly before he got there, they first tiptoed and then raced down the stairs.

The zorel sniffed under the door, whimpered for a moment and then resigned himself to a nap.

As always, Vanar reached the bottom first, his long legs a distinct advantage. Falor's short chubby calves and generous middle were no match for the Ishtban height.

"Wait for me," Falor panted and Vanar, mildly out of breath, obliged. Both entered the training grounds at the same time. Falor uncovered the boxes they had put aside to stand on and they looked over the tall wooden fence.

On the other side of the fence two men covered in thick leather faced each other in a circle, wielding swords. An arm thrust forward and missed its mark while the opponent jumped and landed a point on a shoulder. No blood was spilled during this practice. The swords had protective covers. Vanar and Falor's attentions then turned to the men in the center. Falor was fascinated with the intricate movements of the wrestlers on the mats. Both games ended shortly after the boys arrived.

"Now comes the real fun." Vanar peered over the fence, anxiously awaiting the next segment of practice. A door creaked open and the powerful odor of the beast entered first. Falor shrunk back, but Vanar was undaunted.

"Doesn't that smell bother you?" Falor waved his hand around his nose.

"No." Vanar barely heard the question.

From the side echoed a whinny and a ramek pranced forward with another right behind.

Vanar's heart pumped faster and beads of sweat formed on his forehead. The rameks passed him. He could almost touch them, their long muscular necks, topped with a thick mane, hooves sharp enough to crush and strong enough to break a man. Astride each ramek was a soldier relying on the beast's sturdy thick back to carry him onward.

These particular rameks were different than most. They maintained the same coloring, but had been bred for tameness and controllability and were fed a special diet to enhance those qualities.

Diet and breeding had their effect, but the beast cannot change, and the desire for freedom and strength to work for it, was dampened, not destroyed. The most practiced riders had forearms sturdier than mountain rock. As they rode, only one arm was available to control the animal, the other carried a lance, for the mock battle.

Dirt flew around the ankles of the rameks and their odor permeated the grounds. As the riders dug their heels into the rameks sides and started them charging, Falor's eyes darted back and forth in anticipation of a violent clash or the relief of a near miss. Vanar's body moved in harmony with the beasts.

That night Vanar lay in bed and in his mind rode the beasts across the fields, feeling them as a part of him. More than

321

anything he wanted that, but that, that joy was forbidden. Forbidden temptation is the most alluring of all forbidden things.

Vanar rose with the sun and crept out to the stables, carefully closing the creaking door behind him. Hooves shifted and manes shook as Vanar got closer to the beasts. Sweat formed on his palms, he saw and heard only the long-necked animals, anxious in their stalls. Each stall was a solidly constructed four sided box, each side reaching the average man's chest, which left enough room for the ramek to stretch out its neck and move back and forth.

Vanar walked patiently, studying each one, absorbing their scent. A young brown ramek stretched out its neck and Vanar approached. They studied each other for a moment and Vanar's hand slowly raised to rub its neck. The ramek shifted nervously and its nostrils flared. As Vanar's hand came close to its head, the beast's mouth opened. Vanar was oblivious and was suddenly jerked back and dragged away from the animal.

Shaken out of his entrancement he looked up to see his father's fiery eyes.

"What are you doing Vanar?" Atan spit out the words and did not release the strong grip on his son's arm.

"I wanted to touch them. I want to ride one." Vanar was blunt.

"I've told you before, when you are old enough, you will." Atan's tone only increased in annoyance.

"I'm old enough now." Vanar tried to pull his hand from his father's grip. "I want to feel it beneath me. I've watched, I know how." Finally free, he headed toward the ramek again, whom stood back on his hind legs and whinnied. Vanar still approached.

Atan saw only the danger and grabbed his son. Vanar attempted freedom in vain. Atan pulled him to a nearby stool, bent Vanar over it, picked up a riding crop and proceeded to deliver a short but impressive punishment to the boy's bottom. After the last stroke he threw the crop to the ground and Vanar stood straight.

"That is what riding a ramek feels like, I'm sure you can wait..."

Vanar didn't hear a word, he stared in disbelief at what Atan had done and ran back to his room and locked the door.

Atan stood by the stool, equally shocked at Vanar's reaction. He replaced the crop to its hook and slowly returned to the castle. Neither spoke of the incident that day, but to Raphela their silence clanged as loud as the tower bell.

The sting of Atan's punishment subsided long before dark and the soreness was a minor problem to Vanar, but it did remind him of what happened. Being disciplined didn't disturb him as much as not really knowing why. He still didn't understand the danger. On this day his father was a blind unreasonable brute and he hated him.

Atan rolled over in bed and faced the window. Raphela lay on her back.

"Atan?"

"Yes"

"What's wrong?"

"Nothing." He did not yield easily as she pulled him towards her. Exploring the day's pain did not interest him, avoiding it seemed better. She took his arm and put it around her waist. "Raphela, I don't" He rolled onto his back and stared at the ceiling.

She leaned on her arm, hair falling towards the pillow and she studied the slivers of gray in his hair and the minute crease that enhanced the power of his face. "You can't hide from me," she said softly.

Atan closed his eyes and sunk back into the pillow. She was right. "Vanar and I had a problem today."

"That much I surmised on my own."

Atan looked into his wife's eyes, saw the open door and explained the morning's incident.

"I guess Vanar is very angry with you right now."

"Yes"

Their pain seared through her like a sword. "Atan"

"What?"

"How old were you when you first mounted a ramek?"

"Thirteen."

"Oh." Atan shifted uncomfortably. "And what happened?"

He remembered well and began to blush as the story took blossom in his mind. He had mounted one of the rameks as it stood in its stall. It threw him immediately and only his quick youthful reaction saved him from being trampled. His father did not ride, but the stablemaster had seen the attempt and reported it to Ulfan. Ulfan, no more given to beating his son than Atan, expressed his concern in much the same way. Before he landed the first stroke of the cane he said "fear is valuable, even to you." The first stroke began with the last word. The pain reinforced the words. He was angry for only a few minutes and knew his father was right and later thanked him. Atan squeezed his eyes shut and realized he never gave Vanar the words. Raphela never heard the story, but knew father and son would heal the wound. They did.

Winter petered out and spring melted the snow. Raphela's energy turned to final preparation of Vanar's 12th birthday party, planned for the 35th day of spring. It was more extensive than the wedding, twice as many people would fill the castle and she wanted it perfect, for everyone. By the time the 33rd day of spring raised its head Raphela was so embroiled in the party, little else held her attention. She skipped dinner, for the third time in a week. Atan hunted her down. She was reminding the cooks one more time of the necessity of care in the food preparation.

Atan stood at the doorway behind her. The cooks heads lowered just a bit, forcing Raphela to turn around. She dismissed the cooks. "What is it Atan?" Hurried annoyance ruled her tone.

Atan picked her up, put her over his shoulder, and marched out the front door of the castle. Once on the grass he put her down. "I don't like your tone my lady."

"I don't have time for games Atan."

He took her arm and forced her to walk to the field and the trees. As she felt the chill fresh air tingle her skin, the sense of hurry began to fade. When they got to the trees Atan held her arms tightly in his fingers. "Such disobedience should be rewarded with strong discipline." He did his best to hide the lilt in his voice.

Raphela pushed away his hands and wrapped hers around his waist, pressing her breasts to him, teasing him. "My lord, spank me if you must, but why not have your way with me first."

Lips melded in the passion unique to the Ishtban rulers and take her he did. Neither felt a stone or pebble as they rolled on the lush grass. As she stood to dress he pulled her close, engaged in a last kiss and landed a firm slap on her bottom. "Consider yourself spanked."

Raphela laughed and pressed him against a tree. She could feel him between her legs and he rose even farther as she nibbled on his neck. "I don't believe we've had enough." They played until the moons rose, the cold no competition for their warmth. Sleep was peaceful and when the guests arrived the next day, both were in proper spirits.

Vanar heard the noise downstairs as he dressed. Falor was already with his family. Vanar buttoned his vest, the brown leather fit well on his trim form and would not make him stand out in the crowd. Today was not for being the center of attention, it was for learning. Leather boots slid over his heels and formed closely around his feet. He felt different today. One last moment to put everything in place and as he did at his heels and toes danced the newly sprouted seeds of loneliness, nipping at him as he walked. He shooed the feelings away, in his heart he knew there would be time as the seedlings grew, for all the people on Raalek could not stop their growth in Castle Cordan.

A path opened between the guards and Bertram escorted Vanar downstairs.

In the kitchen Fatell directed servants and service people from town. It was organized yet hectic, but she enjoyed the harmony of many voices. She turned and saw a frail young man leaning in the doorway. "Kind lady, could you spare some food or drink. I will gladly work to repay your kindness."

Well spoken and clear, the words were gentle, yet demanded attention.

Fatell brought him food and drink. His clothes were worn but not yet frayed and his oval green eyes betrayed an intelligence uncommon to beggars. As he ate, first tenaciously and then ravenously, Fatell noticed his arm.

325

He saw her stare and blushed. "Yes, my lady, it is deformed, almost since birth."

Fatell turned away, embarrassed. "I am Fatell, the Lady, is elsewhere. What is your name and what brings you here?"

Fatell sat across the table from him and devoted her attention.

"Mowatt and I am from the far western side of Ishtban. My tale is a simple one. I was born of kind people not willing to destroy a deformed infant. My father was a carpenter, a good solid man, who worked hard to provide for my mother and myself."

As he spoke people began to gather around him, his deep melodious voice enchanting.

"When he died two years ago I tried to do his work, but even with two good hands I would not have made a good carpenter. So I left my mother with her sister and traveled the roads, earning my keep doing small jobs for those whom would tolerate me. I heard that Castle Cordan was to celebrate the birthday of the heir to all of Ishtba. I thought I might find work for a while. I can't do much, but will try anything you ask. My will is strong, at least that is what my parents always told me."

Everyone stood around him, hanging on every word. Fatell saw the man's true talent. "Mowatt, you have created quite an audience with your simple tale."

Mowatt looked at the faces and smiled. "I must admit, many times I have earned my way by telling a tale or two."

"Then you shall entertain the guests at this party. Get some rest. We'll get you some clean clothes and be prepared to speak a great deal tomorrow."

"Thank you, thank you so much. I only hoped for this, Thank you."

Fatell motioned for a young boy who took Mowatt to a room with an empty bed and provided him with clean clothes. Mowatt rested peacefully and prepared his mind for tomorrow.

Vanar, Raphela and Atan had a private luncheon with a few special guests. Raphela's sisters and their families had accepted the invitation to the party. Vanar, anxious to know the few relatives he had, insisted on dining with them at lunch and dinner this day.

Lunch began awkwardly. Vanar and Atan felt like the outsiders and Atan's presence overwhelmed everyone, at first. Yet, as the children began to stir and the wine flowed, chatter started and by luncheon's end the informality of family was almost established.

All day Vanar studied the people and couldn't help but notice the open affection between so many. His parents never touched anyone except him and each other and never in public. But he knew that their passion was beyond anyone else's comprehension, even his own. He put the observance away in his personal mental file.

The morning began with tables of food lined in two rows in the great hall. Sweet smelling juicy fruits and warm breads filled platter after platter. Round trays of smoked meats and even some fish between the bread and fruit completed the array.

Guests lined up, loaded their plates and shared conversation until the day's activities began. Before lunch, adults and older children were escorted to the "Games". Younger children sat on pillows and listened to the cheery tales woven by Mowatt.

In the back courtyard the grounds had been graded at an incline so that rows of chairs could be set up and all could watch the spectacles.

After the wrestling match came the sword fights. This time blades were uncovered and gleamed in the sun and as they met the noise rang through everyone. Guests watched in awe at the well practiced game that seemed so real. Finally one man lost and fell to the ground. Some onlookers cheered the winner, both contestants stood and bowed bringing a wild round of applause.

Mahtso then entered the arena and bade the audience be silent, his chain swinging rhythmically at his side. "Ladies and gentleman, our next event, requires your cooperation and silence," he paused, "for your own safety" he added with a menacing touch.

In the background a drum beat slowly. The crowd heard the hoof beats and saw two rameks enter the ring. Tall and powerful, they whinnied at the crowd. Women shrank back, young boys leaned forward.

The beasts faced each other from opposite sides of the ring, riders holding tightly on the reins of the anxious animals while keeping the long sharp lances pointed towards the sky. Clothed in leather and armor, despite the cool spring air, the sun warmed the men and sweat formed on their foreheads under the shiny helmets. Gloves protected hands and fingers.

The drum beats got louder and faster, the rameks stirred and pulled. At the last boom of the drum, the lances were lowered. Manes flew back and dirt swirled as the rameks charged at each other. Each lance pointed at the opponent's heart. No one noticed the intense odor anymore.   The rameks passed each other by a hair and the lances just touched, both men still astride their mounts.

Again and again they attacked, each time the lances coming a little closer at the meet, each time the beasts a little faster and harder to control. People gripped chairs and hands. Atan, Raphela and Vanar swayed with the pace. Mahtso watched with pride at the culmination of his work. Suddenly a lance struck and a man fell. Quickly he was pulled away and the ramek captured. But the winner turned in circles, lance raised high in victory. The audience rose to its feet as both men took bows amidst the raucous cheers.

By now lunch was ready to be served. Silver trays moved gracefully around the room. Guided by well trained staff, proud to be a part of Ishtba. Raphela and Atan sat in their royal chairs, dressed in flowing black neatly trimmed in green and gold. Vanar, wandering about the room, was similarly attired.

The shutters were opened and spring's cool breezed wrapped itself around the room. Children, despite best attempts at good behavior, could be seen chasing and dashing in good- spirited fun, their laughter lacing the room like spice through a warm breakfast bread.

After a while, fewer fingers reached for the delectable treats on the silver trays and cups of tea and water remained full. The trays slowly disappeared. Three men wove their way through the room, each playing a gently haunting tune, drawing everyone to the front of the room by Raphela and Atan. Most of the people stood, but chairs were scattered for those who couldn't. The breeze rustled the women's gowns and that was the only sound heard. Vanar stood between his parents. Atan's long-fingered hand rested on one shoulder and Raphela's on the other.

"Today my son takes a step towards manhood." Atan's deep voice blanketed the audience. "There is not a day that has passed that Vanar has not made his parents proud and I know it will never stop."

Vanar looked at the sea of faces in awe of his father. He knew it was time to speak. "I am honored that you chose to celebrate this important day with me. I can only hope to earn the respect my parents have earned from you over the years."

The hush was deafening. Raphela's eyes burned with tears. The crowd stared at the father and son whose unrehearsed words were too deep to be treated as speeches. Suddenly someone began to clap and the rest of the audience joined in. Once that settled, Jivad slipped to the front of the crowd.

"Lord, Lady and young lord Ishtba, many of us wish to share our joy at being here by presenting a token of thanks."

Atan nodded as he and Raphela returned to their seats. Jivad had orchestrated this process and it flowed with little ado. Sometimes shy young children shoved a small box in Vanar's hand or a boy his own age proudly presented his fief's honoring. On occasion a boisterous man or woman would include a wordy speech of gratitude.

The gifts were as varied as the guests. Besides clothes, and jewelry were many gifts of food and recipes from the poorer regions of Calcoran. Also paintings and sculptures began to line the floor, canvases as large as Vanar, some splashed with color and design to give a new view of reality and others quiet and serene, depicting nature's bounty. Crystal figures and polished metal sculptures shared space. A few people brought puzzles and games to keep a young man's mind and hands occupied.

Now, Vanar faced an odd looking man, who did not quite reach Vanar's nose. His thick pale hair was incongruous with the shiny grey skin, but the eyes that changed color as he turned somehow made the package right. "Lord and Lady Ishtba and young master Vanar, I, Oolon am honored to share this with you. His hands rested on a box draped with black cloth. "Our province is very old. We have waited many years for this moment. Master Vanar, your parents have created an exciting new world and earned much respect in the process. We believe this gift will help you and Ishtba move on the right path."

His speech bordered arrogance in the eyes of many, but the family Ishtba felt his meaning.

The black cloth was removed. The audience saw only a highly polished gold box, the face was for the eyes of family Ishtba.

All three stared at it. They turned to each other. Oolon's brow creased just a bit in concern. All three faced him and Raphela spoke. "What is it?"

A contented smile began his reply. "This is a Grell. It measures time."

"How?" Vanar squatted down to study it. The Grell was as wide as both arms spread open and as high and deep as one arm extended. Oolon reached for the boy's hand. Bertram jumped but Atan nodded his approval.

"Look at it and feel it."

The face was smooth and polished. In the white background was centered 13 bars, 12 adjacent without a space and one a fingers length away. To the left of each bar was a number, starting with 1 at the bottom and 12 at the top. The 13th bar had 36 sections and numbers above each section. Bars 1 and 2 were gold and sections 1-25 were silver. The bars and sections were black.

Oolon explained. "Many centuries ago our ancestors divided the day into 12 ents and each ent had 36 boks. The sun rises at the first ent and the second moon sets at the last. This varies with the seasons, but it is close."

"This is a generous gift, I am grateful." Vanar lowered his head.

"You are quite welcome. But we have brought a gift for the parents as well." A younger version of Oolon stepped forward, with darker hair and shiny flowing robes. "This young man can build the Grell. He will teach your craftsmen."

"Oolon, your gift of knowledge is as any such gift, beyond measure. We will use it wisely." Atan found the right words and heard only by Oolon and Raphela and that was enough.

The gifts and speeches continued. With permission from Atan and Raphela, Jivad had meticulously planned the order of presenters and took time to arrange for the daughters, near Vanar's age, to present gifts to him. Jivad knew Vanar could eventually choose anyone and that station certainly had no bearing. He also knew that Vanar should be picking from the widest variety of potential mates. So, carefully seeded in the line of givers, spaced apart so that each could leave an impression, were the girls. All those parents watched, even Vanar's. Who would receive a longer glance, a smile, a nod. Vanar found a few that appealed to him and he would seek Falor's council later.

Dusk settled in and the shutters were unobtrusively closed. The gallery of gifts was displayed while people discussed them. Raphela felt her way through the crowd, no special reason, just to know the people.

Oolon felt her pass, towering over him. Their eyes met, words were attempted, but the time was not right.

Falor observed the interaction to the point of staring. Oolon's fingers wrapped around his shoulder. Falor saw golden eyes peering into him. "Questions are answers in themselves, many tomorrows and our doors will open to you. You will be the first." Oolon faded into the crowd.

Round tables placed in clusters made a swirling pattern around the room as dinner was served. Conversations bounced from table to table. Parents attempted to keep children seated, with only moderate success. No one left a table hungry or thirsty and servants made quick work of cleanup.

After dinner yawning youngsters were carried to bed and those adults who tired easily joined them. Drifting to the ears of those who rested were trails of lively tunes, played out by the musicians to tickle the subconscious to begin the foot tapping and shoulder swaying that leads to the dance floor. Jivad and Sonja met the music first and serenely swept the floor with courtly steps. Others joined in and soon the floor swelled with movement.

Falor had little interest in the opposite sex, but knew Vanar did and had learned that Vanar's life needed much guidance. Certainly Vanar was capable of decision making but presenting the options would be Falor's task. He found many young girls for Vanar to dance with that night. Later they would talk and laugh of the plump one or gawky one or the girl who spoke more than a bird could caw. Vanar did learn what he didn't like, but could not yet admit what he did like. Still, the dancing was fun.

Atan and Raphela sat in their chairs peering over their flock like shepherd. They leaned back and allowed their fingers to dance on occasion, but never, despite some prodding, touched the dance floor.

Mahtso and Fatell chose to walk in the moonlight hand in hand, soft content smiles on their faces.

Somewhere between first and second moonrise the crowd thinned out and the musicians slowed their tunes and faded into gentle silence. Guests looked around and saw large comfortable pillows scattered around the floor. Bright torches were replaced with shadowing lumpglows. Couples begin to lean back on the pillows resting heads on shoulders and curling into each other's arms. Teenagers sat cross-legged in small groups. A large bell rang out a single note and all eyes were drawn to the back of the room. There Mowatt stood, dressed in brown robes that covered his lame hand. "I have a tale to tell. Who shall listen?" Everyone turned to the enchanting voice, even Raphela and Atan took notice.

"Tonight I will first tell of a king long ago, who built a castle." He stopped and stared at the crowd. "Without stone or wood and no animal pulled a cart to bring him home."

It was as if the trees and mice wished to hear, so deep was the silence. Mowatt wove his story, it seemed so real, yet everyone knew such things could not be. "Lights without fire, in glass, carts moving without beasts." A wonderful fairy tale most thought.

His first tale ended and the teenagers were shoved off to bed, while Mowatt delivered a tale of lust and passion that warmed the room without the aid of a fire.

At sunrise Raphela and Atan stood over Vanar as he slept. But even in his sleep he sensed their presence and rolled over, rubbed his eyes, and squinted at them.

Atan stared down at him. "Do you expect to sleep all day?"

Vanar rubbed his eyes again and sat up, unsure of his father's tone.

"Get dressed and meet us downstairs in the kitchen." Raphela's tone was flat.

Suddenly Vanar was alone. Very quickly he dressed and met his parents, following them out the kitchen door, grabbing a biscuit to munch along the way.

The reddish ball in the sky shed a glow over the land and the wind lifted the scent of the stables towards the trio. Vanar entered the stables cautiously, his past experience strong in his memory. Atan and Raphela both dressed in riding garb blended well with the woody surroundings and the beasts calmed as they entered. Vanar swallowed hard as his father approached.

"It has occurred to us that we have not yet given a gift to the birthday boy. That needs to be remedied."

Vanar let out his breath and the muscles in his back loosened.

"Vanar," Atan continued. "Your interest in the rameks has led us to believe that you'd like to have one of your own."

Vanar looked from one parent to the other, mouth open in amazement.

"Close your mouth or you'll be swallowing flies," Raphela laughed.

"Yes, mother. Oh yes, father I would love to have my own ramek."

"All right. But there are rules. First, until we feel you are ready, you are not to be alone with him, or ride him."

"Yes sir." Vanar almost saluted. He walked between his parents as they guided him towards his beast. It was a young male, thick brown mane, shiny coat and large white teeth. Its light blue eyes stared into something Vanar couldn't imagine. Atan placed Vanar's hand on the mane. The beast moved its head toward Raphela who matched the touch on the other side of the neck. Slowly Vanar came to meet his beast and learned the

333

rest of the rules. Daily grooming and morning feeding would be his responsibility and the stable master would be watching.

"Thank you, thank you so much." He stroked the beast, that was not yet accustomed to the young boy's touch and shook its mane. Vanar picked up a brush and began long firm strokes on the mane, his parents now a distant memory. "I think I shall name you Twelve." The beast seemed to nod his head in agreement.

Atan and Raphela smiled and pulled their steeds for a ride in the cool morning air. Within two days guests departed and the castle returned to its usual busy state of affairs. Jivad and his family stayed on for a while.

Vanar and Falor explored the many gifts and appeased the adults by writing thank you notes. Posa stood between the boys pushing his large furry head under their elbows hoping for a bit of attention,

"This is so unusual. I've never seen a puzzle like it before." Vanar turned a wooden model of a star with its many pieces fitting together with hypnotic intricacy.

Posa walked to the office door and emitted a few short barks. Vanar and Falor looked up. A young woman, perhaps fourteen or so, stood in the doorway. Her dress hugged her form just close enough to invite a longer glance, past the long thin brown hair and deep brown eyes.

"Rabi wanted to know if you were ready for lunch?" She disregarded Posa sniffing at her feet and he went back to the boys.

"Sure" Vanar stared as he responded.

"Would you like me to bring it to you?"

"Why not. Thank you." Falor gave the nod of approval and the boys returned to their task. Lunch was delivered and the girl was found to have a name, Mareet. Over the next few days she provided many courtesies, all directed at Vanar.

Every morning at sunrise Vanar went to the stables. Twelve whinnied as Vanar moved toward him, bucket of grain swaying in one hand and brush clasped in the other. Twelve's head lowered into the bucket and Vanar began steady strokes that tingled Twelve's thick skin and untangled the knots that inexplicably appeared over night. As Vanar worked the body, he felt a change in the light and saw a willowy form outlined in the doorway. As the form moved forward, the beast began to stir and even before the stablemaster got to the door Vanar was there. "Mareet, what are you doing here?"

Mareet swayed gently with her hands behind her back. "I thought you might like some help."

Vanar shifted uneasily. "No, this I must do myself."

"Oh." Her shoulders drooped as she showed a small pout.

"But you can bring some breakfast and we could share it on the hill." He offered in hopes of bringing a smile.

Mareet cheered quickly. "I'd like that."

By mid-dawn they sat under a tree nibbled on breads, and sipped tea through awkward conversation. Afterwards Vanar gave her a tour of the grounds, describing some landmarks.

Mareet turned her head and saw a man standing about 50 paces from them. "Aren't you ever alone?" She ran her finger lightly down his bare arm.

Vanar shivered inside and looked in the man's direction. "You mean Bertram. I don't even know he's there most of the time. But its his job."

"Can you tell him to go away?"

"Why would I?" Vanar's utter innocence made Mareet sigh.

"No reason, I was just wondering."

Vanar shrugged his shoulders and walked on.

At the castle Falor wandered around seeking his friend.

After lunch Vanar returned, Mareet placed a gentle kiss on his cheek, smiled at Falor and left. Falor glared at the retreating girl. "Where were you?"

"Mareet and I went for a walk. What's bothering you?" Vanar brushed his shoulder against the doorway.

"I don't like her."

Vanar stiffened. "Why not?"

"I just don't like her."

"You're jealous."

"Of what."

"Jealous because I have a girlfriend and you don't."

"Maybe I'm jealous because you don't spend any time with me anymore, but I still don't like her. I don't trust her."

"You just don't want me to have fun with any one except you."

"Not true."

"Yes it is." Vanar pushed Falor back. Falor returned the thrust and soon both boys were rolling on the cold stone floor. Posa barked as fists flew and sweat poured down from foreheads. All talking had ceased. Mahtso saw the altercation and pulled the boys apart "What is going on here?" he demanded. Glaring silence answered. Vanar brushed off his clothes and straightened his hair. Falor tucked his shirt in his pants. "Well?" Mahtso persisted.

Still no answer. "Both of you go to your rooms and cool off." Mahtso ordered.

Mahtso relayed the incident to all parents who chose to let the matter run its natural course. Days passed. Vanar and Falor barely spoke. Mareet became Vanar's shadow. One afternoon Vanar and Falor arrived at the kitchen at the same time. They nodded civilly, but before entering noticed Mareet talking to a man in the doorway leading outside. Hanging back out of sight both listened.

"I'm trying, but he's never alone," Mareet complained.

The man looked around. "Stanton is becoming anxious. He says it's taking too long."

"Do you think I enjoy hanging all over that little brat. Really, Vanar is a child, its quite dull. But that bodyguard or that furry thing or Falor is always there. What am I supposed to do. I can't kidnap him under their noses."

Vanar made a lunge for her but Falor grabbed him and held him back. Mareet and her partner stopped, looked around, saw no one and continued.

"In any case, do something soon."

Vanar fumed, Falor pressed him against the wall. "Vanar, this is for Mahtso to handle, not either of us."

Despite his anger, Vanar knew Falor was right. Falor searched for Mahtso and finally discovered him in the training room. He stared as Mahtso stretched and pulled his body to

336

amazing limits. Mildly annoyed, Mahtso wiped his sweaty forehead and approached Falor. "What is it?"

Falor related the tale. Mahtso immediately directed two men to capture Mareet and her partner.

Falor entered the stables slowly. Vanar poured his anger into the grooming of Twelve, who enjoyed the strength. Falor watched.

"Are you here to gloat?" Vanar sneered.

Falor's head lowered. It was a cruel and uncalled for statement, that Vanar immediately regretted. "Sorry"

"It's all right." Falor shrugged, "I'm sorry for you."

"I feel so stupid, so blind."

"She worked real hard at making you blind."

"But I'm supposed to know better." Vanar worked less intensely and Falor got closer.

"That's why I'm here, just in case." Both boys smiled. Falor fed Twelve and then the boys ran for the fields to work off the balance of their frustration.

Atan and Raphela were brought to the dungeon. Facing the wall and chained to it was Mareet's partner, Alco, his back red from the strokes of a whip, administered simply to prime him. Mareet faced the room, also chained to the wall. Cold air made her feet numb and her skin crawled as Mahtso rubbed the base of a whip under her chin. He smelled of something, evil. Alco trembled as Mahtso approached. Atan nodded and the tip of the whip flew past Alco's ear and left a clean stripe on his back. Mareet cringed.

"Now Alco," Mahtso whispered in his ear. "Where are you from?"

"Don't tell him Alco, stay silent."

Mahtso turned to her. "Children should not speak so or they will be punished." Venom sprinkled over his words. Mareet shivered and shrank back.

Mahtso laid another stroke, this one catching the tip of Alco's ear.

"West Calcoran, far west, Stanton's land." He cried out the words.

"Better, now, why were you instructed to kidnap Vanar."

Mareet began to speak but one glance from Mahtso and her lips never parted.

"To punish the Duke for killing Dahlek."

Atan shook his head. Mahtso made quick business of killing Alco.

Raphela felt an odd sensation as the moments wore on.

Atan moved to Mareet. Mahtso held her chin in his hand as if it were a demon whose escape meant destruction, and forced her to look at Atan, whose grey eyes bore deep into her, expressing a mere shadow of the anger that raged inside him. She felt a trickle of urine leak down her leg. Mahtso's eyes gleamed. Raphela's pulse raced.

Atan leaned close to her and with a whisper that would crack open the earth he spoke. "You will know pain and your Stanton will know agony."

Mareet felt salty tears roll down her cheek, she didn't feel Mahtso's grip yet her skin was ashen.

Atan grabbed Raphela's wrist and dragged her upstairs, both reeling from anger and that unknown feeling of fear. And that unknown was more than either could bear. It demanded attention.

"My lord and master what do you wish?"

Raphela pressed her naked body against him, her words glowing subservience.

Atan's fingers bruised her arms and his tongue forced itself into a willing mouth,

He felt urges arise, urges he had buried long ago.

Raphela's eyes invited him to follow his needs.

Their lust was rough, he pressed into her as if she was a beast and when she knew that wasn't enough for either of them, she pulled away.

Her hand reached for the thick leather belt of his tunic and with sensuality of a true vixen glided it up her leg and handed it to him.

Atan kissed her hard and wrapped it around his hand. Raphela swirled her tongue all over him, arousing him one more time. She wrapped her hands around the bed post and the sound

338

of leather against her soft bottom increased their excitement. Wetness trickled down her leg.

He kissed her hard again and again laid the strap across her bottom.

Raphela let go of the post and slapped him.

Atan's eyes turned to fire.

"My lord, I want you, not your shadow."

Atan's hand rose and the crack of his leather turned her bottom red. He laid three more. She laughed.

He threw the leather on the floor and relieved the hardness he felt, deep inside her wet warmth.

Raphela's arms wrapped lightly around his back.

Emotions exhausted, they slept, with her hair wrapped around his hand.

And in the midst of the night, Mahtso began. He turned on Mareet. In his eyes she saw the self-hatred of a torturer. At this moment his agony was beyond his own belief and Mareet was but a reflection of himself. For her crime, almost committed was blasphemy and only by chance did she fail. Mahtso had failed and for that he found no forgiveness. So, the punishment must begin. His reflection was white and cold with fear, before he even laid a stroke.

With the obsessive care of a madman he removed her clothes, folded them and placed them neatly on the table.

His assault began with a slap, laid hard enough to loosen teeth. Mahtso's brutality exceeded even his own standards and only the royal couple's torrent of emotion blocked the castle residents from Mahtso's anguish.

As the sun rose his sweaty face and hands, reeking of an unsaid evil, no longer felt the rage. His reflection no longer moved and no longer took a breath. Her body was unrecognizable but he saved the face, deceiving Stanton would be the beginning of his agony.

A messenger appeared at Jivad's breakfast table. Sonja and the boys sat quietly as Jivad placed his napkin on the table. Sonja felt the gentle kiss on her forehead and the boys allowed the hug.

He met Atan in the main hall and together they walked towards the fields. Raphela watched the figures fade into the morning light.

"Jivad."

"Yes, my lord."

"We have a problem." Atan's calm was unnerving. "I know."

Both men looked straight ahead, finally stopping at two large rocks.

"Tell me about Stanton." It was more a request than a command and Atan's hands leaned on the brown rock.

"He was a member of Dahlek's outer guard."

"Outer guard?"

"Yes, those responsible for protecting the perimeter."

"I see. Was he close to Dahlek?"

Jivad stared at an insect crawling over his toe. "No my lord, he was not."

"Then why take vengeance for Dahlek's death?"

"I don't know sire."

"Jivad."

"Yes" Jivad heard a voice like his father's.

"Jivad, I do not hold you responsible."

Jivad heaved a sigh of relief and whispered a thank you.

"But, I must know why Stanton did this. Did his father work well with King Samed?"

Jivad searched his mind. "No, as a matter of fact Stanton's father was usually drunk and Samed just allowed him to live on the land. Now, as I think about it, Stanton and his father resented Samed."

"It appears that Stanton needs someone to hate and its my turn."

"Unfortunately I think you're right."

"Then eliminating him will be a service to many."

Jivad pushed some dirt with his foot. "Must we?"

"Must we what?"

"Eliminate him."

Atan turned a quizzical look on Jivad. "What would you have me do?"

340

"Imprison him."

"Where?"

"At Calcoran"

"Why?"

"It seems more humane."

Atan shook his head and rested his hand on his blade. "Jivad, do you really believe imprisonment is appropriate?"

"Yes, he didn't actually kill anyone."

Atan's hand pressed against the blade at his side. "Maybe not, but his ideas and hatred would spread and he would always have the hope of escaping and seeking revenge."

"I don't understand."

"In the books are eons of recorded history. There was a time when people were imprisoned for wrongdoing. At first for life, in cold hard dungeons with minimal food and water. And then some kind soul like yourself" Atan's hand tightened and loosened on the blade, Jivad's eyes opened wide as he noticed the motion, "decided it was too cruel and soon prisons were overflowing with wrongdoers. The prisons had good food, warm clothes and no work was required. And, very few stayed for long. After a while, wrongdoing meant nothing and those who followed the rules lived in fear." He sighed. "Someday it will happen again. But I can't plant that seed while I'm alive. Stanton must die."

Jivad watched Atan's hand wrap so hard around the blade his knuckles turned white, as did Jivad's face, and then the hand opened and rested on the rock again. Jivad wished to argue but knew that besides being very futile, Atan was probably right. "As you wish my lord."

Mahtso led the party to destroy Stanton. The plotter's men were killed quickly and Stanton experienced the agony Atan had promised. Jivad and his family left for home. Mowatt was named Ishtban scribe and began to travel and gather tales and make books. Oolon's assistant stayed on, casting a new wave of thought in the castle.

Chapter 18

"Vanar."

"What" Vanar answered absently as he watched the shapely girl heading away from him.

"Vanar" Mahtso repeated, sharply.

"Sorry, I um."

"I know," Mahtso patted him on the back. Fifteen-year-old boys usually had their minds on one thing. "Are you ready?"

"Sure."

They left the castle wrapped in leather pants and jackets. Autumn's brisk air tingled Vanar's fingers. Mahtso toyed with his chain. Vanar worked to control his pace as his long strides easily left Mahtso in his shadow,

The stable doors were ajar and the rameks odor filtered the air. Vanar's excitement rose. He'd been riding for two years and this year he convinced his parents to allow him to play in the games. This would be his third lesson.

His beast's nostrils flared as Vanar's footsteps broke the silence. Vanar stroked his nose. "How are you boy?" The ramek nuzzled against Vanar's chest. "Looking for a snack?" Vanar reached into his jacket and produced a small fruit. The ramek eagerly wolfed it down as Vanar stroked his mane. "Let's go for a ride, Twelve." He opened the stable door and guided the beast out to the yard where Mahtso was tightening his saddle marveling at the deep connection all three Ishtban family members had with these animals.

They rode the beasts hard to tire them and then began the practice of movement. It lasted well into dusk. Though Mahtso was worn, Vanar needed only a little rest and a snack to catch a second burst of energy. Raphela found him in the kitchen, biscuits effortlessly sliding down his gullet while his eyes moved with the bosoms and bottoms of the kitchen girls.

"Don't you think dinner will fill that bottomless pit of yours?" Raphela teased.

"I was real hungry," he protested.

"Just for food?"

343

Vanar blushed as he wiped his mouth. "What's for dinner?"

Raphela tugged on his ear. "Will a grown donag fill you up?"

"Maybe."

"Let's go. Your father is waiting upstairs."

"As you wish my lady," he grinned impishly.

Atan stood cross-armed by the dining room door. "So, he does still exist." Atan's good-humored sarcasm brought an embarrassed grin from his son.

Dinner conversation was light and easy, though Vanar often seemed to be somewhere else. As the meal ended Vanar grew even more quiet and Raphela sensed it was time for her to leave her men alone.

The "men" sat by the fire. Vanar rubbed Posa's belly while Atan polished his blade and the fire crackled in the silence.

"Father"

"Yes"

"Nothing." Vanar got down on the floor with Posa.

Atan didn't press. He returned the blade to its sheath, leaned forward and studied the flames that licked the pot.

"Father."

"Yes."

Vanar sat on the couch. He looked in Atan's strong gray eyes, and found they warmed him. "Father, how old were you when you first had a woman?"

Atan leaned back and put his feet on the table, not surprised by the question, but hoping to handle it right. "About your age."

Vanar leaned his elbows on his thighs and rested his chin in his palms. "Oh."

"It's a strong urge, isn't it?" Atan closed his eyes and leaned back into his hands.

"Yes." Vanar could have sworn his groin ached constantly.

Atan had the advantage of the concubines and remembered well his feelings at 15. Today there were still three or four women who had chosen to be available for the men. They were monitored for pregnancy and health care on a regular basis and one of them, in her late twenties, Rosa, had been determined unable to conceive. Atan had mentioned her services would be desired for Vanar and asked if she would be willing to teach him. Rosa was ecstatic and considered it an honor.

"There is a woman willing to teach you, if you are interested."

"Teach me? I don't understand."

"Satisfying your urge is simple, but how, when and who becomes the difficulty. She will teach you about the woman's point of view. You must remember your partner has equal footing.

"Do all the boys get teachers?"

"No my son, it is one of the advantages of being the Duke's son."

"Oh" Vanar thought about everything his father said.

"Father"

"Mm."

"I would like this teacher to help me."

"I'll have her find you. Keep in mind her services are not to be abused She is a teacher, not a slave.

"Yes father."

Vanar left Atan to his own thoughts and lay in his bed considering the possibilities of the near future. Atan joined Raphela already dozing in bed. "All is well, I hope." She nuzzled into him.

"Quite." Atan held her close in his arms and let sleep take them both.

At dawn Atan headed for the stables, riding season would be over soon and he took advantage of every day he had.

Raphela made her rounds in the Healers Building.

"What's wrong with her?" Raphela brushed back the little girl's hair.

"I don't know." Aharon rubbed his forehead. "I just don't know."

The frail little girl stirred in her sleep, skin sticky from the fever and body wasting from dehydration.

"What do we know?" Raphela asked.

"We know what it isn't. It isn't from an injury or poison."

"Aharon, there must be more."

Aharon shrugged his shoulders. "Maybe it's an infection." His balding head lowered.

"Infection? Infection!" Raphela threw up her hands. "I'm sick of that word."

Maura, Aharon's aide busied herself opening curtains to let in the warm sunlight and then straightened the sheets. This was a repeat of a previous scene.

"Every time we don't know why someone is sick, its an infection. Just what is an infection?"

"My lady, I..." Aharon stammered.

"I know, something invading the body. But what? Can we see it? Feel it? Even smell it? What is it?" Raphela paced, hands on her hips.

"I have examined the child over and over. I feel nothing, see nothing."

"This is something so small we can't see it?" Raphela calmed and began to think as she turned to stare at the little girl. "Infection is what the ancient healers called something that fed on the insides of a person. Sometimes it was fatal and sometimes not. But how did they kill the "infection"? How do you destroy something you can't see?" Raphela covered the girl and turned to the window.

"I believe the ancient healers found a way to see it and in time kill it." Aharon offered.

"How?" Raphela's frustration evidenced itself in her voice only.

"I've read the word "microscope" many times. The other day I learned that it was an instrument for studying things too small to be seen by the naked eye."

"Microscope. Do we have one? What does it look like?"

Aharon pulled out a book and showed her a clear drawing with descriptions of each part of the tool glared out at Raphela.

Maura shivered at Raphela's sarcastic laugh.

"Even if we had one, we wouldn't know how to use it. So what do we do? She asked, although she knew the answer.

Aharon didn't attempt a reply. Waiting was the only option.

"Make her as comfortable as possible."

The large room was airy and exceptionally clean, "sterile," the ancients called it. White walls and sheets and blankets and bedclothes. Everything was washed and dusted twice daily. As Raphela looked around she wondered if this was right, it smelled empty, despite the herb teas, it smelled of death.

As they waited the girl's mother sobbed in fear and exhaustion until her husband came in and forced her to sleep in the bed beside her daughter. The father held his daughter's tiny hand in his and stroked her brow and told her stories of fanciful toys and imaginary parties.

Aharon crumpled into a chair and buried his head in his hands. Raphela left. Whatever it took, having a microscope seemed imperative. She thrust the task on senior students in the healer's school.

Raphela burst out of the building into the strong sun and biting breeze of fall. Long strides accompanied with deep breaths finally calmed her. Aksi nodded as he passed, walking slowly and decisively, as was his way. Raphela stared at the receding figure, he had answers but would not share them. Occasionally he'd bring some potion to heal a wound or answer a question about the weather, but overall he lived in a well polished shell, no one came in and he rarely came out.

On the hill Vanar strolled with Rosa, she ran a sensual finger down his cheek.

Vanar shivered.

He looked so much like the Duke and had an appeal befitting his heritage. She was drawn to him and wanted to romp and play and romanticize, but that was dangerous. So instead, she took his hand. "Come, let's go to my room."

They passed Atan, who nodded his approval and went along their way.

The duke let the glass door of his plant house click behind him and breathed in the pungent aromas of the clusters of herbs sitting by the entrance. His hand glided over the leaves of plants and the delicate flower petals. They seemed to yearn for attention and to share a harmony he never saw in animals.

At the very end of the long building Atan's kept his special projects, grains and vegetables. He squatted by a stalk that climbed a pole. Large red berries decorated the stalk, which Atan caressed, and then ever so carefully removed one from its pod.

His grey eyes were drawn outside the building, to his wife. Though calm, he sensed her anguish and took a deep breath to avoid getting entwined in a feeling based on a temporary problem. He studied the red fruit in his hand.

"She suffers so, about her work. Perhaps we can distract her." He pulled another berry and stood up. "You will feed twice as many as your ancestors. You've done well, little fruit, grown large and plump. We'll see if Lady Raphela approves."

She heard him coming up the hill but didn't turn until a warm breeze whispered in her ear. "See if this helps." A large plump berry appeared before her eyes.

"I see your experiment is going well." Atan ignored the bitterness.

"Perhaps, but I need a second opinion."

Her wall began to crumble as she reached for the fruit. "Do I just bite into it?" Raphela's finger turned it over and over.

"Yes."

Simultaneously they engaged their berries and laughed as juice dripped down lips and fingers. "Very good." Her smile of approval brought a glow to him.

"I agree. The stalks bear larger and heartier fruit than last year. We can feed more people while taking up less space."

Atan's excitement helped to lessen her own frustration and together they walked back to the castle for dinner.

As autumn began its descent, Jivad and Falor, as tradition now had it, arrived at Castle Cordan. For two weeks Jivad and Atan plotted and planned. Falor and Vanar picked up where they had left earlier in the year.

Before the first snowflake formed in the sky, Jivad returned to Calcoran and Cordan closed its doors on the graying sky and began its bustle of winter activity. Soon the ground was its typical blanket of white and gloss, an innocent villain to any caught in its trap.

In the 'office', Falor and Vanar planned. "Is the market done yet?" Falor scratched Posa's ear while the zorel wallowed in satisfaction.

"Almost. The walls and ceilings are up, but its only a frame. I've been redesigning the inside, but I really need your help."

The boys poured over the designs, measured with accuracy and made with imagination. It only took a couple of days and the redesigning was done. They hung the plan on the wall.

"It looks great," Falor beamed. Vanar glowed and turned to Falor, still a head shorter than him and a little soft around the middle.

"If you had been here all summer it might be done for real." Vanar sighed and then grabbed Falor's arms. "Falor," Vanar spit out the name and breathed with excitement, "Would you stay all the time? Be my advisor, like Mahtso is to my father?"

Falor stared incredulously at his friend and sunk into a chair. "Oh, that's a big job. I don't know. I'm not sure."

"What aren't you sure about?"

"What if I mess up, make a mistake?"

"So what. Don't I make mistakes?"

Falor considered that carefully. "You're right. Yes, I want to do this."

"Great, tomorrow I'll talk to my parents."

The servant girl left the family Ishtba as they breakfasted. Atan poured a second cup of tea as Raphela sipped hers.

Vanar toyed with his utensils. "Father, mother?"

"Yes?" Atan responded.

"I'd like Falor to stay here all the time, become my aide, as Mahtso is to you."

Raphela's eyes opened wide. "What a wonderful idea."

Atan stared at Vanar and turned to his food. "I'll consider it."

"But..."

"I said I'll consider it." Anyone else except Raphela, would have been crumpled on the floor in tears at the stern tone. Vanar shook his head in disbelief. "Yes sire" and with sarcastic obedience left the room.

349

Raphela stared at Atan, still concentrating on his meal. "What is wrong with you?" She demanded.

"There is nothing wrong with me."

"Then why didn't you simply pat the boy on the back and say good choice son?"

"Because I choose not to."

Both voices were raised and the castle folk felt tense.

"Atan, I don't understand you."

"Good! Now go away." He shoved her away with his hand.

"What?!"

Atan stood and pointed towards the door, growling, "Get out of here!"

Raphela slammed the door shut on her way out and heard a plate smash into a thousand pieces as it flew from Atan's hand into the wall.

Vanar took a long time with Twelve, while Falor buried himself in books and kept a shy eye on Cora, one of the serving girls.

Raphela tied her boots tight and wrapped a doubly warm coat around her as she headed out the front door. There was no wind, just the cold thick snow and shiny ice which beckoned to her.

Atan stared at the Grell in his office and felt an emptiness. It was not an ache in his belly for forgotten lunch, but in his soul. Putting aside the books and papers, he looked for Raphela. After checking the usual areas, his ache became panic, quiet and deadly. He grabbed a young servant boy, "Where is Lady Raphela?" The boy trembled as he shrugged his ignorance.

Atan released him, "Get Mahtso, NOW!"

Mahtso appeared quickly. "What's wrong?"

"I can't find Raphela, where is she?" Atan's eyes burned, and his hands almost shaking. This was not fear of disloyalty, but of something much worse.

"I don't know, but we'll begin a thorough search, immediately." Mahtso's chain rattled in his hands, without rhythm. He gave the orders and his men crawled through every space in the castle. People made paths as the men delved into their task.

Atan felt cold. He put on a coat and walked towards the front door. Mahtso grabbed his arm. "Where are you going? She wouldn't be out there."

Atan just stared. Mahtso backed away as his friend and master entered the cold. Atan felt the biting air and the wind had begun its dance. The sun had not yet yielded to the moons and her rays offered hope. Atan's feet crunched the ice as he walked. He didn't have to go far, brown fur, cold and stiff, broke the white sheet. Inside it was Raphela, unconscious, her foot swollen from a fall and her forehead bruised. Atan picked her up and kept the tears from his eyes. As he entered the castle, he demanded Aharon be sent to his room. Fatell watched in terror as Atan carried a stiff cold Raphela up the stairs.

Atan's fingers peeled away the layers of cloth from her skin, his tears falling on her and rolling off her frozen form. He wrapped her hair in towels and replaced the cold cloth with warm thick gowns. She never moved. Aharon knocked lightly at the door. Atan nodded for him to enter.

Aharon swallowed hard as he touched Raphela's white skin and placed an ear next to her mouth and her heart. His eyes turned red and his hands shook as he wrung them together and stared between Atan and Raphela. "My lord, I, I can't, there is nothing."

A silent howl of pain encased all of Castle Cordan, everything stopped. "Go!" Atan didn't raise an eyebrow or look at Aharon, who backed out of the room and shut the door.

Vanar placed himself in the large soft chair outside his parent's bedroom, Posa whimpering at his feet. He sat wide-eyed and empty, praying blindly.

Atan stared out the window, then turned to Raphela. Rubbing his hands together and creating a warmth matched only by fire, he laid his burning skin on his wife, attempting to warm and bring her back to life, but even his intense heat failed.

He paced and thought and the castle echoed with his footsteps. Then he stared at his wife, a lifeless queen. She had told him so much, so much of her healing, but what could it do for her?

Atan climbed on the bed and straddled over his wife. He remembered something, a method the ancient healers used. But how? She told him that if the heart didn't work, nothing would. His palm pressed against the clammy cool skin of her chest and a chasm opened inside him, like a riverbed blown dry leaving its fish and algae to suffocate in the air, widened as the palms got no response to their even movement up and down, matched with the steady breaths carefully placed in her mouth.

For a half a day's journey around the castle, no one moved in the cold stillness, but felt drawn to the castle and its masters tower and the master drew on the life around him and funneled it into his lifeless wife.

After what seemed an eternity of pressing and breathing, he rested his palm against her heart and raised his graying head to the sky. In a whisper bloated with venom he spoke to the Gods, simple words "She is mine". The stillness of night became a frozen picture as the gods turned their back on Raalek and hid behind the veils of snow. In that instant Atan felt the thump of Raphela's heart and a soft mist of breath brushed past his ear.

Raphela lay motionless, but her heart pumped and she breathed.

The cloud of pain thinned and people drained of what, they did not know, finally slept.

Vanar's eyes closed as his head nodded toward his chest and Posa sighed while he fell into deep slumber.

Atan lay on his back and fell asleep with her hair wrapped around his hand and slowly closed the chasm in his soul.

Fatell stared at the papers on her desk, that seemed so meaningless. Even the brightly colored pictures on the walls, gifts from the children were annoying masses of color. Once more she attempted to read the papers, nothing but mottled words.

"Difficult to concentrate, isn't it?" Mahtso toyed with his chain as he leaned over her desk.

Fatell turned sad brown eyes up to the pained pale blue ones. "Are we sure she's even alive?"

"Vanar has seen her and says she is, what more I don't know." Gently he prodded her away from the desk and into the hallway where they could walk. It was quiet in the school, classes were canceled so only the empty echoes accompanied their walk.

"She is the closest thing to a child I've ever had. I feel so lost, so useless. I can't even help." Fatell began to sniffle.

Mahtso squeezed her hand, as much for himself as her. "I know, she's been like a sister to me, so few have ever understood. But we must believe somehow."

They continued to walk in silence, both painfully aware that Fatell, the optimist was drowning in sorrow and Mahtso struggled to compensate.

Falor sat in the kitchen, studying and gathering up the strength to speak to Cora.

Vanar sat by his mother's bedside. Atan looked gray and drained. He leaned on Vanar. "Stay with her, I'll get something to eat."

Atan was only gone long enough to fill a bowl with some stew warming in the dining room and to grab a pot of tea. He barely touched the stew and left the half-eaten biscuit and cold tea for the servants to take away.

He dozed in the bed while Vanar held his mother's hand and spoke of the past and the future. He rambled on and on sharing only the best parts of their lives. Atan allowed himself a small smile; "You can talk, can't you."

Vanar blushed. Atan hugged his son and sent him to find a more cheerful task.

Atan held Raphela in his arms and brought her to the window so that the sun could shine on her face. She didn't move. Her breath was steady and her heart strong, but there was little else.

The sun set and rose again and Atan lived by her side. Fatell was allowed in for a moment, even Mahtso. Vanar took longer watches, but Raphela still lay in her icy sleep.

The sun set and rose three more times and Atan began to pale. Vanar forced him to eat. The moons offered cold comfort, silver shadows of little hope that shone through the cracks of the shutters. Atan lay beside her, hair wrapped around his hand. There was no sleep, only brief obedience to exhaustion.

353

"Atan?"

Atan shook his head and squinted at Raphela, he must have been dreaming.

"Atan," the whisper came again. He sat up, "Raphela?"

Her hand caressed his cheek. "Atan, hold me." He pulled her so close she almost suffocated "What happened?" She asked after a few moments.

He explained the events of the past week. "I'm sorry to have frightened everyone. Could you help me sit up?" She was weak and weary but quite coherent.

Though it was the dead of night, people stirred and began to dream.

Atan heated a pot of tea and insisted she have some. She managed a smile. "Is this an order?"

"Yes," he answered gently.

"I don't take orders well."

"We'll discuss that later, now drink."

"She did and the warm liquid brought life back to her cold blood. They sat and drank tea and said nothing, just held each other until a natural warm sleep took them.

Life began to slowly come back to Castle Cordan. Each day Raphela gained more strength and within a week all was well. Falor was named Vanar's advisor.

After the announcement Raphela and Atan sat alone by the fire in the family room. She was not allowed to go downstairs until her foot fully healed, Aharon's orders. Atan placed a blanket over her, she was still not really warm.

"Atan, why?"

"Why what?" He sipped some wine.

"Why did you have to consider Vanar's request?"

Atan lowered his head. "This is hard, and only you will hear it, but Vanar's choosing an advisor puts him very close to being a ruler. Perhaps I'm not ready to abdicate my position."

"Mm. Come here." She pulled him on top of her and whispered the power into his ear.

"There will never be one to take your place" Her chest heaved up and down. "Not in battle, not on a throne, you stand above, even Vanar is but a shadow."

Atan stared down at the beautiful brown eyes and tempestuous face, his lips and tongue married with hers in the renewal of their passion and power. Their arms like cocoons, clothes though on, were meaningless to this moment, their power melded and the fires of Castle Cordan blazed in every room.

Chapter 19

Fatell stuffed one more small loaf of bread into the already overflowing leather sack. Vanar laughed and pretended to grunt as he slung it over his shoulder while bending down to plant a kiss on top of Fatell's grey head. "You still spoil me."

"Nonsense. I just needed to get rid of all this food before it is inedible."

Vanar shook his head and left, his deep voice echoing a painful reminder that he was no longer a child.

"So it's younger men you've turned to of late." Mahtso whispered in Fatell's ear.

She smiled and turned to him, "At least they don't sneak up behind me. Anyway," she peered around the corner to look at Vanar, "young men have their advantages."

Mahtso picked her up and plopped her on the table between his hands. "And experience has many more." Her arms felt good around his waist while his fingers massaged her shoulders. "I love you," he whispered.

Fatell brushed the hair from his eyes "I love you too." she finished the words with a kiss.

"Now, are you ready?"

"Almost."

Mahtso's shoulders drooped. "Fatell, you've been preparing for two months and we'll only be gone for one."

"I know, but I just want to make sure everything is in order, one final check on supplies and the school."

Mahtso held her hand. "No one will starve and the school will stand without you."

"I know." Her sudden change from light tones to downcast eyes and immediately Mahtso felt miserable, his chain wrapping and unwrapping around his leg.

"All right, I'll be waiting at the front door, take care of your castle.

The peck on his cheek slowed the chain in his hand.

Fatell stopped by Raphela's study. "Haven't you left yet? You said good-bye an ent ago."

"Sorry"

Raphela put her arm around Fatell. "You deserve to go. A trip to Calcoran, just for pleasure, will refresh you."

"I suppose, but..."

"Listen to me. This castle runs like a well-trained army, only better, because the general has faith in the troops. You have made it work so that you can take a break. You can't leave forever, I couldn't stand it. But a few weeks, we'll be fine. Now go before Mahtso leaves without you."

Fatell blushed. "Yes, my lady."

As she walked towards Mahtso she realized how the tables had turned since Raphela's first day at the castle."

Raphela put her papers aside when she saw Falor walk past her door towards the main door of the castle and caught up to him before he reached his destination. "Falor?"

"Yes my lady" He stood at full attention.

"Relax Falor." She studied him for a moment, mature yet still a boy. She straightened his collar. "Keep in mind you are Vanar's advisor, not his bodyguard. Bertram can handle that. And most importantly, enjoy yourself." Falor blushed and muttered his thanks.

He continued his path, Raphela walking with him, and peered into the kitchen hoping for a glance at Cora who walked past without seeing him.

Vanar was waiting. "Are you ready?" He squeezed Falor's shoulder, who nodded.

"Mother." Vanar even had to bend a little to place a kiss on Raphela's cheek.

"Have a safe trip, and listen to Falor."

"Yes mother," he groaned.

She watched the front door close and saw Atan handing out final instructions. Vanar and Falor would inspect the Ishtban fiefs and put time into the marketplace. The door to the carriage closed and the steady clicking of the wheels announced the journey had commenced.

Over the next two weeks the castle became hauntingly quiet. People traveled and families spent time together, Raphela pushed around the food on her dinner plate as Atan watched.

"Is the food that bad? Perhaps I should behead the cook?"

She chuckled and sighed. "I want to do something, something different."

"Such as?"

"I don't know." She left the table and began to pace.

Atan rubbed his eyes and watched her move back and forth in steady steps, much like the waves.

"You're right, that's it!"

"That's what?"

"Waves"

"Waves?"

"Weren't you thinking that."

"In a fashion."

"Waves, Bath of the Gods." Her eyes opened wide and she plopped down on his lap, "Take me there, let me see this wonder," while arms wrapped around his neck.

"Bath of the Gods hmm."

"Yes. Please." She remembered her childhood pleadings to her father, they always worked.

"All right. When do you want to leave?"

"In the morning." Atan felt her breasts rub against him and her lips pressed against his ear, "Let's go alone," she whispered.

Grey eyes stared in wonder. "Alone?"

"Yes," the vixen voice continued. "No bodyguards, no servants, just you and me" Wet lips suckled his neck.

Atan swallowed hard to maintain composure. "That's very dangerous," he protested.

Raphela turned her brown eyes deep into him "So are we."

He resisted no longer and buried his tongue in her mouth. "As you wish my lady."

In the morning Raphela packed two small bags of clothes while Atan loaded the rameks with food and sleeping gear. The beasts stirred as he went for his wife. As they left in the cool rays of the morning sun, those watching were reminded more of two errant children sneaking out to play, instead of the rulers of Raalek, traveling for the summer.

The beasts calmed as the couple approached.

"Are you sure Raphela?"

359

"Absolutely."

Atan mounted his steed "Mahtso would never allow this."

She smiled a cheshirous grin "I know." Then she started the ramek at a slow pace out of Cordan's gates, Atan at her side.

Both wore leather riding gear and Raphela's hair was tied loosely behind her.

Once beyond the gates they dug their heels into the rameks sides and made them gallop. Cool air tingled their faces and washed away the burdens of rule. They rode with the wind, one with their beasts and each other, flying on the freedom of solitude.

At the marketplace Vanar and Falor studied the progress of their plans. Falor's fingers inspected the smooth white wall. The nearby worker grinned "Nice work, huh?"

"Amazing." Falor agreed.

"Yeah, Marco took the mix those students came up with and dressed it up a bit."

"Nice job."

The worker turned his attention to another wall and Falor considered the research done by the students. When the soldiers became workers, one group chose construction. Marco, the team's leader asked the research department and the school to look for a better way to design and build houses and other structures. Among the discoveries was a formula for something called plaster, a new covering for walls. The marketplace was its first use. Time would tell if the rumors of better insulation and decorative flexibility would hold true. For now it looked and felt better than stone or wood.

"Falor, look in here, this room isn't right." Vanar stood with his hands on his hips.

"Where are you?" Falor shouted and then saw Vanar's head. "What's wrong with it?"

"I don't know. It doesn't feel right."

Falor stood in the center and closed his eyes while Vanar stared at the blank walls.

"You're right, two walls are not enough. They should create a circle, not a square. Falor hadn't moved or opened his eyes.

"You're right." Vanar found a large log. A good size for a pillar. His hands felt along the ceiling and open space for the right position. Falor got down on his knees and tried to push the log, his face growing red in the attempt. Vanar shook his head and pushed the log with ease to the right spot and lifted it into place.

Falor sulked as he stood by. "My friend, you must stop trying to be a soldier. You weren't trained for it. I need your brain and your heart, not your hands." Vanar said.

Vanar watched the sunset and then joined the others in the center room. A large black pot, swung gently over the flames in the fireplace as the cook doled out ladles of hearty stew to many shiny metal plates passing through a circle of hands until a plate rested in each pair. A keg of ale hissed open and mugs of golden brew sat beside crossed legs as the steamy stew filled anxious bellies. Easy chatter flowed among the workers, who were undisturbed by Vanar's presence. Falor sat beside and yet behind Vanar, outside the circle, secretly wishing for Vanar's sociability. He sipped at the mildly bitter ale.

One of the men toyed with a small stone and another picked it up. "What's this?" Jared asked.

"Don't know, just found it."

"What's all the funny markings?"

Attention slowly turned to the men and the stone, which began to pass through the group. Hands turned it over with interest and much discussion. Someone tossed it to Falor, who initially dropped it and then did the same study as everyone else. "It's a markerstone," he said almost to himself.

Vanar dragged him forward. "What is it?"

"A markerstone, from Calcoran."

"So what's a markerstone?" a throaty voice demanded.

Falor felt a sudden surge of confidence. "It is a stone belonging to a specific family. Ages ago, each family had its own markings and family members at age 6 received a stone. It

361

was often used as identification when traveling. Of course at that time, only male children received the stone."

He handed Vanar the stone, who also took time to study it.

"Those were the days," a grizzled old man with a voice to match piped up.

"What do you mean?" Vanar's curiosity was struck.

"When women knew their place."

The few women in the room chuckled. Vanar looked at them and then continued his interrogation as he swallowed some ale. "Their place. I don't understand."

Falor tapped Vanar's shoulder. "He means women were uneducated and besides making babies their sole purpose in life was to tend to the needs of men."

Vanar considered this for a moment. "How boring. How could you talk to your wife?"

A general chuckle filtered around the room. "I don't think anyone considered talking." Falor answered.

"Yeah" the grizzly voice joined in. "Women talk too much anyway. They should keep to the kitchen."

Vanar's curiosity metamorphosed into defensiveness. "I don't believe my mother would best serve herself or anything else in the kitchen." The tinge of power in his voice sent a bristle up the backs of those in the circle.

Will, the foreman, put two hands on the man's shoulders. "We must not take Vorlon too seriously. I do believe he is one of the ancients and change is hard."

Jared laughed and the tension broke. The conversation turned to the stew and the weather. Before the second moonrise, plates and mugs were placed in a large vat of water to soak for the night. Heads laid down on pillows and blankets where dreamworlds took over. But everyone had learned something that night. The easygoing lighthearted Vanar possessed a piece of his father's power and had now earned the respect companioned to it.

While Vanar constructed his marketplace Fatell and Mahtso arrived at their destination. Fatell's eyes widened as she took in the sparkle of Calcoran's great hall. Even Mahtso was impressed with the revival.

Sonja glided towards Fatell, her delicate frame blending with the room.

"You look wonderful Sonja!"

Warm arms sparked the kinship and memories of the past and the chatter began. Mahtso offered a peck on the cheek which Sonja permitted and then returned to Fatell. Jivad arrived and patted Mahtso on the back and laughed. "She has waited with bated breath for this moment."

"Indeed," Mahtso's chain swung sadly. Even after all these years Sonja was still afraid of him.

"Let them be Mahtso, I've much to show you."

The women took their time, stopping in the kitchen for fresh tea, while Fatell answered Sonja's mountain of questions about everyone at Cordan. Calcoran's school was inside the castle and Sonja proudly displayed the classrooms.

"You've done a wonderful job." Fatell studied a painting done by a young student.

"I was surprised at how readily everyone accepted the idea. Although most of the older people were reluctant to actually get involved."

"That's fairly typical."

As Fatell walked through, she noticed that everything shined, almost glittered.

"Fatell," Sonja slowed her pace. "How is Falor?"

Fatell took Sonja's hands in her own. "He is doing quite well. He and Vanar are off at their marketplace."

"Oh."

"Do you miss him that much?"

"I think I'm just worried. He's not really adventurous. I just want him to be happy."

"He is," Fatell assured her and changed the topic. "This castle is wondrous, so elegant. You have a golden touch Sonja."

Sonja looked up and studied the ceiling and then the carefully decorated wall. "It is special, but it's not Castle Cordan."

"I don't understand."

"At Castle Cordan there is nothing to fear. I always felt so safe. The Duke's presence was like armor and when Raphela arrived it was as if the very stones had been sleeping and she brought them to life. You know I'm right. There is no place like Castle Cordan."

"If you say so." Fatell had only been away from the castle once before and that was not a fair comparison.

Jivad shared with Mahtso Calcoran's steps to meet Ishtban standards, and the progress was quite good. The stables gleamed with new stalls, framed in shiny steel, and the grounds were impeccably maintained, free of any weed and shaped as beautifully as in the past.

After this expected tour, Jivad took Mahtso to a new place. Servants watched the two men, side by side, walking at equal paces, Mahtso's chain gently swinging, down a rarely used corridor. Mahtso was increasingly curious as they walked down the metal staircase, especially since the metal was textured and rusty, but still sturdy. Their footsteps echoed in the large chamber as they passed through a massive door.

The sterile empty walls were a good match for the spotless floor and empty room. Yet Mahtso could feel something, perhaps the past, his eyes studied the smooth clean surroundings, as he walked slowly behind Jivad. Towards the far end was an object and Jivad led him to it. "This my friend is something special."

Mahtso stared at the mass of intricate pieces made of metal, none of it made any sense. "What is it?"

"It is called a Duplicator."

"A what?" Mahtso's chain revolving lazily began to quicken its pace.

"A duplicator," Jivad caressed it and stared at Mahtso. "We found it two years ago when searching the castle to learn it. That door we walked through was sealed shut, literally. It had no lock, just a soft flexible border around its rim, that proved more than difficult to remove. And when we did," Jivad's eyes opened wide, "the door swung open with such force, it knocked down three of my men and the sound nearly deafened us. And how you see this room, is how we found it and this machine."

Jivad's hands glided over the thing as if it were a woman. "It took us over a year to learn what it is and what it does." Jivad's heart beat faster and his temperature rose.

"This machine can take a woodsheet and by simply turning this handle" his hand rested on an L shaped bar attached to a gear, "make many more to look exactly like the first."

Mahtso stared in puzzlement "show me," he said as his chain beat steadily against his leg.

Jivad took a woodsheet, placed it around the cylinder, attached the gear of the handle and then turned the handle. The sheet spun around and pressed against a second sheet which was forced into a flat bed beyond the cylinder.

"Good concept. But how..." Mahtso began.

Jivad stopped him. "How does the writing transfer from one sheet to the other?"

Mahtso nodded, his chain swinging around his hand.

"It needs a special liquid, called ink. We are still researching the hows and wherefores of this machine. It could change so much of our world."

Mahtso shook his head in amazement. "Should Fatell see this she would fight tooth and nail to own such a thing. I can hear her now, "All the children could have books, not just the teachers. Hmm. Yes Jivad, you have a small miracle here. But why is it here?"

Jivad rubbed Mahtso's shoulder. "I have asked that question a million times. Sonja thought I was going mad the first week we found it. I paced the floor, day and night, looking for the answer. Finally, I decided that fate chose the place and time and the why was not important."

Mahtso peered at Jivad from under furrowed brow. He did not dismiss mysteries so easily. "Perhaps with some help the reason could be found."

"No my friend, I no longer want to know." Jivad was at peace with this so Mahtso let it pass, but stared over his shoulder as they left, still wondering why.

As the sun began to set, everyone prepared for dinner.

Fatell and Mahtso entered the dining room attired in clothes designed and sewn especially for them with simple lines and muted colors but still elegant.

That evening Fatell stared at the chandelier above the table. Its intricate crystal cast out a bright light diffused only by the metal hooks holding the torches. Jivad, Sonja and their son awaited their guests arrival. They dressed very similarly to Mahtso and Fatell but their clothes had a few adornments, gold brocade on Jivad's vest and silver buttons stitched around the neckline of Sonja's gown.

Dinner was a fine meal of fowl, fresh herbs and vegetables, and a wine of intriguing delicacy. Jivad seemed able to adjust himself to any guest, being easy and gentle with Fatell and aggressive with Mahtso. His eyes never wavered when he spoke and Sonja was the perfect hostess.

Mahtso more than once stretched out his hand under the table to Fatell's open palm and his chain jiggled rhythmically in his pocket. When the meal was done they excused themselves and walked outside. Mahtso opened the buttons of his vest and Fatell picked a flower and breathed deep its scent.

"It was a good dinner," Mahtso dropped the chain in his pocket and took Fatell's hand.

"Yes." Uneasy silence accompanied the slow footsteps until Fatell spoke. "It's not like home, is it?"

Mahtso sighed with relief and removed the band holding his hair, Fatell did the same for hers. "I was afraid you might like it."

"It's a nice place to visit, but I couldn't live here."

"Me either."

"But they are very happy together and everyone seems content."

They found a bench and sat and stared at the stars. Fatell rested her head on Mahtso's shoulder and caressed his chest while his fingers massaged her arm. "Mahtso?"

366

"Yes."

"Why have you never asked me to marry you?"

Mahtso stroked her hair. "I can't."

"Is it because you want other women, prettier women."

Fatell felt his arm leave her side as he stood, fingers digging deep into his palms. His voice quivered as he spoke. "I would give up everything for you, I love you so much."

"Then why?" It was half a demand, half a plead.

Mahtso knelt by her and their eyes locked. "It is because I love you." His eyes begged for her understanding, but it would not be that easy.

"No Mahtso, I don't understand."

"Oh Fatell, if I married you, I'd own you and I'd have to destroy you, as anything else I've ever owned."

The wind blew through their hair.

"I don't believe that."

Mahtso fought the rage building inside him. "Believe it, because you can't imagine the pain I feel every time men speak of their wives, that special commitment and I can't."

Tiny tears began falling from the corner of Fatell's eyes. Mahtso's breathing quickened and he grabbed onto her hair, pulling her down, kissing her hard on the mouth. "Years ago I tried. Maybe you remember, a morning you woke with a bruise on your thigh."

She nodded, it was the only time she ever remembered waking up hurt.

"The night before, we had made love and you tasted sweeter than honey from the gods. As you slept I decided I would ask you and as I conceived the thought of having you all to myself, my fingers dug deep into your skin and in that instant I saw the decades of torture I would make you endure. I took my hand and the thought away. Loving you would be all I could give." His blue eyes were set in red tear-filled wells. "I'm sorry Fatell, sorry I can't do what you want. Please, please stay with me, don't go away, don't leave me."

He buried his head in her lap and sobbed. Fatell stroked his hair and cried with him. After a while all eyes dried and the walk continued, hand in hand with a love a bit deeper.

Dim lights caught Atan's eye and the inn quickly came into view. "Raphela."

"What?"

"Let's spend the night at this inn."

Both rameks were brought to a halt and patted gently while Raphela considered the idea. The inn was a small building, but looked safe enough. "All right, let's find a place for the beasts."

Behind the inn a tiny barn, large enough for 2 or 3 rameks stood, with doors open wide and an old man snoring by them. Raphela tapped him on the shoulder

"Huh, what? What's happening?" The old man rattled his chair as he stood.

"We wish to place our rameks here for the night."

The old man rubbed his eyes and stared at Raphela. Atan stayed in the shadows.

"Yes, my lady, of course." He didn't know who or what Raphela was, but anyone dressed like her and riding a ramek had to be special.

The first floor of the inn was a bar. After making arrangements for the room, Atan and Raphela decided to dine. Atan motioned to the barkeep to get them a table. The balding man with a pot belly pointed to the open table, so the royal couple seated themselves at one of the thick wooden tables with sturdy chairs. Raphela felt the air was a bit close as the shutters were closed to keep the cool night air out. A majority of the tables were occupied, mostly by small groups of men, one boisterous group in the back, seemed to be celebrating something.

"I'll be back." Raphela stood and straightened her clothes.

"Where are you going?"

"It's been a long ride."

"Would you like an escort?"

Raphela looked around, it was quiet. "I'll be fine."

Atan sighed and fought arguing, but watched as she left.

She found the facility and made quick work of it.

Atan's eyes and ears studied the people, his subjects, who knew not what he was and realized he did not know them. Most conversations revolved around day to day life, wives and lovers, children and work. There were no great political arguments and no sign of deep unhappiness.

Behind him two men spoke freely of their thoughts. "I know it's a better way," the younger man informed his friend, frustration woven in his voice.

"Why not do something about it?" his friend beckoned to the waitress for another round of drinks.

"I have it on my land and it works."

"So?"

"So I think others would like to know about it, maybe even the Duke would find it useful on other farms." He downed the mug of ale and drew the fresh one closer to him.

"Tell him."

"How?"

The man shrugged and sighed. "Send a letter with a messenger."

"Can you write?"

"No"

"Well, neither can I." The mug hit the table spilling the foam over the side.

"Then go to Castle Cordan."

"Will you tend my farm." Agitation drove the words more than sarcasm.

Raphela returned and saw Atan stand and walk towards the men, she arrived as he began to speak.

"Perhaps I can help." Grey eyes peered down at the farmers whose unblinking eyes and motionless forms could not imagine that it was their Duke, only that this massively powerful being, was speaking to them.

Raphela sighed as Atan looked on, confused, as she spoke. "My husband is very close to the Duke, he could listen to your ideas, write them down and present them to Duke Ishtba."

The men's eyes turned slowly to Raphela. The young man swallowed hard. "What, what if he doesn't like it?"

"Then you'll receive a message of thanks for your ideas and encouragement to continue."

Atan watched in silence.

The friend spoke up. "What if he does like it? You could take all the credit." His voice did not share the bold words.

Raphela smiled gently. "My husband will receive credit for delivering the message, the Duke knows he is not knowledgeable in farming. And so, your friend would then meet with the Duke, here, or at the castle and discuss the idea further. You have nothing to lose, either way."

Both mighty rulers hung on edge, in hopes that this simple farmer would share his knowledge.

The young man, now loosened with ale, agreed and began to describe his concept. Atan wrote feverishly and Raphela had the man repeat, as necessary. The men were thanked and Atan paid for their drinks. The only name shared was that of the young farmer, Rolando, so that the Duke could return a message.

Atan and Raphela returned to their table and put the notes away for later discussion. Atan looked up to see a pair of full bosoms bending over the table and very close to his nose. Raphela sat back.

"What might I get you and the lady? The serving girl smiled widely, but avoided his glance.

"Ales and donag stew for both of us."

"As you wish."

"Attractive young woman" Raphela watched her leave.

"I hadn't noticed." Atan's answer was honest, but not quite enough.

"Really?"

"Raphela."

She stared at the table.

"Raphela, look at me."

Embarrassed brown eyes met his strong grey ones. "Do you know why you are my mate?"

She shrugged, right now, knowing was not enough.

"Because our eyes can meet. Your beauty, is an added bonus, one that grows daily."

She smiled and squeezed his hand.

Everyone felt a warm flush, yet didn't know why. The barkeep delivered the meal and the night played on in simple harmony.

Despite the yearning to stay, Vanar and Falor left the marketplace to continue the task of inspecting the fiefs. Vanar stretched back in the carriage, closing his eyes and thinking of as little as possible as the rain pattered lightly against the glass pane. After assorted bumps and turns he opened an eye and noticed Falor's distant mood. "What's wrong with you?"

Falor ignored him.

"Falor, what's bothering you?"

Falor shrugged.

Vanar sat up and mover closer. "It's Cora, isn't it?

Falor said nothing.

"Have you ever talked to her?"

"Of course I have," He boasted.

"I mean about something other than a cup of tea."

"No. Now leave me alone."

"Falor, if you like the girl, talk to her, ask her to do something. All you ever do is stare."

Falor turned to his friend. "What if she says no?"

"Then you can stop wasting your time over her and go on to someone else." Vanar sounded quite mature for his 16 years.

"Easy for you to say, you're not in love." Falor's shoulders shrunk down. "Damn," he muttered.

"It's no secret."

"You don't like her," he accused, " you think she's ugly."

Vanar lowered his head, remembering his first reaction and became gentle with his friend. "Look, I'm sorry about what I said about her looks, but I never said I didn't like her. I don't know her."

"Mmm"

"And neither do you, so when we get back, talk to her."

371

Falor sighed. "You're right, I'll try. But if she's says no, I'll be devastated."

"She won't say no."

Most fiefs were running well and the boys made meticulous notes about everything. As was Atan's path, the last fief to visit was Merej's." Vanar and Falor knocked on the main house front door, it opened and a lovely young girl with golden hair and deep green eyes greeted them. Falor pushed Vanar in and nodded to the girl.

Vanar stared and she stared back. "It's good to see you again Valeria." His words were choppy, but she didn't notice.

"And you too Vanar." She flushed a tinge.

Vanar felt the blood rushing to his head.

Merej and Norana arrived but Vanar and Valeria didn't notice. Falor greeted them and slowly took Vanar out of his trance.

"Merej, you look well." Vanar finally stammered.

Merej smiled. "And so do you."

Valeria followed her mother to the kitchen, eyes more towards Vanar as his trailed her.

As always, Norana's kitchen was full of life and sweet scents. Vanar did his best to concentrate on the conversation and Valeria tried not to drop the plate of biscuits before it reached the table. After a while she left for other chores and Vanar pressed himself to the tasks at hand.

Merej's fief was always easy and this year was no different. The initial tour revealed the expected growth and some new twists to the operation. By dusk they had been through the closest herd of donags and Norana called them in for dinner.

The large table was laden with platters of hearty fare to be taken at one's leisure. Merej and Norana sat at either end, Falor sat next to Vanar and Valeria across from him with Coty next to her. Vanar did his best to eat, though the food was no match for Valeria's sweet scent.

"Lehcar sent us a letter saying how happy she is at the healers school" Norana passed a plate of vegetables as she spoke.

"Oh yes, um, my mother said to tell you that she's doing very well."

"Good, glad to hear it." Merej chimed in.

A silence, unusual to this group danced around the table. Merej and Norana easily sensed the young people's interest but were not quite sure what to do. Vanar was not the typical young man.

Finally, he spat out a few words, "I um, noticed that uh, you have more male donags this year than last."

"Very observant of you. We do track the numbers, but haven't quite figured out why." Merej polished off the last morsel on his plate.

"I'm sure there is a reason, nature seems to have many."

"I agree. As a matter of fact, Valeria takes great pains to study the differences in the herd from season to season. Her last effort on the females helped us find a better method of drawing milk."

"Really?" Vanar perked up.

"Yes, when she's not painting, she's quite good at her work."

"You paint?"

She nodded. "My father built a small cottage for my endeavor, where little brothers aren't allowed." She tugged playfully on Coty's ear.

"I'd love to see it," Vanar offered hopefully.

Both youngsters turned to Merej for permission and suddenly it was not the Duke's son, but a fine young man at the table. "Go ahead."

"Norana, this was a lovely dinner, thank you." Vanar said as he rose.

"You are more than welcome," she smiled knowingly.

Vanar followed Valeria out the front door. They walked side by side, not speaking at first, then the cottage came into view.

"There it is." She pointed to a small shack, smaller than Vanar's bedroom. He held open the door and sniffed her hair as she walked past and brushed against his arm.

Small pots of paint were scattered around the room on wooden benches. Canvases leaned against the walls and one rested on a tripod. "This is my special place." Valeria placed a swirl of paint on a picture in progress.

In a warm beige dress and golden hair, she was the focal point, as if colors and pictures simply flowed from her fingers and Vanar could feel the paintings around him. He wallowed in it like a parched man rolling in an oasis. "It's all beautiful." He stood a few inches from her.

"Do you really think so?" She carefully studied the canvases.

"Yes, yes I do," he said, but his eyes were not on the paintings.

Her lips curled in a silent pride and ecstasy.

At breakfast the next morning Norana served the usual fare, but with, ice cold milk.

Falor and Vanar stared into their cups and then at their hosts' proud faces.

"Yes, we have found a way to keep milk cold and fresh, all year long."

Falor swallowed a large gulp leaving a white mustache on his lips. "It's very good."

"I'd like to see how you do it." Vanar's deep voice made the request sound like a command.

"Of course."

Merej led the boys behind the house to an open spot with wooden rails of apparently no purpose. Despite the shadowy morning light, Merej easily found and lifted the round cover laying flush to the ground. The sound of running water filled the clearing.

Merej climbed down with Vanar close behind. Falor peered down from the opening. What seemed to be an endless river leaped at Vanar's feet. Nets and poles anchored in the riverbed held a large metal vat.

Vanar leaned over to touch one, its surface felt cold and smooth. "Where is the water coming from and why is it so cool down here?" Vanar asked as he stood and rested his hands on the ceiling just a few inches from his head.

"These questions are as yet unanswered, but we are searching. It's a slow process, without a library."

"Merej, are you asking for something?"

Merej hung his head in embarrassment. He could feel Vanar's' young, but knowledgeable eyes staring down at him and this stocky gentle man, never in need, never in a hurry, never asking for a thing beyond necessity, had a motion of want, and did not know what to do next.

"My parents will be ecstatic, I know they will go out of their way to fill your library, with as many books as possible."

Merej's grey temples and eyebrows covered his blush, only slightly. "I would not have mentioned it, except so many things..." Merej threw up his hands.

Vanar squeezed his shoulder. "It's fine. If you don't mind, I'd like to explore a little."

"Take as much time as you need, and thank you."

As he walked back into the morning light, Merej regained his composure and saw Falor pull his head away. "You can go down if you like," he said to the younger man.

"No, that's all right, I'll stay here." Falor backed up a bit, being adventurous didn't sit well with him.

Merej patted him on the back. "He's fortunate to have a friend like you."

"Why? Because he can look brave next to a coward?"

"You are not a coward. I've seen what you do. He needs your balance and your intuition. They are the invaluable tools of your trade."

Merej left Falor with those words and the young man came to the realization that he had a job.

Vanar knelt down and studied the thick sand by the water. It was dark and rich and as his fingers swirled in the cold water he remembered the first time he had come to this place. He remembered jumping into the pond while Posa barked at the waves and the children splashing. A moment of melancholy overtook him, Posa had died this winter, living about as long as most animals of his breed. He'd been a good companion. The feeling passed and Vanar cleansed his hands and returned to the daylight above.

"So, what are your plans for the rest of the day?" Falor asked as he helped Vanar close the tank area.

"I think I'll ride out with the herders."

"And me?" Falor stared uneasily at the fields.

"Go over the books. I've never really understood that end of it, despite my mother's unending lessons."

Falor laughed. "I know."

"Why do you think I want you around so much? I need someone to explain it to me."

"Uh huh. Anyway, I'll see you later." Falor took his time returning to the house, somewhat enjoying the summer air.

Vanar saddled Twelve and rode out to the fields. Donags grazed lazily ignoring the fast-paced beast and rider who enjoyed the wind passing around them and the ground pushing them on.

Merej's fields were green and lush. The back of the herd crept up on the horizon, a moving patchwork of brown and black bodies, easily 200 across and too many deep to count. Vanar rode the perimeter close enough to touch the back row. Donags moved slowly, their wide bodies and thin legs not adept for high speed.

Vanar had seen a herd run, once, though, and had to admit it was terrifying, the sound of the hooves had nearly deafened him and the thought of being in front of thousands of animals twenty to thirty times his weight was unimaginable.

Two men, about thirty rows in, waved to him. He sighed. Neither he nor Twelve enjoyed being in the midst of this, but leadership had its duties. Calming Twelve they wove their way in to the men.

"Good seeing you again Vanar, I think you grew." Marlin, a short thin man greeted him.

"My mother says the same thing, not always cheerfully though."

"Yup, you sure did grow." Marlin removed his hat and rested it on the saddle of his cull, a small slow-witted riding animal well suited to herding.

"How is your herd doing?" Vanar asked.

Marlin bent down and patted a nearby donag. "Good, real good, wouldn't you say so Yancy."

Yancy, a taller version of his friend, nodded.

"Matter of fact, Merej made this stuff we been puttin' on the grass and in the feed and there ain't so many bugs hanging on their tales and heads. Skins looking a lot better, less of 'em getting sick too. Yup, real good."

Yancy added, "Less bugs botherin us too."

"You're right Yancy. He's right, less bugs botherin us too," his friend nodded.

"I'm glad to hear it and how are you? Are you happy? Any problems?"

Marlin stared right at Vanar's eyes. "Young man, it don't get no better than this. Nobody botherin ya, good food, sleep where we want. Nope, it don't get no better than this."

"That's true, it don't," Yancy concluded sagely.

"Then I'll let my father know his herds and people are happy. Thanks for telling me about the feed, important stuff you know."

"We figured it was too." Marlin's chest puffed with pride.

Vanar turned back towards the perimeter as the older men watched.

"Think we'll have to call him duke, or my lord someday?" Marlin asked.

"Yeah." Yancy nodded.

"Me too, but he's a nice kid just the same."

"Yeah."

Vanar let Twelve make a good pace back to the main house. He thought about the simple men amongst the donags. Most would consider their life, dull, boring, but their contentment left a deep impression, a lesson Vanar would call upon in later years. Raalek's sun began its descent and Vanar knew that Valeria would soon be at hand.

Valeria absentmindedly drew the brush from the top of her head down to the tip of her golden hair over and over again.

Norana stopped in the doorway and watched, smiling. "Are you almost done with that side of your head?"

Valeria's hand stopped mid-stroke. "Oh, mother."

Norana came in and took the brush to the other side with long even strokes. "Would you like to talk about it?" She asked in a gentle and inviting tone.

Valeria took the brush away from her and put it on her dresser and faced her mother. Norana's hair was tied back as always and her apron bore the marks of today's dinner, her plump form sat patiently. "He makes me feel so different, not like anyone I've ever known. I'm so afraid I'll do something wrong. I don't know what to do. I want him to like me."

"I believe he does."

"I hope so. I don't even know what to wear." She looked in her closet, touched every dress before plopping back on the bed. "I'm acting like an idiot aren't I? She walked back to the closet.

"No, just a teenager."

"Well I think I'm being pretty stupid." Her slender arm pulled out a simple blue sleeveless frock with a white bodice. It showed her figure without accentuating it and landed just below her knee. "What do you think?" She whirled for her mother.

"It's perfect. I'll see you in the kitchen, I need help."

"Be there as soon as I straighten up this mess."

Vanar appeared at the table, clean and in a suit befitting his position. The impression on everyone was deeper than he had intended. Pleasant chatter of the day's events passed around the table as easily as the food, though Vanar's words commanded a silence no one else's received.

He was oblivious, noticing only Valeria. Once the last morsel left his plate he turned to Merej. "If it's all right with you, and Valeria wishes, may we take a walk this evening?"

Merej turned to his daughter, who smiled with wide-eyed hope. "Enjoy yourselves and be careful."

"Thank you and Norana, as always, thank you."

Falor watched the couple leave and once out the door, Coty began. "Are they getting married? Will Vanar be my brother in law? Will he Papa?"

"I have no idea Coty, only time will tell."

Norana stood and began bringing dishes back to the kitchen. Falor rose as well and grabbed a platter. "Let me help you."

"Thank you, what a gentleman, you set such a good example." Norana's good hearted sarcasm got the message to Merej and Coty. Both helped to clear the table. Long ago they had decided that servants at the dinner hour were annoying and detracted from the family time.

As Norana put the leftovers away she spoke with Falor. "Does it bother you?"

"What?" Falor nibbled on a drumstick.

"Vanar and Valeria."

"No, I'm really very happy for them."

Norana believed him. She looked around and saw they were alone. "You know, my husband always tells me not to bother guests, but I'm anxious to know of the outside world. I never get to see it. Would you share a tale or two?"

Merej walked in just then and admonished, "Norana".

"Merej, its all right, really. No one ever asks me to tell a story, I think I'd enjoy the chance."

"Are you sure?"

"Yes."

They adjourned to the living room and over tea and sweetcakes, Falor told of his travels.

Vanar and Valeria walked westward away from the building and herds towards the undeveloped land. Raalek's stars shone brightly, guiding them through new paths.

"Would you like to take a ride? Vanar asked.

"A ride?" Valeria couldn't imagine what he meant.

"Yes, on my ramek, Twelve."

She bowed her head and shifted nervously. "I don't think so."

"They are a bit scary to most. Why not just meet him?" This was important to him and he didn't know why.

Valeria stared into his round hazel eyes and shrugged. "That sounds safe enough."

Twelve bucked and whinnied at first. Valeria stayed outside until Vanar calmed him and brought her in. "Here, just pet his nose." She raised her hand, Twelve moved and she backed off. Vanar took her hand and together they stroked the beast. It was just long enough to ensure a comfortable touch and then they left.

"That wasn't so bad, was it?" Vanar realized he could have destroyed something before it even started, if he's forced her to accept the animal.

"No, it wasn't so bad." She smiled, hoping she hadn't made a mistake being afraid.

They continued on towards the woods.

"Do you miss your sisters? Vanar walked with his hands behind his back.

Valeria picked a flower and toyed with it. "Yes, especially Lehcar. She used to tell me stories and we could talk." Summer's fresh scent circled them. "You don't have any brothers or sisters, do you?"

"No." He stared at the ground. "I've always wanted one. But a long time ago I realized it would never happen. We never talk about it." He laughed sadly. "I remember once, my mother told me the gods decided that she and my father were to have only one child and they were blessed with me."

"You sound like you don't believe that?"

He shook his head. "When your mother devotes her life to finding out why everything is the way it is and your father just about makes the sun rise in the sky, its hard to believe the gods have much to do with it. No, I'm sure one of them can't have any more. I think it's my father." Vanar swallowed and stopped walking and took a moment to look in Valeria's eyes. He realized he had never before shared such a personal thought.

"I feel bad for you, it must be lonely."

"Sometimes. There are lots of others my age, but its not like a sibling. Falor is the closest thing to a brother I've ever had. He's my best friend."

"He's so quiet."

"Yes, but he's very smart."

"I believe you."

"Good"

They both laughed.

Vanar's voice took on a serious tone. "I'd never lie to you."

Valeria blushed and pulled up a handful of milkweeds, blowing one into the air and watching the leaves fly into the night. She handed some to Vanar and soon they were surrounded by a white feathery veil.

"I think I'd better stop or I won't be able to see you." His lips pushed the air and cleared it.

Valeria suddenly stopped short, nearly tripping. Vanar grabbed her and looked down. They were at a small stream, too wide for Valeria to cross in one step, but for Vanar, at least a head taller, it was an easy trip.

Without thinking, he scooped her up in his arms. A surprised yelp escaped from her mouth and her arms wrapped around his neck as they crossed the stream.

Valeria's delicate slim fingers sent a tingle through him. She wallowed in his strong grasp, but prayed that her self control would remain in tact.

They returned to the main house as the second moon rose. "Thank you Valeria. I've had a wonderful night." Vanar's heart pounded in his chest.

Valeria's cheeks were warm with desire. "Good, good night Vanar." She closed the door to her room and lay awake for a long while, reliving each moment.

Vanar stared at the ceiling of his own room, remembering the feel of her hand and the scent of her hair.

The next morning she emerged from the hall into the kitchen in pants and a shirt similar to those the herders wore. Her hair was tied up in a bun.

Vanar watched her sit. "I had a real nice time last night."

"Me too." The blush in her cheeks warmed his soul.

"Um, I uh, have to leave today," he said staring at the table.

"Today?" Valeria felt a bit of her world crumble.

"I'm sorry."

"Me too."

The kitchen door opened and Valeria knew it was time to go, it was her day to work with the calves. "Come back, please."

"I will." As the door closed behind her he felt a shadow fall on his life.

"Vanar?"

"Yes Falor" was the empty response.

"Let's pack." Falor said quietly.

Vanar took his time and it was well after lunch before he and his party left. Norana packed almost as much food as Fatell.

"Thank you Norana, you're very kind." Vanar nodded to her as he accepted the basket.

381

Vanar searched for Valeria but couldn't find her.

Before Falor stepped into the carriage, Norana took him aside. "You're doing well, keep it up."

Merej waved good-bye to them as they passed the barn.

Vanar told the driver to go slow, he was in no hurry to get anywhere. Falor didn't need to ask about Vanar's silence, he just let it be. As the sun began to set, Vanar had the party pull off into a clearing to spend the night. Norana's fine rations sat untouched on Vanar's plate while he walked by the trees and stared into the sky. No words ran through his mind, just an ache.

Valeria finished with the calves about the time Vanar left. The carriage had already passed the gates when she came to say good-bye. Her young frame stood motionless in the afternoon sun. "It can't be like this, it's not fair." Without a word to anyone she saddled a cull and followed the carriage. Much as she prodded the beast, he would do little more than trot and it was after sunset when she caught up with them.

Vanar leaned against a large leafy tree and then felt a presence. Turning, he saw someone step up from the shadows. "Valeria?!"

"I couldn't help it. I had to see you once more."

They stood face to face, not a feather's distance between them. Her green eyes melded with him as his long fingers caressed her face.

Tenderly he planted the first kiss, careful not to frighten her, but her warm response full of desire ignited the passion. They buried themselves in each other, lips and tongues and hands moving with the ardor and newness of youth. How they came to lie on the forest floor, neither knew, but the clothes between them were inconsequential. Sparks ran between them like lightning from a spring storm. They took a moment to look into each other, to be sure, to reinforce and then returned to the meeting of lips that answered so much.

Finally, when the young couple had spent their energy, Vanar leaned against the tree and Valeria curled up in his lap.

Vanar felt as if a hole he hadn't known existed had been filled and Valeria felt safer and stronger than she ever had in her life. He had a power.

Bertram emerged silently from the trees and covered them with a blanket. He sent a messenger to Merej and slept nearby. Birds whistled their morning tune and awakened the young couple.

He stroked her hair. "This is a wonderful way to wake up."

Valeria rubbed her eyes. "Mm, yes it is."

Both stood and stretched. "I'll take you back to your parents. We'll ride in the carriage." Vanar draped a cloak over her shoulders as she shivered in the cool morning air.

She sighed. "I guess I have to go back."

"Unfortunately."

Bertram and the driver rode outside the carriage, while the couple talked inside.

"Your parents are going to be mad, aren't they?"

"Yes. But I'm so grateful to Bertram for sending that messenger."

"He's good at those things."

Neither spoke for a while and she rested in his arms."

"Valeria?"

"Yes."

"I'd like you to visit the castle and see my parents. My mother would like you."

"If I'm ever allowed out of my room, I'd love to."

Merej and Norana waited in the living room, doing their best to look stern. They knew where Valeria went and her deep sense of responsibility and dependability more than made up for one moment of forgetfulness.

Vanar and Valeria entered together, hand in hand, eyes downcast, serious and expecting the worst. Silence ruled with a vengeance. Vanar finally broke it.

"Merej, I'm sorry I didn't bring Valeria back last night." He met Merej's eyes without fear.

Valeria peered out from under a furrowed brow, "I'm sorry Papa, I'm sorry Mama. I was foolish, but I..."

Merej walked over to them. He placed a strong finger under Valeria's chin and lifted it up. "What should I do, take a paddle to your bottom? Perhaps, but I doubt it would serve any purpose.

You, young man, you, I happen to trust, but next time, use better judgment."

"Yes, yes I will." Vanar breathed a sigh of relief, as did Valeria.

"Merej, this is a strange time to ask, but I am here." Vanar was rarely sheepish, but now it seemed appropriate.

"What?" His arms crossed and Norana stifled a chuckle.

"I'd like Valeria to visit the castle this fall, spend a week or two, if she has your permission."

"Well Norana, what do you think?"

Norana eyed both Vanar and Valeria. "I don't know, it's a long trip."

"Bu...." Valeria tried to speak but Vanar squeezed her hand for silence. "She wouldn't be alone, we could send a couple of men with her."

Merej and Norana bantered back and forth while Valeria shuffled nervously and Vanar held her hand, only his eyes and ears working.

"Oh, all right." Norana half smiled. "She can go."

"Thank you Mama" Valeria hugged both her parents.

"I thank you too." Vanar nodded.

The young couple walked to the door. "Thank you Valeria." Vanar's arms wrapped around her waist and hers around his.

"For what?"

"Coming to get me."

A light blush filled her cheeks. They kissed as young lovers do and forced themselves to part.

Raphela lifted her head and a unique scent entered her nostrils. Atan rode faster into the wind. Raphela's heels dug into the side of her steed and they raced to catch up with the Duke. "We're getting close, aren't we?" Thick leather reins wrapped tighter around her hand as they sped on.

Atan simply smiled. Soon, not a house or a cottage or even a make-shift tent was in sight. The trees thinned out and the ground began to change. Finally, Atan slowed and gradually came to a halt. Raphela was right behind.

He tied the rameks to two sturdy trees and then they changed from leather riding gear to loose comfortable clothes and carried cloaks on their backs for the cool night air.

The unique scent grew stronger and the breeze refreshingly salted their skin.

"Atan, the ground looks so pale." She bent down and let the fine grains run through her fingers, then removed her shoes, and let the sand move between her toes and cushion her feet.

Atan's hand slipped into hers and the sound drew them like moths to a flame. To their left was the beginning of a mountain and then, it was there, the Bath of the Gods.

Raphela watched the waves curl up and taunt the sky and then gently lap the shore.

Atan felt the unseen life teeming around him and the wind carrying it to him.

"Atan, it is even more than you said. It sounds like thunder wrapped in a pillow."

Tiny waves brushed her feet, the cool water tingled her and she saw odd thick-shelled creatures, crawling along, searching for dinner.

Under the waves they watched the schools of fish and beds of green leaves dancing in the dusk. Soon large waves ventured close to shore, spraying a fine but growing mist.

"Come, let's go to higher ground." Atan took her hand once more and they climbed to the first plateau of the mountain.

Raphela faced the water and breathed in the scent of life and power below as the waves crashed against the base of the mountain.

Atan felt the water heaving back and forth, toying with the wind. His wife's deep brown eyes merged with the waves. "What's out there?"

A wave hit the mountain and shook the rocks loose, the sound more powerful than either Raphela or Atan could imagine. As his eyes joined the water he answered her. "We are."

The waves whirled and danced below, spiraling themselves with the wind. Atan's hand wrapped around her hair and pulled

385

her close. Their eyes spoke thoughts, matched only by the waves.

Raphela welcomed his kiss pressing hard on her mouth. Her breasts heaved upward to meet his muscular chest. She purred in response to the well placed fingers massaging her thighs as she deftly opened his vest.

No more words, no more thoughts, she ripped off his belt and pants and bent down to play her tongue on any part of him that desired her touch.

Atan tore away her gown. Both knelt on the flat stone, skin begging for touch. The starlight silhouetted two forms becoming one. Below, the water banged against the rocks. The gods looked down and lightning struck the waves, fighting the thunderous clash of water and rock. But the water opened up and swallowed the bolts of lightning like a ravenous beast at its prey. Atan and Raphela lay on the rock. Her insides exploding with the power of his lust. They moved with the rhythm of the waves. Atan felt himself burst within her and prayed to do so for eternity.

Thunder bellowed and lightning fought with the stars. Atan and Raphela empowered themselves with all of it, not losing a moment and the gods spat on the waves and turned their backs in blue envy.

"You are mine forever," Atan whispered hoarsely as he pressed into her.

Raphela rolled on top of him. "Remember, the bind is for both. I will not let you go". Their tongues secured the contract made long ago.

Soon the moons took guardianship of the sky and the waves laid down their praise to the round lights of darkness and Raphela and Atan moved with the Bath and their passion waned to intimate blissful sleep. Atan stirred in the moonlight and pulled the cloaks over them and wrapped her hair around his hand. Raalek's sun warmed the air and woke them while the waves moved sleepily to and fro.

"Good morning" Raphela smiled as she sat up and took Atan's hand to stand.

Naked in the morning sun they peered down on the world. The wind avoided them as did everything else except the sun's rays which Raphela swore Atan pulled from the sky for their benefit.

Arms circled waists and lips met for one full-bodied kiss.

"Shall we go?" Atan motioned towards the climb down.

"If we must."

They gathered their clothes, climbed down to the base, and tied their cloaks around them. Slowly they tread the fine sand. Raphela shook her hair loose to feel the last of the water's breeze. Atan smiled. The rameks whinnied as their masters approached. Raphela turned to Atan as he fell to the ground. "*ATAN!*

"I'm fine, I tripped."

Despite an intense desire to interrogate him further, Raphela obeyed another instinct and let it go.

Fatell and Mahtso entered the castle and immediately felt the emptiness. Mahtso grabbed a servant boy, "Where are the Duke and Lady?"

The young boy swallowed hard and trembled. Fatell shoved Mahtso out of the way, shooting him a disciplinary stare. She knelt by the boy and stroked his arm. "Have you seen Lady Raphela?"

The boy shook his head, looked to Mahtso and then returned to Fatell's easy glance. "They went away."

"I see. Who knows a little more?"

The boy shrugged his shoulders and ran.

Mahtso took long determined strides and found one of his men. "Where are the Duke and Lady?" he demanded.

Fatell stood behind him. The man looked at both of them. "They went away."

Mahtso's chain swung wildly and his fist slammed the air. "That answer I got from a boy."

"They went off by themselves, to travel."

Mahtso cocked his head in confusion and concern. "By themselves? Besides Logan, who went along as guard?"

The man shook his head. "No. They went by themselves, no Logan, no other guards. They mounted their rameks and left."

Fatell excused the man. "Mahtso, stay calm."

"Do you know what could happen to them?"

Fatell led him to a bench and looked at him in amazement, his chain nervously jumping from palm to palm.

"You act as if they are children. All our Duke has to do is look at someone and he will shrivel up on the floor and tell me Lady Raphela could not control anyone with a word or a touch. I fear more for those they meet."

Mahtso's chain dropped to his side and swung slowly and steadily. His eyes looked to the ground for help and then to Fatell. "You're right, as usual."

He felt the tender kiss on his forehead. "I'm going to take a long hot bath, I'll see you later."

"Thank you Fatell," he whispered to himself.

Two days later the "children" returned home. The second night Raphela treated Atan to a long luxurious massage, relaxing every muscle from head to toe. He found it a pleasant way to fall asleep.

During the next day's work in the healer's building, Raphela cornered Aharon and dragged him into an empty study. "Tell me about Ulfan and how he died."

Aharon pulled away from her grasp. "He died of the same thing all the Ishtban Dukes died of, a disease that destroys the muscles."

Asking why she wanted to know was useless, no answer would arrive until she was ready, so he waited while her mind absorbed the information and the determination in her heart grew.

"What do we know about this disease?"

Aharon shook his head. "Little more than the generation before, or the one before that. We have history, once it begins deterioration and death are quick."

"What is quick?"

"Less than a year for Ulfan, his father the same, grandfather a little longer, but not more than a year."

Raphela sunk into a chair. "How old?"

Aharon suddenly realized the purpose of the questions and softly responded. "About the Duke's age."

Raphela laid her face down on the table. Aharon waited until she sat up. "Are you sure?"

"Aharon, I know every inch of the man and I know it has begun."

"I'm sorry."

She ignored him. "Listen to me, research is to begin now, for Vanar. You are the only one who knows, if word gets out, I will turn you over to Mahtso without a second thought."

"Yes my lady."

Raphela ate in silence and Atan didn't press. After dinner she put on a cloak and walked towards the hilltop. The moons shone full and bright and the stars twinkled gladly in the clear night sky. Raphela stared up and searched the dome of sky, her cloak fell to the ground as her hands went to her hips. Unmoving in the breeze, hair tied tightly behind her, Raphela searched and saw a light, different than the others, she lifted her hands to the sky.

"Oh Nameless ones, I beseech you to turn to me." The light did not change and the breeze tugged at the bun of her hair. "I will not leave until you hear me."

If the sky could sigh in frustration, it did and she knew the ears were open.

"I have a bargain for you Nameless ones."

The breeze turned to wind and set her off balance.

"Do not laugh at me, I hold the prize behind your laughter."

A gentle brush of air passed her ears.

"Here is my bargain. Keep my husband alive long enough to see his son wed and know that another heir to Ishtba will be born. Then, if you take him, within a moon's cycle, I will offer myself to you as well." She bargained like a merchant, almost a tease to the Gods, but still holding respect.

Atan watched from the bedroom window, unable to hear anything and somehow buried from knowing, he stood and watched, lost but secure.

Nothing moved, the animals in the trees froze to the branches, the leaves could not attempt to meet the nonexistent wind, the stars did not twinkle. Raphela's chest moved up and down in anxious breaths, as the sky remained frozen.

The castle and its inhabitants were locked in a trance as Raphela reached her head up and scrutinized the black and white ceiling above her, the moons offering not even a shadow, the silence was deafening. She waited.

Then behind the black and white ceiling movement and sound undetectable to the world below rumbled. Raphela watched the sky. A star shivered and a breeze worked its way down to her.

Raphela knew the bargain had been sealed.

Chapter 20

The next night Falor and Vanar returned and the following morning the family Ishtba breakfasted together.

"Good morning."

Atan and Raphela looked up at the handsome young man between them. Vanar sat down and reached for the tray of biscuits, putting half of them on his plate.

Raphela shook her head and sipped some tea. "I do believe you've grown, again."

Vanar placed a peck on her cheek. "I do it just to irritate you."

"Of that I'm sure." Raphela smiled and handed Atan a sweet blue fruit.

He leaned back in his chair and swallowed a bite. "How was your trip?"

Vanar gulped half a glass of juice before answering, "Very good." The marketplace should be operational in the spring. Most of the fiefs were producing at top capacity. There were a few problems, nothing of impending doom, it's all in the reports."

"Which I will read carefully, you can be sure," Atan's tone was friendly but firm.

"What did you do while I was away?" Vanar polished off a third cup of tea.

Raphela and Atan smiled knowingly at each other. "Nothing much, just a little traveling." Raphela laid her napkin on the table and savored a bit of the tea.

"That's nice. Oh, by the way, I've invited Valeria to spend a few weeks here this fall."

Atan sat up straight and turned his attention to Vanar. Raphela's teacup clattered as it met the saucer, its contents jumping off the rim onto the saucer below.

"That's very nice Vanar." Raphela's distant voice brought questioning glances from both men, but Atan returned to Vanar.

"Valeria is Merej's daughter."

"Yes, she is so beautiful and smart, and strong. You'll like her Mother, you really will."

"I'm sure."

"Anyway, I'm going to groom Twelve, see you later."

Atan watched Vanar leave and waited until he was out of earshot, before speaking. "What's wrong?"

Raphela straightened the napkin by her plate. "What do you mean?"

"Raphela"

Breath moved heavily from her chest through her nostrils. "I suppose I'm just not ready, he's so young."

"You have to let go eventually Mama."

"I know, I just need some time."

The following day Atan called for a meeting. No longer was it the trio of the past, scheming for battle victories and training spies. Now a conference room was established with a round table, around which sat Fatell, Mahtso, Vanar, Falor, Atan and Raphela.

The windows were open and Ishtban's fresh air swirled through on the bright rays of sun. Atan noted that every one had woodsheets and scribes.

"Mahtso, you may begin."

Mahtso absent-mindedly toyed with his chain. "First, we have four new Ramek colts, three male and one female. One shall be used for the games, which are growing in popularity in Calcoran. We noticed the children wrestling and playing at sword fights. Calcoran's fiefs are becoming more productive, but the land is different. I've assigned a team to travel around the fiefs and see what can be done. The Calcorans have a lot of knowledge from the ancients, but no one knows how to use it, yet." He explained Jivad's discovery concluding, "I'm sure there's more."

"All in good time my friend." Atan soothed Mahtso's impatience. "Fatell, what did you find?"

Fatell addressed the audience with simple confidence. Raphela warmed at the woman's growth over the years. "Sonja has done a good job with the schools, but I 'd like to send two of our more experienced teachers. I think they need to master the next step of learning."

"As you wish"

"Thank you my lord. Their healers are slowly giving up secrets. The east has so much to offer, but it will take time. I don't know why they won't share, they just won't."

"I believe they know what they're doing." Raphela made notes as she spoke.

"Vanar, Falor, it's your turn."

"The marketplace is in the final stages of completion. Workers will stay this winter to complete the inside of the structure." Vanar checked his notes.

"Are you sure that's wise?" Atan had no doubts, but wanted to be sure Vanar had none either.

"I've made certain there are twice as many provisions as they will need. No one staying has any reason to be anywhere else."

"We know who everyone is and where they are from." Falor joined in.

"That sounds thorough." Atan nodded for them to continue.

"Yes, we'd like to have a healer there in the spring, in case of any emergencies. We left one person who has some training, but not full knowledge."

"I'll take care of it." Raphela made a note.

Discussions continued on. Raphela remembered their stop at the tavern. "Fatell, it came to our attention that beyond the immediate area surrounding Cordan, no one is getting an education." She and Atan repeated the events of that evening. "I'd like you to create a team of teachers willing to travel and establish schools. We cannot expect to grow if we can't communicate the knowledge."

"Absolutely my lady. I'd be delighted."

"And Fatell," Atan spoke

"Yes sire?"

"Have your agricultural department delve into the man's idea and send the results and a deep note of thanks, including a gift to him and his family."

"As you wish sire."

Mahtso and Raphela beamed with pride at Fatell's ability to handle the demands. Though her hair was quite gray, it was lustrous and her posture had improved over the years.

The meeting lasted for two days. With plans set work began.

Vanar and Falor began their list of desired merchants in the marketplace and spent much time developing and refining it. By late in the afternoon both had had enough. Vanar took off for the stables to ride Twelve for a while. Falor headed for the kitchen, where he sat and stared as he had done so many times before.

Cora's hand reached for the cup by Falor. He cleared his throat and Cora stopped. "Did you want something?" She asked.

Falor's heart pounded and his mouth was dry despite the many cups of tea he had consumed. "Would you, um," he took a deep breath, "take a walk with me?"

Cora sighed and stared at the floor. "Sure"

"Really! Oh, I mean um, I'll meet you by the kitchen door."

"All right," her bored response flew over Falor's head or he chose to ignore it. All he knew was that she had said yes.

Wildflowers filtered through the patches of grass by the backdoor, making many a colorful spot amidst the green. As Falor paced back and forth, hand constantly smoothing his hair and clothes, he noticed the flowers and decided to make a bouquet for Cora. Gently he pulled the prettiest, freshest ones he could find and then tied them up with a stem. He heard the door open and he quickly put his hand behind his back.

"Hello Falor."

"Hello Cora."

Both stood waiting, Falor remembered the flowers and almost shoved them in her face. "These are for you."

Cora's mouth opened and her eyes didn't blink. "For me? Flowers?"

"Yes, I hope you don't mind." Falor felt his chest ache, he had goofed already. She hated him.

"Oh no, they're so beautiful, no one has ever given me flowers."

Falor breathed a sigh of relief. "Well I'm glad to be the first."

"Thank you" A trickle of warmth in her voice made Falor's spirits soar.

They began to walk.

Cora smelled the flowers and caressed the petals.

"Do you like working in the kitchen?"

"Yes, its fun." Her words were honest, yet something was unsaid.

"What would you rather do?" Falor wanted to know her, all about her.

Cora stared and shook her head. "I'd rather work the books. Sometimes Rabi lets me track the inventory and costs. It's so fascinating." Her tone took on a spark. "I even figured out how to inventory things so that we didn't run out and spend less time counting" Cora's mouth took a turn down, "until my father found out."

Falor chose not to press the last comment. They walked on and came upon a long flat rock, that offered a perfect view on a clear evening like this one.

"Let's sit." Falor climbed up and offered a hand to help, but Cora heaved a sigh and did it herself. He sat cross-legged with Cora beside him. She put the bright bouquet down and noticed the contrast between it and her dull brown frock. Falor watched as her fingers moved towards the buttons of her blouse and with cold practice began undoing them.

"What are you doing?" Falor's eyes questioned as much as his voice.

"Isn't this why we're here?" Cora continued undoing the buttons.

"I don't know what you're talking about."

"To touch my breasts and look at them and the rest of me."

Falor leaned over and began to button her blouse. "Close your shirt."

Tears began to form in Cora's eyes. "Am I that ugly?"

Falor took a deep breath. "Cora, I think you're beautiful. I asked you to take a walk with me so that I could get to know you better, not play with your body."

"I don't understand."

"Neither do I. What made you think I wanted that?"

Cora put the last button in the hole. "Because it's what all the other boys do."

"The other boys?"

"My father told me that I should let boys do that because I was too ugly for them to look at my face. He said maybe someone would want my body." Her head lowered in embarrassment at her own vision of imagined ugliness.

Falor felt both anger and a passion rise inside him, like a cloud about to burst forth its load of water. "Your father is wrong. I never want you to do that again." Falor held her chin firmly in his hand. "I want to know you. Maybe, someday I'll be lucky enough to touch you, but I'll wait until we're both ready and we both want to."

Cora broke into tears and sobbed. Falor pulled her into his lap and held her until the tears dried. "No one has ever been so good to me, you're so kind." She whispered.

"No, I'm selfish. For months all I wanted to do was let you know I was alive, to talk to you, be near you. That feeling grows every minute."

He helped her down off the rock and they walked back to the castle in serene silence. He took her to her door. "Tomorrow, will you walk with me again?"

She sniffled and nodded.

"Good."

A few days later Atan sent a carriage to Merej and two men carrying letters to Valeria. Over the next few weeks Falor and Cora spent more and more time together. He'd tell her of his travels and they'd read the tales of days gone by. Falor began to notice that Cora wore one of two dresses every day, and decided to embellish her wardrobe. One evening, along with the daily flower he presented her with a box.

"What's this?" Cora shook it, curiously.

"Open it."

She laid it on the kitchen table and cautiously lifted the lid off the box. Her hands lifted the dress, a toasty maroon fabric sewn in, with simple lines, long sleeves and a high neck.

"It, it's beautiful, but I can't." She carefully returned it to the box and stared longingly at the warm color reaching out to her.

Falor sighed. "Why not?"

"You know, my father, he..." She threw up her hands.

"Cora, he may not want you to have anything, but that can't stop the rest of the world."

The small seed of confidence Falor had planted, managed to subdue her desperate fear.

"All right, I'll be right back." She slipped away to change, shyly re-emerging a few minutes later wearing the dress. "You look wonderful Cora."

"You think so?"

"Yes, I do," he smiled. "Turn around."

She obeyed.

"You look more beautiful than ever."

Cora threw her arms around him and placed a warm kiss on his cheek. "Thank you." Falor felt as if he had conquered the universe.

They walked slowly, so as not to mar the new dress, which Cora studied at every chance. As always Falor brought her to her door. She closed it carefully, hoping her father was asleep, he was.

Over the next week Cora wore her dress more than once and the glow in her cheeks grew. Falor enjoyed watching her walk among the trees. One evening as they sat together Falor studied the ground. I'm going to visit my parents next week." He announced suddenly.

Cora's flower stem made a path in the dirt. "I'll miss you."

Neither looked up.

"Not if you come with me." Falor swallowed afraid of her response.

"I, I couldn't could I?"

"Absolutely. Please." Falor could feel his heart pump and he leaned forward.

Saying no to Falor was like trying not to breathe. "Yes, I'll go."

"Wonderful, we'll start the rest of your wardrobe tomorrow."

"No Falor, you've done enough."

397

Falor took her hand. "Cora, my parents will like you in rags or jewels, but you will not be comfortable without new clothes, take my word for it."

"If you insist."

They returned home, anxious to begin plans. The next day was spent with the dressmaker. Finally, Falor brought her back to her door. Her father was waiting when she entered. Falor did not rush to leave.

"Where is my dinner?" he grunted.

"I'm sorry."

"And what's this?" He flung her new dress on the floor.

"It was a gift." Cora's voice trembled.

"Nobody gives an ugly thing like you, such a gift. You stole it, you'll pay for this. You're a no good bitch like your mother."

Falor heard the first slap. As he opened the door his heart pounded and his stomach tied in knots. Neelon, as tall as Vanar and heavier had Cora hard in his grasp, in his other hand was a thick wide belt that came down on Cora's back.

Falor didn't think about the next move. Racing to Neelon his fist landed squarely on the man's jaw, forcing him off balance and then to the ground. The distinct odor of ale announced the reason for Neelon's mood.

Neelon rubbed his jaw and stared at Falor.

"If you ever lay a hand on her again, I'll have Mahtso use you as the example in one of his disciplinary sessions."

Cora lay on the ground frozen in fear and shock. Gently, Falor got her to her feet. "Come, you're not sleeping here tonight."

Cora's eyes moved from her father to Falor and back many times, finally she followed Falor.

They passed the guards quarters. Falor asked that Neelon be watched and not permitted to leave his room. Falor rarely took advantage of his status, but he knew that now was the right time.

Cora walked in a trance, not because of her father, but because of Falor. They ended up at Fatell's room.

The older woman asked no questions as the sight of Cora's bruised face.

"Cora, Fatell will take care of you, no one can hurt you here."

"Why Falor, he could kill you?" Cora rocked back and forth as she sat on the bed.

Falor caressed away the tears that still flowed as he sat beside her. "Don't you know, you silly girl?"

Cora just stared.

"I love you and that means I'd do anything for you, anything." It was too much for her to absorb, she sobbed herself to sleep under Fatell's watchful eye.

Fatell stayed with her the next day. By lunchtime Cora was calm enough to sit in the kitchen and share a meal.

"Cora"

Cora's back stiffened as Neelon, sober and placid approached. "I'm sorry Cora. I was wrong. I won't do that anymore."

Cora stared up at him and said nothing.

Fatell motioned quietly for someone to get Mahtso.

"Come home Cora, everything will be fine."

Cora was accustomed to the abuse and false apologies, but now she had a chance to break the cycle and she took it. "No," She whispered.

"What?" Neelon's voice developed an edge, contradicting his supposed repentance.

"No, I think I'd like to stay away for a while." She swallowed hard and cringed.

"You belong to me," his hand wrapped tight around her arm.

Fatell stood between them. "She doesn't want to go, leave her alone."

"Mind your own business woman."

Neelon's growl didn't intimidate Fatell, but it did anger her. "I said, **leave her alone!**"

Neelon turned away from Cora, without letting go. "I don't care who you are, mind your own business." He shoved Fatell back into her chair and yanked Cora out of hers.

The other people in the kitchen gasped quietly at the scene and prayed Mahtso would arrive soon.

Cora resisted. As Neelon backed up he felt his knees buckle, his grasp loosened as a second blow from the flat edge of a sword pounded his stomach, bowling him over. Two men tied his hands and feet at Mahtso's command.

By now Falor was at Cora's side, Vanar stood between them and Neelon. Atan and Raphela were on their way.

"Take him downstairs." Mahtso drooled inside at the future, but turned and kneeled by Fatell who still sat at the table. "Are you all right? Did he hurt you?" Panic waved in his blue eyes. Fatell caressed his cheek. "I'm fine, let's talk to the Duke."

Cora sat with Falor and Vanar while outside the kitchen the adults discussed the situation.

"This is not news, I presume." Atan's annoyance made Mahtso a little uneasy, his chain wrapped and unwrapped around his leg.

"I've had my suspicions."

"I see. What should we do now?"

Deadly silence held the foursome. Mahtso broke it. "I'll resolve it."

"Ladies, are you in agreement?"

Fatell and Raphela exchanged glances.

"Yes, but wait until next week. Falor is taking her to Calcoran. I think it might be better if she weren't here." Raphela was strictly business and received no argument.

Fatell took Cora to her room and there they sat for a while, saying little. Fatell busied herself with needlework while Cora stared blankly at the walls.

"Fatell" A strange calm in Cora's voice brought Fatell's full attention.

"Yes."

"Did you know my mother?"

"Only a little. She was a hardworking young woman, very shy. She took up with your father when she was about your age, no one saw much of her after that." Fatell sighed. Hindsight could be depressing.

"How did she die?" Cora's gaze remained fixed on the wall.

"I'm not sure, I heard she fell and broke her neck." Fatell maintained a level tone.

"I want to know, I have to know."

"Do you really want to torture yourself with all that knowledge?" Fatell feared for the girl's sanity.

"Fatell, the only way to get rid of a monster, is to know its name. My monster is anonymous. When I know its name, I can rid myself of it."

Fatell felt the determination, there was no sense in arguing. She made arrangements with Mahtso for Cora to see her father.

Even in the summer Cordan's dungeon was cold and damp.

Mahtso removed all the sharp objects before Cora entered. Her father swayed from the ceiling, hands above his head, shirt gone and ankles bound together. He stretched his neck to see who entered.

She trembled at first.

"Oh, its you." He sounded tired, a bit weakened. "Let me down please."

Cora circled him in silence, overcoming years of fear, she flinched when he moved and he knew he still had some power over her.

"I have learned Cora, I never should have done that to you."

Cora listened to the rational man, the one who was her only companion for years-- her torturer, and her companion.

"If you leave me, you know what will happen to me" Cora shivered, but began building a wall, for survival.

"We've had good days Cora. Remember the doll."

Years ago he had given her a doll, as a birthday gift, frilly and delicate. She treasured it, slept with it after every beating. But soon his taunts about her looks made her envious of the pretty doll and it collected dust and her pain. The doll no longer mattered.

"How did she die?"

"Who?"

"My mother."

"She fell and broke her neck." He swayed as the words, coldly rehearsed and repeated so many times in the past, left his lips.

"I don't believe you." Cora felt her lungs fill and release air. Her nostrils flared and her voice grew louder.

"You were a child, what did you know," he sneered.

"I know she was bruised from head to toe. No fall could do that much damage" Cora circled him like a vulture.

Neelon twisted to meet her eyes. "You know nothing."

"No, I know a lot." Cora's monsters broke the locks of her gate and as she circled Neelon, she found a stick, long enough to reach his shoulders.

"I know she cried more nights than not." Cora landed a firm stroke on his back.

"I know she crawled into bed with me so many times I began to believe that was normal and I know we cried together. You hid us from the world. You lied, you said you loved us." Cora began swinging the stick wantonly, sometimes striking a blow, sometimes striking the air, but her hands kept the rhythm of movement.

"And now I remember that night." Cora felt sick to her stomach but an anger and fear ten years old would not yield. Her eyes and ears could hear it, she could smell his breath and her mothers blood. "You beat her, beat her to death, calling her a worthless bitch over and over again." Cora raised the stick with both hands and began an assault on the monster, whose name she knew.

"Yes, yes I did it" He spat it out. "What of it? The only thing either one of you was good for is end of my fist anyway."

Cora's barrage of strokes began to leave welts and bruises. **"I HATE YOU! I HATE YOU, I HATE YOU, MURDERER, MONSTER, I HOPE YOUR SOUL ROTS IN THE GROUND!**

Mahtso watched, enjoying the event. When Cora had spent her anger and was simply striking out of habit, he stepped in and gently removed the stick from her hands and brought her to Falor, waiting outside the door. They returned to Fatell's room.

Mahtso hung a chain on Neelon's ankles, spreading them and attaching him to the floor.

Neelon caught the scent of Mahtso and saw in his eyes the madman of legend and felt his skin turn white and prickle in fear.

"You are alive Neelon, only because I will not let your daughter live with being a murderer, she is too good for that. Now, me on the other hand, it is what I live for."

Neelon howled as the first barbed whip tore away at the skin on his chest.

"Good, I like that sound." Mahtso's pulse raced.

Cora was given an herbal sedative and fell asleep in Falor's arms.

Fatell covered her and kept watch for two days, when she finally rose from sleep in the early morning. "Fatell"

"Yes Cora."

"I think it's time I go on with my life, if he'll still have me."

Fatell stroked the girl's hair. "He can't wait."

A few days later, they left for Calcoran. Falor tread carefully, not sure how to support her. Fatell said Cora had nightmares and probably would for a while. During the night she slept in his arms, whimpering at times and curling up close to him.

Around midday they crossed into Calcoran land. Cora stared out the window for a long time, while Falor dozed. Then she moved beside him.

"Falor," she whispered in his ear.

"Mm," was the groggy reply.

"Falor"

He rubbed his eyes and faced her. "Are you all right, is something wrong?"

Cora's warm smile sent an odd feeling through him.

"Nothing is wrong." she leaned forward and kissed him on the lips.

Falor stared and then returned the kiss.

Cora leaned over, pushing him into the corner. Falor's arms searched to wrap around her. Frenzied passionate kissing and touching followed, the kind from two people who have waited too long to share themselves. They did not venture beyond lips and arms, but it lasted almost until the castle's doorstep.

They sat up and refreshed their appearances. Before they left the carriage, Cora took Falor's hand, "I love you too."

Falor floated to the doorstep.

Jivad and Sonja greeted them with warm hugs. After brief conversations between Falor and his parents, Sonja whisked Cora away to a guest room. Cora sat on the bed, in awe, studying her bright surroundings. Sonja had chosen a white room laced with burnt orange trim. Cora was almost afraid to touch anything and quickly understood why Falor had insisted on new clothes.

"I'm so excited to have you here, Cora, I'm the only woman in the family so I have no one to share with."

Cora came out of her trance and stared at Sonja. "Thank you, I'm honored Falor brought me along."

"I love your dress" Sonja made Cora stand and model it.

Falor got it for me.

"You mean he told the dressmaker to make it for you." Sonja half laughed.

"I guess."

"My dear, Falor is a wonderful boy. He has no taste in clothes. But his instincts for people are infallible."

Cora blushed, Sonja's words were meant as a compliment but they were also true. Sonja knew Falor would always choose the right people.

Cora and Sonja took a small walk around the castle. Cora learned some of the history of Calcoran and Sonja caught up on the gossip at Cordan.

Falor shared Cora's tale, in depth, with Jivad.

"She's a strong girl Falor, but I doubt that she'll ever truly forget the past." Jivad walked with his hands behind his back.

"I know, I only hope I can make it easier for her."

"If anyone can, it's you."

Jivad's confidence in him was important. Despite Falor's outward appearance of strength, he was still unsure. "Thank you, she means so much to me."

"Do you love her?"

"Yes." Falor did not hesitate for the answer.

"I see." Jivad left it at that and the conversation went on to summer travels and such.

Geho took some time with Cora and found he approved of his brother's choice.

After the first week, Sonja dragged Cora to a closet, larger than the apartment Cora had shared with her father. Sonja pranced like a school girl, while Cora wandered in confusion.

"I've waited so long for this." Sonja took Cora by the hand. I have all these clothes, half of which Jivad says I am too old to wear. I want someone special to give them to. I started picking out the outfits that I thought you would like the best, but choose anything you want, that includes the shoes, coats, hats, anything." Sonja's eyes were wide with excitement.

"I can't believe this. Just pick anything?" Cora's hands glided over the racks of clothes.

"Anything."

It took a while for Cora to get into the spirit of it, but she did and the servants packed three bags full of clothes.

"I am so happy Cora. Finally, another woman around the house."

"I think I got the better end of this arrangement." Cora stood in front of the shiny metal mirror and smoothed the wrinkle of a new dress, and then sunk into a chair.

"What's wrong Cora?"

"Nothing."

"Cora, no one looks so unhappy over nothing."

"It's just that these clothes are so pretty and well, I'm, so, so, unattractive."

Though Sonja could not honestly tell Cora she was beautiful, it wasn't important. But Cora's lack of self esteem, evidenced by her constant rounded shoulders and attempts to hide her face, was important.

"Cora, you have a problem." Sonja felt like a mother and a teacher, it was a good feeling. "Listen to me, you are living with the most beautiful woman on Raalek, the world has standardized beauty to her."

"You mean Lady Raphela?"

"Yes, but you must realize that these standards are set by shallow people, not those whose opinions really matter."

"I know." Cora sighed heavily. She'd heard all this recently from Falor and Fatell and even Vanar.

Sonja could see her words were not enough. "But, we can make you feel better."

"What do you mean?"

Sonja smiled, an impish secretish smile. "Come to my chambers, I'll show you."

Sonja's room had a table with a large mirror. She dug behind it and pulled out a box. "A long time ago, when I was in the harem, we used to fix each other's hair and work on our faces, it was fun." Sonja's tiny hands dug deep into the box and her face nearly buried itself.

"Harem? What's a harem?" Cora ignored the box and Sonja dropped whatever she found and plopped down on a chair.

"Oops, I forgot." Sonja had Cora bring a chair close by and the two women faced each other. Sonja said nothing for a long time.

"Cora, I'm going to share some history with you and trust you'll know when and with whom to explore what you've learned."

Sonja explained the conditions at Castle Cordan just prior to and immediately following Raphela's arrival. She omitted details directly regarding Atan and Raphela, that would be saved for another day. Cora found Sonja's tale full of nostalgia and she warmed to the past, the harem had its advantages.

Then Sonja pulled out her magic. "This is makeup. It cannot hide who you are, or change you, but it can enhance your best features."

"You mean I can look prettier?" Cora's blood raced, an opportunity to be attractive drew her to the box like a kitten to warm milk.

"In a way. Would you like to try?"

Sonja did her best not to make promises and Cora worked at not expecting miracles. They did however, spend most of the afternoon revamping Cora's appearance,

"You look incredible!" Sonja declared. She put one more pin in Cora's hair and added a touch more color to her cheeks.

When they appeared at the dinner table, Falor stared and said nothing, but Jivad and Geho offered profuse compliments. Cora felt beautiful, though somewhat uncomfortable with all the trimmings. After dinner she and Falor walked around the gardens, summer's air still and quiet as their mood.

"Falor, what do you think of the new me?" Cora tried to look in his eyes, but he avoided her.

"It's nice."

Her shoulders and face sunk. "What's wrong?"

Falor stretched his shoulders and moved his head from side to side, hoping the right words would come to him.

"Cora, I fell in love with you, not a painted face and pinned up hair. Honestly, I find all the colors confusing. I can't see the real you."

"You don't think I look prettier?" Cora didn't accuse, she was truly curious.

"I think the rest of the world might like the 'new you,' but for me, it's like a veil hiding you and I like <u>you.</u>" Falor fought anger with himself and the situation.

Cora felt a surge of self worth she would never have believed she could have. "You really love me, for me, don't you?"

Falor lightened. "Of course I do."

Cora took the pins from her hair and put them in a pocket and then wiped off the lipstick. "Kiss me."

Falor sat on a bench and pulled her onto his lap. "For as long as you want." And they did for sometime.

On the way back to the castle they struck an agreement.

"In public places and parties, I'd like to wear the makeup and put up my hair, but between you and me, it will never happen. All right?"

"It will cost you something."

"What?"

"A hug." Cora paid on the spot.

Cora slept well that night and thought about the early spring when two dull dresses and a pair of sandals and tear-filled nights were all she had. She thanked the Nameless ones, many times.

Vanar forced his hand around the brush and stroked Twelve firmly and evenly. The ramek responded by staying calm. But Vanar felt anxiety rise inside himself, for today Valeria was to arrive.

Twelve got a thorough grooming and feeding, if for no other reason than it took up sometime.

When he was done, Vanar bathed and changed and paced. In exasperation Atan sent him to Mahtso but two hours of exercise did little to calm him. He bathed again and walked to the gate and back more times than he could count.

Valeria did her best not to ask the men when they would be at the castle. By midday the sun had warmed the carriage enough for her to remove her coat and she began to count the trees and birds, to pass the time.

Vanar closed the door behind him one more time and then opened it at the next sound. Was it some animal scampering in the trees or carriage wheels?

The steady click relieved most of his tension, he stood in the doorway, deciding if he should be in or out.

Valeria brushed her hair and straightened her dress.

Vanar closed the door and waited inside, sending word to his parents that she was here.

Finally the door opened and despite practiced calm, both Vanar and Valeria flung their arms around each other mixing tears with kisses.

"I missed you so much Vanar." Tiny tears rolled from the corners of her eyes.

"Not as much as I missed you."

Atan and Raphela arrived and waited patiently for the greeting to end.

Raphela studied the blonde-haired girl, bronzed from working in the summer sun, young attractive and strong and obviously deep in Vanar's favor. She offered Valeria a cold peck on the cheek. "Hello."

Valeria held back the tears and warmed a little at Atan's smile. Both men avoided Raphela. Vanar took Valeria to her room. Atan considered questioning his wife but chose to let it go, for the moment.

Raphela took a walk to the hilltop, hiding her tears until only the sky could see. Finally she spoke to the trees and the birds whose ears did not lead to voices.

"What do I do? I like her, she'd be good for him. Do I deny him happiness to keep my own? Is it fair that Atan should lose? Can I doom my son to eternal loneliness if no one else is right? Maybe someone else will be, yes maybe." She rested with that and pictured the young couple's greeting and soft words. "Perhaps I can stretch the time, yes make them wait to marry." She laughed a bittersweet laugh. "It won't stop anything will it." She noted to a bird hopping by her. Raphela turned and walked slowly back to the castle and a breeze arose from nowhere and ended the same place. She muttered under her breath, "Yes, I know you're there."

Vanar diligently removed the clothes from Valeria's bag, while she, with little interest, put them in the closet.

"She hates me." Valeria's quiet words burned Vanar like scalding water.

"No she doesn't." He took the last blouse and put it in the closet himself. Valeria sat on the bed and smoothed the covers. "Why does she hate me?"

"She doesn't hate you."

Valeria turned unbelieving eyes to her young man.

"She really doesn't, she's been acting a little strange lately."

"Uh huh."

Vanar could see his words were useless. "Why don't I take you to see your sister?"

"Tired of me already?" she teased.

"No," He pushed her down on the bed and they rewarmed themselves.

"Lehcar will be glad to see you."

"And I her." Valeria adjusted her clothes as they headed to the healers building.

Lehcar closed the door behind her and nearly knocked Valeria down.

"By the gods, you're here!" Lehcar wrapped her arms around her younger but taller sister and both blond-haired girls danced around in a circle.

"You look so grown up." Lehcar brushed the hair away from Valeria's face.

Vanar said good-bye and left them to visit.

When they were alone Lehcar said, "And you also look unhappy. Why?"

They walked outside and toured the grounds, breathing deep Raalek's brisk air. "It's Lady Raphela." Valeria answered at last.

"Yes?"

"She hates me."

Lehcar looked into the sky. "Not possible. Lady Raphela doesn't hate anyone."

"She was so cold to me." Valeria picked a weed and shredded it as they moved on.

"I'm sure she had her reasons, but hating you wouldn't be one of them." As far as Lehcar was concerned Valeria was over-reacting.

"Are you sure?"

"Yes, now, what's happening at home?"

Valeria began the gossip from home and soon both girls chatted easily and talked until dusk.

Before dinner Vanar met Valeria at her door and bowed when she came out. "You look lovely my lady"

Valeria blushed. They walked hand in hand to a small informal dining room. Valeria felt her stomach tie in knots and sweat form around her chest. "I'm so nervous," she whispered.

They stopped and he turned to her. "You have nothing to fear. In truth, the stronger you are, the better." These words of wisdom were political and firm, given in gentle love.

"All right." She took a deep breath. "Let's go."

They entered the small room. Atan and Raphela sat caddy corner to each other. They stopped in mid-conversation as Vanar and Valeria entered.

"Valeria, come, sit next to me." Raphela patted the chair and her warmth shattered any ice or fear that lingered.

Dinner flowed with pleasant small talk and a growing bond. As the plates were removed Raphela turned to Valeria. "Tomorrow you and I will tour the castle."

"Yes, my lady."

"Good, and" she smiled at Vanar, "I'll share some wicked tales about my son."

410

Valeria immediately caught the tease. "Lots of juicy stories I hope."

"Mmhmm"

"Mother!" Vanar turned on an air of rightful indignation.

"That's right. I'm your mother and I can say or do as I please." She grinned. "Valeria, would you like some tea?"

"Thank you my lady, that would be nice."

"Let's go to the other room. When the men can push themselves away from the table, they can join us."

Valeria giggled and followed Raphela. Vanar began to move but Atan held him back. "Father?"

"Vanar, the women need this time, let it be."

Vanar sighed. "If you insist."

"I do, just long enough for them to sit together a bit and then we can join them."

"What ever you say," he replied miserably.

Atan rubbed Vanar's shoulder and smiled, someday he would understand.

Valeria rose early, took a hot bath, and spent what seemed an inordinate amount of time picking her clothes of the day.

"Why do I do this? It's so silly, but I can't help it." She placed a fourth outfit against her body and gazed in the mirror to see how she looked. Finally she chose a pale green dress with a gathered waist, not severe but responsible.

After brushing her thick long hair she carefully braided it so that it lay down the middle of her back.

Once more Valeria took a peek at her reflection as a light rap at the door told her it was time to go. Vanar took her hand.

"Where are we going?"

"To the kitchen."

"Kitchen?"

"You didn't really want to eat breakfast with my parents, did you?"

Valeria felt her jaw loosen its lock and her teeth didn't ache anymore. "No, thank you, no."

"Good. Anyway, food in the kitchen is more interesting."

"Why?"

They turned the corner and entered the warm kitchen. People were just beginning to move about and the smells were enticing.

"My parents eat pretty much the same thing all the time. But here," Vanar sniffed the air and smiled, "Rabi experiments"

They sat at a table obviously prepared for two. Rabi, a short strangely thin balding man, who rarely left his stove and prep center, appeared and smiled widely. "So glad to see you Vanar, and this lovely young lady must be Valeria."

She nodded gracefully.

"How is it that the Ishtban men get the most beautiful women?" Rabi eyed her up and down, not so much as a man, but more like an uncle watching out for a favorite nephew.

Valeria did her best not to blush under the scrutiny.

Vanar placed a friendly hand on Rabi's shoulder and brought the older man's ear close to his lips "It's because we are the handsomest men."

"Well, in that case, I'll see if some day your mother's healers can change my face,"

"Whatever you wish, as long as you continue filling our bellies."

"Without a doubt." He poured some tea and disappeared. Returning quickly he produced a large round pastry drizzled with fruity syrup. "A special surprise."

Vanar sliced through the soft thick shell and a deep red filling oozed out, its scent permeated the air. Valeria's eyes widened as the exquisite looking treat was placed on her plate. Rabi waited anxiously as her lips closed around a forkful of the warm tart. Its delicate and unique combination of flavors swirled around her tongue and slid easily down inside her. "Oh Rabi, this is incredible!"

"You really liked it?" His thin fingers trembled.

"Let me tell you, my mother is an excellent cook and baker, but I've never tasted anything like this."

"Thank you, thank you." He waved his hand and a young girl placed a pitcher on the table.

Vanar poured from it and Valeria watched the thick white liquid fill her glass. She took a sip. "Cold milk"

Genuine satisfaction painted her face. She stood up and gave Rabi a big hug. "Thank you, you've made me feel so much at home."

Rabi blushed and scuttled off to his stove.

Vanar beamed, she knew exactly what to do.

Breakfast was indeed good and they made it last as long as possible, but finally Vanar pushed away his plate. "Are you ready?"

"I guess so." She shrugged.

Her hair felt good under his palm and she smelled fresh as his lips met hers for a brief kiss. "You look wonderful."

Valeria met Raphela in the healer's building.

Raphela gave some final instructions to an aide and walked Valeria back to the castle. "Your sister tells me you do a very good job with the calves on the ranch."

Valeria stood next to her, feeling tiny, though Raphela was only half a head taller and certainly did not outweigh her by much. "Yes my lady."

Raphela smiled and placed a strong arm on Valeria's shoulder. "You are not my slave, no one is, there is no need to cower."

"Yes my lady" she whispered.

"That's a lovely dress, it suits you well."

"Thank you, I uh, made it myself." Valeria sparked and Raphela grabbed onto it.

"Do you make all your own clothes?"

"Yes my lady, I design them as well." She lowered her head.

"Really, certainly a talent I've never possessed, though it would have pleased my father. I did have a good friend who was a seamstress." The touch of melancholy in her voice matched the words and eased Valeria.

"I enjoy sewing and designing. I like clothes so much, my mother says the talent wasn't wasted."

"I couldn't agree more. What else do you like to do?" Raphela took her through the large dining hall and Valeria marveled at the grandeur and strength she felt, here and throughout the castle.

"I like to paint." Valeria's hand studied an intricately woven curtain of green and gold hanging in the great hall.

"Paint?"

"Yes, pictures, mostly of flowers and animals." While she spoke she envisioned the room in which they were standing reproduced on canvas.

"Do you ever paint pictures of people?" Raphela's honest fascination made Valeria feel at home.

"Sometimes, but people are complicated."

Raphela listened to the carefully chosen words and liked them. "Perhaps one day" Raphela was interrupted. "My lady, there is a woman from the town, she says she is supposed to meet with you today?"

Raphela sighed "Is it that late already?"

"It's early afternoon my lady."

"Well Valeria, so much for the tour. I suggest you grab some lunch before Rabi growls that he has to cook again. Oh, you're free to roam the castle."

"Thank you"

"It was a lovely morning, we'll do this again before you leave."

"Yes m'lady"

Raphela hurried off to her appointment and Valeria made a graceful dash for the kitchen. Servants bustled, cleaning up after themselves and who ever else had wandered through.

Valeria stood amidst them and almost got knocked over by one of the women.

"What do you want dear?" The woman forced herself to be courteous, despite the interruption of the routine.

"Just some lunch, I'm really hungry."

"Of course." She sighed with annoyance, "Leeann, bring some food out for this young lady."

Valeria took the platter from Leeann and found herself utensils and water. She wolfed down the first few bites and then nibbled and watched, doing her best to blend in with the activity. It was definitely different than clearing the dishes at home.

Once done, she found where the dirty plates belonged and slipped out of the still busy atmosphere.

Cordan's ceilings were tall and most places open and airy, but Valeria found a narrow hallway, towards the back of the castle and a door. She turned the knob and it creaked open. Without creating much of a chasm between door and its frame, she could see a dark stairwell. Her eyes tried to focus. Suddenly the door shut. Valeria jumped and turned around.

"You don't want to go down there."

Valeria stared and then regained her composure. "Is that Mahtso's workplace?"

"Yes."

"You must be Fatell."

"Very good, yes I am." Fatell was impressed.

Valeria looked down at the mature woman, gray hair tied back, eyes full of untold secrets. A feeling of desire crawled over Valeria, one she had never sensed before.

"Fatell, I'd like to paint a picture of you and Mahtso, together, please." Valeria's chest heaved up and down with excitement and hope.

"Me? Mahtso? You want to paint a picture of us?" Fatell made no attempt to hide her shock.

"Yes, I just feel so much about you and he's there, please." Valeria threw decorum away with the first request.

"Why not the Duke or Lady?"

She mellowed a bit. "Because they have a wall, you don't. Please let me do your portrait." Valeria's request was little different than a child asking for a special favor, it had the same innocence and boldness.

"If Mahtso agrees."

"Wonderful, let's find him."

Fatell laughed as Valeria took her hand, this girl was a bit like a young Raphela.

Mahtso reacted much like Fatell and would have refused if not for Fatell's prodding. The sittings would begin the next morning. After dinner Valeria explained her plans to Vanar.

"You got Mahtso to do this?!" Vanar glanced in the cave as they walked past it.

"I had a little help" Her sheepish reply brought a grin to his face.

415

"Even so, I'd love to watch."

"No." Valeria responded without hesitation and firmly.

"Just like that, NO? Why?" Vanar wasn't sure whether to be hurt or offended.

She made him sit down on a large rock and plopped down on his lap, wrapping her bronze arms around his neck and blowing gently in his ear. "When you and Falor created the Marketplace, did you have an audience?"

Vanar held her tight and easily lost focus on his question. "No." He attempted a kiss but she backed off.

"Then don't expect me to have one either."

"Whatever you say." This time she couldn't avoid him and he pressed her down on the rock and kissed her willing lips.

In the morning Valeria found a room with white bare walls. Fatell and Mahtso sat side by side, dressed in muted grays and greens, her hands under his.

With their permission, Valeria studied their faces with her fingertips, sensing every line, the texture of their hair. She kept her eyes closed to avoid distraction and didn't open them until after her brush first struck the canvas.

Quite accustomed to the smell of paint, Valeria ignored it. Her models often wrinkled their noses, but otherwise were quite still. By lunchtime all three had had enough.

Every morning for the next three days Fatell and Mahtso sat, while Valeria worked.

As the morning session drew to a close, Vanar waited outside the door. First he leaned casually against the wall, then engaged in a variety of exercises of leg and arm stretching, bodybending and twisting, even short sprints. Once he'd done two or three rounds of that, he took to counting the tiles on the floor and jumping at every noise.

Finally the door opened to find him leaning against the wall, as if he had always stood there. Valeria almost missed him. "Oh, Vanar, there you are."

Doing his best to sound interested "How was the session?"

"A little tiring, but good."

416

They walked outside to the cool fall air. Vanar covered Valeria in a wrap he had brought. It didn't take long to reach their spot for the picnic lunch Vanar had also carried along.

"Are you done?" Vanar's attempt at being nonchalant barely masked the anxiety in his voice.

"Almost, one more day." Valeria's mind was slowly winding down and Vanar was simply a voice at this moment.

"Oh." Vanar watched a bug crawl over the blanket.

Valeria suddenly realized the silence and empty plates. She doled out bread and meat and poured juice into the mugs.

Vanar toyed with the food on his plate. Valeria took a huge bite of bread and watched Vanar's continuous moping.

"It's only one more morning." She endeavored to abate his frustration.

"I know."

Two pairs of eyes stared onto the horizon, while plates of food tempted the senses of small animals, surveying the situation learily from holes in the trees and crouched by nearby rocks. Valeria rubbed her arms when the wind motioned through the leaves. Vanar picked up a stick and made meaningless drawings in the dirt. On occasion Valeria would gaze at Vanar, but he would not return the glance. She brushed away a little bird and thought about how pleasant Vanar's summer visit had been. He'd talked of his travels and the Marketplace. The Marketplace, hmm.

"Vanar"

"What?"

Valeria considered leaving, his annoyed response not what she had hoped for but years of sibling interaction trained her otherwise. "Would you let me decorate the Marketplace?"

"Decorate the Marketplace? What are you talking about?"

Valeria moved closer and put an uninterested hand between her two. "This wonderful place you've built, let's make it beautiful."

"How?" He treaded cautiously, like a tot coming out of the punishment corner.

"Put pictures on the walls and fabric and...."

He felt a surge of excitement and considered the possibilities. "Would you really do this?"

"Yes, I'd love to. From what you've said, I could start with the Common Room, where the vendors set up their stands."

Vanar listened and soon they were gobbling up lunch and drawing plans. By dusk a lot of ground had been covered.

Walking back to the castle, hand in hand, Vanar took a deep breath and stopped them. "Valeria, I'd like to ask you a question, but I want an honest answer."

"It's the only kind I give."

"Decorating the Marketplace, is this real for you, or are you appeasing me?"

Valeria gazed up into his hazel eyes as his thick brown hair rustled in the breeze.

"I'm not good at appeasing. Initially, I wanted to cheer you up, but as we started to talk, I knew it would be a marvelous project, if you let me do it."

"Thank you." His hands cupped her face and the sun cast a glow on the tender kiss and Vanar's heart filled with the knowledge that she understood him.

The next morning, as promised, Valeria completed the portraits. No one, not even the subjects, were permitted a peek until the finishing touches were done. That afternoon, a draped easel was brought to the main hall.

Before dusk, when the sun's rays would still do justice to the work, everyone gathered. Raphela stood on one side of the canvas, Atan behind her and Valeria on the side, Vanar behind her. Fatell and Mahtso faced the canvas, hand in hand, Mahtso's chain made circles around his leg as he squeezed Fatell's hand. Her fingers pushed away hair on her face that wasn't there and straightened her dress almost as often as the chain circled Mahtso's leg.

Valeria was serene, a consummated project, an illustration, of people, of all things she did, for this she needed only her own approval.

The crowd grew and formed a great wedge by the painting. Raphela raised her hand for silence. The graying hair by her temples flowed into the grey trim of her blue dress. She smiled, as proud owners do.

"We have in our midst, an artist. She has given a great deal of her time to create a portrait, and has graciously given it to Castle Cordan as an eternal remembrance of two of our dearest people."

Valeria blushed and stepped forward on Vanar's push.

"This is Valeria, she is the artist and now, with her permission, we shall unveil her work. May I?"

Valeria swallowed hard and nodded. This was a great deal more attention than she anticipated.

Raphela's hand reached to the bottom of the brown cloth and gently raised it, revealing the portrait. Gasps from the audience, captured Raphela's attention before she even looked at it. Fatell and Mahtso moved closer to touch the canvas.

Valeria leaned into Vanar and observed the crowd.

Atan and Raphela finally viewed the illustration. Troubled blue eyes and strong brown eyes stared back at them. Each line in Fatell's face drawn with the compassion that made her the perfect mate for the man whose nervous hand clutched hers while his chain lay over his wrist. Valeria had captured them, almost as if their very souls were in the paint.

Vanar's eyes moved between her and the canvas. "You are amazing. It's, it's, perfect."

"Do you really think so? I like it, but it could always be better."

Raphela put her arm on Valeria's shoulder. "I don't think so. Someday, I would like one of my husband," she whispered in Valeria's ear.

Valeria gazed unblinkingly in Raphela's eyes and could not explain why right now, that seemed so impossible.

Atan did not leave the portrait for a long time, hands behind his back, standing straight, eyes bent on learning what he saw and already knew.

Valeria took her accolades, from everyone at the castle, with dignity and girlish charm.

That night Atan sat on the bench by the window, The stars putting on a show for him, or so it seemed and Raphela caressed his shoulders.

"She's very good, Raphela." Atan didn't turn but made sure to gently grasp his wife's hands.

"I know."

Deep inside, both rulers were volcanoes, rumbling, yearning to spill out the feelings, spit out the words, like hot lava. The molten mass of years of building and caring churned inside them, but neither could speak.

Atan's finger studied her face as Raphela's ran through his hair. Lips and tongues moved in the silent explosion that had to replace the words neither could find. It was only lips and tongues and fingers. Conversation without the constraints of verbage.

And at the bottom of the volcanoes buried under the scorching stones was the cold fear of never being able to touch again.

Valeria and Vanar lit a fire in a small room and cuddled up on a large pillow from long ago. Vanar felt drunk from the scent of her hair and as she nestled so close beside him, her dreams were nothing more than reality.

Fatell lay awake, trying not to toss and turn so much as to wake Mahtso. Finally, tense muscles drove her to rise. She wrapped a robe around her and tiptoed out. Groping along the walls, until her hands found the storage closet and a lumpglow. After breaking it open, she used its warm light to guide her to the great hall and there, it cast its dim illumination on the painting.

Fatell studied her face, it showed so much of the strength she denied.

Mahtso rolled over to the warm spot. His palm felt the emptiness and his eyes squinted open. He took the same steps as Fatell, knowing full well where she'd be going.

"A little eerie, isn't it?" Mahtso's voice startled Fatell, but his presence was no surprise.

"She was very gracious, I don't look that good." Fatell spoke to the air.

Mahtso rubbed her arms. "To me, you look better." A contented smile crossed his face as her head leaned into his chest.

He was awed at how well Valeria had captured the turbulence in his soul. It was as if the paint were drawn from their own blood.

Both stayed until they knew nothing was missing from inside themselves.

Vanar kept Valeria to himself all of the following day and late that night Cora and Falor returned. In the morning Vanar and Valeria sat in the kitchen over hot tea and biscuits. Vanar looked up, saw Falor, and jumped to greet him. "You're back!"

"Yes, and glad to be." He pulled a chair up to the table and the boys began to chat while the girls sat and stared, first at them then at each other. It lasted but a moment and Valeria made the first move.

"Hello, I'm Valeria."

"I'm Cora."

They looked at the boys. "It's nice to know we're so important."

Valeria's sarcasm hit Cora just the right way. She leaned towards Valeria. "Let's get a really good breakfast," she whispered.

Valeria smiled "Lead the way"

Cora guided them toward the three cooking hearths. She peered over the shoulders of everyone working and wrinkled her nose in frustration. Then she saw him.

"Rabi?"

"Cora!"

Instantaneous mutual hugs made Valeria feel a little awkward.

"Stand back, let me look at you." Cora wore one of Sonja's dresses, a bright blue frock with a white lace bodice and her hair was tied back with a wide shiny ribbon. Rabi held her hand at arm's distance and shook his head. "You look wonderful."

"Thank you" Another hug and Rabi returned to the pot on the stove.

Cora rocked back and forth on her heels.

"What do you want Cora?" Rabi didn't look up.

"Something special. Please." Her little girl voice, wasn't necessary, but it helped.

"Something special?"

Valeria shrugged her shoulders. Cora crossed her arms and thought. "I know, you'll love this Valeria. Rabi, your wheat soup, with my favorite sauce.

"You would make me start another pot. Well, get what we need."

Cora began digging through cabinets for a pot and the foodstuffs.

"Can I help?" Valeria meekly offered what she knew was unnecessary assistance.

"Just get a couple of bowls, spoons and stools and then wait."

Valeria obeyed.

Cora climbed on a stool and pulled a canister down from a high shelf and instinctively poured two portions into a large bowl while Rabi filled a small pot with water and placed it over a flame. Cora attacked a second cabinet clanging metal cans together, never knocking one over or disturbing anyone else's work. Her hands did the digging rather than her eyes and finally her fingers worked through the maze and latched onto the right one.

Rabi turned to the pot and saw large bubbles traveling from the bottom and ultimately breaking free on the surface, popping and releasing a stream of mist. Slowly he poured the grains from the bowls into the water and stirred, gently slapping Cora's hand when she tried to get involved. "Sit down and behave like Valeria is doing."

"Whatever you say."

The easy banter made Valeria feel good for Cora. Vanar had relayed the events of the past few months.

Soon the hard solid grains filled with water and took on a chewy mushy texture. Both girls sat, bowls in hand, necks stretching, feet dangling.

"Cora."

"What?" She watched Rabi while she answered Valeria.

"What is wheat soup?" The accent on "is" caught Cora's attention.

"I'm sorry. About a year ago, Rabi and I were experimenting. We took some of the wheat meant for bread and chopped it up instead of grinding it down.

"Yes."

"And then we did what you see here. I love adding flavors to food so I found a sauce that I liked and put it in, some people like fruit, some people even like it plain."

"Can I taste your sauce?"

"Definitely"

"All right girls, come over here with your bowls." Rabi ladled the thick mixture into the bowls. Cora got the sauce and swirled it around the top.

Valeria watched the rich brown goo drizzle around her meal and took a whiff of the new scent. Cora returned the jar to the cabinet, before she and Valeria took a stool and delved into breakfast.

"This is really good." Valeria swallowed a second hot spoonful. "What is this sauce?"

"We call it mud sauce?

"Well it's delicious. My mother would love this kitchen."

Rabi smiled, but made sure no one could see.

Falor turned his head. "Isn't that right Cora," and saw the empty chair. "Vanar, where did they go?"

Vanar and Falor twisted themselves in all directions. Finally, Vanar pointed to where the girls sat, now chatting and eating.

"I guess Rabi didn't need my good looks after all." Vanar stood behind Valeria, whispering the good-natured tease in her ear.

"Good looks can't compete with this" She shoved a spoonful in his mouth.

"It's good, I've had it before."

"I haven't."

"Enjoy it, but enjoy it at the table."

Valeria pretended to ignore him.

"Please. I'm sorry, I was rude."

Valeria sighed and looked at Cora "Should we give them another chance?"

Cora finished her breakfast. "I suppose so, they're not all bad."

The girls giggled as they walked back to the table.

"Cora." Rabi beckoned to her with a finger

"Yes."

"Tomorrow, I want you to start something new."

"What?"

"Be my assistant. I'm getting too old to take care of all these people and tasks myself. And there's a lot that you already do."

Cora threw her arms around Rabi's neck and placed a kiss on his cheek. "Thank you."

Over the course of the next few days Cora and Valeria got to know and to like each other. The foursome spent a lot of time together.

When Valeria prepared to leave Cora was almost as sad as Vanar to see her go.

Valeria stood by the carriage as her bags were lifted up and tied down to the top, Vanar stood with her. As the last knot was tied and the driver took his place Vanar pulled Valeria close to him. "I'm going to miss you so much." His fingers ran through her hair and he felt her arms squeeze his waist.

"Not as much as I'll miss you."

"In the spring, we'll meet at the Marketplace, the 40th day. Right?"

Vanar's heart pumped hard, he couldn't let her go. Valeria felt tears escaping from the sides of her eyes.

"Right."

Warm wet lips met and refused to part for ever so long, avoiding the inevitable. Finally Vanar whispered, "Until the spring," as his fingers indulged in one last touch and she climbed into the carriage and waved good-bye.

As the large door shut behind him the shadows settled over him.

Chapter 21

Vanar lay on his stomach, his muscles tighter than reins on a wild ramek, gazing at the stars whose light reflected off the clean white snow. It was the middle of winter and he missed Valeria more than ever. Despite a rigorous training schedule and working early morning until dusk with Falor, the ache inside him never ceased, and wondering if she felt the same way was even worse.

Falor and Cora spent most evenings by the fire, reading or talking. Her father's apartment had been cleaned out and refurbished, there Falor left her every night.

Raphela's sensuous fingers kneaded the muscles in Atan's calves and steadily worked her way up to his thighs.

Her fingers warmed the firm muscles and although Atan relaxed, he was also thinking and before Raphela's hands reached his buttocks, he rolled over and sat up.

"Don't you like my touch?" Raphela mocked hurt.

Atan's hands encased hers. "I'd be a fool not to. The question is why are you being so generous with it?"

"Do I need a reason?"

The gentleness of their voices skirted the real issue.

"Raphela, for over 17 years we've shared a bed and a life. In that time you've honored me with six thorough and delicious massages."

"So?" For the first time she couldn't meet his glance.

"So, three have been in the past three months."

"Perhaps I realized you enjoyed them." She toyed with the sheets.

Atan placed his hand on her chin. "Let's be honest. Your massages are thorough enough to be exams."

Raphela lowered her eyes.

"Raphela, in case you weren't sure. I do have my father's disease." Atan's deep voice was as steady as his grey eyes.

Raphela felt her eyes fill.

"It began last spring, but after our trip, it stopped progressing. You must know that I will never deny the truth and," his voice took on a determination Raphela hadn't heard in a long time. "It will not possess me, though I know it will win in the end, it has a tough battle ahead of it."

Atan the warrior pierced beyond Raphela's fear as he rolled on top of her. Her arms stretched out above her head, Atan's hands met hers. "The only fool here, has been me," she whispered.

Along with a nibble on her neck came soft words, "I forgive you," followed by the powerful kiss of the warrior.

They rolled in the passion, savoring every moment, denying the future its grasp, at least for now.

Though Raphela and Atan would have welcomed a few more weeks buried under the snow, the spring would not wait, much to Vanar's delight. He watched the first storm in ecstasy, followed by an increased exercise schedule and plans for his trip.

Falor got dragged into the exercise room with him. Vanar made ten passes around the track and stopped, hands on his knees, to catch his breath. Falor, after five rounds, came up behind him, panting and then leaned against a wall, eventually sliding to the ground.

Vanar tossed him a towel. "That wasn't bad for warm-up." He stretched his arms, doing a series of toe touches.

"Warm-up?" Falor panted. "Are you trying to kill me?"

"No, just keep you in shape. You wouldn't want Cora's eye to rove would you?" Vanar teased.

Falor bolted to his feet and grabbed Vanar's arm "Is there someone else? Is she looking?"

Vanar squinted his eyes in quizzical wonder. "What are you talking about?"

"You said..."

"Falor, Cora is madly in love with you. I'm just trying to keep you healthy."

"Are you sure?"

"Yes, about both. Now, let's get back to work." Vanar shook his head and began the next round of calisthenics.

Cora finished labeling the jars and Nomi, a girl about 2 years older, helped her put them away.

426

"You look really nice lately, Cora." Nomi handed her the last bottle.

Cora stepped down from the ladder and brushed the dust off her hands. "Thank you."

You and Falor are really lucky. You have each other."

"Mm."

"It's lunchtime, where is he?"

"Working out with Vanar."

"That's good, he should stay in shape for you."

Nomi's chattiness confused Cora, but she let her continue. "How about having lunch with me?"

"Sure"

The girls whipped up a lunch and sat at a small table.

"Nomi, can I ask you something?" Cora pushed her plate away.

"Ugh huh" Nomi swallowed the last of her meal.

"Why are you talking to me, having lunch with me?"

"Why not?

"Because you never did before."

"Oh." Nomi didn't hide her embarrassment. "I guess I was afraid to before, we all were, all the girls."

"Afraid? Afraid of what?"

Nomi's eyes met Cora's. "Your father. We were afraid he might hurt us, but even more, we were afraid he'd destroy you."

Cora sank back in her chair, mouth open in astonishment. "You knew?"

"We guessed, we just didn't know how to fix it."

Large tears rolled down Cora's cheeks.

"I'm sorry I didn't mean to upset you." She handed Cora a cloth.

"Nomi, you've made me so happy. I always thought everyone hated me."

"Not a chance, you're too nice." Nomi smiled widely.

Cora discovered a new world. The girls who had always been at arm's length now treated her like a part of the team. After a while her spare time became divided between them and Falor.

While Vanar had no problem keeping Falor occupied, he did notice a certain somberness, even more than usual, about his friend.

It was five days before they were to leave. The "office" was a mass of boxes and cartons, all items for the Marketplace.

Vanar reviewed their list of vendors and as he rattled off the names Falor nodded but stared off into space.

"Next vendor, Mashta the Donag."

"Uhhuh."

Vanar stopped and waited.

"Oh sorry, was that a test?"

"What's been bothering you?" Vanar put the list down and leaned forward in his chair.

"Nothing." Falor tapped his foot nervously.

Vanar just waited in the edgy silence.

Falor stared at the floor. "Vanar?"

"Yes"

"What do you think about bringing Cora along?"

"I hadn't. But I don't see any reason why not. Valeria will probably like the company."

Both boys silently pondered the concept until Vanar spoke again. "As a matter of fact, it's a great idea."

"Why?" Falor became suspicious.

"Well, as much as I'd like to have Valeria with me constantly, I know that it can't happen. Taking her to all the fiefs will make her and the people there uncomfortable. If Cora comes along they can stay at the Marketplace, Valeria can decorate and Cora can probably set up the supply room better than we can. What do you think?"

"Considering that having Cora come along was my idea, I think its great." Falor's voice lost its gray veil and his eyes focused, temporarily.

"What does Cora think about it?"

"I don't know." He mumbled.

"You don't know. You mean you haven't asked her?"

Falor covered his eyes with his hands and took a deep breath. "No. She's been so busy, I hardly have enough time to say hello."

Vanar leaned back in his chair, his tone now somber like his friend's. "So that's why you want her to come along."

"I miss her. I'll ask her tonight. She's supposed to see her friends after dinner, but maybe she'll change her plans."

"I'm sure she will." Vanar offered kindly words and felt a little helpless at having nothing else to say.

Falor and Cora ate in the kitchen at a small table, Cora had long ago set up just for them.

Falor picked at his food.

Cora finished half of her meal and pushed the plate away. "You're not eating much lately," Falor said as he looked at the plate.

"I'm watching my weight." Cora had developed a little glow. Her hair was softer, with the help of a cream from the healers and she dressed perfectly, every day.

"You look perfect to me."

Cora squeezed his hand and cocked her head to look into the sad eyes of her love. "I always want to, just for you."

Falor permitted himself a smile. "Really?"

"Of course silly, where would I be without you." Cora shivered at the direction her life would have taken if Falor hadn't stepped into it.

"Cora, don't go with the girls tonight, come with me please."

"Sure."

They bundled up and walked outside. The snow was almost gone, but the air kept its winter chill. Cora kept close to Falor as they walked.

""In a few days I have to leave," he said.

"I know.' She dropped his arm, her head raised and big eyes concentrated on a bird bringing food to a nest.

This would normally send Falor into a realm of worry, but today it made his heart beat faster in joy. "Come with me," he blurted out the words.

"Where?"

"Everywhere, almost. Valeria's coming to the Marketplace. Why not you too."

"Do you really want me to come along?" Cora sniffled in the cold.

Falor wrapped his well-covered arms around her waist and pushed back their hats so their eyes could really meet. "Of course. Nothing would make me happier."

Cora hugged him hard and kissed him with a passion she had saved for just a moment. He replied in kind. Their faces reddened and tingled, but it wasn't important.

"Did you ever think I didn't want you by my side?" Falor came back to his normal state of concern.

"Not really, I just figured you and Vanar worked together and that it wasn't my business." Cora wasn't offended, it was a simple fact.

"You're right, to a point. But you're part of everything."

Cora took Rabi aside the next day to tell him. He made a face and crossed his arms in annoyance. "I'm getting too old for this you know, you in and out all the time. Pretty soon I'll have to chain you to this place. After all, I can't leave and when you take my place, you won't either."

Despite his growling, Cora knew Rabi understood and gave him a peck on the cheek. "I'll bring back a chain and a lock so that I can't go anywhere."

Rabi just shook his head and sent her away with a fatherly pat on the bottom. "Behave yourself."

"Yes Rabi." She giggled and ran off to begin her preparations for the trip.

For the next few days the three young people planned and anxiously waited for *the day*. Finally it arrived and they climbed into the carriage. All three slept the first leg of the journey, as none had for a while.

Vanar did his best not to push the drivers and the beasts, despite the gnawing at every inch of him. At long last it came into view, the great round building, gray stones stood strong in the light gathering up all the roads to its growing belly.

For a moment Vanar forgot his anxiety and watched a few carts move in and out of the Marketplace. His pulse quickened, for his dream was now a reality.

"Look Falor, its alive." Vanar woke Falor from a comfortable rest.

Falor and Cora sat up and peered out the window. "There are people there." Falor's amazement brought a chuckle to the trio.

"Wasn't that the idea?" Cora continued to stare out the window,

Vanar ignored her as they approached the main entrance, its regal frame proudly crowned with the Ishtban crest carved into the stone and splintered with gold and black stones.

The rameks barely came to a halt before Vanar scrambled out of the carriage. Falor helped Cora and slowly they followed their friend. Vanar's hand admired the finished walls, he even knelt to inspect the floor. The building was whole, ready for traffic and trade.

Cora wandered throughout the maze of rooms, while Falor, ever efficient, reviewed work orders and details. She found the grayish white walls easy on the eyes, but knew Valeria's touch would be an improvement. It was still quiet here, mostly workers, only one or two tradespeople. Vanar prayed that would change, that all the people that promised to set up shop here would do so.

Each of them found a room and after a day of inspecting, settled down for a good night's sleep.

In the morning Cora found a room she could turn into a kitchen. Everyone woke to a zesty aroma of hot tea and spice bread.

Before Falor found his way to her, a few workers hovered in the doorway. Cora smiled and gave permission for them to enter.

One young man came close to a pot of fruit stew and Cora. "Smells good." His nose drifted between her and the stew.

"If you find a table, chairs, plates and spoons, you might get some." Cora smiled, accustomed to control in the kitchen, but oblivious to the boy's flirtations.

Falor arrived as people lined up for breakfast, at first observing with pride Cora's confidence. Then his smile drooped and his brow creased.

The boy with the wandering nose hung at the back of the line, waiting to be alone with her. "You're really a good cook." His big eyes and wide smile hoped for more than a splash of tea.

431

"Thank you." She blushed, beginning to catch on to his meaning.

Falor swallowed hard and moved quickly. "Good morning Cora." He placed a gentle kiss on her cheek and stroked her hair.

The boy took his food and slipped away. Cora turned her head and watched. Falor's chin dropped to his chest. "Falor, what's wrong? Are you sick?" Cora felt his cheek with her palm.

"No, no I'm fine." He forced a grin.

"Good. Will you have breakfast with me?"

"Absolutely."

They sat by the pots, Cora frequently rising to direct and aid the last stragglers of the morning, including Vanar, who joined them.

"Good bread Cora."

"Thank you."

"I hope Valeria will arrive today."

Falor watched his friend tap his fingers on the table and twist his head this way and that. "We all do."

Cora stood up, her hand slid under the plates, but Falor's fingers wrapped around her wrist. "Sit down, someone else can take care of this."

"But..."

"Please."

"If you insist" She plopped back down into the chair and nervously waited for someone to begin cleaning up.

Falor quietly motioned to a couple of boys, who satisfied Cora's need. Though it wasn't her kitchen, technically, it wasn't anyone else's either.

"Cora?" Vanar tapped her on the shoulder

"Huh, what? Oh sorry. Vanar I just wanted to make sure"

"Cora, why don't you take charge of the cooking and food supplies. Now that the construction is done, there are a number of people looking for things to do. Why not choose three or four and train them to be your staff?"

"I don't mean to take over."

"Sure you do, any way, someone needs to."

"Thank you." She placed a grateful kiss on Vanar's cheek.

432

Falor began coordinating the few vendors who had arrived and studied the movement of the people, what rooms they drifted to most, and why.

Vanar made a weak attempt to plan his travels but often found himself pacing the floor.

Raalek's sun set in the south. Vanar stood at the southern entrance, far from people, allowing the purple rays of the sleepy sun to warm his face as he questioned himself and his decisions.

His eyes were drawn to a furry sloth, creeping along the branch of a tree. The slow, practical movement of each paw provided a hypnotic view, a distraction Vanar welcomed. He observed each brown muscular paw move inch by inch up the branch, the animal's body like a dead load, attached for the ride.

A soft warm breeze brushed by Vanar's ear, he jumped and turned.

Valeria smiled and their arms drew them close. He kissed her so powerfully she had to catch her breath. They didn't let go, two sets of young eyes locked. "I was so afraid you wouldn't come.'

"You're a fool. But so am I. I was afraid you'd send me away."

She laid her head on his shoulder and his strong gentle hands began to massage her shoulders and back. Valeria's fingers explored his muscular frame and her breasts pressed against his chest as his hands discovered her round firm bottom. Vanar's chest heaved and they kissed with a passion neither knew existed. He felt himself grow and yearn to be inside her and she didn't resist sharing the excitement. Vanar sucked on her neck and his fingers lifting her skirt. Valeria stroked his well-defined back, feeling the tight skin that sent a shiver down her spine.

Suddenly, Vanar broke away, his lips wet, staring at her for a moment and then ran to the hills.

Shocked, Valeria gazed at the receding form, unable to speak or cry.

Bertram, in the shadows, as always, considered approaching her, but knew his duty was to follow Vanar, that he did.

Falor, looking for Vanar anyway, saw Valeria, standing motionless.

"What's wrong?" He stood behind her. She didn't turn.

"I don't know. He, he, just left. Why Falor? Why did he go?" She faced him, feeling more confused than anything.

"Come inside, its cold out here."

Valeria allowed him to guide her to a chair by the fire where Cora joined them.

Valeria's long blond hair flowed over the chair, her face pale and her hands trying to explain what her voice couldn't. Cora wrapped a blanket around Valeria's shoulders, pulled up a chair and took Valeria's hand. "Tell me, what happened."

"I don't know. We were together, holding, kissing. I never felt so good, and then, he stopped and ran away. What did I do? What did I do wrong?"

Cora stroked her hand. "I doubt you did anything wrong."

Cora turned to Falor for support. But he was racing through his mind trying to understand his friend's behavior and finally coming to what he believed was the solution. He disengaged himself from the trance.

"So do I. Just sit here. Someone will bring you some tea and I'll see if Vanar has returned."

Cora sat with Valeria, neither saying much.

Falor wrapped a coat around himself, took one for Vanar, and began the search.

Vanar and Bertram walked back to the Marketplace together.

"She's going to hate me, how can I face her?" His head shook back and forth in self-beratement.

"You did the right thing." Bertram's hand on his shoulder was reassuring.

"I know. But if I weren't me, I wouldn't have had to do the right thing. I could be like any other boy." He stared at Bertram. "Sometimes I hate being heir apparent."

"I know and I don't envy you."

"Thanks," he sighed deeply. "I just hope she forgives me."

"She will, but I'm not sure about me. Here, catch."

Vanar instinctively raised his hands and caught the coat from Falor. "Is she really mad?"

"Vanar, you confused her something awful." Falor fell into step beside Vanar, who stuck out above Falor and Bertram.

434

"I'm a fool."

"Vanar."

"What?"

"Was it self control?"

"You know me too well."

"Then you're not such a fool."

"I'm afraid that's for Valeria to decide and I can't even tell her. I'm not ready yet."

Bertram squeezed Vanar's shoulder. "You may have a very long night ahead of you."

Valeria and Cora had set a table for dinner. Bertram wandered off and the boys joined the girls.

It was a quiet meal, after which Falor and Cora slipped away to watch the stars.

Vanar and Valeria sat across the table from each other, first watching a server remove the plates and soon it was just a table and chairs and them.

Vanar saw his fingers follow the cracks in the wooden table, Valeria did the same.

"I'm sorry." He couldn't look up.

She heard the words, but somehow it wasn't enough.

"What did I do? What did I do wrong?" She tried to make him look at her. It worked.

The pain on her face sent him reeling. He wished Mahtso were there to dole out some kind of beating that could put her pain on him and leave her well.

"Will you walk with me?"

She shrugged a yes and did not shrink back when he took her hand.

They walked to the north entrance and watched the clouds pass by the moon. Vanar leaned against a column and held her hands so she would face him.

"You didn't do anything wrong, you couldn't have done anything more right."

"Then why?"

Honesty and reality are hard partners and few people, especially young men, can deal with both equally, but Vanar had been trained and had sprung from special loins. His eyes never

435

left hers, didn't avoid the painful stare. "I can't tell you. It isn't right for me to tell you."

She pulled her hands away. "It's not fair for me not to know."

How do you tell someone you believe you love that you're not 100% sure, just because you're the son of the Duke? How do you say, "I can't make love to you, unless I know. I can't let you bear my children, unless I'm sure. Is that fair? Though much of Atan's past was shrouded in mystery, his attitudes were as clear as the stars. He had instilled in his son, that no child of Vanar's would survive, unless, Vanar had made a commitment to the mother, as a partner for life.

Valeria's green eyes burned. No young girl should make love with a threat over her head. She didn't know the rules and could not be told.

"I'm sorry, I just can't tell you." The muscles in his throat ached as he spoke the words.

Valeria felt an anger rise inside her. It had no words, simply a black feeling of frustration. She tried to understand, but there was nothing to understand. Vanar didn't flinch at her stinging slap.

"I hate you Vanar." She ran off to Cora's room and cried into a pillow.

Vanar allowed the tears to fall down his cheek and cursed his life.

Cora found Valeria sobbing in the bed, her eyes red and cheeks blotched.

"Want to talk?" Cora sat down and faced her friend.

Valeria sniffled and sat up. "He won't tell me anything"

Cora handed her a hot cup of tea and just listened.

"If I knew why, it would be all right. I feel like an outcast, not permitted to know the truth." Valeria stopped sniffling and began honing in on her words. "I just don't understand. We were getting so close, it was incredible. Cora, he made me feel so alive. I tingled all over, and then suddenly, he stopped. It was like, like breathing and someone taking away the air."

"How awful"

Valeria closed her eyes and allowed a few tears to escape. She whispered, "I told him I hated him and then I, I slapped him." She began a new round of tears.

Cora felt helpless, as Valeria cried she had no wisdom for her friend, no advice. She thought long and hard about what she knew of Vanar and found a slice of hope to share. "Valeria?"

"What?" She wiped her eyes and blew her nose.

"I don't know why all this happened, but I do know he cares about you so much. He paced this building all day, waiting for you."

"Oh Cora, I love him, but will he hate me now? Did I ruin it all?"

"I doubt it. Vanar is not put off that easily."

"I hope not."

The girls chatted a little longer until both fell asleep.

Vanar lay in bed, dazed, not knowing what to do. Did he lose her? Were all those feelings telling him there should be no more doubts? Finally exhaustion forced him to sleep.

In the morning Valeria woke early and passed by Vanar's room on the way to the washroom. Bertram stopped her.

"Valeria, I don't intrude in Vanar's life, but now is when parents might help, but they aren't here, so I'll make an attempt to say the right thing. Remember that Vanar is not just any boy, his life now and later is unique."

Bertram made sure their eyes met as he spoke. She nodded and left.

Was her anger of value enough to hold on to it? She knew Bertram was telling her something important and even if the words were fuzzy to her, she knew she had to decide whether or not to accept the "unique" person's situation.

The cold water felt good on her face and cleared her mind. She arrived at the breakfast table, as Cora was setting it. "How are you doing?" She handed Valeria some glasses.

"Better."

"Good."

Falor arrived and placed a flower by Cora's seat and a kiss on her lips. Vanar showed up soon after, head bowed. Valeria felt tears well up in her eyes.

Before he had a chance to sit, she stood in front of him and looked up at the sullen face. "I love you Vanar."

The answering hug said so much, she felt his tears in her hair as hers stained his shirt. He stroked her hair and whispered, "Be patient with me, please, I want you more than you know."

"Shh, let's just take it day by day." Valeria felt his tongue mix with hers and their lips joined in warm forgiveness.

Breakfast metamorphosed slowly from quiet conversation to exciting plans. Over the next few days Cora chose a staff, created a schedule for them and worked with them to build menus and to control food supplies.

Each time Falor passed her she looked contented. He noticed more people drifting toward the dining hall. It had, like many kitchens, become a place to gather.

Cora had decided to keep tea, biscuits and sweetcakes available from sunrise to sunset. Once the flow of people extended to travelers and shoppers, she had a plan for recouping costs and making a profit.

Valeria traveled from room to room with two aides, all three pulling carts laden with paint and cloth. Vanar watched her smear paint on a wall or nail up a piece of cloth. Then all three would move around the room and generally determine if the hue was right or wrong.

Meanwhile, he and Falor checked in on the few traders who had arrived and asked a multitude of questions of everyone there. What more was needed, what less, how to make everyone want to flock to the Marketplace. Their itinerary for travel was about complete and the boys would soon have to be on their way.

It was five days since Valeria's arrival. Cora was tearing apart a supply cabinet while a young man stood patiently by her side.

"I know its here, I can't believe I didn't bring any mull spice." Cora's carefully combed and tied back hair had begun to fall out of place and her knees hurt from resting on them while she searched. Finally she sat on the floor in frustration and looked up at the young man. "It's not here." She sighed and moved to stand. He offered a hand which she accepted. Falor, unseen, watched.

As she stood, Falor swore the young man held onto to her for a second or two longer than necessary. Cora turned her head, but Falor vanished before she could see him.

Valeria helped her set the table for dinner.

"You look bothered. Is something wrong?" She placed a basket of rolls on the table.

"Nothing really. I just wish we had some things that we don't."

"Why not ask the boys to take us to town? It'll be a little adventure and any way tomorrow is supposed to be a day of rest." Valeria's eyes sparkled, at the prospect.

"Good idea. Here they come."

Respective lips received gentle kisses, followed by the sound of chairs moving back and being occupied,

"Smells good Cora, what masterpiece have you dreamed up today?" Vanar stuck his nose in the air.

"Nothing very exciting." She laid the platter of meat and vegetables sautéed in a sweet sauce, on the table.

The boys immediately dug in.

"Falor?"

"Mm, what Cora?" He washed down his food with a large gulp of water.

"I'd like to go to town tomorrow." She approached the statement cautiously, although the request was reasonable.

"All right, but why?"

"I need some supplies, spices and such."

"If that's what you want." He shrugged.

"I do."

Valeria opened her mouth and turned to Vanar.

"Yes, we'll go to." Vanar said before he could speak.

She landed a playful slap on his leg. "Oh you." She pouted. He responded with a kiss,

After dinner the couples went off separately. Vanar and Valeria choosing the brisk spring air for a walk, while Falor and Cora curled up by the fireplace.

"You look so good Cora. I'm so proud of you, of everything you do."

The fire crackled and popped sending sparks up the chimney sharing a part of its warmth with the couple. But Cora still sat on his lap and wrapped her arms around his neck. "None of it would be, without you.' Warm honest eyes demanded his attention. He tried to avoid them, but her hand pulled his chin up.

"Why are you here with me?" he asked suddenly.

Cora moved her head back in surprise and then leaned into him with a long sensuous kiss. "Because I love you, you foolish boy." She tickled him and again he tried to avoid her, but in the end couldn't resist playing. They rolled around, sharing passionate kisses and longing touches.

"I love you so much Cora." He lay on her, wishing there were nothing between their bodies.

Cora engaged him in one more lengthy kiss. "Not as much as I love you." They parted for the night on that note, though neither wanted to leave the other.

It took half a day to ride into town. The drivers were a little unsure of the way, but after only one wrong turn the array of shops and houses came into view. The community was about the size of Milson.

The young couples walked hand in hand down the cobblestone streets, anonymous among the townspeople, enjoying each other and the quiet day.

A small red building, at the end of one street that beckoned with exotic scents and a curious window design. The shopkeeper lifted only an eyebrow as they entered and left them alone to explore his trinkets.

Valeria picked up a jar that reflected the light, upon removing the cap she was greeted with the aroma of flowers.

"Cora, come see what I found." Both girls hovered over the bottle.

The boys took stock of the unusual inventory and both had the same idea.

Vanar approached the man. "Good day. I am Vanar, son of Duke Ishtba." He spoke casually, but the man still dropped the stone in his hand.

"Young sire, I'm honored to have you here. What may I do for you." His graying curly hair went well with the gray stubble on his face and his deep blue eyes.

"My friend and I were wondering if you'd consider opening a second shop?"

Vanar studied a small bottle marked POTION.

"A second shop?" He cleared his throat. "Where?"

"At The Marketplace."

Nostra, the shopkeeper, was aware of The Marketplace, but knew little about it. "Perhaps my son could do this for you. Omar, come here."

Omar, a year or two older than Vanar was explaining his fathers unique items to the girls. He brushed some of the liquid scent on each of their wrists. Falor felt his chest heave up and down as the boys fingers rubbed into Cora's fresh skin.

Omar put the bottle back in its place and walked to his father. "Yes father?"

"This is Vanar, son of Duke Ishtba and his associate Falor, they wish to discuss a business proposition with us."

The men spoke briefly and it was agreed Omar would open a shop at the Marketplace, and Vanar would provide his food and shelter until business was good enough for self-support.

The girls purchased a bottle of Aroma, which Falor tolerated and Vanar ignored.

Broad leaves shaded the streets and the young couples strolled casually past the doors enjoying the sights and sounds of the simple town. Falor paid more attention than the others to each window, inspecting the goods thoroughly enough to keep the pace slow.

Finally he stopped at a jewelry store and without examining the window fare entered with Cora tightly in his grasp. The other two, shoulders shrugging, followed.

"What might you have for this lovely girl, a bracelet perhaps?" Falor spoke to Egan, the shopkeeper.

Cora stared at him. A bracelet? More than a simple trinket.

Vanar and Valeria stood quietly in the background.

Falor examined the selection of gold and silver in the case and chose an intricately carved gold bracelet, speckled with greenstone, and placed it by her hand. "What do you think?"

Cora held onto the counter for balance and croaked, "I don't know."

He put it back. "Pick something."

Vanar squinted his eyes and shook his head. Falor never gave commands.

"Falor, I..."

"Cora" His fingers intertwined with hers. "If there is someone else, I'll go away, but if not, stay with me, forever." Command mellowed to truth and emotions beyond words.

Cora looked deep into his eyes and her hand moved to the glass counter. "Those, the rings."

Egan pulled them out. "You have a fine eye. These are special, a matched set for certain. The only ones in existence to my knowledge. They are braided gold and silver. The tale is, only young lovers, destined to be together can wear them. Those untrue will suffer the pain of their spell. It is said the rings will burn the skin of the undeserving, as the undeserving burn the heart. I have had them in my shop for over a year. No one has yet been brave enough to try." The man swallowed hard, fearful of losing the sale, but his large brown eyes trembled with honesty.

Vanar and Valeria squeezed each other's hands, but remained silent.

"Let's find an elder." Cora handed one ring to Falor and kept one for herself. Both were placed carefully in pockets.

Upon Valeria's insistence, the boys were sent on a mission to purchase the spices and other items for which they had originally come.

She took Cora to the local cloth merchant. "You must have something special to wear." Valeria studied a bolt of blue velvet fabric as she spoke, putting it up against Cora's face and then returning it to the table.

"Val, I really don't care what I wear."

"Shh. It will be something to keep, forever, to pass down to your daughters." Valeria placed another swatch of cloth by Cora's face, this one a mauve silk.

"Excuse me" Valeria beckoned to the merchant.

"Yes?" He smiled at the girls, one so exuberant, the other so embarrassed.

"What do you think? Is it right for her?"

The man stood back and evaluated the match. Cora stood helplessly in Valeria's control. "Excellent choice of color, but I have a thicker material that will do better."

He drew out a rich shimmery cloth. Even Cora's eyes lit and Valeria's lips curled up in ecstasy.

"Yes, that's perfect. Don't you agree Cora?"

She just nodded.

"May I borrow a needle and thread and shears. We need to create this cape now."

He laughed. "Young girls, they never change." He produced a sewing kit.

Valeria measured Cora and immediately began her work.

"You have a good friend. But what is the occasion?" The man straightened the bolts of cloth Valeria had sorted through and watched a woman walk by his shop.

"I'm getting married." A tiny blush crept into her cheek.

"Let me guess, today?"

"Mmhmm"

The man looked at Valeria feverishly creating the cape, a beautiful young girl and by outward appearance a more than likely candidate for marriage then her plain friend.

Another customer began browsing around the shop.

"Well, best of luck to you."

"Thank you."

The girls paid for the cloth and the shopkeep pressed an object in Cora's hand and whispered, "It's good luck for the bride."

When they arrived at the Elder's house Cora looked in her hand and saw a simple but elegant, silver broach.

Valeria gently rapped on the door. A young man, not much past twenty, with rounded shoulders and curly hair peered down at them.

"Can I help you?" His words soothed the air.

"We are here to see the Elder." Both girls met the man's glance, Valeria with determination and Cora with longing.

"That would be me." He ushered them in.

Valeria explained the reason for their presence. The Elder, Nomac, frequently studied Cora, who sat quietly and inventoried the few simple artifacts around the room.

Once the explanations were complete Valeria waited outside and Cora took a little time to prepare herself.

Valeria paced back and forth, watching the sun and the shadows it cast, move and change.

Finally, the boys appeared, Falor toting one heavy sack and Vanar laden with two.

"Give Vanar your sack" Valeria sounded much like a mother readying her children for an outing. Instinctively, Falor obeyed. Vanar sagged with the additional weight and wondered how the next Duke could be in this position of pack animal.

Valeria fitted Falor with a sash to match Cora's cape and adjusted it until she was satisfied it looked right.

"Valeria, these bags are getting heavy" Vanar moaned and the cool air was beginning to put an ache in his neck.

"There, you look wonderful," she announced, stepping back.

"Thank you. Can we go inside now?" Falor asked anxiously.

"Of course." Valeria smiled indulgently and¹ led the way. Vanar deposited the bags by the door.

Cora was not in the room but the Elder greeted them.

Vanar looked long and hard at the man. "Are you sure you're an elder? You're so young."

Nomac smiled. "You look familiar, have we met before?"

"No"

"Mm." He placed a hand on Vanar's shoulder. "You are Vanar, son of Lady Raphela and Duke Ishtba."

Vanar's mouth opened in shock. "How did you know?"

"Your features and your stance. I am honored to have you in my home. By the way, I am an elder. Unlike at the castle, where

444

the elders are limited in their usefulness, the towns are more dependent on our help. Age is of less importance than the ability, to use wisdom handed down from the ancients and to lead the people and help them in their daily struggle to live happy lives." Nomac didn't boast, if anything his soft spoken manner painted a picture of honor.

Falor caught a whiff of dinner cooking. "Have we come at a bad time?"

"Not at all. Now, come to the sanctuary." He led them to a small room, draped in heavy cloth and lit by candles in twelve places.

"Valeria and Vanar, will you be witnesses?"

They nodded and walked slowly towards the podium, feeling somehow small and unimportant, yet very safe.

Falor saw Cora waiting, head bowed, and exercised every ounce of control not to run to her and hold her. Vanar and Valeria stood to the side. Nomac took his place at the podium.

Falor's feet turned and his eyes gazed deeply at Cora, dressed in the simple clothes he adored, the cape an incredibly sensuous addition. Her hair flowed behind her clear, clean face, free of any adornment. Falor's skin tingled, his heart beating faster than ever and his desire to be inside her mounting like a snowball swelling on its way down hill.

Cora saw nothing but Falor and his yearning drew her to him willingly and wantingly.

"Falor of Calcoran" Nomac forced their attention forward.

"You choose Cora to stand by you and to bear your children until the gods shall part you. Is this so?" The soft-spoken voice was demanding, almost harsh.

"Yes, without question."

Nomac turned to Cora, who no more looked at him than Falor had. "And you Cora of Ishtba, you would bear his children and share his life?"

"It is all I wish for."

"Friends of this couple, would anyone object to or see as unfit this union?"

Valeria and Vanar each whispered, "No".

"Do you have a bracelet?"

445

"No."

"Then I..."

Falor raised his hand and stopped Nomac. "Cora, together forever" he slipped the ring on her right forefinger.

Nomac gasped in silent recognition of the rings and his lips moved in silent prayer.

"Falor, together forever" she slipped the ring on to his finger.

The silence deafened even Nomac, who finally found his voice. "I decree by the gods wisdom that you be husband and wife."

Falor pulled Cora so close she felt his heart and his desire. "I love you," she whispered as they kissed.

"Not as much as I love you." He breathed in her ear.

"We have a room for newlyweds, my wife will show you," Nomac smiled.

A short plump woman guided them to a small room furnished with a bed a table a jug of wine and a loaf of bread.

Nomac turned to Vanar and Valeria. "Perhaps you two would join us for dinner?"

"We'd be honored." They followed him to a modest dining room.

At the other end of the house Cora's cloak gently fell to a chair, her hand moving with a grace Falor didn't believe possible as the candlelight accentuated every movement. She stood in front of him and began undoing her buttons.

Falor pulled her hands to his lips and brushed them with a kiss. "Let me."

Cora nearly melted at his tenderness. Deftly, slowly, his fingers slid the buttons from their tight places until her bodice just barely covered her breasts.

Cora loosened his belt and his pants slid to the floor.

Her nipple hardened as he cupped it in his hand. Her bodice left her as their eyes and lips met.

"You are so beautiful," he whispered as he bent his head and sucked on her breast. Cora grabbed his naked buttocks and pulled him close.

For a long time they explored, not rushing to the bed, just learning. Falor's hands felt so good on every part of her and Cora's lips on his neck sent him soaring.

As the moons took there places in the sky Cora lay on the bed. Falor climbed on top of her, caressing her with his tongue.

Before he took her, his hands held back her hair and his eyes demanded hers. "Are you afraid?"

"I don't know," she whispered.

"I won't hurt you, I know I don't want to."

"I know." She stared at him, and then pulled him close for a kiss. "Make love to me." she whispered.

He penetrated her cautiously. She felt unbelievably warm and wet and wonderful. Cora felt her tension give way to an excitement she had only dreamt possible.

They loved over and over again, stopping just before the sun rose and sleep took over.

Vanar and Valeria shared dinner with Nomac and his wife Irma.

"You are very handsome young people. My father always said the Duke would have a handsome son, He was so right, wasn't he Nomac?" Irma waited long enough for him to nod and then continued. "My father saw the Duke once, a long time ago, very tall he was, and strong. And that Mahtso, was with him. Do you know Mahtso?" She didn't wait for an answer. "Of course you do, how silly of me to ask. Anyway, Mahtso frightened most of the people in town. Your father was simply beyond understanding. You seem like a gentler fellow. Don't you think Nomac?" Nomac smiled and nibbled on a vegetable. "My sister would never believe you were here. She'd say, Irma you've been drinking gramma's wine. I know she'd say that."

Vanar and Valeria listened politely, amazed that Irma could actually eat and keep up the pace of conversation.

"But perhaps you could write a note, make her believe. She's never been far from home, just over the hills you know. But it is a long trip even to town. A note would be a prized possession. Only if it's not too much trouble of course. I wouldn't want to trouble you."

Vanar found the exact second that Irma would take a breath to respond. "I'd be happy to leave a nòte as proof of my appearance." His patronization, not cruel, yet unavoidable, went undetected by Irma and ignored by Nomac.

"Oh thank you so much. Do you believe it Nomac? My sister will be so proud. I'm so excited." Irma continued on well into dessert and ended with a gentle nudge from her husband.

"Perhaps you'd like to take a walk. It is a beautiful night." Nomac opened the front door and took in a breath of fresh air.

"That sounds like a good idea, what do you think Valeria?" Vanar felt meeting one's bride on the wedding night would have been less awkward than this moment.

Valeria shrugged indicating her agreement and with a wrap provided by Irma, the two young people crossed the threshold into the night.

Vanar slipped his arm through hers as the front door closed behind them. Above them the sky sparkled with stars and the shadows of Cora and Falor were silhouetted in the window.

Both glanced in that direction and quickly turned away.

"Irma certainly can talk." Valeria rubbed Vanar's arm.

"Yes she can. I suppose it takes the patience of an elder to be married to her." Vanar hid a sigh.

"I suppose." Valeria's pretense of cheer crumbled with her words.

Vanar felt his chest ache at not knowing what to do.

They walked long past the house and came to a pond surrounded by trees.

Valeria threw a stone and watched the water ripple while Vanar snuck a whiff of her hair and leaned against a tall old tree sprouting broad leaves on thick branches.

Valeria, as lost as Vanar watched the stones roll down the gentle slope toward the pond, and brushed away the early night flies from her face. Then her feet, as if without guidance, moved to Vanar. She leaned into him and despite self-made promises his arms circled her waist.

Nothing ever felt as good, as her soft sweet skin inside his large hands. Valeria's head rested easily on his chest and again she felt safe, content. Yet, the touch between them was not whole, like an unfinished song whose writer wandered lost in a sea of notes.

For the moment, though, this would have to do.

Before the sun rose, Falor writhed in pain and sat up so straight he looked like a board. Cora turned and stroked his leg, eyes barely open and voice only capable of a groggy whisper. "What's wrong my love?"

Falor stared at the wall and squeezed Cora's hand, his forehead a waterfall of sweat and his mouth as dry as the embers of an old fire. Finally he turned to her, taking a deep breath and relaxing the muscles in his back. "Just a bad dream. I'm fine."

"Are you sure?"

He lay back and held her close to him, stroking her hair, "Yes, I'm sure."

He forced a smile as they lay down together. She fell asleep in his arms. But he lay awake until his eyelids gave in to exhaustion.

Before mid-morning both couples were in the carriage, headed for the marketplace, Falor and Cora stealing kisses for no reason and displaying the affection expected of newlyweds.

Valeria lay her head on Vanar's strong shoulder and his hand gently caressed her hair and arm. Both chose to attempt sleep and to avoid watching the newlyweds.

The marketplace was open, but not bustling. The few vendors who had arrived had only each other for customers. The basic operation was ready to go, it just needed people.

Vanar and Falor convinced themselves that it was early in the year, so business would be slow.

Valeria and Cora were busy establishing their own realms. So the boys, bored after two days packed to leave and visit the fiefs.

Falor and Cora clung to each other until the last possible moment.

Vanar gripped Valeria's hands so tight they hurt, she said nothing, as their eyes searched for answers neither had. Their parting kiss was long and full, yet as incomplete as that of a few days before. Both wiped tiny tears as they parted.

Cora wished she had something to offer her friend, but wisdom comes with age and youth was still her gift.

Falor didn't prod Vanar, but carefully discussed fief business and soon they both avoided personal questions.

Raphela sat on the bed while Atan pulled up his pants and then searched for his tunic. She held it before his eyes and snickered.

"Humph." He turned his back and tucked the shirt into his pants.

"Have you packed everything? Extra clothes?"

"Yes."

Her tone bespoke more than concern about clothes. "Be careful, don't take any stupid risks." She stood and handed him a jacket, receiving an "are you done?" stare.

"Sorry. I'm just concerned."

"Good. Then my plan to add a few gray hairs to your head is working.

"There are plenty without your help." Raphela put her hands on her hips. "Why do you want gray hairs on my head?"

Atan wrapped his arms around her waist. "So no one will think I'm robbing the cradle."

"You can't steal what's already yours." Raphela felt the words barely escape before their lips met and her eyes burned with tears at the rare tender words. They held each other for a long time. Then she brushed away the tears as she fixed his jacket. "Behave yourself."

"I promise."

"Thank you." She smiled and swatted his bottom as he left.

Atan climbed into the carriage where Mahtso was waiting. With a gentle click of the reins they were on their way.

"It's been a long time my friend, hasn't it?" Atan leaned back and put up his feet as he spoke.

"Yes, when riding in a carriage generally meant a trip to Calcoran, for a gala."

450

"Indeed. When you were trying to find a mate for me, ever so diligent in your task."

"I'm glad you ignored me."

"So am I," Atan smiled.

Raphela and Fatell sipped tea together in the kitchen.

Raphela swirled hers around, observing the gentle waves lick the side of the cup.

"Is something bothering you?" Fatell bit down on a crunchy biscuit.

The skeleton summer staff made little noise and much effort to avoid the two women. Though the kitchen was a place for open talk, important people said important things, not for the ears of lesser folk, at least that was what the staff perceived, a baffling concept to those 'important people'.

"No, you know how I feel. They're both gone." Raphela's tightly tied hair matched her pent up mood.

"Mmhm." Fatell sensed there was more but knew not to push. "Mahtso drew a map for us and the drivers. It should be an exciting trip."

"I'm sorry Fatell." She squeezed her friend's hand. "This is important. I wonder how receptive the general public will be to this new idea."

"Mowatt has been asking and the response has been good."

Raphela smiled. "So, now you have Mowatt to do your research. When did you ask him?"

"I sent him word last fall and got a message just yesterday." Fatell sipped her tea and exhibited a confidence she long deserved.

"Good. When do you want to leave?"

"Three days?"

"As you wish. But will you be able to leave?" Raphela teased.

"Its hard, but I'll try."

They both laughed and studied the map. Three days later they climbed into the large carriage. It left slowly, with another tagging along behind full of woodsheets, scribes and books.

Atan signaled the driver to stop just as they passed the main gates of Calcoran Castle.

451

Though the door closed gently, Atan heard nothing but that door. "It's very quiet, don't you think Mahtso?" He eyed the area as he spoke.

Mahtso chuckled. "Not everyone is up at dawn my lord."

The driver smiled, accustomed to his Duke's early ways.

Atan nodded and the driver took the carriage and rameks to the stables.

Mahtso and Atan strolled side by side, casting a shadow that moved in easy even steps. A tiny bird glided overhead and broke the silence. Rows upon rows of brilliant flora layered the land like a carpet carefully woven and meant for hanging. The scent circled them and the bees hovered over a distant patch doing their fair share to keep the land alive. They didn't linger too long with the flowers and garden there would be a full inspection later.

When they arrived at the front door, it swung slowly open as Mahtso knocked. Both men immediately transformed from visitor to soldier. Their eyes studied the terrain and both leaned against the wall of the building.

Atan's nose picked up a familiar scent, of days long past, Mahtso's nostrils were not immune. Ever so slowly Mahtso pushed open the door, just enough to allow them entrance. The main hall was deserted, except for the trails of blood on the floor.

Taking small quiet steps they proceeded. Fingers wrapped tight around the handles of their blades.

Mostly the walls were solid and open, displaying many portraits, narrow areas were concealed by heavy curtains. Atan lightly stabbed each curtain before approaching it. As he stood in front of one, he felt a tug at his pants. Immediately his blade was ready to thrust downward. As it began its descent, a large pair of mahogany eyes beneath a mop of curly hair looked up at him. The young boy shrank back to avoid the blade.

Atan lowered his head, replaced the blade to its sheath and knelt to the boy, signaling Mahtso to watch his back.

"What has happened here?"

The boy stared at Atan's face, evading his glance. "My lord, it was barbarians, they came last night, killed and captured many."

"How did you know I was not one of them?" Atan was gentle.

"Your shoes. The barbarians didn't wear any."

"All right. Are they still here?"

The boy swallowed. "Yes, upstairs and in the kitchen."

"What of Jivad?" Maintaining the calm the child needed from him was difficult, Atan gripped his blade and squeezed hard.

The boy bowed his head. "Dead my lord. They killed him first. But Sonja, she's alive and so is Geho, he's hiding."

"You've done well. What is your name?" Atan didn't have time to analyze this curious lad, but he would, soon.

"Telep, sire."

"Telep, would you be able to sneak out and get to the stables?"

"I think so my lord." Telep quivered, but only a bit.

"Then tell my men to bring help and send one to me." He kept his voice mellow, like a warm fire. The boy obeyed without question.

Mahtso and Atan continued on, hugging the walls as they went, all senses attuned to any change. Mahtso passed a closed door and stopped, silently motioning to Atan. Both heard the faint sound of breathing. Atan opened the door slowly while Mahtso waited, sword in hand.

In the darkness behind the door the breathing grew clearer, but there was no movement. Atan's sword cautiously brushed the air until it tapped something other than a wall.

"Whoever you are, come out slowly," The command left no options.

As the figure emerged Atan closed his eyes and sighed. It was Geho staring up in gratitude and hope.

"Are you hurt?" Atan studied the boy, clothes glued on by nervous sweat, his hair stuck to his forehead, just a few dry strands way at the top.

Geho replied with a silent, "no."

"Then return to your hiding place until Mahtso or I return. You've done well."

Geho crept back and leaned against the wall, wrapping his hands around his knees as the door closed.

"Mahtso," Atan drew close to his friend and whispered "I'm going to explore upstairs, you finish here."

"But..."

"We have no choice, time may be critical."

Atan's skin tingled and his heart beat with a sense of adventure and danger reminiscent of days past, as his fingers tightened around the sword, sharp and gleaming, now an extension of himself. With each step towards the bedroom his sense of a presence grew and it lit the warrior in him. Silently he passed the first bedroom, empty as was the second, but from the third, the master bedroom came an odor and a sound of footsteps Light shone through windows, almost into the hallway, well lined with torches. Atan saw him, broad, tall, clothed in animal skin and obviously in need of a bath. He didn't see or hear Atan step through the doorway. But halfway to the bed his nostrils flared and the big bushy head turned from its interest to Atan.

Eyes locked for a moment of study. One man seemed lean and wispy, but experienced, not to be taken lightly, the other was a beast by size and definitely a leader, but every chain has a weak link. Atan met the man's heavy blade, whisking the air around him, with the knowledge that victory has many avenues.

Uneven yellow teeth bared themselves, "First battle," he smiled with delight.

Atan easily stepped away from the sword, while trying to ignore the stench and Sonja, lying still and naked in the bed.

The barbarian grunted and moved more quickly, raising his sword for a more direct blow. Atan's blade met his and the ring of steel against steel signaled battle.

Atan made no aggressive moves, allowing his opponent to take action, while he learned. The large beastly man was much quicker than his appearance suggested.

The swords met time and time again, each man turning and twisting to defend and attack. Under deep bushy brows the barbarian's eyes followed Atan, again baring the yellow teeth, "Good fighter" he growled and missed Atan by a hair.

454

Atan's blade swooped under the barbarians, pushing the large man off balance, but only for a moment. He responded with a strong thrust, hair bouncing as he moved, and followed with a frustrated sweep of lateral moves, forcing Atan to remain on the defensive, his face feeling the beads of sweat forming and his back already wet.

They circled each other, both leaders, both waiting for the right moment. Atan's sword reflected off the morning sun, forcing the barbarian to squint and to bring his blade down in a fit of frustrated anger. Atan didn't bother looking at the shirt as it tore, or his flesh as it broke, he turned his attention to the dispenser of the damage and thrust his sword deep into his belly.

With a thud the man fell to his knees and before he could come to his end on the floor, Atan's blade swept through his neck. So the body lay, twitching in incomprehensible short-lived pain while the head, for a split second watched itself perish.

For just a moment Duke Atan Ishtba reveled in his victory, then he approached Sonja, covering her bruised body with the silky blanket. "Sonja, can you hear me." So gentle a whisper, a babe would have cooed in its warmth.

Sonja stared at the wall, breathing, but still. He didn't press.

Atan sheathed his sword and then stuck the barbarian's blade into his neck and lifted up the head. Careful not to alarm any true Calcoran resident, he covered the head, until he found Mahtso, in the kitchen, not faring so well.

Arms soaked with blood and a knife just making its way across his cheek, Atan saw Mahtso barely wince as the blood began a trail to his neck. Atan slammed the door behind him and the stocky men, with more hair than skin and fingernails that twisted and gnarled around themselves, turned their swords to the new intruder. But their eyes and hands reacted together, knives quickly clanging to the floor as bloodshot eyes and foul smelling mouths opened wide at the sight of their beheaded leader.

Despite Mahtso's deep desire to torture both men, wisdom ruled and one was killed while the other was honored with Mahtso's interrogation. The howl as his skin was slowly peeled back brought a fire to Mahtso's eyes.

Atan questioned the man, calmly, holding the leader's head casually, allowing it to come within inches of the man's face. "How many others?"

The man shrugged and screamed as Mahtso toyed with the soft red exposed nerves of his hand. Struggling to count, he held up the other bloody hand and showed four fingers.

"Better, let's find them."

Atan's men were now, in the front hall, two dead barbarians laying in the main entrance.

"There are two more, find them."

With little trouble, the task was done and the bodies brought to the back and burned. Though the barbarians attack was brief, it was deadly and one more time Calcoran's barely healed scars were opened.

Atan's sigh as Jivad's broken body was brought to the funeral altar, was an echo, of the very walls of Calcoran Castle. Jivad and Sonja had brought life and pride back to the once great kingdom and with the stroke of a sword, Calcoran fell under a familiar veil of uncertainty and aimlessness. Mahtso stood by his Duke, steady, obedient, waiting for direction.

Winds whined lightly through the trees in the dying sunlight of the day, even the flowers paled and the green grass stained with blood somehow brazened itself to the eye.

"He was a good man," Atan said more to himself than anyone and nodded as the men wrapped Jivad's body in white linen.

The men climbed down from the altar. Mahtso and Atan walked slowly back to the castle. The funeral would wait for Falor, already summoned by Atan's men.

Castle folk shuffled around, making dinner. Atan's presence gave a thread of reason to maintain routine. It kept them from simply collapsing into uncaring anarchy. Telep ran errands for Atan and appeared less affected by the trauma than the others.

Mahtso and Atan ate in a small dining room, by the light of one candelabra, it fit the mood.

"Mahtso, you will return to Cordan. You and Fatell must handle its operation for a while. I want Raphela here with me."

"As you wish." Mahtso's left hand toyed with his chain his right pushed the food under the blank stare of his eyes.

He felt Atan's firm hand on his shoulder. "My friend, in battle I want no one else but you by my side. And there is no one I trust more with my home than you."

Mahtso pushed the vegetables on his plate.

Atan continued. "But you cannot deny me my partner. Raphela could do battle, but I would have a hard time winning. You could help me here, but Raphela is the better choice. Keep Castle Cordan safe, I'll be back before winter." Atan's fatherly tone was hard to fight, especially when he was right.

Mahtso's shoulders rose and fell. You're right, I know."

In the morning Mahtso mounted his steed and rode back to Cordan. Atan spent the next few days exploring the castle, with Telep's help. Sonja remained catatonic and Geho was little better.

At the Marketplace Cora and Valeria toiled in the kitchen.

"Hand me that jar Val."

Valeria passed over the heavy jar loaded down with dried meats. As it opened both girls shook their heads at the pungent, intense spices.

"I am guessing we use very little of this?" Valeria kept the jar as far away from herself as possible.

"You're learning. It isn't that hard is it?" Cora teased. She had been trying to teach Valeria the basics of the kitchen. It was a slow process.

"No harder than teaching you to sew," Valeria teased back.

"I'll give in on that. Let's set the table, the boys should be home soon."

Valeria placed a cheerful gold linen cloth on the table and created a centerpiece of fresh flowers. The dishes were not a matching set, but the table looked quite appealing anyway.

"That looks great."

"We each have our talents."

Both girls smiled at their work.

Vanar and Falor followed their noses to the girls.

457

Cora nearly knocked Falor down when she saw him. He held onto to her forever so long. "I missed you," he whispered. Her kiss was enough response. They headed to their room.

Valeria caressed Vanar's cheeks. She felt his hazel eyes on her.

A young boy, red-faced and out of breath tugged at Vanar's tunic.

"What, what is it?" He let go of Valeria's hand.

"Falor must leave." he panted, "Right away."

"What are you talking about?"

The young lad did his best to ignore Vanar's annoyance, but did shrink back a step just the same.

"A message from your father. He sent someone to take Falor."

Vanar pushed breath hard from his nose and patted the panting boy's shoulder. "Thank you, I'll take care of this."

Vanar went immediately to Falor's room, Valeria at his heels. His hand stopped the door from closing as Falor peeked around.

"Is something wrong?"

Cora stretched her neck over Falor's shoulder.

"I suppose there is. A carriage is waiting to take you to Calcoran. One of Cordan's guards is on it."

"Why?"

"I don't know," Vanar snapped. In that moment, the other three felt the Duke hovering silently in the air and discussion was over.

Falor and Cora said good-bye to their friends and met the guard at the carriage.

"Falor" The guard, Remo, about 30 years old and just a bit taller than Falor stopped him.

"Yes?"

Remo sighed and paused as two sets of eyes rested on his.

"Falor, I'll be riding with the driver." Small beads of sweat formed on his forehead. Relaying bad news was not part of his standard day's work, and this was more than just a lost crop of grain.

"And" Falor knew there was more, and pressed gently.

"Falor, I'm afraid there's been a serious incident at Calcoran." Remo took a deep breath. "Your father has been killed."

Cora gasped and leaned on the carriage.

"And my mother?" Falor rolled out the words with less emotion than if he had been requesting a glass of water.

"Alive but not well, your brother is not much better."

"Thank you Remo."

Remo nodded and climbed up with the driver, unsure if he had made himself clear.

"Are you all right?" Cora regained her composure and stroked his cheek.

"Yes" Again the blank emotionless voice fell from his throat.

She placed her foot on the carriage rim.

"Cora"

"What?"

Strong fingers massaged her arms and a frighteningly calm face stared into her own. "You don't have to come with me."

Stinging tears sat on the rims of her eyelids and she held back a sniffle. "You don't want me there?"

"I want you with me more than anything else, but the burden to be faced is not, not normal. It wouldn't be fair to you." In his mind Falor took deep calming breaths, but outwardly he simply wrapped his fingers around Cora's hand, half afraid she would take his offer.

"I'm your wife, if I can't handle the bad, it won't be much of a marriage. I want to be by your side, no matter what."

"Thank you," Falor whispered as he held her close.

The sun gave them its last few rays as they began their journey to Calcoran. If not for the clacking of the wheels and whinnying of the rameks, Cora would have believed she was deaf, for the carriage cabin was coated in silence.

Falor's straight back did not lean against anything while his passive hands were crossed in his lap. The intense yet vacant stare in his brown eyes sent Cora to sit by herself, feeling every bump of the long journey.

Raphela's carriage broke the silence of the night as rameks hooves hit the ground, but Calcoran residents were nestled safely in their beds and most were oblivious to the disturbance.

In the dark hush Raphela climbed the short flight of stairs surrounded by the spacious hall. Without the glitter of daylight, it felt like a home. The handrail was cool and smooth, she stopped and felt the people. No longer was she Lady Raphela of Castle Cordan, now she was Lady Raphela of Raalek. For years she knew it, but now it finally had meaning. It meant not that her place was above the others, but to provide the emotional shelter and guidance she and Atan had promised to the people and to themselves long ago. Yes, this was the place for her to be.

She undressed quietly, slipped into bed beside Atan, and felt her lips spread into a warm smile as his fingers wrapped around her hair.

"It's about time" he whispered.

"Yes my lord, it is."

Breakfast was shared in a small yet elegant room created for just such meals. Breakfast was also shared with news from Telep. He stopped in midstep, dropped to one knee and lowered his head. "My lady, welcome to Calcoran Castle."

Raphela's shoulders twitched just slightly and her eyes moved between Atan and the wisp of a boy kneeling at her feet. Atan wondered what honored his wife so much. Neither were sure about the right response. How to be kind, without patronizing, this was delicate. Raphela chose the most queenly tone she could find inside herself. "Thank you so much, please rise that I may view this courteous young man."

Telep blushed.

Her eyes looked into a boy full of wonder and a mystery of his own.

"You are even more beautiful than they say my lady."

She smiled and nodded.

Atan coughed and brought Telep back to reality. He took up a soldier's stance of at ease and delivered a wide variety of messages from all corners of the castle. Each one conveyed with the feeling intended, and none with the aid of a written note.

"Telep?"

"Yes my lord." He lowered his head, despite Atan's gentle voice. He counted the stones on the floor and inhaled the aroma of the tea.

"Do you know how to read and write?"

"Yes my lord." Telep hoped this was a correct answer, honesty had to be the best way.

"Yet you write none of these messages. You remember each, in detail even to what the person truly intended at that moment. How is that possible?" Atan did his best not to sound like an interrogation.

"I, I don't know sire." Telep's hands felt sweaty and his mouth dry.

"Very well then, you may go,"

"Yes my lord. Good morning to you Lady Raphela." He smiled praying only for a reflection, and relaxed as his prayer was answered.

Raphela stood and waited until he was out of earshot. "There's something different about him."

"I agree, but what? I've checked the information he brings. He is accurate, but even the people sending them don't remember dispersing all that information. Yet they admit that he is flawless in his reporting."

"Mm. I'll keep my eye on him."

"That should prove easy, he appears to be quite taken with you," Atan teased.

"I suppose I have that effect on younger men." Her lips curled up.

"Indeed." He placed a kiss on her forehead. "Now, I must tend to the men."

"What are you doing?"

"Reteaching security. I've given them a few days to recover and with you here I can concentrate on my tasks."

"I'm going to start with Sonja."

"Raphela" Atan's grey eyes bespoke a thousand words his tongue could never form.

"I understand." Fingers twined together. The edge of Calcoran's pain softened.

Sonja's well-lit room smelled of sweet spring flowers.

461

"How is she?" Raphela spoke to the bun, neatly tied behind the caretaker's head.

Wrinkles, gently folding onto themselves, surrounded sad eyes as the old woman turned to the voice. "The same my lady. The same as yesterday and the day before. She doesn't move, she doesn't speak." The gentle old woman allowed a few tears to fall as she stepped aside for Raphela.

Raphela swallowed hard and held back her own tears. Sonja's perfectly clean face and shining hair carefully laid on the pillow reminded Raphela of a doll she had seen many years ago. It was during one of her many walks. A shopkeep had placed his newest arrival in the window. Raphela had studied it so carefully, for its ability to imitate life, with tiny fingernails, thick eyelashes, even teeth teasing behind pretty pink lips. But the eyes offered only a blank stare, no thought. Raphela looked at Sonja, possessing the same blank stare. She had tired of the doll quickly, but this was not a doll.

Raphela's strong hands stroked Sonja's hair and tested her forehead for fever and found none. "Has she been examined by a healer?"

"Yes my lady, there are no broken bones, or, or, I can't remember what he said, oh"

"Internal damage?" Raphela prodded.

"Yes my lady, that's it, no internal damage."

"Thank you. You're doing an excellent job. Perhaps this care will heal her soul as well as time has healed her body."

"I hope so my lady, I hope so." Her full figure stretched to cover Sonja with a blanket and then she sat and began to read out loud.

Raphela left quietly.

A casual tour taught Raphela that most people were at least functioning and their warm gratitude was not lost on her, but no eye sparked, no foot took an unnecessary step.

The kitchen smelled of ordinary tea and bland vegetables. A small child stood by an old man as he handed her a candle.

"You must light this." Tired pained eyes matched the gentle sigh in his voice.

462

"Grandpa, where's Papa, did he go away?" Her bittersweet voice matched the pale young skin and tiny frame.

"I've already told you. Papa went to be with your mother."

Her little head shook back and forth. "No, take me to Papa, he's just hiding." She peeked around Grandpa's legs, big blue eyes searching for a clue.

"I wish he was, I wish he was." The old man felt a tear run down the wrinkle in his face.

"I want my Papa." She began to cry.

Grandpa picked her up and felt little hands hold onto his neck. Aching fingers stroked the long curly hair as she sobbed into his chest and the curly hair grew wet with his own tears as they rocked back and forth in mourning. After a time she calmed, wiped her nose on a sleeve, and he did the same as he put her back down on the floor.

The tall candle dwarfed her but she held it steady as he lit it and with his help she lit the one beside it. In whispered prayer they honored her dead parents and the gods protection of their souls.

Raphela stood hypnotized until the last whisper faded, then hurried out to the garden. She sat on a stone bench and her heart swam in a burning pain she'd never felt before.

Light breezes blew wisps of hair around her face as the sun, bright in the sky, did little to warm her. She didn't hear him come up from behind, yet she didn't flinch as the long fingers massaged her shoulder. Atan met her desperate gaze and sat beside her.

"I, I, I don't understand. Are the gods angry with Calcoran? Is it cursed? How can so much sadness weave its way through a place. Even the flowers seem pale."

A pair of tiny birds circled above, curious about the visitors. Curiosity soon satisfied they sought out the sweet nectar of a nearby assortment of flowers. Atan squeezed her hand and sighed. Raphela had to question, tear away at veils of mottled words until a clear crisp answer shone through. But there was no answer, no single thread. She knew it, but that made it all the harder. Atan's chest was a good pillow, if only for a moment or two, in the quiet afternoon with only the garden for company.

463

Both heard the soldier's steady footsteps long before he reached the bench.

"Raphela?"

Brown eyes stared up at him.

"Calcoran's sadness happened yesterday, today can start the joy. If anything Calcoran's wound, its ease at being defeated, is its breath in the past. Keep that in mind."

He didn't hear it when she said, "You're right," but he felt it.

Raphela brushed a few leaves from her dress, took a deep breath and returned to the castle, it was time to put the past to rest.

Calcoran was still owned by Samed. His personal tastes in decor, food, and style of dress, permeated the fabric of living. So how to remove the caked on layer of yesteryear without destroying the foundation? Raphela paced the halls and with each step her mood lightened as the answer began to take shape.

Raphela stepped over the threshold of the grand hall whose very essence bellowed of Samed. She soaked in every detail of the room. The only sound came from her dress brushing the smooth floor as she approached the throne, still covered in the white lace of grief. With bowed head she knelt by the impressive chair and whispered her honor while removing the lace. Her lips curved up in an odd smile. She neatly wrapped Samed's robe which had been casually placed, still patiently waiting for his return. Raphela stood, with the bundle in her outstretched arms. She searched for a room, hidden from daily life, one that could be locked. Finally she found such a place, in the lower levels and began the storage of Calcoran's past in a small dark room.

On her way back she passed the courtyard, where Atan both taught and surprised the guards. Well toned men, practiced at hand to hand combat, throwing and tossing an opponent when possible.

Atan tutored two young men in swordfighting. The scent of the men's sweat permeated the air as each tried time again to mimic the master. Atan, bare to the waist, moved his sword through the air as gracefully as a bird swooping down from the sky and his thrust had the strength of a ramek as it tore through the mock body hanging before him. The young students jumped at the sound of tearing cloth, so much like skin.

Raphela couldn't help herself, taking in every sight and scent. She left unnoticed.

Before sundown Atan returned to the room and noticed the door slightly ajar. Slow steps brought him over the threshold, inching the door open. Once inside one hand pushed the door shut while another reached for his blade. Suddenly a long stick whisked by his face and Atan's knife was at the attacker's throat.

Raphela laughed and then purred. "You are so good."

Hard breath pressed out of his nostrils, grey eyes opened wide. The knife fell to the floor and his fingers wrapped tight around her arm. "I could have killed you."

"I don't think so."

Despite his logical urge to be angry, her well exposed breasts and thick hair tugged harder.

"Pick up the blade," he commanded.

"As you wish." She teased and bent over to pick it.

Her very short gown exposed a bare bottom, as her hand grasped the blade Atan didn't resist temptation and landed a stroke bit harder than love tap.

Raphela pouted as she handed him the blade and rubbed the offended area. "Is that for being naughty?"

"Perhaps." Atan's hands squeezed her cheeks. "But I should turn you over my knee and paddle you."

"Maybe later" Raphela's lips sucked on his neck

It didn't take long for skin to be on skin. Soon Calcoran felt the passion of Ishtba and its flame touched even the most melancholy.

Atan and Raphela reveled in touches of power long forgotten by years of safety. Skin tingled and breath grew short. Raphela gloried in the power that brought her to the Duke so many years before.

Passion waned but Atan lay on her still, eyes full of a thousand words, Raphela read everyone and then kissed the lips that could not speak a one.

Falor could smell the Calcoran gardens as the carriage rolled up to the main door.

465

Cora leaned on him as they exited the carriage.

He faced the white veils over the doors, if not for Cora he would have landed face first on the castle doorsteps.

"Falor, are you all right?" His arms were cold to the touch and his blank stare did not ease her concern. "You haven't slept in so long. I'm worried."

"I'll be fine." Emotionless grey tones were all he had as the door creaked open for them.

Cora felt the difference but had no time to think about it. Her eyes focused on a curly haired boy.

Telep locked onto Falor's eyes, both entered a trance until Telep's jaw dropped and his eyes rested on Cora. "Your wife?!" He croaked.

Cora started to speak but Raphela arrived. Cora dragged her gaze from Telep to Raphela who said nothing but caught the silent conversation between all three.

"Falor it's good to see you." Raphela said gently.

"And you my lady." Though his ashen skin hid it, he was relieved she was here.

"Cora, I'm glad you were able to join him." Raphela left an opening for further commentary.

"My wife felt it only right to be by my side, my lady." Practiced syllables worked hard to leave the lips. Raphela chose to treat them as the adults they would need to be.

"Of course."

"I'd like to see my mother." Falor's calm was like a cloud, ominous and quiet, ready to spew forth a torrent. Raphela prayed for Cora's strength.

Falor marched with evenly paced steps. Cora felt each stone and pebble of the stairs, her hand clinging to the handrail.

Despite it being late in the afternoon, torches kept Sonja's room bright, though shadows filled the corners. Falor's finger's tightened around Cora's until they were bloodless and white. Cora held fast and took in the well-scrubbed scent of the elegant room.

The young couple beheld the same picture that Raphela had the day before. Falor brushed Sonja's cheek with a kiss, no

466

response. The aged caretaker watched the silent reunion with a growing sadness.

Cora stared at a plate of cold soup, still layered with a film of sitting for too many hours, accompanied a crumbling roll, both untouched and never to be. Falor didn't speak, just held his mother's hand and closed his eyes. After a while he whispered something in her ear and left a kiss on her forehead.

Cora straightened the covers. "Sonja, we're here now, you must get well soon" Cora barely finished the words before she started sniffling and left.

Geho sat legs crossed, a tower of brightly painted blocks tenuously standing before him. He jumped up when Falor entered, crashing the tower at the same time. "Oh no, I'll have to start all over again." He pouted only for a moment. "Oh well. Where have you been Falor? Mama and Papa went away on a trip, I think to Castle Cordan." He sat down and launched a new effort on his tower.

"Geho, what's wrong with you? Why are you acting like this?" Falor's angry tone slid off his younger brother.

"You are always so serious. Help me build this." Innocent ignorance, blind ignorance, Falor wasn't sure what spell had possessed his brother, but it had to end. He bent down and pulled the boy to his feet and began shaking him. "Wake up Geho, you're not five years old anymore, you're a teenager." Geho's hair shook and his eyes began to fill with tears.

"You're scaring me Falor. I'm not a teenager. I'm seven years old and you're nine. Come on, let's play something."

"I don't want to play. I want you to be you."

Cora heard Falor's resounding words in the hallway and hurried to Geho's room. Locked in Falor's firm grasp Geho paled in fear, Falor shouted and shook his brother, venting irrational words and angry feelings, all for naught.

Cora pried the tight grasp of fingers from Geho's arm. "Falor" She barely broke a whisper, "Stop, its no use."

Falor stared at her as if a stranger had intruded, but after a moment calmed himself and slumped into a chair and stared at his brother.

467

Cora held Geho and comforted him until his tears stopped. "Who, who are you?" Red eyes and trembling lips questioned her.

"I'm Cora, I'm Falor's wife."

"Wife, Falor is too young to be married."

"No, you forgot. He grew up and we met a while ago." She was as gentle as a summer rain.

"Can I play with my blocks now?"

"Of course, and later on we'll see what you've built."

"All right." He returned to his toys without another word or thought.

Cora helped Falor to their bedroom. It was as he had left it years before, but change was now inevitable. He reached out for Cora's hands. "What am I doing here?" What is going to happen? What if the Duke wants me to take my father's place? What will I do? I can't run Calcoran?" Falor rambled.

The castle was quiet and the room deadly silent but for Falor. Cora listened patiently.

"Cora?"

"Yes?"

"I'm frightened."

"Me too," she admitted.

"What are we going to do?"

"I don't know about tomorrow, but for now, let's get some rest. Neither of us have slept much." She began removing his clothes. He offered no resistance. Soon both caved in to exhaustion and found a restless sleep. After a while Cora's eyes squinted at the failing torch and she turned to look at the window and saw but a shadow of light. Sliding noiselessly from the bed, she dressed for dinner and rekindled the torch.

Falor squirmed in a cocoon of covers, moaning with each movement and Cora sighed and let him sleep, it was better rest than none.

She closed the door without a sound and wandered through the castle, of course eventually coming to the kitchen.

The cooks walked with steady paces, as measured as the food they prepared. Though the fires burned the kitchen was not warm and odors were pale.

Picking up a long spoon, Cora stirred a gravy. The cook, a tall lanky man, twice her age, stood back, uncaring.

"Excuse me, what is this?"

Both looked down into the thick brown mass as its lazy bubbles popped to the surface.

"Gravy for the roast."

"I see. Would you mind if I added a little something." Cora could never serve such a lifeless meal.

The cook shrugged his shoulders and led her to a cabinet filled with bottles of herbs and spices. Cora discovered the appropriate amenities and insisted the cook assist her.

Despite the gray mood, he, Carmine, ventured a smile at the enhanced sauce. "It's good."

"Yes, we did well." Cora returned the spices to the cabinet and left to arouse Falor.

"Telep?"

"Yes my lady." He stopped short in mid-race to somewhere.

"Would you please see if Falor and Cora are ready for dinner?"

"They will be soon m'lady." He smiled widely, eyes never leaving hers.

"How do you know?" Raphela had been watching Telep and knew he hadn't been anywhere near their bedroom for sometime.

Telep swallowed hard. "I, um, I, I, I saw Cora. Yes, Cora was in the kitchen." Telep shifted from foot to foot, brown curly hair framing an anxious face.

"All right then." Raphela nodded. He sped away. Raphela sighed, frustrated at a mystery she knew existed, but couldn't prove, much less solve.

Fresh cut flowers were placed in the center of a table large enough for six, but feeding only four. Atan leaned back in a tall chair, watching Cora and Falor sheepishly take their seats and stretch themselves to see over the centerpiece. Raphela watched Atan and motioned for a servant to move the flowers to a less interfering spot.

The older couple kept a respectable distance from each other, enough that an outstretched arm might allow contact. Falor

469

scooted near Cora at the far end of the table, his eyes bloodshot but open. Cora 's hand rested on his leg, out of sight.

The servants placed platters of steaming food in the center of the table and dished it out to the silent group.

Atan tasted the wine, cut a small piece of steak and chewed slowly, still observing the young couple, who did their best to look casual despite their fears.

Raphela kicked Atan, a small reminder that scrutiny was not the best method for the moment.

"This is one of the better meals we've had here. Cora, do I taste your hand?" Raphela wiped a spot of gravy from her chin.

Cora blushed. "Yes my lady."

"Have you gotten some rest Falor?" Atan swirled the wine in his glass.

"A little my lord." He looked deeply into the round green vegetables swimming in the gravy on his plate.

Cora and Raphela did their best to maintain the conversation, but it soon died and when dinner ended all left the castle to begin the funeral.

White flames broke the dark night. Falor refused to leave the pyre until the last spark was done.

Cora waited, with unflagging patience, by the door, entwining her fingers with his as they made their way to the bedroom.

She closed her eyes while Falor shared his tears with the darkness and when he finally closed his eyes, Cora's fingers squeezed his and both truly slept, at last.

It was time to continue with life. Servants arranged teapots and such in a large room, simply decorated with muted colors. A small table ready for the foursome.

Atan and Raphela surveyed the setting.

"It is right," she said.

"I agree." He ran his hand along the back of a chair.

"I'm glad Cora is here, she's a strong girl."

"I suppose." Atan stared out a window,

"What's wrong with you?"

"Nothing."

Raphela placed herself a footstep from his face. "You lie poorly."

Grey eyes turned down at her with a bitter smile. "I was just wondering how many more times I'd have to do this."

"I think you're getting old."

"What do you mean?"

"You never worry, never get lost in the melancholy."

Raalek's sun shone in her eyes, he felt the flood inside him dry. Her cheek, soft as the day they met, unchained the tension in his face. Lips almost met, but for the door.

They quickly took their seats, immediately joined by Falor and Cora.

"Are you feeling better today Falor?" Atan questioned with the concern of a father.

Falor and Cora stared at the royal couple. The Duke's silver hair and weathered skin in tandem with the Lady's shimmering streaks of gray added a dimension of strength that sent a chill of respect and awe through both young people, even though they had known them all their lives.

"Yes my lord, much. Thank you."

"Good. Falor, I am not one for long-winded speeches or explanations and I can't soften the blow of circumstances, so I shall get to the point. We are unfortunately again in a position of needing someone to govern Calcoran."

Cora's jaw tightened as Falor's fingers turned her hand white, both maintaining as mature a calm as they could.

Atan continued. "You would be my first choice Falor."

Falor's shoulders slumped back and his eyes didn't leave the table. "If you wish my lord," he mumbled and then instantaneously, with relief blurted out, "I have a choice?"

Atan and Raphela sunk back in disappointment. "Of course Falor, it is your decision, forcing anyone into such a situation would be disastrous. You simply are the best choice."

"Yes my lord, I understand birthright." The tension had lifted from his voice and he now listened more rationally.

"It's much more than birthright."

"Then I don't understand sire."

471

Atan began walking around the table. "You have the fortune of carrying Ishtban blood as well as Calcoran and more than that, you have lived the Ishtban way. I would have a governor trusted by his people, a close descendant of the King and a man already wise to my methods. Besides" Atan placed a hand on Falor's shoulder. "You have displayed an intelligence and wisdom beyond your years."

Falor felt Atan's strength flow through him like the sun melting the ice on a cold winter's day. "My lord, you are generous." He turned to Cora and squeezed her hand, gently. "To be honest, I'm frightened."

Atan smiled. "That's good. Fear warns of danger, as long as it is not an obsession."

Falor's heart beat like the hooves of racing rameks and his mouth dried making him suddenly yearn for moonstone tea. He swallowed hard. "My lord."

Raphela touched his hand. "Falor, why don't you and Cora take a moment. After all, she is a part of this decision."

Atan and Raphela walked to the shadows.

"I suppose we knew this was going to happen," Falor sighed nervously and looked over his shoulder.

"Yes we did." Cora's heart, soul and very breath of life was with him, her eyes as steady as trees on Cordan's hills. Nothing could move her.

"It's our destiny isn't it." Falor reached into the part of himself that knew more than he cared to know.

"Yes it is."

"I can't do this without you."

"I wouldn't have it any other way."

Lips met and shared a support meant for those years older.

Atan and Raphela returned.

"My lord, I accept. My wife and I accept the position you have offered."

"I'm pleased. The only loss is that Vanar must find a new advisor."

Falor forgot that this meant separation and considered taking it all back, but stopped himself. "He will choose well."

"Yes. I'm..."

Telep burst into the room. "Falor, here is the tea you wanted." He laid the tray on the table, panting, and then noticed that all eyes were on him, except Falor's whose face was buried in his hands.

Telep turned to leave but Raphela grabbed him, and sounding much like a mother investigating a broken vase commanded, "Sit down."

He bowed his head and obeyed.

"How did you know Falor wanted that tea?"

"He um, likes it."

Again eyes bored into him. His stare begged Falor for help.

"My lady, Telep knows a good deal of what I like and want and think." Falor took a deep breath. "He and I are," he paused, "mindseers"

"What?" She squinted and cocked her head.

Cora began to comprehend a good deal very quickly.

Atan felt like Raphela, lost in the woods.

"A mindseer." We know what people are thinking without hearing them speak." Falor shook his head, years of secrecy gone and who knew to what end.

"Do you know what I'm thinking?"

"My lady, you and the Duke are the only two people whose minds are totally closed to either of us."

"Tell me more" She leaned forward, sternness giving way to curiosity.

Telep relaxed.

"I learned of my ability when I was young and felt quite alone. When I met Telep we immediately connected. I had trained myself to not invading the privacy of anyone's mind. But I did train to listen beyond the spoken word. I have tried to teach my young friend, but he is a bit verbose."

Telep cocked his head in confusion.

"That means you talk to much," Falor said helpfully.

"Oh" The young boy lowered his head.

Atan observed as Raphela pressed on. "Must you be in the building, to be, um, connected?" Raphela's doubt regarded her terminology.

473

"No, my lady. In truth, I knew of my father's death, when it happened.

Cora turned to him. "Your nightmare."

He nodded.

Silence dominated, young people and old alike unsure of consequences, of this disclosure.

Atan broke the hush. "Are there others like yourselves?

"I don't know my lord. But I've heard other minds reach out, but it is difficult to be sure."

"If Telep were to live at Castle Cordan, while you remained here, would Vanar be able to reach you immediately, with Telep as intermediary?"

"I suppose so sire." Even as the words left his lips Falor began to see Atan's idea and felt the tingle of a new concept take its first breath.

Atan and Raphela shared a glance. She spoke. "Telep, you may leave."

He scurried out as quickly as a 10-year-old boy could.

"Falor, how much do you trust Telep?"

"Only a bit less than Cora."

"Would you know if he was lying?"

Falor sighed. This would be the burden of leadership, constant surveillance, always a slice of doubt. "Yes my lady, I would know."

"Would he willingly leave Calcoran and then be able to be the link between you and Vanar?"

Cora watched the gentle curves of Falor's lips as they tipped upward. "For such an honor. Telep would lay down his life."

"So it shall be." Atan's deep voice rocked the room, and shattered the momentary diversion of Falor's impending life.

"My lord," he swallowed hard.

"Yes Falor."

"Will you be staying here, at Calcoran?"

"Lady Raphela and I will stay until we feel everything is under control." Atan gave an answer, but he knew it wasn't to the real question on the younger man's mind.

"I see." Falor ran his hand along the table top, studying his fingers as they moved.

Atan and Raphela waited.

"Sire, might I be permitted an advisor?" A light blush of embarrassment filled his cheeks, but the royal couple understood that this was a large responsibility, for which Falor had never been trained.

"Who would you choose?" Asked Atan.

"Oolon, my lord." Even Falor was surprised at his lack of hesitation.

Cora smiled. Falor spoke of Oolon often.

"Hmm. He is very unfamiliar with Ishtban ways.' Atan tried to avoid questioning Falor's judgment.

"My lord, Oolon has a unique wisdom, one I respect. Although he is not Ishtban, I believe he can guide me towards maturity."

Raphela's eyes were glued to the boy. He didn't sweat or quiver and his voice did not waver from its conviction.

"You are quite sure of this then."

"Yes my lord."

"As you wish, if Oolon agrees."

"Thank you my lord."

Oolon did agree and a few weeks later Calcoran was in order, allowing Atan, Raphela and Telep to journey to Cordan.

Vanar distractedly picked at his dinner.

"Can I help?"

Vanar looked into her clear green eyes and saw the most beautiful compassionate face he'd ever seen. It made him ache inside.

"No. My life and the lives of so many have been turned inside out by a stupid act of barbarism. I don't even know what should be done."

Valeria pushed her plate away and they both left the table. They tried to talk, but moving a stubborn beast would have been easier.

Time did not heal the gap between them. Vanar traveled to the fiefs while Valeria managed the marketplace. Their accomplishments were adequate, but without color. Few travelers arrived, leaving Valeria bored and Vanar disappointed.

Before summer ended Valeria decided to return home. Vanar was coming back to the marketplace that night. Her bags were packed, sitting at the front entrance by noon.

Vanar arrived early, he fed Twelve and boarded him up at the stable.

As he walked towards the main building the trees whispered in the wind but he couldn't understand the words. Smells of dinner trailed from the kitchen, subtle standard fare, not as interesting as Cora's meals.

Men passed by, nodded to Vanar, some coming, some going. He noticed a new vendor and took a moment for small talk, then his eye caught the bags at the door. The conversation ended abruptly as he sought out Valeria.

She sat on a bench, long blond hair like a cloak around her shoulders. Vanar knelt by her side, green eyes turned to him, full of frustration and pain. He ached, more than he thought he could.

"I have to go," she whispered.

"I wish you wouldn't." It was a weak reply, barricading a torrent of feelings and needs she couldn't see.

"I'm sorry."

"I'll see you later this summer."

The agony in his eyes, so well reflecting her own, almost convinced her to stay, but the loneliness was more than she could bear. She knew nothing would change.

The carriage pulled up and the door opened. Vanar loaded the bags and held her closer than he had in a long time. She hid her face and her tears as she left and he let the last strand of her hair fall from his grasp as slowly as he could.

People, smells sounds all faded along the narrow path to his room. There he locked the door and many other things as well.

Valeria moped around at home, sharing little with anyone, painting as often as she could, Vanar's face always a shadow somewhere in the picture.

When Vanar visited that summer no new bridges were built or walls destroyed between them. When he left for Castle Cordan, his heart locked in his chest, Valeria resigned herself to her loss.

Parents still away, not knowing quite what to do, he wandered the castle and grounds, a deep unsatisfied hunger festering inside.

Vanar's eyes followed Rosa as she walked through the kitchen and out the back door. His feet soon brought the rest of him. Rosa's pace was casual and easy. Vanar caught up to her quickly and wrapped his arms around her waist, planting his lips deep on her neck.

"What, who?" Rosa turned to see the heir of Ishtba, staring down at her, arms holding her close.

"How about a little romp with me?" Firm fingers crawled up the back of her legs and rested on her buttocks, pulling her even closer. "You smell sweet today."

Rosa stared into Vanar's eyes and saw his animal desire. She shrunk back. It was not a new look, but one so strong it frightened her. There was no thought in those eyes, not even a feeling, just a need.

"Not, not now Vanar, perhaps later."

Her words fell on deaf ears as his grasp tightened. He reeked like a beast. Rosa struggled to free her arms and began pushing him away. "Please Vanar, not now."

"Aren't you supposed to service my needs," he hissed.

"You are not in your right mind. Stop it, just stop it." Her fists beat futilely against his chest.

Vanar laughed and squeezed her bottom as he sucked her neck. Rosa kept trying to push him away but with little success.

"VANAR!" A voice bellowed.

Vanar stopped, but held her tight.

"What are you doing?" Bertram pried Rosa from his arms.

"None of your business," Vanar snapped.

"You had better leave, find something else to do," Bertram ordered.

The young man snorted and sulked away.

Rosa shook like a leaf and began to sob. Bertram held her close until she calmed. "Are you all right?"

"I suppose so."

"Now the question, what do you want me to tell his parents?"

She leaned back against a tree, eyes glazed, for a moment. Lady Raphela was a mystery to her. The Duke would be angry with Vanar, but would he not also be angry with her? Perhaps she did something to encourage the behavior. Soft brown eyes turned to Bertram.

He saw the confusion and took her hand. "Rosa, you have done nothing wrong, Vanar is totally at fault here."

"Thank you," she whispered. Though not thoroughly convinced, she knew Bertram was right and that the duke would probably unleash a resounding punishment on his son.

"I think, we should keep this between us. He did no harm and he's a young boy. Young boys do foolish things." She persuaded herself even as she spoke.

"Are you certain. I will stand behind you on this." Bertram needed to be sure she felt comfortable with her decision.

Rosa went on her way and Bertram, not so certain, sought out Vanar, who had taken to the training room. Bertram leaned in the doorway and watched Vanar mercilessly beat the overstuffed dummy hanging before him, each stroke a slice of frustration.

Bertram said nothing and Vanar persevered. After a time Bertram turned to leave.

"What do you want Bertram?" Vanar didn't stop and he spat out the words.

"At least you haven't lost your awareness along with the rest of your mind."

Vanar concentrated on the stick and the dummy, each blow making a delightfully fulfilling sound.

"Rosa has chosen to forget today's incident. But I'm not so sure I have."

"Do whatever you want." He didn't move his eyes or miss a beat.

Bertram's hand wrapped around Vanar's wrist and stopped it mid-swing. Though shorter, Bertram matched Vanar in strength. "Listen to me young man, you have a problem and for months I have watched. If you cannot solve it with me, speak to your parents or ride off to Calcoran and speak to Falor, but this mood of yours is getting dangerous." Bertram forced eye contact with

Vanar. Both held the look. Vanar turned first and pulled his hand away, returning to the dummy.

Bertram sighed and left, still with no answers.

Vanar had already been home a few days, but his parents didn't find out until the day after they themselves arrived.

Castle Cordan was refilling with people returning from visits and vacations, its sounds and smells a hint away from the norm.

Raphela caught Vanar, late in the afternoon, wandering about, apparently without purpose.

"Vanar."

Cloudy eyes and an emotionless face looked at her.

"What's wrong with you?" Her motherly hand held his chin.

He pushed it away. "Nothing."

"Where are you going?"

"Out."

"Out where?" Raphela demanded, growing irritated.

"Just out."

"We'll see you at dinner." Raphela resigned her self to no response.

"But"

"We will see you at dinner." Each syllable was pronounced clearly and offered no option for rebuttal.

"Yes mother." He mumbled and shuffled away.

Raphela felt an ache rise inside her and did all she could to deny it.

Dinner was no more friendly than the afternoon encounter. Atan was surprisingly more patient at one point squeezing Raphela's leg under the table, to stop her questioning, which she begrudgingly did. When he finished Vanar left and closed himself off in his room.

"What's wrong with him Atan?" She asked in frustration. They strolled the castle grounds as dusk turned to darkness and fireflies danced in the breeze that sung in the leaves.

"I don't really know, but pressuring him won't help." His fingers locked together behind his back as they walked.

"I know." A worried sigh woven in her face and voice.

"He's a young man and growing up is hard."

"Am I getting so old that I can't remember?"

479

Atan cringed at the rarely heard doubt in his wife's voice and cursed himself for not having an answer better than, "No".

They walked back to the castle in silence. Raphela crawled into bed and slept more out of depression than exhaustion.

Atan turned the handle to Vanar's room and peeked inside. Vanar stared at the ceiling.

"Would you like to talk about it?" Atan took a casual stance in the doorway.

Vanar's eyes did not leave the ceiling. "There's nothing to talk about."

"Is that why you're so solemn, because of nothing?" Atan kept his tone even and quiet.

"Will you just, I..." Vanar stopped himself. "I'm just tired."

"Oh. Then I'll let you sleep."

Neither slept well and for the next few days Vanar's presence was scarce.

One evening he walked outside and passed a few of the men sitting around, sharing easy chatter and a large keg of ale.

"Vanar, join us."

It had been a long time since Vanar talked to anyone. He found a rock, sat, quickly downed a glass of ale and began another. By dark the others became part of a typically raucous group sharing exaggerated tales of bravery and conquests over the opposite sex.

Both moons shone down and the group began to thin, men stumbling in the darkness. Vanar and three others were the last to leave. Vanar leaned against a tree and burped loudly. "I'm going to take a ride. Who's with me?"

A large hairy hand rested on his shoulder. "Vanar, we've all had a bit too much ale, ride tomorrow."

Vanar shook off the hand. "Cowards."

The men watched Vanar head towards the stable. One relieved himself in the woods and then all returned to the castle.

Bertram heard a knock at his door and was greeted with the odor that trailed from outdoors.

"What is it?" Bertram tied the robe around his waist.

"Bertram, I thought." The man held back some foul smelling sound. "You should know, Vanar has had a bit to drink, quite a bit and he's out riding."

"By the gods. Thank you."

"Mmph," the man groaned and shuffled away.

Bertram's wife sat up in bed. "Where are you going?"

"Vanar," he said simply.

"Be careful."

"I will."

Vanar saddled Twelve, who whinnied more than normal. "Shh, you'll wake the others." He laughed as the slurred words left his lips. Finally, after three attempts he mounted his beast and was on his way.

Bertram took one of the slower beasts, hoping Vanar didn't get too much of a head start. It was a short ride.

Twelve nudged at Vanar's motionless form, sprawled out on the ground.

Bertram forced himself to approach with care, but his feet yearned to lunge at Vanar, it seemed a lifetime to take only a few steps and at last grab the beast's reins and tie it to a tree.

He knelt by Vanar, heard a breath, and smelled it, though that was no matter now. There was no blood, as far as he could see. With the gentility of a mother, he laid Vanar across his beast's back, slowly walked back to the castle, and headed straight for the healer's building.

Aharon, now a full time resident there, was awakened immediately to examine the heir apparent.

As Raphela headed downstairs after breakfast, Aharon cornered her and brought her to Vanar. Mahtso did the same for Atan.

Vanar lay quite still in the bed, moaning when he moved. Raphela ignored Aharon's report and examined Vanar herself.

"No broken bones, just a few scratches. That's a nasty one by his eye."

"Yes, Bertram couldn't even see it in the dark. The poor man nearly fainted when they got into the light."

"Why didn't you wake us immediately?"

"My lady, what would have been accomplished. Vanar would not have been any different."

"You're right, Still."

Vanar looked up at the blurred image he knew was his mother, and closed his eyes in shame.

Raphela sat by the bed. "You foolish boy, angry as I am at you. I still love you. Just come to your senses." She placed a gentle kiss on his cheek, pulled up the covers and left, meeting Atan on her way out, nearly knocking her over.

"Raphela, is he all right? Any permanent damage?"

Yes and no. He'll be fine. I examined him myself."

His sigh of relief coated a castle on edge, without even knowing why it was on edge.

Atan sat by his son's side, vigilant, through the morning and just past noon when Vanar finally stirred and attempted to sit.

Looking his father in the eye was impossible.

"How are you feeling?" Matter of fact question without emotion.

"Not so good."

"Aharon says you're bruised, but the ale, though causing your fall, probably relaxed you enough to save you any broken bones."

"Fall?" Vanar rubbed his head and groaned.

"You don't remember much, do you?"

Painful as it was to do so, he shook his head.

"Now, would you care to talk?" Only a small taunt arrived with the question.

"Where's mother?"

"She's been in and out all morning. She's having a difficult time."

"She's very angry with me, isn't she?"

"No, not really. I don't know what's troubling her at all."

Vanar finally looked in his father's eyes. "I miss her so much and I want her so much."

"Valeria?"

He nodded. "But I'm afraid. I don't know what to do. How to." His fingers massaged his throbbing temples.

"Its more than Valeria, isn't it?"

"Yes. How can I be you? You are, like, like a god, a legend. The world trembles at your thoughts."

"You can't be me. I am not so great as you think. I've done many deeds I'd rather forget and my fame will fade with time. It is a different world now Vanar and when you rule, the people will look to you just as they have looked to me, but with more trusting eyes.

"No father, you and mother are not like other people. I can't do what you do."

"I'm not abdicating my position so quickly."

Vanar leaned his head back and realized the fears that had surmounted inside him. They made him forget that choosing a wife, did not make him the Duke. "I am a fool."

Atan smiled. "All young men are fools. Though most don't take quite the stupid jaunt you chose."

"I'm sorry."

They shared a moment of silence.

"Would you choose Valeria as a wife, as mother to your children?"

"Yes" Vanar didn't need to think about the answer.

"Then, when Aharon and your mother allow, go to her."

Vanar closed his eyes and dropped his head on the pillow. "If she will have me."

"If it is meant to be, she will forgive you. Women forgive." Atan considered his wife for a moment. "Yes, women forgive."

Raphela made Vanar stay in bed for two days and despite his pleadings two more confined to the castle.

At dawn on the fifth day, Atan and Raphela bade him goodbye.

"I've padded the carriage, stop as often as you need."

Vanar bent down and placed a kiss on his mother's forehead. "Mother, I think you need a rest. I've never seen you this worried."

Raphela laid a loving tap across his bottom. "I'm just trying to make up for your lack of common sense."

The carriage door closed, Vanar, for all his bravery, still ached and said a quiet thank you as he lay down on the pillows.

Merej's fief drew closer and the scent of cattle warmed him, but even as he knocked at the front door, Valeria was too far away.

"Vanar, how nice to see you." Norana smiled, her warmth took a little edge off his fear, but he still looked and felt like an anxious young man.

"Good morning Norana. May I see Valeria?"

"She's in the barn."

"Thank you."

Vanar took many deep breaths as he approached the barn. A light breeze pulled the hair away from his eyes and he swore Valeria's scent floated over everything.

She tugged at one of the calves until his foot was freed from the stall door. "You naughty creature." She rubbed its neck and turned to the next task when she noticed the shadow in the doorway. "You're blocking my light." Her hand ordered the shadow to move. "It didn't."

Valeria walked to the door and saw Vanar, straight, tall and handsome. Every fiber in her wanted to run to his arms, but her head kept her feet at a slow pace. "Hello Vanar."

"Valeria."

Neither said anything for a moment. "Would you take a walk with me?"

His sheepishness took Valeria by surprise. "All right." She brushed off her hands.

The land was flat and both stared at the rising sun. Vanar stopped by a tree. Their eyes met and locked. Valeria felt beads of sweat form on her neck. Vanar's palms were moist and both were wrapped in the scent of each other.

"I've done a lot of stupid things these past few months. Can you, will you forgive me?"

She studied a butterfly lighting on a flower. "Is there any way I couldn't?"

Vanar took a deep breath and caressed her cheek "Enough to marry me?"

Valeria's eyes opened wide, it felt like eternity until her arms wrapped around his neck and her lips meshed with his.

"I'll take that as a yes."

For the first time since the marketplace, their passion was unleashed. They fondled and touched, breath hot and fingers searching, but their clothes stayed on. Valeria caressed his hair. "I love you," she whispered to a welcome ear. His kiss was like lightning from a spring storm. Just being this close, inhaling the odor, feeling the skin, that was enough, it lasted well into the morning.

As they walked back to the house, Vanar stopped. "I must ask you something. You said you'd marry me, be my wife, mother of my children, my friend. But, will you marry the Duke's son?" Vanar's shoulders were straight and regal, making Valeria suddenly realize the meaning of his question.

"The Duke's son, hmm."

"Someday, you would be Lady of the land, more than my wife, you would be my advisor, and the one to rule should anything ever happen to me."

Valeria had fantasized about all this. "Vanar, I've never done anything halfway. I don't know that I could be as good as your mother, but you will always have my best." A kiss sealed a pact laden with commitment and sprinkled with fear.

"Now, how to tell your parents."

"What do you mean? We just tell them. Anyway, your the Duke's son, you can do what you want."

"No, my position doesn't give me the right to steal someone's daughter."

"Vanar you're not."

"I know. But your parents deserve respect. I'll think of something."

"She smiled. "I'm sure you will."

Norana had a large lunch spread out. Platters passed from hand to hand. But before anyone actually began to eat, Vanar stood. "Merej, Norana, I have asked your daughter to marry me."

Both parents looked up, not in surprise, but in curiosity, at how would he continue. "We would like your blessing," he ended in a near stutter.

Merej took on a stern fatherly countenance. "Hmm, I don't know."

Norana kicked him under the table. "Of course. We're happy to have you as part of the family." She jumped out of her chair and hugged Valeria and then Vanar, with Merej right behind her.

Raphela's breakfast sat picture perfect on her plate, cold and untouched, just like her dinner the night before.

"What is it Raphela? What's wrong?"

Raphela could not meet his glance. "I'm going to Milson today."

"Milson? Why?"

"To find some answers."

"Why can't you..." His frustration gave way to maturity. "It may be a good idea."

She breathed a sigh of relief and rose to go.

"Raphela?"

She stopped and looked not in his eyes, but at him. Atan lowered his head and silently kicked the table. "Be careful"

"I will."

From the bedroom window Atan saw Raphela's carriage. It pulled away from the castle like a tired animal.

For him solace and answers were elusive, better sought elsewhere, the glass plant house.

Atan had never seen a jungle, or knew such a place existed, but he had created one. The plethora of life sprouting and growing at will left little room for human company. But Atan had a special spot, where the leaves respected the stool, framing it, but not hiding it.

There he sat, between two deeply rooted herbs amid aromas intertwining around the room as much as the vines clinging to each other on the windows. Sheer habit took Atan's fingers to the dead leaves, as he gently pruned the foliage and patted the soil. Soon he was on his knees, digging into each one, his hands working like an artist. "You are so simple, why can't she be like you? What can I do for her? What have I done wrong? I haven't harmed her, have I? Is there something I've said or done?" From a sturdy stalk he pulled a large brown leaf, dry and crumply. It disintegrated in his grasp. "If there is, I don't know about it."

A small furry animal crouched under a leaf. It twisted its head at the odd sounds from this giant and then scurried by

Atan's feet, stopping by a tasty berry, which it pulled off and nibbled on. Atan ignored the creature and turned to the trees yielding tiny fruits, a new species created by nature's cross pollination.

"What questions so deep and personal that they can't be shared with me?!?" He suddenly roared in a voice so loud it shook the glass walls.

Mist from his breath clouded the windows. His eyes caught a patch of brown, at the other end of the house. Slow determined steps drew him to the flowers and his knees folded to bring him closer to the colorful plants. Tears rolled freely down his face. Blooms reached for the sunlight, while leaves withered from neglect. Most gardeners would have seen a few extra stalks and leaves to prune, perhaps a little more water to the roots. Atan Ishtba, mighty duke, caressed a paling bloom and gently laid a dead leaf by his side.

"Raphela, it is not what I have done, but perhaps what I haven't done. Mahtso has told me what women need to hear, but the words are so hard for me. Have I neglected to let you know just how beautiful and special you are to me?"

Atan diligently cared for the flora and swore they were brighter when he was done. Then he plucked the most brilliant ones and bundled them together. Saddling his ramek, the flowers tied to the horn, he slowly began the journey to town, each step of the rameks hooves bringing a clearer thought.

Raphela arrived at Nabus' door just before lunch. A customer stared at her as he left. Nabus' fingers trembled as she stepped over the threshold, her cloak flowing as she walked.

"Good morning Nabus."

He took a deep breath, "Raphela." He noticed her red eyes, as she lay her cloak on a chair.

"Oh Nabus." Raphela broke into tears and rushed to him, burying her head in his chest. Despite his promise not to touch her, he stroked her hair and found his arms wrapped around her waist.

"I'm so frightened Nabus." She sniffled.

He closed the door and looked out the window hoping no unnecessary eyes were inspecting this scene. "Sit and tell me about it."

"I made a bargain."

"A bargain?"

She took in the air of the shop and didn't look up. "Yes, a bargain with the gods."

Nabus sat back, considered her words, then leaned towards her, taking her hands. "From any other woman or man, I'd pat you on the head and say 'certainly, my dear'. But, from you, I believe this. Go on."

"I can't give you the details, but it's about my husband and my son and I'm so afraid. I've ruined everything, for everyone. Oh Nabus, what do I do?" She pushed the words as if they'd disappear.

"It's difficult to answer when I don't know anything, but, Raphela," he lifted her chin "Let's explore your ruination."

She sniffled and nodded.

"Has anyone died?"

"Almost."

"Does that mean on death's door now or permanently injured for life?"

"Neither."

"Good. We've eliminated fatality."

She had to chuckle at the sarcasm.

"Is anyone's life proceeding differently, for the worse, than it should?"

Her hair bounced as she shook her head no.

"So, why is this woman, who is second only to the Duke, in ruling our world, babbling like some foolish teenager?"

Raphela had all these answers before she arrived, but hearing it from someone else was much better.

"Thank you so much." She threw her arms around him and planted a kiss on his cheek

Nabus returned the hug and suddenly dropped his arms, as the door had opened.

"My lord I..."

"Shh. Raphela?"

Large brown eyes met his intense grey stare.

"Raphela, these are for you." Hope swayed in his eyes.

Raphela dissolved into tears once more and broke their unwritten rule, falling into his arms.

Nabus felt himself stumble back as they touched, arms tightening in a circle. He left the room.

"Whatever I have not done for you, I, you are all there is. I don't know how..." He fumbled, all his carefully planned words.

Raphela put a finger to his lips and then kissed him as hard as she knew how. Nabus couldn't see but reeled in the other room.

Raphela whispered, "Where is a whip to punish me now, for the pain I have caused you. You have done nothing wrong, no man could do more right. Forgive me."

Atan pulled her so close her tears wet the hair on his chest and all they could do was share their breath with lips too close to part and hands to glad to let go.

After a time the grip loosened and Nabus returned. They sat and sipped hot tea.

"Atan, as long as I'm in town, I'm going to visit my sisters," she said suddenly.

The look on Atan's face told Nabus that Atan did not wish to share in this venture. "What a shame he said quickly. I was looking forward to some company, I so rarely get visitors."

"Raphela, Nabus has done us a service. I will return the favor and stay with him." For a leader of the known world, Atan edged his words with a little more sugar than necessary.

Raphela's hands moved to her hips as two pairs of hopeful eyes met her own suspicious ones. "I don't know about this. Can I trust the two of you alone?"

"We'll behave, I promise." Nabus said and Atan nodded his agreement.

"All right then, I should be back before dark.

Raphela felt their eyes follow her, but she just smiled to herself and walked on.

"Thank you Nabus," Atan said when his wife was out of earshot.

"My lord, I understand." He smiled.

489

"You may call me Atan."

"As you wish."

Both men sat at the table suddenly caught in the grips of an uncomfortable silence.

Atan turned his head toward the door. "She is so beautiful. I wonder if she knows?" The words slipped out in subconscious whisper, perhaps seeking an ear, which it found.

"That she's beautiful or that you think she is?" Nabus placed a tall slender bottle on the table and two glasses.

Atan didn't answer, just lowered his head. He heard the thick liquid fill his glass and watched the glass slide towards him.

Nabus continued. "The answer is yes, to both."

"I never tell her, shower her with gifts. I do nothing." Long fingers turned the glass around in a circle.

"Drink, I have saved it for a special occasion."

Atan raised the glass, breathed in the aroma, and took a large swig of the pungent liquor. It distracted him for a moment. "Interesting drink."

Nabus took a long sip. "Ahh. Yes it is." He closed his eyes and smiled.

Atan swirled the liquid in his glass and downed the rest. Nabus refilled it.

"Let me tell you a story Atan, a story of a young girl. Her days were spent in the shops and by the workbenches of everyone in town. Most were happy to share what they knew and she was more than anxious to learn. As a teenager, this comely young woman still sought knowledge. Any man in town would have laid out his finest for a peek at a breast or brush from her lips. She never offered, nor did she ever ask for so much as a sweetcake from the baker. She came to me one day, as she had many others." Nabus finished his drink and poured some more.

Atan now sipped at his. Listening was easier, with his own thoughts blurring a bit.

"For a smile, I would have given my entire shop. But trinkets and material things, they were of little value to her."

Nabus swallowed a large gulp and the glass hit the table hard. "No, nothing so simple as a broach or a necklace. No" Nabus' voice raised and the words were not so crisp as before.

Atan, warmed by the drink, didn't notice.

"No trinkets. Teach me she said, I wish to learn."

Atan looked, Nabus didn't need to say about what.

"Atan, if at 16 she didn't care about gifts or the flowing words from men's lips, today they would mean even less."

Atan nodded his head. "Then why, why come here?" He couldn't step into the frightening territory that somehow his own touch was not right and she was seeking someone else.

Nabus put a loaf of bread on the table, they each pulled off a piece.

"Because she can't bear the thought of life without you. She's worried. Foolish woman."

"What are you talking about?" Atan heard the words, but wasn't sure how they left his lips.

"Damn it, I don't know. She babbled on about nothing."

Atan stumbled as he walked out to relieve himself and then plopped back down at the table, downing more liquor and nibbling on the bread. "People speak of my power, but it is nothing compared to hers."

"I'll drink to that.'

The only two men who had tasted of her power continued on, Nabus rambled, words clinging together like a jumble of pins, and Atan's tall form swayed more with each drink. Finally Nabus poured the last few drops and both sighed. The bottle was done.

"It was a good occasion, mm." Nabus opened his back door and let the excess leave his body. "Come Atan, let's go into my house, there we can talk in the living room, on soft chairs and couches."

Both swore the rooms had grown incredibly large and the floor moved as they walked. But as promised the seats were quite comfortable.

Raphela returned at dusk. the shop was closed, so she went to the house. There they were. Nabus' feet were on a table as he sat in the enormous chair with his hands hanging down and his head back. Atan lay sprawled out on a couch, one arm by his side, the other sweeping the floor. They snored in harmony.

"I knew I couldn't trust them alone." She shook her head, found blankets for each one and despite their disobedience, placed a gentle kiss on each forehead, before she found a bedroom and dozed off to sleep.

At Castle Cordan Mahtso paced the floor while his chain made wild swings around his hand. Fatell sipped her tea and watched. "Where are they? Why aren't they home? I don't understand," he snapped.

"Mahtso, they can take care of themselves." Serene and pleasant as always Fatell did what she could with a hopeless cause.

"What if they've been ambushed, or the rameks are injured?" A fly landed on a nearby wall. Mahtso smashed it with violent accuracy.

Fatell flinched and stood, wrapping her arms around his waist. "Whatever it is, we can't change it now."

The ice blue eyes that terrorized grown men, softened as Fatell's fingers brushed back a loose hair and his lips pressed gently against hers. "This doesn't mean I've stopped worrying," he grumbled.

"I know," she smiled. "But you'll do it quietly."

They went to bed. Mahtso tried to sleep. But when he thought Fatell was asleep he crept out of bed and paced until the ache in his legs made him stop.

Atan rolled off the couch and was rudely awakened by the hard floor. Nabus stirred at the thud. Raalek's sun peeked in the windows and both men groaned and rubbed their heads. From the kitchen rose an odd scent. With squinting eyes they walked to the doorway.

Raphela poured steaming liquid into two cups. "Quite a pair you two are. I'm ashamed of both of you. Now sit down and drink the tea."

Humbly they obeyed. Whatever herbs were in the foul-tasting brew cured the pain in their heads.

"Good morning Raphela." Atan's schoolboy glance almost melted her, but she was enjoying her role.

"I'm surprised you know my name."

He lowered his head.

Nabus opened his mouth but didn't get a chance to speak.

"YOU! I don't know what got into you Nabus. You said I could trust you, you wanted some company."

"I did," he squeaked.

"Well its time for your playmate to go home."

"Yes my lady."

"I'll get my things." She left them, more so they could commiserate than anything else.

"Do you think she's really angry?" Nabus craned his neck to be sure she was gone.

"I hope not."

"This is one day I'm grateful she's yours."

Atan thought for a moment. "I pray it never changes." They shook hands and Atan prepared to leave.

Logan took Atan's ramek back to the castle while Atan and Raphela rode in the carriage. Raphela worked at maintaining her stern stance, though Atan saw through it.

Once back both realized that Mahtso would be beside himself. As they entered the castle Atan's face broke into a mischievous grin. It was still early, no one was in the hall. Their footsteps echoed on the stone and Raphela breathed deep the smells of home.

Atan whispered in her ear. "Let's take some mud and dirty our faces. Tear your dress, even make a little scratch on my chest, just enough to trickle some blood." His eyes lit up at his plan.

"Just to torture poor Mahtso." Raphela landed a hard swat on Atan's bottom. "You've been naughty enough." She pulled the front of his shirt so that he had to bend close to her. "March up to your room young man and wait for me, we'll discuss this in a moment." The schoolmarm seductiveness steeped in her voice made him gladly submit.

She found a servant to relay the message to Mahtso of their safe return and that they were not to be disturbed.

Atan stood by the bed shirt pulled outside of his half open pants, looking very much like an arrogant schoolboy.

Raphela closed the door to the outer room. Atan's playful arrogance slipped away as she drew close, hair barely covering her naked breasts and legs moving with her unique sensuality. His nostrils begged for her scent as his fingers yearned for her skin.

"Drop your pants," she ordered and produced a long switch from behind her back.

He obeyed and stepped out of his pants, shirt just barely covering his bottom. Atan's eyes moved with the rhythm of the switch as it lightly tapped her hand.

"I require satisfaction young man. What kind shall it be?" Brown eyes, oozed the companion of what moistened the lips between her legs.

Atan felt himself rise and turned his back on her, removing his shirt. The muscles in his back danced a slow sensuous dance and Raphela's breath sped up. "My lady, come close."

Raphela's breasts rubbed against his back and the switch moved slowly up and down the inside of his thighs. His head turned for a kiss, she obliged. "Take your satisfaction," the words came as a sensual whisper. "Teach me. Teach me what drives my friend and even skirts your fancy. Teach me the pleasure of pain."

Raphela sucked on his neck "As you wish my lord."

She stepped back and laid a stroke on those well-defined muscles. The sound excited her and the sting made his blood race. He asked for more, drank in the sting, and then turned. The fire in his eyes became a beastly desire. Pouncing on her like a cat, he stretched her arms above her head as she lay willingly beneath him feeling him push inside her with the force of a sword through stone.

Her back arched. "Kiss me or I shall tear your heart out," she growled.

The castle folk tiptoed that morning, lost in a mix of strange feelings while the master and mistress explored a new realm ending in a deep and comforting sleep.

Raphela stirred little when Atan awoke. Gently he rubbed her shoulders. "The world awaits us."

She didn't bother to open her eyes. ""The world always awaits us."

494

"True." He considered it for a moment. "But today it will be at our doorstep.

A broad, contented smile, one almost lost from Atan's memory, filled her face and opened her eyes. "Indeed, they are coming today, aren't they."

He didn't answer. Both luxuriated in a long hot bath, while Mahtso paced the main hall. Finally, their footsteps, moving in perfect time together, broke the silence of Mahtso's mind.

Despite all the chastisement he had intended, none left his lips. Atan as always, the king, somehow most royal and calm and Raphela, more sensual than ever, with hair splayed like a gleaming carpet on her back, appeared.

"My lord and Lady, it is good to have you back." He bowed and smiled.

"Enough torture Mahtso, how soon before my son arrives." Atan brushed away the mock honor offered by his friend, whose chain immediately began twitching.

"According to Telep, they should be here this afternoon." Raised eyebrows were the perfect fit to his tone.

Atan shook his head and headed for the training room. Raphela stared at Mahtso, whose eyes conveniently found the ground. "You don't like him much, do you?" Her words were like a gentle rain.

"I don't know." How does one not like or trust a child.

"New ideas are hard and don't worry, he won't get near you."

A melancholy seeded long ago, groomed and pruned and rooted in honest cause, curled Mahtso's lip. "No one ever does."

Raphela's stomach knotted like a fist. She felt for him. They had an unspoken tie and were in many ways, kindred spirits. This summer began so well for him, a chance for he and his friend to relive old times. To have it ripped away by a barbarian, by the stain of wanton destructions for the simple want of a finer roof and more food, was callous. His pain tore through her like a fire in the dry woods. He felt a kind caress on his shoulder. "Not everyone my friend, not everyone."

495

Why this eased him, he didn't know, but the chain that furiously punished his leg broke its train of thought and moved to lazy circles in the air.

The fist in Raphela's stomach loosened its grip. "Now, we must prepare for the future."

Ice blue eyes locked onto her gaze. "Yes, my lady we must."

Castle Cordan's shadow lay long on the land as dusk approached. Inside the call sounded, Vanar's carriage approached, before the sun set, he would be home. Atan made his way to the hall as did Raphela and Mahtso. Fresh flowers filled the well-polished brass vases that topped the five pillars around the main hall.

Raphela brushed an infinitesimal piece of dust from Atan's jacket. He leaned towards her and whispered, "Raphela". She looked up. "Calm down."

She nodded and sighed but still fixed the flowers and her gown more times than he could count. Suddenly she whirled around. "Where's Fatell?"

Mahtso shrugged his shoulders. "I was wondering that myself."

Raphela shook her head and marched out the front door. Mahtso attempted to stop her but Atan shook his head and they both stood by as she disappeared.

Her skin prickled in the brisk afternoon, but a quick pace brought her to the building in short order. Following the path of torches, Raphela found her.

Fatell sat at a desk, falsely engrossed in some book.

"Why aren't you at the castle? Vanar is almost home." Raphela took a few deep breaths.

Fatell closed the book but didn't look up. "I don't think I belong there."

Raphela plopped into a chair and rubbed her forehead, peering up at Fatell. "Why not?"

"I'm not" she hesitated, " family."

Raphela had seen Fatell fall into the trap of insecurity bordering on self-pity, she wished that Fatell had not chosen this instance to slide.

"Not family? Who is? Just his parents?"

Fatell swallowed but still found the desk a safer view.

"Fatell" Raphela smoothed her voice, to almost a melody. "Are you not the person I entrusted with his life? Have you not fed and clothed and cared for him? Dried his tears, snuck him cookies, even swatted his bottom when he needed it? And aren't you the only person he calls Moofie?"

Fatell blushed and despite her best efforts found herself smiling. "How did you know that?"

"I know about a lot of things Moofie. Doesn't that mean Aunt in some ancient dialect?"

Fatell nodded in embarrassment.

"Then come, he'd be so hurt if you weren't there to greet his future wife."

Raphela heard the soft clicking echo of Mahtso's heels on the stone floor.

"He will never stop pacing." Fatell smiled as she left Raphela to be close to her love.

At long last the wheels came to their creaking halt. Vanar climbed out of the carriage first, followed by Merej. Valeria's slender arm extended from the coach and Vanar grasped it watching her dress flow behind her. Norana stood at the edge, looking down such a big step. Vanar stretched out his arms and lifted her out.

"Oh my," Norana felt dizzy, but quickly caught her balance.

"Are you all right?" Merej took her hand.

Norana nodded and stared at her daughter, who was admonishing Coty for something or other. The castle's door opened like the entrance of another world waiting to absorb new inhabitants. Vanar held Valeria back as her parents and brother entered first. Raphela held her breath, it seemed an eternity until her son crossed the threshold.

Vanar and Raphela shared a glance that washed away all the fears and tension. "It's good to be home." He bent down and placed a kiss on his mother's cheek, which she returned. "It's good to have you home." She answered.

Vanar and Atan exchanged a manly hug while the women exchanged warm embraces and kisses.

Vanar picked up Fatell and whirled her around. "Thank you for being here."

Mahtso received the firm back slap and handshake deserving a mentor.

Bertram watched and smiled and with a nod from the Duke took to finding his wife.

Present and future royal couples climbed the stairs.

Mahtso took Merej on a long deserved tour.

Norana stared in wonder. From outside, Castle Cordan was a foreboding fortress, eyes poking and prodding, wondering why you wanted to enter. But once through the door a new dimension opened its arms. She marveled at the stone walls, not smooth like the floor, but textured, creviced and polished and even in the dusk the entrance hall, as large as her house, was bright and warm. The last time she was here, so were a hundred others and the beauty was lost on her. As she looked around she saw the painting and warmed inside at Valeria's work.

"Would you like to visit Lehcar?" Fatell assumed Norana had enough time to soak in the edge of her daughter's new world.

"What? Oh, is she here? I thought she was assigned to a small village near Calcoran."

"She isn't leaving until tomorrow."

"Wonderful."

Norana's hands nestled in her shallow pockets and she looked ahead as she walked through the dust free gleaming halls that glared down upon her.

Pastel curtains gently swaying in doorways hid most of the building's business, one curtain leaned against a doorway and Norana couldn't help but notice the frail gray haired woman, laying so still under the crisp white sheets, the only movement her chest as breath moved in and out.

Norana shivered as they walked on and finally arrived at a large reception area, still clean and shiny, but with soft chairs and a small plant, breaking the blinding glare from the walls.

Lehcar grinned broadly. "Mother!"

Warm hugs and tears gushed.

"You look marvelous Lehcar."

"I live well."

Norana looked around. "Do you really like all this?"

"I love it."

"I always knew you would." Merej's mellow tones took all of them by surprise.

"Papa!" Lehcar threw her arms around her father.

Fatell began a quiet retreat, passing Valeria as she left the building. Mahtso leaned against the great stone wall by the main door. A long-legged insect crawled up the wall, and froze in time as Mahtso brushed a flake of dirt from his shirt.

Fatell moved slowly towards the castle, focusing on the blades of grass and tiny pebbles in her path. Mahtso lost patience and walked to Fatell, the stars framing her diminutive figure. Fatell didn't see his feet and her nose found his chest before her eyes did.

"Try as you might, you can't walk through me," he said.

Fatell forced a smile.

Mahtso wrapped his hand around hers. "Dinner awaits you."

While Merej and his family shared the happy chatter of reunion, and family Ishtba renewed their bonds, Mahtso and Fatell dined in candlelight, silence an intrusive third wheel.

Mahtso toyed with his chain as Fatell toyed with her food.

"Rabi said this was your favorite meal, I thought so too," he finally said.

"The food is fine."

"Perhaps the company is making you so cheerful." He rose from the chair.

"Please stay."

"I never intended to go. But tell me what's wrong."

Fatell made a thousand paths in her head, trying to find the right words, only one left her lips, "Family."

Mahtso bowed his head, The lack of children, was like a sore that never healed for Fatell.

He took her hand and they walked under the stars. "Fatell my love, if I could drag the gods from the sky and force them to give you a child I would."

"I know."

Mahtso placed himself on a large flat rock and pulled Fatell on his lap. She curled up. He rocked her like a baby, her tears staining his shirt and shearing his heart.

The second moon's rays guided them back to the castle and where they lay close until a secure sleep found them.

Atan's arm rested on the edge of the couch, in his hand, a smooth silver cup, the hearty wine inside lazily licking its smooth sides. Raphela stared into the fire, her head against Atan's shoulder.

At the other end of the couch Valeria mixed her attention between Vanar and his parents. Vanar, toyed with her hair as they spoke in whispers and light giggles.

Raphela occasionally turned her head to smile at the young couple but soon nestled against Atan's chest, while he downed the last drop of wine and dozed peacefully.

A log on the fire crackled loudly, crashing into the ashes rousing them both. She nudged him "Let's go to sleep."

"Good night you two."

As the door shut to his parent's bedroom Vanar moved to the couch and pulled Valeria on his lap. "I thought they'd never leave." He stole a kiss.

"I'm glad they did." Valeria draped her arms around his neck, their mouths drawn together like magnets. Her dress rustled as wet lips and anxious hands worked together.

Laying on the couch and looking up at her sent a shiver of excitement down his spine. Valeria's skin exploded into a tingle as Vanar's fingers worked their magic through the layers of cloth. Her breasts pressed against his chest. Valeria's tongue swept over his throat and even through the folds of her gown she felt his excitement. An irrepressible urge to lay naked with him swept over her.

Warm breath lit her skin, bringing seduction ever so close while Vanar swimming in the ecstasy of her scent, lost in the softness of her skin, found his hands climbing up her legs resting on an oh so appealing bare bottom.

Valeria pressed herself into him and took a deep breath. For a split second, Vanar loosened his grip and she slid to the floor.

Vanar's face wrinkled in hurt, Valeria heard his silent whimper as the fire relinquished its fight to the cool breeze flowing down the chimney. Her lips took a gentle upward curve while her fingertips kissed his lips.

Vanar rolled on his side, revealing his bulge. Valeria took a deep breath and turned her attention elsewhere. "Tomorrow I must meet with Fatell, and our mothers. Is there anything you want, for the wedding?" Words trickled out like bare feet walking on hot stones.

Vanar rolled back, his arousal diminishing, but his eyes still soulful. "Why did you stop?" He whined.

There is a look in one's eye when an answer would be more than unnecessary. Valeria shot him that look and like a naughty boy he lowered his head. "Thank you."

He knew more everyday why she was right. His own vow to remain celibate until the wedding night could so easily be broken. No one else would care, even if she were pregnant at the altar. But he would never forgive himself.

"Vanar, the wedding?"

He broke from his reverie. "Do I want anything? Just you."

"I know."

The torches cast ghastly shadows on the wall, good entertainment for the moment.

"Val"

"Mm"

"There is something."

Slim arms propped a lithe body on the small table and then green eyes turned to him. "What?"

"I want to change something."

"Change something? You're hedging around this, are you afraid I'll be angry?"

"Afraid, I'm not afraid of anything." He sat up and pushed out his chest in mock bravery.

"Is that so?" Cross-armed and smiling she took the upper hand.

"Well, you know I..." Vanar stumbled around a thought.

"Yeess?" Her smile teased and loved all at once.

501

"How is it that women don't rule the world?" He asked in frustration.

"We do."

"So it seems." He agreed with resignation.

"Vanar," slim fingers pulled his hand to her lips. "What do you want to change?"

"Instead of the bracelet, I'd like to have two rings, like Cora and Falor."

"What a wonderful idea."

Vanar sank back into the couch, breathing a sigh of relief.

Valeria's smile dissipated and she quickly found a small stone to busy her eyes and hands.

"I thought you liked the idea?"

"I do."

"Then why do you have such a sad face?"

"Parents, yours especially."

"Oh, you think the great Duke and Lady will send us to the dungeon for breaking a tradition?" It was his turn to tease.

"You needn't be melodramatic. I just don't know."

Vanar lifted her chin and saw the fear. "Let's take a walk."

After insisting she take a cloak they moved quietly down the stairs and out of the castle. Hand in hand they walked until they stood between the school and the healers building, Night creatures peeked at them from behind large leaves and rocks. The moon and stars directed a serenade of light while fireflies sparkled the air.

Vanar pointed to the two simple structures framed by the trees. Valeria knew them, thick layers of gray stone, unimpressive shells by the naked eye. Yet, within, activities blossomed such as Raalek had never before known. Valeria felt a strong arm around her waist and warm breath in her ear. "Tell me how much more tradition can we break than that?"

As anticipated all parents dealt with the changes well and plans were made and solidified. After a few days Merej and family bade good-bye to Castle Cordan and their youngest daughter.

Chapter 22

Autumn's leaves layered the ground and crunched under the wheels of the carts bringing the cold weather staples. Soon Cordan's winter cocoon began winding its way around the walls.

Twelve's snort misted the morning air as his head nuzzled under Vanar's arm. "Are you looking for a snack?" Vanar pulled the brush through a small knot, almost falling over as Twelve became more insistent.

"All right, all right." Moving around a stall full of fresh hay was slow. The bucket of overripe fruit, saved specifically for the rameks, was just a few steps outside the stall. Vanar picked up two pieces and turned around very slowly. Motionless and silent the small figure waited.

"What are you doing here Telep?" Vanar's tone bordered on accusation.

"Just watching." Undaunted, Telep moved closer.

"Watching?" Are you sure you weren't trying to see into my mind?" Vanar felt like kicking himself as soon as the words left his mouth.

"No." Telep seemed untouched. "But I was looking into Twelve, he likes you very much."

Vanar plopped down on a nearby stool. Twelve, still insisting on his snack began nibbling at the fruit that Vanar readily handed over. He wiped the animal's slobber off on his pants.

"How can you look into something that has no mind?"

Telep came close, his thin hands gently stroking the beast who was unperturbed by the young boy. "Oh, he has a mind, just no words, only feelings."

Eye contact, the open door between all creatures, locked between the two boys. Sitting down, Vanar was as tall as Telep standing.

"My parents tell me that with your help I can contact Falor." Vanar said.

Telep's eyes opened wide and his skin took on a sheen. "Yes, would you like to talk with him."

"Do you mean now?"

"Yes".

"All right. How? What do I do?" Vanar hid neither his confusion or concern.

"Just sit there." Telep closed his eyes and reached out to Falor.

Barely awake Falor rubbed his eyes and sat up, feeling a tugging at his mind. He heard the silent words, "Falor, Vanar wants you."

Messages traveled on some unknown current between the three. Vanar sent codes to be sure Falor answered. Nothing of major importance was expressed, just simple greetings.

Vanar found the thoughts begin to fade and noticed Telep's eyes closing and his head nodding. He sent a hasty good-bye. Before they left the stable Telep was asleep in Vanar's arms.

Telep's bedroom door closed with a quiet click. Vanar saw Fatell at the end of hallway, observing like a deserving child denied the prize so many others took for granted.

As the day wore on, every moment his mind wasn't occupied, the vision of Fatell's face was there.

That night was one of two a week that Vanar and Valeria dined with Atan and Raphela.

The table was set and plates already layered with first helpings. Vanar breathed in the steam of the roasted fowl and saucy noodles. His eye turned to the small plate, covered with layers of crispy green leaves drizzled with a tangy dressing. They received the same disdainful look given to a dose of bitter medicine.

Valeria smiled, her green eyes danced. "It won't bite." She picked up a forkful and crunched it down in her mouth. "See"

Vanar pursed his lips and wrinkled his nose in annoyance.

Raphela stifled a chuckle while Atan did his best to ignore the situation. Many years of cajoling, badgering, "You won't leave this table until" and once something closely resembling a spanking regarding the eating of salad, all to no avail. It was a battle Atan had lost.

504

Vanar swirled noodles in sauce and savored a mouthful washing it down with a cold swig of water. "I was in touch with Falor today," he said suddenly.

Atan now looked up. "With the help of Telep I assume."

"Yes."

"Did he have any news, any information?" Despite his even voice Vanar knew his father and mother were hungry for news and deeply curious about the procedure.

"We only had time for a brief encounter, Telep tired quickly."

"I expected as much." Raphela wiped her mouth and pushed away the plate decorated with a thin layer of sauce and a few stray noodles.

The servant girl stoked the fire, rewarming the chilly room.

"I know." Vanar sighed.

"Vanar, how did Telep do it?" Raphela's expression changed from acceptance to plotting.

"What do you mean?"

All eyes were drawn to her. "Did he tell you what Falor was thinking, did he say what you were thinking or was it totally silent?"

"He was silent."

"And he tired quickly?"

"Yes"

"Would it be easier if he spoke Falor's thoughts instead of sending them to you?"

"I suppose it might."

"And what if Falor read your thoughts directly, then Telep would only need to be in contact with Falor." Raphela felt a world opening and solutions laying themselves out in neat order and the lilt in her voice displayed it well.

Atan's noncommittal lips curled up, just a bit.

"I will ask him Mother, first thing tomorrow." Vanar considered patting his mother on the shoulder the way one patronizes a doting parent, but he knew better.

"There is another issue I think we need to consider." Vanar allowed himself a small burp.

Valeria seeing empty plates pulled her chair from the table out of habit to clear them away. A gentle stroke of Vanar's hand on her leg reminded her again that there were servants to do that task. She lowered her head and blushed. Vanar continued. "I noticed Fatell shadowing Telep a lot today."

Raphela sighed. "I've seen it."

"It seems to me that Telep needs a mother and Fatell wants a child."

"Are you suggesting that we put Telep in Fatell's direct care?"

"Yes."

"What an excellent idea. Don't you think so Atan?"

"Yes. Good observation Vanar."

Valeria's eyes moved to each speaker, listening and watching.

Vanar took the situation to the next level. "Mahtso could be a father figure, there would be a family."

The word had importance and coated the room like icing on a cake.

Raphela noticed Valeria shift in her seat.

"Does Mahtso being involved make you uncomfortable?" Raphela was curious.

"My lady, it is not my place to say."

Raphela stared at Vanar and then turned back to Valeria. "If you are some day to be Lady of Ishtba, then you must say, it is important."

"Yes, Mahtso, is... well, different."

Atan's grey eyes took time to place themselves in Valeria's direction. "And anyone outside this castle would be wise to utter such concern."

Valeria's shoulders loosened their grip on her back. The duke understood.

He continued. "You have not lived your life with this man... I will assure you of one thing, if Fatell wished to care for Telep and for Mahtso to help her, he will die before any harm will come to the boy. Telep will receive the same affection, teaching and discipline of any other child, nothing less."

Atan could have told Valeria poison would save her soul and she would have swallowed a goblet full and thanked him as she died, so powerful were his words, delivered softly, even gently.

And so it was decided that Fatell would finally have her family.

Valeria finished her routine of hair brushing and straightened out the covers on her bed. It would take a long while to expect someone to do it for her.

Vanar's door was ajar, he was gone. At the top of the stairs a young guard stood at ease, nodding politely to her.

No one else in sight or sound. The silence was difficult. She was accustomed to the flurry of activity which she knew exploded on the floor below, and from which she was now distanced by necessity.

Vanar had promised her a studio, a place to paint. "If it's what you need, pick a room, anywhere in the castle, as long as it's available, it's yours." It was time to accept the offer. Winter was around the corner, she'd need something to do.

Valeria opened a door to the room farthest from the stairs, looked around and closed it. Not right, neither was the next one. Her hand turned the round cold knob of the third, it didn't budge. She jiggled and peeped through the hole.

"Can I help you?"

Valeria's throat tightened as she stood and backed up to the wall, eyes wide as the hole she had peered through. "My, my lady."

"Can I help you Valeria?" The question so simple and genuine Valeria felt her cheeks flush as she shifted from foot to foot, her simple green dress stirring at her ankles. "I, uh, was looking for a, a room."

"A room?" Raphela's hair, wrapped around her head, shimmered like a crown.

Valeria stumbled through an explanation.

"Well this room remains locked and should be so. But I think the next one would do well."

Valeria opened the door and Raphela waited on the threshold as Valeria explored, rag in hand, to uncover what hid under the thin layer of dust. Despite dark wood shutters, the sun was determined to enter this place. Through seams, cracks and slim spaces between window sill and shutter light forced itself through. Drawn to the power of the light, Valeria drew back the shutters allowing the sun to flood the room with brightness and warmth. Carefully with the rag, she wiped clean a spot on the window, but the view demanded more than a sliver of sight. She opened the window, leaned on the dusty sill, and peered out onto the vast diverse land of Ishtba. The chill air turned her skin white, but she didn't notice. Trees, birds, animals-- all the world had to offer danced before her, titillating every sense, sending her soaring into realms of imagination.

Raphela smiled and stepped into the room, about the size of her own. An old tapestry woven with as much dust as thread hung on the far wall. Empty cobwebs clung to the ceiling corners and the solid wood floor had lost its sheen.

Valeria finally moved from the window and looked around. It was as if she floated to the wall, its intricate carvings like a magnet to her eyes and hands. At least five different kinds of wood were used to tell the tale. A Gilfon with unfolded wings boasted a kingly place at the top. Beneath him animals, though carvings in the wood, scurried under his eyes. Valeria's slim fingers delved in the intricate curves of a bird's plume and she squatted as her hand came to the flared nostril of a ramek, its mane, flowing in an invisible wind. She traced down its back.

Raphela stood in the middle of the room taking in the simple surroundings, the only furniture a small stool.

A sound, like distant thunder cracked the silence. Raphela turned to the wall that sent it. Valeria was sprawled on the floor. Raphela was there instantly. "Are you all right?"

Eyes laden with fear and surprise turned to her for support. A mother helped Valeria to her feet and held her, for just a moment, unperturbed by dirty hands and trembling legs.

Valeria gently broke from Raphela's hold. "I'm fine." She swallowed hard and brushed away a tear.

Both women stared into the blackness that had been a wall.

Raphela ventured forth and stuck her head beyond the opening, she encountered only darkness, but knew there was more. "Valeria, bring that stool here, let's keep this open," she ordered.

Valeria obeyed while Raphela retrieved two torches.

Side by side their footsteps followed the flames that broke the darkness into shadows. It wasn't long before their eyes adjusted and the full complement of the room showed itself. Torches were laid in wire racks, obviously designed for such things, allowing the women to gaze in wonder at the eclectic compilation of furnishings.

Valeria drifted to a chair, a most unusual piece, its tubular metal frame, polished enough to show her own reflection. Valeria smiled at her distorted face. The seat felt odd, like thick flexible animal skin, yet she knew it wasn't skin.

Raphela was drawn to a desk, its deeply grained wood, pieced together with the passion of a craftsman. The drawers didn't creak as they opened and smelled sweet, like the wood flowers of the autumn.

Above the desk were layers of wood planks, evenly spaced. On the first three books rested against marble slabs. Raphela gently pulled one out and sat in the cushioned armchair by the desk. So little dust touched the leather-bound hard cover that Raphela had to take a moment to look around at the rich colors of the room. It was unmarred, by any intrusion from the outside.

She opened the book and began to read.

Valeria handled the brocade on the walls as if the gods had created them in her presence. Then she found the closet and the oddest array of clothes she'd ever seen. Each required close inspection, from a dress resembling her grandmother's wedding gown, to a sleek robe of shiny fabric.

Raphela discovered the first book she picked up was a diary, written by Atan's great grandmother. She skimmed the pages and replaced it for later reading.

A black book, no decoration, stood alone on the third shelf. This she also pulled down to read. It was in the ancient tongue, written by hand, it too was a diary, each page a lesson of some kind. Raphela wiped silent tears away so as not to stain the paper

509

and stifled a chuckle or two so Valeria wouldn't hear. At morning's end she had finished and replaced the book.

Valeria hung all the clothes back in the closet, where they had escaped hungry moths.

"Valeria?"

"Yes my lady?"

"Please call me Raphela."

"As you wish."

"Valeria, this has obviously been hidden for many years and must remain a secret between us."

Valeria considered asking why, but the haze in Raphela's eyes and the softness in her voice was answer enough. "It will be our secret," she agreed.

"Can you read the ancient language?"

"Only a little."

"You must learn it. There are lessons in this room that can change our lives, but it will be in your time, not mine."

"I don't understand."

"You will, someday you will."

The room was left exactly as it was found. They discovered that the mane of the ramek opened the door and its saddle closed it.

"My, um, Raphela, I would like this room as my studio."

"Good choice." She smiled broadly and wrapped her arms around the girl, placing a wise kiss on her head. "Let's clean up and have some lunch."

Telep sat silent, as usual in the back of the classroom. A shadow grew daily under his big brown eyes, now focused on the picture-laden wall.

"Telep, spell 'ramek' despite the teacher's expectations of catching him off guard, Telep stood without hesitation.

"R-a-m-e-k"

The teacher licked her lips in embarrassment "Very good, you may sit."

Telep looked around, saw all eyes on him and quickly returned to his previous view.

During the breaks he would stay alone in the classroom, avoiding the other children. After a few weeks the teacher

510

insisted he join the others. Little girls giggled as he walked past, trying to find a solitary spot. His shoulder brushed against an older boy.

"Watch it curly!"

Telep walked on, head down. The large hand shoved him from behind. ""I said watch it." Cold blue eyes matched the throaty growl.

"Sorry." Telep continued his slow shuffle.

The red face and long blond hair that accompanied the voice put itself an inch from Telep's face and other faces took their niches in a growing crowd. "That's not good enough."

Telep looked up with big brown eyes and didn't say a word. Silence rippled through the gathering.

In less time than the teacher could notice, Telep turned his curly haired head and walked away, leaving a mesmerized schoolmate, staring at thin air. The boy refused to answer any questions and soon the cluster of children dispersed and returned to routine. Telep found his solitary spot.

Fatell made weak attempts to observe Telep nonchalantly. At first she took his solitude as adjustment, but no rationalization worked for long. Finally one night she broached the subject at dinner.

Telep dangled the soft, white noodle swinging gently on his fork. A bubble of gravy made its way to the tip of the noodle and landed with a splash on the plate.

With the untethered methods of youth, Telep sucked on the noodle leaving a ring of gravy around his toothy grin. "I got to play with the zorel pups today. They licked me all over."

"How many were there?" Fatell raised the decanter to pour more juice for Mahtso, who silently turned down the offer.

Telep used his fingers and after three attempts arrived at an answer. "Six. There were six pups. Can I have one? Please."

Mahtso raised his eyes and chewed on the inside of his lip. "We'll think about it. Now wipe your mouth."

Telep obeyed.

"How are you getting along with the other children?"

"Fine." Telep searched for something to look at, besides Fatell.

Mahtso's chain began to dance as Fatell worked at being stern. "Your teacher tells me that you're having a difficult time."

"I said I'm getting along with them just fine." The frustrated child displayed itself with the clang of a fork on a plate.

Mahtso felt the hairs on the back of his neck bristle and his chain's speed moved up a notch.

Only a thin layer of Fatell's calm remained. "She said that you don't play with the other children."

Pounds of air moved through Telep's lungs and his face turned red. "I hate them I hate them all. I hate this place, I want to go home. I want to go back to Calcoran." The chair wobbled as Telep ran from the table to his room

Fatell made no attempt to control her tears as they gushed down her face. Through blurred eyes she stared at the table. It didn't look any different than last night. A trail of crumbs led to half a loaf of bread and three plates swirled with dried gravy sat in their proper places. The empty platter held two lonely strands of noodles and a stray vegetable. Yes, it looked very much like last night.

Mahtso stood and placed a kiss on Fatell's head. "I'll talk to him." He was calm as a summer day.

"Mahtso."

He leaned against the table and placed her chin between his fingers, blue eyes wide open for inspection. "Trust me"

She nodded.

Torchlight entered first. Telep, far too upset to actually look into anyone's mind, curled up in a safe corner of his bed, stirred as the scent of the flame sifted through the room.

Mahtso raised the torch so that he could see the boy as the door creaked closed. "Telep?" Still as a rock, Telep remained in the corner. "There's no need to hide."

Telep wished to rest on his fear, but Mahtso's voice was a gentle wind, not a torrent of rain. His legs scooted out and then his face. "Are you going to punish me?" The words came through a latent sniffle.

Mahtso considered the question. "I should, just because you hurt Fatell so much."

Telep's head lowered in shame. " I, I didn't mean to..."

"Mm, let's take a walk."

Castle life was yawning and few people were about. Those who were had to notice the pair, walking side by side, legs moving in unison. Telep's head lowered, seeming to count each step as he walked. Mahtso's ponytail displaying a few loose hairs far above the hands locked behind his back.

Mahtso opened the window to the small room he found, allowing winter's breath to surround them. Telep shivered before Mahtso wrapped his arms around him and they peered out at the stars twinkling above.

Telep avoided looking into Mahtso's mind, less out of fear than lack of desire to hear his words.

"It's hard being different. I know."

Telep buried himself a little deeper inside Mahtso's warmth. This was a statement that had no argument.

Telep took a long time to form the right words. Mahtso waited, patiently. "How did you do it?" he finally asked.

Mahtso found two chairs, closed the window, and pulled the seats close to the torch on the wall. Both took in the sweet mixed scent of cold and flame. "I was lucky, not as lucky as you. No one found me until I was 13. Another boy, Atan Ishtba, befriended me and helped me learn to live with myself. And Fatell is the web that keeps me together."

"I don't feel so lucky. Fatell is so wonderful to me, but the children are so hard."

"Why?" Blue eyes would not release Telep's glance.

Tears formed and dotted his cheeks. "All those thoughts at one time, in one place. It's like, like being attacked by a hive of stinging bees, buzzing in my ears." Telep's breath got shorter and his thin chest heaved.

Mahtso pulled him on his lap and held him close. Two different worlds, two different agonies, somehow meshing and melting in a common sea. Both shared a sense of safety and relief rarely felt. After a time Telep began to yawn.

"Telep, let's ask Fatell to change your schedule, less time with the children until you learn to shield their minds from yours."

Telep smiled. "That's a good idea." Curly brown hair rested comfortably in Mahtso's firm chest, as Telep was carried back to his room. Anyone seeing Mahtso would have sworn he'd been possessed by a satisfied grin and warm thoughts.

Fatell watched him tuck Telep into bed and smiled. That night Mahtso's touch was a thick coat on a cold day and his lips sweeter than spring fruit.

Soon Cordan was cocooned in snow, no different than any other winter. Vanar squinted at the pale morning light and the grell that stared down at him. He needed no encouragement to wrap the covers tightly around him. The grell had not yet demanded he awaken.

Few people abided by the structure of the timepiece and Vanar cursed it and himself for being one of the few.

His efforts to regain slumber were weak against his energy as he kicked the covers away.

The sun, still innocent in the day's young sky, shadowed the landscape below. Vanar leaned against the cold windowsill and studied the white crust. The wind laughed at the sun, and sent funnels of snow dancing around the world.

One last tug and his boots were wrapped around thick socked feet. Vanar saw the light in his father's study, ignored it, and plodded down the stairs, avoiding the few people that were awake.

The tunnel to the barn kept the snow at bay, but the cold tingled his cheeks and numbed his fingers. Twelve whinnied in delight as Vanar came close. The routine of feeding and grooming took place in total silence.

Their brief ride in the indoor corral was intense and demanding on both. Rameks care little for conversation. Vanar was glad.

As he returned to the castle Vanar considered putting his energy into the training room. He looked in, stared blankly at the equipment and left. All the exercises and training for hours at a time had not relieved the energy and yearning that grew in him every day.

Valeria peeked in Vanar's room, which she found empty and retreated to her work. His wedding suit needed just a little more attention and it would be done. It glimmered at her, strong and smooth, the gold and green so perfect for him. His footsteps broke her reverie. She ran to the stairs to meet him. He continued walking.

"Vanar, I finished, come look." Green eyes pranced with joy and her fingers pulled at his hand, which he quickly pulled away.

"Not now, don't bother me," he grumbled

She mocked a sigh of annoyance. "You have been awful for days now. Just come look. This will cheer you up."

"I don't care."

The guard at the top of the stairs did his best to ignore the louder tone.

"What do you mean you don't care. You asked me to make the changes. How can you not care?" more annoyance than hurt reflected back at his grumbling.

"I said I don't care, go away!"

"I will not." Valeria's hands rested firmly on her hips.

She didn't see the back of his hand as it struck her face. She stumbled back and grabbed onto the couch to keep from falling and then touched her face. Two pairs of eyes stared at each other in disbelief. Vanar opened his mouth. "Valeria, I'm..."

She was in her room before he could finish the sentence.

"Sorry," He whispered.

Valeria sobbed into her pillow.

He knocked at her door. "I'm sorry, please, open the door."

"Go away, I never want to see you again." The words came between sniffles.

Vanar slid down beside her door and leaned against the wall, his knees against his chest and his hand rubbing his head. "What have I done. How could I?"

How long he sat, he didn't know or care. When he looked up, Atan's shadow was over him. "What's wrong?"

Fire blazed from Vanar's eyes. "You! It's your fault I did this!"

Atan stepped back as Vanar stood, ranting.

"What are you talking about?"

"I hit her."

"Let's go to my study and talk about this." Atan attempted to put his arm around Vanar, whose brutal reaction wounded Atan's feelings more than his son could imagine.

"I won't leave her alone."

"Your mother will take care of Valeria, you're not doing her any good."

Vanar considered arguing more, but the guards didn't need to hear all this.

Raphela closed the door gently. Valeria's face red and blotchy felt more tears roll down it. Raphela's arms were strong yet soft. It didn't take long for the girl to stop shaking.

Raphela caressed her hair and finally was allowed to get close to her face.

The tender pale cheek was turning purple and blue, but fortunately it was only a bruise.

"Tell me what happened."

"I don't know. I was talking to him. He'd been grumpy but I... He hit me. Why? I just wanted him to see the suit. I was so excited I thought maybe it would brighten his mood." Valeria sipped some hot tea and then wiped her face. "Why did he hit me. I hate him. I can't marry someone like that. I want to go home." She began sobbing again.

Raphela sighed and let her cry a little longer. "He cares for you, very much."

"Really. My father loves my mother, he doesn't hit her, never." A spark of anger came through the hurt and self pity.

Raphela jumped on it. "Vanar, is not your father."

"That is a fact. But because he is the next duke that doesn't give him the right to hit me."

"Very true, it doesn't. Did he apologize?" Raphela pulled back the curtains to allow the warm sunlight to enter the room.

"Yes, through the door. But that won't remove the bruise on my face."

"Valeria, he's a young man with a great deal inside him."

Valeria cut her off. "Why are you defending him? Because he's your son?"

"I'm not defending him. I'm teaching you." Raphela maintained her patience.

516

"I don't think I'd make a good student right now." Bitter tones passed through a sneer.

"Do you love him?"

Valeria buried her head in her hands and cried again. "Yes."

"Then you must learn. You are here not so much to learn duties but to learn more of what you are going to marry."

Valeria curled up and leaned against a wall, staring at Raphela with frightened eyes.

Raphela sat beside her and squeezed her hand. "When he holds you, what does it feel like?"

Valeria wiped away a tear and remembered the strength of his embrace. "Safe, as if nothing could ever harm me."

Raphela half smiled. "And his kiss?"

Valeria blushed and swallowed hard. "Like flames dancing in my blood." It was an odd question from her future mother-in-law.

"That is his passion and his soul and if you will take his embrace and kiss, then you must deal with his dark side."

"I cannot allow him to hit me."

"True, so you must learn when to stay away."

"Why? Why should I have to stay away?"

"Because we all have our weaknesses. Did he search you out? Demand that you stand there and take his abuse."

"No."

"You didn't heed his warning, true?"

"I suppose. But it's not my fault." Valeria felt suddenly defensive.

"No, it's not, but if he tells you his self-control is behind his passion, then you must stay away."

"Is that what you do?" Slowly Valeria realized Raphela was not handing out blind wisdom.

"Sometimes."

"But the Duke never hits you. You don't know what it's like. I can't just..."

"Valeria, I do know."

"What?"

Raphela had decided that a time would come when the past would need to be opened and the door was ajar, she had to walk

517

through. She loosened her bodice and let the back of her dress fall, exposing the scars. Valeria stared, even raised a finger to touch, but shrank back. "My child, you cannot imagine the depth of passion that brought these scars. It is more than Vanar will ever have. But he is the son of the man who did this."

Valeria forgot her own situation.

"Why would he..." The words couldn't reach her tongue.

"Why would he nearly whip me to death? It's a long story and if you can listen, I will start at the beginning."

She nodded yes. Raphela wove her tale from the day she arrived at Castle Cordan until the death of king Samed.

"I can't do this Raphela. I can't live this life." Valeria imagined the violence of the past, of Rayna and Fakrash, and shivered.

"Valeria, we never shared this with Vanar or anyone in your generation because it is history and we are leaving you a world that needs the charm of your art and the vigor of Vanar's drive for commerce. But remember, the strength that brought Vanar to this world is in him and he will deal with it. But as his wife, you must know who he is, or you will not be able to rule beside him.

Somehow the bruise no longer seemed so awful. "So I must forgive him?"

"You must do whatever is in your heart. But do not let him believe he can do this again. He had no right to strike you."

"Thank you." Valeria brushed a tiny tear and enveloped Raphela in a warm hug.

While Raphela spoke with Valeria, Vanar began his tirade. "It's all your fault. I inherited this from you. How could I do this? It has to be because of you!"

"Why?

Vanar snarled at him. "I know about you. How you used to beat mother. I've heard the stories, you cruel sadistic..."

Atan slid into a chair and closed his eyes. For all his care to keep the past from hurting him, his own son stabbed him with it. "What did you hear?" He resigned himself to clearing the air.

"You beat and whipped her, tortured her. I heard all about it. And now, now I'll end up doing the same thing." Vanar paced, his hands rising and falling with each word.

"Sit down and hear the truth."

"The truth after years of lies? Why should I believe you?"

"Vanar" Atan's voice, always the champion, "Sit down and listen."

Angry eyes stared into Atan's sad grey ones and the fire began to cool.

"I have not lied to you, I have kept history from you. Truth, truth is I did strike your mother. Twice. Once, just like you and once, once my son I took your mother, chained her to a wall and whipped her until she was almost dead."

Vanar stared in disbelief. He knew the servants and soldiers had exaggerated and his anger doubled any tale he heard, but the cold hard facts sent him swaying. "How, how could you?"

Atan lowered his head. "I have asked myself that every day for eighteen years. I don't know, anymore than you know why you lost control and struck Valeria."

"How could she forgive you?"

"I don't know that either. But your mother is unique and that is why she's your mother. Its time you knew much more about the past.

Atan relayed the tales to Vanar as Raphela had to Valeria. When he finished Vanar studied the lines in his father's face and gray hairs ruling his head. "I understand more, perhaps more than I want to. Will I ever have to live as you did?"

"We have struggled over the years so that you wouldn't. Your time will be different. But know this, you were wrong today. Should I find out you did this again I will personally show you what it feels like." Atan did not threaten, he promised.

Vanar buried his head in his hands and wished somehow that his father would at that moment dole out some punishment to relieve his guilt. "Yes father."

Raphela and Atan chose a light dinner, downstairs in a cozy room. Vanar pondered the day and found himself at Valeria's door, it opened slowly and fully. The scent of her skin made him shiver until his eyes rested on the deep purple bruise of her cheek. Gentle fingers raised to caress, but she flinched and the tears trapped inside him flowed forth, a silent stream.

Valeria tried to avoid his glance, but was gathered in like a leaf whirling in the wind. Deep in his brown eyes lay a guilt so encompassing that her own pain and anger felt foolish, tears gathered in the corners of her eyes.

Yet his lips were still, not a whisper, barely a breath. Held tight in his eyes. Valeria knew this more than any other was a time of decision. This man, whose love knew no bounds, knew not of sharing it with words. He never learned and it was not a part of him, could she live in the silence? Learn to wallow in the touch? Raphela learned and loved it, but she was not Raphela. Could she teach Vanar to give her the words? His eyes begged a forgiveness and sorrow his speech could never match, but was it enough?

He felt the cool fingertips caress his cheek, the feel of his skin answered all the questions. They would learn some how, they would learn.

Vanar swore he could feel her heart beating against his chest as she moved to the safety of his arms. Green eyes turned up at him.

"I love you Valeria."

Tongues married in the success of a hill overtaken. They watched the fire die and fell asleep on the couch, nestled together, warmed by a blanket that mysteriously appeared.

Atan lay under the covers and watched his wife slip into the warm clothes of night, her hair shining after the nightly routine of brushing. Her hand laid the brush down with a gentle tap.

"Have you ever forgiven me?" His deep voice broke the silence.

"Forgiven you?" Raphela ignored the tingling scent of burning logs and night air. "For what?"

Atan said nothing, just stared at her.

She sat on the edge of the bed, her hand resting on his knees. "There is nothing to forgive."

"For eighteen years you've been silent, is there no anger?"

"No" She stood and walked to the wall, took down the whip and laid it by his hand. "No, for if being by your side required I live it over again every night I would." Raphela's blood began to race, her breasts forming a soft moving mountain on her chest. "I could not be full just tasting the sweet, like everything else, I want it all."

Neither was sure if her tantalizing voice and cattish turns of her bottom were intentional or instinctive, but soon Atan felt himself deep inside her, satisfying her demand for his power. Like a vampire she sucked on his neck, titillating them both. Nothing felt so good as he pressed inside her, his heart rested on hers. Together they beat like the hooves of a ramek dancing in the freedom of flight.

For a moment he paused to stare down, strong fingers pulled his ear to her lips. "I would walk the Gods' fire for you, if this was my reward."

He buried his tongue in her willing cheeks, and then circled her neck and laid a soft whisper in her ear. "Gods fire be damned, I am yours, for eternity."

Raphela sipped at the lukewarm tea, lost in a fuzzy thought, while a nervous young girl cleared the breakfast table. The fire below the water pot crackled to its end as the sun forced its first rays through the split in the shutters.

With practiced care the girl, about Vanar's age, picked up Atan's cup and saucer, then turned to see what else could be moved. The cup, not so inclined to turn, dove from the saucer and crashed to the floor. Raphela jumped, disturbed from her reverie. The girl stared in utter fear and scurried to the floor to clean the mess, slicing her skin and drawing blood.

Choosing to ignore the cut, she continued to clean, but Raphela noticed the stain on the cuff of her blouse. "Come here Ula."

Despite the gentility, Ula broke into tears. "I'm so sorry my lady. I didn't mean to, I really..." She began to sob uncontrollably.

Raphela sat her down. As blood trickled down the girl's finger Raphela wrapped it.

"Hold your hand up," she commanded.

First aid done, she handed Ula a cloth to dry her blotchy red eyes and then waited for the heavy sobs to fade.

"I'm so sorry my lady. I know you're disappointed. Please, please forgive me. Will, will the Duke be angry?"

Raphela sensed no fear of reprisal but something obviously upset the girl. "Over a broken cup, I think not."

"But he will be disappointed, won't he?" Long brown hair dipped below her shoulders as her head lowered.

"No. What makes you think so?"

Ula wiped her nose and sniffled. "My mother told me what an honor it was to care for the Duke and Lady and that I should be careful to do everything right, or I'd have to find another job to do."

"Do you enjoy this work?"

"Oh yes my lady, it is what I have always wished to do." Eyes sparkled with emotion, but little else, which spelled to Raphela the girl's limited abilities and desires.

"If it is what you wish, then you shall do it. Your only fault was fearing failure. Just be the best you can be."

"Yes my lady. Thank you my lady. I shall tell my..."

Raphela's hand went up. "Shh" The clicking of carriage wheels echoed, even up here. "I must go."

Atan stretched out his legs and read an old book. His sitting room always comfortable.

"We have company my Duke." Raphela's light tone brought a raised eyebrow and sigh.

"I suppose that means I must dress properly to receive guests."

"Indeed, I think the winter has spoiled you."

He followed her and soon both were ready. Raphela tied her hair up and took one last look at herself.

"Raphela." Atan stood behind her and the word was as much a request as statement.

A smile, gentle as the spring breeze outside the window, met his soft grey eyes and leaned into the touch of long fingers. Lips and cheeks brushed, saying more in silence than what most attempted in a sea of empty words.

"Come, come my Duke, our guests await."

They straightened hair and clothes before heading downstairs.

Despite Falor's protest Cora climbed out of the carriage on her own two feet. "You are so stubborn," he growled before knocking.

"And you worry too much."

Stepping over the threshold calmed them both, especially as Vanar and Valeria were there to greet them. Atan and Raphela watched from the stairs.

Pensive lips turned to broad smiles as Valeria and Vanar gazed at Cora's large round belly. Cora was nearly knocked down by Valeria's hug.

"How wonderful! I'm so excited for you." She studied her friend up and down. "You look incredible."

Cora smiled. "Thank you."

"How do you feel?"

"I feel great." Cora's eyes betrayed to Valeria what her voice and words denied.

"Great or not, I'm changing your room to one downstairs. Let's find one now." Cora breathed a thank you.

Vanar took charge of Falor, slapping his back firmly. "Congratulations, you must be thrilled." Both looked towards the slowly receding figures of the girls.

Falor stared at Cora, her belly hidden from his view. "I'm glad to be here. Honestly, we almost didn't come, but she'll get the best care here."

"Well I'm glad you made the trip and as always you worry too much."

"I know."

"Let's get a snack."

Valeria opened the door to a large room with a more than ample bed.

As her eyes saw the bed Cora felt her shoulders loosen and suddenly her jaws were no longer chained together like beast and master. Her relieved smile gave Valeria a sense of satisfaction, almost like a mother with a happy child.

"Thank you, thank you so much."

"Just get some rest."

"I will."

523

Valeria closed the door and Cora closed her eyes. Valeria met the boys in the kitchen.

"Where's Cora?" Falor jumped out of his chair.

"Resting, relax Falor."

Falor sank back into his seat.

A servant boy laid a cup of tea on the table for Valeria.

"It smells good. Are you sure Rabi isn't here?"

Vanar sighed. "Trust me, he has no idea they've arrived."

"Good. Cora really wants to surprise him." She took a sip of tea and listened to the bustle of the kitchen.

"Why didn't you tell us?" Vanar pushed away his cup and leaned towards Falor.

"Superstition I guess."

"Superstition? Well that makes sense, for you."

"Thank you." Vanar's snide remark received an equally sarcastic reply.

"Now boys." Valeria smelled an argument. "Are the flowers blooming at Calcoran?"

"Yes" Falor was slow to change his mood, but Vanar quickly dropped the matter.

"Is Cora happy there?" One last bite of cookie met its end in his mouth.

"I think so. Everyone seems to like her and she has her own kitchen." Falor smiled at his wife's pleasure.

"I can tell." Valeria poked gently at Falor's stomach.

"He's just not getting enough exercise." Vanar jumped to his friend's defense.

"He's getting exercise, just not the right kind." Valeria's tease brought red to Falor's cheeks.

"I don't need to take this abuse." He rose to go, only half as angry as he acted.

"I'm sorry Falor, I didn't mean any harm." Her apology was real.

"It's all right. I want to check on Cora anyway."

"We'll see you later."

Vanar laid a quick kiss on Valeria's cheek and headed off to chores, she did the same. Falor meandered down the hallway, tiptoed into their room, and settled into an overstuffed chair, just a bit more than an arm's reach from the bed.

Disturbed by a familiar sound, Cora reached to the other side of the bed. The cold empty spot forced her eyes open. She sighed in frustration, though her neck lifted her head, it still couldn't push far enough for her eyes to see over her belly. After a few gyrations, she managed to sit up. There was Falor, chin resting on his chest, snores arriving at regular intervals. For a while she sat and listened, but her bladder was not so patient.

"Falor?" It was a peaceful sound. When he didn't respond after a third try, she picked up a pillow and tossed it at him.

"What, huh?'

"Falor."

He yawned and seeing his wife immediately changed modes. "Cora, is, is it time?"

"No, I just need some help."

"Sure." More than happy to lend support as she slid from the bed to stand.

"Thank you.

Soon the rested couple headed back towards the kitchen. Telep met them halfway, his hopeful eyes easy to read.

"Go ahead Falor. I can handle this alone."

"Why didn't you tell me?" Telep demanded of his friend.

"Hello to you too." Falor's social reprimand did its job.

"Hello Falor. I'm sorry. But..."

"Telep, we were keeping it a secret from everyone outside Calcoran Castle.

"I would have kept..." Telep stopped and shuffled his feet, Falor's eyes said it all. Telep's record of keeping secrets was not good.

"You seem happy, happier than in the fall anyway."

"Its nice having a family. It took a while to get used to, but Fatell is the best mother I could ask for.

"And Mahtso?" Falor searched the boy's mind and studied his body.

"Mahtso is not half as bad as everyone thinks. He's sad a lot, but we get along real well." Telep did not work to convince Falor, so his friend was satisfied.

525

Cora took her time, soaking in the feel of Castle Cordan, its strength and safety.

Rabi sipped the steaming sauce from the spoon.

"Not enough yellow root." Cora grinned as Rabi spun to see her, spoon falling back into the pot and sprinkling sauce in the air.

"Cora, look at you." His wide-open arms searched for a way to hug her and finally he just did it. Then standing back held her hands, reviewing her from head to toe. "You look marvelous! How do you feel?"

"Pretty good actually." Cora looked around and nodded to the other members of the kitchen staff, walking by and wishing her well.

"Sit down, what a fool I am, keeping you standing." Rabi ushered her to a seat.

"I'm fine, really."

"I know, I know, even if you weren't, you wouldn't say." Underneath the bright eyes his thin face smiled.

Cora blushed. "It's not fair, you know me far too well. But I really am fine."

Rabi listened to the confidence in her voice. "I believe you."

"Good. How have you been?"

Rabi began a litany of inconsequential complaints, just for her.

By the morning Valeria realized she had a task before her and waited, somewhat impatiently for Cora to emerge from her room.

"What are you doing here?" Cora stretched and rubbed her belly.

"Do you remember when I had Telep send a message about your measurements and Falor's?"

"Yes, but I never did understand why."

"Can you handle a climb up the stairs?"

"I don't know if she should do that." Falor's fingers intertwined in hers.

"I'm sure I won't give birth on the way. Let's go."

Falor sighed with frustration. "Can I come too?"

"You must." Valeria chuckled and guided them to her studio.

526

Cora was glad their room was downstairs.

Neatly stacked bolts of cloth, sat by carefully organized spools of thread and a rack bearing an assortment of wedding garb.

"You've been working hard this winter." Cora fondled the clothes, envious of her friend's talent.

Falor sniffed the air, it smelled more like a garden than a sewing room. Finally he saw it, her studio, tucked away behind a curtain. He walked over to peek behind the colorful drape, his fingers just wrapping around the edge.

"That is forbidden territory." Valeria tried to sound light hearted but the guard dog in her voice was in control. Without argument Falor returned to the business at hand.

"Try this on Falor." Valeria handed him a jacket made of rich green cloth, subtly trimmed in gold, matching green pants and a pale yellow shirt, all fitted to be slimming and elegant.

Falor obeyed, heaving a sigh as he modeled for his wife and friend. The suit, pieces of cloth planned to work in unison, transformed his appearance. Cora looked up and saw the man Duke Ishtba had chosen to manage Calcoran.

"Oh my," was all she could say.

Valeria made him look in the mirror. Falor turned back to his wife. "Is this really me?"

"Um hm."

Falor stared at himself, amazed at what Valeria had created. "What is this for?"

"The wedding, of course. You and Cora will stand by us, won't you?" It never occurred to Valeria that they wouldn't.

"Of course we will," they replied in unison.

"But why this?"

"Because everything will be coordinated in color and style. Now take that off and hang it up. Cora, I need to make some adjustments on your gown."

And so the morning was spent. Falor, finding his way to Vanar, was forced to exercise while the girls adjusted Cora's gown.

With Raphela's encouragement and Falor's insistence Cora agreed to an examination by Aharon. The Healer's Building was clean and sterile as ever. Cora expected the crisp white sheets on the exam table to crack as she climbed up and lay down.

Falor paced nervously outside the room while Aharon did his job. Cora felt experienced fingers glide over her skin, from head to toe. He looked in her ears and eyes and nose and mouth, for what, she never knew. Cool palms rested on her naked belly and flinched only slightly as a tiny foot expressed its annoyance at being disturbed.

"Busy little fellow in there." Aharon laughed. "You appear to be in excellent health. To be honest better than I would have anticipated. Who is caring for you at Calcoran?" Aharon turned his back as Cora dressed and then helped her off the table.

"Summitra is the healer, but in truth, Oolon has had a very active role in my care." She spoke cautiously.

"Oolon, really. Why? What does he know?" Aharon was neither pleased nor displeased, but just curious.

"He said it was important that I cared for myself and the child. He gave me a packet of herbs for every morning to have with my tea. When he arrives tomorrow I think he'll show you what's in it, because I haven't been able to figure it out and he won't tell me. But I feel really good most of the time."

"Then I am looking forward to his visit."

Evening arrived as did dinner, a shared occasion of the two young couples and Atan and Raphela.

Cora leaned against the tall back chair, finally finding a comfortable position.

The dining room, usually reserved for entertaining guests, possessed enough formality to force the young people to consider their positions. The carefully polished silver bowls dressed with delicate flowers framed the elegant display of finely carved tables and chairs.

Vanar looked around and then across the table at Falor. All four felt like the teenagers that they really were, not the future rulers of Raalek.

"It's been a long time since I've been in this room." Falor studied the chandelier above his head.

Vanar looked at the painted vase by the window and his eyes lit. "Falor, do you remember what happened here?" His cheshirous grin brought the girls attention and Falor's curiosity.

"What are you talking about?"

"A long time ago, we were about 11 years old, my mother..."

"Oh that."

"Yes, that."

Valeria looked to Cora who shrugged her shoulders. "Vanar, tell us what happened."

"Well, Falor and I were exploring. My mother told us to stay away from the great hall, some other formal rooms and, this room. At first we did, then we got bored."

Falor interrupted. "You, got bored."

Vanar smiled. "Anyway, we ended up here. I don't know why but I was chasing Falor and we were running around having a generally good time."

"It was a good time all right." Falor shook his head.

"Go on" Cora pressed.

"Suddenly, Falor runs right into that vase, the big one by the window." All heads turned. "Just as my mother walks by the door."

"Which I told you to close." Falor chastised.

Vanar ignored him. "Fortunately, it didn't break, but my mother did catch us."

"And she was mad, quiet, but mad."

"That's true. When I saw her finger silently call us I knew we were in trouble."

Falor took the next portion of the tale. "She took us to this dark little room, with just one torch on the wall, a table and a very ominous looking paddle."

"My mother is very good at setting a mood." Vanar chuckled.

"I was scared to death." Falor didn't crack a smile.

Vanar picked up the story. "She looked at us long and hard, arms crossed, then spoke. "Well boys, I'll give you a choice. You must be punished for disobeying me. But shall I punish you or should I leave it to the Duke?" I closed my eyes to think about it, but you, you just jumped right in with an answer."

"How was I supposed to know?" Falor defended himself. "I figured your father would beat our bottoms black and blue."

Vanar shook his head. "To continue, Falor says "My lady, I will take your punishment." So we were stuck. My mother said "All right boys, I have a two fold punishment for you. First turnaround." Which we did and received one very solid wallop of the paddle."

"Your mother is quite strong."

"I know. But then, she doled out the rest. We had to scrub the entrance hall floor until it shone."

Falor buried his head in his hands. "Oh how my knees hurt. Tell them the rest."

"Well, my father comes by to watch. Standing over us, grinning, he said "Perhaps my punishment would have been easier. So I..."

Vanar stopped as the dining room door closed with a gentle click.

Atan and Raphela took their places at the end of the table.

Atan grinned "Yes Vanar, you were saying."

Vanar caught his breath as Atan finished the sentence. "So, he stood up and offered me his bare bottom and said, is it too late?"

The girls burst out laughing while Falor's cheeks grew rosier and Vanar shot his father a "Why did you do that" look.

Despite the embarrassment of not being able to complete the tale, dinner moved on in a pleasant wave. Teenagers soon felt like adults and parents warmed at their growth.

Telep whispered the impending arrival of Valeria's parents to her early the next morning. She paced by the door, ignoring the plants and food and people moving about the bright hallway. Finally, when her feet were almost callused, the great door opened. They were barely inside when Valeria flung her arms around all of them. Coty squirmed away, with Norana, in tears, and Merej warmly returned the hug.

Vanar's hand rose in the background and he joined in the group welcome. Raphela kissed their cheeks and shared in a hug. Atan smiled with his hands tightly clasped behind his back.

"Mother, I have so much to tell you." Valeria slipped her arm through Norana's elbow. "Would you like to see your room or take a walk or get some tea or..." Her lips outpaced her breath.

Norana laughed. "Let's get a cup of tea, but you must slow down, I can barely understand you."

Valeria took a deep breath. "I'm sorry."

"She hasn't changed." Merej shook his head as his wife and daughter walked away.

"Merej, join me for a drink." Atan made the offer, easily acceptable.

Telep stood by to drag Coty off for some fun, leaving Raphela and Vanar staring at each other.

Vanar held out his arm for his mother. "Care to take a walk?" Genuine charm oozed from Vanar as power did from Atan, both were irresistible.

"I'd be honored."

Raalek's sun's next few passes over the castle showered a steady blossoming of activity. Guests arrived all day and well past moonrise.

Valeria dragged Norana to the great hall, guards standing by the closed doors. Norana couldn't help but stare at the trim and serious young men, who nodded in silent obedience as Valeria had them open a door, just enough for the two of them to squeeze through.

Norana walked around the room, as if in a museum, her eyes unable to focus anywhere special in the glorious surroundings. The walls clothed in pale gold cloth, shimmering in newness and beauty, guarded by elegant twists of cloth, looking much like thin waisted royal ladies. These ladies, deep green velvet cloth banded at the center with blackstone, staring out like the eyes of wisdom.

Row upon row of identical tall straight-back chairs, crafted of fine black wood and upholstered with green satin laced with gold, waited patiently to serve a purpose. All eight windows welcomed the light, yet were prepared to lock out the night eyes with black drapes emblazoned with the golden Gilfon.

Norana held her daughter's hand. "Did you do this?"

"Not all by myself, but Raphela allowed me to design it as I wished."

"It's magnificent. Have they seen it?"

"Do you mean the Duke and Raphela?" Valeria uncreased a curtain, and looked for flaws with the ease of an artist, putting one last brush stroke on a painting.

"Yes." Norana stared at the flowers, all so perfectly placed.

"Definitely and yes, they fully approved, even liked it. And yes, so did Vanar."

Norana hugged her. "I am so proud of you, this is amazing."

Valeria beamed, receiving that which every child yearns for, parental approval.

Amidst the fervor and excitement, Fatell found herself guiding lost adults and shooing curious children out of harms way, more often than she imagined she could.

It was late afternoon and she had just completed one more "shooing" from the kitchen, she leaned against a cabinet and sighed.

Cooks and servants worked around her as kettles boiled and cakes baked.

"I do believe this is more difficult than the battles of long ago." Her words were meant for no one, just a need to leave her lips.

"And there kind lady weaves many a tale."

Fatell turned around and finally saw the figure in the doorway, finely clothed, leaning casually, bearing a warm grin.

"Mowatt"

"At your service."

Hands grasped each other, tightly, kisses pecked all cheeks.

"You look wonderful."

"And I owe it all to you."

Fatell felt the warm redness rise in her cheeks. "Come in, sit down. Would you like some tea or wine?"

"No, just a chance to share my tales."

"And not a moment too soon."

As Fatell spoke, two more children, about 8-years-old zipped past her.

Mowatt's hand grabbed the shirt of one. "Come here, what's your hurry?"

Dumbfounded at the stranger, the boy stood silent and his playmate soon turned, realizing he was alone.

"Now, boys, gather all your friends and go to..." Mowatt hesitated, Fatell jumped in,

"The purple room."

"Good, the purple room and I shall tell you a tale you'll not soon forget." Just the tone of his voice was enough, the boys scurried and found many children with willing ears.

"I see you are right as always."

"Thank you so much." She looked up to the sky. "And thank you too."

Dusk settled in and the children were kept occupied with various activities while the adults attended a pre-wedding reception, an opportunity for everyone to become acquainted, and for security to achieve a strong handle on who was there.

Servants carried trays of drinks and hors d'ouevres, winding their way through the crowd. Clusters of guests loosened and reformed as some flitted about while others clung to their spot.

Gorotnik, tall blond, well chiseled looks, sipped at the freshly poured wine, his hand steady and eye roving.

"What are you looking for?" Mishka, also about 40 years old, prodded.

"Shh. Is that her?"

"Stop pointing and if you mean Lady Raphela, the answer is yes."

"Even better than I'd heard." Red liquid swirled in his cup.

"She's an incredible woman." Mishka's admiration echoed the general feeling.

"She's not so special. I'm sure she and the Duke have their faults." Gorotnik's eyes slowly undressed Raphela.

"Only the Gods are perfect, but what are you thinking?" His reply was tinged with a bit of horror.

Guests flowed past, paying little attention to these two or anyone else, not directly of interest.

"I'll bet she has lovers and he must too." Gorotnik finished his wine and put the glass on a tray of a servant walking past.

"You are not going to flirt with Lady Raphela, are you?"

"Why not? I'll bet you I get what I'm after." Gorotnik still stared at Raphela, watching her every move.

"You are insane."

"So be it. But will you take the bet?"

"All right, five head of cattle."

They shook hands and Gorotnik wove his way through the crowd, Mishka trying to keep an unobtrusive distance.

Raphela bade goodbye to a woman and turned to find Gorotnik, a few inches in front of her.

"My lady, your beauty outshines the stars in the skies" He bowed his head, lifted her hand and kissed her fingers.

Suddenly, he noticed a shadow to his left, Logan, tall, broad and quiet, looked down and simply shook his head.

Raphela stared at Gorotnik, his action reminiscent of a time long gone. Her cold stare matched her words. "Thank you." Logan followed her into the crowd.

Gorotnik, shocked, didn't move.

A soldier of Castle Cordan, there when the Duke first built the army, leaned towards Gorotnik. "I wouldn't do that again," he advised quietly.

Gorotnik looked at the old man. "What?"

"I wouldn't do that, hand kissing, nah." He shook his head and took a swallow of ale. "Do you know what happened to the last man that kissed her hand?" The soldier's lips worked to a grin.

Gorotnik, still shocked, shrugged his shoulders.

The soldier leaned into Gorotnik's ear, "Knife, right in his back, base of the neck, and his captain," the soldier drew a finger across his throat, slit his throat. Logan, the shadow over you, was there, told me all about it. He patted Gorotnik on the back and walked off.

Mishka brushed past and whispered, "I'll pick up the cattle this summer."

Gorotnik shot him a dirty look and grimaced at the embarrassment.

Falor took notice and made a mental note to remedy the man's unhappiness and avoid any retribution.

Raphela wound a ribbon through her hair, for the third time and pulled it out for the third time. Her face contorted in silent disgust.

Atan observed, his fingers deftly buttoning his jacket, considering all the complements he could give, useless as they would be.

The brush attacked Raphela's hair as it cascaded down her back, thick and beautiful as ever. After numerous attempts she wrapped it in a way that somehow satisfied the moment and turned to Atan.

"Are you ready?" It was a weak attempt at conversation.

Atan held her close valuing every tear that marked his jacket. She regained composure in short order.

"You are the picture of stature, as always." Her words warmed him.

"I have no choice, Lady Ishtba must have the best by her side."

"I think Vanar must be waiting for you by now."

"I'm sure he is."

Atan left and Raphela allowed one more tear before waiting in the hall for her men.

Falor handed Vanar his belt, heavy with a ceremonial sword.

"Thank you."

"Are you nervous?" Falor wiggled in his suit.

"Just anxious."

"I'm not surprised." Atan's deep voice received all attention. "She's a special girl." His eyes rested on Falor for a moment, impressive in his fine clothes and then he turned to Vanar. Fully dressed, he bore his royalty with the passion and control born to him. Atan's face boasted a pride irreplaceable with any verbal sound.

Vanar glowed. Both men shared the warm hug belonging to family Ishtba.

Raphela paced the hallway, listening to the guests downstairs, finding their way to seats as musicians practiced a wedding march one last time.

When the men emerged Falor slipped away to Cora who waited outside Valeria's room.

535

"Vanar, you look so grown up." Raphela allowed the tears to fall. The Duke, his Lady and their son joined together for the last time as family, sending a wave of incomprehensible feeling throughout the castle.

They arrived at the great hall as the last guests took their seats. Falor and Cora were waiting by the podium.

They walked the simple path with the dignity and strength everyone expected.

Norana primped her daughter's hair one more time, holding back the tears, that threatened to fall.

"Mother please." It was a gentle exasperation.

"Are we ready?" Merej slipped his arm through Valeria's and Norana did the same.

"Yes Papa." A calm smile was the signal, Merej nodded to the guards and the grand white doors to the great hall opened.

The chairs, empty for so many days, now did their job. Valeria reviewed the back of the audience, a myriad of color and size. Golden spring flowers mixed well with the people, the room was alive.

Once past the doorway, people began to turn and watch the bride walk her path. Valeria took slow, practiced steps, stopping every three. Oohs and aahs rose above the blend of whispers.

"She is so pretty."

Valeria turned to the tiny voice on the aisle. A little girl, perhaps 5 or 6 years old sat on her mother's lap and stretched to touch the gown. Her mother pulled her back. "Yes she is and I'm sure very smart as well. She has to be, she is the next Lady of Ishtba."

Those words swam in Valeria's head, a tune that refused to leave. At the end of her path stood Cora and Falor on one side. Vanar on the other. He was so much, no woman could hope for more. Behind this handsome intelligent man, were the parents, Duke and Lady Ishtba, the very symbols of life and breath for all Raalek.

Sweet flutes and wispy harps encouraged the walk. Tiny beads of sweat took shape in her palms. The eyes of the world were on her. Her heart began to beat faster, one side of her yearning to rush to the safety of Vanar's arms, the other ready to run back to the simple life on her parents' ranch. If not for her parents' guiding hands, the ranch might have become home.

At long last the altar was but a few short steps away.

Vanar's eyes never left his bride. Only years of training to do the right thing at the right time kept his feet in place.

Norana held her tears no longer as she let go of her daughter's arm.

Deep blue robes swayed in unison as the Elder and his assistants chanted an ancient hymn while Vanar and Valeria stood before them.

The Elder's words meant little more than the chirping of a bird, neither bride nor groom heard him. They had rehearsed so many times, it was almost instinct to perform the rituals. But when the elder finished his task, Cora and Falor took their places by the bride and groom, each presenting a tiny pillow bearing a sole gold ring, a matched set.

Vanar looked deep into Valeria's green eyes, caressing her arm as he lifted it. Cool gold slipped over her finger, Valeria swore her heart stopped.

Soft skin lifted his palm and the ring fell into place, both hands were raised to announce the union.

Somewhere, in the back, an old man, with two strong hands brought them together in the ritualistic rhythm of the marriage.

Vanar smiled and responded by pulling his bride close and engaging her in "the kiss." Valeria gave no argument and the crowd joined the old man and were soon on their feet.

The path out was quicker and noisier. Children followed them to the edge of the stairs. As the door to their room closed Valeria leaned against it and sighed. Her headdress soon lay on the table. "Oh look, look at what Falor and Cora left."

Vanar smiled at the loaf of bread, a jug of wine and note, "For a special night."

"They are so kind. Cora is such a thoughtful girl." Valeria paced, her gown swishing on the floor, her words choppy.

Vanar laid his jacket on the chair.

"I must remember to thank them." She prattled on.

"Valeria."

"Hm, what?" She swallowed.

537

"If you're not ready, I will wait." Not a hint of disappointment escaped his lips, only support, as a pillow breaking a fall.

Tears took shape in the corner of her eyes. "Oh Vanar, I want you so much, I'm, I'm..." she took a deep breath "I'm just frightened."

She paced again and Vanar sunk back into a wall, pain was all he could show or feel.

"I swear to you, I will not hurt you." It was a hoarse whisper and as the tiny voice sent her to fear, this pain gave her a light. In an instant she was by his side, caressing his cheek. "My love, my dearest love, you don't frighten me."

Vanar did not yet move closer.

"Vanar, it isn't you, it's the world, I, I..."

His arms closed around her, she felt his hands massage her bottom.

Words faded as her fingers studied the firm muscles under his shirt. As he unbuttoned her gown, it slid to the floor, revealing a translucent shimmering slip, clinging to her slender form, announcing her nipples.

Vanar's pants joined her gown and very soon two naked forms stood together.

Valeria could not have imagined so perfectly shaped and toned a body, each muscle sculpted as if by an artist. Vanar cupped her breasts, soaking in the ecstasy of her freshness. They nibbled and kissed and touched as they had for a year, but without the chains of cloth.

Valeria lay back on the bed. "Come to me."

Vanar's chest pressed against her as he stole a long luxurious kiss, encouraged by excited fingers, rubbing his buttocks bringing him ever so close, as her leg wrapped around his.

"I love you Valeria."

She heard the words, but didn't need them as he pressed into her. Her kiss was like none he had ever tasted as they rocked up and down. She felt power and strength, it owned her, she was willingly its slave. "Never let me go," she whispered in his ear as she rolled on top of him, her breasts dangling in his face.

"You couldn't make me."

Finally, Vanar felt complete as Valeria curled up in his arms, fearing nothing, resting better than she ever had.

She awoke to his kiss.

"Make love to me."

In the sunlight, they loved as youngsters do, exploring, giggling, rolling in the newness of life. The marriage had been sealed in the moonlight, now it was time to play.

Despite an attempt at a quiet entrance, Vanar and Valeria were spotted and greeted by a warm round of applause. Atan beckoned them to join he and Raphela. The royal chairs had partners, smaller versions for Vanar and Valeria. In the background, a round of chimes announced the commencement of the gift presentation.

While the tables laden with food invited the guests, many people walked with plates and glasses listening carefully for their turn, wiping greasy fingers and handing off plates at the proper time.

It was an interesting event. When invitations to the wedding were sent out, a note was included. "NO GIFTS OF MATERIAL VALUE (SUCH AS CATTLE OR GRAIN) WOULD BE ACCEPTED, ONLY THOSE ITEMS, PREPARED, DESIGNED OR CREATED BY THE PERSON OR PEOPLE GIVING WOULD BE ACCEPTED." Vanar and Valeria saw no reason to take precious supplies they didn't need. So, the hall was lined with gifts of breads and cakes, quilts and clothes, and even a few innovative items to be explored later and most especially, no guest felt outdone. Finally, the last gift had been laid by the feet of the wedding couple. The once heavily laden tables sat half-naked, displaying the remnants of rolls and gravy stained cloths. Musicians watched as people walked about, trying to look busy. The lead musician nodded and the tune began.

Vanar took Valeria's hand and began a genteel dance, small steps, in a pattern everyone knew but couldn't quite name. Then his arm, wrapped around her waist bringing them close enough to feel each other's breath. Not quite touching, he guided her around the dance floor, Valeria's long green gown, moving in time with his brown leather boots.

Precision and artistry never mated so well and as Mowatt cast the dance to words, a young woman driven by the voice that lives in the minds of all creators took her personally crafted tools from a hidden pocket and put in color the picture before her, to remember the beginning of tomorrow. The music faded, the young couple honored the audience with a bow and then, then they took control.

Vanar extended his hand to Norana, standing at the inner circle's edge. Blushing cheeks and all, she took uncertain steps and joined him on the dance floor.

Amid a round of applause the music commenced. Valeria took a deep breath, with bowed head she stood before Atan. He had avoided these encounters for years, but now, there was no alternative. "My lord, would you honor me?"

His fingers touched the top of her hand and they took to the floor.

Unlike Vanar, Atan did not clasp her hand tightly in his, or pull her close. Her fingers rested lightly on his palm. Even the light touch sent storms through her blood. If not for the previous night of love with Vanar, she would have collapsed.

Merej and Raphela joined the music as well. And with a bow, when the tune broke, so did the couples, changing partners.

Norana trembled as Atan rested his fingers ever so lightly on her waist, not even attempting to touch her hand.

Vanar and Raphela whirled to the music, in tandem with Valeria and Merej. The crowd swayed with the music and the show. Necks craned to catch a glimpse.

Once more the musicians ceased the sound. But the gathering was infected and a demand began, as a whisper.

Norana, thankful to be in her husband's arms, muddled through another few steps, but the guests' hunger was far deeper. Atan and Raphela turned to each other, accepting the inevitable. Merej and Norana slipped into the circle. Atan and Raphela locked in a glance and the room lost its sound, as his arm wrapped around her waist and her fingers interlocked with his.

Music began, not the sweet whimsical melodies of the previous dances, but a pounding haunting beat. Not a foot shuffled, no tongue moved to speak, not a morsel of food was devoured. Their steps were large and firm, each one a tale unto itself. The young artist could not find a color, even Mowatt's scribe was still.

They moved as one, and, if for an instant they whirled away, their hands remained locked and their return glance was like thunder. Soon the musicians realized that the royal couple did not dance to the music, but the music danced to them.

Atan and Raphela saw and heard nothing except each other. When they had enough, the music came to a halt and hypnotic silence ruled.

A voice broke through, wise and strong. "Hail to the Duke", and then another, "Hail to the Lady." Hands and feet moved in rhythm, rippling through the crowd. Young men stepped forward, lifting Vanar and Valeria high in the air. "Hail to Vanar and Valeria, hail to the bright future!"

Stamping and shouting and clapping stormed the hall, and Ishtba had taken another step forward.

After a time the abundance of excitement waned and conversations began. Valeria took a moment to study the Duke and Lady, their moment on the dance floor burned in her mind for now until she could put them to canvas. Her reverie was interrupted by the vibrant melodies that began again from the musicians and the room swirled with celebrants. She was introduced to her first act as the next Lady.

Gorotnik's fingers rested gently on Valeria's waist as a new tune began. "You're from Calcoran, the western province, right?"

"Yes my grace, the far western province."

"I understand it is very cold there, most of the year." Valeria permitted eye contact.

"This is true, it is why we have the best fur in the world." Gorotnik's chest puffed out a bit.

"That would make sense."

"Do you like fur?"

"Of course."

"Then I shall have my brother create the finest coat on Raalek for you."

"I'd be honored."

Gorotnik took the next dance step with a sense of pride.

Raphela's smile faded when her eye caught Gorotnik and Valeria dancing amid the crowd.

Vanar found himself stuttering an apology as Raphela dragged him away from conversation. "What is going on?"

Vanar learned at an early age to respond seriously to that tone. "I don't know what you mean."

"Look" She guided his eyes to the dance floor.

"Oh that" His eyes found the floor and he wished Falor was there. "Um, it was Falor's suggestion."

"Falor?" Her voice increased a few decibels and Vanar cringed.

"Yes, your incident with Gorotnik could have been damaging in the long term."

At this point Falor walked up behind them and Vanar's eyes begged for help.

"My lady."

"Falor will you please explain."

"Yes my lady." Falor revealed a new maturity, capturing Raphela's full attention. "Gorotnik is a shallow man and easily turned to vengeance. Yet, he and his brother produce the best furs in Calcoran. Dancing with Valeria healed his bruised ego and avoided any incidents, perhaps, even made him feel better about Ishtba." Falor's logic bordered on salesmanship and his eyes never left hers.

"I don't like it, but I will accept it, for now."

"Thank you my lady."

She headed off for other guests.

Vanar's broad smile was a welcome sight. Falor felt his shoulders curl and his mouth turn dry. "That was one of the hardest conversations I've ever had."

"You were great. I can't believe you were so convincing." Vanar's open admiration brought a smile to Falor's pale face.

"Thank you, I hated it."

"It's a shame, you're good at it."

Falor opened his mouth but nothing escaped.

"There you are." Lehcar grabbed hold of Vanar's hand. Her effervescent mood, unavoidable. "You must dance with me."

542

"Oh well Falor, I must fulfill my tasks." Both boys grinned as Vanar was whisked away.

Raphela finished a chat with Alato, and in the brief moment she was alone felt a gentle whisper tickle her ear. Her chin brushed her shoulder and her lips crept towards her eyes, nodding to another guest she wove her way through the room to the front door. There he stood, breathing deep the night air. As her hand slipped into his, all the joy Atan felt soaked through her soul like fine wine through fresh warm cake.

By the crest of the hill they paused and stared out onto the land. No words spoken, and though they would deny a mental link, their thoughts mirrored each other in perfect clarity. To see the vastness of the empire they built and know it would have new guardians, to tend and cultivate, had meaning beyond mere words. Once the empire surrounded them, they became as one, so much so the Gods saw but one being in the starlight.

Chapter 23

Slowly the castle emptied, no longer bulging with noise and movement. Within a few days life returned to its normal state.

Norana and Merej, last to leave, bade their daughter goodbye.

Valeria looked up at her husband, a tired smile on her face. "I suppose we really are married, the party is over."

Vanar held her close.

Falor and Cora remained at Castle Cordan, not wishing to chance any danger. Cora was now two days overdue. She tasted Rabi's soup and groaned as she sat back in the chair.

"Are you all right?" Rabi jumped to her side.

"Oh yes just fine. I simply feel like I've swallowed a donag, whole."

Rabi stirred the soup, its spicy scent tempting his nostrils. "Where is Falor?"

"I finally convinced him to spend some time with Vanar."

Rabi smiled as Cora rolled her eyes. Falor had hovered over her like a zorel with its pups. She had to have some space. "I see."

That night Cora paced until the second moon rose, while Falor feigned sleep. At last she crawled into bed. Falor allowed his exhaustion to take over, despite the twisting and turning of his partner.

Cora's eyes closed, as the moons winked above and as they began their descent. Falor was wakened by a tight grasp around his arm.

"Falor!" She croaked.

"Cora, Cora what is it?"

"It's time." Sweat began to form in her forehead and the shriek of pain at the next contraction shook Falor out of bed.

Aharon was awakened and according to Vanar's orders, so were he and Valeria. Robes wrapped tight around their waists, they arrived at their friends' room.

Falor paced outside the door, wringing his hands, mumbling. Valeria went inside.

"Falor, what are you doing out here?" Vanar shook his head as if he were dreaming.

"I'm, I'm waiting.'

"For what?"

"The, the baby."

An assistant healer hurried past them with a pile of clean sweet smelling towels.

"Why are you out here? Why aren't you with Cora?"

Falor stopped pacing and swallowed hard. Only Vanar could do this with him. "I'm frightened. What if something goes wrong? What if I do something wrong, hurt her or the baby? I, I couldn't live with myself." He began to pace again.

Vanar put two strong hands on his friend's shoulders. "Falor," he was gentle, "you love Cora more than anything or anyone. You can't do anything wrong except to leave her alone."

Whether it was the tone, the words, the friendship or all those things, Falor listened and knew Vanar was right. "Thank you."

He cringed as Cora bellowed in pain and gladly shared it as she squeezed his arm.

Valeria closed the door behind her and joined Vanar, planting a gentle kiss on his cheek.

What did I do?" He asked.

"More than I ever hoped for."

Vanar stared at her as if he were a lost puppy.

"It's comforting to know what you will do someday." Warm words and a silky sound sent a blush to his cheeks. He didn't know she had heard.

The sun broke through and Cora writhed in pain, Oolon and Aharon providing all the soothers they had. Falor never left her side.

Vanar and Valeria paced, sipping hot tea outside the door.

Atan and Raphela kept to themselves and prayed.

Rabi prepared every type of broth he knew for Cora, and burned breakfast for everyone else.

Aharon pressed on her stomach, while Falor held her tight. Oolon pushed the medicine through her lips.

Her knees and thighs ached from being spread for so long and the pain inside her was beyond any words.

Birth has a scent all its own and for all his years, Aharon was swayed at its entrance.

Cora emitted a shriek and Aharon at last saw a small head pushing its way through the passage. His hands reached in and ever so gently guided the infant into the world, Cora pushing as hard as she could, too hoarse to cry out any more.

Falor, face as stained with tears as Cora's, and Oolon, sat back exhausted.

The bed sheets were red with birth as Aharon lifted the baby, whose welcome cry trumpeted loudly in the small room.

Proud parents caressed the infant, laying on Cora's still swollen belly. An aide brought towels and cleaned the baby boy, wrapping him in warm blankets before returning him to Falor's arms.

Aharon washed his hands and sunk into a nearby chair.

"Cora, look, look at our baby."

She sat up with Oolon's help and smiled weakly. "He's beautiful, just beautiful."

Little hands struggled through the blankets and waved in the air.

"You're wonderful Cora, look what you did."

She just nodded.

Soon she and the bed were cleaned. Vanar and Valeria were invited in, for just a brief look, then the new family was left to rest by themselves.

Falor and his family wove their bond in the tranquillity of a room off limits to the world.

After a few days, when the baby had opened his eyes and Cora was rested, they emerged into Castle Cordan.

There was no lack of caretakers. Telep studied the infant, though avoided trying to hold him. Fatell cooed and cradled the babe, whose only reaction was to search for food.

Raphela arranged a small meeting room for people to slip in and out of to view the fresh face. Falor cradled him with comfort, as Vanar sat down beside them.

"Good looking baby."

"He's smart. Watch.' The proud papa waved a finger in front of the infant and watched as tiny eyes followed the moving object.

"How do you feel Cora?" Valeria squeezed her friend's hand and sniffed the aroma of fresh cut flowers.

"Tired but good. He is one hungry baby." Cora grimaced a bit as her hand brushed against her nipples.

"Are they sore?" Valeria knew, but somehow hearing it from Cora was more real than anyone else.

"Yes, but I hear it gets easier."

Falor handed the baby to Cora, his tiny head searching for lunch, and fists were tightening into a demand.

Vanar, embarrassed at what was to be, pulled Falor to the safety of the hall. While accepting congratulations from passersby, Falor tried to concentrate on his friend.

"Falor, my parents..." Vanar stopped as someone halted to pat Falor on the back.

"My parents," Vanar continued "would like you and Cora and the baby to have dinner with us tonight. There, I finally said it." Vanar breathed a sigh of relief.

"Dinner?" Falor had only been half listening.

"Yes, remember, food." Vanar shook his head in frustration. "Of course, only if Cora is up to it."

"I'll ask, but I'm sure she'd love to."

"Good, we'll see you later."

Unlike the last dinner, this dining room was small and the table just large enough for the six of them, with a little extra squeezed for the newest guest.

Vanar passed the platter to Falor who gladly filled his plate, and Cora wasn't shy either.

"I see you do remember food." Vanar teased.

"Aharon says the baby is doing very well." Raphela sipped her wine.

"Yes, he's already gained weight."

Easy conversation coated the room, as if the people were any group of friends. Once bellies were full the table was cleared and the star of the evening took his place.

Raphela pushed away blankets to look at the curious youngster and with a nod from Cora lifted him into her arms. Even Atan took a moment with him. His tiny dark eyes studied the face and in the cradle of Atan's arms turned to restful sleep.

"What have you named him?" Raphela toyed with the fine dark hair.

"Jivad, after my father." Falor peered over the table and smiled.

"A good name." Atan leaned back, baby sound asleep in the crook of his arm.

"We have a gift for Jivad." Raphela stood and brought a box to the table.

One believed the whispers of the past pleasantly hummed around the room, enjoying the scent of new life.

"There are three books here, one to read to him, one so he may learn to read and another to read and add to, for the history of Calcoran."

"My lord and lady, you are too generous." Falor caressed the books, Cora felt tears in her eyes. One book was a treasure, three was beyond measurable value.

"No, you and your child are worthy and deserving."

"Thank you so much." They replied in unison and shared a glance, Falor spoke. "We have a request of all of you." He stood and all eyes exchanged questioning looks.

Falor took a deep breath "All our lives, my lord and lady, you have created families. As the Gods should have it, Cora and I have been blessed with a child. But, he has no grandparents, aunts." Falor stopped, closed his eyes and allowed the pain inside him to subside. "If you would agree, we would like all of you to become our Machatenum"

Silence overpowered the pleasantness.

"Machatenum?" Valeria searched her mind out loud.

Atan leaned forward and watched Jivad purse his tiny lips. "Machatenum is the ancient word for special family, one that is not blood, but chosen to be just as close. It is quite an honor you bestow upon us."

"It is we who would be honored, if you would accept." Cora found her strength.

549

Vanar squeezed Valeria's hand and Atan nodded to Raphela. "We accept your honor and hope to live up to it." Raphela spoke for all.

"Thank you."

Vanar poured six glasses of wine and a silent toast sealed the honor.

Atan slipped between the cool covers, closing his eyes to the world. Raphela snuffed out the miniature torch flame and watched the gray smoke spiral up and dissipate. The pillows were soft and full as always, she leaned against them and looked down at the lines in her husband's face.

"Cora and Falor truly appreciated the gift."

"Mm" Atan groaned and rolled to face the window.

Raphela stared at the firm shoulder peeking out from the covers. "It is a deep honor they've given us."

Resigned to conversation he rolled back. "Yes it was."

"I never realized how alone they felt." Raphela spoke half to herself.

Atan just kept an open ear as the night birds cast shadows of their flight and the wind sprinkled a fresh scent in the room.

"And who knows, perhaps, some day, we may really..." She couldn't finish and he began to roll towards the window, but her warm gentle fingers were like an undemanding yet irresistible string and he was pulled by it.

The two rulers of the land lay facing each other, needing no light to see the stinging salty tears on each other's cheeks. Their faces brushed and the two streams of tears melded to a single path as their arms encased each other in the silent night.

After a time Raphela pulled away, toying with his hair, allowing herself one last sniffle.

"Do you know what I'd like to do this summer?"

"What would you like to do this summer?" He patronized her, while his fingers began twirling her hair.

"Climb the Blue Mountain of Calcoran."

"Indeed. Do you plan to do this alone?" he teased.

Raphela breathed in the night air. "Well, if my husband won't join me, I'm sure I can find some strong young man to climb with me." The glimmer of white became a broad grin and then an open tunnel accompanying wide eyes as Atan delivered a playful but firm slap on her bottom.

"You should be careful of what you say, the next time you might get a real spanking."

Atan smiled, rolled on his back and closed his eyes.

Raphela leaned on her elbow for a moment and then pounced on him. "We have not settled this."

Atan wrapped her hair around his hand and attempted to be annoyed. "Raphela" She grinned down at him.

He sighed. "You would have me tell Mahtso and deal with his reaction?" Atan knew his friend would cluck like a mother hen.

"Am I not worth it?"

Even at forty, her face remained that of a temptress, but he kept still, just looking back at her big brown eyes, in quiet refusal.

"All right, I'll tell him myself."

Atan rolled over on top of her, hair wrapped tightly in his grip, eyes full of life. "You are still fearless."

It was her turn for a silent answer.

The smile that had coated his face faded to a warmth that glowed. "And that is why I will never let you go."

Lips moist and full met his with the only response she had. Their kiss had the passion that strengthened the very seeds of Ishtban land.

"The Blue Mountain of Calcoran will meet the Lady this summer." He caressed her face. "I hope its ready."

Raphela enjoined him for one more kiss before they both found a peaceful sleep.

Raphela bade good-bye to her son and daughter-in-law as they headed off to visit the fiefs and marketplace. Fatell waved to Telep who obediently waved back, but was obviously feeling too grown up to show much emotion.

"Fatell, let's get a cup of tea." Raphela drew her friend back inside the castle.

"I hope he took everything." Fatell traveled her mind, considering what might have been forgotten.

"If he didn't, he'll make do with whatever he finds. Now let's close this door, its still cool outside." Raphela shut the door and rubbed her arms.

"I'm sure I packed all of it." Fatell continued disractedly.

"Fatell, we need to plan our own trip, remember?" Raphela's firm yet gentle prod brought Fatell back to reality.

"You're right, I'm sorry."

"Don't worry about it. I plan to take Chana with us." Raphela wrapped her fingers around the warm teacup.

"Who is going with Mahtso and the Duke?"

"Patar. It seems that he, Chana and Telep have a very strong connection. We should be able to contact anyone at anytime."

"My lady," Rabi brushed flour off his hands onto his apron. "I hope I'm not interrupting."

"What do you need Rabi?" Raphela always liked him, though she knew he felt intimidated by her presence.

"I was wondering how Cora and the baby were doing. I haven't heard since she left. It was about a month ago, wasn't it?"

"They are fine. Telep spoke with Falor just yesterday. The baby is growing like a weed and Cora is feeling like herself again. I'll have Telep send the message that you asked."

"Thank you my lady." He disappeared as quietly as he arrived,

"He really misses her." Fatell looked over her shoulder as she spoke.

"I know. He's had a hard time finding someone to do her job, besides missing her friendship."

"Mm."

"Anyway, will we be ready to leave tomorrow?" Raphela teased. Fatell always had a hard time leaving.

"Yes my lady."

"Good. I believe Atan and Mahtso are leaving tomorrow as well."

"Yes, the two boys are looking forward to old times, as it were."

Both women laughed imagining their men playing in the past without the women to get in their way.

"Calcoran is a big place, I'm sure they will find much to explore, besides checking on the fiefs.

"True." Fatell studied the warm bustling kitchen and then returned her attention to her friend. "How many schools do you think we can open?" Fatell was excited, but skeptical.

"I don't know, but if we open just one, it will be a good start."

"I agree." Fatell took a short breath and put down her cup. "Raphela"

"Yes?"

"Are you really going to climb the Blue mountain?"

"I hope so." The far away voice and wishful tone told Fatell her friend was serious.

"Then I suppose we must leave tomorrow, lest the men get done quickly. I would hate to keep the Duke waiting and Mahtso will need a strong hand."

"He worries far too much."

"I know."

Warm soil, teeming with life settled under Oolon's nails, filling the fine lines of his palms and coating the skin of his hands. Such was the joy of intertwining one's self with the seeds of life. The carriage that casually rolled past him only briefly interrupted his reverie.

Atan peered out and allowed his lips to curl up at the peacefulness residing inside the gates of Calcoran's castle.

Falor shooed away some children, who had gathered around trying to get a peek at the famous Duke. They giggled and hid by a large door.

"My lord, it's an honor to have you here again." He bowed with the ease of a master of his home. Cora, beside him smiled with pride.

"Its good to be here."

Mahtso instinctually surveyed the room, his chain swimming lazily in his pocket. Atan's nose picked up a familiar scent of spice tea and freshly baked sweetcakes. Cora watched the subtle movement of his nostrils..

"My lord, I have freshly brewed spice tea."

"Well done Cora. I'll have it in the garden. Falor, join me there." It was more request than command and Falor was happy to oblige. "Mahtso?"

"I think I'll stretch my legs a bit." His blue eyes were clear and calm, but he had learned to choose his wording for "verifying security" so that the average person wasn't alarmed.

Atan nodded. He and Falor settled into comfortable chairs amid the flora of Calcoran's front yard. Steaming tea and the sweetcakes waited for them on a table.

"Tell me Falor, of the business of Calcoran." Atan leaned back, his cup making the slightest of noise as it met the table.

Falor retrieved from his pocket a plaque, just a bit larger than his hand. Its surface smooth as glass and it gleamed in the sunlight.

Atan peered over as Falor tapped a finger on his first note. "What is that?"

Falor looked up to see eyes, anxious as a child's, staring at him. "This my lord?"

"Yes."

"I found it in the lower levels, odd item and yet quite useful. Watch." Falor maintained his calm but felt elevated at the Duke's interest.

Pulling a cloth napkin off the table he moistened it and rubbed the words on the tablet and both men's eyes grew wide as the words disappeared. "And now." he pulled a large wide scribe from his pocket. Atan could see the ink barrel placed tightly in the instrument. Falor scribbled some words on the empty spot and then removed them as he had before.

"Amazing! Are there any more?" Atan caressed the tablet that Falor hesitatingly placed in his hands.

"I don't know, but I can certainly look."

Atan returned the plaque. "Do so before I leave, I'd like to have one."

"My pleasure my lord."

"Falor."

"Yes my lord."

"Let us dispense with formalities while in private."

"Yes my..." He stopped and smiled sheepishly.

"To return to the original question, tell me of Calcoran."

Falor perused his notes and relayed what he knew. Atan listened patiently as a great deal more than appeared on the plaque was revealed.

"Well done Falor."

"Thank you, " he paused, searching for a word, finally choosing "sir". Falor lowered his head.

"Sir will do I suppose. I know it's difficult to change," he smiled tolerantly.

Falor blushed.

"You've turned this castle into a home, I'm pleased."

"Cora is the one," Falor stopped as a shadow arrived at his side. "Baal? Falor, I'm sorry to interrupt." The gentleman, a bit older than Atan, spoke professionally, with the manner of one accustomed to waiting on royalty. This inner polish shone with pride.

"Thank you. My, um, sir, I have been expecting two men from a distant fief."

"Falor, I put you here to handle business, do your job."

Falor nodded to the servant and rose to go. Before he took a step Atan rose as well and placed a fatherly hand on Falor's shoulder. "Your father built a good foundation and as Vanar must build, you must too. Don't be afraid to take the next step."

Falor smiled and nodded before heading back to the castle.

Atan stretched, took in the clean air and out of the corner of his eye he saw Oolon.

Oolon, still kneeling and digging in his garden, ignored the Duke as he walked past. Atan squatted by a row of lilac flowers, his long fingers gently caressed a petal.

"You have roots with the quiet ones, sire." Oolon did not lift his head.

Atan watched a bird soar overhead, observing the triangular crowd of wings that followed. "The quiet ones?"

"Yes sire, plants, we call them the *Quiet Ones*. Their voices seldom used, reach but a few."

"I see. You have quite a garden here." His hand studied a hearty head of cabbage incredibly close to the lilacs.

"We provide each other mutual pleasure." Contentment infiltrated every carefully chosen word and tone. Oolon pointed to a silvery tool by Atan, who without a word handed it over. Oolon smoothed out the dirt and stood, brushing the loose soil from clothes and hands.

Atan did the same.

"I'm going to take a walk, join me?" Atan offered well earned respect.

"As you wish my lord."

Oolon was barely as tall as Falor yet showed no discomfort beside Atan.

"Are you comfortable at Calcoran Castle?"

"It is where I should be sire"

"Does that mean your personal pleasure or comfort is of no importance?"

Oolon's semi-evasive answers were well practiced and accepted, but Atan's eyes betrayed his annoyance.

Oolon bowed his white haired head. "I am sorry my lord, we are not in the habit of discussing our an personal needs. But to answer your question, I am quite comfortable."

"Good. Falor relies on you and to this point whatever guidance you've provided has done well."

"Thank you sire." Oolon worked at keeping pace with the Duke. Though the larger man walked slowly, Oolon needed two paces to Atan's one.

Atan sighed. "Have I asked too much of Falor? How is he really dealing with his position as Governor?"

Oolon wanted to look into the eyes of this man, yet he had not the strength. "My lord, you are blessed with the gift of making good choices."

A gentle wind brought the well-blended scent of the gardens and both men breathed it in deeply.

"And Falor has chosen wisely, a wife worthy of him and his position and aides to advise or simply be his eyes and ears when he can't. Falor will not take upon himself more than he can handle, a trait rare in one so young." Oolon's even tone betrayed an inkling of pride, that satisfied Atan more than the words.

Oolon turned as a tiny creature scurried past and he caught sight of a tool left in his garden. "My lord, I must go."

Atan gave his silent approval and headed back to the castle. Somehow the grand entrance hall was not so gleaming as before and many of King Samed's possessions were out of sight. The castle folk walked with purpose again.

Atan was drawn to the sounds of a wailing infant. A plump nursemaid wrapped up the last corner of the diaper, but the child was not appeased.

"Perhaps he's hungry." Atan stepped through the doorway into the cheerful playroom. The woman jumped in surprise.

"I believe he is. Although poor Cora I think has been suckled dry. We insisted she take a nap."

"What do you do with a hungry baby then?" His tall sinewy figure leaned against the doorway arms crossed, eyes a pool of concern.

The woman paced, trying to calm the crying babe in her arms. "We would give it a little mush with fruit juice," she whispered.

Atan held out his arms. "Give me the child and make the mush."

Despite the wailing the woman stopped pacing and stared at the open arms of the Duke. "But my lord, I, I couldn't ask you, you, um, are, a, a, man, to care for..." She stuttered and stumbled with the words.

Atan took the child. "In Ishtba, men care for children too."

The woman continued to stare but now because the young Jivad ceased his crying, resting his tiny eyes in the Duke's powerful glance, as the strong arm cradled him.

"Go woman, get the food." It was a good-natured command, quickly obeyed.

Young Jivad wallowed in the strength of his Machatenum and Atan allowed himself to surface and played grandfather, for just a while.

Dust settled quickly as Raphela's carriage slowed to a halt. This was the third village, definitely larger than the others.

Logan held Raphela's hand as she stepped onto the dry rocky road. Fatell and Chana received the same assistance. The foursome strolled casually down the main street, exchanging friendly nods with shopkeepers and customers alike.

One man, Olaf, hawking his wares more loudly than most, pulled them to his stand. "Ah, fine ladies, could I interest you in a new cloak, made of the finest cloth in all Ishtba?" With the flare of his speech the round man displayed a bold green cloak sporting an array of gold decorations. "Beautiful isn't it?" Despite his overbearing manner, his wide smile had a charm.

Raphela tested the cloth "It is fine material."

"As a lady of your stature would know. Lady Raphela herself uses this very cloth for her best gowns." Olaf could smell the sale.

"Imagine that Fatell, Lady Raphela, herself." Raphela made no attempt to deny the mischief in her eyes.

Chana stepped back and hid her face, trying not to expose identities too early.

Fatell also tested the cloth, her small frame enrobed in a tailored blue frock, which caught Olaf's attention. He licked his lips. Fatell looked up. "My lady, I don't recognize this, do you?" Her matter of fact tone made her words almost blend into the conversation, but the "my lady," was not lost and Olaf backed up, grabbing onto the table for balance. "My humble apologies, my lady, I meant no disrespect, truly I didn't." Beads of sweat dotted his brow and his hands grew moist as he subconsciously wrung them together.

"It's quite all right, although I'd be more careful about my research if I were you."

"Yes my lady."

"Now, will you direct us to the village elder."

"Of course my lady." He pointed to a house just a short walk away.

"Thank you." Raphela began to walk and then turned back and placed a small object in the man's hand. After she was out of sight he opened his hand to find a coin with Raphela's seal engraved in it, a coin that would never be spent.

Logan knocked on the door of the elder's house, a teenage girl answered.

"Who is it?" A crackled voice spoke from the background.

Raphela stepped forward, graceful as she had ever been. "It is Lady Raphela. I would like to have an audience with you."

The tall lanky girl by the door lowered her head as an old man, leaning heavily on a cane, made his way to the door. He breathed heavily, wheezing as he stood in the doorway. He studied Raphela up and down through squinting eyes, the few scraggly hairs on his head surrounded by freckles.

"Well if you are not Lady Raphela then you should be."

"Father!" The girl chastised.

"I apologize, please come in, Devon show them in."

Raphela and company entered the worn but clean living room and took seats as offered. Amos, the Elder, slowly returned to his chair, taking some time to catch his breath.

Devon brought a tray of tea and took a seat by her father.

"What brings you so far from home my lady?" He coughed and pushed away the cup Devon offered.

"We at Castle Cordan would like to see that all of Ishtba receives the same education that the inhabitants of the castle have been afforded."

Amos did his best to sit up straight, his mood softened. "Education?"

"Yes" Raphela felt a flush as she always did during this part of the conversation. "To be sure that everyone learns to read and write, count add, subtract and more if they choose." Her eyes lit. Amos was drawn willingly to the flame. "Everyone, including the women, right?"

Raphela smiled broadly. "Everyone."

Devon felt his wrinkled hand squeeze hers. "My lady, do you know how to read and write?" Amos asked the question knowing the answer.

"Yes, we all do."

"You see Devon, it is not something to be ashamed of, even the Duke must approve."

Devon blushed.

"My lady, years ago I taught Devon to read and write. We have kept it our secret, but now..." He trailed off as he tried to hold off a cough.

"This is good news. We discovered a building perfect for a school. Devon, would you be interested in taking on the job as teacher?"

"Could I my lady? Truly?"

"It would make our task easier, one less teacher to send out from the castle."

"Oh thank you!" Her spirit rose and descended instantly. "But, we have no books, nothing to write on, or with."

Fatell jumped in, "All of that will provided along with a team of workers to refurbish the abandoned building."

Amos sunk back into his chair, wheezing a bit, eyes closed, dozing into a catnap. Devon looked at him, all joy left her face. "You will need to find another teacher, I can't leave him alone, I'm so sorry."

Fatell lowered her head while Chana grimaced, there was no need of her services but the girl's pain was even more apparent to her.

Raphela shook her head. "Nonsense, we will send someone to care for your father while you work. Caretakers are far more abundant than teachers." Amos snored. "Anyway, I believe he would prefer you to teach."

"But"

Fatell took Devon's hand. "You don't want to argue with Lady Raphela, even the Duke knows better." Her gentle and strong smile settled the issue.

That evening Raphela sat outside the inn and watched the stars, Logan ever silent by her side. Chana and Fatell joined her, wrapping shawls tightly around lightly covered arms.

"Chana" Raphela continued to study the sky. "Does Amos have anyone in mind to take his place?"

"No my lady. As a matter of fact that is why he believed you had come to him, to relieve him of his duty."

"Mm." Raphela sighed. "Fatell, go to him tomorrow, alone. Find out who he might take under his wing. He's a good man, but I doubt the caretaker will be needed next spring when the school actually opens."

"I will take care of it."

On that somber note they turned in for the night.

Atan stirred with the light of the sun, stifled a moan as he sat up, gently massaging his calves.

Mahtso nodded politely at the girl who poured his tea, his shoulders pushing and pulling muscles in his back. Atan caught sight of the gyration as he joined his friend.

"It's good to see that age affects us all," he teased.

Mahtso looked up from under a furrowed brow. "I have managed to deny this for some time, especially to Fatell, you needn't remind me."

Atan just shook his head. "Are you ready to leave?"

"Anxious." His words were clearly supported by the steady but quick threading of his chain through his fingers.

The rameks whinnied, eager as their riders. The stablemaster breathed a sigh of relief as the two men took off towards the rising sun. Swift hooves broke the ground bringing the wind to the petals of the flowers, the weak ones tugged away from home and circling above the ground until the still air returned.

Thick forests flourished under the bright sun, occasionally sprouting a conclave of homes, but few towns were revealed in the first day of the journey. As dusk approached so did a small inn.

Once the rameks were in good hands, the dusty riders entered. It smelled of ale and something else. Mahtso pointed towards the ceiling and thin wisps of smoke. Atan studied the men at the corner table, the source of the smoke. Two held short, thick brown rods, not much longer than a man's finger, though a bit thicker.

The bar keep noticed his new patrons. " 'Ave a seat, gentlemen."

Before they had a chance to move two men approached, weaving as they walked with an odor to match the walk. "Ain't you fancy ones." The taller one stopped a few inches from Atan. "Lots o' coin, don't ya think?" He turned to his friend.

"Most definitely," his companion grunted.

Atan and Mahtso watched in amazement as both men pulled long poorly made knives from their belts.

The barkeep did his best to ignore the situation, as did everyone else.

The tall one, shirt hanging below his waist, looked up at Atan, trying to raise his blade to Atan's throat. Mahtso's man found a pointy edge by his jugular, even before his elbow bent up.

Atan's man looked in the Duke's eyes. Not a sound was heard through the room, except for the echo of a blade striking the floor as the tall man felt his urine take a path down his leg and his skin turned whiter than the froth on the ale sitting in his glass, oh so far away.

Atan turned his head. "Go."

Both men literally crawled out of the inn. For another moment all eyes were on the strangers and then returned to drinks.

Mahtso and Atan took seats at the bar.

"Ale on the 'ouse. First blokes to ever rid me of those two nasties." the barkeep placed overflowing mugs on the bar.

"Thank you." Mahtso took a sip, his blue eyes letting the barkeep know that they were always prepared.

Atan studied the room as he sipped the ale, its taste a bit sweeter than Ishtban brew.

The barkeep, as was his nature, engaged Mahtso in talk. "Your friend is a man of few words." His hand finished drying a glass.

"He doesn't need many." Mahtso finished his glass and signaled for another.

"You ain't from 'ere, are ya?"

"No, we're from Ishtba."

"Ishtba ya say." He nodded to men that left, laying a practiced eye on the table, to be sure the coin was beside the empty glasses. "I hear its pretty there."

"It is."

"You wouldn't be knowing the Duke would ya?" He laughed.

Atan still watching the people placed his empty glass on the bar, his insignia ring shining like a beam in the night.

The barkeep stared, jaw almost touching his chest. His head turned to see the mischief in Mahtso's eyes and smile, silently keeping time with the chain that circled his hand. Much as he considered asking if the ring was real, he knew better. Why be foolish?

Atan turned around. "Do you serve food here?" it was a simple question from an irritated man.

"Yes, yes my lord we do. But it ain't nothin' fancy." He swallowed hard, feeling the blood drain from his face.

Do you eat it?"

"Yes, me wife cooks it, has for 10 years now."

"Well if you have survived 10 years of her fare I imagine I can survive one meal. Bring it to the table by the window."

The tavern was slowly emptying and Atan began to relax. The barkeep trembled as he set the table. Shortly, a tired woman, obviously trying to make the best appearances of the food and herself, lay two bowls of steaming stew before Atan and Mahtso.

The barkeep refilled their glasses and kept his distance.

Only one room was available for guests, fortunately it had two beds. Both men slept soundly. A tray of biscuits and tea sat outside their room when they awoke.

Atan left a heavy bag of coins on the bar as they left.

The barkeep stayed out of sight, but when he heard the clank of coins, peeked onto the bar. After counting the generous payment he ran out the door, towel wrapped like an apron around his waist. "Thank you my lord, thank you."

Atan nodded and they were off.

Over the next two weeks Raphela and company traveled and made assorted arrangements. The carriage pulled into the last town on their route. As always Raphela picked a spot not too deep in town to stop, so she could get a feel for the place. As they walked in the noonday sun, few people raised their heads from tasks at hand. Children sat quietly. Chana shivered.

"Are you all right?" Raphela put her arm around the girl.

"Yes, it's just quiet."

"I agree."

Logan hung especially close.

Fatell, upon Raphela's instruction approached a local merchant. "Please direct me towards the home of the town Elder."

The merchant looked up from, his work, moving only his eyes. "Two streets down, the big house."

"Thank you." Fatell waited for a response but the emotionless directions were apparently all she would receive.

Chana sighed and shrugged her shoulders, as Raphela looked to her for some information.

As Logan raised his hand to knock at the door, it opened seemingly on its own. No one moved, especially with Logan blocking the doorway.

Finally, a young boy, no more than 10, peeked out from behind the door. "Come, come in" he squeaked.

Four pairs of feet entered cautiously into the immense yet stark room. Six straight-backed hardwood chairs and a simple rectangular table were all that occupied the space except for the Elder, hands crossed in his lap, his plush velvet seat overwhelming his scrawny form.

"So, the great Lady Raphela has arrived." He sneered. "Oh, please do sit."

Raphela squeezed Chana's hand, lending her an inner strength.

"From whose mind did you pull my identity, Brucello?"

Black eyes worked at her and in disgust gave up. "The fat one."

Chana fought back her tears. Her weight, putting her well beyond pleasantly plump, had always been a problem, unfortunately detracting from an attractive face. Her mindseer gift lifted her past appearance, most of the time.

"Since I've matured past name calling perhaps you could be more specific."

"Chana, then. Boy, get me a drink."

The young boy scurried away.

"I see. It appears you have the ability to see into people's minds."

"What of it?"

"I don't know, why would I make an issue of this gift?" Raphela's calm offensive continued to keep Brucello off balance.

"Why are you here?"

Logan losing patience, snorted and placed a large firm hand on Brucello's shoulder. "You will address Lady Raphela with respect, or I shall you teach you manners." All three women stared at Logan, not known for such venomous speech.

Brucello, having no more success with Logan than Raphela, acquiesced. "My lady, what brings you to our village?"

Obviously he hadn't had time to discover this through mindseeing techniques. "It is the Duke's command that all people become educated, learn to read and write and count."

"That is nonsense." Brucello looked up at Logan, "my lady. Farmers and women have no need for such knowledge, even merchants need know only how to count."

"We disagree"

"Then ask the people yourselves, my lady, they will tell you."

"I'm sure they will agree to whatever you've said, however when they can no longer trade outside the village and their children are ridiculed for being unable to read, their needs will change."

Brucello's nostrils flared and his fingers turned into his palm creating a bony fist. The scraggly hair by his lip curled up with the contortion of his face.

"Go then, create, your, your"

"School" Raphela calmly offered.

"School!" His fist slammed on the arm of the chair.

"We shall." Raphela rose and began to leave.

Brucello stewed and then regained his composure, "But my lady, you will not be here and even if you send your mindseer, she will not be able to protect the entire town, even you will find that a task. So create your school, it's meaningless as long as I am here."

"Perhaps you're right, we will discuss the details tomorrow."

He smirked in victory and a silent shocked troop followed Raphela out the door, Chana made contact with the boy as the door closed.

"My lady"

Raphela put a finger to her lips, sensing Brucello staring at them from the window. Once a safe distance Chana spoke again.

"My lady, how could you let him believe he's right?"

"There is nothing to let him believe, he is right."

Not a word was spoken as Raphela led the way, very slowly back to the village inn, still watching the people peek out windows at the strangers.

Halfway to the inn Raphela turned to Chana. "Did you see anything in the boy's mind, just a brief view perhaps?" Raphela was hopeful.

"The boy as everyone else is in terror of this man, but in both the boy's mind and Brucello's mind was a name, Lemot."

"Good work Chana. Let's get some lunch and then Logan and I will find Lemot."

Fatell sat by Raphela as they ate.

"What is going on Raphela?" Fatell's eyes demanded the explanation her voice couldn't."

Raphela's eyes had a glint that sent a shiver down Fatell's spine. It mirrored a little too closely the familiar view of Mahtso.

"We try not to interfere with the ways of the people. It only creates resentment, but in this case we have a leader who is abusing not only his power but his gift as well.

"Gift" Fatell shook her head.

"He is using it to control the town."

"He should be stopped. Even the ever-patient Logan was pushed."

"He needs to be eliminated." Raphela sipped at her tea.

"You wouldn't really..." Fatell swallowed hard.

"No my friend, unfortunately having Logan slice him in half, a happy thought for Logan, is no longer acceptable." Raphela shook her head.

"You have a problem yet you seem pleased. Why?"

"The challenge. Our esteemed Elder gave me a clue."

And"

"He said that any mindseer I send could not protect the town, that even I would find it a task."

"So?"

"So obviously I unknowingly can shield the people around me from his power. Isn't that true Chana?"

"Oh yes my lady, but I didn't know you were..."

"I am not. I simply must possess another type of gift. But somewhere in his tone was a thought that someone else was outside his realm and Lemot must be that person."

"So Lemot can make him stop?" Fatell felt as if she were blindfolded.

"No, I don't think so or he would have done so already."

Chana was enticed. "Then why is he so important?"

"My friends, if my healers must go further than removing a splinter to cure an ill than we must know its cause. Lemot may know the root of this illness."

No one was quite sure what Raphela would do, only that she had to succeed.

Lemot responded to the knock on his door as he always did. "I beg your patience." He opened the door to see Raphela. His old gray eyes opened wide. "Have the Gods sent me a messenger?" Such hope in his words as Raphela had never heard forced her hand to extend and rest on his.

"I don't think so. Are you Lemot?"

"Yes, yes I am."

"May I come in?"

"My apologies, please come in."

Raphela and Logan waited patiently in the cozy parlor as he took each painful step.

"Please sit. Join me for tea?"

"You don't need to go to any trouble for us."

"It is rare I receive visitors, much less one as lovely as you."

"All right, but allow Logan to assist you."

Soon all were settled in the comfortable brown chairs by a fireplace.

"I am Lady Raphela and have come to this town, as to many others, to establish a school so that all of Ishtba will be literate."

"What a wondrous thought my lady." the old man warmed his hands on the teacup and answered more in distant reverie than reality.

"Lemot, I have come across a problem in this village."

The reverie dissipated and the cup lost a bit of liquid as it met the saucer. "I presume you mean our Elder."

"Yes and you are the only person willing to say more than here is your meal."

"My lady, I have heard tales of the Duke and yourself and your powers, I tell you, if they are needed anywhere, they are needed here." Lemot betrayed his passion.

"How did Brucello come to be Elder?"

Lemot sighed. "My brother, my dear dear brother." The old man took a sip of tea and leaned back. "When Brucello was young his parents had a difficult time and often asked my brother, Surat, then the town Elder, for advice. Surat offered what he could, but by the time Brucello was a teenager he was unmanageable, his ability to see people's minds disturbed the entire town. Surat agreed to take the boy into his home and teach him, perhaps change his ways. For a while Brucello was under control, as a matter of fact it was a number of years. But then my brother's health began to fail. He lost his hearing and eventually his voice and in my heart I know, in the end, his sensibility. As tradition has it our Elder chooses his successor. Despite my attempts to dissuade him, Surat chose Brucello."

"What a shame. If Brucello were to leave, what would the town do?"

Lemot shrugged his shoulders, "Choose some one else. But how could that happen?" Brucello is far too comfortable to leave."

Raphela's tea made gentle waves in its cup. "What if the Duke insisted?"

"My lady, you have met this man, yes?"

"Yes I suppose my question is more could the town be convinced that Brucello was leaving of his own free will?"

Lemot studied the regal woman before him. "Not to be blunt my lady, but should you or the Duke care what the town thinks?"

Raphela smiled. "Lemot what is worse, the monster you know or the one you don't?"

Lemot nodded.

"We don't want to frighten the people, just make their lives better. But it must be done correctly."

"Mm" Lemot closed his eyes to think.

"Lemot, a question."

"Yes my lady."

"How is it that you are not afraid, do you possess the gift?"

"No, but my brother was careful to instruct that no harm was to come to his family and the town knows this. Any discomfort on my part would give reason to revolt. Without any proof any thought to harm Brucello is met with dire consequences by his personal guards."

"I see, is there anyone else under such protection?"

"No"

Raphela walked many routes to resolve this situation. "How many people in the town?"

"About two or three hundred"

"And how far does his power extend?"

"What do you mean?"

"If someone left the town would he have a few days travel before going beyond Brucello's reach?'

"I don't know."

"Can he really see everyone's mind at once, or has he simply convinced the town that he is ever present in their minds?"

Lemot stared at Raphela as if she discovered the names of the Gods. "I think you may have the answer."

Together they created a plan.

Midmorning the next day Raphela arrived at the center of town, flanked by Fatell and Chana, followed by Logan, in whose arms rested Lemot.

Under the warm sun a crowd began to gather as Logan gently placed Lemot in a large comfortable chair.

Raphela swore a few people actually smiled when greeting the man and children fought for a hug or turn on his lap.

Once the town square had enough bodies to meet Raphela's requirements, she began. "I am Lady Raphela, wife of Duke

569

Ishtba, ruler of these lands." she wore formal clothes, trim and brusque as her tone.

All eyes turned to the command. Her wings of protection spread and those under them felt a certain freedom. A velvet voice, firm as the land, safe as a mother's womb addressed the crowd. "I have made an offer to Elder Brucello. He says you are not interested. Yet one of your most respected residents says otherwise. We offer you education, the right to learn to read and write. To know the Laws of the gods by your own eyes." Raphela stopped. She had learned this was a religious town.

Heads moved, but voices did not venture. Raphela turned to Chana, no thoughts yet.

"Sadly, you are chained by your fears. I cannot change your world, but I can empower you to do it yourselves. Is there not one among you who permitted themselves a thought and went unpunished?"

Feet shuffled, eyes moved and finally a voice. "My lady" A middle-aged man stepped forward, despite the clinging of a wife and children.

"Your name?"

"Elrod"

"Tell us Elrod, about your thought."

He looked around, licked his lips. "I, I wished Brucello would leave."

Gasps from the audience and one body slipping away, but Logan brought him back."

"And you didn't suffer?"

"No my lady."

"Surely Elrod is not the only one"

A few more hands raised.

"This is good. Now you can see Brucello is not omnipotent, he has played on your fears."

A buzz of thoughts and words trickled forth.

Raphela smiled. "So, now I ask you, do you want the education we offer?"

Elrod took a proud step forward. "Yes my lady"

Many others stepped up behind him.

"What of Brucello?" Raphela would not let the joy override the root of the problem.

A woman, about Lemot's age stepped by the old man. "I say we choose a new Elder, I say we choose Lemot."

It took little encouragement for the crowd, now more than a hundred strong to make the decision."

Brucello paced in his house, head spinning from the onslaught. Driven by a growing madness he stormed to the town square. "How dare you defy me. I shall make you pay, all of you." He ranted and raved, desperately trying to take one mind.

Gradually the crowd changed, all thoughts and eyes were on Brucello.

Raphela watched.

Brucello stood frozen in fear. Chana whispered to Raphela as the crowd turned away from the catatonic Brucello. "They had but one thought. It was amazing. They all told him to go away.

"And in his mind he has, hasn't he?"

"Yes my lady"

Raphela stepped out of town leaving Fatell and Chana to make the arrangements.

Many years ago Atan had planted the seeds of growth, ordering the creation of villages near fiefs and occasionally a fief by a lone village. Small villages grew to towns and fiefs enjoyed a break from the monotony of unchanging scenery. They stopped here and there along the way, breathing in the scent of the thick forests, always nearby. The ultimate goal, was to reach the mines. Calcoran wealth lay not in its forests or fiefs, but in its mines.

While Ishtban's fertile soil always filled the bellies of its folk and more, Calcoran struggled with its few fields of grain, poorly managed as well. This had been Atan's advantage, though Ishtba had little ore, making steel weapons, a precious commodity, it could easily supplant its supply by trade with Calcoran. Samed enjoyed Atan's rule for that purpose, and

571

gladly shared the wealth of his mines to ease the clamoring of hungry people.

Finally the border of the mining town was upon them. They wasted little time stabling the rameks and heading for the mountain.

Atan entered the mountain cavern, immediately sensing the change in air. His eyes focused on the textured walls while metal carts creaked up and down the pathways carved out of stone.

Mahtso followed a footpath, parallel to the carts and was soon out of sight.

Atan surveyed his surroundings. Though the mountain was above him and light only shone in from the entrance it was not as dark as he anticipated, the walls sparkled with the elements.

Only men moved about. Women would stop by to drop off food and it was then that he truly noticed it. The men's faces and hands, were so sprayed with dirt, they appeared to have been rolled in black flour, that after a while the smudged faces looked natural.

Ore was brought to a foreman, who inspected a cart for purity, Atan was told, and then was on to the next phase. Atan did not venture very deep. Although the consistent sound of hammer against rock fascinated him, the people held a deeper attraction. No one paid attention to the Duke. Few words were spoken or needed. The men operated with the same efficiency as an army, each one knowing his task and completing it.

At day's end Atan saw the men gather in work teams and there the talk began. Their voices seemed especially loud.

"Look, look Jonah, I finished four loads today and good stuff, fine for sword making." A wiry man with a booming voice made sure Atan heard of his accomplishment.

"Four loads, good job, Refa." A foreman slapped him on the back, increasing the view of Refa's dirt-stained teeth and gums.

"Jonah, come look at the quality of this cartload."

Words like this passed back and forth. Jonah, the inspector, responding with some sort of praise each time.

The foreman took Atan on the side. "Every day we measure the loads, examine each for purity. The teams compete for a monthly prize. It makes for a better product. This is a dull job, daily competition keeps them on their toes." the foreman, unsure of his leader, stopped at that point. But Atan listened carefully and heard the unspoken words and said it for him. "Its good for morale."

The foreman smiled. Both men relaxed in the knowledge the other slated people's feelings as important as production.

It dawned on Atan that he hadn't seen Mahtso since they entered the mountain. "Have you seen Mahtso? Atan's head moved from side to side, not waiting for the answer.

"I believe he worked with the blue team today my lord."

"Blue team?"

"Yes my lord."

Atan nodded and sought out the blue team, passing assorted groups as he walked.

"Where is the blue team?"

A grimy face looked up "Over there, got a new man today, pretty good I hear."

"Not good enough." A teammate banged a glass of ale against that of his friend's and leaned over. "Eh, my friend."

Atan ignored them and walked on, finally seeing the carts with the blue stripes. The "team" consisted of five or six men, all about Mahtso's size and build, which Atan realized fit the description of almost everyone he saw. His eyes scoured the group, but could not discern Mahtso, immediately.

"My lord, over here." Mahtso beckoned with a dirt caked finger. But it was not the grime that shadowed him but the broad smile and joyous eyes.

"Mahtso?!"

"Yes, come look at what I found."

Atan wove his way through the carts. The team hung tighter like wildebeests near a watering hole.

"He got the prize, he did." Another toothy grin accompanied the boast.

Mahtso held out a small rainbow stone. "They say only one is found a year."

"Its very pretty." Atan looked at the brightly colored rock with polite interest.

573

"I will take it back to Ishtba and have Nabus make a necklace for Fatell."

"Says he's got a good woman, eh sire?"

The men were all a bit under the influence of ale.

"Yes he does."

"It's what every man needs."

"I couldn't agree more."

"My lord" A third man spoke, turning to Mahtso to be sure he spoke correctly. "Mahtso, being the winner and all, gets the prize today."

Atan just squinted his eyes in confusion and tried to avoid the dust clouds that popped up as men walked by.

"My lord," Mahtso suppressed a belch. "The prize is dinner with my friend."

"I see."

"Me wife is the best cook in town."

"Then I hope you enjoy it Mahtso. Now, I have other matters to attend to."

Atan left the group of merry men, his friend staring after him, like a child at the first day of school, anxious for the new experience, yet unsure about leaving home.

Atan walked away, feeling much like the parent, letting go. His feet took him towards the inn, where he had made arrangements. It was empty except for three young women sitting at a corner table. Scents of herbs faintly toasted the air, even to the doorway where he stood.

A matronly woman, hair tied back in a bun showed a generous helping of cheeks and chin above large sagging breasts and round stomach. She was well covered by a simple cotton dress and apron, designed to work well with the kitchen or serving room. She approached.

"My lord, what can I do for you?" She curtsied politely.

"A warm meal and cool wine."

She took no offense at the curt answer, it served the purpose.

"Choose any table sire." The low pitched voice matched well the mature face and hearty arms.

Atan found one by the wall. Leaning back into the seat, he rubbed his calves and let his fingers loosen the muscles in his neck. He slipped into a quick reverie of Raphela's touch then, brushed the feeling away he had worked to avoid, the growing emptiness inside him.

Before long the wine appeared, soon joined by a thick steak and vegetables. Atan picked at the food, although it was good. He ignored the women, whose whispers and giggles were obviously directed at him. From a table by the kitchen, the hostess waited, occasionally closing her eyes, as hard working people do, towards the end of their day. And, like a mother, knowing a child is done with a meal, though half of it sat swimming in cold sauce, the hostess removed the plate but did not turn to leave.

"My lord, if you would permit, I have prepared a dish in your honor." Despite her hardened appearance, she still sought approval.

Atan raised his hand in acceptance.

On a plate far too delicate for this place of heavy wooden tables and benches, she displayed her offering. Atan stared down at the golden lattice of spun sugar protecting a mountain of swirled custard and mouth watering fruit. A clean fork was placed in his hand. Dipping into it more with curiosity than hunger, Atan placed a forkful in his mouth. The dish's delicate flavor was enhanced by liqueur.

"This is amazing."

She beamed with pride and relief. "Thank you my lord, it's my special recipe."

"Very good and it would go well with a cup of tea."

"Oh yes my lord." She fetched the tea and as she did, Atan noticed a letter, framed and hanging on the wall. It had Samed's seal.

She laid the cup on the table.

"Tell me, is that letter from King Samed?"

"Yes sire, he too visited this place and wrote a letter of thanks. Would you like to see it?"

Atan thought about it. "Yes."

She put it beside his teacup. He read out loud, "To Catarina, my complements and gratitude for a fine meal."

Atan looked up with his eyes only. "A nice letter."

575

She returned it to the wall and asked if he needed anything else.

"As a matter of fact, I was wondering if you might give me the recipe for tonight's meal. The meat was different."

"Korob steak sire."

"Korob? The little grazing animal?"

"Yes, it's too hilly to raise donags here, so we use korobs my lord."

"That makes sense."

"My lord, would you like me to write the recipes for you?"

Atan smiled. "Yes I would."

She pulled up a chair and did just that. Atan had sensed she was literate.

"Can everyone in town read and write?" He watched her hand move comfortably with each letter.

She didn't look up as she answered. "Well, all the women of course."

"The women?"

"Yes my lord, is that a problem?

"No, but why only the women?" Curiosity was inspiring at the moment.

"What use would men have for reading? You don't need to read in the mines, To operate the shops and handle money, one must know how to read and count."

"How unusual."

The woman's fleshy face filled with question and a tinge of fear. "Why my lord?"

"In the rest of the world, those who are literate are usually the men. Lady Raphela would be pleasantly surprised here."

"She would?"

"Yes. But, we would like all our citizens to have knowledge. Perhaps someone could teach the boys as well as the girls." He held back a laugh, remembering the opposite prejudice he grew up in.

"If you insist sire." She lowered her head in frustration.

"I will not force you, but in the long run you will find it best."

She nodded as he went to his room.

Sleep evaded him for oh so long. His body ached and the emptiness he fought battled back. It was getting harder every day to be away from her. And for the next few days even the distant contact via the mindseers was not an option, as they were given some needed time on their own.

Sleep arrived, restless and wanting, but doing some good. Waking's partner was the same as sleep, stiff unyielding muscles and the loneliness he had locked out found a crack in his armor and seeped in, hooking on to that tender spot that gnawed at him.

His hostess prepared an ample and tasty breakfast. As he sipped his tea he wished for a healer to ease the ache in his bones. Steam passed his nostrils and he remembered something, just before leaving the castle Raphela pressed a small packet into his hand and said, "A little magic."

Digging long fingers into his pocket, he found the lump and pulled it to daylight. With the care of any healer he opened the tiny packet and saw the magic, fifteen tiny leaves, green, spiked and aromatic. Five were swirled into the hot tea, which swept through Atan and the aches lost their battle. He whispered a thank you, but the loneliness suckled on his ease and spread like cold thick syrup, slow but sure.

By midmorning he regrouped with Mahtso and together they toured the rest of the village. Their presence at the weekly gathering that evening made it special.

Around the town center the golden, orange flames of sturdy torches fell on rows of tables, laden with hearty food and fine drink. Children sucked on long sweet sticks while parents gathered in knots talking. A loud bell clamored and all attention was drawn to the circle's center where Atan and Mahtso stood beside the town leader and his wife. Mahtso's chain slid nervously through his fingers, reflecting, the mood of his master more than his own.

"My lord," the leader began, "we are honored that you chose to visit us. We have prepared gifts for Mahtso, you and your family. While we know little of the world, we take pride in our swordmaking." His wife turned, presenting a long heavy blade on a blue velvet cloth. "This is for Mahtso, perhaps a long lost brother of ours." Mahtso accepted the gift, nodding his gratitude and studied the intricate pattern etched along the length of the blade.

"My lord, for your son." The woman handed over a second blade, thinner, than the first, its gold handle glimmering with a complex mosaic of black and green stones.

Now his wife stepped forward, curtsied and then revealed a dagger, its gold handle softly curved, one side a pattern made of flat black stone, communicating knowledge and power. On the reverse side was the image of jar and herb, the healer's symbol. Atan knew, only Raphela's hand was meant to carry that blade.

"For you my lord," the leader spoke reverently.

A sword of such precision as he had never held, so balanced and polished it reflected the stars. Its handle gold with straight powerful lines and on both sides a Gilfon, black, deep green eyes set above a gold embossed body.

"Your craftsmen are blessed and all will appreciate your gifts." Atan's words sent a chill and warm glow all at once, through the crowd. A man began a tune on a flute and was soon joined by others. The party had begun.

Atan slipped away, fighting the growing hole inside him.

Mahtso, hoping also to avoid the crowd was dragged in by his team and joined the festivities, his chain never at peace. He finally escaped and found a quiet spot, closer to the woods. A young girl, not much older than Valeria sidled up to him. Her bodice almost overflowing with soft young breasts teased by strands of long blond hair.

"You are Mahtso, eh? Sultry lips and eyes were ill matched to the young face and voice.

"Yes." Mahtso tried not to stare and took a step aside. Undaunted, the girl brushed against his shoulder.

"Shouldn't you be with your friends?" Mahtso stiffened but his chain made wild spins around his hand.

"I like you better."

Mahtso took a deep breath. "I really think you should leave me alone."

"Don't be silly. If you want to be alone, just be alone with me." Her tongue circled his ear.

He turned, eyes a muddy grey where blue used to be. His hand stroked the ever present whip by his side, while his fingers squeezed her forearm as he pressed her against a nearby tree. "You don't know me," he hissed

The young girl's eyes opened wide, her fear a sound that wouldn't leave her throat. His body pressed against her, his excitement, obvious. Tears formed in her eyes as his whip caressed her chin.

"It's been a long time, a very long time." He almost drooled, his dark side, drew on her fear like fire on dry wood.

"Oh, but it would be so much fun and you like me so much."

Tears rolled down her face.

"There you are Baritsa."

Mahtso heard the deep voice and turned.

"Father," she whimpered and ran to him. Father studied Mahtso for a moment. "Has she disturbed you?" He asked, finally.

The shadow inside him retreated, "No, no she was simply trying to learn a bit more about our ways."

"Mm. Well I imagine she's learned enough for one night."

"I agree."

Baritsa and her father moved away a few steps. "I should have let him have his way with you. How many times have I warned you about approaching men with that attitude of yours."

Baritsa still shaking stared between her father and Mahtso. "Never again, father, never again." For the first time she spoke the words truthfully.

Raphela climbed into the carriage, paying no attention to her surroundings and leaned back into the seat. A silent signal to Fatell to proceed when ready was the only communication she sent.

Fatell sighed.

Raphela listened to the wheels slowly creak as the gray clouds forced their way in front of the sun.

579

Chana felt her teeth clench together and looked to Fatell for support. Little could be done.

The week's journey to Calcoran was painfully slow.

Raphela's skin turned gray as the sky and her eyes held back the tears that the clouds amply provided. The carriage pushed through the mud, rameks as weary as the drivers by each day's end.

Atan moaned in his sleep. The herbs had lasted but a day.

Patar, pressed too often to reach Chana, by their arrival at Calcoran, could do nothing but sleep.

Mahtso paced, his chain digging deep into his palms and legs.

Raphela, desperate for the peace of sleep, tried again and again, but every bump or caw of a bird took her back to the empty wakefulness she endured.

Fatell prayed as she watched her friend sink into a black void whose tentacles wrapped around all who traveled with it.

Chana, unable to meet Patar's calls and avoid Raphela's mood, slept in self preservation and ever-faithful Logan stood watch over his Lady, devoted as a zorel pup.

Atan's hollowness coated Calcoran Castle, slowing activity almost to a halt. He walked in agony, shoulders beginning to curl, eyes dull.

By the time Raphela reached Calcoran, her hair was as brittle and dry as parched grass. She saw and heard nothing.

Once the carriage stopped, Mahtso ran to greet them.

Raphela was the last to emerge, her cold hands sending Mahtso into an even deeper frenzy. But he knew too much to say anything about it.

"Raphela he's..."

She raised her hand, "I know where he is."

Careful steps took her towards the back garden.

How she knew Mahtso never understood.

Atan stared into the dull moonlight of the still night. No breeze, no nightlife stirred. Raphela saw his silhouette, gray hair reflecting off the metal bench.

Atan breathed deep her scent as she approached from behind.

Raphela, just a few paces away, saw the back of his hand fly out. She didn't flinch and although it intentionally missed her, she crumpled to the ground.

"Why so long," he muttered "why did you stay away so long?"

Raphela wept openly, tears staining a gown already crusted with mud from the journey, splayed around her like a crown.

Atan looked down, tears welling in his eyes. With little effort he scooped her up and carried her to their room. Raphela nestled her head in his chest.

Atan settled into a large comfortable chair. She curled up in his lap and both slept.

As the second moon began its descent, Raphela stirred. As she tried to stand, she realized her hair was tightly wrapped around his hand.

He woke and stared at her.

"Am I prisoner?" The playful words and tempting smile tightened his grip.

"Do you think I'd permit you to be out of my grasp?"

She turned and straddled his lap, lifting her gown so that her bare bottom rubbed against his legs. Then her fingers tugged at the lace in her bodice, loosening it.

"What are you doing?" Any remnant of sleep slipped away.

"Well my lord, aren't all prisoners inspected, checked for weapons?"

"Good point! If you promise not to leave, I will let you stand." The sternness of his tone took her aback, but not enough to stop.

Atan watched the sensual dance of cloth sliding from her. Once all was bare, she stood a breath away, lifted her arms and turned slowly.

Atan's desire for her pounded inside him. Raphela unbuttoned his shirt and felt strong fingers wrap around her wrist.

"I'm not done inspecting." the whisper was a fresh breeze in her ear.

As he removed his shirt her fingers discovered her breasts and then she turned, stretching down, while his pants fell to the floor. She caressed her thighs, breath becoming shorter.

He bit his lip, savoring the moment until the show was over and then, he grabbed her. They smelled like lust and passion and need and desire.

"Atan," she croaked as he sucked on her neck, "I have missed you so." Tears raced down her cheek. He licked each one between kisses long and deep.

Moments were taken to drink in the view. Her skin tingled while he caressed and squeezed and then he lay back as Raphela's tongue renewed every inch of him.

No other woman could have held his desire as he pressed into her with the force of a wild ramek. It sent shivers through them, each push sparked again and again their power and their passion.

To think that to have Raphela's moist inside wrapped around him only once was ludicrous. They planted and reaped their passion over and over until the moons wearied and the sun was past the yawns of rising. And when they were whole again, they slept, her hair wrapped tightly around his hand. They did not leave the room for a day, yet all felt the stony cold seep from the castle and the sun took control of the sky once more.

As always, he arose with the sun and Raphela watched as he shed the baggy threads of night. His lean form still sculpted with muscles dancing as he stretched. In the corner of her eye she caught a basin of steaming water and before his hand touched the cloth beside it she was washing off the last flakes of the grime and pain of the past weeks.

When she was done, the cloth swam in the lukewarm liquid while her fingers dried and massaged through a thick towel. And then, she wrapped him in a warm robe, tying it tight around his waist. The gentle caress of her cheek drew her close and she sank in the strength of his arms that encased her.

After breakfast they walked through Calcoran Castle, less like people, more like royal beasts.

By the next morning the rameks were saddled and laden with supplies. Hooves tamped at the dirt, anxious to fly over the stony paths ahead. Raphela stared up at the blue mountain, its white crest peaking above a layer of clouds, trees bundled around it, green and thick.

Atan began with a soft click of his tongue. The beasts took to a trot and soon sped by the lesser creatures of the forest, who were happy to watch from a distance.

The two-day journey to the mountain was full of joyful silence. Near the mountain's base was an inn, where the rameks were left in good hands.

Raphela smoothed the leather pants sitting close to her skin as Atan put on his shoes.

"My lady, if you are ready?" He held out his hand, gladly taken.

"Lead the way my lord."

Despite its massive size the slope was gentle. Many before had climbed this mountain. Atan looked for and found firm footholds. Raphela, by his side, followed his path.

The sweet fresh scent of summer leaves drifted down from the towering trees. Raphela's cheeks took on a blush not seen in years.

Atan breathed deep the clean air.

They stopped midday for a light lunch.

"Fatell as always has packed enough food for an army." Raphela nibbled on a piece of cheese.

Atan leaned against a tree and tossed a crust of bread to a small waiting creature. Nothing ached. Such peacefulness was rare in his life. "Raphela?"

She turned, more to the mellow relaxed tone than to her name.

"Thank you, Raphela."

More rosy color came to her cheeks, but not from the climb.

By nightfall they were a third of the way up and made camp for the night.

"This place is even more beautiful than I anticipated." Her finger wiggled over the dying campfire.

Atan looked around, feeling the eyes in the trees and then the tug at his pants.

"Sit with me"

Atan obeyed, pulling her close. "When Vanar traveled with me he'd insist on a story, something from long ago Papa, he'd say."

Raphela leaned into him.

"And he'd be asleep before the tale was done." Thick hair found its way around his hand.

Raalek's moons were bright that night, chaperoned by a thousand twinkling stars.

"Vanar loves the stories." Raphela gazed at the sky. "How many people are on those stars? We can't be the only ones in the universe."

"So you've told me."

Both enjoyed his cheek burying itself in her sea of hair.

"I'm right you know." She twisted her head up to make the point.

"Of course you are." He teased while giving into the temptation of a long kiss.

Soon both were tucked in the oversized sleeping blanket, ignoring the nightlife around them.

Raphela stirred in her sleep, dreaming some great tree had fallen on her chest. Waking with a start, she opened her eyes to see a pair of large, round orange eyes, staring down at her. Lifting her head ever so slowly she could make out a wide furry face and long whiskers, obviously attached to the weight perched on her chest.

She squeezed Atan's hand. He smiled in his sleep and rolled over to hold her, only to find a hairy lump.

"What?"

"Shh" Raphela did not want to alarm this creature, for despite its youth and padded paws, she sensed powerful claws hidden between the furry spaces. It gurgled at her, rubbing its face on her chest.

Atan leaned on an elbow and took in the scene, somewhat amused. "I believe it likes you." He stroked the soft fur on its back, encouraging more gurgles.

"Well and good, but its adoration is making it difficult for me to breathe."

"Oh" Slowly and gently Atan lifted the creature which attached itself to him.

Raphela sat up. "No loyalty."

Its tiny brown nose moved all about, searching.

"I think it's hungry." Raphela scratched under its neck.

The intriguing scent of charred wood was no match for the goodies in their packs, as far as this creature was concerned. Raphela reached over and offered it a piece of dried meat.

It sniffed, inspecting and then gingerly taking it, pulling away from Atan. It rested on the ground to enjoy its snack.

Suddenly, a throaty growl emanated from the very air and a much larger version of the hungry creature crouched by the pair of humans.

Baby pranced over to its guardian, showing its snack and receiving a shove, but no glance. The guardian's eyes were frozen on the strangers.

Atan's hand cautiously went for his blade, but Raphela signaled to be still. Her eyes met the guardian's and in some silent agreement, the guardian turned and took its charge.

Atan stared at Raphela, who for a moment watched the creatures fade into the darkness, and then turned to Atan, "Mothers agreement," she said simply as she lay down and returned to sleep. Atan just shook his head and joined her.

It took another day and a half to reach the mountain's top. There were far fewer footsteps to follow and the air became quite crisp. The trees thinned out and overhead birds danced and swooped down for a meal of mouse or for a better look at the invaders.

The special shoes Atan had purchased for both of them were a true blessing on the stony paths, grabbing onto the solid ground as tiny stones tumbled below.

Raalek's sun beat down on the icy cap, which was a little too smooth for even this adventurous pair.

They paused on a sturdy ledge, staring out at the world. Floating in the distance, the lush green fields of Ishtba. Raphela's gaze passed through the white fluff of a cloud, her skin tingled and blood raced through her. Atan drank in the glistening mountains of Calcoran while breathing deep the incredible scent of the sky.

Hand in hand the two handsome rulers of Raalek stood, knowing that if they wished they could pluck a god from the sky, but why bother. All they needed and wanted at that very moment was in their grasp.

A roll of thunder and blink of light answered their solidarity and strength; the gods grew annoyed. No matter, Atan pulled her close, their eyes mirroring their souls, their lips meshing and tongues dancing. No crack of thunder or crackling lightning bolt would break this.

Chapter 24

Valeria scooted up doing her best to enhance the noise of the crisp bedsheets.

Vanar snored on, like a ramek.

"Vanar."

She would have gotten a better response from the wall.

"Vanar!" Her gentility gave way to demand, but fell on deaf ears, even with a slim finger tapping the muscular shoulder.

Valeria sighed and slipped out of bed. "You never change," she muttered.

Furry slippers slid onto her feet as a thick robe hung loosely over the pale blue gown.

Vanar rolled on his back, exposing a hairy chest, moving up and down with each breath.

Valeria's green eyes lit and her hand reached outside the window, pulling in a ball of freshly fallen white snow.

The rumpled covers moved as Vanar squirmed, and then were kicked violently off as the fresh cold snow plopped down on that warm chest.

It melted quickly, streaming down, still cold and wet.

Valeria stifled a laugh as Vanar squinted in the morning light and brushed the remaining moisture in her direction.

"Ooh," she squealed as wet sprinkles hit her face.

"Ooh? Just ooh? How do you think I feel?" He demanded.

"Cold and wet." Her laughter killed any anger that considered entering his mind.

"Do you hate having me in bed that much?" he teased.

"Only when you snore."

"Snore! I don't snore."

"Yes, you do."

"Really. What does it sound like? Like this, chch, chch?" He made a variety of animal noises, chasing her around the room. She let out joyous squeals of laughter, ending with her back against the wall and Vanar pressing his hairy chest into her soft breasts.

"If I had time," he whispered and caressed her cheek.

Long soft arms rested on his shoulders. He smelled oh, so good and she couldn't resist one luscious kiss. There was no resistance.

Soft lips brushed his neck. "We must dress." She slipped out of his grasp.

Digging through her closet Valeria found the gown for the day, but still sought Vanar's approval.

"It's beautiful, but I like you better without it," he grinned wolfishly.

Next time wake up earlier."

The thick green grown slid over her slim form. Before she had a chance to pop her head through the top Vanar's hand landed squarely on her bottom.

"OW!" she protested.

"That's for the snow". He tightened his pants around his waist.

"Just think about the next time." She grinned and led him to breakfast.

Atan raised an eyebrow as the young couple entered. Raphela shook her head.

"You're almost on time". She teased.

"I'm working on it." Valeria pulled up a chair and shared a grin with Vanar who simply lowered his head.

"After breakfast you'll join me for a tour of the Healer's Building." Raphela finished her tea.

Valeria's grin faded. It was not a command, but she had avoided this responsibility for some time. As much as her sister loved the work, it frightened her. Though Raphela had told her she only needed to understand, not practice, the building itself made her skin crawl.

"Yes my lady," She muttered as a strong hand rubbed her shoulder.

"You'd think I'd told you to bend over for a paddling. This is not so bad."

Valeria moaned. "I'd rather be paddled." She pushed away the food.

"Come, let's get this over and done with early."

"All right."

Both women placed gentle kisses on their respective husband's foreheads and left.

"She's working on it?" Atan asked, cocking a speculative eyebrow.

"It's not what you think." Vanar poured another cup of steaming tea.

"Oh?" Atan leaned back and waited.

"Ummmm." It was a long sigh. "She delicately dropped a ball of snow on my chest."

Atan laughed out loud. "Good girl. It sounds like something your mother would do." He sipped some tea. "But I wake up early enough to avoid such torture."

Vanar buried his head in his hands, but only for a second. "How about a visit to the stables. I think a ramek bite would be less painful than the past meal.

Both chuckled and headed for the stables.

It was midweek and that evening after dinner was scheduled for "counseling". As time had passed the Duke and Lady were less available to resolve the problems of a growing population on an instantaneous basis. So one night a week they took to their royal chairs and attempted to satisfy the wronged and answer the needs of those who felt that normal channels were unsatisfactory.

Atan took his place, as did Raphela. Mahtso and Fatell were always there and Vanar and Valeria were required to attend as well.

"My lord, before you is Kali and Soren." Oram had fallen into the position of organizing the pleaders of the evening.

"Kali insists that Soren lied to the supervisor and was therefore given the choicer tasks."

"I see" Atan studied that both men, who had their eyes to the ground. Neither seemed pleased at being here. "And what does the supervisor say?"

"Only my lord, that he can neither prove nor disprove Soren's statement."

"Mm"

"Kali," Atan said, less like a ruler and more like a father.

"Yes my lord."

"What is it that Soren said?"

Kali's mouth felt dry. "He, he told Toneno that I was late for the third day in a row."

"I did not." Soren's voice burst forth like a child wrongly accused.

"You will have your turn Soren." Raphela said sternly.

"Yes my lady." Even grown men fall into place at a mother's admonishment.

"Were you late as Soren said?" Atan continued, evenly, undisturbed.

"Only one day, my lord."

"One day, so Soren told an exaggerated truth, it seems."

Kali blushed and said nothing.

Soren stood a little straighter and then heard his name.

"Soren, did you tell Toneno that Kali was late three days in a row?"

"No my lord." He spoke with pride that trickled away under Atan's eyes. "I told him two days, my lord." Soren swallowed hard.

"Was Kali late two days?"

"No my lord, just one."

"And did Toneno know he was late one day?"

"No, sire".

"Why not Kali?"

Kali swallowed hard. "I managed to avoid being caught my lord."

Grey eyes traveled between the two, obviously feeling an inordinate amount of guilt for their pettiness. Yet Atan and Raphela knew that pettiness unpunished festered into backstabbing and worse.

"You are both wrong. Oram, give the following instructions to Toneno. Both men are to spend a week at the worst task, together. After which they may return to their normal duties and all will be treated as if nothing occurred.

Oram made his notes and the men left. Before the next case arrived Atan also made note that Toneno was to come see him and discuss the situation. Atan's concern was Toneno's lack of awareness of the problem.

590

Valeria's hand slipped behind her and pulled out a pad and drawing coal. Her hand moved the coal and put on paper the Duke and Lady, just outlines, but she bottled the air and feelings with each stroke.

Vanar listened and learned, praying someday he would be so wise.

Mahtso's chain circled his leg as he stood by, obedient and faithful. Fatell calm and content stood by his side.

And so the evening wore on.

Winter was settled in and had built its slanted fortress around the castle. Over the next few weeks the fortress grew and the people settled into the busy and standard cold weather routine.

Vanar and Valeria each taught a class at the school as was required of everyone under the age of 25, They also continued to learn more about their future responsibilities.

Vanar dove into more intense development of the marketplace and Valeria pressed on the arts.

Raphela spent a morning with Aharon in the research department.

"Are there any new applicants worthy of the task?" She leafed through the applications.

Aharon closed the door to his office and rubbed his balding head.

"Meeting your standards makes 'worthy' an inadequate word."

Raphela peered over her nose with a stern look. This was not a new discussion. Raphela had created strict requirements for researchers. Dedication, an obsession with thoroughness and cleanliness. Detail oriented down to the size of a speck of dust, if it could be measured. Thirst for knowledge tempered only by the ability to throw one's self into the task at hand and find the answer. These were only the guidelines; the interviews were worse. Yet the researchers were exceptional and everyone in Calcoran and Ishtba knew that those standards were the reason hundreds of people were alive today, who, years ago would have died.

"Well?"

"I found two. I have scheduled interviews for tomorrow morning."

"Good. And, the healers?" She caressed an ancient herb manual lying on his cluttered desk.

"One." Aharon had talked with so many people his head ached. To be a healer was almost as important as being a researcher, but he understood their requirements better. The ability to heal was a misnomer, to diagnose was the key. He had always known that and Raphela leaned heavily on that philosophy. Researchers had the cures, or learned them.

The healer's task was to find the ailment without alarming the patient and to administer a cure, if known, without creating panic. The attention to detail was a requirement, but compassion was the key, for without that, the patients would rather die.

"You've done well." She replaced the book and laid a caring hand on his. "Thank you."

"You're welcome my lady."

Raphela returned to the castle, her steps taken with purpose and unquestioned direction.

Atan made careful notes in dribs and drabs on the slate that Falor had sent as a gift.

Raphela plopped down on the table right next to the book.

"I'm busy Raphela," he said without looking up.

"I know I haven't seen you for three days," She admonished.

"We had dinner together last night." He didn't leave the book that displayed an intricate drawing of some form of wheat.

She walked around, taking a whiff of the fresh cut flowers in the deep heavy vase by the windows.

"Considering the length of the meal and conversation, I'd count that for a nod of the head while passing in the hallway."

"Umm." Atan closed his ears.

"Atan, I miss you, we go through this every winter. You curl up into a shell and I can't talk to you. Are you listening to me?"

Atan read on.

"Don't you care? Aren't I..." She stopped. Her words and tone made her feel like a shrew.

Her fingers caressed the back of the chair and she leaned over to his ear.

"Since I have lost my appeal to you," she began a sensuous whisper. "I'll lick my wounds with some other interest."

It wasn't the words that pushed his hand to grab her wrist, but her hot breath.

Raphela didn't face him but allowed herself a wry smile.

"You could be punished for such insolence" His eyes still rested on the book.

"Oh my duke, are there not better things to do with me."

He stood up and pulled her close, remembering her same words of years before and hair cascading down her back. "For now, I will taste the 'better', but a full meal will be required later." Lips were sealed in the emotion of years of caring and passion, enough to warm the room.

Valeria often used the library to look up the art of the past and on this slow day, it seemed a good place to be. Her foot got over the threshold and she felt a wall of heat like none ever experienced. Her hands grabbed onto the doorframe and her eyes rested briefly on the entwined figures of Atan and Raphela. Valeria slid into the hallway and sat on the ground, catching her breath.

Fatell, seeing the girl, walked over. "Are you all right?"

Mystified green eyes looked up. "I, I saw them kissing." Like a child seeing her first sunset Valeria struggled with the words.

Fatell helped her to stand and walk her away from the room. You have seen something, no one except perhaps Vanar has seen since the wedding. I'm sure it was overwhelming."

Valeria stopped, regained her composure and relived in her mind, at a safe distance, her experience and grabbed Fatell by the shoulders. "I can do it, do both, all, oh Fatell, this is so wonderful."

"What..." Fatell didn't get a chance to finish.

"I have to tell Vanar." Valeria vanished and Fatell shook her head, and smiled. To be young.

"Vanar, Vanar, where are you?" Valeria tore into his office as he turned the corner.

"What is it?"

Air moved in and out of her lungs a few times as she caught her breath. He felt her energy and its radiance shining on him. All he could do was grin.

"I can do it, I can really do it now."

"What can you do?"

"Their portraits."

"Whose portraits?"

"Whose portraits? Your parents silly boy." Her green eyes blazed.

"But I thought you already started the portraits."

Valeria's fingers squeezed his hand. "Only the portrait of the Duke and the Lady, but now, I can do Atan and Raphela." Mysticism clouded her voice and Vanar knew it filled her thoughts.

"Why can you now?"

"I saw them kiss. No, I saw and felt them kiss. They didn't know I was there. Library, I was going to the library, but they were already there. It was incredible, amazing." She placed a gentle kiss on his cheek "I must go, just send food to my room, I'll come out when I'm ready."

"But..."

"I love you." She said as she disappeared.

"I love you too," he whispered.

Valeria labored for two weeks, not seeing anyone. She crawled into bed as Vanar dozed off and was gone long before he stirred in the morning. Finally he dragged her out one afternoon and insisted she rest and eat. She obeyed, but fidgeted and escaped as soon as he gave up.

As the third week came to a close Valeria emerged, beaming with a contentment rarely seen. She snuggled under the covers and whispered in Vanar's ear, "It's done," and fell into a deep sleep.

The next afternoon the portraits were unveiled. The crowd gathered. Atan and Raphela on one side of the portrait, Vanar and Valeria on the other side of it. A hush settled over the crowd as the mottled cover was removed. Gasps and oohs and aahs circled the room.

The brilliant strong colors of Ishtba stood like a stage on the canvas. The Duke and Lady, main players of the show, sitting in their chairs. The Duke leaning forward, grey eyes, a stone wall of strength surrounding the precious soft pillow of wisdom. His lips ever straight to match the grey hair that crowned the weathered face while his hands clasped together in thought in his lap. The Lady, sitting back, listening, understanding, revealing a gentle smile on her lips and firm resolve in her eyes. It was as if a piece of each had been sprinkled in the paint.

Once all had a good look Valeria revealed a second canvas she called "Atan and Raphela".

Not a sound escaped the crowd because no mouth could open. Skin tingled, palms moistened but all eyes were glued to the canvas.

Raphela's hair caressed her shoulder as Atan's fingers caressed her cheek. Fingers intertwined like braids in a young girl's hair. Two sets of eyes, so encased in passion and possessed by devotion, they saw only each other. Their forms slowly softened and meshed, swirled together, amid crowning golden flames.

Atan moved towards his daughter-in-law. Raphela took her other side.

"Valeria has done an excellent job, she is to be congratulated."

Fatell began to clap and soon the crowd joined in hearty approval.

"The Duke and The Lady" was hung in the main entrance hall, while "Atan and Raphela" adorned the family room.

From that day forward no one entered the castle without knowing why life existed as it did.

Raphela dug through the basket for her favorite muffin. It smelled as aromatic as the tea.

"The stablemaster has a problem. I've been meaning to discuss it with you," Atan said as he poured a cup of steaming tea. He sniffed it before he took a sip and listened to the world outside the window. The silence, deceptive, as the snow ruled, building its fortress, patiently, like ants marching into a hill.

Raphela's teeth sank into the sweet soft muffin, allowing the crumbs to fall. "What kind of problem?"

"The rameks are losing patches of hair."

"Have they been checked for insects?" Raphela considered the possibilities.

"Yes."

"Has yours contracted this condition?"

Atan leaned back. "As a matter of fact, he hasn't. Neither has Vanar's or Mahtso's."

"Mm, and have they ever had this before?"

"I don't know." Atan scooped up a mound of eggs onto his fork and suddenly, it clattered to the plate. Atan stared at the splattering of food. Raphela's eyes opened wide.

His fingers struggled to grasp the fork, his jaw clenched and eyes focused. Finally his fingers pressed onto the instrument and raised it to his lips. Atan never looked up at Raphela.

Raphela's eyes closed, her lashes moist from the tears that were kept at bay. She took a deep breath. "I would say that the stablemaster needs help so that all the rameks receive the same care."

She closed her eyes and prayed. The uncomfortable silence haunted them both and breakfast ended quickly.

Raphela paced outside the classroom door. Finally, dozens of feet poured out of the room amid a stream of young chatter.

Raphela held back until a head, far above the others appeared. "Valeria?"

She turned, blond hair swinging with her. "Raphela?"

"Are you done teaching for today?" Brown eyes, all business, waited impatiently for an answer.

"Yes."

"Good, let's go." Raphela grabbed her hand, almost jerking her along.

"But this is the way to the Healer's Building," Valeria whined.

"I know."

It was a short walk, especially at Raphela's pace. The heavy door of the building closed behind them.

"Valeria"

"Yes" It was a meek reply.

"When was your last cycle?" Raphela's pace slowed to normal, as she looked around, peeking in various doorways.

"Um, uh, I don't know." Valeria blushed.

Raphela stopped, hands on her hips. "Don't you keep track of your cycles?"

The young girl shrugged her shoulders and shook her head no.

Raphela dropped her head and sighed in exasperation as Valeria squirmed in her pristine surroundings. "Well you must think back and figure this out. NOW!"

Valeria swallowed hard and thought and counted on her fingers.

"Umm, six weeks, no seven weeks ago, I'm sure."

"Much as I suspected. Here we are."

They entered a small room with an examining table.

Valeria considered the flurry of activity of the past few minutes and stared at her mother-in-law. "Raphela?"

"Yes?" Her annoyance was clear, but its basis, unknown. "Where is he?" she muttered to herself, then to Valeria, "What is it?"

"Do you, ugh, think I'm pregnant?"

Raphela took a deep breath and softened her mood.

"Yes I do. Now sit down until Aharon arrives so he can verify..." She didn't finish the sentence.

"Verify what?" He closed the door behind him.

"That Valeria is pregnant."

"That will be a pleasant task." He took Valeria's hand. "Now, lay down."

Aharon performed his examination. "Sit up Valeria."

Valeria obeyed and straightened her gown.

"My lady, you are correct." He grinned broadly.

"I'm going to have a baby?" Valeria sounded blurry with the news. "When?"

"By what you've told me and your last exam, I'd say late summer."

Valeria's hand rubbed the tiny bulge of her tummy, the glaze in her eyes fading only a bit. "Is that why you insisted Aharon examine me before the wedding?"

"One of the reasons."

"Valeria, you must watch your diet. I will expect to see you at least once a month and towards the end, every week," Aharon said.

"Here?"

Raphela and Aharon stifled a laugh as she whined and stared at the cool white walls. "If you promise not to tell anyone, I will come to your room. If Lady Raphela permits," he said gently.

"I suppose a pregnant woman should have some leniency." Raphela sighed and gave in.

"Thank you." The sweet wet lips that pressed against Raphela's cheek spoke more than gratitude and Raphela worked at holding back tears.

"Isn't there some one you should tell about this?" Raphela was as brusque as she could muster.

"Vanar, oh, yes." Valeria scooted off the table, moving quickly and then slowly, unsure of what was best.

"Thank you Aharon." With bowed head and polite words Raphela left.

He raised a hand to call her back, but slowly lowered it, not even sure why.

Vanar, arduously at work in his office didn't hear Valeria enter and the tap on his shoulder made him jump. She stood by his chair, creamy white cheeks blushing in just the right spot. "Stand up Vanar," she said.

"As you wish" He stood and bowed, thick brown hair falling by his eyes and the scent of him filling the room.

Valeria took his hand and placed it on her stomach. "Do you know what's in here?"

Vanar looked into her eyes and cringed, feeling somehow he should know and didn't. "Um, a beautiful woman?"

Valeria warmed inside. "You are so sweet, but something else."

"Breakfast?" Raised eyes and shrugged shoulders begged for help.

"That and..."

"Oh, um, um, " Vanar crinkled his eyes and sighed like a puppy. "The most sensuous smooth skin I've ever touched."

"Under that."

"I'm sorry, I just don't know."

"Take a guess."

Gestures of helplessness flowed forth, but no guess.

"Ahh" She sighed, pushed up on her toes and leaned to his ear "It's a baby."

"Baby?"

Her blond hair moved as she nodded.

"We're going to have a baby? Really?" Vanar felt his heart pound and encased her tight to his chest. "This is amazing, it's incredible." No touch could have been more tender as his fingers fondled her face and pulled it close for a kiss. "I love you so much, Val"

"I love you too."

Young eyes anxious to please, naive and wise bonded in a silence that padded the room.

"Who else knows?"

"Your mother and Aharon. I imagine by now, your father."

Vanar scooped her up and began towards the stairs.

"Just what are you doing?" She hung onto his neck.

"Do you think I'll let you strain yourself? Not while I'm here."

"Put me down." It was a gentle order, which he obeyed.

"Haven't you been around your mother enough to know that pampering of that sort is foolish".

"I know, but I have to do something. Don't worry, I'll find something for you to do."

"As you wish." He teased, as hand in hand they went downstairs.

Raphela caught Atan just as he was entering the training room, and blocked the door. "I have news."

Two men nodded as they passed their Duke.

Raphela's face, yielded no sign, lips still and eyes softer than he had ever seen. They walked to the side.

Pulling on an inner strength her lips curled up ever so slightly. "Duke Ishtba," she began.

"Duke Ishtba?"

"Duke Ishtba, your realm is now expecting a new heir." So serious and slow were her words their meaning was almost lost. But her eyes spoke more.

"Valeria, she's pregnant," he said finally.

Raphela nodded.

"So soon? It happened so quickly. This is a miracle."

" A wonderful miracle."

Raphela turned and saw Vanar, beaming.

Atan pulled Vanar to him and these rulers of the world hugged like two long-lost brothers.

Raphela's touch was not so full, but loving all the same and as Atan's arm lay on her shoulder Valeria swore the baby inside grew at his touch.

Raphela made sure Fatell and Mahtso were part of this joyful gathering. Fatell broke into tears and Mahtso clapped Vanar on the back and wished them all well.

Fatell, as she had done years before, gathered the castle folk to announce the news, which was met with the same excitement as Vanar's impending birth.

Atan found a quiet corner and slipped into reverie. His chair leaned back and his eyes closed. He remembered the day Raphela announced her pregnancy and how he cursed himself for not having convinced her, that she was the one. But the change it made in their lives was more wonderful than he had anticipated. And so he reminisced in silence.

Vanar and Valeria vanished to somewhere private.

Raphela wandered the halls aimlessly and found herself sitting in Corin's old room. She had insisted it remain untouched, except for dusting. Sunlight and snow cast tiny rainbows and the bottles of herbs sat patiently while the sun faded their labels and the dust, unreached by shorter hands, rested comfortably on the caps.

Books still lined the shelves and the same gray blanket Corin loved warmed the cot. Raphela swore it still smelled of him,

600

wordless thoughts meandered in her mind, barely taking shape and then fading away.

"Good man Corin."

Raphela stared blankly out to the hall.

The crackling voice belonged to a man well matching the sound, his bald freckled head reflecting the light and his hand resting heavily on a dark cane.

"Yes, he was."

The cane moved forward and then one foot. "My lady, I understand congratulations are in order."

"What, oh yes." She offered a polite smile.

He went on, ignoring her mood. "He would have been so pleased. This baby, is quite a miracle. The Duke, the first one since my great grandfather's time, to know that a grandchild was to be born. You must be so happy, what a blessing." He sighed and Raphela stared in wonder. "I had always hoped for grandchildren, but, ah, well, congratulations." Now he moved on, slowly.

Raphela stood at the doorway, ready to chase after him and then leaned back, arms crossed. He had made a point and she remembered that death had not yet come, why give it a feast when it already fed too soon, too often.

Raphela strolled to the training room and he was there. Slipping in soundlessly she watched the others slow down their exercise and leave, dinnertime was approaching.

Atan worked on; torso twisting with the same elegance as the stick mocking a sword that broke the air. Legs taking long deep strides, each movement revealing the control. She caught sight as a bead of sweat crept out from his shoulder and blossomed into a tiny ball, skiing down the curving muscles of his arm. Her breath jumped.

As most people disdain the odor of the ramek, so do they the scent of human work, but to Raphela it was a beckoning finger.

Atan knew she was there, if only by the smell of her hair.

Each time his arms raised and stretched, her skin grew a bit moister and soon her gown lay on the floor. Her breasts easily moving the light slip that remained as she moved towards him.

Both lithe forms moved in perfect unison to the beat of a drummer that wasn't there, not touching, yet knowing the next step, the muscle to flex.

And then, when their palms met and eyes locked, her breasts under their satiny slip tickled the hairs on his chest. And for a moment everything halted except the deep breaths between them. Raphela's hands drew a trail from his shoulders to his waist, the lightest and most feathery of touches. His lips brushed away the strap of her slip so he could fully enjoy the sweet taste of her skin. Raphela felt her slip rise past her buttocks and over her head.

What better response could she find than to return the favor? Sinking to her knees, her fingers pulled down his pants, not missing any opportunity to touch along the way.

Atan's hands wallowed in her hair and she sucked hard. Her tongue whispered at just the right spot and soon he too was on his knees. Lips grabbed and tongues meshed and the floor was barely large enough for the rolls of passion it endured. Finally she pulled him on top of her, the moistness between her legs an invitation no longer worth resisting. He drank in every touch, every kiss as she swam in his power. At long last their energy dwindled and passion was forced to retreat.

Raphela lay on her back and smiled. "Good dinner, I think I'll skip dessert."

Atan grinned broadly. Both slept well that night.

Woodsheets decorated the table like flower petals on a field. Vanar poured over the receipts and comments of the summer. Silently, Valeria placed a tray of sandwiches and tea on the one clear space she could find and turned to leave. Under the rustle of her gown, her belly had grown just large enough to advertise her condition.

"Where are you going?" Vanar didn't look up from his work.

"I don't know."

"Stay. Please." A chair miraculously appeared and Valeria placed herself in it.

"What are you doing?" She stretched her neck to look over his notes.

"Planning." A sandwich was quickly downed and followed by a deep swig of tea. "That was good."

"What are you planning?"

Vanar, though lost in the ideas that swirled in his head, was drawn to the innocent voice. "I want to do more with the marketplace. This year was better, but the potential is overwhelming."

Neither paid attention to the guard who walked past the room. Valeria had become accustomed to the security and Vanar took it for granted. Green eyes focused on him, fascinated by the incredible concepts that they knew would explode forth. They awaited the hypnotic and magnetic string, waited as it spun its web.

"In order to bring the marketplace to its potential, the leaders must put more emphasis on its use," he said.

Strong hands drew her to the map on the board he had used since he was a boy. "Look, we have filled over half the slots available for vendors. But it is still little more than a glorified way station for travelers."

Suddenly she felt his fingers encompass her palms and looking into his eyes was all she could do. Flaming in clear brown windows of his soul was a piece of his father and that chained her, willingly.

Vanar took a deep breath and whispered. "I want to build you a house, there, at the marketplace. It won't be as grand as the castle, but it will be the best. Say yes. Say you'll work with me to build this new world. I must be there, from the time the snow melts until the skies fill with gray and white. I promise you winters here at the castle, but... "

Two soft fingers pressed against his lips. "Shh. It could be a roofless shack and I would still go with you."

"You can decorate it any way you choose," he still sounded afraid she'd turn away.

"I love you Vanar and wherever we live and whenever we live there is fine with me."

"Really? You, you don't mind?" This tall and powerful young man, with the right and ability to command, had to be sure his pleading worked.

"Believe it or not, I am your wife and being with you is more important than almost anything else in the world," she whispered as she leaned into his embrace and answered his kiss.

"I have an idea. I would like everyone to bring their taxes to the marketplace." Eyes glazed over with the thoughts of future that forced the words from his mouth

"But how will the taxes get to the castle?" Valeria remembered the vast train of carts and wagons that delivered the collected supplies. It took over a week to just bring it into the castle and two more to inventory and store.

"If taxes are collected over three or four months instead of one week, it won't be so difficult to have a team of men, traveling back and forth delivering the goods. And with more and more people paying, each needs to give up a little less. We almost always have an overabundance of everything. Since each payment is less, it will be that much easier to transport." Those deep brown eyes begged for approval.

"It's a wonderful idea, but what about your parents? What do they think?"

Vanar brushed off the question. "They will be fine with it." He wished to avoid thinking about their future, his father's condition a constant shadow to every thought and plan.

"Then do it," she said simply.

"Good." He marked her approval on his board. "Oh, you do know you'll be doing the bookkeeping for those months" He cringed in mock fear, but didn't flinch as her palm caught his shoulder.

Valeria placed her hands on her stomach and looked down. "Did you hear that? He just wants me there to do the bookkeeping. I should have known. I'm sure he'll find something useful for you to do as well." She teased.

"Be glad its that and not cooking."

"That could be grounds for leaving you."

The smile faded from Vanar's face as his fingers clasped her face, with a frighteningly strong grip, enough to keep the blood from coloring her cheeks.

Valeria stared at him in shock.

"Don't say that, not even in jest."

She nodded her head and felt his fingers loosen their grip.

Vanar pulled a coin from his pocket and placed it on the table. Valeria approached cautiously.

"Do you know what this is?" The excitement that had possessed him a few seconds before had returned and despite her wariness she was drawn.

"It's a coin.'

"Yes, and there are not enough of them to build our economy."

"I don't understand."

"The merchants have coin and occasionally one or two fall into the hands of a fiefholder or farmer. But for the most part, all they do is trade goods. That means if someone doesn't want what they have, they can't trade for the other persons goods. This leads to frustration. If Castle Cordan purchased the goods available after taxes were paid and provided coin to the farmers and fiefholders more people could get what they wanted, making everyone happier. And, we could in turn, sell those goods for a small profit to those interested. And this way the fiefholders wouldn't be tied down to working at the marketplace. They could purchase their supplies without worrying about losing any profit."

"You are amazing." Valeria shook her head in wonder.

Vanar shuffled some notes and stared at the table. "I love you." He croaked it out in a guilty whisper.

Sweet wet lips caressed his cheek with a kiss and his head bowed down.

"Vanar"

He looked up in time to feel the sting of a hard slap across his face. She said nothing, the tingle in his cheek told him that she would not tolerate such behavior. For that he was glad.

Atan's eyes focused blankly on the rough surface above the bed, his long legs tucked under the covers.

Raphela stirred, her scent wavering by him, reminding him of the joy of life. She stretched and sat up. "Well, its about time." Her soft pink gown hid only the view but not the feel as she leaned over him.

"Time for what?"

605

"For you to let me get out of bed first." Caring lips placed a tiny kiss on his forehead. "But I won't let you be lazy." Her hands reached out for his and with the aide of his firm grasp she helped him to sit. "And now I simply must devote some time to choosing a dress." The gentle sarcasm forced a grin as she disappeared toward the closet.

This gave him time to allow his fingers and toes and legs to wake, ending the tingle of stubborn nerves. Finally he made his way to the hot bath that awaited. Walking was not as hard as sitting up.

Atan and Raphela descended the stairs, royal as ever, yet an observant eye would have seen his strong grasp, each slow step an effort. The stairs were little easier than sitting up.

Mahtso's chain beat the banister slowly, blue eyes harboring the thinnest of veils as Atan joined him for a trip to the training room. He had increased his time there, forcing his body to feats beyond any expectation. Yet, he could no longer best the young soldiers and they carefully avoided him.

"Mahtso, are you tired already?'

Mahtso rubbed his face in a towel and raised his hand as he caught his breath. "For someone supposedly suffering, you have more energy than I. What is Raphela feeding you?"

"Don't patronize me, it doesn't suit you." Atan sat by his friend, sticky sweat coating his face and arms.

Mahtso threw down his towel is disgust. "What would you have me do? Wallow in misery? You are stronger than any man I've ever met and that's the truth." His chain beat the wall behind him, and the smell of someone's blood crept into his nostrils, his chain beat harder.

"I will not give in to this disease. It taunts me and drains me, but I am not ready to bend to its will." Struggling with his clothes Atan buckled his belt and the two men, after an entire morning in the training room, left to attend other matters.

The veil of humor Raphela danced before him simply eased the facts, but it did not change them.

Atan strode slowly yet proudly, using his father's walking stick only when necessary, though the sturdy smooth wood felt good in his palm. He, like each of his predecessors, hoped it would simply gather dust. None had been so fortunate.

Vanar dispatched a messenger to the marketplace and patiently waited for his father. The hallway echoed with Atan's footsteps, solid and reliable.

Atan entered, followed closely by a servant. Though he demanded his independence, Raphela arranged for silent guardians throughout the castle, distant eyes that assured Atan would never be stranded. If he knew of this tender web, he said nothing. Little escaped the master of the house and Raphela assumed he simply chose not to argue.

"My lord, your special tea." The servant laid a pot of steaming brew by Atan as he sat. Atan nodded his acceptance.

"I see mother has been delving into Corin's remedies," Vanar chuckled as he pulled up a chair.

Atan raised the teacup to allow the steam to reach his nose that wrinkled at the bitter smell. He sighed and sipped it. "I just wish she'd find one that tasted a little better." Atan drank the brew, despite its bitter taste. It did alleviate much of the discomfort.

"When are you leaving?" He asked his son.

"As soon as the snow melts. I've already started the architects designing the house."

Atan smiled with pride. "You have a strong vision. It's good."

"Do you really think so? Are we taking the right direction? Am I moving too fast? It's so different from anything you've ever done." Vanar didn't plead, yet Atan realized how young Vanar really was and the tremendous responsibility he had thrown himself into. Approval from father meant so much.

"Vanar, you can't repeat my work and I couldn't work your vision."

Vanar looked deep into his father's eyes, soaking in the strength and support, hoarding it like a man knowing a drought is about to come.

"But, along with your Marketplace don't neglect the fiefs and towns that make it necessary."

"Yes, I know." A new wave of excitement flooded his face. "I've managed to talk with Falor, with Telep's help, and I've chosen four people, three men and a woman to visit the fiefs. With four, each can really get to know the details. If there is a major problem I will ride to the fief myself. Falor is doing the same. He feels it's working." Vanar took a breath.

Atan nodded his approval.

"Then, early this fall all of them will come to Cordan and meet and discuss what they've seen. Falor and his people as well. Then you can listen and guide us, teach us what we've missed."

"I would enjoy that." He winced with a flash of pain.

Vanar turned his head.

Atan sipped the lukewarm brew in his cup. "I'm proud of you Vanar. One more thing, with this new house of yours." He finished the tea. "Be sure Mahtso sends a strong security team to protect you there."

"Of course, of course." Vanar indulged his father's concern. "I'll be sure to take care of it. But then we..."

Vanar jumped back as Atan's fist slammed on the table. "Do not make so light of this issue young man."

Vanar swore flame came from his father's mouth with the words.

"To be lax is deadly, it almost killed you once and if that is not enough to remind you, remember you have no advisor because his parents are dead. They too saw little need for protection."

Vanar sat back in his chair and stared.

A shiver went through the castle like chalk on a board. Raphela, sitting with Fatell looked up to see her friend's face drain, but she sat back and smiled. The power of his passion, how it warmed her.

Atan probed hard into his son's eyes, "You, my son, are the tomorrows and your wife carries the most precious of all things, next year and a thousand years from now. "He took a breath and leaned back, somber and solid. "For two decades we have built this world. It is an infant for you to take into childhood. You are to be more than a ruler or a king, you will be responsible for everyone. Much as we like to believe that the world is here to cater to us, without our strength and guidance the world is no better than the anthill, droning day in and day out. We are protected not for ourselves, but for everyone."

Vanar sank down in his seat. This was the lesson he had feared. It stung more than the switch at the stable, but he valued it, that much more. "Thank you father."

Atan saw Vanar's throat gulp on the nothingness that fear generates, but knew the thanks was genuine. Once the necessary silence lost its hold, Atan spoke. "You and Valeria have not had a meal with your mother and me in over a week, it is time."

"I agree, dinner tonight."

Fatell recovered quickly, in time to notice Raphela smile. Her head shook in continuing wonder.

"We have six teams ready to leave, two teachers and four builders per team."

"Supplies?"

"Packed, but we are short on woodsheets." Fatell made notes as she spoke.

"What are you going to do?

"I already have done it. I had Telep contact Falor and he is sending a fresh supply directly to the new schools."

"Well done, as usual Fatell."

They chatted a while longer and then parted for other duties.

Atan stood in the great entry hall. He looked to twenty years before and remembered the castle, well kept, ordered and lifeless. Then came Raphela, and now there were smartly covered white plaster walls. This room remained in stone but not the dreary gray rock as before. Raphela had found someone to run veins of sparkling greenstone to weave around the room. It had taken the workmen two years but there was no place like it on Raalek. One knew that this was an entrance to a new world. Each vein of green beckoned and the black and gold plates inlaid in the walls spilled the power of Ishtba.

As Atan drank in his palace, Raphela drank in Atan. Silvery gray hair crowned him better than any golden band. Though he leaned on the walking stick, she saw no weakness, only strength so deep the roots of the trees hoped to meet it. She was no less drawn to him now than the day he rode by her in Milson so many years ago.

"No man has done more." The warm whisper in his ear brought a smile to his face, as she slipped her arm through his. Their eyes met and lips yearned but the shuffle of castle folk sent them on a slow journey up the stairs. There in the seclusion of family quarters Raphela found a wall cool and smooth. Atan's palms rested above her shoulders and the yearning was filled, a joining of lips and tongues, a simple refresher of what was felt.

Atan slid into the chair at the top of the stairs and nodded for the two men at the bottom to bring him down.

Fatell watched as the thick rope around the pulling mechanism moved with the rhythm of the muscles of the men. She was amazed at how many people had sought out ways to ease her Duke's pain. A student found the design for this chair two years ago and started building it as soon as the Duke became ill. It took a great deal of strain off both the Duke and Raphela.

In the shadows of the upper level, Raphela, seemingly calmer than ever, observed and slid back as her husband arrived safely at his destination.

Sturdy fingers wrapped around the cane, and he took special care that his eyes and face were as steady as his fingers.

This eased Fatell's mind very little as he said his good morning and passed her with slow, determined paces.

Each day Fatell crumbled a little inside. This man had given her reason to rise in the morning, freedom to grow from the time she was a teenager. Fatell was not ashamed to say she worshipped him and loved him. His agony felt as if the world itself were disintegrating.

The world should have been his servant now, but he never asked and Raphela demanded no one change their lives. He was a man, his needs accommodated and no more. Yet she rarely left his side and arranged all the accommodations herself. There would be no early mourning, no waiting for death. Life was not so quick to make room for a partner.

Atan walked on to the training room, but not to exercise, to teach. Young men milled around the room, trying each other's strength and skill. Atan's entrance needed no announcement. As soon as he sat they were by his side.

These men, Vanar's age more or less, hailed from Calcoran and Ishtban. Word had been sent, through mindseers and eventually more conventional methods, that Defenders were needed, those willing to risk their lives to protect the citizens of Raalek. The word 'army' was not mentioned, but those capable of using a sword were especially welcome. Many arrived and many turned away. These men had walked through a long road of tests to be in this room and the physical part of their training had yet to begin.

Atan's grey eyes studied the group of fresh faces and began telling them why they were chosen and what lay ahead. Every word was gospel. They hung on each syllable as if the sky would fall if missed. What honor they had achieved, not spoken by Atan, or anyone else, just amongst those who tried. To be sitting so close to him, to the man who made this world. Close enough to touch, though none would dare. They saw no infirmity, only legend, the deep voice ever powerful-- Lord Duke Atan Ishtba, ruler of all they knew.

And, secretly each wished to look in his eyes, to be able to withstand the briefest of glances. Atan completed his lesson of defense. Now he waited for questions. One hand raised warily, Atan nodded.

A short stocky boy rose, hair cropped close to his head, the same as his comrades. "My lord, do you truly believe that peacefulness and defense is the way?" The boy tried to look in his Duke's eyes but failed, yet he did question the man and this gained respect among his friends.

Atan sipped his special brew of tea, breathing in its soothing scent. Mahtso hung by, the mother hen, chain sliding through his fingers as Atan stretched his back muscles and wiggled in the chair.

"What way should we follow? One of aggression?"

"Was is not your way my lord?"

"It was another time, the world was a different place."

"But there is so much beyond our realms. Can't we conquer again and spread Ishtba even further?" The young man spoke with the passion of youth.

"I suppose we could, yet there is a cost to everything we do." Atan hoped he would jump at this, he did.

"I don't understand."

"Mmm. "You, " He pointed to a boy at the back of group. "Get the pail of stones in the corner. Now, you, what is your name?"

The pink fresh skin turned white and his eyes took on a veil of fear. "Melot my lord."

"Do you think I am angry?"

"I, I, I don't know sire."

"Youth. I am not angry. I am here to teach. Hold out your hands."

Melot trembled as the top of his hands were placed in front of Atan, expecting a lesson of pain, for what, he wasn't sure, but he must have done something.

"Turn your hands upwards.'

"Yes my lord."

The pail of stones sat by Atan. His hand rumbled around inside it, the noise of rock against rock the only sound in the large room, it echoed ominously. Finally his hand emerged from the pail, capturing a large handful of the gray rocks. He placed four on Melot's palms. "Tell me Melot, is that difficult to hold?"

Melot, whose eyes had been closed, looked down. "No my lord."

"Very well." He added a few more. "And now?'

Melot closed his fingers around the rocks that filled his palms. "No my lord."

Atan slowly added more and more stones. After a while Melot's fingers stretched just to keep the rocks balanced, closing his fingers was not an option. Soon after that the stones began to drop off one or two at a time. Finally, Melot's hands so overflowed that all the stones fell to the ground except three of the four originals.

"Men, can anyone see why it is no longer time to conquer?" Atan sat back, doing his best to hide exhaustion. Mahtso breathed unevenly as his chain made deep impressions in his hand.

Faces turned to each other and the walls and floor. A long hand reached up, Atan nodded. "Your name?"

"Solomon, my lord."

"Do you have an answer?"

I believe so my lord." Bushy red hair and deep green eyes, content to look in the Duke's direction but not so anxious to meet the glance, seemed incongruous with the confident voice.

"Speak then."

"It seems sire, that if one conquers too much, one can lose it all." All heads turned from Solomon to Atan, who rewarded Solomon with a smile

"Well said. For those of you, and by your questioning glances, there are many, I will explain further. As Melot's hands filled with stones, he first could not protect the newest as his reach could not extend any further. Without a large enough base, developed and totally self-sufficient, Ishtba cannot hope to reach out and hold onto more, lest the new lands go unprotected and that is not acceptable. And if more lands were to be gained and they were not only unprotected but also beyond our control, they would fall as the stones fell from Melot's hands and eventually bring down everything. No, it is time to grow and make strong the base, plant good roots."

"My lord." Solomon, still standing, spoke again.

"Yes?"

"If we are not to conquer, are we, what the ancients called 'Policemen?' Curiosity and the need to know were strong in this boy.

"You are well read. Does anyone else know what a policeman is?"

Heads shook in denial.

Atan sipped his tea and coughed. Mahtso bit his lip but didn't move. "A police man is one who enforces the rules and brings to the elders those who break the rules. To answer your question, I hope you will not need to be policemen, although sadly in the future they will probably be necessary."

"My lord, why?"

"Why will they be necessary?"

"Yes my lord."

"Solomon, I think you already know the answer. Try."

Solomon took a moment to consider, ignoring the hush. "Policemen are needed because people are breaking the rules too often."

"That is a good answer. Why would people do that?"

"Too many rules." The response was a loud whisper from the corner.

"Stand up, whoever said that."

A frightened young man, shook as he stood, "I'm sorry my lord, please forgive me."

Atan sighed, fear was a sad thing. "Don't apologize for thinking, just work with the system. You are somewhat correct. Too many rules and some will be broken. Remember that as you grow up, don't make it too difficult or you will spend your lives looking for people breaking some foolish law that no one believes in anyway. What other reason?"

"There is no reason to follow them, no punishment for the crime." Solomon rejoined the conversation.

"Excellent. There are few rules-- do not steal, do not kill, do not abuse anything living and don't destroy for the sake of destruction. To break any of these laws brings swift and fierce reprisal. True?"

Each man looked to the ground; enough tales had been told, though few had personal experience. One young man remembered the shrill cries of woman whose husband lay limp in the town square. He had brutally murdered a merchant, swearing he had been cheated. The merchant, not wrongfully accused, suffered a punishment worse than his crime. The Duke declared that murder of this sort was unacceptable and had the man slain, quickly and publicly. It was a lesson no one forgot.

"Once reprisal is gone, the fear of breaking the laws is gone. Most people need no laws, common sense dictates right and wrong. But for some, who straddle the line on following the right path, they need the laws and the punishment. So, for now, being a policeman is not your task. To protect the towns and fiefs from nomads and wild wanderers and predatory beasts, that is your job. Should some army arrive to challenge us, then you will become soldiers."

Atan sank back in the chair and Mahtso directed everyone to the trainer. "It is past time for you to begin your exercise." The bald muscular man smiled at Mahtso and immediately began a regimen of bending and twisting, demanding the young men join him. They were immediately on their feet and in tune.

Atan signaled to Mahtso. "Bring Solomon to me."

Solomon stood by his Duke, looking clumsy and awkward.

"Why did you ask for this job?"

"I don't know. It simply felt like the right thing to do."

"I see. Did you meet Vanar before he left for the Marketplace?'

"No."

"You may return to your exercise."

"Yes my lord."

Atan and Mahtso left. "When Solomon is done with this basic training I think he should stay on and become Vanar's advisor."

"I agree, he is much like Falor."

Both men knew the need for that type of balance

"Get Telep for me so that I can discuss it with Vanar."

Mahtso left Atan in his downstairs office and did as bade.

"I know you are a busy woman, I hate to bother you with such minor problems. But to me, you see, it is not so minor. I hope you understand, I really need another set of chairs. It is so rude to keep customers standing. You do understand." The little man maintained respect for Valeria, while trying not to whine.

Valeria smiled as politely as she could. "Of course, I will speak to the craftsmen. I'm sure we can do something."

"Thank you, thank you." He bowed and backed away.

Valeria continued her stroll through the building.

"I have told you over and over, we cannot do that. It is against the rules." A shrill- voiced woman dressed in a colorful blend of cloth loosely bound around her body shook a finger at a man weary of her voice. "There is Valeria, we should ask her."

Before his lips could part the woman was upon Valeria. "Baal Valeria, " she curtsied, "Please settle this question for us."

The man pleaded in silence.

"Are korobs permitted inside the building?"

Valeria closed her eyes and rubbed her stomach, avoiding the overwhelming blend of odors surrounding her. "It is preferred that all animals, excepts pets, such as zorels, are left outside."

"There, you see I told you," she droned on.

"Yes dear." He nodded to Valeria, grateful for the somewhat ambiguous answer.

Valeria shrugged her shoulders in sympathy.

A few more requests were dropped on her shoulders as she made her way to the entrance, Gondor, her bodyguard, close by her side. Once outside she took a deep breath of the fresh air, it held only the faintest hint of what lay inside the walls.

For a short while peace reigned. Then she felt a tap on her shoulder. A face painted with exasperation turned, and then changed to joy. "Lehcar, I thought you'd never get here." They shared a sisterly hug.

"I had to wait for my replacement. Let me look at you." Her hands stretched out to Valeria's, which took them gladly. "Growing well I see."

"Yes."

"I noticed the mass of people hanging about you. Where is Vanar?"

"He had to visit a fief." Valeria sank into a nearby chair. "It seems that the crops had a problem and someone besides the newly created Visitors were needed to solve it."

"So you are left here to manage the marketplace."

"Yes I..."

She was interrupted by the panting of a boy, chosen to run errands and messages. "Baal, there, there..."

616

He was stopped by a well-dressed man. "You take too long boy, I can deliver the complaint myself." He shoved the boy out of the way.

Valeria took a deep silent breath and waited.

In the type of demeaning tone that the family Ishtba had never permitted he continued. "Who is in charge?" He turned to Gondor, who came within a finger's reach of the man and nodded towards Valeria. The man moaned under his breath, "A woman. If that is what I must deal with." His polished speech could not cover his irritating voice. "My ramek is ill and your stableman, obviously an incompetent oaf refuses to aid me in restoring her to health. I demand assistance, now." His nostrils flared.

Valeria stood and looked the man almost straight in the eye. She remembered Raphela's lesson of dealing with this sort person. She met his stare, unblinkingly and with a calm beyond her years. She spoke not to him immediately, but to the errand boy. "Nola, ask the stablemaster to come here, please."

The boy, feeling vindicated by Valeria's respect, walked with pride past the man.

"I told you..."

"I know what you said. I will hear what my stablemaster has to say before I do anything."

The man paced until the stablemaster arrived, sweaty and trying to straighten his work clothes before presenting himself to Valeria.

He bowed and waited for her to speak. The stranger began. "Ah, here at last. I tell you..."

Valeria raised her hand for silence and turned to the stablemaster. "Is this man's ramek ill?"

"Yes Baal, but..."

"One answer at a time. Have you refused to help him?"

"Yes, but"

"Why?"

"Baal, his ramek is in such poor condition. She is in desperate need of rest and water and food. He wishes me to patch the bruised spots on her back and allow him to leave." The stablemaster's genuine concern for the beast touched Valeria and the stranger became defensive.

"It is not his concern. His task is to do what I ask, nothing more."

Valeria turned on the stranger. "I do not know where you come from, but now you are under the auspices of Duke Atan Ishtba and he has rules which we follow. One of the most important is the care of living beings, person or animal. The stablemaster is doing his Duke's bidding and is under no obligation to you for anything. It is a courtesy we offer to care for truly ailing beasts. As of now I will not release the beast to you and the stablemaster will take the necessary steps to bring it back to good health."

"This is ridiculous, there must be a man I can speak to."

Gondor moved closer and the stranger backed away from Valeria.

"When my husband returns you may speak with him, until then, my word is final." Neither voice nor eyes wavered.

"Aaah." He threw his hands up in disgust and went inside the marketplace.

Lehcar stared at her sister in amazement, "You handled that so well."

"Thank you."

The stablemaster and errand boy slipped away.

"I think I'd like to go to my room for a while."

Lehcar took her sister's arm and walked her back to the room, shooing away any annoyances. Gondor's silent presence assured the privacy.

Once behind closed doors Valeria flopped onto the bed, leaning back into the wall and pulling up her knees as close as the baby allowed. Lehcar sent Gondor to retrieve some hot water for tea, the herbs were in her bag.

Neither woman spoke, Valeria rested her forehead on her knees and as she lifted it the red tear filled-eyes brought Lehcar to tears as well.

"This is so hard Lehcar, I hate it sometimes." Valeria wiped away tears as new ones fell. "How does Lady Raphela do it? She handles so much. I will never be able to take her place. Vanar will hate me. This is awful."

Lehcar allowed Valeria to spill out the feelings. No answers were really expected, just a sympathetic ear.

"Every day is like this. This one is short a supply, those two can't agree on a price, it never ends." She put her head back towards the wall, long blond hair cascading behind her.

"How long has Vanar been gone?" She placed the hot teacup in Valeria's hand and forced her to drink.

"Three days. When he's here its easier. He handles a lot of the problems, but there is so much."

"When will he be back?'

"Tomorrow. Chana got that message from Telep."

"Good. It's getting late, the sun has almost set. You will have dinner in your room and then sleep."

"Oh no, I still must take care of the marketplace. What if..."

"I assure you the marketplace will survive without your in-depth attention for one evening." She sounded a great deal like Norana at that instant.

"But..."

No buts. If there is a major emergency I will notify you, I promise."

Valeria slid down on the bed and smiled. "Thank you."

Before long she was asleep and didn't even wake up for dinner.

"You did well Telep. I think we solved their problem." Vanar patted the mindseer on the back.

"It gets easier each time we reach out."

Bertram walked along side Vanar and Telep, a little tired and glad to be back at this temporary home.

"If you don't mind, I'm going to my room." Telep yawned.

"Of course, even you look weary Bertram. I think you're getting old," Vanar teased his long-time friend.

"Just weary of your chatter," he shot back, grinning widely.

Vanar now halfway through the marketplace looked up and saw Valeria's arm wrap around his neck. "I'm so glad you're back." She said his arms around her waist like a coat in a storm.

After kiss long enough to bring a bit of blush to Lehcar and Gondor's cheeks Vanar looked in her eyes and saw a great deal. "Bertram, you and Gondor need some rest, I think we can take care of each other."

"It's about time. Come Gondor, I hear there's a tavern at the west end that serves the sweetest of ales."

"I'm ready."

Both men disappeared down the halfway.

Vanar and Lehcar shared a hug. "It's good to see you again. Maybe Valeria will heed your advice. She certainly doesn't listen to me."

"My first advice is that the two of you spend a quiet evening together."

"I won't argue with that," Valeria squeaked.

"Good. I'll see you later."

Lehcar strolled the quiet halls of the market place. Once the sun faded, people usually slipped away to their rooms with family. She realized she hadn't eaten all day and searched for a good meal, or at least a filling one. Most shops were closing their doors, except the one or two open for mature entertainment. Lehcar walked on and caught sight of a small place, just three empty tables and a young man staring distantly at the wall. More than her eyes, her nose drew her to a unique aroma, emanating from that very place. After standing for a moment unnoticed she sat and peered over at the man.

Finally, he turned saw and nearly fell from his perch on a high stool.

"I am so sorry, I didn't see you."

"That's all right. I noticed the most wonderful smell."

"You did?" His surprise almost made her giggle.

"Yes, is it the food?" Lehcar's smile lightened the room.

"Oh, yes. It's my special recipe. Would you like some?"

"I would love something to eat."

The young man dashed away, returning quickly with a plate, utensils and a thin vase with a golden flower. Lehcar sat back and watched as he disappeared into the kitchen and reappeared carrying a steaming plate of something. It sat before her, tiny brown grains sprinkled with a myriad of vegetables and iced with a most remarkable blue sauce. It smelled perfect. The young man stood by, obviously waiting for her to eat. She obliged.

"Mm. This is wonderful. I've never had anything like it." The joy on her face made him feel ten feet tall.

He pulled up a chair and sat across from her.

"You really like it?"

"Mm, hmm," was all she could say with a mouthful of the grain.

"I'm so glad. By the way my name is Anton."

Lehcar sipped some water before responding. "Lehcar. It's nice to meet you"

"I haven't seen you here before."

"I just arrived yesterday."

"Really."

In this instant their eyes met and their courtship began.

"Yes, I'm here, visiting my sister." Lehcar spoke slowly, hypnotized by the deep blue eyes, peering into her.

"Your sister?" He could barely form the thought to speak the words.

"Valeria, my sister."

"Valeria?"

Neither spoke for a while, they just stared, amazed that after years of searching a soulmate had appeared so simply.

Finally Anton broke the silence. "Vanar's wife Valeria?"

She nodded.

"You're a healer."

"Yes I am."

"You are very good at it."

"But I haven't done anything."

"Yes you have." He squeezed her hand. "If you're done, we could take a walk."

"That sounds so nice."

"Good."

Together they closed his shop and walked and talked and wallowed in the new found wholeness.

The smooth skin over his sculptured arms sent a pleasant shiver through Valeria as Vanar removed the sweaty clothes of the day. Despite his half-hearted argument, Valeria insisted on

621

providing a hot sponge bath. Both relaxed as the water dripped down his back and as it cooled Vanar pulled her palm to his lips. "Thank you."

He wrapped himself in a warm robe and began to massage her shoulders. His fingers kneaded muscles as tight as any fist. "Tell me about the last few days."

Under his strong fingers and gentle voice Valeria's words came slowly, like cold honey and then spattered like hot wine. Finally she cried in the comfort of his arms.

"I'm so sorry Valeria, I'll never leave again. I promise."

Valeria lifted her head, revealing red eyes and blotchy cheeks. She sniffled. "No, that would be wrong. This was hard." She sat up and clasped his hands in the flickering torchlight. "I have to learn. I never knew you did so much."

"I've grown up knowing I would, training to do all this, you haven't, it's too much to ask."

"It wasn't too much to ask of your mother."

Vanar slumped back. "What do I do? Here you are sobbing in my arms and suddenly you're demanding the right to visit the reasons that made you cry all over again. I don't understand."

"I'm sorry for not being strong enough, but I'll get better. Lehcar will be here to help." Valeria's guilt battled on even ground with Vanar's

He pulled her close and held her in silence. "Whatever pleases you my love, that is what I shall do. Yes that is what I shall do."

Moonlight laid them to sleep, blissful, restful sleep.

Cora's lips felt the soft pink stick glide over them one last time. Finally satisfied, she plopped her make-up into its bag.

One last check of clothes and she nestled the make up bag into the suitcase and peeked out the bedroom door. With the hallway clear, she lifted the large bag and walked towards the stairs. She managed but a few paces and found the way blocked by a guard who stared at her from under a shaggy blond mop of hair.

He stood not much taller than Falor but could still look down at her and did, with a stern grin. "You know that Falor doesn't approve of that," he taunted.

Cora dropped the suitcase and sighed. "I am quite capable of carrying my own bag."

"And a lot more, but that is why *we* are here." He lifted the bag and continued towards the front door.

Cora shook her head, she hated people waiting on her but now she could take care of Jivad. The morning light hadn't disturbed his sleep and even diaper changing brought little more than a wave of the hands.

Again she began the trek toward the stairs, Jivad in contented sleep on her shoulder.

"There you are." Falor extended his arms and Cora reluctantly handed Jivad over to him, though as they walked she was grateful not to have the ever-growing weight in her arms.

The carriage door opened as the castle door closed and soon they were on their way to the Marketplace.

Though it looked as it had two years before, both Cora and Falor could feel the difference, even before they walked through the doorway. Scents wound their way to the entrance and the bouquet of sound caught Jivad like a magnet. Despite Falor's attempts to keep the baby settled in his stroller, Jivad did his best to stand and look around. Finally Falor picked him up and to Jivad's delight rested him on his shoulders.

Cora looked around and finally, spotted a swatch of blond hair and then the green eyes to go with it. "Falor, that way."

The two couples met in the middle of a busy hallway and found a quiet corner. Hugs were exchanged all around and Jivad studied the new folks, especially when placed in Vanar's trust. The baby looked at the new face for a moment, unsure and then quickly decided that, yes, this was a good spot.

"Look at how big you've grown." Valeria shook a strong little hand.

"Look at how big you have grown." Cora rubbed Valeria's round belly.

"Did you think we'd let you have all the fun." Valeria teased back.

"Let's take them to their room." Vanar, upon Jivad's demand, carried him on his shoulders.

After Falor and his family were settled in, they strolled through the marketplace taking in the new sights.

."It's amazing, it really happened." Falor counted each full shop.

Cora pushed Jivad in his stroller, nodding to strangers, soaking in the fulfillment of her husband's plans. After a while the baby was returned to his room for a nap.

Vanar and Valeria waited for Cora to return.

"Would you like to see the house?" Vanar walked beside Falor while the girls followed.

"Is it done?"

Valeria piped up joyfully, "Almost, you've got to see it."

The two couples walked a little beyond the Marketplace and came upon a house larger than most but not so large as a castle.

Walking through the unfinished structure one could taste Ishtba even without a single bed or couch. Walls were being painted in the toasty colors of autumn leaves and the wooden floors seemed alive.

"It's beautiful." Cora looked up at the huge living room ceiling.

"I can't wait to decorate it," Valeria beamed.

"How are you feeling?" Cora asked.

"Good, Lehcar hangs over my every breath."

"I didn't know she was here."

"Yes and I'm glad."

Vanar stepped through what would soon be the master bedroom. "What do you think?"

"The house is great, but the Marketplace is incredible," Falor said. "How did it get so busy?"

Both young men sat down and leaned against a wall right beside a window.

"To be honest, I had very little to do with the success. Kito stopped in last spring and made it his business to tell the world. And, of course, Mowatt has written a tale or two." Vanar explained.

"There you are," Valeria accused.

"We were waiting for you." Vanar defended himself as both he and Falor stood up.

"What do you think Cora?" Valeria asked her friend.

"I think they just wanted to sit and talk while we tired ourselves out looking for them."

"I'd forgotten how abusive they can be when they're together." Falor placed a kiss on his wife's cheek.

Cora looked out the window. "How is your father?"

"You know we're planning a vegetable garden, right outside that window." Vanar pointed at a spot.

Cora and Falor shared a concerned glance.

"Vanar, they need you at the Marketplace," cried a young boy who burst into the room, delivering a very important message as far as he was concerned.

"Is someone ill or hurt?" Vanar assumed it was a minor problem, but had learned never to neglect the possibilities.

"No."

"Good. Now take me to the problem." He smiled and waved goodbye.

Valeria stared out at the future vegetable garden and sighed. Cora and Falor stood on each side of her.

"Valeria, how is the Duke?" Falor sounded much like a brother-in-law laden with care and love.

Valeria swallowed hard. "Not good." A little breeze fanned her hair.

"Vanar is not willing to admit that, is he?"

"No." Her long fingers wrapped tightly around the windowsill.

"Valeria, you are needed." Another young boy, a little more shy than the last, guided Valeria away.

Falor and Cora walked slowly back to the Marketplace.

"Falor?"

"Yes."

"How ill is the Duke?" Cora looked straight ahead,

"I don't know exactly, but the mindseer at the castle indicates he worsens daily."

" I feel sorry for Valeria."

"I agree. She is going to have a difficult time with Vanar. He hasn't changed, denying the inevitable."

They squeezed each others hands and walked on.

By dusk the foursome rejoined for dinner, at Anton's, with Anton and Lehcar. Easy conversation circled the table as a large platter was placed at its center.

"Now watch." Anton placed his finger on one edge and the platter spun gently. This simple tool delighted everyone. The platter had seven compartments, one in the center and six around the circumference. Each compartment held its own tempting dish and the center steamed with a vibrant sauce.

Jivad crawled around the large play area by the table. Despite his colorful toys he was far more interested in people. Very soon he shook the walls of his play area and jabbered until Anton lifted him from the enclosure. Wide eyes stared at the stranger and lips began to tremble, but a smile from Mama told him all was well.

Jivad's fingers reached for the whirling platter as he bounced on Anton's knee. With permission, Anton provided a sweet hard stick for Jivad to suck on.

After a time Cora looked around and realized it was dark. "I think we should let Anton and Lehcar clean up, its late."

Valeria agreed. "I 'm getting tired."

Even Jivad yawned, though he fought nodding off to sleep.

"Falor, why don't we head to the tavern. It's at the other end of the Marketplace." Vanar rubbed his friend's shoulder and smiled broadly.

Both wives, standing and ready to go, cast stern glances in their mates' direction.

Boyish grins and pleading eyes returned to them." We won't stay too late, we promise."

"What do you think Cora?" Valeria teased as Cora scooped Jivad up from his play area.

"I don't know."

Lehcar and Anton put dishes away and hid smiles.

Vanar showed a bit more tooth.

"Oh, go ahead, just don't complain in the morning."

Valeria and Cora took a leisurely stroll back to their rooms.

In the shadows of lumpglows and lingering scents of dinner Anton pulled Lehcar close, lips met and their silhouette would have warmed any soul.

In the morning Valeria didn't even try to wake Vanar. Cora was already on her way to breakfast.

"Would you like some company?" Valeria came up behind her in the hallway.

"Absolutely. Especially since neither of my men will wake until noon." Both laughed.

"Somehow I think Vanar and Falor were naughty boys."

"Mmhmm."

One shop opened early, serving tea and biscuits just right for starting the day. The girls chose a small table towards the back.

"We have a new tea today, red berry. Would you like to try it." The woman placed shiny white cups and plates as they sat.

"I think I'll stay with my usual brew." Valeria sighed, new taste hadn't been a good idea during her pregnancy.

"I'll try it." Cora sniffed the air. "It smells good here."

Fresh sweet biscuits and hot tea appeared shortly and the girls were left alone. Few people wandered the halls yet. The sun just peeked through the windows, allowing eyes to adjust to a new day.

"Cora?"

"Mm". Cora finished a biscuit. "What?"

"I need your help." Valeria stared down into her cup.

"Are you all right?" The briefest tinge of panic skirted through her.

Valeria's long fingers wrapped gently around her hand. "I'm fine. It's Vanar."

Cora still studied Valeria, just in case.

Valeria continued. "The Duke has found someone who would most likely be a good advisor, bur Vanar is avoiding the issue. He feels guilty, as if he's betraying Falor."

Cora shook her head. "Men are such fools. Falor moans every day about how he abandoned Vanar. How fortunate he is to have Oolon and poor Vanar, well, you understand."

"They are fools, aren't they?" Valeria sipped her tea. "Perhaps Falor could speak to Vanar, say something. He needs another ear and voice, besides mine."

Cora didn't need to look at Valeria to know the pressure she felt. Oolon was as much a blessing for her as Falor. "I'm sure Falor will know just what to say."

"I hope so."

Raphela tried to ignore the gray strands of hair in her brush and peeked around the corner to see Atan sitting at the edge of the bed. Curly hair, once deep brown now silver, covered his chest, but for all the changes, his eyes possessed the same power as the day they met.

Two boys poured the last buckets of steaming water into the tub and rapped gently on the bedroom door before they scampered off. Despite Raphela's urge to help Atan walk to the tub, she resisted. He managed the short walk fairly well.

She listened for the soft click of the door to open and close, and as it did, she continued dressing. The lightweight dress, sitting close to her form was just right for bathing Atan, loose enough for comfort, tight enough not to get soaked.

She opened the door to the study where the tub was located.

"Atan?" She didn't see his head above the rim of the tub. "Atan!" Her voice rose and then she looked down.

He was sprawled on the floor motionless. Flinging open the outer door, she shouted to anyone who was there. "Get Mahtso and Aharon, NOW!"

The guard at the top of the stairs, raced away.

Raphela knelt down, gently lifting his head. Her heart was beating fast enough to feel it. Atan's skin was cool, but not grey. Raphela looked down, afraid of what could be, afraid that the closed eyes might never open, but she had to know. Taking a deep breath, she lay her ear on his chest and allowed a tiny tear to fall. He still breathed, his heart still beat.

"Atan, oh Atan." Whether or not he felt her fingers caressing his temple, she didn't know, but she would not leave him.

Quick long strides could be heard coming towards the room. Both men were out of breath. Mahtso turned the white color of death at seeing his Duke, Aharon closed his eyes for just a moment.

Raphela looked up at them. "Help me get him to the bed."

Mahtso lifted Atan by himself, cradling him like a baby and placing him ever so carefully on the bed. Atan stirred.

Raphela covered him and made room for Aharon to examine her husband.

"He hit his head. We need something cold to bring the swelling down."

Mahtso stared in fear and then rushed out of the room, ordering some young boy to bring the necessary items.

"I think he'll be fine." Aharon placed the cold pack behind Atan's head.

"Thank you Aharon."

He left and Atan turned to Raphela. "We're alone at last."

"Atan, you're awake!"

"Yes." His eyes focused clearly on her and his tone betrayed his true mood.

"I'm sorry, I should have been there. I took too long to dress."

"It's not your fault."

"But I..."

Atan's fingers wrapped around her wrist. "Raphela, it's not your fault that my arms have become as weak as my legs. All you could have done was avoid the bump on my head."

Raphela swallowed, trying to hold back her tears and caressed his face. His hand held hers close to his cheek, both soaked in the comfort of that simple touch like hot tea on a cold day.

They shared breakfast, and after a time Atan tired and dozed off. Raphela stood by the window and swore the sun was not as bright as before. She busied herself with folding clothes that were already neat and tidy, fidgeting with curtains and doing her best not to suffocate her sleeping husband with attention.

"My lady?" The words were accompanied by a knock at the door.

"Yes?" She opened the door to Logan.

"My lady, there are two men who wish to see you." He was calm and forthright with a business-as-usual tone.

"Not now Logan" She turned to look at Atan who moaned.

"My lady, it is important."

She sighed. "If you insist." She closed the door gently.

Two men were outside the study, she recognized them immediately, Leon and Koon, twins, about ten years younger than herself. She remembered them as children, always wearing different color shirts so people could tell them apart. It was the same today, both had close-cropped sandy hair, dark brown eyes, and different color shirts. But between them sat a chair.

"My lady, we hope this will help the Duke." Bittersweet smiles and devoted eyes met her grateful glance.

The chair had wheels, large enough for the occupant to push or be pushed by someone else.

"The Duke and I are more than grateful for this gift." She caressed the wheel and held back tears.

"My lady," Leon spoke.

"Yes."

"There is another chair, just like this to be used downstairs."

"Thank you." She turned away, no longer able to control the emotion welling inside her.

Logan escorted the men, overwhelmed by her gratitude, back to their workshop and then returned to his Lady, sitting in the Duke's outer room. He knelt by her. "Will you be all right?"

Raphela wiped her nose and eyes with the white cloth in her hand. "I never realized how much everyone cares for him."

Logan looked to her with silent acknowledgment and then rose to go.

"Logan?"

"Yes my lady."

"How did they know? How did you know? And the chairs?"

"Aharon told them. He knew of the chairs. They have been building them for sometime."

"And you?"

He smiled. "I am never far from you my lady." And with that he left.

Raphela pushed the chair beside the bed and waited for Atan to open his eyes. It was early afternoon when he did.

"Raphela?"

"I'm right here."

"So you are." Soft grey eyes smiled.

"There is a gift for you." She pushed the chair by his hand.

"What is this?"

"It's a wheel chair so that you are not tied to the bed."

"Who?" He wondered at this gift.

"Leon and Koon. There is a second one for use downstairs."

"Help me." The words were curt and hard, but she knew they were even harder to say.

She dressed him and with her aid he sat in the chair.

"Perhaps I have been right," he muttered.

"What are you talking about?"

"Nothing, just a little introspection."

Raphela didn't push, it wasn't important. He was alive and semimobile. Though life pressed on, no one could miss the grey shadow that moved about, never really settling anywhere, yet never out of reach.

Raphela never left Atan's side, dressing and bathing him each morning. Each night removing his clothes and preparing him for bed. Once he was safely tucked in, she climbed onto her side and rolled away so he wouldn't see the tears.

On this night Atan pushed out his hand to touch her, but she was just beyond reach. He sighed and stared at the stars and the moons in the black night sky.

"I don't blame you," he barely whispered.

But Raphela rarely slept anymore and heard his every breath. "For what?"

"For staying so far. It must be hard for you."

"For me? I don't understand." She sat up and met his eyes as she always had.

"For you not to have the powerful man you once did."

Raphela lowered her head and her tears and breath moved in harmonious spurts.

"Have I lost you? Am I no longer important to you?"

Atan forced himself to sit, groaning as he did and then grabbed hold of her hair, wrapping it around his hand, forcing her to come close.

"You are my life, for eternity you will be, but it is you who seems to have lost interest, now that I..."

Raphela put two fingers to his lips. "I am a fool. Every night I ache, longing just to be in your arms." She held his hand between her own and kissed it. "But I am so afraid you will feel as if you are depriving me, so I thought it better to stay away."

Atan pulled her down. Passion poured from his lips, Raphela encased him, savoring each moment, warming him with her touch. They lay close that night, her head resting on his chest. Both slept until dawn, safe and secure from reality.

Falor and Cora spent a week at the Marketplace. The last day was full of good-byes and see-you-soons."

Vanar and Valeria waved goodbye as the carriage pulled away.

"It was wonderful to see them again." Valeria rubbed her belly, which seemed to be moving on its own.

Vanar stopped walking and bent down to be close to it. "You've been very busy today. I think you're making mama very tired, why don't you take a nap." He whispered the words and stroked the little foot that kicked out.

"He can't hear you." Valeria said, embarrassed at Vanar's actions.

"How do you know that? Maybe he can." Vanar bent down once more. "She just doesn't understand." He smiled and they walked on.

"Jivad has gotten so big."

"Yes he has." Vanar nodded to a shopkeeper. "I've sent for Solomon, I'd like to get to know him."

"I'm glad." Valeria smiled more inside than out.

"I know and I'm grateful. I couldn't do this without you." He looked straight ahead, but squeezed her hand.

On the way to Cordan Falor met Solomon. They spoke and Falor shared some insight about his friend. They didn't spend much time, long enough for a meal, long enough for both to feel content.

632

Falor's carriage moved on. "He's a good man. He'll serve Vanar well." The tinge of jealousy had its hour and left. Cora ignored it, it was best that way.

Cordan, as always was a welcome sight. They arrived at night and fully enjoyed the comfort of a real bed. The next day they roamed the castle, Rabi doted on Jivad as Fatell had Vanar.

In the evening Falor and his family joined the Duke and Lady in the upstairs family room. It was warmer than usual. Falor noticed warming stones in various spots and the torches were quite bright.

Jivad raced to Atan, crawling up onto the chair and standing in the seat. Raphela stayed and signaled for Falor and Cora to sit. Jivad giggled and looked into the eyes of the great Duke Ishtba whose face brightened as the baby demanded his attention. Jivad then plopped down on Atan's lap and proceeded to jabber in some incoherent yet fully understood language explaining toes and fingers and all sorts of things. Soon both tired and nodded off to sleep.

Cora put Jivad in a crib and Raphela covered Atan with his blanket.

The young couple did not know what to say or do. Raphela had become accustomed to the uncomfortable silence with so many people and learned how to break it.

"How is Vanar?" She asked

"Well, very well. The Marketplace is amazing, so many shops and customers."

"That's wonderful, and Valeria?"

Cora answered this one. "Also well. Lehcar keeps a close eye one her."

"Good."

The silence crept in again, but Cora stopped it. "Lehcar is engaged."

"I didn't know that."

"Yes, he's very nice."

"What's his name?"

"Anton."

All three worked at the conversation for a while, but when the silence finally pushed its nose in, it stayed and all retired to their rooms.

The next morning Raphela opened the shutters to sunlight and Atan squinted.

"Are you ready?" She sat by him, hands caressing his arms.

"For you, always."

She pulled him up and took advantage of a hug.

"I look forward to our grandchild." Atan forced his hand through the sleeve of his shirt.

Raphela struggled with his pants and said nothing.

"It will be a joy to hold," He continued.

Raphela buttoned his pants and rebuttoned his shirt.

"Aren't you excited Raphela?" He asked.

"No" Her answer bordered anger.

"What's wrong with you?'

"You will not see any grandchild."

For all his weakness, the back of his hand still hurt as it struck her face. "How dare you deny me that thought."

"It's the truth." She spat it out.

The wind rustled the curtains.

"Are you a God now, that you know I will not see my own grandchild?" He demanded an answer.

Raphela's long buried frustration, fear and anger about her bargain burst forth.

She pulled the dusty whip from its spot on the wall and threw it at him. "Since you are in a striking mood, listen on. I made a bargain, three years ago, with the Gods, so yes, I know." She lowered her gown, baring her back.

He sat back stunned and curious. "What kind of bargain" His deep voice threatened and cut as his fingers grasped the handle of the whip.

She lowered her head, the venom gone, only the pain was left. "To keep you alive, long enough to see your son wed and know another heir to Ishtba was to come."

Atan's eyes scrutinized the air. "And at what price?"

Raphela shivered inside. "Within a month of your death I told them, they could have me."

634

The whip didn't draw blood and the sound echoed only in the ears of Atan and Raphela. It was only one stroke and she enjoyed it, feeling it well deserved for some reason.

"Get out of here." He croaked the command.

She raised her robe over her shoulder, stood, and walked towards the door.

"Raphela," he whispered.

She stopped but didn't turn.

"Come here."

Raphela sat by his side, eyes overflowing with anguish. His hand caressed her cheek and lifted her chin. "For three years you've held this secret?"

She nodded and buried her head in his chest, sobbing. Atan stroked her hair.

"You are mine, forever, forever."

Falor and Cora spoke with Aharon and learned the full gravity of Atan's condition.

Falor sent a message to Telep for Vanar and Valeria to return soon. If not for the need of Calcoran to have Falor, he would have stayed until Vanar arrived. But his own duty called and he and his family returned home.

Solomon had barely settled in when Telep knocked on his door.

"I understand you're to be Vanar's advisor."

"I hope so." Solomon folded a shirt and placed it in a dresser. "Where is Vanar, I haven't met him yet."

"About this time of day the shop keepers are offering a variety of suggestions and complaints," Telep chuckled.

As Telep said Vanar and Valeria were surrounded. It was not an angry mob, just people who wanted answers. The voices were friendly, just not clear, more like a choir out of tune. Some woman shoved a bag in Valeria's hands. "Its good for the baby.

A polite smile and nod was enough and the woman left. "Vanar, will the harvests be brought here this year?" another voice asked.

"I haven't decided that as yet."

"But when?" a voice in the background popped up.

"Later. At this moment I have had enough questions for today." He stood and took Valeria's hand.

Amid a few grumbles the crowd dispersed.

"But Vanar, when will you decide?"

"I already said." His exasperation was blatant.

"I heard." Solomon offered a wry smile.

The unmistakable red bushy hair was all Vanar needed. "You must be Solomon."

"At your service," he bowed.

Valeria held out her hand "How do you do, I'm Valeria."

Solomon bowed again. "I'm honored to meet you."

Valeria learned a lot from a handshake, a gift Vanar was learning to appreciate. A brief glance told him what he needed to know. They both agreed he would do well.

It was but a few days later when Telep received the message.

"Vanar, I must talk to you." Telep interrupted a discussion between Vanar, Bertram and Solomon. Valeria was at Telep's heels.

"What is it?" Vanar stood, towering over the boy.

"You must go home, back to Castle Cordan." Telep was not prone to panic, his words and tone were carefully chosen.

"Why?" The question was unnecessary and received no answer. "We'll leave in a few days." He turned away.

"We should leave tomorrow." Valeria's hand rested on her husband's shoulder. He brushed it off.

"She's right." Solomon added quietly, yet firmly.

Feet shuffled and those not directly connected with this scene felt bristles rise and gave space. Vanar looked around and saw no support. "Then you all turn your backs on me!" It was not quite a shout, yet the power that made most cower at his father, sent the few lingering souls on their way.

Valeria's green eyes opened like a snake's jaw. "How dare you!" The slap echoed in his ears and down the hallway. "These are your friends. I'm leaving tomorrow."

Her blond hair swayed as she walked away. The men stood in shock and then faded from the table, leaving Vanar very alone.

With focused determination Valeria folded her clothes and packed them in the large suitcase

"Valeria."

"What." She snapped to the tender tone and immediately cursed herself, but didn't turn.

"Please." He stood behind her, yearning to reach out, but held his place. He remembered laying in a bed, aching all over, a foolish midnight ride, his father sat patiently at his side. All the support he needed was in those grey eyes.

Valeria turned. She watched the puzzle of emotion whirl inside him, praying to put the pieces in place, praying for a hand to help. He looked down and into the net of strength and guidance.

Vanar's "thank you" was lost in his kiss, one that took them away from the world, her face wrapped by the hands that tingled her skin. This plane, one step closer to what they must be, for love would not be enough.

Raalek's sky changed as Cordan rose on the horizon, looking much like a faded frayed robe, long past repair or revival, even by the best seamstress.

Valeria reached out to Vanar. "I love you."

She didn't expect an answer, nor did she receive one. His hand around hers would have to do.

Patar announced their arrival before they rode up the hill.

Mahtso opened the door and greeted both with a big hug. "It's good to have you back."

Fatell took Valeria's hand. "How are you?"

"A little tired." Valeria's eyes betrayed the wear of the trip.

Vanar's arm wrapped around her and his lips pressed gently on her head. "Fatell, she needs a good bed to sleep in."

Vanar watched Valeria walk towards the room and noticed the inordinate number of people around the castle for this time of year. "Where are they?" He still surveyed the room and didn't turn to Mahtso until Valeria closed the door behind her.

"Your mother took him outside for a while." Mahtso's fear and pain beat him with his chain in hard and steady beats. He looked to Vanar like a child seeking answers.

637

Whether he drew on Cordan's strength or actually had his own, Vanar wasn't sure, but he rubbed Mahtso's shoulder as he spoke. "Thank you Mahtso, thank you for everything." It was not the Duke, but close enough to lighten the beat of the chain.

Vanar didn't need to ask where outside, he knew. They were at the crest of the hill.

Atan turned his face to the bright warm sun as Raphela rubbed his shoulders, passing through him the strength to clasp her hand and feel the life within her.

"A beautiful sight on a beautiful day, isn't it?"

Raphela smiled, not enough for a grin, enough for contentment and turned the chair around.

"Vanar, it's good to see you."

Inside Vanar trembled to see his father's form, skin hanging on muscles withered by disease, but the voice hadn't changed and his face was still strong, especially the powerful grey eyes and there Vanar rested. "Its good to be home."

"Where is Valeria?" Atan moved his head to look around his son.

"Resting."

"That's good."

They chatted a while and when a light breeze tickled the trees, Raphela turned towards the castle. " I think its time we went inside."

Atan shivered under his clothes and nodded agreement.

"Mother, you should walk next to father, I can push. You've never been good at following."

She didn't argue or answer, but gracefully took her place beside her husband whom had nodded off to sleep.

During the quiet walk back Vanar saw how the grey more than sprinkled her hair and the way her pace was slow even without pushing the chair."

He carried Atan up the stairs and gently laid him in the bed. Raphela sat in a chair, caressing his hand.

"Mother, I'll stay with him. Go have some tea, sit by the fire, relax." Vanar covered Atan.

"Vanar, you of all people should know better." She redid the covers and brushed a few stray hairs from Atan's face. "I can't leave him, not for a moment." In her voice was exhaustion and yet desire, that need, that bond.

Vanar shook his head. "All right. But can I bring you anything?"

"No, we'll rest."

Vanar left as his mother dozed off.

Later she served him soup. Each spoonful carefully brought to his lips. They ate alone now, always.

After dinner Valeria came to the door, spoke with Raphela and left.

"Atan" Raphela sat on the bed.

"Yes."

"It seems that a show has been prepared in your honor. I know you've been out today, but perhaps?"

Atan's need for seclusion had been compounded by his disability. The fawning of servants had increased and was even more disturbing. But Raphela would not ask on a whim.

"If they wish," he said.

Raphela dressed him while everyone waited.

Mahtso paced with his chain.

Vanar cornered Aharon. "How is my mother? Does she ever leave his side? Does she eat? Does she sleep?"

Aharon sighed and pulled Vanar to a seat, looking around and leaning towards him. "I wish I knew the answer. They live in that room."

"Aharon, she looks terrible."

"I know. But tell me, can you get an answer from her. You're her son."

Vanar buried his head in his hands.

"They're coming." Valeria whispered in his ear.

Smiles painted all faces. Atan and Raphela entered the main hall where a crowd waited and cheered. Every member of the castle was there, man, woman and child. Atan was placed in his chair and Raphela took her place beside him.

Solomon stepped forth. "My lord and lady, we present to you an evening of pleasure."

The youngest children paraded in front of them, carrying pictures, each carefully drawn by tiny hands, to create a scene of the castle and its people, with the most prominent drawings being the Duke and Lady.

Atan stared in wonder. Raphela gasped, totally shocked at the display.

Older children sang songs and told tales of the great Duke. The room smelled of all the flowers and plants the Duke kept in his glass house. Those handy with yarn and needle covered Atan with a thick quilt blazing with the colors of Ishtba.

During these displays he called Fatell to his side. "Fatell, you have done wonderful things here, I am so pleased." He patted her hand. Fatell mumbled a thank you and escaped so that she could burst into tears alone.

As a finale the soldiers put on a show of exercise and mock battle to rival any Atan had ever seen. Mahtso, always by his side nodded approval to the leaders.

"Mahtso?"

Mahtso knelt by his Duke. "You know Ishtba would not be as it is without your help. I and everyone else am grateful, my friend."

"Only by your guidance my lord, only by your guidance."

Mahtso lowered his head and Atan stroked it with the caring that hadn't changed in more than thirty years.

Atan drew everyone's attention. "You have honored me beyond any way I could imagine. May the gods bless you."

Bowed heads hid the tears. Everyone slipped out of the room. Fatell and Mahtso escaped to their privacy and each other.

Vanar and Valeria remained in the vast and silent empty hall.

"Children, come."

Valeria squinted her eyes in confusion.

"Yes, you are my child too."

Chairs were pulled close.

"You must," he wheezed and coughed. Vanar stood, but Raphela's hand brought him back to his seat, "take care of each other and that wonder that grows inside you Valeria. But also remember, you are Ishtba, care for it and the people as you would the child. The reward is tenfold."

For an instant Valeria looked up and shared a glance with Atan. The veil that separated him from the world was lifted and the blinding power rose inside her like the sun breaking the night sky. She reached to Vanar's hand. "We will," they answered in unison.

"So I believe."

Vanar pushed his father back to his room while Valeria and Raphela walked together.

Vanar closed the door to their room. Valeria sat on the bed, still dressed, eyes red, lips trembling. He lay down and pulled her into his arms, tears not hidden, simply shared.

Atan lay in bed and stared at the ceiling. "Raphela."

"Yes my lord." The tender passion in her voice added a spark to a rekindled spirit.

She rolled towards him, eyes full of the power and passion he had pulled from the sky the day he was born. He drew her in and demanded lips and tongue dance and they did as their hearts beat as one. For a while tears in the castle dried and the stars actually twinkled in the sky.

A little after sunrise Raphela rose and opened the shutters. Atan still slept, so she dressed quietly. After brushing her hair, she saw him stir.

It had been weeks since his arms would do their job and raise him up, but his patience was in tune with his power, he could wait for her.

"Would you care to join me for tea?" It was a small game they played, to ease the pain.

"Only if you pour." He smiled.

Raphela fluffed the pillows and he sat. They shared a cup of tea and she began to read out loud some of the notes from the evening before.

Fingers rustled her gown, a touch to stop anything. "Raphela."

She scooted onto the bed and leaned close to the warm voice. "Raphela", his eyes had her chained to him. "I love you."

Through tears she whispered, "And I love you."

The world stopped. The birds didn't fly and the wind was at bay. No living thing took a breath and it is said the sun turned black at that instant for those were the last words Duke Atan Ishtba would speak and hear.

Raphela lay on his chest, crying in silence and shock, all the foreknowledge still had not prepared her for this moment.

After a time Vanar came in, with, Mahtso. They were both calm, knowing this would not be an easy task.

"Mother, its over. You must stop. Go rest in your room.

Raphela clutched onto Atan's lifeless form. "No, no, I can never leave him."

Never had anyone seen desperation in Lady Raphela, never panic, never fear until now and it frightened everyone.

"Mother, you will always be with him, but for now, go rest in your room."

"No, no I can't."

"Raphela, just for a while. He won't be taken anywhere, I promise." Mahtso took one arm and Vanar the other. Both guided her to her room where Fatell waited to sit with her friend. Logan stood by the door.

Aharon verified what everyone already knew and the fleeting shadow that had circled Cordan spread its wings and covered all Ishtba.

Fatell stayed by Raphela's side all night, dozing and waking as Raphela suffered through a mire of restless sleep. Aharon had sneaked a potion in her tea to induce sleep, for what little it accomplished.

In the morning Fatell crawled into her own bed. Raphela returned to "the" bedroom and Atan was unmoved, as Mahtso promised. She opened the shutters and sat by him, caressing the cold cheek. She didn't sit long. Life was beginning to stir, outside the doors of this room. A gentle kiss was placed on his forehead. As she closed the outer door she nearly bumped into Valeria.

"Raphela, would you like to have breakfast with us?"

It was a quiet walk to the breakfast table. Vanar looked to Valeria whose eyes spoke only confusion. The teapot held a crown of steam and the basket of breads smelled of spice.

Vanar as always filled his plate with breakfast meat and sweet rolls. Valeria broke a roll and dipped it in her tea.

Raphela stared blankly at the pot hanging over the fireplace. "When will Falor and Cora arrive?" Her tone was as emotionless as her eyes.

"Tomorrow." Vanar's gentility surprised even Valeria, but was lost on his mother.

"Who is handling the arrangements?"

Valeria swallowed hard. "Lita."

"As it should be, she is well trained. Your father has a white suit prepared. You may move him whenever you're ready."

Both young people shivered. How does one deal with cool rationality, no, cold logic? They didn't know.

Raphela left and spent that day and next sitting in her room.

There were a few more people than expected, but not a crowd.

When the sky turned dark and a pale moon shone, it began.

Atan was placed on the mound, shrouded in white. The Elders commenced a round of prayers in a moaning tone, chorused by the circle of people whose white arm bands made a pattern of light in the darkness.

Raphela stood nearest the mound, closely guarded by Logan, Mahtso and Fatell. Valeria stood near her side. Vanar stood draped in the same white sash as his mother. At the appropriate moment took long slow steps in the deadly still night up the mound and lit the pyre. Quickly he was between his mother and his wife. Haunting songs died as the fire took life. Flames blazed high, stretching up, lighting the sky.

All around their world, people stood on hilltops and roofs to share in this one last moment of the great Duke Atan Ishtba. Each hoping for one small sight of flickering flame. None were disappointed, for as the flames rose, they multiplied, building upon themselves like a ladder, reaching towards the stars that had hidden for two nights. Now they seemed to reach down with luminous fingers welcoming the flames and what was carried in them. The moon boasted its light offering all a chance to share in the welcome of Duke Atan Ishtba.

Raphela stared at orange and white swirls of hot light and walked towards them, entranced. Slow steps, so slow at first no one noticed, but Logan, always wary, saw and pulled Mahtso and tried to drag her back.

"I must. Don't you see, I must go." She strained even them.

But with Vanar's help, she was turned back. And in Vanar's strong arms she stayed, sobbing wildly at times, silently at others, safe in the shield of her son's arms.

Vanar stared at the fire, unsure of anything. Valeria slipped her arm through his and watched as a man she had worshipped since childhood disappeared from her life, forever.

Mahtso and Fatell entwined their fingers and held the fire in their eyes until the flames finally had no more fuel. The flames died after the second moon paid its due and sat like a guardian in the sky.

All retired for the night. Raphela was guided to her room. No one believed "the" room was a place for her to be. She didn't argue and lay in bed, never sure if sleep came, but she didn't leave there until the rest of the castle was well under way.

She did her best to be unobtrusive and walked past most people unnoticed. She knew she would be found, and by the right person. It was simply a matter of time.

As the lunch hour passed, Vanar realized he hadn't seen her and the search began.

Raphela didn't hear, but knew. The guards would comb the grounds. Fatell would have everyone else search the main level, while Vanar, Valeria, Falor and Cora searched upstairs.

Mahtso would come downstairs, only Mahtso, so she waited until the door upstairs shut and the stairs creaked. Raphela smiled as he entered.

Mahtso stopped and leaned on the table, he had to stare.

"I'm so glad you came." Her voice, sensuous and purring, matched her clothes-- what little there were. Tight green cloth wrapped to accentuate the most voluptuous parts of her. But the cloth left little to the imagination, revealing much soft tempting skin and Raphela was even more woman now than ever. She leaned forward, breasts almost tickling his chin. "Do you like it? It evoked from Atan very much what I want from you. Take me, it's what you have always wanted."

Mahtso's chain was still, his heart beat hard enough to feel and his palms grew more moist with each word.

"Raphela, this is wrong."

"Oh Mahtso." It was a purring whine. "Have you not longed for me? Drooled over me?" Raphela pulled a small whip from the table and glided it ever so slowly between her legs. "Have your way with me Mahtso. Tear flesh. I'll be silent, I'll scream, I'll meet your every desire. No woman can handle you as I can."

Mahtso felt himself rise, yearn as she drew on every thing he had buried for a lifetime. Suddenly the whip wrapped around his hand and she stood before him, lips wet, inviting. He pulled at the handle of the whip. His fingers caressed her cheek. His breath grew short as she stepped closer. His fingers curved and held firm around the back of her neck. The whip handle slid to his hand and tauntingly caressed her thigh.

"Yes, yes begin." He looked at her one more time, then pushed her away. Seeing her robe, he threw it at her. "Go away."

"Please," she pleaded and tossed the robe aside. "I beg of you Mahtso." Raphela faced the wall and grabbed the chains. "I am your willing victim, desperate for your attention. Punish me, tear at me, I deserve it." She wailed at him.

He stood firm, breathing heavily, clasping his chain hard enough to draw blood. "Raphela, get dressed." Tears filled his eyes. "I have loved Atan Ishtba all my life and you most of it. If you care for me at all, I beseech you, leave."

She knelt before him. "Mahtso, help me."

He wrapped the robe around her. "Go Raphela, because I will not have control much longer, please go."

By now Logan had decided to investigate the lower level as well and found them.

"Logan, take her, now."

Logan brought his Lady to her feet and took her upstairs.

As the door closed on Mahtso, a howl escaped to chill the bones of Logan and everyone else in Castle Cordan, except Raphela. She heard, felt and saw nothing.

Fatell curled into a ball and closed her mind.

Before Logan brought Raphela beyond the stairwell door, he removed the robe that hung haphazardly over her shoulders. To straighten the robe was intended, but also to be sure that Mahtso had not strayed. Once satisfied Logan announced Raphela's safety and left her again in her room, with a little addition, Fatell as chaperone.

Raphela sat on a chair and stared. Her hair hung flat against her back, gray as the sky, eyes blank as the wall. On occasion she'd spout a few words-- my fault, never again, alone forever. Single words and phrases, not a tear, not a whimper.

At dark she lay in the bed and closed her eyes. Fatell dozed, yet knew her Lady did not truly sleep.

In the morning Valeria escorted Raphela to breakfast. Fatell crawled into her own bed.

Raphela sat obediently, dressed in the palest of yellow gowns, as close to white as possible. Vanar and Valeria did their best to maintain a light conversation.

"How could I?" Raphela broke into the middle of a conversation.

"How could you what?" Vanar prayed for an answer. Valeria held his leg.

Raphela didn't answer.

Both young people sighed and pushed away whatever was left of the meal.

Vanar left the room. Valeria sat passively with a woman who had become a stranger.

Outside Raphela's door Vanar cornered a guard. "Scour the room, remove anything dangerous."

The guard, a good ten years older than Vanar, could not simply obey. "It is Lady Raphela's room. I have no right."

Vanar's voice raised, as did his stature. "I have given you an order. Make that room safe for my mother.

The guard nodded his head. "As you wish, sire." The obedient words carried a less convincing tone. But he did as bid.

Falor caught the interaction, made note and walked on.

Vanar turned to a young errand boy. "Stoke the fire, Lady Raphela keeps complaining of the cold." He barked the order and went downstairs.

Raphela spent the morning in the family room with Valeria and by lunchtime Cora took her post at Raphela's side.

Vanar stormed around the castle, inspecting every nook and cranny. He looked around the entrance hall and saw a shroud beginning to droop. A girl, perhaps fourteen or so passed as he saw it. "You, come here." He grabbed her arms. "Why are the shrouds in such disarray. Can this place not be kept properly."

Wide brown eyes stared in fear, her body shook.

"Answer me!" He growled like a frightened beast.

"Child, get Lita and have her take care of this." The mellow voice belonged to the hands that freed her.

Vanar turned to Solomon. "What?!"

The girl ran.

"Let's take a walk." Solomon's incredible calm somehow left Vanar no choice.

As they walked, Solomon nodded to a guard. Soon they were in a small room, away from everyone and were joined by Falor and Mahtso.

"We need to talk." Solomon closed the door.

"I don't have the time for this." Vanar moved towards the door but was blocked by Solomon.

"Yes, we do." Mahtso sat. His tone, that of mentor, commanded the respect and Vanar sat.

"You have been moving around the castle like an ogre," Solomon began.

"I have taken control."

Mahtso's chain ran between his fingers as he leaned back in the chair.

"Who are all of you to speak this way to me?" Vanar demanded.

"He's right." Falor spoke softly. "And we are your friends."

It was Solomon's turn. " I have been here a short time, but you had the respect of everyone. I see it fading.

Vanar's face contorted in pain.

"Your parents never raised a voice or touched a servant, you know better." Falor's voice rang deep, for he knew.

Vanar sank back into the chair. "I didn't even realize."

"It's all right as long as you do now." Mahtso's blue eyes focused on the young man.

"I do."

"Good, there's another matter at hand. Your mother." Mahtso continued.

Vanar slammed his fist on the table. "I will protect her from herself if I must."

Falor and Solomon sat back, this was not their place.

"Do you really think so." Mahtso leaned forward, the evil inside him wavering in his eyes enough to grab Vanar into silence. "Lady Raphela, your mother, is the most powerful woman Raalek has ever seen. Do you think your father married her just for her lovely face? Yesterday she tortured me. Me! She took me to a place where I almost became all that everyone fears, because it what was she wanted. If not for my love of both your parents I would have gladly answered both our desires." His malevolent tone turned all of them white. "So, do not think, even briefly that you can protect her. No locked door will stop your mother. She is capable of twisting anyone in this castle. If she wishes something, it will be. Don't waste your time." Mahtso sat back, his voice turned soft, eyes now a clear blue. "All you can do is be there for her, it is all any of us can do."

Vanar buried his head in his hands and took a deep breath and looked at the three men whose wisdom kept him from Dahlek's fate. "So, what do I do?"

Falor placed a hand on his friend's shoulder. "For one thing, grieve. I know you too well, stop avoiding it."

Vanar stared into his friend, one who had always known him so well.

"And take care of your wife." Solomon joined in. "She's a good woman, but she's young."

"He's right, Valeria has been at Castle Cordan less than two years. Cora would have an easier time with this state of affairs." Falor's harmony with Solomon pleased Mahtso.

Vanar looked between them and sat back, realizing how he had ignored his wife.

Mahtso spoke as gently as if Fatell were in his arms. "Vanar, she carries your child and Ishtban's future. Losing Atan is hard enough, for she loved him too. But to bear the responsibility of her new life in the shadows and alone is a strain. Pregnant women, often deliver babies far too early when under strain. That can be fatal to mother and child.

"By the Gods, what a mess I've made."

"No you haven't, not yet. Take some time. The castle will run for a few days on its own." Solomon, new as he was, did understand.

"All right. Give me a little time alone."

He had his request and found Valeria trying to organize dinner for some guests. He took her hand and walked with her out the kitchen door.

"Vanar, why?"

"Some good friends gave a kick and put my brain back in my head." He smiled just a bit.

Her hand felt good in his and they walked to the mouth of the cave, just far enough to be out of view.

Despite the dull gray day, the air was still clean and refreshing. The two young people stood face to face, seeing a mirror in each other's eyes. Exhaustion, fear, pain, all a thick coat, clinging but not stuck.

Valeria leaned her head on his chest and their arms wrapped around each other. Slowly the feelings loosened their grip, not leaving, but not ruling either.

Silent words on his tongue "I don't deserve you" never found his lips while her throat couldn't release the "Can I do this, please you?" but for now, that too was all right.

They found a large stone and sat.

Vanar tried to speak and as much as she wanted the words, they would never be right.

"Just hold me." She whispered.

He did and soon so much of the fear and pain slipped away, carried by the breeze and dissipating into the air, harmless to anyone.

For two days, Raphela mumbled and sat in stone silence. Fatell so often by her side, tried to break through at any chance. It was dusk and Raphela stared out her window.

"The bargain, how foolish, how could I, the bargain."

"What are you babbling about Raphela?"

For some reason she caught an echo of Fatell's voice and looked at her.

"If you would only speak more maybe I could help. Talk this out Raphela." The mother, the friend, touched her cold hand.

"Talk it out?" The words were spoken as if foreign. But then, her eyes changed, not so dull and empty. "Talk it out, yes, of course. All of it, what did I promise?" Raphela showed more life than she had in days.

Fatell sat patiently.

"What did I say. I said, "You can have me too. Have me too. I never said alone, never said without him. Yes, there is hope, there is hope." Raphela smiled, contented for some reason. Fatell still didn't understand, but it seemed better.

Raphela lay down and closed her eyes.

Fatell stayed until she was convinced that Raphela was asleep.

As the door closed, Raphela rose and turned to that secret passage between rooms. She slipped through and closed the door.

As she had ordered, nothing had been touched, yes it was still their room, His belt hung on the post, sword carefully sheathed. She could feel him still there. The bed opened itself to her. Sheets laden with his scent. She swore he touched her.

Raphela lay down under the covers as the first moon rose. Her breath still quick with excitement. But it slowed and her lips curled up in contentment. Her heart slowed more each moment and the air lost importance. As the second moon took the sky, her heart and breath, slowed, waned and ceased.

Torches flickered and the dark sky turned pitch. The moons fought for their lights.

Vanar jumped up from his sleep.

Fatell and Mahtso woke slowly. Every mindseer, living in agony since the Duke's death, felt a wrench of change that seared their souls.

Vanar raced to his parent's room. How he knew was a mystery to himself, but he knew. Mahtso was right, she could will anything, even death.

Vanar allowed his silent tears and left when Valeria covered Raphela. Aharon did his duty, no more necessary than before.

All the castle was awake, it had to be. Two years before Raphela had decreed that her funeral take place before the next sunrise after her death. They made quick work of the preparations. Vanar stumbled to the mound and lit the pyre, clasping Valeria as he returned.

The flames circled her and danced, everyone swore the flames danced. Suddenly a roll of thunder broke the night and all the world awoke. The flames leapt up, but it was the sky that lit. Great balls of lightning painted the sky like a spring storm blew across the horizon. It looked like daylight. Eyes and mouths opened in wonder. The smoke from the torchlights moved towards the sky. Color upon color, cracks of thunder to deafen, the sky itself was ablaze.

Vanar swore he saw his father, large as a mountain, standing in the sky, sword in hand, laughing as he battled six ever-changing shapes. And then he knew his mother stood behind him. Her smile wide and proud, hand brushing Atan's shoulder.

A voice, a song, filled the air. Atan turned and knew she was there. He lunged and the shapes pushed on, spitting forth the balls of fire and spears of light. But the Duke and Lady, were not strangers to battle. They laughed and blew the balls back. Raphela caught a jagged pole of light and tossed it into the stars. Atan lunged forth, pushing and pushing until the shapes retreated back behind the stars.

The last roll of thunder rang like a bell and the stars shone amidst a swirling rainbow of light. Anyone alive that night swore that a new constellation was born-- two forms entwined in each other, spiraling together, silhouettes in the sky, so much like a man and woman the Elders had no choice but to say the Duke and Lady had joined the Gods.

The moons shone bright and when day broke, the sun beamed joyfully down on Raalek, the grass was green again and the flowers bloomed. Raalek would prosper well under the new bright sky.

Mowatt closed the book to the usual cheers and tears and joy of the spring audience.

651

These tales are handed down from the Mowatt family, originally taken from the diaries of the Duke and Lady and other members of Castles Cordan and Calcoran of that time, as well as the writings of the first Mowatt scribe.

For further study of this period, visit or call the library at Akar province,

The diaries of Duke Atan and Lady Raphela Ishtba can be viewed at Castle Cordan during daylight hours.

For an in-depth interview with any member of the Mowatt family, contact the head of the history section at Calcoran Castle.

About The Author

Andrea Sharkey was born and raised in New York City and then transplanted to Northern Virginia a bit more than two decades ago.

She is a widowed mother of 3 almost grown children. She'll tell you that while raising her family and working full time plus, she wrote this book to save her sanity.